Great Stories of
Mystery
and
Suspense

CONTENTS

The Tiger
in the Smoke

A CONDENSATION OF
THE BOOK BY

Margery
Allingham

ILLUSTRATED BY STAN HUNTER

A killer's escape from prison sets off two days of terror in the "Smoke," as the city of London is sometimes called. It begins in a very odd way — with a dead man's widow receiving a series of recently made photographs of her husband seemingly alive and well. The widow seeks help from her cousin Albert Campion, amateur sleuth extraordinaire. Suddenly Campion finds himself one jump behind the rampages of the "tiger," one of the most vicious criminals ever encountered in either his or Scotland Yard's experience. As the fog swirls around London, so does the massive manhunt for the killer. Only Campion knows where the "tiger" is headed, and why. Can he possibly overtake him in time to prevent one last death?

Along with Agatha Christie and Dorothy Sayers, Margery Allingham is among the high priestesses of mystery fiction. Her creation Albert Campion has been a favorite with fans of detection for nearly 60 years.

Chapter One

"IT MAY BE only blackmail," said the man in the taxi hopefully. The fog was like a saffron blanket soaked in ice water. It had hung over London all day and at last was beginning to descend. Already the traffic was at an irritable crawl. By dusk it would be stationary. The taxi crouched, panting, in a traffic jam south of the great railway station. The fog oozed in to smear sooty fingers over the two elegant young people who sat inside. They were keeping apart self-consciously, each stealing occasional glances at their clasped hands resting on the shabby leather seat between them.

Geoffrey Levett was in his early thirties. He had a strong-featured uncommunicative face and a solid, powerful body. His brown eyes were intelligent and determined, but not expressive, and both his light hair and his sober clothes were well and conventionally cut. There was nothing in the look of him to show the courage of the man, or the passion, or the remarkable gift he had for making money. Now, when he was undergoing the most grueling emotional experience of his life, he appeared merely gloomy and embarrassed.

Meg Elginbrodde sat beside him. He was much more in love

with her than he had ever believed possible, and every social column in the country had announced that she was about to marry him. She was twenty-five years old, and for five years had believed herself a war widow. But ever since her engagement had been announced, she had been receiving through the mail a series of photographs taken in the city streets. They were all recent snapshots, as various landmarks proved, and in each of them there had appeared among the crowd a figure who was either her late husband, Major Martin Elginbrodde, or a man so like him that he must be called his double. On the back of the latest picture to arrive there had been a roughly printed message.

"It may be only blackmail," Geoffrey repeated, his deep voice carefully casual. "That's what your cousin Campion thinks, isn't it?"

She did not reply at once and he glanced at her sharply, accepting the pain it gave him. She was so lovely. She had flax-white hair and wide eyes, lighter than Scandinavian blue and deeper than Saxon gray; a short fine nose; and a wide softly painted mouth, quite unreal, one might have thought, until she spoke. She had a fashionable husky voice, but her intonation was alive and ingenuous. Even before one heard the words, one realized that she was both honest and not very old.

"That's what the police think. I don't know about my cousin Albert. No one ever knows quite what he thinks. Val certainly doesn't, and she's his sister. Amanda may, but then, she's married to him."

"Didn't Amanda talk of it at all?"

"I'm afraid neither of us did," she said. "It was rather a beastly meal. Daddy kept trying not to say what was in his mind."

"The canon thinks it's Martin, doesn't he?"

She began to speak, then laughed uncertainly. "Oh, dear, I nearly said, 'Daddy always thinks the worst,' and that's terrible! It isn't at all what I meant—either about Daddy or about Martin."

He made no comment and the cab leaped forward a foot or so, only to pause and pant again, frustrated. Geoffrey glanced at his watch. "You're sure it's at three thirty that you're meeting Campion and this inspector?"

"Yes. Albert said we'd meet in the covered yard at the station. The message on the back of the photograph just said, 'Bath train, three forty-five, November eight,' nothing else."

"It wasn't in Martin's handwriting? It was in block capitals?"

"I told you."

"You didn't show it to me. Why?"

She met his glance calmly with her wide stare. "Because I didn't want to very much. I showed it to Val because I work for her, and she called up her brother. Albert brought the police into it, and they took the photograph—so I couldn't show it to anyone else."

Geoffrey's face was not designed to show exasperation or any other of the more helpless emotions. His eyes were hard as he watched her. "Couldn't you tell if the photo was like him?"

"Oh, it was *like* him." She sounded helpless herself. "They've all been *like* him, even that first one, which we all saw. But they've all been bad photographs. Besides, I've never seen Martin out of uniform except for a short time on his two leaves. We were only married five months before he was killed—I mean, if he was killed."

"And dear old Canon Avril seriously believes that he's come back to stop you from marrying me five years after the War Office cited him as 'Missing—believed killed'?"

"Daddy fears it. He always fears that people may turn out unexpectedly to be horrible or mental or desperately ill. He's afraid Martin may be alive and mad."

"And how about you, Meg? What are you hoping?"

She sighed and leaned back. Her eyes were entirely candid. "I knew you'd ask that, Geoff, so I've thought it all out. I love you. I really do. But I did love Martin when I was nineteen, and when I knew—I mean when I thought—he was dead, I thought I'd die myself." She paused. "Somehow I think I did. Your Meg is a new girl."

Geoffrey Levett discovered with horror that he was in tears. At any rate, his eyes were smarting. His hand closed more tightly over the slender gloved one. "I'm a damned fool," he said. "I ought not to have asked you that, my dear, dear girl. Look, we'll get out of this somehow. It'll be all right, I swear it, Meg."

"No." She had the gentle obstinacy of her kind of woman. "I want to tell you, Geoffrey, I want you to know so that whatever I do—well, at least you'll understand. In an hour I may find I'm talking to Martin, and I've been thinking how horrible that'll be for *him*. You see, I've *forgotten* him." Meg bowed her head. "I didn't really know him, I suppose. I never saw him out of the war."

The last word faded and ceased uncertainly. The taxi started again and, seizing an opportunity, swung sharply into the station approach.

"Are you coming with me, Geoff?"

"No." The disclaimer was altogether too violent, and he hastened to soften it. "I don't think so, do you? I'll telephone you about five. You'll be all right with Campion and his bloodhound. I think you'll be happier without me, won't you?"

She hesitated too long. "I'm so muddled I just don't know. I'm sorry, darling."

"You go along." He kissed her lightly and had the door open before the taxi stopped. As he helped her out, she clung to his sleeve. The hurrying crowd on the sidewalk snatched her and bore her away from him into the dark archway of the entrance, which was festooned like a very old theater proscenium with swathes of fog. She was swept on out of his sight as he stood watching, still with the cab door open.

MEANWHILE Albert Campion stood waiting in the covered yard of the southern end of the station with Divisional Detective Chief Inspector Charles Luke, father superior of the second toughest police division in metropolitan London and proud of it. Apart from bleaching him, the years had treated Campion kindly. He was still a slim, elegantly unobtrusive figure exactly six feet tall, misleadingly vacant of face and gentle of manner.

The easiest of men to overlook or underestimate, he stood quietly and surveyed the crowd through his horn-rims with casual good temper.

His companion was a very different kettle of fish. Charlie Luke looked like a heavyweight champion in training. His dark face with its narrow diamond-shaped eyes and strong nose shone in the murky light with a radiance of its own. His soft black hat was pushed to the back of his close-cropped curls and his long hands were deep in his trouser pockets. He was some inches taller than Albert Campion, but his thickset build made him seem shorter. He conveyed intense but suppressed excitement and rigidly controlled physical strength, and his bright glance traveled everywhere.

"It may be just some silly woman playing a game," he remarked. "Weddings are funny times."

"There's a man involved, at any rate," objected Campion mildly. "How many photographs have you got of him—five?"

"Two taken in Oxford Street, one at Marble Arch, one in the Strand, and then the one with the message on the back. That's right, five." The chief inspector buttoned his coat and stamped his feet. "It's cold," he said. "I hope she's not late. I hope she's beautiful, too. She's got to have something if she can't even recognize her own husband for sure."

Campion looked dubious. "Are you certain you could recognize a man you hadn't seen for five years from those snapshots?"

"Perhaps not. Those old street photographers—mug fakers, we call 'em—don't use very new cameras or very good film. I'm allowing for that. But I should have thought a woman would know her own husband if she saw the top of his head from a bus. If it's blackmail—and it probably is—I don't see how the bloke expects to collect anything out of it, do you?" His eyes were snapping in the smoking mist. "If it had been her wedding that had been announced rather than her engagement, it might have made sense. 'Pay me off or you'll be up for bigamy.' Even so, what's the point of sending her one picture after another and giving us all this time to get on the job?"

Campion nodded. "How are you coming with the street photographers?"

The chief inspector shrugged his shoulders. "They all take several hundred snaps a day. They all remember photographing someone exactly like him, only it wasn't quite he. My boys are still working on it, but it's a waste of time and public money. All five pics show the same bleary figure in the street. Nothing to help at all. This last one with the train time on the back is the craziest of all, to my mind." His glance scanned the hurrying travelers. Almost at once a soft but unmistakable whistle escaped him. "This is our young lady, I'll bet a pound. Am I right? What a smasher!"

Campion glanced up and started forward. "Clever of you. That is Mrs. Elginbrodde."

Meg saw them bearing down upon her. In her hypersensitive mood they appeared monstrous. There was Campion, the amateur, a man who never used his real name and title. In appearance, a middle-aged Englishman typical of his background and period: kindly, unemotional, intelligent and resourceful. Perhaps also very brave, or very erudite.

The man behind him was something new to her, and at first glance she found him frankly shocking. He came bounding forward with the unaffected acquisitiveness of a child spying a beautiful cuddly pet. His eyes were flickering and his lively shrewd face expressed boundless interest.

Campion performed the introduction and Chief Inspector Charlie Luke studied the girl cautiously. She was obviously worried, so torn by her loves and loyalties that her genuineness was unquestionable. He shut off his magnetism regretfully.

"I was so sorry I couldn't find you any good snapshots for comparison," she said earnestly. "My husband didn't live in England before the war, so none of his things were here."

Luke nodded. "I understand that, Miss—I mean Mrs. Elginbrodde. He was in France, wasn't he, brought up by a grandmother? And he wasn't very old when he died—twenty-five, I think it was?"

"Yes. He'd be thirty now." She looked around as she spoke, nervously and yet not entirely unhopefully. The movement was quite subconscious, and it struck both men as pathetic. It was as though the war years had peeped out at them suddenly. To add to the illusion, the dreary thumping of a street band on Crumb Street reached them faintly through the station noises. It was the ghost of a wartime tune, not recognizable, yet evocative and faintly alarming, like a half-remembered threat.

Luke hunched his wide shoulders. "The studio portrait and the passport didn't really tell us much, you know. But as far as our experts can determine from the measurements of the features, it's not the same man."

Her face was both disappointed and relieved. Hope died in it but also hope appeared. She was saddened and yet made happy. "I did find this last night," she said, turning to Campion. "I'm afraid the whole thing is very poor, but it's a snapshot a child took of a dog we had, and that's Martin in the background. I don't know if it's any use at all."

She brought a little faded square from the depths of her big handbag and gave it to him. Chief Inspector Luke looked over his shoulder at the overexposed snap of a plump dog wallowing on a London lawn, and far in the background, laughing, with hands in pockets and head thrust forward, a young man wearing a braggadocio mustache. There was nothing definitely characteristic there, except perhaps his spirit, and yet the picture shook them both and they stood looking at it for a long time.

At length Luke said, "Tell me, Mrs. Elginbrodde, did your husband have any young brothers or cousins?"

"No, none I ever heard of."

"Now, look"—Luke became conspiratorial—"the only thing you've got to do is keep your head. It all depends on you. It's a million to one that this will turn out to be the usual blackmail by a man with a record as long as a train. He's behaving altogether too cautiously so far, and that may mean that he's not sure of his ground. He may just want to look at you, or he may risk talking to you. All you've got to do is let him. Leave the rest to me, see?"

"Time is getting on," put in Campion.

"I'd better go to the platform." Meg turned as she spoke and Campion drew her back.

"Not yet. That's where he'll look for you. Don't move from here until we spot him."

She was surprised. "But I thought the message meant that he was coming *off* the Bath train?"

"That's what he wants you to think," Luke said. "He wants you to watch the train so that he can pick you out at leisure. The postmark was London, wasn't it? He doesn't have to go to Bath to be on that platform."

"Oh. Oh, of course." She stepped back, her hands folded. In spite of their escort she looked lonely, peering out anxiously, waiting.

The fog was thickening and the glass-and-iron roof of the yard was lost in its greasy drapery. Only the occasional plumes of steam from the locomotives were clean in the gloom. From where they stood, they could see all the main-line gates, and over on the left the main entrance from the street with its four twenty-foot doors and the bright bookstall just beside it. The afternoon rush was in progress, and wave after wave of hurrying travelers jostled onto the departure platforms. Away to their right was the drive leading from Crumb Street, and behind them was the tunnel to the Underground.

Luke was watching the main entrance with misleading idleness, while Campion kept a discreet eye on the tunnel to the Underground. Neither was prepared for the sudden cry beside them.

"Oh! Look! Over there. There he is. *Martin!*" Meg stood transfixed, pointing like a child and calling at the top of her voice.

Fifty yards away a neat soldierly figure had appeared. He wore a distinctive, well-cut tweed sports jacket and a green pork-pie hat, and had just turned in smartly out of the drive from Crumb Street. He had a brisk, purposeful step and was not looking about him. Even at fifty yards the shadow of a large mustache was discernible. Behind him in the distance, as though designed to enhance the somewhat theatrical militariness of his bearing, the rowdy street band thumped out its violent marching song.

"Martin!" Meg broke away before they could stop her. There was something in the cry that reached the man through the noises of the station. Campion saw him start violently and pause frozen for a moment. Then he ran.

He fled like a deer down the first avenue of escape, through the open gateway of the suburban-line platform, where a train stood waiting. He ran as though his life depended on it, blindly, knocking strangers headlong, leaping over suitcases. Luke shot after him, charging through the crowd like a bull, shouting the familiar "Mind your backs, please!" of the station staff. Campion's hand closed firmly on Meg's wrist. "This way," he said urgently and swept her toward the next platform immediately behind and parallel to the stationary train.

There Campion and the girl found themselves practically alone. The suburban train, still unlit, was separated from them by a second row of rails.

"Martin ran away," Meg began huskily. She was very white and her hands were shaking.

But Campion was not looking at her. He was watching the dark train, and at last the moment he waited for arrived. A door halfway down the train opened abruptly and a dark figure dropped onto the tracks. The man stumbled across to the platform, only to find its stone rim level with his shoulders. He sprang at it and clung there, his head turned from them, as he peered anxiously down the track. Any incoming engine must crush him, but at the moment there was no sign of one.

Just as he slipped back to make another effort to hoist himself onto the platform, Campion's lean arm shot out and caught him by the collar. At the same moment Luke appeared on the platform and the train became alive with spectators. Windows rattled open, heads were thrust out and the shrill clatter of voices broke over them in a wave. Luke dropped onto the tracks with unexpected lightness, caught the stranger by the waist, heaved him into Campion's arms, and vaulted up beside him, his hat still in place.

A white face with narrow black frightened eyes looked up at them. All the soldierliness had vanished. The mustache looked enormous and ridiculous. He made no sound at all but stood shaking and twitching, ready to run again the moment the grip on his arm should relax.

"Oh . . . oh, I'm so sorry. How crazy of me. Now that I see him up close, he's not even like Martin."

The men had forgotten Meg, and her wondering voice took them by surprise. She put out her hand to touch the tweed jacket sleeve and the prisoner leaped away.

There was a momentary struggle, and when they overpowered him again, Luke jerked the man toward him so that their faces all but met. "You're losing something, mate," he remarked with ferocious good humor. "Look at this. It came off in my hand." The movement was too swift to be resisted. The mustache had been lightly gummed, and now the skin on the long upper lip was pale where it had been. Luke tucked the piece of hair into his vest pocket. "Nice one," he said shamelessly. "I'll take care of it for you."

Without his mustache, it was difficult to believe that the stranger had ever resembled any other man closely. He had a distinctive mouth, marred by a scar and a broken tooth in the center front. There was an air of slyness about him, which at this moment was overshadowed by a terror quite out of proportion to his crime, at least so far as it was suspected.

Meg put her hand up to her cheek, then turned away abruptly. Luke peered down the platform. Two heavy men in raincoats were running toward them.

"Your men?" Campion sounded relieved.

Luke nodded. "I put them on the entrance doors in case." He turned to his prisoner. "Well," he said cheerfully, "don't get the idea this is an arrest. It's just a friendly invitation to a quiet talk in a nice warm room. You may even get tea. Understand?"

The man said nothing, but there was a tenseness in his body. He was still ready to make a dash for freedom.

Luke handed him over to the two policemen, who had arrived breathless and unsmiling. "No charge. Held for questioning." He might have been delivering a parcel.

Meg and Campion walked down the shadowy platform together, Luke beside them. The two policemen escorting the prisoner formed a solid knot in front. The crowd that had gathered parted for them, and they quickly moved out of the station.

The girl was silent for some time. Campion watched her out of the corner of his eye. "You'll have to put this out of your mind, if you can, you know," he said. "I think you'll have to face the fact that it was only a performance from the beginning."

She paused on the street and faced him. "You mean you're quite certain it wasn't Martin in the photographs?"

"Oh, no, it was this fellow every time. That's practically sure."

"Practically sure." Her wide mouth twisted and her eyes looked darker. "Martin is dead—again. I've been remembering him. He was a very sweet person, you know."

A wave of old-fashioned black anger swept over Luke's face. "That's the thing which makes me wild," he announced with a bitterness that startled them both. "A chap gives his life, and as soon as there's a chance for happiness for the woman who is the only thing left of him, a pack of ghouls come scrapping around, looking for a penny's worth of gold out of his eyeteeth."

"A pack?" she said dully. "Are there more of them?"

"Oh, yes. I've seen that quivering little mug before somewhere. He's nothing. He's the tailor's dummy. If he'd been on his own, he'd have done a bit of talking. I'm not the one that lad is so frightened of."

"Then Martin might—"

"No." He spoke with unexpected tenderness. "No, lady, no. You've got your own life and you go and live it, as no doubt he'd like you to. Go home now. Will Mr. Levett be there?"

"No. He brought me here and went on to his office. He's going to ring me at five. He has some sort of business appointment this evening." She saw his expression and smiled to reassure him. "Oh, I shall be all right. My father is home. In fact, there are quite a lot of people in the house."

"Fine. Now we'll put you in a cab just over here . . ."

Luke was still fierce when they closed the taxi door on her some minutes later and caught a last glimpse of her face as it changed after her parting valiant smile. As they walked up the drive to Crumb Street, Campion was struck both by the chief inspector's power and by the unexpected emotional depths he had revealed. Luke was as moved as if Elginbrodde had been his own brother. It made him an alarming enemy for someone.

Crumb Street, never a place of beauty, was at its worst that afternoon. The fog slopped over its low houses like a bucketful of cold soup over a row of dirty stoves. The shops had been mean when they had been built and were designed for small and occasional trade, but since the days of victory, when a million demobilized men had passed through the terminus, each one armed with a parcel of government-presented garments, half the establishments had been taken over by opportunists specializing in the purchase and sale of secondhand clothes. Every other window was darkened with displays of semirespectable rags. The fine new police station on the corner was the chief ornament of the district, and the chief inspector advanced on it with the tread of a proprietor. The impatient traffic was moving a little now, and they were held up for a moment on a street island. As they waited, Campion heard afresh the distinctive noise of the irritable, half-blinded city—the scream of brakes, the abuse of drivers, the fierce hiss of tires on the wet road.

Just above it sounded the thumping of the street band. The knot of men who were playing were half in the gutter and half on the sidewalk, and the rattle of their collection boxes was as noisy as their tune.

Luke jerked his chin toward them. "See that? Demanding beggars. We can't touch 'em. 'Keep moving,' that's all we can say. They're ex-service, and they tramp all over town, wearing placards around their necks saying 'No Pension,' 'Invalid' and

'One Arm.' Nothing's known against any of them, but they're not pretty to look at. Still, they've got a fine old ex-service song. Remember it?"

"I've been trying to. Was it called 'Waiting'?"

Luke stood listening, an odd expression on his face. The band was moving very slowly. " 'I'll be *WAI*-tin' for you,' " he sang suddenly just under his breath, " 'at the old oak tree-ah! I'll be *WAI*-tin' for you, just you wait for me-ah!' Most poetic. But those aren't the sentiments those boys down there are thinking. You can tell by the way they're playing."

The band and its bellow had become hateful and menacing in the bone-chilling fog. Suddenly there flashed out for an instant the reality of the thing that had been chasing them all afternoon. For the first time Campion recognized it, and it sent a thin trickle down his spine. "Violence," he said aloud.

"That's it, chum." Luke had seen their chance and they were edging through the traffic. "It's always here. You can't miss it. I shouldn't be surprised if we don't get a whiff of it the moment we get inside the station. That shady little mouse we just caught was frightened of somebody, wasn't he? Hullo, what's up?"

Campion had paused when they reached the sidewalk and was looking over his shoulder. "It was nothing," he said at last as he moved on again. "I thought I caught a glimpse of Geoffrey Levett just then. I must have been mistaken."

Luke turned into the narrow archway of the police station. "Everyone looks alike in the fog," he said cheerfully. "If Mr. Levett is here at all, he's probably inside, asking a few important questions. Now, Mr. Campion, we'll have to treat this lad very gently. After all, we haven't a thing on him—yet."

Chapter Two

THE FOG WAS THICKER than ever over in St. Petersgate Square, but there its brown folds hid no violence. Rather it was cozy, almost protective. St. Petersgate was one of the smallest squares of its kind in the city, and well hidden even on the brightest of days. In its center a magnolia, two or three graceful laburnums and a tulip tree had overgrown unmolested.

The square was a cul-de-sac. There were seven houses on each of two opposite sides. On the third side was a wall that shut out the steep drop into Portminster Row and the shops, and on the fourth were the sharp-spired church of St. Peter of the Gate, its rectory and two small adjoining cottages. The only road led in by the wall, but for foot passengers there was a flight of steps at the other end between the church's stone yard and the rectory. They led up to a wide residential avenue behind.

The rectory was a pleasant cube of a house possessing two main stories, a half-basement and a fine range of attics just above the cornice. Canon Avril, Meg's father, lived on the ground floor very comfortably, while his old verger, William Talisman, made his home in the basement with Mrs. Talisman, who looked after both men. In the fine rooms on the second floor Meg had her self-contained apartment, and the attics had been converted into a pleasant dwelling for tenants of whom everybody was fond.

Canon Avril was standing on the Persian rug before the fire in the living room. It was the room he had brought his bride to thirty years before, and since then nothing in it had been changed, including the rug, which had been a wedding present from his younger sister, Albert Campion's mother. The canon was a big man with a great frame, untidy white hair, and the ease of manner of one to whom every stranger is probably due to become an old friend.

At the moment he was brokenhearted. When Meg had returned from the train station with her story, he had found it so bewildering that his incredulity had made her cry. She had gone upstairs and left him sorrowing, but still very puzzled. His books were in his study, waiting for him to return to their sanity and peace, but he was resisting them valiantly. His distress was poignant. Normally he was the happiest of men. He asked so little of life that its frugal bounty amazed and delighted him. The older he grew and the poorer he became, the calmer and more contented his fine gentle face appeared. He was in many ways an impossible person, with an approach to life that was clear-sighted, yet slightly off-center. No one feared him, simple people loved and protected him, and other churchmen found him disconcerting. He believed in miracles, and nothing astonished him. His imagination was as wild as a small boy's, and his faith ultimate. "She *saw* him," he repeated, his voice urgent. "She saw and recognized him. You heard her say that, Amanda."

The only other person in the room, the Lady Amanda, sister to the Earl of Pontisbright and wife to Albert Campion, sat in a high Queen Anne chair, embroidering. Her red hair was cut neatly around her small head, and under it her brown eyes were thoughtful in her heart-shaped face. She had explained the business very carefully to him twice already, but her clear voice preserved that quality of adventurous common sense that was her chief characteristic. "But when they caught up with him, Uncle Hubert, he wasn't Martin at all."

The old man shook his head uneasily. "But when she first saw him, she was sure," he insisted. "Unless by chance there were two men."

"No, Uncle. There was only one man, and he was not Martin—though he looked like Martin from a distance and wore clothes like Martin's and must have moved and walked exactly like Martin, or Meg would not have been deceived. No, Martin is dead. He was killed in the war. This man who is impersonating him must have known him before."

The canon sighed. "Yes, perhaps so. And what about this photograph." His eye had caught the new copy of the *Tatler* lying open on the couch before him, and he bent down to retrieve it. "This is the same man in the same masquerade, is it?"

For the first time Amanda frowned. "That really is bad luck," she said. "The photographer simply saw Bertie and May Oldsworth on the racecourse and went over to snap them. There were two or three other people standing near who got into the picture, and as he did not recognize them, he asked them their names. He remembered Elginbrodde because he asked to have it spelled."

"The man gave his name as Martin Elginbrodde?" The canon peered at the small figure on the extreme edge of a picture of a group of racegoers. " 'The Honorable Bertie Oldsworth,' " he read aloud, " 'in the paddock with his wife. Also in the picture are Mr. and Mrs. Peter Hill and Major Martin Elginbrodde.' It's so like the boy as I remember him. Upon my soul, Amanda, I can't believe a stranger would have given Martin's name to the press."

"But of course he would if he was impersonating him, Uncle Hubert. He must have been following the photographer around, waiting for a chance to slip into a picture."

"Why should he be so cruel? What could he hope to gain?"

Amanda had no answer. She was genuinely worried and her embroidery lay quiet in her lap. "People we know have been ringing up ever since, asking if Meg has seen it," she said slowly. "There'll be a lot more calls this evening. Meg's going to hate that. Just now she's expecting a call from Geoff. I hope I did the right thing in putting Sam on to it."

"Sam? Just the man. He knows all about newspapers." The canon's face brightened, as it always did when he spoke of Samuel Drummock, who was one of his tenants on the attic floor. That elderly and distinguished sports journalist and his wife had lived there for many years, and the relationship between the two men was cordial.

Amanda sighed. "He's sitting in the hall upstairs with the phone and a mug of beer. Meg has left her door open, and the moment it really is Geoff, Sam's going to call her."

A key sounded in the lock of the outer door, and a moment later Albert Campion and Chief Inspector Charles Luke appeared in the hallway.

"Ah, Albert my boy," the canon said, "come in, come in. Good evening, Chief Inspector. I'm afraid we're giving you a lot of trouble."

Charlie Luke came swinging in behind Campion, filling the room to bursting point by the mere size of his personality. He shook the canon's hand, greeted Amanda and glanced about him. "Where's Mrs. Elginbrodde? Did she get home in good shape?"

"Yes. She's upstairs in her own rooms. I'm afraid I upset her." The canon wagged his head regretfully. "This has appeared too." He took up the *Tatler* as he spoke and the chief inspector nodded.

"We saw it at the station. It's going to cause a bit of trouble, I'm afraid. Well, it's an upsetting time, sir. I think I ought to see the young lady, though."

Amanda rose. "We'll all go up. Did you find out anything?"

"A little. Nothing conclusive," murmured her husband, who seemed unhappy. "Come on, Charles. This way."

Meg Elginbrodde's living room, immediately above the one they had just left, was as different from the canon's traditional English setting as could be imagined. Between the damasked gray walls and the deep gold carpet there ranged every permissible tint and texture, from bronze velvet to scarlet linen. On an elegant side table between the windows there were evidences of Meg's own art—sketches of dresses, swaths of material, samples of braid and beads. Since Campion's famous sister, Val, had acquired the controlling interest in a fashion house, she had sponsored several young couturiers, and Meg Elginbrodde was one of her most successful discoveries.

When they arrived, she rose to greet them. "Who was he? Did you find out?" She spoke directly to Luke as if to a friend.

"His name is Walter Morrison, commonly called 'Duds.'" Luke indicated an exaggerated outline of his own clothes by way of defining the nickname. "Does that convey anything to you?"

"No," she said slowly. "Ought it to?"

"Not particularly. He got out of jail just six weeks ago. He was in for a holdup—thug stuff—with another man. The other man got the full ten years for robbery with violence. But the charge against Duds was reduced to 'assault with intent to rob,' and he got the limit of five."

Meg said softly, "Is that all you know about him?"

"Oh, no. From 1932 to 1940 he was in and out of prison for various offenses. After that, he vanished for nearly five years, which suggests that he was being taken care of by the Army."

"Did he serve with Martin Elginbrodde at any point?" asked Amanda.

"We haven't established it. He says he never heard of him, naturally. His story is that he's an actor by profession."

"He certainly had a most professional mustache," murmured Campion.

"How did he explain the mustache?" Meg asked Luke.

"Oh, he said he used to wear one but lost it in stir, and didn't like to turn up among his pals without one. After we let him go—"

"You let him go!" Meg looked at him in amazement.

"We can't hold a man because a lady thinks she recognizes him as her husband." Luke sounded scandalized.

Campion did his best to explain. "If the police arrest a man, they're bound to bring him before a magistrate as soon as possible," he said gently. "Habeas corpus and all that. That was why we hoped he'd speak to you. Once he had asked for money, or uttered threats, it would have been different."

"We were only within our rights in marching him off for questioning because the chump ran away," Luke announced inelegantly. "However, we're on to the blighter now."

Meg sighed and sat down. Luke stood looking at her with the half-ferocious, half-condoning knowingness that was the essence of the man. He had clearly made up his mind to come clean. "Mrs. Elginbrodde," he demanded bluntly, "just how well did you know that husband of yours when you married him?"

Campion's face became misleadingly blank, and Amanda looked up, surprised and wary. Her eyes were hostile to Luke, and he was aware of it.

"You see how it is," he went on. "Now that I've talked with Duds, I can see he's a smooth piece. Nice voice. May have come from a good home. May easily have had a very good war record."

Canon Avril, who had been sitting very quietly in the darkest corner of the room, now leaned forward. "I didn't know Major Elginbrodde from boyhood. He was introduced here by a young nephew of mine soon after the war started. I thought he and Meg were young to marry, but then life was shorter in those days. Youth is relative, after all."

The chief inspector hesitated. Then his eyes smiled at the canon. "As long as you satisfied yourself about the chap, sir," he said, "as long as you did check up on him—"

"Check up?"

Luke sighed. "Neither Mr. Campion nor I ever met Mr. Elginbrodde. Today we questioned a man called Duds Morrison. There are five years in Morrison's life which from our point of view are unaccounted for, and it was during those same five years that Elginbrodde met and married your daughter. I'm just trying to make quite sure they're not the same man."

Meg gaped at him. In her amazement she didn't hear the trill of the telephone in the hall outside. "But I saw him too."

Luke regarded her stolidly. "I know you did," he said, and added with an irritable gesture, "You're human, aren't you?"

"But of course." To everyone's astonishment the canon got up, crossed the room and took his daughter's hand. "Of course," he repeated. "The chief inspector must make sure, Meg."

Luke smiled broadly at the old man. "That's all right, then. You might take a squint at him yourself, sir—"

"Is there a chief inspector of po-lice in there, Meg? Name of Luke?" Sam Drummock's bellow from the hall cut Luke short and sent him hurrying to the door. "Divisional Headquarters, urgent."

Everyone listened to the ensuing conversation, but it was not revealing. "Where?" they heard Luke demand after a long silence, and then: "I see. I'll come there now. No good sending a car in this fog."

He came striding back into the room. "I'm afraid it'll have to be tonight, sir," he said to Avril. "And I'll have to ask you to come out again too, Mr. Campion, if you will. I haven't been very bright. They've just picked up Duds in an alley off Crumb Street. He's what you might call thoroughly dead."

Campion slowly rose to his feet. "So soon?" he murmured. "I didn't envisage anything quite so—prompt."

"Are you saying he's been murdered?" Meg was very pale.

Luke smiled at her from the midst of his preoccupation. "He didn't die of neglect."

The canon got up. "We must go at once," he said.

As THE FRONT door closed behind the three men, Meg paced in the apartment upstairs. "I love Geoffrey," she said. "I love him unbearably, but I don't know him at all."

"I don't expect he's very knowable at the moment," Amanda observed. "Getting married is always rather complicating, don't you think? I know it's useless to say don't worry, but I feel you must wait. Waiting is one of the great arts."

"Suppose Geoff *doesn't* ring. He was supposed to call at five."

"Eh, he'll telephone, lass." The door had been kicked open a little wider by a soft-soled shoe and Sam Drummock came cautiously into the room carrying two large overfilled tulip glasses. He was a round man with a round bald head, small shrewd eyes and a red face. At the moment he was clad in a high-collared shantung jacket worn over tidy gray flannel trousers, and his small round feet were set in neat and shiny red slippers. His entire appearance managed to suggest the highly conventional costume of some unknown land. "Gin sling," he explained, handing each of them a glass. "I mixed it myself. It's a pick-me-up. You need it. Wait till I get my drink. It's on the stairs."

He moved very quickly and lightly, like the boxers he admired, and was soon back again, a shining pewter tankard in his hand.

"Well, I listened," he announced cheerfully. "It's murder, eh? Well, that's bad. Still, cheer up. Thank God it's not us." Sam raised his tankard. "Meg, that girl in Geoff's office rang again. She wants him to phone the moment he comes here." Sam was worried. The anxiety peeped out of his kind little eyes and was gone again. A hopeful idea had occurred to him. "But maybe he's gone and had a drink or two, eh?"

"That wouldn't be like him."

"No," he admitted. "If it was Martin having a few, I wouldn't give it another thought. That *would* be like him."

Amanda hesitated. "I never knew Martin, of course. Was he a wild person?"

"Martin?" Sam put his head back and crowed aloud. "Oh, a lively, dashing, smashing sort of a lad. But we don't want to talk about him, poor fellow, do we? That's done. My Meg's going to be happy with a grand chap. She's going to have a good, steady, sensible manly sort of a husband. One of the best. A straight clean fighter."

This last was clearly the highest praise the old sportswriter could bestow. He hesitated, glanced at the door and back again, and said with exasperation, "But if he's *not* flat on his back under a bar table, why the hell doesn't he ring up?"

Chapter Three

IT IS NOT EASY to tell when enmity first begins, but it was on that freezing walk to the police station that Charlie Luke caught the first wind of the man who of all his many quarries was to become the chief enemy of his life.

At the moment he was chiefly angry with himself. He was the best of policemen, which is to say that he saw his job as first to locate the malefactor and then to bring him in alive. It was his responsibility to protect as well as corner a man like Duds Morrison, so the fact that he had ignored the terror that he had seen so plainly in the man's face and had sent him out alone to die made him furious. It had been a professional slip of the worst kind and he hated himself for making it. Yet behind his self-criticism there was something more: a sixth sense that he was about to encounter something rare and dangerous. The whiff of tiger crept to him through the fog.

The walk itself was an experience. Without old Avril, who knew his parish blindfolded, they might never have achieved it. The fog was now at its worst, rolling up from the river dense as a featherbed. However, the canon plunged into it with complete confidence, walking very fast. He led his nephew and Charlie Luke to Crumb Street by a series of shortcuts, and they followed with their fingers crossed. They came upon their goal unexpectedly. A last spurt through a pitch-dark mews brought them not a stone's throw from the police station. Here the canon paused and looked around at them. "Now, where is this poor fellow?"

"Pump Path," said Luke promptly. "Up here on the right, past the Feathers."

The chief inspector assumed the lead here, and they walked swiftly past the shuttered shops. It was no night for strolling and there were few people about, except for the inevitable group lounging around the dark entrance to the alley beside the Four Feathers public house. Behind the saloon window a row of heads turned to peer at them curiously as they swept by. At the alley's dark mouth a constable saluted as he recognized Luke.

"The trouble's at the other end, sir, near the Bourne Avenue entrance. You'll need a flashlight. It's very thick in there."

Luke had already produced one, but even so, progress was difficult. The stone way was very worn and sloped sharply from each side to an open gutter in the center, while the high walls that lined it leaned together, their dark surfaces blank as cliffs. At the end of the walls was a crooked wooden fence. Some little way behind it the square of a small window shone orange in the mist.

"Back garden of Thirty-seven Grove Road," said Luke over his shoulder. "Last of its kind. There used to be a row of 'em here, but they've all been built over, except that one which is kept tidy by the caretaker of the solicitors' office. It's quite a sight in the summer. Four marigolds in a fancy flowerpot. The old man has nuisance-by-cats on the brain. Goes down to the station to complain every Friday. I wonder if he heard anything tonight. Look out, there's a bit of a bend here somewhere. . . . Ah."

The beam turned and, following it, they came upon the scene of the trouble. It was a dramatic picture. Some resourceful policeman had unearthed an old naphtha flare, which is the only real answer to fog. It spat and hissed above the heads of a knot of men.

"Chief?" The brisk voice of Sergeant George Picot came to them from the dark mass. "Can you get by? There's not much room."

They advanced cautiously, the little crowd parting for them.

Duds had died in a hole. In a narrow angle where two walls met, there was a space perhaps a foot wide and eighteen inches deep, and into this his body had been crammed in a sitting position, the legs drawn up, the chin on the breast. It seemed impossible that any human being should take up so little space, but there he sat, a heap of unwanted rubbish. A red shadow of blood had spread out over his tweed sports jacket like a bib. He looked very small and negligible.

Luke squatted down on his heels and Picot bent toward his chief. "One of our own men found him at six forty, but he may have been here an hour or more," he murmured.

"What was the exact time he left us this afternoon?"

"Well after five, sir. I came along as soon as I got the report, of course. We've had the photographer and made the survey. Here's the doctor, sir."

A plump figure appeared at the region of the chief inspector's elbow and a clipped schoolmasterish voice remarked, "Any sort of examination in these circumstances is quite useless, Chief Inspector. If you'll have the body sent along, I'll do the postmortem at nine tomorrow."

"Righto." Luke did not turn his head. "But before you go, Doc—all that blood? Throat cut?"

"Oh, no. The hemorrhage is from the nose. It's nothing."

"It's nothing? You mean he had a nosebleed and just sat down and died?"

"Not unless by so doing he cracked himself over the head with sufficient force to fracture his skull." The prim voice was smug. "I have no intention of committing myself now, but I should say that the blow was done with a boot. We shall know in the morning. Good evening." He trotted off and was swallowed by the fog.

Luke turned to Sergeant Picot. "Can we get this face fit to look at, George? I've got someone to see it." He broke off abruptly as Campion touched his shoulder. Old Avril was wiping the blood very gently from Duds's face with a great white handkerchief. He betrayed no trace of distaste but kept at his ministrations quietly and inexpertly, making a considerable mess of himself. It was clear that blood had no terrors for him.

"There," he said at last, apparently to the corpse, and pulled the lids down over the dull eyes. As he took up the dead man's hands to fold them, the jacket sleeves caught his attention, and for the first time he became puzzled. He lifted the right arm and ran his hand up to the elbow.

"Some light, please," he commanded gently, and Luke's flashlight shone down for him at once. It fell on a neat leather patch on the elbow and on a smaller one nearer the cuff. It was good amateur work, an army orderly's job.

"Seen him before, sir?"

Avril did not answer but finished folding the dead man's hands. Then he rose and leaned over to Luke. "Where are you taking this poor fellow? Can we go there?"

"No, sir, we'll go along to the station. It's just around the corner. The body must go down to the mortuary."

"I want that jacket," said Avril. "I want to take it home."

"Very good, sir." Luke did not bat an eyelid. "George, we'll have all the clothes down at the station as soon as possible."

Picot stepped back to give an order. The atmosphere of the entire proceedings had undergone an abrupt change. The query had gone out of it and life and bustle had returned.

"Detective Slaney there?" Luke inquired, and a shadow hurried in out of the dark. "You know Mrs. Gollie, don't you, Bill? Nip over to the Feathers Pub and see what you can pick up." He looked around. "Detective Coleman?"

"Here, sir." The young voice just behind Campion was unsteady in its eagerness and a heavy figure brushed past him.

"Zeal, energy, that's what we want, Coleman. Only don't tread on Exhibit A!" Luke smiled in the dark. "Just down behind us at Thirty-seven Grove Road, there'll be the damnedest old man you ever saw, called Creasey, a caretaker for a solicitors' office. If you can get him to tell you if he heard or saw anything unusual in this alley between five thirty and six forty tonight, you may grow into a detective. He's sure to have been in. He's got a bedridden old mother he can't leave. Got it?"

"Right, sir."

The crowd of detectives was thinning and the mortuary attendants had appeared. Luke took Campion by one arm and the canon by the other and moved them gently away. "We must get over to the station," he said. "The chief might be there by this time."

Avril looked back. "That poor fellow."

"This way, sir," Luke said, still guiding gently. "I think you want to talk to me. Did you know him?"

"No. He was a complete stranger." The canon sounded regretful. "This poor boy was not at all like Martin in feature."

"But the jacket," Luke began, and Avril nodded.

"The jacket was Martin's, and it came from my house."

"Did it, by Jove! When did you last see it?"

"Some weeks ago, perhaps two months."

They had reached the station and Luke led them through the Criminal Investigation Department room to his own modest office beyond. Even here the fog had penetrated, but the light was quite good enough to show the younger men something they had not noticed before: the canon was in no fit state to be sent home uncleansed. The only occupant of Luke's office, Detective Constable Galloway, a round-faced young man who was Luke's clerk, sprang up from his desk at the first glance, supposing no doubt that the canon was a murderer caught red-handed.

"Yes, well," said Luke, eyeing the old gentleman with

incredulity, "we'd better continue this conversation in the washroom. Has the chief phoned, Andy? He hasn't shown up yet, I suppose?"

"No sign of him, sir. There have been several calls concerning Mr. Geoffrey Levett, though. It appears he was to speak at a dinner tonight, and he hasn't turned up. Both his secretary and Mrs. Elginbrodde suggested he might have contacted you. They seemed very worried."

Luke and Campion exchanged glances, and then Luke shrugged his shoulders and touched Avril's arm. "You'd really better come along with us, sir," he said, and in the washroom, while they attended to him with considerable efficiency, the interrogation continued.

Avril stood talking in his shirt-sleeves as the chief inspector scrubbed the front of his coat with a wet towel. "That particular jacket of Martin's has been hanging in the cloakroom at the rectory for years, and it was there quite recently."

"How do you know, Uncle?" Campion asked.

"Because I saw it when I took my heavy coat from over it on the first cold day of the autumn. That's less than seven weeks ago. I always hung something over it, you see, and I looked around for something else to cover it with."

"Why?"

"Because I thought Meg might go into the cloakroom and see it. It always reminded me so vividly of Martin, and I saw no reason why she should have the same experience. I might have folded it and hidden it in my study, but I didn't. I just left it there and covered it up again."

Luke's face grew a shade darker. "You see what it means."

"Of course I do, my boy." Avril struggled back into his coat. "Someone very close to us indeed must be involved, and it's a very curious thing because, as I see it, this strangely cruel deception is aimed directly at Meg. That's why I must have that jacket and I must take it home."

"You think you can find out who took it, do you, sir?"

"Oh, yes," said Avril, "I shall find out."

They had been longer than they thought and Sergeant Picot was waiting for them in Luke's office, his horrible parcel open on a table and each item, neatly labeled, set out upon it. Avril pounced on the stained jacket and spread it before them. "It's what we used to call 'loud,' " he observed. "The tweed is loud. That's what Meg recognized in the station, do you see? The pattern stuck in her mind and was associated with Martin."

Luke said, "It was the patches you recognized, though, wasn't it?"

"Yes." The canon turned the jacket sleeve over and found them again. "Those two patches. I used to wonder why there were two. Why not put a large piece of leather over both holes?"

"Perhaps the holes were made at different times, sir."

Avril was unconvinced. "It may have been that, but I do wonder. I sometimes feel that all these very small things have a purpose. Now, if you'll wrap that up, I'll take it home and find out how it came to be where it was."

"I'm going to send Sergeant Picot down with you, sir," Luke said. "Do you mind?"

The canon frowned. "I'd rather do it alone. Everyone in the house has lived there so long it will be like dealing with my family."

"Exactly." Luke was handling him with affection. "That's why I want to give you George. He's my senior assistant, a quiet, discreet sort of man," he added firmly. "Besides, it's evidence, you see. Got to be produced in court. We can't let it go."

The canon gave way gracefully. "In that case, Sergeant, you and I must make good friends. Come along."

As the door closed behind the unlikely pair, Campion offered Luke a cigarette and took one himself. "You are trusting the canon quite amazingly," he remarked. "You're right, of course, but I don't see quite why you decided to."

"Don't you?" Luke thrust long fingers through his hair. "I know his kind," he said. "All you know is that you can trust 'em where you wouldn't trust your ma. He'll come back with the truth about that jacket whatever it costs him. He's got to."

Campion's eyes had grown dark behind his horn-rims. "But who in all that household," he demanded, "could have smuggled that jacket out to Duds Morrison?"

"Who could, except the girl?" Luke said slowly. "Either she, or that new chap of hers, who seems to have disappeared."

"You're wrong."

"I hope so." The chief inspector smiled. "Perhaps it was a miracle."

"Perhaps there's another card in the pack," said Campion.

Chapter Four

MRS. GOLLIE, owner of the Four Feathers pub, came into Luke's office as if she were hastening to the scene of some terrible personal disaster, or perhaps merely going on the stage. There was drama in every curve of her splendid young body. Her well-dyed black hair sat neatly around her head in stiff waves, but her fine eyes were ingenuous and her mouth, for all its bright paint, was kindly and innocent.

"I had to come down, Chief Inspector Luke," she began without preamble. "I saw him, you see, and you want to know, don't you?" She had a gentle voice.

Luke waved her into the chair in front of his desk and winked briefly at Campion. "Okay, then," he began, "you saw the deceased, did you, duck? When?"

"It was just when we were opening. I was getting my keys for the spirits when both men came in—"

"Both?" Luke's eyebrows shot up.

"I was in a hurry, see, so I didn't notice them particularly right then. The other man—not the one who was killed—gave the order. Two small gins, they had."

"Were they alone in your little bar?"

"I've just told you so. We were hardly open. They came in together, talking very quietly, confidentially, as if they had business. When I came back, from talking with Bert, I was just in time to see the smaller man—that's the one with the well-cut jacket and green pork-pie hat—shoot out through the door, pulling his arm away from the other chap."

"Pulling?"

"Yes, you know, shaking him off. The other chap started after him, remembered me and shoved ten bob down on the counter. Then he went after him."

"Did you hear anything they said?"

"I didn't, Chief Inspector. I didn't listen, you see. Besides, there was such a row going on. There was a band in the street, bawling."

"What did the second man look like?"

Mrs. Gollie clicked her tongue against her teeth. "I wish I'd looked, but I never thought of a murder, see? He was tall and he was clean, sort of scrubbed-looking. A thoroughgoing gentleman."

"Was he fair or dark?"

"I couldn't say. He had his hat on. He had brown eyes, and although he was young, he looked important. Respectable— that's the word I've been looking for. He wasn't this district at all. He wore a good dark overcoat, black hat and white collar. And he had a navy tie with two little stripes on it, very wide apart, silver-gray and sort of puce. There was a sort of flower with a bird's head coming out of it, very small, between."

"Had he, though?" Campion sighed. "I wondered about that." He leaned over Luke's shoulder and wrote on the blotter: *Phoenix Rugger Club tie. Geoffrey Levett?*

Luke stared at the scribbled words for a moment before he straightened his back and stared at his friend. "You thought you saw him outside here this afternoon, remember?"

Campion looked unhappy. "It hardly proves—" he began.

"Lord, no, but there's a healthy supposition there. Hullo, Andy, what's that?" The final remark was directed to the clerk, who was hovering at his elbow, his round face shining with excitement.

"Going through the deceased's effects as directed, sir, I found this in his wallet. Note the postmark, sir."

Luke took the used envelope from him and turned it over. It was addressed to G. Levett, Esquire, at the Parthenon Club, and on the back an address with a telephone number had been added in pencil. The postmark was unusually clear and the date was the current one. The letter had gone through the mail that morning.

Luke showed it to Campion. "Is that Levett's handwriting?" he asked, pointing to the pencil-written address.

"I'm afraid it is. And that's his office address."

They looked at one another for a moment, and Luke put the thought into words. "Why did Levett give Duds his address, and then run after him and—? That won't wash, will it? I could do with a chat with that young man."

"Well, have I helped?" It was Mrs. Gollie, glowing with excitement. "I mean, I—"

Luke turned to her and then stiffened. The door behind her was opening and a tall sad figure came quietly into the room.

Assistant Commissioner Stanislaus Oates, chief of Scotland Yard, had not changed since Campion had first met him over twenty years before. He was the same shabby dyspeptic figure who peered gloomily out at a wicked world from under a drooping hat brim. But he brightened a little at the sight of his old friend and, after nodding to Luke, who was standing like a ramrod, came forward with outstretched hand.

"Hullo, Campion, I thought I might find you here. Just the weather for trouble, isn't it?"

A great reputation has many magical effects. In a matter of seconds Constable Galloway escorted Mrs. Gollie out of the office without her uttering a single word, and then returned and faded into the recess that contained his desk.

Oates took off his ancient raincoat, laid it carefully over the back of a chair and sat down. "I thought I'd slip in and see you myself, Charles." He had a sad voice. The words came slowly. "You may have a little more on your plate than you realize. How far have you got?"

Luke told him, reeling out the essential details with a minimum of gesture and the precision his training had taught him. When he was done, the assistant commissioner picked up the envelope and turned it over. "Humph," he said.

"Levett must have been waiting for Duds outside here." Campion spoke thoughtfully. "When we let Duds go, he must have followed him, taken him into the first pub, tried to get the tale out of him, failed, given him his office address and then— what?"

"Duds wasn't working on his own," Luke supplemented, "so as soon as he got a chance, he ran. Levett started after him, but lost him when he paused to pay his bill. We know where Duds ended up, but what happened to Levett? Where is he now?"

"Mr. Levett seems to have planned quite an evening," Oates said. "Telephone calls over half the world, an after-dinner speech at a banquet and a business interview after that. None of his friends can find him, and they want to know why we can't."

"Medical opinion, for what it's worth, is that Duds was kicked," Campion said. "I don't see Levett doing that, you know, I really don't."

"Do you see him killing at all, Mr. Campion?" Oates asked.

"Frankly, no."

"But on the other hand, do you see him missing all his important appointments like this?"

"It's odd." Campion was frowning. "Geoffrey is a punctilious, solid sort of chap, I should have said. Unadventurous, even."

Oates's gray face was puckered into a faint smile. "That's what most people think, but he's not, you know. I've been hearing about him. He's Levett's Ball Bearings and one or two other very sound old-fashioned companies, and he's a very rich man. But the original money came from gambling on the Exchange. For two and a half years after he came back from the war, he was one of the biggest gamblers on this side of the Atlantic. He quadrupled his fortune. Then he stopped. Levett is not unadventurous. He's not a man who doesn't take risks."

Charlie Luke strode restlessly around the little room. "Duds wasn't alone," he said. "He was terrified in the train station, and he was terrified in here. And it wasn't me he was frightened of, and it wasn't Levett. He couldn't have been working *for* Levett, because if he had, Levett wouldn't have needed to write down his office address for him. Levett *must* have given him that in the pub. The envelope was new. It only went through the mail last night."

"Seen any police bulletins tonight, Charles?" Oates asked.

Luke pulled up sharply. "No, sir, can't say I have."

"A convict called Jack Havoc has made a getaway from the Scrubs hospital. When I heard that, I put on my hat and came down here."

Luke drew a deep sigh. "Havoc. That was the man who Duds did the holdup with. So that's it. I wondered when we were going to see a little daylight."

Oates did not respond immediately. "It's very unsatisfactory," he said at last. "Your people picked up Duds Morrison's body at six forty, but at six forty-five Jack Havoc was only just making his break halfway across London. He was killing another friend of his, as a matter of fact. I received the two reports side by side."

Oates leaned back in his hard chair, his legs stretched out. "I remember Havoc. I think you'll be finding traces of him here in your precinct, and I'd like to talk to you about him. Both you and Campion were overseas when we jailed him last, so you missed him. You missed quite a phenomenon." He repeated the words softly: "Quite a phenomenon."

Campion found himself fascinated at this departure from character. No one had spoken with more force or at greater length than Oates on the stupidity of creating a legend around any wrongdoer. It was his theory that every crook was necessarily a half-wit, and therefore any policeman who showed more than a kindly contempt for any one of them was very little better.

Oates caught his expression and met it steadily, if not with ease. "Havoc is a truly wicked man," he said.

Charlie Luke hastened to bring the conversation to a more specific basis. "Are you saying he's a born killer, sir?"

"Oh, yes. He kills if he wants to. But he's not casual about it, like your gangsters. He knows exactly what he's doing. Take this latest performance of his. He killed Sir Conrad Belfry—"

Campion sat up. "C.H.I. Belfry?"

"That's the man. Distinguished doctor. About half past six tonight Havoc throttled him and slid off down the fire escape. The guard, who—against regulations—was sitting outside the door of the consulting room, heard nothing."

"Good lord! Where was this, sir?"

"In a second-floor consulting room on Wimpole Street. After badgering the authorities for weeks Belfry had got Havoc out for an experiment." Oates leaned forward as he spoke. "I believe Sir Conrad's murder was planned before Havoc even knew the man existed. When Havoc was sentenced, he was sent to Parkhurst. No one but a mug tries to break out of Parkhurst because of the water."

"So he went sick and got pushed up to the Scrubs hospital, I suppose, sir?" Luke could not help making a leap in the story.

"You're underestimating him, Charles, my boy," he said. "He went sick, but in a most ingenious way. Three years ago he developed a compulsive neurosis concerning the number thirteen." He lifted his eyes, caught sight of Luke's expression and laughed outright. "I know. It was so hopeless, so silly, but in the end he got clean away with it. He did the thing not only thoroughly but progressively. He went sick on the thirteenth of every month. When he found his cell number added up to thirteen, he starved himself until they moved him. He was always polite and apologetic. He explained he knew he was being silly, but said he couldn't help it. It's a well-known phobia, I understand." He looked at Campion inquiringly.

"I have heard of it."

Oates went on placidly: "It took him eighteen months to get himself moved up to the Scrubs hospital, where they've got a psychiatry unit. He was so docile and intelligent that they seem to have made a sort of pet of him. Sir Conrad had nothing to do with the unit, of course, but one day last month he went down there and was taken around the exhibits. Havoc took his fancy and nothing would satisfy him until he got the man up to Wimpole Street to examine him. Havoc was sent to him just after six tonight. Two prison guards went with him, but one stayed in the hall downstairs and Havoc was not handcuffed to the other. For a time the second guard stayed in the consulting room, but Havoc appeared so oppressed by his presence that old Belfry at last persuaded the chap to sit outside the door. The rest of the story is just what you'd think. By the time the wretched guard got nervous and made up his mind to take a look, it was all over. Belfry was lying on the floor, the window was open, Havoc had vanished."

Campion frowned. "Are you absolutely serious when you suggest that the thing had been planned so long?"

"I take my oath on it," said Oates, "and it wouldn't surprise me if he had timed the attempt for November, just on the off chance of a fog like this." Oates felt for his pipe. "Well, Luke, Havoc fits somewhere into this puzzle of yours. Havoc was the man Duds feared, but I don't see how he could have killed him, since he was in Sir Conrad's consulting room when Duds's body was found."

The chief inspector said nothing. Despite his veneration for Oates, at that moment Charlie Luke did not altogether believe in Jack Havoc.

The immediate development, therefore, gained considerably in drama. When it came, the wave of outrage spread through the Crumb Street police station in the same electric way it would later spread through every newspaper office in the country. The message arrived in Luke's little office over the telephone on the clerk's desk in the corner, but afterward no one there could have sworn on oath that it had not been shouted in their ears.

"A nasty job just down the street at Holloway and Butler's, Solicitors, sir, Thirty-seven Grove Road. Someone broke in the front and rifled the office on the ground floor. Creasey, the caretaker, who was in the basement at the back talking to one of our own men, young Coleman, must have heard something, so he and Coleman went up, leaving the bedridden old mother behind. They're all dead, sir—the old woman as well. Knifed. Blood everywhere, the witness says. He's Mr. Hammond, an elderly employee of the firm who lives alone in the attics. He took his time getting downstairs, which was wise of him. Whoever did it got clean away through the little bit of a garden at the back, which leads to Pump Path."

The chief inspector did not speak when he heard of Coleman's death, but a grunt escaped him, a sound of rage, and he stood momentarily arrested, one long arm outstretched, warding off realization. Then he swung into action, snapped out the order to call up all the police units that make up the machinery of detection.

Campion's response to the news was of interest. "Holloway and Butler were Elginbrodde's solicitors," he said. "Meg mentioned it the other day." His eyes met Luke's own. "Elginbrodde's jacket, Elginbrodde's solicitors—?"

"And Elginbrodde's successor!" said Luke. "There's still no sign of Levett."

Oates had gone out to the Criminal Investigation Department room, where the first reports from the detectives who had raced to the scene of the new crime were just coming in. Now he stepped back into Luke's office for a moment. "All three victims have clean, expert wounds," he said briefly. "Over the collarbone, into the jugular. Schooled professional stuff. This is where Havoc has been."

Chapter Five

EARLIER THAT afternoon, when Geoffrey Levett had accosted Duds Morrison some thirty yards up the dark street from the police station and persuaded him into the Feathers by the simple process of thrusting him through the door, one great anxiety was lifted from his mind. This man, whoever he was, had never been married to Meg.

From Geoffrey's point of view the afternoon had been a nightmare. He was by nature a participator in events rather than an observer. Acting on impulse, he had paid off the cab near the station and had followed Meg at a distance because he wanted to see for himself the man who was threatening his happiness.

The result was that he found himself hanging about outside the dreary Crumb Street police station. Above all he wanted to make sure that Elginbrodde had not returned from the dead. Therefore, by the time Duds stepped swiftly out of the police station, Geoffrey was in the mood for reckless action.

He hurried after the man, caught up with him and took him by the elbow. Duds made a futile effort to escape, but the bray of a street band starting up not far behind them seemed to devitalize him. He struggled once more halfheartedly and gave in.

Geoffrey pushed him on down the street and into the doorway of the first pub they reached. The little bar parlor was deserted and dim with fog, and from the street the cacophony of the band came ever nearer.

Geoffrey fixed the stranger's dull black eyes with his own. "Listen to me," he said distinctly. "Get it well into your head from the outset. This may be worth your while." He noted the faint flicker of interest. The tenseness in the arm he held slackened and the stranger stood more firmly on his heels.

As the woman behind the bar came over to take their order, Levett drew out his wallet and pencil, still keeping an eye on his captive. By now the street band was immediately outside the door and the noise was so great they could not hear themselves speak. Levett scribbled on the back of an envelope and handed it to Duds, who took it dubiously and read it. When he raised his eyes, Levett took a bank note from his wallet and handed it to him. The band passed by.

"The rest when you come to see me."

Duds regarded him sulkily. "What do you want?"

"Only the story."

"Newspaper?" All Duds's terror returned and he made a move toward the door, but something seemed to check him. He glanced back uncertainly.

Geoffrey shook his head violently. The abominable band had returned, and until it repassed the door, he was forced to be silent. "No," he said at last. "It's purely for my own personal information." He took hold of Duds's coat sleeve. "Who employs you?" He saw the white face grow wooden.

"No one. I'm unemployed. I'm an actor. I'm not working."

"I don't mean that. I only want to know one thing. Who instructed you to get your photograph taken in the street?"

The man's leap for freedom took him by surprise. Duds jerked his sleeve out of Geoffrey's grip and flung himself at the door. Geoffrey slammed down a ten-shilling note and shot after him.

He was on Duds's heels, but the street had darkened considerably, and for a second he thought he had lost him in the fog. But almost at once Duds reappeared, running back, darting into an unsuspected opening between the houses. It did not dawn on Geoffrey that some other enemy must be after his quarry. He merely saw his man and went blindly after him into the alley, led by the sound of his flying footsteps.

The noise behind him did not register on his mind for several seconds. He was within inches of Duds before he became aware that they were both being overtaken, and an instant later a violent blow on his shoulder sent him reeling past Duds and against the wall.

Then a tide of men swept over them, pinning them close in the dark. At first there were no voices, no words, only heavy breathing, the slither of soft feet on the stones and the chink of something that sounded like metal. Very near to his shoulder Duds whimpered. It was a shred of a sound, high with fear.

"Where's the Gaffer, Duds?"

It seemed to Geoffrey, spread-eagled against the wall, that the inquiry came from many lips. Urgency was in it, and menace. "Where's the Gaffer? Where's the Gaffer?"

"Inside." The word arrived explosively. "Parkhurst. Been there years."

"Liar. You always was a liar, Duds." The blow that followed passed so close to Geoffrey's own face that he felt its wind. Then he felt Duds sliding down slowly at his side. Panic swept over him and he struck out. Instantly he was seized and lifted bodily off his feet. A hand found his mouth, and something hard and round hit him above the ear so that blackness denser than the fog descended upon him and he fell.

HIS FIRST CONSCIOUS thought was that even for a nightmare it was extraordinarily cold and uncomfortable, and the noise was incredible. Soon he realized that he was awake, but in such an astonishing position that he doubted his sanity.

He was wedged tightly into a little wheelchair, his arms pinioned to his sides under an old khaki mackintosh fastened behind him, and his cramped legs drawn up and strapped to the undercarriage of the chair. His mouth was sealed with a strip of adhesive tape. He was wearing a knitted-balaclava helmet that covered his entire head save his eyes, and he was being wheeled swiftly along a foggy gutter in the midst of a rabble of marching men who kept time to the thin music of a mouth organ.

Having made certain that he really was helpless, he concentrated cautiously on his kidnappers. There were ten or a dozen of them, drab, shadowy figures who kept shielding him with their bodies from passersby. From where Geoffrey sat, very close to the ground, they towered above him, and he noticed with a shock that there was something odd about each one of them, although for people with such emphasized disabilities they seemed to move with surprising freedom and lightness. The only heavy feet were the boots that stamped immediately behind his chair.

The man directly in front of him was leading the way. He was tall and made monstrously so by the fact that on his shoulders he carried a dwarf, a small man whose normal conveyance was no doubt the little chair now occupied by the prisoner. It was the dwarf who played the mouth organ. Geoffrey's own dark hat sat on the back of the little man's bulbous head.

It was the tune that gave Geoffrey the essential clue. He remembered it as a sentimental dirge of the Second World War

called "Waiting." He had been hearing it at intervals all afternoon, played execrably by an "ex-servicemen's" band up and
down Crumb Street. This was the same band.

The group had haunted him all through his nervous vigil
outside the police station. He saw now that it must have
been his own quarry for whom they had been waiting. But what
they had done with him he had no idea. He decided that the
business was doubtless some kind of minor gang warfare, and by
mistake he had been collected instead of the man they had
called "Duds." They were probably taking him somewhere
now with the idea of questioning him.

The Gaffer. The words returned to him suddenly. That was it,
of course. He was on the track of Duds's employer at last. In
spite of his discomfort, he felt a deep satisfaction. He had made
up his mind to solve the mystery that had been upsetting his life,
and now he seemed well on the way. The thought that he might
be in actual danger did not occur to him. He had every confidence that he would be able to deal with the situation—unless,
of course, Elginbrodde proved to be alive.

The little procession halted abruptly. It took him by surprise and jerked him forward in the chair. The mouth organ
squealed and was silent, and he was aware of nervousness all
around him.

A silver-crested helmet loomed out of the fog and the voice of
the law, casual and consciously superior, drawled at them.
"Packing up for the night, Doll?"

"That's right, Officer. It's a nasty night. Warmer at home."

Geoffrey recognized the courage in the new voice, which
came from behind him. It belonged to Heavy Boots, he decided.

"You're right about that." The law spoke with feeling. "What
have you got there?"

Geoffrey achieved a snort and at once an iron hand closed on
his shoulder. He was aware of the stink of fear reeking all around
him, but Heavy Boots seemed quite equal to the occasion.

"It's only poor Blinky, Officer." And then with dreadful con-
fiding: "Fits. He has 'em."

"I see. Very well. Good night, all." The law moved on with steady dignity.

The procession was now moving at speed, and Heavy Boots swore softly for a little while. His suppressed savagery was startling. As an introduction, the incident was revealing. Geoffrey understood that Heavy Boots was the leader.

The dwarf was playing the mouth organ merrily again by the time they turned out of the dark street into a lane ablaze from end to end with light and bustle. It was one of those small markets that still dotted the poorer parts of the city. Ramshackle stalls roofed with flapping tarpaulin and lit with naked bulbs jostled each other down both sides of the littered road. The band kept to the middle and closed very tightly around the little chair. For the first time Geoffrey was aware of their faces, and he recognized some of them from having seen them in Crumb Street that afternoon. There was a hunchback, taller than most of his kind but typical. A one-armed man strode close beside him, while a flying figure swung himself between a pair of crutches just in front.

The end of the journey came suddenly. At a gap between two stalls the group swung sharply and they plunged into darkness again, through a doorway beside a greengrocer's shop.

The hallway was narrow, chill and pitch-dark. Geoffrey and his little chair were swept on until an inner door swung suddenly open and he found himself at the head of a dimly lit flight of cellar stairs. There he was stopped, held precariously on the top step, while the rest swept past him, bobbing and weaving with ease down the dangerous way.

He found he was looking into a cavernous shadowy room, warm and smelling unexpectedly wholesome. He was struck first by its neatness. There was order, even homeliness, in its arrangement. Its size was enormous: it took up the whole cellar of the building. The walls were clean and whitewashed up to a height of ten feet. A mighty iron stove, very nearly red-hot, stood out in the room, and around it was a circle of junk-shop chairs. Three plank tables placed end to end, covered with clean newspapers and flanked by packing-case benches, stood waiting, and far away against the farther wall was a row of couches stacked with army blankets. The whole effect was one of military discipline.

Geoffrey's scrutiny was cut short in a most terrifying manner. The men below him scattered. There was a shrill scream, wild and ecstatic, from the dwarf, and at the same instant the hands holding his chair were suddenly withdrawn, so that it began a dreadful descent down the steep stairs.

There was nothing he could do to save himself. His weight sped the little wheels, but by some peculiar adroitness in the method of launching, the chair did not overturn when it touched ground but rather sped through the whooping crowd to crash into a pile of paper-filled sacks stacked against the wall. Their position was too lucky to be accidental, and he realized even before the dwarf had ceased his delighted yelping that this cruelty must have been practiced on the little man himself many times.

He felt deathly sick—the adhesive tape was suffocating him— but the sound of heavy boots was clattering across the bricks toward him and he made a great effort at control. A man approached and bent down.

Geoffrey looked up and for the first time set eyes on his persecutor, the man called Doll. He saw a big shambling figure, stooped and loose-jointed, middle-aged but still very powerful. The startling thing about him was his color. He was so white that he was shocking, his close-cropped hair so much the color of his skin that the line of demarcation was scarcely visible. The black glasses that hid his eyes explained him. He was an albino, one of those unlucky few in whom the natural pigmentation of the body is entirely absent.

Doll was seeing his prisoner for the first time. The dim light suited his weak eyes and he swung the chair around slowly to get a better view. He pulled the woolen helmet from the prisoner's head, and the others came closer. They were a strange company of "ex-servicemen," of whom six at most could possibly ever have been in the armed forces. Geoffrey particularly noticed the tall man who had carried the dwarf home. He was a thick-featured, mild-looking youngster with a strangely dazed expression. An older, shorter man, who resembled him so closely he was obviously his brother, and the ragged acrobat who had now laid aside his crutches and was moving with ease without them—these could well be ex-servicemen. Most of the rest were oddities, collected no doubt for their freak value. The albino Heavy Boots was the declared leader and main personality.

Geoffrey was liberated from all his bonds except for the cord that bound his hands behind him and the tape over his mouth. He made an attempt to rise when his feet were freed, but he was too numb to move. After the mackintosh was removed and his expensive clothes came into view, Heavy Boots turned to the smaller of the two brothers. "Now, Roly, who's that? Who is it?"

The man called Roly stepped forward and looked earnestly at the captive. "I ain't never seen him before."

"Ain't that he? Ain't that the Gaffer?"

"No, no." The pronouncement came from the tall brother and caused something of a sensation. Geoffrey understood that it was unusual for him to speak at all.

Heavy Boots motioned to the acrobat. "Bill, come here, boy. Now, look steady. Who *is* it?"

The ragged man peered down and laughed. "Search me. No one I know. Friend of Duds, I suppose."

Heavy Boots ripped open the prisoner's overcoat and thrust his hand into the breast pocket. Geoffrey sat quiet, waiting stolidly, and the search yielded little remarkable: his wallet, a checkbook, his driver's license, and the letter he had taken out of the envelope he had given to Duds. The only unusual item was a set of miniature military medals he had been intending to wear to the banquet that evening. Heavy Boots studied these with great interest. It was clear he understood the history they told, and he touched them with respect.

There was no talking whatever as the albino continued his unhurried examination of Geoffrey's things with the dignity that springs from complete authority. The checkbook and driver's license interested him, but the trophy that turned the day was an unexpected one. The letter that had arrived in the envelope Geoffrey had given to Duds happened to be a charity appeal from the Royal Institute for the Relief of the Orphans of East Anglia. It was a dignified letter beneath a heading that incorporated a list of patrons, led by royalty. The effect it produced on Heavy Boots was startling. He removed his dark glasses and held the sheet very close to his red eyes. His lips moved soundlessly as he read the words over and his hand shook a little.

"Here," he burst out suddenly, swinging around on the company, "what ruddy fool's made this mistake, eh? I've kept you all out of trouble, haven't I, up till now? Who's got us into it proper this time?"

His alarm was infectious. The company swayed away from him. Only Roly, the older brother, showed any truculence.

"You can talk," he began, "you can talk, Tiddy Doll, you always could. What's the matter, eh? Who is he?"

Tiddy Doll spat. "He's only my dear Mr. Levett, friend of Gawd knows who. That's what this here paper shows. Come on, step on it. Get the cords off him. Who was so silly as to make the mistake, that's what I want to know?"

"But he was *with* Duds, Tiddy. They both ran when they saw us, first into the boozer and then down the alley."

"Shut up, Roly. I'll see you get your time to talk." Tiddy Doll was having trouble with the rope on Geoffrey's wrist. "A moment, sir, I shan't be long. There's been a mistake in the fog." He got the knot loose and ripped off the cord with searing speed. "I saw service same as you, sir." The time had come for the adhesive tape to be removed. Despite his anxiety, Tiddy Doll could not resist the opportunity to hurt. He tore it off so suddenly that the excruciating pain took Geoffrey by surprise.

"That's better, ain't it?" Doll smiled. "We was only playing a game on a friend, sir," he went on hurriedly. "I never had such a shock in all my life as when I saw you down here in the light."

Geoffrey struggled painfully to his feet. "Where's the man I was with?" he demanded.

"There you are, Tiddy." Roly was eager to justify himself. "Him and Duds was together. They was friends."

"I met him for the first time this afternoon." Geoffrey turned a chilly eye on the speaker. "You mobbed us, and one of you had the infernal impudence to knock me out." It was stilted talk, but as he remembered from army days, it was the language of authority, which they all understood perfectly. "Where is the man I was with?" he repeated. He took a chance and picked on the elder of the two brothers. "You there, what's your name? Roly? You called him a liar."

"No, that wasn't me, sir. That was my brother, Tom. Young Tom's funny, sir. He got blowed up and has never been the same since. Tom knew Duds. Duds was the corporal, see?"

Geoffrey thought he did. He had a moment of inspiration. "And the man you call the Gaffer was the sergeant, I suppose?"

"That's right, sir," said Tiddy Doll, who could not bear to be left off center stage for long. He had put his dark glasses back on, and Geoffrey thought that much of his impressiveness lay in that concealing half-mask.

"Were you under him?"

"No, sir," Roly cut in eagerly. "Tiddy wasn't with us. Tiddy never saw the Gaffer. There was only me and Tom and Bill. We are the only three left who was with him at the time."

"Well, where is this sergeant?" Geoffrey demanded.

"That's what we want to know, sir," Roly said. "We've been looking for him for close on three years now. A few weeks ago we see Duds all dressed up in Oxford Street and we lost him. Then today we see him again and we followed him. Then you came up to him and we followed you both and waited outside the pub. When he come out, he ran right into us, and Tom, who hasn't noticed nothing for years, caught sight of him and started after him as if he'd come to himself all of a sudden. When you both went down the path, we started after you. We hardly noticed you, sir, to tell you the truth."

"Of course we noticed the gentleman," protested Tiddy with exasperation. "We thought that he was the Gaffer."

"But I told you he weren't the Gaffer," said Roly with passion.

"Tiddy thought we'd got the officer." It was the high flat voice of the hunchback, and he giggled.

The remark was so obviously true that it took the whole company by surprise. It was Tom, the young brother, who spoke first. He lifted his head and looked steadily at Geoffrey with eyes that betrayed a fleeting reawakening. "Major Elginbrodde," he said slowly, "that's who you are."

"He ain't!" Roly was startled and protesting. "Major Elginbrodde were a little dark fellow. Besides, he's gone, poor chap. No one knows that better than you, Tom." Roly turned back to Geoffrey. "Major Elginbrodde and Tom was together when they trod on the mine," he explained. "That was on the beach in Normandy, four months after our own little job. The major were wiped right out, but Tom wasn't touched—or so we thought until we found out he'd gone strange. He's a proper fool, Tom is, now. He weren't at one time. When he were young, he was proper smart, Tom was. We were fishermen, had our own boat. That's why we was chosen, you see, sir. That's why the Gaffer picked us. The Gaffer found the men for the raid."

"Nark it, chum!" Tiddy Doll's warning was frantic. "The gentleman doesn't want to hear your life history nor your brother's, Roly. The gentleman's got his own position to think of."

The threat was an open one and Geoffrey wheeled to stare coldly at the dark glasses. "You've considered your own, I suppose, Doll?"

The albino regarded him steadily. The situation was relatively simple. Geoffrey knew that unless they actually murdered him, they must at some point permit him to go free. Since he appeared to be a person of some standing, the business must eventually resolve itself into a question of whether or not he would lodge a complaint. If he did decide to complain, the future of the band would not even be problematic.

Tiddy Doll was not without cunning. "There are some gentlemen who wouldn't like it to be known they was mistook for friends of persons they wasn't friendly with," he essayed.

"There are also gentlemen who could not care less," said Geoffrey. "But," he added carefully, "they are usually reasonable people who do not want to do others any harm if they are sensibly treated and their questions answered." He turned back to Roly. "Which raid are you talking about?"

"It didn't have no name, sir. It was secret."

"Four months before D Day?"

"Yes, sir."

"To the Normandy coast?"

"I don't rightly know, sir. We were took over by submarine and put off in a little boat that me and Tom managed. We didn't go up to the house, not even Bill here. Bill sat on the beach with the light to give the signal should we need it."

Geoffrey glanced at the ragged man who had used crutches in the street and needed none indoors. He made no attempt to join in the story but was remembering it with pure pleasure. It had been an hour of utter and appalling danger that he had enjoyed to the point of ecstasy. It went through Geoffrey's mind that the Gaffer, whoever he was, had chosen his men intelligently if not orthodoxly.

"Who were the others?"

"There was only Duds and the Gaffer and the major. Duds didn't go into the house. He stayed below."

"Who were you after?"

Roly shook his head. "We never knew for sure. Duds said it was a spy."

"I see. And the Gaffer was expected to go into the house and take care of this spy?"

"Well, they reckoned there was a woman there too. It were only a little house, all by itself. Sea and rocks on one side, private road on the other."

Geoffrey nodded. He believed the story. Some very strange things had been done along the French coast in those months of waiting before the great invasion. Five men and one officer: at such a time a small force was well worth risking to remove a single dangerous man.

Roly's voice was still droning on. "The Gaffer done the job all right—both of 'em, we reckoned. Duds told me later the Gaffer was in stir—that's prison to you, sir—but Jack was too smart for that. Even if they catched him, they'd never hold him. We know better than that. Jack has collected the treasure and he's living on it in glory, while his mates are tramping the gutter. That's why we're looking for him."

"Now you've said it," Tiddy Doll burst out. "Now you've given everything away."

Geoffrey ignored him. The story was taking shape. Elginbrodde certainly appeared to be dead, but in that case Duds's impersonations were even more inexplicable. He tackled Roly again. "You said Major Elginbrodde went up to the house?"

"Of course he did. It was the major's house. He'd lived there as a kid. It was an old place, a kind of little stone castle. They would never have got up the rocks so quiet in the dark save that he knew the way. That's why he was chosen."

"What happened to the major's family?"

Roly looked blank. "I don't think there was but one old woman, his Granny. She went away and the Germans left the place as it was. Then the spy we was after put his lady there, but they never found the treasure. That was still there when we went, because the major went to look."

The inflection upon the operative word "treasure" was not lost upon Geoffrey. As he glanced around the ill-assorted group, each face was solemn, engrossed, avid. Treasure—it was holding them together as nothing else could have. "The sergeant described it all to you, I suppose?" he inquired.

"The Gaffer didn't say too much." Roly spoke bitterly. "But he knew it was there, and you can bet he went back for it as soon as he knew the major had met his fate."

"And he's living on it now," added Tiddy Doll. "And don't forget the souvenirs. You all had a taster, didn't you?"

There was a moment of hesitation and then Roly went over to his brother and, after a muttered conversation, came back with a package wrapped in a rag.

"Major Elginbrodde give us each a souvenir," he explained to Geoffrey. "The rest of us have had to part with ours at different times, but Tom's kept his." In complete silence he unfolded the parcel. He might have been about to display a holy relic. It was an early miniature, beautifully painted on wood: a man's head surrounded by a full wig of chestnut curls. Geoffrey could see that it was fine work and obviously genuine.

"It used to have a frame—solid gold, set with little bits of colored glass. A fellow on Walworth Road gave Tom seven pounds ten for it."

This history was cut short by a curious interruption. At the far end of the room a folded newspaper suddenly appeared through the ceiling and floated down the wall. The cellar was built a few feet out under the roadway, where there was a grating that was used as a letter box by some obliging news vendor.

"Late night final," exclaimed the dwarf cheerfully as he hurried off across the bricks to retrieve it.

"What did you say the sergeant's name was?" Geoffrey began gathering up his possessions.

"Jack Hackett," said Roly. "At least that was the Gaffer's army name. He was a man with many names, I reckon."

"You can lay bets he won't be Hackett now," put in Doll contemptuously. "He's a lord by this time. But you'll hear his history all right when we catch up with him. What was you thinking of doing, sir?"

"Doing?"

"About our little mistake."

"I shall forget it." The educated authoritative voice carried conviction. But Geoffrey realized they expected a warning from him, so he gave them one. "But if I hear of any similar incident—if you make a silly mistake again, Doll—then of course I shall consider myself free to speak. Do you understand?"

"Yes, sir." It was a smart military answer and the man drew his heels together.

Throughout this performance no one was watching the dwarf. He was sitting on a box, the late edition held close to his eyes.

His startled burst of words shook everybody. "Bloke found murdered in Pump Path. That's Duds. He's a deader."

"That's a lie." Tiddy Doll swung across the floor to him to peer at the line of print.

"You done it, Tiddy." Roly's face had become green, and he and the others huddled together, shrinking from Doll. "You done it when you went back. You said you give him something to go on with."

The albino crushed the paper in his hands. "If one of us done it, we all done it," he shouted. "That's the law." He turned savagely and pointed at Geoffrey. *Him as well.*"

Geoffrey was just too late. There were eight men between him and the stairs.

"Don't be idiots!" he cried out to them. "Don't be fools. Pull yourselves together. If this is true, you've only got one hope. A statement to the police now, at once. It's your only chance."

"That be damned!" Tiddy's roar filled the building and he bent his head for the charge.

Chapter Six

ACROSS THE CITY in St. Petersgate Square it had been one of the most unusual interrogations of Sergeant Picot's experience. But by eleven o'clock that evening he was prepared to admit that the chief inspector had known what he was doing when he let "the old parson" have his head.

As an extractor of the truth Canon Avril was remarkably efficient. He had begun with his nearest and dearest—his daughter, Meg. She had been subjected to a catechism that had not only satisfied but scandalized the sergeant. Tenants Sam Drummock and his worried wife had received the same treatment. Miss Dot Warburton, a pleasant spinster who lived in one of the cottages next door, had been shaken up. And now, after William Talisman, the verger who lived in the basement, had exhibited a somewhat spineless innocence, his wife, Mary, stood before the canon's desk and at last they were getting somewhere.

The tweed jacket in which Duds had died lay folded on the desk. The canon's spectacles were pushed up high on his broad forehead, and his eyes, naked and inexorable, looked out sternly from his kindly face. "Your husband has already told me," he was explaining, "that he saw you wrapping up this jacket in a piece of brown paper on the kitchen table about a month ago. Don't lie."

Mrs. Talisman was plump, carefully coiffured and possessed of a foolish pride, which showed in her face. "Oh, I did!" she exclaimed at last, giving up in a flood of wretchedness. "I did. I took the major's old jacket and I gave it away."

"Well, then." The canon sighed with exasperation. "To whom did you give it? Some poor fellow at the door?"

Mrs. Talisman made a helpless gesture with the palms of her hands. "I gave it to Mrs. Cash."

"Mrs. *Cash?*" The listening Picot understood that, whoever Mrs. Cash was, this was a revelation. Unless the sergeant was very much mistaken, Avril was dismayed. The old man rose and put his head out of the door. "Dot!" he shouted.

"Yes, Canon." Miss Warburton's high cheerful voice floated down the stairs from Meg's room.

"Please fetch Mrs. Cash."

"She'll be in bed, Hubert."

"Then fetch her out of it." Having settled the matter, the canon shut the door firmly. "Now, Mary," he said as he reseated himself, "think this out very carefully. Did you offer this coat to Mrs. Cash or did she ask for it?"

"I—oh, I don't know, sir."

To the sergeant's astonishment, the old man seemed prepared to accept this statement literally. "Ah, yes," he said, "I see that. Now you go and make yourself a cup of tea and sit in the kitchen and don't move until I call you. Understand?"

"Yes, sir. Yes, I do." Mrs. Talisman took out her handkerchief and wept herself out of the room.

Who is this Mrs. Cash? Picot wondered. The old boy had been taken aback when her name was mentioned. What was there between her and the canon? He'd like to see the lady, he thought.

His desire was granted almost immediately. The front door opened with a burst of Miss Warburton's cheerful noise. "*Come* along, Mrs. Cash, *come* along. *In* you go."

The study door opened next and Miss Warburton came in. "Here she is, Canon," she said. The other woman was still invisible behind her.

Avril nodded and smiled at her. "Thank you very much, Dot. Come in, Mrs. Cash."

Miss Warburton withdrew and Mrs. Cash entered. At first sight of her, every experience-sharpened wit that Picot possessed came smartly into play, yet there was nothing outstandingly peculiar about her. She was a sturdy little person near sixty, and very tidy. Her very good black coat was buttoned up to her throat and finished with a collar of very good brown fur. Above her massive face a sleek flat hat sat on thick coils of iron-gray hair. She carried a large black bag, holding it squarely on her stomach with both neatly gloved hands, and her eyes were round and bright and knowing.

"Good evening, Canon. You wanted to see me about the jacket?" Her voice was like the rest of her, bright and bold and not very nice. "I'll sit down here, shall I?" She moved the small armchair before the desk and sank into it.

The canon was on his feet, looking at her gravely across the desk. "Yes," he said. He made no apology for summoning her so late, and the watching Picot realized with a shock that these two were old enemies. "Mary tells me she gave it to you some weeks ago. Is that true?"

"Well, no, Canon. I bought it. Three pound ten of good money. Of course, I felt sure she'd had it given to her. You know me well enough for that after I've been in the second cottage six and twenty years."

The old man pressed on. "And after you bought it from Mary, what did you do with it?"

"That's my business, Canon." She was reproving but still affable. Picot guessed that her round eyes were laughing.

"Of course it is," Avril agreed. "You will recognize it, though, and that will be a great help. Come over here and look at it."

Picot moved so that he could see her face when she first caught sight of the terrible stains. As she bent forward and shook the jacket open, the appalling lapels curled stickily before her and her busy hands in their tight gloves hesitated, but her face did not change at all.

"I don't suppose that will clean," she remarked. She refolded the garment and put it back on the desk. Her voice was perfectly easy. "Yes, that's the jacket I bought from Mary."

"The police will want to know what you did with it," said Avril.

"Then I must tell them, mustn't I?" She seemed very sure of herself. "I must look it up in my little book. I think I put it in the lot I sent down to the tailor, Mr. Rosenthal, in Crumb Street." She swung around in her chair so that she came face to face with the hovering Picot. "I'm not a rich woman, but I like to do my bit for the church. I sometimes have to take a little percentage for my trouble, but that's only reasonable, because if I can't live, I can't give, can I?"

"You deal in secondhand clothes, do you, Mrs. Cash?" The sergeant thought he knew the sort of handling she needed.

Eyes quite as sophisticated as his own met him squarely. "Well, I'm not an old-clothes woman, if that's what you mean, young man," she said complacently. "You know the sort of district this is. A lot of very good houses going down, a lot of very good people going down, too. Old ladies needing money more than jewelry, and not knowing how to go about selling it. So I trot around helping. Sometimes I buy and sometimes I sell. And sometimes I have things given to me for charity, and I turn them into money and send a small check to one of the societies."

"And you put it all down in your little book," said Picot, smiling.

She echoed the smile exactly. "I put it all down in my little book."

"It's the jacket I'm interested in at the moment."

"Yes, I can see you are. Someone's had a nasty accident in it, haven't they? Well, I will help you if I can. I'll look in the book."

"I'll come with you."

"There's no reason why you shouldn't." She hoisted her big bag onto her knees. "I feel certain it went down to Mr. Rosenthal. His shop is quite near your new police station."

"Yes, I know Rosenthal." The sergeant's expression was rueful. "He keeps books, too."

"Wait." Old Avril intervened at last. "Mrs. Cash, I wonder if you'd mind going to the kitchen and asking Mrs. Talisman to come here. Stay there, if you will, for ten minutes, and then Sergeant Picot will come to get you. Will you do that?"

"Of course I will, Canon. Young man, you come and fetch me, and then we'll go to my little house together. Good night, Canon."

She rose very lightly for one of her build and trotted out. A few minutes later Mrs. Talisman crept in, drowned in tears.

"Oh, sir!"

"Did the three pound ten cover it?" Avril demanded. "Speak up, Mary. Was three pound ten all you owed her?"

"Yes, sir. On my soul, sir. It was only a pound at first, you see. They had some lovely white shirts at the stores, and Mr. Talisman is so particular about his shirts that when Mrs. Cash offered me money, I—well, I took it and bought the shirts. It was only a pound."

"The rest was interest?"

"Yes, sir. Five shillings a week. It mounted up so fast. She didn't bother me right away, but then she started coming around. I offered her several things of my own. But she wouldn't take anything except men's clothes, she said. Then she asked me if Miss Meg hadn't given me any of Mr. Martin's things, and—oh, sir!"

Avril sighed. "Run along, Mary. But don't do it again. Silly old women like you encourage wicked old women like Lucy Cash."

"Twenty-five percent per week," said Picot as the door

closed. "That's coming it a bit, even in her business. It *is* her business, I suppose, sir?"

Avril raised his sensitive chin in the air. His eyes were half shut. "For nearly thirty years I've seen Lucy Cash trotting about these streets. As the houses have grown shabbier, she has grown sleeker. As she passes down these great airy streets, window curtains tremble, blinds creep down, keys turn softly in locks. When you go to her house, look around you. You'll find it full of knickknacks, every single one of which·has been treasured by someone. They look to me like petrified morsels hacked out of living pain."

Picot shrugged his shoulders uneasily. "I suppose she does make these donations to charities from time to time, sir?"

"I'm sure she does." Avril sighed.

"Of course, it could have happened like that," said Picot. "A coat picked up secondhand. It's not likely, but I can see it's going to be very hard to prove anything different. All the same, I'll collect the old dear and see what I can find out."

He broke off and looked around. The door had opened and Miss Warburton, tiptoeing exaggeratedly, came creeping in. "A most extraordinary thing, Hubert," she said. "I thought I'd better report it at once." She seated herself on the arm of the chair vacated by Mrs. Cash. "Meg and Amanda have slipped out to the new house. Meg pretended she wanted to fetch something, but I think she just wanted to show Amanda the place. I was left in charge here. Well, a Mrs, Smith phoned in a tremendous state. After a lot of cross-purposes, it emerged that she was Mrs. Frederick Smith, the wife of Martin's solicitor on Grove Road. Her husband had been called out from a party she was giving, by the police. Apparently something terrible, something quite dreadful, has happened at his office." She took a breath and her candid eyes rested on the sergeant. "She thought Albert Campion would probably be here. She'd heard of Albert and believed he might help her, but of course he's with the police, as I told her. Then I came down to tell you two. But you were busy, so I went into the kitchen to wait, and there I found Mrs. Cash drinking tea. She told me she was waiting for you, Sergeant. I said I very much doubted if you'd be able to bother with her tonight because I expected you'd have to go straight over to the solicitors' office. Three murders in one house! They'll need every man they've got, I said."

"Murders?" Picot and the canon spoke together.

"I certainly understood Mrs. Smith to say murders. Do you know, Mrs. Cash was really upset? It's the first time I've ever seen her show any feeling whatever. She actually jumped and spilled the tea, a whole cupful, all over herself. She went running off to change, and she said if you wanted to see her, Sergeant, you must go around and knock."

"I think if you'll excuse me, sir," Picot said, "I'll go after the old woman at once. I'll take the jacket, if you please." He stepped over to the desk and began to repack the tweed jacket in the brown paper in which he had brought it.

Miss Warburton was openly disappointed. "Won't you ring up your headquarters?"

"No, miss," Picot said. "If I was wanted, I'd be sent for. Mrs. Cash's house is the second cottage, isn't it? Two doors from here on the left?"

"I shall come and show you," Miss Warburton said. "Our little houses are built right under the church wall." She hurried the sergeant out so fast that he had time only to nod to Avril and grasp his parcel.

When she returned a few minutes later, Avril was standing by the window, staring out into the square.

"Mrs. Cash has the light on in the attic, Hubert," she said. "That means she doesn't want any other visitors while the policeman is there."

"You say these things, Dot," he exclaimed. "How *can* you know?"

"Because I make it my business to," she said softly. "No one ever visits Lucy Cash when that light is on in the attic. It's a signal to certain people to keep away."

"Certain people," he mimicked her. "What people?"

"Business people, I suppose," said Miss Warburton.

The canon did not speak for a moment and his face was still hidden. Presently a shudder ran through his broad flat shoulders. "I hope you're right, Dot," he said unexpectedly. "On this occasion, do you know, I hope you're right."

Chapter Seven

IT WAS ONE OF the most pleasant things about Amanda Campion that she had never lost that outlook that regards the wildest illogicalities of human behavior as perfectly normal. Therefore when Meg proposed to drag her out at past eleven o'clock at night to inspect the partly furnished bridal house in which the power was not yet connected, it struck her as the most natural move in the world. She was relieved that it was no farther away than the other side of the square, but she would have gone out to the suburbs quite cheerfully had she been asked.

On inspection, the house proved to be a delightful place. Even when seen in the beam of flashlights held in very cold hands, it displayed enormous charm. They had come at last to the object of the exercise, Meg's own studio at the top of the house where the attic had once been. Parcels of Meg's belongings, still to be unpacked, were stacked against the walls.

Meg gave up pretending suddenly and dropped to her knees before one small wrapped bundle. "I wanted to find these and burn them," she said without looking up. "I wanted to do it at once, right away, tonight. They're Martin's letters."

"Jolly sensible of you." Amanda made Meg's purpose sound infinitely reasonable.

"That's what I thought." Meg had uncovered a battered leather case and was emptying it hastily onto a sheet of packing paper. "I haven't looked at them for years," she went on, "but tonight, when I was thinking about Geoff, and—well, needing him, I suppose—it suddenly seemed terribly important that they shouldn't stay in his—I mean our—house. Tonight the whole thing crystallized, and no one but Geoff existed anymore for me.

I can think of Martin objectively now as an ordinary person. I never could before."

As the letters spilled out on the brown paper, something hard and bright fell out with them. Meg held it to the light. "Oh, yes," she said slowly, "I suppose I ought to keep that. There was something awfully queer about it, a secret, something to do with the war."

She handed the discovery to the other woman. It was a miniature: a girl's smiling face in a golden jeweled frame, a frame worth rather more than the few pounds that the dealer on Walworth Road had given a soldier for its fellow.

"How beautiful!" Amanda shone her flashlight on the painting.

"Martin gave it to me a few weeks before he went overseas for the last time. He'd just been away for a little while on some trip he couldn't tell me about. He came in one night, tired and excited, and pulled it out of his pocket. He said it had had a companion but that he'd had to give it away. Then he told me he remembered looking at this through the glass of a cabinet when he was a child." She paused and added thoughtfully, "I've often wondered if he could have gone back to Sainte-Odile somehow when the place was occupied. That sort of incredible thing did happen during the war. It was right on the coast, almost in the sea."

"Sainte-Odile? His grandmother's house?"

"Yes. She had to clear out very quickly at the beginning of the war. She died down in Nice just before he was lost."

Amanda returned the miniature. "What happened to the house?"

"Oh, it's still there, deserted but almost intact. I had to go over and see it some time ago. Martin left a will with a firm of solicitors here on Grove Road that was full of the most specific instructions. For some reason he was terribly anxious that the *contents* of the house should come to me eventually. He didn't seem to mind about the building itself, which was being claimed by some cousin of his in East Africa, but everything inside bothered him enormously. Smithy—that's the solicitor—told me he thought there must once have been something of great value there, or at least something Martin set great store by. It was left so that I could claim everything movable, but of course the place had been pretty well ransacked by the time we got there. We held a dreary little sale, and now the house is going to pieces waiting for the cousin from East Africa."

"How sad," said Amanda. "Was it a pleasant place?"

"It may have been once." The young voice had a shiver in it. "But something horrible had happened there during the war. The locals were very discreet about it, but apparently some enemy bigwig had installed a mistress there, and one night either they killed themselves or were murdered. The place was stripped of everything interesting, let alone valuable, and there had been a fire in one room. I didn't like it, and I was awfully glad Martin never saw it that way. Anyway, I'm so pleased I came and got these letters, Amanda. I'll take them home and burn them. I know Martin would approve."

She was scrambling to her feet with the parcel in her arms when a thin hand caught her shoulder and held her still. "Wait," whispered Amanda. "Listen. Someone has just come into the house."

For a moment they held their breath. The dark house lay quiet, shrouded tightly in the damp swaddlings of the fog. The street outside was deserted.

It was the draft Amanda had noticed first. It crept up from the ground floor, chill from the outside air. The sounds came later—a swift patter of feet, a door opening cautiously, the nervous ring of metal, the squeak of a chair on the parquet.

"Geoff." Meg was whispering, but the word was happy and excited. "No one else has a key. He's got back at last and come to look for us."

"Listen." Amanda was insistent and her hand was still firm on Meg's shoulder. "This person doesn't know his way."

They waited. The sounds grew and came closer. Someone was stumbling through the ground floor with a restless, fumbling eagerness, looking for something. The sense of urgency was violent. It reached up to them through the dark, unmistakable and frightening.

"Ought we to go down?" Meg's whisper sounded breathless in the cold airless room.

"Where's the fire escape?"

"Just behind us. On this window."

"Could you get down to the next house and call the police? You mustn't make a sound or he'll hear you. Meg, could you?"

"I think so. What about you?"

"Hush. Try. See if you can."

On the ground floor a door slammed with startling noise. It was followed by utter silence. Then at last there were footsteps again in the hall, receding now, ceasing and going on again.

"Now." Amanda gave the shoulder a little push. "Shut the window after you and—not a sound."

Meg did not hesitate. She rose silently and tiptoed to the casement. The house was well built and her lightly shod feet made no sound on the boards. The window opened easily. Amanda saw her dark figure silhouetted against its pallid square of light for an instant. Then she was gone.

Amanda remained where she was, listening. There was a long silence, followed by a movement in the bedroom immediately below her. The intruder must have come up the stairs to the second floor without her hearing him. She stifled her breath and suddenly she heard him again, very close this time. He ran up the first few steps of the attic stairs outside and paused. A thin pencil of light penetrated under the closed door of the room in which she sat. It touched her foot and vanished, and there was silence.

Very slowly she rose and stood waiting. He must have decided that the top floor was unused. After a long interval she heard him down on the ground floor again.

Amanda considered the fire escape but changed her mind. It seemed a pity that the burglar should get away without being seen. She decided to go down.

The first flight of stairs seemed to promise the only difficulty, but she moved gently, feeling her way. The second-floor hall was very dark, the small circular window little more than a blur. But she remembered the design of the house and, by following the wall, came softly to the top of the graceful winding stairs to the ground floor.

He was in the little study, whose door was immediately to the right at the foot of the stairs. A trickle of fear touched her, but she ignored it resolutely. The study door was wide open, and through it candlelight, very faint and unsteady, crept out across the hall to touch the bright casing of a chest and the mirror hanging above it.

Amanda edged down the stairs until she was just above the open door. Glancing across the hall, she saw that a patch of the room was reflected in the mirror. The burglar had his back to her and was wrestling with something on the desk. She could not see it, but she guessed it was the small cabinet that Meg had earlier shown her with such pride, bewailing the fact that the key had been mislaid. The burglar appeared to be wrenching it apart. She heard the scrape and splinter of the wood. What was he opening the thing with? She was never certain if she saw the knife, if it caught the light and flashed in the mirror, or if she merely heard the blade biting into the fragile wood, but she was suddenly very cold.

With a final squeal of protest the tiny doors of the cabinet split open. In the mirror Amanda saw the man's shadow contract and then grow large, and she heard his intake of angry breath. Then the empty ruined cabinet shot through the door into the hall at her feet, and immediately, as though at a signal, the whole world became alive with noise.

The hammering on the front door was like thunder. From all sides came the sounds of feet, heavy and hurried on stone, and the unmistakable voices of policemen demanding admittance.

Close to Amanda, there was sudden and utter silence. Then the candle went out, and the stranger fled recklessly past her up the stairs. After that it was pandemonium.

Campion found his wife huddled against the wall on the bottom stair, while the thunder of police boots made traffic around her. He drew her roughly into the comparative safety of the study doorway.

"How damned silly!" he exclaimed irritably.

Amanda was very startled to see him and for the first time it occurred to her that this avalanche of official aid could hardly be the outcome of Meg's telephone call. "Oh," she said with sudden enlightenment, "he was being chased!"

"He was, my dear, and they've now got him, I should think. Oh, you are an idiot! Why didn't you come out with Meg? It was because you were in here that we had to rush him. Otherwise the police would simply have stayed outside until he walked into their arms."

"You got Meg's call, then?"

"Good heavens, no!" He was contemptuous. "We came up just as she reached the ground. Don't you understand, my dear? The moment Luke talked to the solicitor we all began to see daylight. A man was sent down to watch the rectory and another to keep an eye on this place. Their two reports came in almost simultaneously. Naturally we were half out of our minds. The fellow must have arrived just after you came in. Our man outside missed you completely."

Amanda only understood that Albert was more badly rattled than she had ever seen him. "Let's have some light," she suggested. "There are some candles on that wall."

Campion produced his lighter, and when the candles cast an elegant radiance over the wreckage of the pretty room, Amanda considered the damage. "What a shame! And also silly. There were no valuables here yet, no silver or anything."

"He wasn't looking for silver," said Campion grimly. "He was looking for papers. He didn't find them at the solicitors' office, so he came here. Hullo?"

The last word was directed to the doorway, where a drooping figure in a disgraceful old mackintosh hesitated.

"Stanis!" Amanda sounded delighted.

"My dear girl." Assistant Commissioner Stanislaus Oates, chief of Scotland Yard, came forward and shook her hand warmly. "Well, well, young woman," he said, "you've frightened us all very badly, you know." He pulled a chair out and sat down, wiping his gray forehead.

"Have they got him?" Amanda asked.

"Eh? I don't know." He smiled his wintry smile. "But even if he slips through their fingers now, it won't be long. It was you I was worrying about."

"Oh, forget her," said Campion testily. "Where's Luke?"

"Skipping about the roofs or halfway down the drain. That fellow's angry, Campion. He's been touched on the raw."

A moment later the chief inspector himself appeared, coattails flying. "Lost him," he announced. "Twenty-five men of various branches, and what happens? The bloke slides out of the bathroom window—the only one in the house that didn't have a man sitting under the sill—and leaps into the fog!"

Oates cocked an eye at him. "Did anyone see him?"

"Two uniformed men saw a shadow and went after it. But he melted. It's like looking for a flea in a featherbed."

Oates nodded. "He's got nerve and he's got quality, I grant him that."

"We underestimated him." Luke spoke grudgingly. "We just weren't thinking in his class. I don't suppose the lady happened to see him?"

Amanda shook her head regretfully. "No, only as a shadow in the mirror. My impression is that he had a round, tight sort of head. The thing I do remember is that he was so urgent—rather like you, Chief Inspector."

"That's Havoc," exclaimed Oates. "He's an extraordinarily vital animal. He's got force."

Luke hunched his shoulders. "I don't know about force," he said bitterly, "but he's leaving a trail. We're bound to get him before dawn. Meanwhile there are four people dead who ought to be alive. One of them a famous doctor, and another of them my own man, one of the best young detectives who ever lived."

"That man murdered four people tonight? You didn't tell us. Meg and I might have been killed!" Amanda shivered and glanced behind her in the shadows.

"Luke will get him soon," Oates said with certainty. "The animal is trapped. Now that the machine has gone into action, the odds against him are lengthening every hour. Nothing can save him."

Luke was breathing heavily. "But we ought to have taken him tonight. This was our best bet. He'll keep away from Mrs. Elginbrodde and her friends now, whatever he's looking for."

Amanda was astonished. "Why Meg? What is he looking for?"

"Some documents," said Campion. "Something to do with Martin. He was after Martin's file at the solicitors' office."

He made the explanation briefly, sketching in the story of Havoc's escape and the triple murder at the office. She nodded, but her next question was unfortunate. "What happened to Geoffrey?"

"You may well ask." Luke's eyes were keen. "There's another person who can vanish like smoke."

"My dear," Campion murmured, "Meg has been taken to the rectory, where there are a dozen good people anxious to comfort her. You and I are going home now. If Luke needs either of us, he knows where to find us."

"Good idea," said Amanda quickly, and she slid her arm through his.

They left the sad little house to Luke and his minions. Magers Lugg, Campion's personal servant, was waiting in a car outside. He was a large globular person, with a vast white face, small beady black eyes and a drooping mustache.

"Hop in the back," he said briefly, his moon face scowling at them through the choking gloom.

Amanda climbed into the car with relief, and Campion followed. Magers cast a baleful glance at his employer and pulled out silently into the fog.

"Now," said Amanda, "what about Geoffrey?"

"What indeed?" Campion answered. "He was certainly with

Duds Morrison the last time the man was seen alive, and they were then only a few feet from where the crook was subsequently found dead. From that moment Geoffrey Levett appears to have wandered off and lost interest. It's not good."

"But Luke doesn't really suspect Geoffrey of kicking Duds Morrison to death, or does he?"

"No. I don't think he does. But I simply can't understand Levett fading away when he ought to have gone to the police to report his meeting with Morrison. We shall have to tread very softly in this business, Amanda."

"Yes, I do see that." She echoed his seriousness. "Geoffrey must be made to go to the police, that's vital. Isn't there a chance that he may not know what has happened yet? Do you *know* that he went down the path after that man Morrison?"

"The evidence suggests that Morrison didn't run down the path alone. That young detective Coleman, who was stabbed at the solicitors' office, was interviewing the caretaker there when Havoc disturbed them. Coleman had taken down a long statement in which the old man said that he heard footsteps running down the path which skirts his garden just about the time when Duds and Geoffrey are known to have left the Feathers. He referred to 'the rush of many feet' and 'I heard a number of men.' The detective seems to have queried him but couldn't shake him." He hesitated.

"Yes?" encouraged Amanda.

"Well, the other thing is rather ridiculous. It looked very strange written down. The caretaker said he heard chains. The precise words were: 'I heard the rattle of heavy chains as the men ran past, which made me wonder.' "

"Chains," said Amanda thoughtfully. "What sounds like chains?"

Campion stiffened at her side. "Money," he said suddenly. "Coins. Coins clattering in one of those heavy wooden collecting boxes."

Through all the excitement of the day a recollection had returned to him. He saw again the perambulating group of musicians in the gutter and heard the echo of a song, urgent and ferocious.

"I say," he said softly. "It's an outside chance, but I wonder if I've got something there."

Chapter Eight

GEOFFREY LAY on the cot farthest from the stove, in acute physical misery. He had not surrendered, and his overpowering had been a grim business. His hands and feet were tied with the same cord, which was drawn up with agonizing tightness behind him.

It was in the small hours long before daylight. Tiddy Doll alone was on his feet. He was standing before the stove, peering into its red depths, and he was burning his boots. He went about the task methodically, hacking the solid leather into strips with a knife and dropping them one by one into the mouth of the iron cylinder. So far it was the only sign of fear he had shown. Doll knew that laboratory technicians employed by the police can do remarkable things with blood. They can find it on a heel, and can type it and swear to it and weave it into a rope to hang a man.

But if Doll was afraid, his fear was prudence compared with the abject quaking of the others. The cellar had become a pit of mindless terror.

In the earlier part of the night Geoffrey had had an opportunity to learn something of the company that the albino had collected about him, and he had soon realized that the bond holding them together was the shiftless dependence that had made them beggars. Roly, Tom and possibly Doll were the only exceptions, and they had no illusions about the rest. Doll had let Roly outside, taking the risk because he figured the man had more to lose in flight than to gain. The ex-fisherman had gone down the alleys into Fleet Street to pick up a morning paper and to bring back some food from the all-night fish-and-fry.

Doll continued his task steadily. He needed to get the job done before Roly came back and saw what he was about. The others did not worry him. None of them seemed to realize that he was destroying the only valid proof that he was the particular one among them who was actually guilty of murder.

Tiddy Doll had set himself to finish his boot burning by four at the latest, and he achieved it almost to the minute. He threw the last piece of leather into the stove and glanced down at his feet with satisfaction. They were lightly shod now in a pair of cracked leather shoes that he kept for his leisure hours. He reckoned he was safe.

But at ten minutes after four he began to worry. Half an hour later he was beginning to sweat, and as though his alarm had made a sound, the men heard it and grew restive. Only Roly's brother, Tom, the young soldier who had seen Martin Elginbrodde disintegrate before his eyes and had never been the same again, slept soundly.

By a few minutes before five the emotional atmosphere in the cellar had become electric.

"He's gone. You won't see Roly no more. He's left you, Tiddy." Bill, the ex-soldier to whom fear was an excitant, spoke with glee from the shadows. "He'll turn King's Evidence, you'll see."

Doll turned on him, the muscles of his neck swelling. "There's many a ruddy fool thought of that, Bill, and made the last mistake of their lives. Them as trusts in the police gets all that's coming to 'em."

"When's the grub coming?" complained the dwarf with nerve-racking abruptness.

"Shut up!" the albino roared. "Listen, can't you?"

A step sounded in the passage above. "There," Tiddy Doll said, his voice hearty with relief, "what did I tell you? Here's Roly. What happened to you, mate? Got lost?"

Roly did not reply immediately. He was descending the stairs very steadily, a large grease-soaked newspaper parcel in his arms. Doll met him as he reached the ground.

"Spirits!" he exploded. "You've been drinking spirits at the all-night boozer. Who've you been gassing to, eh? Who've you been squealing to?" He had taken the man by the shirt collar and was shaking him.

"Stop it," Roly said briefly. "I just had one to steady my nerves. I got something to show you, Tiddy." His sharp-featured face was eager with news.

"Save it," Doll commanded, and maintained his superiority. "Give us the grub first." He took the parcel and set it on the table beside a pile of clean paper.

While he was superintending the division of the warm fish, Roly slid over toward Bill. The whole company scrambled to get near him. Tiddy Doll reached the center of the group a second too late. The headlines in the morning paper streamed out across the page:

KILLER ROAMING LONDON FOG

FAMOUS DOCTOR STRANGLED

THREE FOUND DEAD IN SOLICITORS' OFFICE

Police Cordon Thwarted as Convict Patient Escapes

Doll stared at the paper, then snatched it and strode out under the light with it. He read out each word with equal emphasis, moving his head with the type. " 'At a late hour last night the picked men of London's crack Criminal Investigation Department had to confess that an escaped convict, who is possibly one of the most dangerous criminals this country has ever known, was ranging the fog-bound streets of their city, possibly with a still crimson knife in his hand. Meanwhile, in a solicitors' office in the western area, three innocent people, one of them a detective officer, lay murdered, each, so say experts, butchered with professional skill with an identical weapon. Earlier in the evening, on the other side of the metropolis, the well-loved physician Sir Conrad Belfry, whom men called the Kind Healer, lost his life. . . .' "

"Tiddy. Look down. See the pictures?" It was Bill who

pointed out the two photographs from the police files. "This is the man the police are seeking," ran the legend above the photos, "Jack Havoc, age 33."

Roly began to chatter in his excitement. "That's him, Tiddy! That's the Gaffer. He's changed his name from Hackett."

"The Gaffer!" Tiddy Doll said, aghast.

"That's right," Roly said. "He's been inside, in prison, like Duds told us, but he got out and done the murders."

The news sank in very slowly, but it got home at last and the revelation had the paradoxical effect of raising the morale of all the party. Roly reached the heart of the matter with his next remark.

"There's only a couple lines about Duds. They don't care about Duds no more. They've got the Gaffer to think about. The streets are full of coppers, but they ain't looking for us. We're almost in the clear."

"Perhaps the dicks think the Gaffer done Duds as well as the others," said Bill.

"And perhaps they're right," Tiddy Doll said loudly. "So the Gaffer's been in jail all the time. He didn't get no treasure."

"No, he didn't get it." Bill was thoughtful. "It says here he done five years of a maximum sentence for robbery with violence. That means he must have got nabbed when we thought he deserted."

The albino made a sudden decision. "I say that ain't the Gaffer at all," he declared. "I say the Gaffer has picked up the treasure and he's living on it like a lord, and one day we'll come across him. As it is, there's this other chap in the paper who must have done poor old Duds in after we left him, so the best we can do is to go on like we always have, taking our money and keeping our eyes open."

As he finished, the snag in this happy program occurred to him and he glanced over his shoulder toward the bundle on the bed in the corner. "There's no telling what a bloke like this here bloke in the papers might do still," he said under his breath.

At that moment there was a diversion. From where Geoffrey

lay he could look up and see something happening to the grating through which the news vendor had thrust the evening paper. The iron had been lifted quietly, and through the dark square a pair of legs in well-pressed trousers had appeared. Suede shoes accompanied them, and above there was the suggestion of an expensive tweed jacket.

Everyone in the group around the paper became aware of the intrusion at the same instant. The circle of upturned faces froze in their astonishment. Then the iron grate dropped back into place, the legs kicked out and a man swung lightly to the ground before them. Every man in the cellar saw the tragic face, the forehead, the coarse hair and the steady eyes regarding them boldly as he looked around for men he knew.

"Dad's back," he said, and his voice was smooth and careful. Only the shadow flitting like a frown across his forehead, and his pallor, which was paperlike, betrayed his weariness. His spirit danced behind his shallow eyes, mocking everything.

The silence in the cellar was absolute. No one breathed. Helpless in his far corner, Geoffrey was aware of the tension but by no means clear on the true cause of it. He had not seen the paper and had not been able to catch much of Roly's story. He lifted his head painfully in an effort to see the newcomer, but he was careful to make no sound.

Inside the circle the stranger was dusting himself off. He was just under six feet, with long bones and sloping shoulders, most of his phenomenal strength in his neck and in the thigh muscles that moved visibly under his sleek prewar clothes. His beauty, and he possessed a great deal, lay in his hands and face and in the narrow neatness of his feet.

His hands were like a conjurer's, large, masculine and shapely, the bones very apparent under the thin skin. His face was conventionally handsome, the nose straight and short, the chin round and cleft. His eyes were a deep blue, with very long thick lashes. As much as could be seen of the brown hair under his black beret betrayed an obstinate curl despite the prison cut, and jail pallor could not destroy the fineness of his skin.

He was a magnetic man who must have been a pretty youth, yet his face could never have been pleasant to look at. Grief and torture and the furies were all there naked, and the eye was repelled even while it was violently attracted. He looked exactly what he was—unsafe. He nodded to the three men he recognized. "Hullo, Roly, hullo, Bill, hullo, Tom. Mind if I sit down?"

He dropped onto the box at the head of the table, where Doll usually sat, and, with a grin at the dwarf, took a fried potato from the little man's sheet of paper and ate it. "Duds been in yet?"

The inquiry was casual, but to his hearers the words had a superstitious horror. With a warning glance at Roly, Doll began to edge backward toward Geoffrey, while the ex-fisherman burst into nervous disclaimers.

"No, he ain't. Duds don't come here, Gaffer."

Havoc stretched out his long fingers for another potato. "I didn't know that. He let me have the word on you, of course. That's how I knew where to look you up, actually." He paused. "I've not seen him yet. I've been on the run."

The step behind him was light, but he turned so quickly that they all scattered, and Bill, who had been sidling toward him, squealed as he sprang back.

Havoc laughed in his face. "Bill, you old iron, don't do that," he said. "I've been under a doctor for my nerves for so long I've begun to believe in them myself. You don't know."

"But we do know, Gaffer. We do know. That's what I'm trying to tell you. We were all reading this when you came in." Bill laid the limp wreck of the morning paper on the table.

The sight of it already in their hands was a shock to the newcomer. His magnetism faltered for a moment, like a current switched off and on. Then he bent forward to take a handful of potatoes and dropped them on the headlines contemptuously. "That?" He looked around him. "I've been reading that myself."

"Did you read it all, Gaffer?" Bill asked. "You ought to, because there's a bit about old Duds in it. He's dead. He's been done in. It says so."

"Duds?" Again there was the same strange sensation of shock

and faltering power, more marked this time. He read the paper.

In the far corner, where he had been bending over Geoffrey, Tiddy Doll noticed the reaction. A strong self-preservative sense kept Geoffrey quiet while Doll swiftly applied a new piece of adhesive plaster to seal the prisoner's mouth.

"When did you see Duds last?" Havoc asked.

Tiddy Doll spun around. "We seen him this afternoon. He come out of the station in Crumb Street and we followed him, but he give us the slip. That's right, ain't it, mates?"

The lie came out glibly. It was the old leader reasserting himself, and they responded at once, relieved at the proffered escape.

"That's right, Gaffer," Roly affirmed. "We seen him once in the West End, but we ain't *never* spoken to him."

"He saw you more often than that." Havoc's weariness was beginning to show, but he had great reserves. "Duds was busy—working for me, as a matter of fact. I got the news from him—indirectly, of course—but I heard all about Tiddy Doll here and Tom's bit of trouble. And you've all been looking for me, I hear." The small regular teeth showed in a smile. " 'Living like a lord.' "

"Who gave us away?" Tiddy Doll's bewilderment was destroying his caution.

The man who sat in his place at the head of the table considered him thoughtfully. "Your name is Doll and you come from a country town in Suffolk called Tiddington," he remarked pleasantly. "After being rejected on medical grounds by every regimental depot, you attached yourself in the middle of the war to the transit camp at Hintlesham as temporary unpaid hanger-on. After some time your willingness, cleanliness and talent for organization got you into the company and you even got a stripe. Do you want to hear any more?"

Doll could not speak. He stood gaping.

Havoc turned his head away and returned to the others. "You silly fools," he said, "stomping up and down the streets making a God-awful row. Do you think no one sees you? Every bloke in the town knows everything there is to know about you. You're no mystery."

The company was startled but Roly was impressed. His thin face was flushed and he looked younger, more the soldier he once had been. "You ain't really forgot us, then, Gaffer?" he said proudly. "We thought you had, me and Bill and Tom. Tom's very funny," he added confidentially. "I don't reckon he knows you."

The tall boy, who was still lying on his bed, raised his head. "I ain't forgot him," he said. "I know you, Gaffer. I know the state you're in. You're like you were that night when you came back to the boat—you know, after you'd done them that time."

The directness of the statement and its simple implication brought the whole terrifying situation into key. Havoc glanced down at the newspaper headlines, still visible through the potato grease.

Doll grasped his chance. He sat down at the table and put his elbows on it. "Lister, Gaffer," he said, "I reckon you didn't come here to find Duds at all. I reckon you came here because you figured we wouldn't see the paper until morning, and you wanted a quiet lie-down. You've come here because you ain't got nowhere else to go."

The broadside was annihilating and the ring of truth in it clear. Slowly and gracefully Havoc leaned back in his chair. No one saw any other movement, but as their glances traveled down from his face to the table, they saw that a knife had appeared in his hand as if by magic.

"So what?" he said softly.

This time there was no faltering. All trace of weariness was gone. No one stirred an eyelid.

"Perhaps you'd like me to give you a demonstration?"

"No, Gaffer, no, no!" Roly was frantic. "No, we've seen your demonstrations. Put it up. Tiddy don't understand. We're with you, Gaffer. Besides, we've got reasons of our own to think of."

The fatal admission was out before he could stop it. Havoc's flat blue eyes came to rest on him. "Oh? What reasons?"

Roly appealed helplessly to Tiddy Doll, expressionless behind his dark glasses. The albino sat solid and still. "We've got private affairs, like other people," Doll said at last. "We don't want the police around here just now, not on any account. Just lately we had a little accident, so we ain't doing nothing out of the ordinary, not for a week or two." He hesitated and no one knew if his red eyes behind the dark glasses were peering at the weapon on the table. "We're keeping quiet and keeping to ourselves."

Havoc glanced around him with casual arrogance. "They told me that you were clean in your habits, and I hand it to you, Corporal. I don't know how you do it."

This inconsequential piece of flattery was an inspiration.

"The Queen could eat off the floor," Doll said with enthusiasm. "We got our rules. We got comfort too, and good grub."

The tired hagridden tiger in the good clothes allowed his glance to stray toward an empty cot next to Tom, but he remained a tiger. Doll was feeling his way.

"But I'm not saying we're all quite so strong upstairs." He tapped his forehead significantly. "You can see for yourself, Gaffer, there's plenty of us to make mistakes."

There were noises from the market above now, if no actual daylight. The city was awake and stretching itself.

Doll looked at the table. The knife was gone. The Gaffer's hands were resting there, his fingers drumming very lightly on the board. Doll took a long breath. "I was thinking, Gaffer, there's enough of us for a bloke to hide among, even in the street, supposing he wanted to get from place to place."

"Your mind works." Havoc was condescending but friendly. "I like that."

There was no more bargaining. Both men were feeling the strain, and each understood the other remarkably well.

Havoc stretched himself, and when he spoke, it was in conscious imitation of the British junior officer in the field. "I rather think we should have a conference, Corporal, don't you?"

Tiddy Doll sighed and played his master stroke. "Pick your officers, Captain," he said.

Chapter Nine

AT FIRST GEOFFREY was the only person to notice Tiddy Doll's peculiar maneuver with the conference table. The albino arranged some orange crates with a great deal of care, so close to the prisoner's bed that the gagged and helpless man would be able to overhear the talk perfectly. It was such an extraordinary mistake that Geoffrey was astounded until the explanation occurred to him. Doll might have qualms at removing an unwanted witness in cold blood, but Havoc would have none.

The newcomer still sat at the head of the main table in a pool of light from the single swinging bulb. From the way they were all treating him he might have been a genuine wild animal sitting up there, fascinating and uncertain.

He watched the fussy preparations with growing annoyance and, as usual, it was Roly who precipitated matters. Having noticed what he thought was a serious mistake, he made frantic signals. Havoc caught him and at once the whole interest of the gathering was centered on the bed in the far corner.

"What have you got over there, Corporal?" The languor in the careful voice deceived no one. Doll was ready for it.

"That's our bit of private trouble, Gaffer," he said, lowering his voice to a murmur. He made a subservient gesture, bent over the bed to pull the blanket higher to cover Geoffrey's face, and then bustled the full length of the room. "Our little accident I was telling you about. He's spark out, only just breathing. Been like that two days and a night now."

The lie brought tremendous comfort to the two men lurking in the background because it seemed to put them in the clear with the Gaffer. The admiration of Roly and Bill for Doll became almost affectionate. "That's right," said Roly.

Doll shrugged. "Anyway, he's harmless, Gaffer."

"Who is he? One of you?" Havoc sounded as if he were being forced to listen to the troubles of children.

Tiddy Doll hesitated. "No," he said finally. "He's a fellow

who was brought down here when he was blind drunk. He had a bit of money on him. We shook him up, and there he is. We didn't know if he'd been missed."

"So that's why one of you went out early to get a paper?"

"That's it, Gaffer. That's how we come to see your picture. It gives you the creeps, don't it, how it all fits in?"

The flat blue eyes rested on him darkly. Then Havoc got up and swaggered across the room.

In the darkness under the blanket Geoffrey lay still. He had no idea what was going to happen to him. One thing he did know was that he was helpless. His feet and hands had been numb for some time, and the gag was nauseating. But he could breathe, for the blanket, although covering his head, was carefully loose about him.

They ignored him and sat down, Havoc with his back to the bed, the albino on his right, and Roly and Bill on his left.

Tiddy Doll's voice sounded in the prisoner's ear, it was so close. "There'll be no trouble with our lot, Gaffer, if they're handled right."

Havoc made an impatient noise and Roly intervened nervously. "You can't tell the Gaffer nothing about men, Tiddy. He could always size a bloke up. That's what we noticed in the Army."

"That's what I was coming to." Tiddy took over firmly. "The Gaffer's a judge of men, you say. Well, then, he'll know I'm right. We all know too much about this treasure no one has spoke out about yet. We've been thinking of it, dreaming of it, for years. The Gaffer has shown he knows we know. 'Living like a lord,' he said. Well, that's what we all want to live like." He made a sudden movement. "We've got to be in on it, Gaffer."

"But I always meant that you should." Havoc was graceful even when giving ground. "You can take the place of Duds, Corporal. I always felt that the men who were there ought to share. The rest—"

"I ain't thinking about the rest," said Doll, keeping his voice down. "They'll do what I say, and I'll look after them same as I always do. They'll live like lords' pals," he added sardonically.

"So I imagine." The faint drawl was amused. "I let Roly into this thing long ago. He and Bill and Tom were with me, serving under me. I chose them."

"That's right, Gaffer. You was never one to let your mates down." Roly spoke with hearty sententiousness and was unprepared for the reaction, which was instant.

"Cut that." There was an alarmed note in the outburst. "I chose you because I needed you. I need you again, so I choose you again. I face things. I know if it didn't suit you to be trusted, I couldn't trust you. That's how I've got on, see?"

"That's sense," Doll said cautiously. "As long as it's worth my while to go along with you, I'll go along. That's me, Gaffer. That's fair."

"It's the living truth," said Havoc. "You can forget the fairness."

"Did you see the stuff, Gaffer?" Despite himself, Roly could not keep quiet. "You never said. Did you see the treasure?"

Havoc clicked his tongue against his teeth. "No, of course I didn't see it. It was well hidden. That's why it's still there waiting for us, if we can pick it up quickly. Listen, this is what happened on the raid. After we'd done the job, we were alone, Elginbrodde and me, in the house. The orders were that I was to do the necessary and he was to verify they were dead. He didn't like it, he wasn't that sort. He wasn't yellow, but he hadn't got what I have and he wasn't expected to have. He got me into the house, and I went to the bedroom and did the job while he waited. When I came out, he went in. He came back white, but quiet, as he always was, and gave me the okay. We had one or two other things to do, and when they were done, instructions were that we were to come out at once and get back to you on the beach before anyone came up the road. When we reached the little garden behind the house, he stopped me."

As he listened, Geoffrey caught the stillness of the spring night, the noise of the sea, soothing and forever, and behind, the two in the bedroom, still warm, the dreadful necessary thing.

Havoc was still talking. "Elginbrodde said to me, 'Keep a lookout a minute, will you, Sergeant? I just want to have a squint at something to see it's still all right.' He left me standing there, but presently I saw he had gone into a sort of stone hut by the garden wall. I went after him because I didn't want to miss anything. There he was, moving a little flashlight over the stone. The place was empty as a poor box. He told me afterward it was an icehouse. There was a drain running through it, and a garden statue at one end of that. There was nothing else, so I said, 'They got it, sir, did they?' He laughed and he said, 'No, it's safe. They'll never find it now unless there's a direct hit, and then it'll hardly matter.'"

"But he brought out some of the treasure." Roly's anxiety was pathetic. "He give us all a souvenir. Don't you remember, Gaffer?"

"That stuff was from the house." The voice was soothing. "We had to make the Germans think it was a burglary, not enemy action. The place was full of lovely stuff, so I knew that if there was something hidden, it must be damned well worth hiding. I said, 'What have you got in the icehouse, sir? The family plate?' 'No, Sergeant,' he said, 'that's the Santa Deal treasure there, and it's still all right. I didn't know about it until I was twenty-one, or I'd have got it out of the country. But then it was too late for that, so I had to hide it. I'm the last of the family. No one knows now but me.' I did my best to make him repeat the name, but he wouldn't. It sounded like a ship's treasure to me."

The secret of a ship's treasure handed down in a wealthy family to an orphan boy at twenty-one electrified the men around the table. Roly and Bill were past speech and Doll's mouth was dry. Havoc's murmur, forceful with the weight of years of dreaming, held his listeners spellbound.

"Then I asked him what was going to happen to it if he got hit. 'In that case it stays there forever, I suppose?' I said."

"What did he say?" Roly was trembling.

"He said the damnedest thing. He said, 'Then it'll be up to the man my wife marries. I've left full instructions in a sealed envelope, and he'll get it on his wedding day. She couldn't manage it alone, but she'll choose someone like me, always.' "

Lying on the sacks, his head not three feet from the speaker, Geoffrey felt his heart turn over slowly and painfully. He heard an incredulous rumble from the others, but he had recognized the unmistakable ring of truth in the reported words. Of course that was what Elginbrodde had done. It was exactly the bold, simple, but unobvious step that in similar circumstances he would have taken himself. Elginbrodde had been so right. They *were* alike: practical but imaginative, conventional but ready to take a chance. All the jealousy Geoffrey had ever felt for Martin died outright like an exhausted flame. He felt freed of it suddenly, as Meg became, mysteriously, entirely his own.

Meanwhile, his immediate danger was becoming more acute. Havoc was growing practical. "Now," he was saying, "the first thing to do is to get the envelope Elginbrodde left. That's vital. The raid was a top secret job. None of us knew where we went, except Elginbrodde. We thought it was France, but it might have been anywhere along the whole west coast of Europe. We've got to have the exact location of the house. There'll be legal documents, too, papers giving the bearer permission to take the stuff away. Elginbrodde will have thought of that."

Tiddy Doll sat motionless, his chin raised, the dark glasses hiding any expression in his eyes. "Who'd Major Elginbrodde give the letter to?" he said at last. "His wife?"

"No. She'd open it. Any woman would. I didn't worry about that. I was certain that he'd left it with his solicitors."

It was the first time the word had been mentioned and at once the atmosphere became tense. Doll wet his lips. "You went to their office tonight to see, didn't you?"

"Yes. As soon as I'd seen a contact of mine and changed my clothes, I went down there." Havoc paused and in the respite Tiddy Doll did a terrifying thing. He slid out a foot and kicked the bed on which Geoffrey lay. He did it very stealthily, but it was a definite movement guaranteed to call the occupant's attention to anything about to be said.

"That's where you went on the bash, ain't it, Gaffer?" Doll prompted gently.

"Yes."

After a long silence Doll asked, "What makes you so certain the treasure's still there after all this time, Gaffer?"

"Because it's waiting for me." The conviction in the tone was absolute and it impressed them. "I'm meant to find it. I knew that as soon as I heard of it that night. I was chosen for that mission because I was special, see? They needed someone who was athletic, combat-trained, reckless, able to climb and not particular. I was under guard waiting for court-martial. They fetched me out, restored my rank and paired me with Elginbrodde. While I was training with him, I found he was a man I could always keep my eye on. I knew someone who was close to him, see? That's why I knew that what he said was important to me and part of my life. Call it the science of luck, that's my name for it. There's only two rules in it: Watch all the time, and never do the soft thing. I've stuck to that and it's given me power."

"That's right, Gaffer, you've got power all right." Doll spoke hurriedly. He knew men were often a little strange when they came out after a long prison term, but he was frightened all the same. "You've been able to watch Elginbrodde's wife while you was inside?"

"Of course I have. I've watched you all. You can hear more in stir than you can out, if you give your mind to it. I knew she was going to marry again before the engagement was announced."

"Marry again?" This was news to them all, and Roly sat back, ludicrous horror on his sharp-featured face. "You're not tellin' us she's done it? The new bloke ain't got the envelope?"

"No. He doesn't know about it yet, but he will, and that's the hurry. When I got the news, I couldn't make my break immediately. So I got the word out to Duds, and he's been doing the stunt that we arranged if ever this should happen while I was inside. It was a beautiful idea and it was working like a dream. My contact expected the wedding would be called off. But now

Duds has come unstuck. Perhaps the girl's new bloke got him."

As Geoffrey waited for the next words, the stabbing pain of fear took his breath away. One of the three *must* put two and two together now.

But when Doll spoke, his mind was still on the envelope. "And it weren't at the solicitors'?" he said thoughtfully.

"No. I made sure of that." Havoc sounded introspective. "I shall get it, though," he said. "I tried one other place tonight. It was an address my contact had given me when I got out. I went to the new bloke's house, the one he's getting ready to take the girl to when he marries her. It was no good, though. They hadn't moved in properly. There weren't any papers in the place at all." He laughed abruptly. "I nearly walked into trouble there and I had to jump for it. There was someone in the house. A woman. I smelled her face powder."

Geoffrey's scalp was crawling and his lips moved helplessly against the gag.

"She couldn't have seen me," Havoc was saying. "She was out on the stairs when I was in one of the rooms. I didn't waste any time on her. It wasn't because I went soft. The police cars had turned up by the time I noticed her, and I had to slip off."

"It must've been her," Roly said. "It must have been the major's widow."

"What?" The question sounded appalled.

"It must have been the major's widow," Roly repeated. "If only you'd bashed her, we'd have had all the time in the world."

"But I didn't know, I tell you." Havoc's voice was high.

Tiddy was wagging his head. "That ain't sense, Gaffer, and you know it. You knifed three people at the solicitors' tonight just because they'd seen and might recognize you. You ain't gone soft, you've gone wild." His tone was smug and mocking. He was trying to make the man angry, prodding him. They were all aware of it, but only the prisoner, helpless behind him, realized its purpose. "As you've started, so you'll have to go on."

"Tiddy!" Roly could bear the strain no longer. "You've gone out of your mind, mate!"

"But he's dead right." The voice was no longer smooth. "I ought to have seen to the woman in Levett's new house, whoever she was. I—"

"Whose house?" Tiddy Doll forgot every other consideration as the name hit him in the face. "Whose did you say?"

"Geoffrey Levett's." Havoc's suspicion flared and he swung around. "Levett. He's the new bloke. He's the one the envelope is to go to. Why? Speak up, Corporal. Why? Have you ever heard that name before?"

MEANWHILE, JUST above in the street market, the morning fog was thicker than ever. Twenty-four hours of city vapors had given it body and bouquet, and its chill was spiteful.

Inside a shop, the owner, a stout, irritable woman, spoke her mind to two men who had just confronted her with a polite request. "But we've *been* measured," she protested. "We was done last week. I don't care if you're the government, we've *been* measured for the rates. If they go up again, I can't pay them."

The taller of her two visitors, a thin, mild-looking person who had changed his horn-rims for Health Service-issue spectacles for the occasion, regarded her anxiously. Albert Campion's position was delicate. He had been forced into making the inquiry without police aid, since he was still half convinced that Levett was engaged in some misguided business of his own. This had involved getting the band's address from some very unofficial quarters, and now that at last he had it, it proved to be unspecific. He had understood that the entrance to the cellar was through the back of the shop. He was regretting that he had chosen to introduce himself as a surveyor from the rating authority, but his chief worry was a premonition that urgency was vitally important.

He glanced at his companion, and Magers Lugg, impressively immense in raincoat and derby, took it for an invitation to assist. He thrust a sheaf of old income-tax forms at the lady. "You're goin' to be helpful, my dear," he said.

"Go on and measure, then," the woman grumbled.

Campion coughed. "It's the cellar, ma'am," he began in a confidential tone. "Our people forgot to enter the measurements of the cellar. That's why we've had to come back."

"No, I won't give you the key. It's not my place to. My tenants leave their key with me when they go out to work. There it is, hanging on the wall. You touch it and I'll call the cops!" She paused blankly and they all stood looking at a large and naked nail sticking out of the wall. "It's gone!" she exclaimed. "Who's took it? Police!" she shouted at the top of her voice.

To her intense embarrassment a constable heard her. He was standing immediately outside the shop, his smooth blue back not a yard away. He turned at once and stepped inside.

"Now then, what's going on here?"

The shopkeeper's anger vanished and she became reasonable, if overanxious to justify herself. Her explanations were voluble but perfectly clear.

When she had done, the constable glanced from the officials to the nail. "What gives you the idea the key's lost at all?" he inquired placidly. "Are they out yet? I've not seen them go by."

This was altogether too much of an anticlimax. The woman's hand flew to her heart with the easy histrionics of her kind. "And it's past nine! Oh, Officer, that stove! I've warned them time and again. I saw a bit in the paper once. A whole family dead in the morning, suffocated from a coke stove just like that."

"Don't say that, don't," the constable protested. "They're much more likely having a lay-in. I don't blame them on a morning like this."

Mr. Campion saw his chance. "All the same," he said firmly, "I think you'd be justified in looking, Officer." He added in the confidential whisper of one servant of the state to another, "I'd just like to run a tape over the place if I could."

The constable hesitated. "I can't admit you, you know that," he muttered to Campion, "but if you was to follow me, I don't suppose I should stop you."

He turned on his heel and Campion and Lugg followed him.

DOWN IN THE CELLAR Tiddy Doll had just thrust back his box and clattered to his feet.

Havoc was leaning toward him, his strange eyes dark with eagerness. "Have you? Have you heard the name before?"

Doll was speechless, but his mind was working. The staggering success of his plan was overwhelming. The awkward witness to Dud's murder was as good as dead already. But there was one little difficulty to be overcome first. If the Gaffer should decide to talk to Geoffrey Levett before he settled him—and he very well might in the circumstances—the dangerous subject of who killed Duds was certain to arise.

He was still standing there, hesitating, feeling for the safest lie, when the door at the top of the stairs swung slowly open and every man in the cellar save one sprang to his feet and stared upward.

A policeman in uniform and two officials in regulation raincoats stood at the top of the steps. They made no attempt to descend, but simply stood there looking down.

In the first frozen second Tiddy Doll felt his arms being gripped from behind by hands whose strength was a revelation to him. He was moved bodily and set squarely between Havoc and the newcomers. He was being used as a shield.

Then he kept his head and rose to the occasion. "Hullo?" his voice rang out, clear and belligerent. "What d'you want? We're all at home."

He might have got away with it—the constable was already muttering an apology—but the band did not have their leader's mettle. When the first moment of stupefaction passed, the whole feckless rabble surged forward into the body of the room.

The albino began to roar at his people, forcing his authority upon them. "Form up! Line up, can't you? There's no need to panic because you've overslept. The grub will still be there. Got your music? I can't wait all day. Look alive."

The dwarf scuttered past him, shouting shrilly in his excitement. Doll caught the little man by the back of his clothes, lifted him bodily from the ground and thrust him behind to Havoc.

"Here, you carry him across your shoulders, mate," he said.

The long hands seized him and the little man was swung up into his favorite position high above the heads of his persecutors. Doll could have offered his leader no better disguise, for naturally all eyes turned on the mannikin rather than on his steed.

Doll strode forward and looked up the stairs, his dark glasses peering blankly at the intruders. "We're just going out to have a bit of breakfast," he announced. "Any objections?"

The constable waved him up and retreated back into the fog himself. Campion and Lugg remained at the top of the stairs, however.

Doll did not like the look of them at all. "We're coming up if you *don't* mind," he shouted warningly.

At his words, the band pressed around and past him up the stairs and out into the passage. Doll came hurrying up last of all. He had no time to listen to the intruders. At the first word, when he discovered they were not plainclothesmen, his interest in them vanished abruptly. The Gaffer was too far ahead as it was. He could just see the dwarf silhouetted against a murky square of light that was the open doorway to the street. If he lost him now, he lost him forever, and everything else besides. He sped out into the fog after the band.

"Blimey!" Lugg said. "What d'you know about that?"

"Not enough." Campion was already descending the stairs. "I don't care for it at all, do you?"

Lugg caught up with him as he reached the ground. Then Campion moved down the line of beds, stripping any suspicious-looking humps among the blankets. He worked with the peculiar thoroughness of one who is afraid of what he may find, but in spite of his care he might have missed the cot in the far corner. The "conference table" had been left in a disorder that hid the bundle swaddled in its dark blanket, and one box had been thrown on top of it by the resourceful Roly.

Having peered into the recess under the stairs, Campion lifted his head. "Geoff!" he called aloud on impulse. "Geoff, where are you?"

The two stood listening, and then they heard it—a stifled snort from the corner. Slowly, as the man on the bed heaved himself with an effort that tore his cramped muscles, the box on top of him wobbled, and toppled onto the bricks.

Chapter Ten

WHEN CAMPION telephoned Meg from the Crumb Street police station, where Geoffrey had been taken to make his statement, she went there at once. Just before four, she rang the rectory back and Sam Drummock took the call.

"Right," he said at intervals. "Don't you worry. Leave it to Sam. . . . The lad's all right, though, is he? That's all that matters. . . . Thank God for that. . . . Good-by, love."

He hung up and, wriggling back onto his chair, pushed his glasses up on his forehead. He had a lot to do. He saw that. He got up and went over to the fireplace. Above the tiled grate there was a glass-and-mahogany mantelpiece whose natural somberness was enlivened by a festoon of invitation cards, press clippings and letters. He surveyed these doubtfully for a time, then fetched a chair, mounted on it and peered over the top of the collection. As he knew perfectly well, there was a considerable space between the wood and the wall. He rubbed the heads of the screws that kept the whole contraption in place.

THE MURDER STORY, which had excited Londoners at breakfast, had shocked and startled them by noon, when they had digested it. For obvious reasons, the police had not released Geoffrey's story, and to the ordinary Londoner the affair remained a manhunt for an escaped convict gone berserk in the mist. It was very unnerving.

At the end of the second day, the fog had become thicker and dirtier and more exasperating than any in living memory. In the streets passersby walked quickly, hugging the lights. Children were hurried home from school, and the outgoing suburban trains were crowded from four o'clock on.

The Crumb Street station remained the headquarters of the investigation, but backing it up was the whole beautiful mechanism of detection at Scotland Yard. The police were keeping the St. Petersgate Square angle dark, and so far no one from the newspapers had discovered the inner story behind the prison escape. The quiet square remained deserted, therefore.

Inside the rectory the atmosphere was curious. Old Avril's home was a place so loved and comfortable that violence in any form was apt to seem incredible when viewed from its quiet precincts. Now, however, it had come too close to be discounted, and the whole house had developed a startled and piteous appearance, as Amanda summed it up.

She and Meg were sitting on the rug before the fire in Meg's living room, leaning as close as they dared to the comforting blaze, and Campion stood beside them, one lean elbow on the mantelpiece. Meg shook her long yellow silk hair away from her face and appealed to them openly. "The whole thing seems utterly insane to me. A man in prison scheming to get another to impersonate poor Martin, to prevent me from marrying Geoff. And then, because it didn't work, breaking out and doing all these frightful things. He's a maniac."

"I don't think he's mad," said Amanda. "He just wants the treasure. That may be wrong, but it's not insane."

"But, Amanda, there can't *be* any treasure." Meg sounded helpless. "The family had been wealthy, but they lost it all in the First World War. Don't you see, this murderer is making a fearful mistake? Martin must have said something to him which he completely misunderstood. He's been brooding on it all these years, and now he's raging about the place like a man-eating tiger, killing recklessly and all for nothing." Her pretty voice quavered and she rose impulsively. "I'm rattling away. Forgive me. I think I'll go and see how Geoff's getting on."

As the door closed behind Meg, Campion said to his wife, "I should like to wrap you in cotton wool and send you down to the country tonight. Do you mind?"

Amanda's calm brown eyes flickered up at him. "Scared?"

"A little. Luke isn't happy. Geoff says Havoc has an outside contact on whom he relies, though he doesn't admit that he overheard anything which could connect him with this house."

Amanda frowned and her lips formed the question: "Who?"

Campion shook his head. "God knows. I can't see it myself. There's no odor of anything but sanctity about this family. All the same, let me send you home, old lady."

"Are you staying?"

"Yes, I think I'll stick around."

"Then that settles that. I'll stay with you. And now I'll see if I can fetch us something to eat."

Left alone, Campion felt that the room had grown darker. He sat down by the fire and felt for a cigarette. He did not like the situation. Havoc and Doll and the three men who had been on the original raid had vanished too completely. The rest of the band were being brought in one after the other. They were pathetic figures, most of them, unable to help and frightened to try. But the ringleaders were gone, as though the earth had swallowed them, and they were tricky quarry: five experienced men driven by a dream and led by something mercifully unusual in the humdrum history of crime.

For Oates had been right. Havoc was that rarity, a genuinely wicked man. He was no lunatic, but a much more scarce and dangerous beast, the rogue that every herd throws up from time to time. The last message Luke had given him stuck in Campion's mind. The dwarf had been fished out of the Thames just before dusk, too late to save his life.

Campion's thoughts were interrupted by the sudden arrival of Geoffrey, who looked somewhat bizarre in an undersized gaudy dressing gown loaned to him by Sam. He still bore traces of his rough treatment, but his strong body was taut under the silk and his jaw stuck out belligerently. A less shrewd observer might have thought him angry, but Campion diagnosed an unusual emotional experience and Geoff's first words proved him right.

"So there you are," he said with relief. "Look, this is the damnedest thing. What do you know about this?" His eyes were hard and dark and his hand shook a little as he drew two folded sheets from the pocket of his robe and held them out to Campion. "It's a letter from Martin Elginbrodde."

Campion sat up. "Really? Where did you get it?"

"Sam. Can you believe it?" Geoffrey was looking at him with open appeal. "He's had it all the time. He says he intended to slip it to me after the ceremony, as he promised Elginbrodde he would, but Meg said something to him on the phone this afternoon which gave him a clue, so he unearthed the letter from behind the mantelpiece in his living room." Geoff sat down on the opposite side of the hearth. "Read it, Campion. This is the thing Havoc is looking for."

As Campion unfolded the sheets, the deep pleasant voice went on, by this time a trifle huskily. "It must have been written just before the kid went out on the raid, and evidently he was still full of it when he spoke to Havoc. It was addressed to Blank Blank Esquire, and marked 'Personal.' "

Campion began to read.

Visitors' Club, Pall Mall, S.W.1.
February 4th, '44

Dear Sir,

I fear I cannot call you anything else but I feel very kindly disposed toward you. Meg is such a thoroughly splendid person that she deserves a real life with a man who is batty about her. I know you will be [crossed out] are, otherwise she would never have married you. Please understand that I realize that my intrusion into your life at this point is rather "much," to put it mildly, but there is something you have got to do.

In the old icehouse of the garden of the house at Sainte-Odile-sur-Mer (Meg will know the place; I cannot leave it to her because it is not mine, but the contents *are*, and those I have left her) there is the Sainte-Odile treasure. It is for Meg to do as she likes with, so long as she sees it is kept safe. Safety is all that matters. If I go—and I shall have gone, of course, if you get this—our Sainte-Odile line will have ended and someone else must take over.

101

I am handing you the job because I am conceited enough to believe that you will be the same sort of chap that I am, and will just go and get it the instant the thing seems at all possible. The old women in the country around Sainte-Odile used to say, "One truly loves only the same man." They meant, as I take it, that a woman only *really* loves the same sort of man all her life. I am betting that Meg will only marry when she really loves again, so my guess is that you and I are rather alike in important things. As I am now going off on a sticky assignment, this is a great comfort to me.

The treasure is portable, but it will require great care. I will put where it actually is in the icehouse on a separate piece of paper. I do not know why I do this except that it seems safe. I hid it myself, which is why the whole thing may look a bit odd. Be careful how you break in.

Of course I appreciate that all this may be a waste of time. The place may have been looted already, or it may get a direct hit. If so, forget it; it can't be helped.

But in that case, please do not tell Meg about the treasure. I have never told her about it because if she cannot help, she will only worry, and I feel she has worried enough.

That is all. Please go and get it the instant you feel it is practicable for you to do so, and give it to Meg.

Give Meg my love, but do not tell her it is mine. Over to you, chum.

Yours very truly,
MARTIN ELGINBRODDE,
Major

Campion sat staring at the signature for some seconds before he turned back to read the message once more. The room was quiet. Geoffrey was looking into the fire.

When he had completed the second reading, Campion's pale face was blank and his eyes shadowed behind his spectacles. Geoffrey took back the letter and handed him a third sheet. "This is the enclosure."

As Campion read the single line written neatly across it, his brows rose. "Odd," he murmured, "but quite clear. Yes, I see. What are you going to do now?"

Levett crushed the flimsy sheets into three tight balls and threw them one after the other onto the red coals. Little blue flames leaped out to devour them. "After all, it was a personal letter," he said, his eyes meeting Campion's for an instant. "I don't see a pack of officials breathing over it, do you?"

Campion did not speak at once. He was thinking how surprising the man was. He had grown to like him enormously during the day, but he had not suspected this sensitivity. He realized with a little shock how right Martin had been, how discerning Meg's heart.

"Oh, I agree," he said aloud. "And now?"

"Now we nip over and get it right away, just as he asks." Geoff had become his familiar self again, brisk, purposeful and capable as they come. "There's no point in hanging about. We'll settle things with the police, and we'll all four go—you, Amanda, Meg and me. We'll drive to Southampton tonight and catch the first boat to Saint-Malo, taking the car with us for the trip down the coast. I feel that if Meg gets away from here, it will be safer for everybody. And the job ought to be done, so let's do it."

The more Campion considered the proposal, the more he liked it. He felt that Havoc was "police work." And as for Meg, Geoffrey was right. The farther she was from the scene of action, the better. He glanced at his watch.

"Luke is due soon," he remarked. "Get your clothes on and we'll tackle him. If I know him, he'll be fascinated. What exactly are you expecting to find, by the way?"

"I haven't the faintest idea." Geoffrey stood up. "Anything. It's fragile and portable, that's all anyone knows. A crystal candelabrum, perhaps, or a tea service even. Something they thought a lot of when Elginbrodde was a kid. Families do have the most extraordinary treasure. But it's not a question of intrinsic value at all. The point is that it was *his* treasure and he wanted Meg to have it and keep it safe. I shall be quite prepared for a bust of Minerva or a set of andirons, and in the circumstances I'd risk my life to get them for Meg. I've got to. It's over to me. Why, you weren't thinking of pieces of eight, were you?"

Campion laughed. "No," he said, "not exactly. That notion may occur to Luke, though, and I shouldn't disillusion him."

Geoffrey was eyeing him curiously. "He'll let us go, won't he?"

"I think so. It's good orthodox procedure. Phase One, recover loot. His only anxiety as far as you are concerned is that you may be shielding someone here—Havoc's contact."

He made the suggestion lightly, but his eyes were inquisitive. Geoffrey met them steadily. "Havoc spoke of a contact, but there was no suggestion that it was anyone in the house. Who could it be? Are you worrying about the safety of my future father-in-law?"

"No. Quite frankly, I feel to do that would be presumptuous. Someone else looks after Uncle Hubert. Very well, then, I'll see you downstairs soon."

Geoffrey's gaudy dressing gown vanished through the doorway and Campion was left frowning in a fruitless effort to remember something. Somewhere, at some time—in an old guidebook perhaps—he had heard tell of the Saint-Odile treasure before.

Chapter Eleven

AN UNNATURAL peace had settled over the house when late that night Luke sat in the study with Canon Avril. The four treasure seekers had left sometime before, groping through the fog in an attempt to catch the first Saint-Malo boat out from Southampton. The rectory was quiet without them, although it was by no means empty. Sergeant Picot lolled on a hard chair in the front hall, while in the basement two of his men made half-hourly rounds, after dispossessing the Talismans, who were now asleep in the two little rooms beyond the kitchen. Under the roof Sam was working on an article, and in Meg's elegant bedroom Miss Warburton, who had been induced to leave her lonely cottage for the night, brushed out her limp hair before the mirror.

In the study, where the coal fire burned softly, Luke was at the desk. As Campion had recognized when he first met him,

Charlie Luke was destined to become one of the great policemen. He possessed the one paramount quality that appears in all the giants of his profession: utter persistence. The man hunted his quarry with the passionate patience of a devotee hunting salvation. After thirty-six sleepless hours, his red-rimmed eyes were bright as a bird's.

Sergeant Picot and his men had been working on the St. Petersgate Square angle all day and they had gleaned only a little. Luke had digested the scraps they had given him and now he was talking to the canon about Jack Havoc, expending the precious minutes deliberately, feeling his way, letting his intuition stretch out beyond where his rational mind could take him.

Old Avril was listening. He sat in a worn chair, his fingers folded across his black vest. He looked both wise and good, but there was no telling what was going on behind his quiet eyes.

"Usually, you see, sir," Luke was saying, "we know these lads like our own brothers. We know their families. Havoc is an exception. We know nothing of his life before his first conviction in 1934. He was sixteen then, or so he says, and that seems to be all they ever got out of him. It's not his real name, of course."

"No?" Avril did not appear surprised, merely interested.

"I should say he invented that, as a boy might, trying to sound big. Anyhow, it was as Jack Havoc that he first went to prison, and as Havoc, Jack, that he's down in our files. He said he came from nowhere, no one came forward to claim him, and from our point of view, his life started then. All I know about him is what I've been able to get from the records. For five years he's been safely in jail, and for some time before that he'd vanished, presumably into the Army. The outstanding thing about him, as I see it, is that he's been able to disappear before in his life, just as he has now."

The canon nodded. "You feel that he must have friends among the people the police do not normally walk hand in hand with. I understand."

"It's obvious, isn't it? How did he get the clothes he's wearing so quickly? Who was waiting for him to make his getaway?"

Avril sighed. "Sixteen years old, and no one came forward to claim him. How very terrible that must have been."

"Very likely, sir," Luke agreed bitterly, "but he doesn't sound like my idea of a lovable kid. He and two other boys stole a laundry van, ran over a postman, maimed him for life and pinched his bag, leaving him in the road. Then they smashed up the vehicle while fighting over the mail. One young brute was killed outright, the second was seriously hurt and Havoc was arrested trying to run away."

Avril said nothing. His chin had sunk on his chest, and his eyes stared unseeing at the polished wood of the desk pedestal.

Luke went on cautiously. "Mrs. Cash—the woman who lends money. We had great hopes of her, you know."

"Ah, Martin's jacket. I thought you might. Where did that lead you?" Avril's direct intelligence was comforting.

"Not very far," Luke admitted. "Her story was that a dealer asked her to get it for him, and that was confirmed by the man. He says that Duds came into his shop and asked if he could get an old coat or suit of Martin Elginbrodde's, and he mentioned this address. He explained that he was an actor and that he was due to give an impersonation of his old officer at a reunion dinner. The dealer saw no harm in it, and he knew that Mrs. Cash, who did little bits of business of the kind, lived in this square, so he got in touch with her."

Old Avril nodded. "Ingenious," he said unexpectedly. "Mrs. Cash is not involved."

Charlie Luke eyed him curiously. "I understand you've known her for a long time, sir."

The canon agreed. "My wife persuaded me to let her live in that little cottage twenty-six years ago."

"And she was a widow then with one child, a little boy. Is that right?" Luke hoped he was not sounding heavily significant.

"Perfectly. Did she tell you that?"

"No, that came from your Mrs. Talisman. We haven't worried Mrs. Cash since last night. Since then, we've merely kept an eye on the place. She hasn't been out today."

"So she told me. She seems to have a cold."

Luke sat up. "When you called on her this afternoon?"

"Of course," Avril said. "That was the only time I saw her. I asked her if she could possibly come and hunt for the minutes of the last meeting of the Diocesan Education Committee. She couldn't. She said she had a cold."

Luke stared at him blankly. "I see," he said at last. "I suppose that your work has to go on, whatever happens around you." He brushed the incident aside and returned to the heart of the business. "This son of hers—do you happen to remember, sir, exactly when he died?"

Avril hesitated. "Not the year," he said at last, "but it was just after Epiphany—that's early January."

"Mrs. Talisman says it was 1935, and the boy was then fourteen or fifteen, but well grown." Luke was about to test the one and only theory that had occurred to him, though its flimsiness dismayed him. "My information is that the child died down in the country, where he had been for some time, and his body was brought to his mother's house for a night on its way to the cemetery. You were sick in bed, but your wife, the late Mrs. Avril, went in to see the mother for you. Now, sir, this is the question I have to ask you. Mrs. Talisman is certain that when Mrs. Avril returned, she mentioned that she had seen the body. She knew the boy well and she said she saw him when he was dead. Do you happen to remember that?"

"Yes," Avril said. "My poor Margaret." His face changed only for an instant. The grief upon it passed like the shadow of a leaf in the wind, but its intensity was great.

The chief inspector was taken aback. He had no wish to torment his new friend, whose regret for his dead wife was quite clear, so he shelved his "substitution of the child" theory. It had been a forlorn hope that had come to him when Picot was telling him about Mrs. Cash. It had occurred to him then that a self-centered widow who was making money in a shady way under cover of respectability might have preferred to let her neighbors believe her son was dead rather than to allow him to become a permanent danger to her—especially if she was then free to do what she could for him secretly. The actual substitution would not have been easy, but not, he had thought, impossible for a woman with so many impoverished folk beholden to her.

It had been the dates that had interested him most. In May 1934 a boy went to prison, and about the same time another boy was "sent away to the country because he was difficult," and in the following January he had died. However, if Mrs. Avril had actually seen the dead child, then that was the end of it.

The chief inspector took up the official photographs of the wanted man, which lay before him on the desk. He pushed them across to Avril, who glanced at them and handed them gravely back. "That's the bird we're after, sir."

"And when he is taken, what will they do with him? Hang him, I suppose, poor fellow."

The epithet stung Luke and anger shone out suddenly from his eyes. "That man," he exploded, "has killed a doctor who was trying to help him, a caretaker old enough to be his father, an invalid woman in her bed and a boy I'd give my right hand to have here with me on the job. That man is killing mad. He's got no right to life. Of course they'll hang him," he said savagely.

The old canon had been watching the other man's rage with a look of acute apprehension. "If you'll forgive a great impertinence," he said apologetically, "but it comes within my province, and it might be helpful just now. Beware of anger. It deadens the perceptions."

He spoke so earnestly and with such obvious goodwill that it was impossible to be offended. Luke liked Avril and would have been delighted to go on being surprised by him, but there was a night's work waiting for him at Crumb Street. Presently he left the rectory and strode away through the fog.

WHEN CANON AVRIL had made sure that the front door was locked—to the amusement of Sergeant Picot, who was seated in front of it—he would have gone to bed had not Miss Warburton appeared with a cup of steaming milk in her hand.

"So there you are at last!" she announced loudly. "Sitting up until I don't know when, chatting to policemen. Here, take this and do drink it down. It will help you sleep."

Avril looked down at her kind plain face and smiled at her with great fondness. He thanked her gravely for the milk, which he had no intention of drinking, and took it carefully into his bedroom, which was just behind his living room. She lingered in the doorway, dying to gossip, but quite incapable of taking a step inside.

"Hubert," she finally said briskly, "suppose this murderer comes here looking for Martin's letter? He might kill us all."

"The man will not come here." The canon spoke with complete authority, but she was loath to let the subject drop.

"How do you know?"

Avril frowned. He was wondering what she would say if he explained that he knew Havoc would not come to the house because he, Avril, seemed to have arranged that he should not. He could imagine her face changing, just as Mrs. Cash's face had changed when he had knocked on her door that afternoon and made the unprecedented request that she should come and hunt through his house for some "papers" he had mislaid.

He could still see the look, first of incredulity and then of fear, on that broad bold countenance, and the knowing smile that had followed. He heard again the abominable words: "No, Canon. I won't come out. I've got a cold. But you needn't worry. We'll take your word for it that there's nothing to read at the rectory."

The speed with which she had given a meaning to his request still shocked him. Why had he made the move? He honestly did not know. There had been no plan in his mind, of that he was certain, for now he came to think of it, Martin's letter *was* in the house at that time, although he had not known it. The idea of taking such an extraordinary step had come to him without ulterior motive as soon as he had heard the story of the letter from Campion, and he had acted upon it there and then. It was only after Mrs. Cash had reacted that he had wondered at himself and her.

Miss Warburton bore with his silence but misunderstood his expression. "Oh, you *are* worried, aren't you?" she said with concern. "That's why I want you to sleep. Drink that milk."

"You run along, or you'll catch cold," he said. "Good night."

He began to remove his jacket, and she hurried off at once. Left to himself in the dark little bedroom, he covered the cup of milk with a book lest he should forget and drink it inadvertently. He did not want to sleep. Now was no time to deaden his perceptions. He had just seen how Luke had been hampered by anger. Avril approved of Luke. He thought him sound and shrewd and very likable. How amazingly close the chief inspector had come to the truth—always supposing it was the truth.

Avril remembered his dear Margaret, sobbing out her confession before she died. What a silly wayward little tale it had been! The changes in money values during the First World War had taken her by surprise, so Margaret had borrowed. It had been such a trivial sum, and the woman Cash had made her pay so much, not only in money but in agony. He had been angry at the time, and his anger had deadened his perceptions and he had paid for it. He was still paying for it. He could not remember exactly what she had said as she lay sobbing on his shoulder. Had she said that she had actually seen another child in the open coffin, or merely that she had been told to say that she had seen the boy when she had not, and so had suspected that it wasn't he? Avril could not remember. All he could remember was her pain.

And as he stood remembering, he felt himself growing angry again. It terrified him and he prayed against it lest he should lose his understanding. Avril had only one prayer that he used in private nowadays. As he climbed out of his clothes, he repeated it, drawing the blessed sense out of every word.

"Our Father . . ."

When he came to the part that was most important to him that night, he paused and said it twice.

"Lead us not into temptation, but deliver us from evil."

That was it. Lead us not into temptation. But deliver us, take us away, hide us from evil. That was his prayer, and tonight it was not going to be answered.

He got into his thick dressing gown, which looked like a monk's robe. Meg had made it for him, and the simplicity and warmth of the garment pleased him. All his household were used to meeting his cowled figure striding down the passages, but Sergeant Picot had the shock of his life when, on turning at a sound, he saw a "a black monk" behind him. The canon was carrying the cup of milk. He was most anxious not to hurt Dot's feelings by letting her find it untouched in the morning, and was preparing a little guiltily to pour it away. He handed it to Picot with relief, delighted to find a good use for it.

The sergeant was not a milk drinker, but he had not eaten since a belated lunch and had a long cold night in front of him. He took it as a very kind thought of the old gentleman's and drank it down, unaware that Miss Warburton had added two barbiturate tablets to the milk because she wanted Hubert to have a good night's rest. Before long, Picot was nodding peacefully at his post.

Once back in his room, completely ignorant of what he had done, Avril pottered about, waiting for something, he knew not what. He recognized his own mood. It was one that had come on him very seldom in his life, and always it had preceded some experience in which he had been called upon to play a principal part. Its chief characteristic was a strange sense of absolute peace. He was not frightened because he knew that with the danger would come the courage.

The small clock in his room said ten minutes after one. The house was silent. He switched off the light and felt his way over to the window that looked out onto the stone staircase between the rectory and the church. The fog seemed to be lifting at last. He peered up to see if the familiar triangle of sky, just above the high wall and bounded by the church spire, had stars in it. He could see none. But the corner of his eye caught something else. It was faint and very brief, and when he looked properly, it had gone, but he knew at once what it had been.

111

He had caught a flicker of light from high up inside the church. The beam of a flashlight had passed along the east window, catching the azure robe of a saint in stained glass. Avril stood transfixed. He knew as clearly as if someone had just informed him of them all those facts that his subconscious mind had known all along.

For instance, he knew that when Mrs. Cash had shown Sergeant Picot over her little house she must also have shown him the backyard coal shed, whose door was situated in the wall of the very foundations of the church. Even if the sergeant had opened that door, Avril thought it unlikely that he would have stared beyond her small stock of fuel to the heavy door behind it.

Twenty-six years before, he had given Mrs. Cash permission to make a coal shed out of the service entry to the unused crypt of the church. As landlord, Avril had paid for the alteration himself and had stipulated at the time that the door to the crypt should be kept locked and the key given to Talisman. For the first time it occurred to him that that had never been done, and the crypt must have stayed open for Mrs. Cash to enter and use as she chose.

He went on to think of the men the police were hunting for and where they were hiding. It was so easy, so convenient. They must have approached it from the church itself, entering not from the closely guarded square but from the avenue behind. Once in the church, it was simple for one who knew the way to go down to the crypt from inside.

He also found himself perceiving that his visit to Mrs. Cash that afternoon, by conveying to her—and through her to the man behind her—that Martin's letter was not in the rectory, had also conveyed that he knew where it was, and in fact had hidden it somewhere else.

Avril knew where Havoc would look for it. Doubtless he was there now, rummaging through the old black folder the canon kept under the lectern in his pulpit. He·must have felt he was safe in the small hours, but his flashlight had betrayed him, if only for a second.

Suddenly Avril saw what he was about to do. Events had so arranged themselves that he had no choice. He went quietly out of the room and down the corridor.

Picot's snores were loud in the hall and the canon let himself out quietly so that he should not wake the weary man. The fog was clearing rapidly and no one was about. The detective on duty outside had only that moment entered the kitchen, and for the first time that night the coast was clear.

Avril crossed the stairs to the avenue, and passed around under the high wall to the church gate, traversed the paved yard without stumbling in absolute darkness, and made his way to the vestry door. It was unlocked and he let himself into the blackness inside. His long robe brushed against the woodwork of the vestry wall. He pushed open the inner door and stepped into the misty darkness of the great building, paused and looked around into the dusk.

"John Cash," he said, "come out."

THE BEAM OF Havoc's flashlight cut through the darkness like a blade and found Avril where he was standing in the side aisle. For an instant it trembled there, transfixed, and recollecting his dressing gown, the old man pushed back his hood and let the light play on his face.

"Come down, my boy," he said in the slightly schoolmasterish tone he always used when he wanted something done quickly. "There's nothing there for you at all."

As soon as he spoke and his voice was recognized, the beam shot away from him and sped to explore the entrances one by one. It was a series of startled flashes seeking out a trap, but the doors stood steady and the silence was absolute.

During one of the flashes, Avril had noticed a pew beside him and now he felt for it and seated himself, folding his hands in his lap. His body was afraid and trembling, but his mind was peaceful, relieved and extraordinarily content. He felt at home in the church, as he always did, and presently he cleared his throat with a loud pre-Litany "Hur-ump!"

"Shut up!" The whisper was the most violent sound the old building had ever heard within its walls. The flashlight beam died, and in the darkness there was a scuffling, light footsteps on polished wood, and then silence again. The soft laugh when it came astonished Avril because it was so close to him. "You're alone." The whisper had incredulity in it as well as amusement.

"Of course I am," said Avril testily.

"You've telephoned, though. You've put out a warning." The man had ceased to whisper, although he spoke very softly. His voice was more mature than Avril remembered it, but it still aroused the uneasiness in him that it always had. It was a false voice, every true thing in it hidden rather cheaply.

"No," he said. "No one knows that you and I are here. Come and sit down."

There was no immediate reply, only movement so soft that it could have been the scurry of a rat over the tiles. Avril smelled fear, and with it came a portrait of the boy as he remembered him at fifteen, and as he had half fancied he had discerned him under the hard shadows and unrevealing highlights of the police photographs. He saw again the disfiguring stamp of tragedy on the young face with the flat blue eyes that had nothing behind them.

The man was very close behind him now. "What's the big idea, Padre? Not Prodigal Son stuff, surely?" The menace was unmistakable. "Ma said you *knew* this afternoon when you came around to her, and she swore you'd never let on. We didn't risk it. We made her get us another place. But I came back because I remembered you used to hide things in here—"

"Not hide," protested Avril. "Keep."

"What are you up to, coming in here to find me?"

Avril made no answer because he had none. The danger was apparent to him, but he pushed it away and ceased to tremble. He was glad of that because he felt a hand brush over his shoulders, feeling for exactly where he was.

"Are you my father?" The inquiry came out abruptly in the night.

The enormity of all it implied was not lost on Avril. "No," he said, and he sounded matter-of-fact, regretful even, "not your parent. I am, or ought to be, your spiritual father. I'm your parish priest. I don't seem to have been very successful in that. The man who begot you died, poor fellow, fighting in a public house. Your mother was left a widow, and after some little while my wife found her her present cottage to get her out of the district where the tragedy occurred."

"And your wife was paid for it later, I suppose?" The sneer was very bitter. The boy was disappointed because he had been searching for a reason for the canon's charity toward him and it was not the shameful one he had chosen.

"I suppose she was," Avril said sadly. "In those days respectability seemed to matter very much."

"Don't I know it! Ma buried an empty coffin for the sake of respectability. Think of it, a whole funeral procession costing pounds, and all it did was give me a hold on her. She didn't think of that."

"I wonder. She held you, too, if only in that way."

"Cut it out. Look, why are you here? You're not trying to save my soul, by any chance?"

"Oh, no." Avril gave the little grunting laugh that showed he was genuinely amused. "My dear boy, I couldn't do that. The soul is one's own affair from the beginning to the end. No one else can interfere with that."

"Then why the hell did you come?"

"I don't know," said Avril, and struggled on, making the truth as clear as he could. "All I can tell you is that I had to."

To his amazement, the explanation appeared to be understood. Behind him he heard the man catch his breath.

"That's it," said Havoc, and his voice was natural. "The same thing happened to me. Do you know what that is? That's the science of luck. It works every time."

"The science of luck?" Avril said cautiously.

"I'm one of the lucky ones. I've got the gift. You have to watch for chances, and then you must never go soft—not once, not for a minute. You mustn't even think soft. Once you're soft, you muck everything, lose your place and everything goes against you. I've proved it. Keep realistic and get places fast. I discovered it when I was a kid."

Avril turned around in the dark. "The pursuit of evil—that is what you discovered. It is the only sin which cannot be forgiven because when it has finished with you, you are not there to forgive. On your journey you certainly get places. But in the process you die. Suppose you had got to Sainte-Odile—"

"Where?"

The sudden eagerness did not warn the canon and he went on steadily, throwing away what he felt was worthless information in his anxiety to make the truth clear. "Sainte-Odile-sur-Mer. In English, Saint Odile on Sea. A little village west of Saint-Malo. Supposing you had got there and uncovered treasure worth a king's ransom. Do you think that would have satisfied you?"

Havoc was not listening. "Is that the name of the house or the village?"

"Both. But you must put that out of your mind. Geoffrey Levett has gone there tonight."

"Has he? By sea?"

"Yes. But the fog is lifting. He will be there by tomorrow, or the day after." Avril was impatient. "You must forget that. That is over. The ports are being watched and you are being hunted, my boy. Now is your last chance to think of yourself."

Havoc laughed aloud. "Got it!" he said. "The science of luck—it's done it again. That's why I came back, see? You've told me the only thing I want to know, and I came to hear it. You don't even know why you came, you old fool. Go home to bed—"

His voice died abruptly. He was hesitating, a torn and wasted tiger. In the silence the chill grew so intense that it was painful. Far above them the ghostly figures on the stained-glass windows had begun to take shape as the morning light strengthened.

The long fingers closed around the bones of Avril's shoulders and the trembling force of the man shook his whole body.

"Look, swear. Swear you'll keep quiet."

Avril saw the temptation into which he was being led. "Oh," he said wearily, "you know as well as I do that I can swear and you can let me go, but as soon as I am gone, what will you think? Will you feel confident or will you think you have been soft? That is no good, John. The time has come when you must make a full turn or go on your way."

"You fool, you fool, what are you doing? Do you want it? Are you asking for it?" Havoc was weeping in his weary rage and the tears fell on Avril.

"I want very much to stay alive—much more than I could have believed."

"But you've done it, you've done it, you've put the doubt in my mind. You know I daren't go soft."

Avril bent forward to put his head in his hands. His resignation was complete. "I cannot help you," he said. "Our gods are within us. We choose our own compulsions. Our souls are our own."

He had reached the end of his secret prayer when the flashlight blazed and the knife struck him.

The fact that he felt it at all was significant. For the first time Havoc's hand was doubting, and because of that, it had lost some of its cunning.

Chapter Twelve

THE LATE-MORNING sun was shining through the newly cleaned windows of the chief inspector's office in Crumb Street as if no such thing as a London fog had ever existed. Charlie Luke sat at his desk and considered the situation with that complete detachment that arrives with exhaustion.

Three days of rushed and unrelenting work, and nothing, not one useful clue. Havoc, Tiddy Doll, the brothers Roly and Tom, and Bill had vanished as utterly as if the sewers had swallowed them.

This morning Stanislaus Oates, the chief of Scotland Yard, was at the Great Western Hospital, hoping to get an interview with

Canon Avril. The old man had been out of danger since mid-night and it was hoped he would be able to say a word or two as soon as he awoke.

Dear, *silly* old fool. Sam Drummock had saved his life. He had come down in the very early morning and had found Picot asleep, the front door unlatched and Avril's bed unslept in. It had taken the frightened household twenty minutes to find the old man where he lay on the church floor. The actual nature of the wound was one of those miracles that Luke decided he would never understand. Why a man of Havoc's skill should suddenly miss his mark by inches, so that the collarbone took most of the blow, or why, having surely known he had missed, he had not struck again, completely defeated him.

Oates would get nothing from Avril voluntarily. Luke was sure of that. Besides, what news could he tell? They knew Havoc had been his attacker. His prints were all over the blessed church. As to the rest, Luke could hardly suppose that the chap would have had a chat with the old man before he did his handiwork, much less mention where he was going.

Luke had taken the church apart, and the crypt, with its clear signs of recent occupation, had been gone over with a fine-toothed comb. The miserable Sergeant Picot, still woozy from the drug (and what a fantastic piece of bad luck that had been!), had found the way out through Mrs. Cash's coal cellar.

Luke sat staring red-eyed at the notes before him as he checked every point. Mrs. Cash was in a detention cell down-stairs, held on an accessory charge. She had refused to speak all yesterday, and he was giving her until the midday meal before he tried her again. Luke did not think she would crack yet, if she did at all. Perhaps there had been something in his "substitution of the child" theory, after all. Mrs. Avril could have been mistak-en. Certainly something was giving the wicked old girl in the cell downstairs a remarkable amount of courage.

He sighed. All this was getting him nowhere. Routine—that was the only thing. There was plenty to do. His desk was stacked high with confidential memos containing news and gossip from informers. The crime fraternity was leaving Havoc strictly alone, by all accounts. The underworld had never liked him and now considered him dynamite.

As he put out his hand, the papers on the right side of the desk toppled over and slid to the floor. He dived after them, but one sheet eluded him and he had to lean over under a chair for it. As he fished it out to place it with the rest, he glanced at it, and one paragraph caught his attention. It was a reply to a query about Roly and Tom that he had personally put to the officer who had been reporting on Havoc's companions.

Why, Luke had asked, did these two fishermen spend the war in the Army when all such men had been directly instructed to join one of the two sea services? It was a minor point and he had forgotten making it, but after enormous difficulty the officer had identified the two as Roland and Thomas Gripper of Weft, near Aldeburgh, Suffolk, and the paragraph in his report that had caught Luke's eye said simply:

> On leaving school the two brothers joined their father, Albert Edward Gripper, who owned a fishing boat, and worked for him until he was convicted of smuggling, imprisoned and severely fined. The boat appears to have been sold to meet the fine, and the brothers then left the district. The evidence is that they were simple, ignorant men who had spent most of their lives on the water, and it seems possible that they felt it safest to disclaim any knowledge of their former calling—hence their appearance in the Army soon after the outbreak of war.

As the chief inspector finished reading, the telephone on his desk rang and Assistant Commissioner Oates's familiar voice came through to him.

"Charlie? . . . Good. Listen. Canon Avril spoke to Havoc and told him (a) that the name of the place where the stuff was hidden was Sainte-Odile near Saint-Malo, and (b) that Geoffrey Levett had gone after it. I have nothing else so far. The old gentleman is very weak, but they say he'll live. Anything new with you? . . . No? . . . Very well, keep at it. Good-by."

Luke's hand was still on the receiver and the expression of incredulity was still on his face when Picot appeared.

"Chief Inspector," he burst out as he slammed a file on the desk, "a small van was found abandoned at Tollesbury in Essex. First reported ten p.m. yesterday and just traced to a family called Brown who run a little bakery on Barrow Road here. Old Mrs. Brown, who owns the shop, is on Mrs. Cash's books. She owes her three hundred pounds."

Luke sat looking at him. "Where's Tollesbury?"

"You must know Tollesbury. Yachts, oysters, fishing boats—"

Luke jerked to attention. "Is it on the sea?"

"The estuary, only forty-odd miles from London. It's littered with little seagoing boats. If anybody should want to pinch a seagoing craft, it would be the one place on earth to get away with it. Chief Inspector, *suppose those lads tried to stage the raid again?*"

"Anyone down there lost a boat?"

"Nothing's come through from Essex yet, sir, but it's early. I don't suppose a man would notice for twelve hours or so that his craft had gone, and then he'd think she had broken away."

Luke stretched out a long arm. As in most other professions, the one certain way of cutting through red tape in police matters is to have a private word on the telephone with a very old friend in another department. Superintendent Len Burnby of the Essex constabulary had walked a beat with Luke in the far-off happy days when they were both prepared to put the world right; within a few minutes the well-remembered voice was drawling over the wire.

"Charlie boy, how are you? See you've kind of mislaid someone up there in the fog. Never mind, it's a nice drying day today. . . . What? . . . Boat from Tollesbury? That's a very strange question—are you trying to confess? I just got the report on my desk this minute."

Luke spent a few precious moments in lucid explanation.

"It could be," the other voice said briskly. "You may be on to something. This is an eighteen-ton boat, the *Marlene Doreen.*

The owner's son missed her yesterday afternoon about three. Until dawn this morning they thought she must have fouled her anchor. They finally notified the Tollesbury police an hour ago. Customs has been informed. Anything else you want?"

Luke mentioned the abandoned van. "Wouldn't five strangers be noticed on this marsh of yours?" he added.

"Not on a November morning if they knew where they were going. Owners and their agents are always popping up and down that road." Burnby's voice had not quickened, but some of Luke's own rising excitement was echoed in its drawl. "Charlie, I've seen that van. I've been down there this morning. It was quite empty except for one thing our chap happened to find on the floor. He showed it to me, but we didn't think there was much to it. It was a lens out of a pair of dark glasses. Wasn't one of the five wearing dark glasses?"

Charlie Luke's spirits rose so violently that they took his breath away. The luck had come.

Burnby was still speaking. "I'll have the van tested for prints and rush 'em to you, to be on the safe side. Meanwhile, I'll get the water people out. The *Marlene Doreen* will be sitting on a mudbank by this time, unless your blokes are fisherfolk born."

"Two of them are. Suffolk folk from Weft."

A thin whistle came over the wire. "That's torn it. She only carries a crew of two. Where will they make for? Do you know?"

"Sainte-Odile, near Saint-Malo."

"Ha, they'll be there by now, then."

"What?"

The violence of the exclamation startled Superintendent Burnby. "Well, they must have taken her out on the tide yesterday morning," he quickly explained. "That gives them a twenty-six hour start approximately. If their luck held, they should be there just about now."

"Are you sure of this, Len? It matters."

"Saint-Malo from Tollesbury? Yes, twenty-six hours with luck. It's been ideal weather since the fog cleared, so she could make speed. Depend upon it, they're due about now." He paused and, as the silence lengthened, laughed apologetically. "Well, I see you've got plenty on your plate, boy, so I won't detain you. All the best. Let me know if there's anything you want."

Luke hung up. It was not often that he found events outstripping his mental speed, but now he found himself staggering rather than rising to the occasion.

"The French police," he said to the startled Picot. "Radio the French police. Here are the details. And get me Commissioner Oates at the Great Western Hospital."

He cocked an eye at the window, which showed a square of limpid sky, and his dark face began to glow again as the fires of his energy reddened once more. "If it's a good day for boats, Len, you old so-and-so," he murmured, "it's good enough for flying, isn't it?"

MEG ELGINBRODDE sat in the front seat of a touring car stopped on a coastal road in Brittany. The November afternoon was as mild as early autumn, and in the sunlit stillness the neat French countryside lay like a scarf of purple and green and soft gold under a sky of pearl. Beside her, Geoffrey lit yet another cigarette. At the head of the growing line of traffic, they and the Campions waited for the tide to recede from the road so that their car might pass.

In the backseat, Amanda nodded toward the dark wedge-shaped hill before them. "We can see it, anyway."

"Every vehicle in which I have set foot in the past two days and nights has stopped dead for an hour or two when just in sight of its goal," said Campion, sitting beside her. "The thing that amazes me, if you'll forgive me, Meg, is why you thought to tell us everything about this doubtlessly delightful village except that it was an island."

Meg did not turn her head, which was all but lost in the fur collar of her traveling coat. "When I was here, it wasn't an island," she said. "This only happens at high tide."

"Which is twice a day," murmured Geoffrey, his hand tightening over hers. "Feeling happier, beautiful?"

"Much." She smiled at him. "I've been happy since last night. Suddenly, just about midnight, everything seemed all right. I'm sorry I made such a fuss. It was that boat being so late after all the delay at the beginning, I suppose. I wanted to get on."

"You didn't, you know," said Amanda. "You wanted to go back. I think Geoff was wise not to wait at Saint-Malo. Of course the tire trouble at Les Oiseaux was utterly unforeseeable."

"And for some hours irremediable," muttered Campion. "Where are we going? To the village first, or straight up to the house?"

"Oh, the house." Meg turned around to him. "It's so late, nearly two. It'll be dark if we don't. The road divides when we get across here, and the village is down there to the west. If we take the east road up the hill, we'll be there in ten minutes."

Campion's reply was drowned in a hysterical outcry of hooting behind them, and a black car shot past them through the traffic and took to the shallow water like a duck throwing out a wake on either side.

Geoffrey glanced after it with interest. "See that?" he said. "The gallant gendarmes. Quantities of them. The police, can we never get away from them? They're across, by Jove! Yes, there they go, away down the west road. We go east, do we, darling? Right, well, now for it. We'll take it steadily." He moved the heavy car smoothly into the receding tide.

On the other side the road forked and they edged up the narrow way, leaving the rest of the traffic to take the main track to the village. The hill rose steeply between high hedges, and the air was clear and peaceful save for the buzzing of a little silver scout plane that flew low across the sky, swooped and turned back again.

"What's *he* doing?" murmured Campion, but no one was listening.

Meg was sitting forward, her eyes eager. "It's somewhere here, Geoff. A white gate. You turn in and drive for a long way up to the actual house—nearly a mile, I should think. Yes, here we are."

They turned off the road into a lane that ran up across a broad bank of meadow, bare and desolate. There was no cover anywhere, no tree to break the arc of earth against the sky. The house appeared suddenly, and with it the dark green sea and the ragged broken line of coast, lace-edged with surf, stretching out to the horizon on either side.

It was a little stone house, squat and solid as a castle, with a single turret and a wall around it. Until they were almost upon it, it looked neat and circumspect, but as they passed under the arch leading to the courtyard, they saw it was deserted and in bad repair. There was no glass in the windows, and grass had grown through the crack that split the stone before the nail-studded door. The house was dead, a casualty of war.

They climbed out of the car in silence.

"I hate this bit of it," said Meg. She crossed the small courtyard to a door in the wall. It creaked open, and they followed her into what once had been a formal garden sloping to the edge of the cliff. Opposite them, through many breaches in the garden wall, the sea gleamed dangerously far below.

Meg and Geoffrey paused before a small stone building that crouched in an angle of the wall. This was the icehouse. It was not large and was constructed in a pit, so that only half its walls and its conical roof were visible above the rank grass surrounding it. The two stepped inside, and Amanda and Campion followed them.

The interior was a surprise, for it was light. The whole of one corner had fallen away, with part of the outer wall, so that now there was a ragged window at breast level looking out over the cliff to the sea. The effect was unexpectedly enchanting. Sky and sea merged on the horizon, and the afternoon sun streamed out over the green water, while violet shadows and plumes of surf made marblings between.

A little boat lying at anchor bobbed in the foreground. At that distance she was no larger than a matchbox, and her name, painted boldly in white on her dark side, was unreadable.

"How very lovely!" Meg spoke with delight. "There's smoke,

too. A little bit of smoke on the horizon. Can you see it? Otherwise she's absolutely alone."

Geoffrey laughed. "First sign of life since we turned east," he said. "Nice to see it. I thought we'd come to the end of the world. Now, Campion, the great moment."

They looked at each other, and for the first time since the journey began admitted to themselves the sadness and absurdity of the quest. All save Meg were past their youth, and the pathos of the little legacy hidden in this crumbling tomb touched three of them at least. Meg alone was radiant.

"Geoffrey, you say it's andirons, and Albert, you say it's something you've heard about but forgotten. And you, Amanda, say it's a set of priceless glass," she said, glancing at each of them in turn. "But I say that whatever it is, it's mine, and I shall love it very much. Now then, Geoff, no more secrecy, we're all alone. What have we got to do? Get the floor up?"

"No." Levett was looking at an uncompromisingly Victorian cement garden figure that kept a mildewed guard over the icehouse. It was an insipid shepherdess, much too large for life, seated on a formalized tree stump. She was now crumbling badly.

"It's in here, whatever it is," Geoffrey said. "The enclosure in Martin's letter simply said, 'The treasure is hidden in the statue.' I think our best way is to pull it down, Campion, so that we can see the base. Shall we try?"

Together the two men took the figure by waist and shoulder and tipped it slowly back. It was heavy, but they lowered it very gently to the moss-grown flagstones.

That they had found the hiding place was obvious immediately. The statue was hollow, but its underside had been plastered over inexpertly. There was a fold of some sort of cloth—a blanket possibly—just visible in the white mass. Campion tried it with his fingernail and marked it slightly.

"It's soft, but not quite soft enough," he said. "I think we need expert help with this, you know, since the treasure inside is supposed to be fragile. It's not three o'clock yet. Suppose we go down to the village and get the local mason. We can't possibly get at it without tools."

"Isn't there something in the car?" Meg asked.

"No," Geoffrey answered. "Albert's right. It's delicate. The letter stressed that. No good coming all this way and smashing the thing. We'll all go down to the village. You and Amanda can get us rooms at the hotel while we hunt out the mason. I think it might be easier— What's up, Amanda?"

"Nothing." Amanda replied. "I thought I heard something, but it was only the courtyard door swinging. Let's go down to the village, shall we?"

"You three go," Meg said earnestly. "Amanda can see to the hotel. Let me stay."

"I shouldn't if I were you," said Amanda promptly. "You'll only get cold, if you don't fall over the cliff."

"But I'd like to stay with my treasure. Do you mind, Geoff?"

A fleeting flame of jealousy flared on Geoffrey's face and died of shame. "Do anything you like, my dear," he said awkwardly at last. "Stay if you want to. It'll make us hurry back."

She was as delighted as a child. "I'll just sit here and look at it and wonder what the Sainte-Odile mystery can be."

The Sacred Mystery of Sainte-Odile. Campion finally remembered. He had been ten years old, standing in a church at Villeneuve, struggling to translate the rolling phrases booming from the official guide. It went something like:

"This work of art miraculous without something-or-other alone in the world except for a sister in the custody adoring of the family private of one of the most big gentlemen in France. They call it the Mystery, the Mystery Sacred of Sainte-Odile-sur-Mer."

"This is going to be interesting," he said suddenly. "Let's go to the village and get a truck and cart the whole thing down to the hotel. You stay here, Meg, since you want to, and we'll be back in under a half hour." He swept Amanda out with him.

Geoffrey turned, hesitated and kissed Meg. "Are you going to be all right?"

"Don't be silly. Hurry back and we'll see what it is."

"Right. Twenty minutes. Don't go too near that hole in the wall."

"I won't."

Meg sat down on the empty plinth and extended her hand to the base of the statue. The place was exquisitely peaceful now. She heard the car start quite distinctly and listened to the sound of the engine dying gently away until it was lost in the deeper and more caressing growl that was the sea. The sun was shining, making tinsel streaks on the water so far below. The little boat was still there. There was another boat, too, far away as yet and beetle-sized. It was dark, with a long white tail of foam that showed its speed. The roar of a plane passing very low over the garden spoiled the peace, and she resented it mildly.

She was very anxious to see her new responsibility, and she ran an exploring finger over the plastered underside of the statue. As she rubbed, some plaster flaked away, exposing a deep rift. She was so interested in its possibilities that she did not hear the soft rustle of the bushes outside in the garden, and by the time she had opened her bag and unearthed a long nail file, nothing could have disturbed her.

Her fragile steel wand probed the weak spot cautiously, and unexpectedly a whole chunk of the powdery composition came away, disclosing a dusty bulge covered with some woolen material. She worked on and very soon had a cavity nearly a foot deep and wide enough to admit her hand.

She was so excited that the step on the stone behind her was purely welcome. She turned her head briefly to catch a glimpse of a blue jersey and beret dark against the bright doorway. "*Bonjour,*" she said politely and, returning to the work, went on without looking at him. "*Qu'il fait beau. Est-ce que—?*"

"Speak English."

"English?" she said. "What luck. I wish you'd appeared before. Do you work here? Or no, I suppose you're fishing. Is that your boat?" Another lump of plaster came away as she spoke. She set it down carefully beside her and put in her hand for

more, still chatting with the easy friendliness of her age. "Doesn't it all look wonderful from here?"

Havoc did not move. He had slept for an hour on the boat, no more, and was nearly exhausted. The final effort up the cliff had drained his resources, but he had made it.

He put one hand on the doorpost, spoke, and was frightened by the lifelessness of his own voice. "What are you doing?"

The question was ridiculous. He could see what she was doing, and its significance was not lost on him. The science of luck had ceased to be a mere series of opportunities that he could seize or miss. It had revealed itself as a force that had swept him on without even his connivance. The sequence of events had been dreamlike. The van ride along the deserted roads, Roly knowing the way, the dinghy already afloat at the lapping water's edge. Tom had greeted the *Marlene Doreen* with a cry of recognition. She was the same sort of boat as his old man's, and on her smooth planks he and his brother stood taller and became different men.

They were on her now, sitting there expecting him to return, the fools; blissfully trusting him, even though Bill, who was lying sick as a dog in the bows, was swearing pitiably at them for their idiocy.

They would still be sitting there when the police launch came up. From all he had heard, the French coppers carried rifles on a job like this. One way or another, they would all be busy for quite some time. The old science was certainly holding. The luck was more than just with him: he couldn't go wrong.

There was only Doll still to be considered. Havoc had seen him drop into the water and come after him while he himself was lying panting on the cliff after the climb. The old brute was shrewd and he was game, and the treasure had got him. But he'd never make the cliff. He must be somewhere on the face now, just under that second overhang perhaps, clinging there with only one eye open behind his broken dark glasses.

Meg's voice had taken Havoc by surprise. It reminded him of her voice when she was a child, clear and kiddish and with an irritatingly better accent than his own. He remembered, too, her complete absorption in whatever she was doing, which struck him as fantastically ridiculous now when she should have seen that she was in danger.

"I'm trying to get something very fragile out of here without breaking it," she was saying. "It's something which has been left to me and I don't know quite what it is. I've got to get all this packing out. You wouldn't care to have a go at it, would you?"

He lurched forward, stumbling as he let go of the doorpost. He was much weaker than he had thought. He saw her horrified look as the light from the breach in the wall fell on him, and his first thought was that she had recognized him from their childhood. But her exclamation dispelled that flattering illusion.

"Good heavens, are you all right? You look most terribly ill. Please don't bother about this. The others will be back in a minute, anyhow. Can I do anything for you?"

There was no power in him. He noticed it and thrust the thought aside just as he thrust aside the hand she put out to steady him. "Get out of the way."

She rose from the plinth and he dropped onto it and put his hand into the cavity she had made. He worked feverishly, his fingers breaking away the plaster and clawing it out.

The hard core of the discovery—a bundle wrapped in several thicknesses of cement-soaked blanket—began gradually to take shape. It appeared to be roughly cylindrical, about five feet long, with a base not quite two in diameter. Twice he made attempts to drag it out bodily, but it resisted him and he returned to his feverish scraping and shoveling. The white dust covered him, turning his hair and the blue jersey he had found in the *Marlene Doreen*'s locker to matted gray.

Meg eyed him dubiously. He looked so ghastly, his eyes so dull within their caked rims, that she saw no tiger there. She was not afraid of him, but for him, and she was relieved to hear the vague buzz of activity that was becoming slowly more and more noticeable both from inland and the sea.

A plume of spray streaking across the seascape caught the

corner of her eye and she turned just too late to see the craft whose wake it had been. The little boat was no longer visible either. "Your boat has moved," she said.

"It's not mine. Pull the side of this thing."

The command had come back into his voice and it surprised her into immediate obedience. She took hold where he indicated.

At that moment there sounded very faint and far away from the sea below a splatter of sharp little noises, followed by a long bodiless cry like a seabird's. It was only just audible. Havoc heard, but his busy hands did not falter. Rifles. He thought so. Doll's pallid torso must have made a wonderful target.

The whole incident had passed clean over the girl's head, he noticed. The science was not altering, the luck was holding. He could feel it sweeping him on.

At last the bundle moved. "Pull," he commanded, "now."

She had as much strength as he had, he realized, and it bothered him fleetingly. The flaking mass slid forward on the slippery powder.

"Pull," he repeated, unaware that he whispered. "Pull."

"No. Look, it's caught. There. See? It's this jagged bit here, that's what's stopping us. Wait a minute." She tried to dislodge it with her ridiculous nail file.

"What we really need," she said, splitting the words as she made her futile efforts, "is a good—strong—knife."

She was not looking at him, and anyway, his face did not change. He felt under his jersey. His fingers found the familiar sheath, and he sighed as the knife handle slid comfortably into his palm.

Meg laughed aloud when she saw the blade. "What luck!" Her voice sounded joyful, like a child's.

"I am lucky," he said, and struck.

The fang of plaster and the bright steel blade split together and together fell to join the debris.

"Oh!" She was concerned at his loss. "I'm so sorry."

He did not hear her. He was listening to the rhythm of gasoline engines, still too far away to be anything but an undercurrent to the breeze blowing up from the valley. He flicked the useless knife shaft over his shoulder and tugged at the bundle with both hands.

"Take care, oh, please take care! It's very, very delicate."

She bent forward to help him and he permitted it, because he knew the thing must surely be too heavy for him to lift alone. Together they set it down softly on the moss-padded stones.

The roar of an airplane swooped down through all the other noises that were converging on the icehouse. As it began to circle over the smooth pasture on the cliff top, its clamor drowned the revving engines in the valley and the shouting from the sea. Neither of the two in the house in the garden heard it at all. The stiffened blanket around the bundle had rotted and fell away easily from the main structure, which lay before them.

It was a wooden chest, white and seared with age, but hooped like a barrel with iron. For a moment its impregnability was too much for the man, and his hands flickered over the gnarled surface with awful helplessness.

"It opens here. Look, there's a hinge and a catch." The girl stooped over the box and lifted the rounded lid. Inside there was a mound, covered with cotton wool, pounds of it rising up absurdly like whipped cream on a cake. Very cautiously she drew back the covering, and the Sainte-Odile treasure lay regarding them. It was a Virgin and Child in ivory, a fourteenth-century work carved out of a single curving tusk so that the main figure bent slightly as if the better to support its gentle load.

It was not quite the twin of its more famous sister at Ville-neuve-lès-Avignon that Campion had remembered. That exquisite work of art had been damaged. But this, the unknown master's other surviving work, was perfect. Its serenity flowed up naturally from the breathtaking drapery at knee and hem to the medieval face, not yet a saint's nor yet a child's.

For a full minute the two stared at it in a silence that nothing could penetrate. Meg sank down on her heels in the dust and her eyes grew slowly wider and wider until tears formed in them. As the drops fell on her hand, she turned apologetically to the man who had helped her.

"I didn't expect it," she said huskily. "I didn't expect anything like it. It must be the most beautiful thing in the world."

Havoc did not move and she was spared the sight of his face.

It was typical of him that in that moment of disaster he remained realistic. He saw his position immediately and with perfect clarity. The science of luck was an impersonal force, relentless as a river winding down a hill. The only human, and therefore blamable, element in this whole catastrophic mistake was himself.

There was no other treasure. The figure filled each crevice of the ancient case, which had been hewn to fit it. There was no space left for a secret cache of jewels or other lesser trove. All there was lay before him, open to his hand.

Havoc scrambled to his feet and swayed over the girl. "What will it fetch?" He was clutching at a straw, and he knew it.

Her reply only just reached him. "Who could possibly buy it?"

That was the answer. He could hear any of the dealers giving him that one. He let a fantasy creep into his mind. Didn't they hide things in images in the old days? Perhaps there was something worth having buried inside it.

"I'll smash it," he said aloud.

He saw her swift upward glance, in which there was no fear. Then, very smoothly and with much more control than he possessed himself over his movements, she closed the lid of the chest and quite calmly sat down upon it.

"You're ill," she said, and the authority in her voice was frightening. "You listen to me. You've helped me, and I'm very grateful to you and I'm going to pay you back. But I don't think I ought to have let you exhaust yourself."

He found he could only just see her. She looked strong and quiet and the power in her was greater than his power because he was so tired.

"You've broken your knife, too," she was saying. "Let me square up with you for that."

He still stood before her. He could see her bag and guessed that it contained not much money. There was her coat, of course, which looked all right if he only had somewhere handy to sell it. Her hands were so covered with the plaster that he could not see if her ring—and she only wore one—was any good or imitation.

He shook his head and motioned to her to move. He did not want to have to touch her because he needed all the strength he possessed and time was short. All the same, he thought he would smash the ivory. There might be something in it, and smashing it would be a satisfaction anyhow.

The girl was still sitting there like a fool, and he let her have it. "Get up!"

She seemed to be much farther from him than he had thought, for the blow missed her entirely and all but overbalanced him. Her sudden laughter was the most terrible sound he had ever heard, for he knew what she was going to say a fraction of a second before he heard the words.

"You remind me of the boy next door, John Cash, who took my toy theater and tore it up to get the glitter out of it, and got nothing, poor darling, but old bits of paper and an awful row. Do lie down. Then you'll feel better."

Old bits of paper, yellow and red and thick tinny gold, lying on the coal-shed floor. It was not even a new mistake. He had made it before.

He turned from her blindly, shambled across the floor and staggered out into the overgrown garden.

Now the whole hillside was alive with noise and from down on the rocks hoarse exclamations floated up as men fished for a pallid body in the shallow water.

The man who fled lurched against the door into the courtyard. It did not give because it opened the other way, and that was lucky for him. He heard a footstep on the stones beyond and had just time to drop down behind a dark bush beside the post before the door swung inward and Luke, followed by his opposite number from the French police, came charging through on his way to the icehouse.

At the same moment a touring car and a police car raced each other into the yard.

Havoc edged a step backward, missed his footing and rolled over into a ditch that had been completely hidden by the long grasses. His luck was persisting. It was soft and cool in the ditch and he could have slept where he lay, but he resisted the temptation. He crawled a few feet and found that an old conduit pipe, quite large enough to take his lithe body, passed under the wall and out onto the open hilltop.

As he emerged, lifting his head wearily amid the weeds, he discovered that he was in a disused waterway, a deep narrow fold in the open plain, with the house to his left. He could stand in it, without his head showing above the dry grass on its edges.

Behind him the noise and commotion, the shouting and the signals from cliff to beach, were all receding, and as he stumbled painfully on, they grew fainter.

He could not tell where he was going, and the curve in the hollow was so gradual that he was never aware of it. He moved blindly and emptily, asking no questions, going nowhere except away. The ditch wound around toward the cliff edge, where the coast was deeply indented, dropping to a tiny bay two hundred feet below.

Havoc paused. A great beam, placed across the ditch to save any unfortunate animal swept away by the rains, supported him at breast height, and he hung there for some minutes looking down.

Beyond the bay the sea was restless, scarred by long shadows and pitted with bright flecks where the last of the autumn sun caught it. But the bay was quiet and very still.

It looked dark. A man could creep in there and sleep soft and long.

It seemed to him that he had no decision to make, and now that he knew himself to be fallible, no one to question. Presently he let his feet slide gently forward. The body was never found.

The
Uninvited

The Uninvited

A CONDENSATION OF
THE BOOK BY

Dorothy Macardle

ILLUSTRATED BY BEN WOHLBERG

Cliff End, a beautiful house
perched high on the coast of Devonshire,
seemed the dream house
Roderick Fitzgerald and his sister
Pamela were looking for, when they
decided to forsake London for the country.
But once they moved in, their
happy dreams turned into a nightmare —
full of unexplained sighs and moaning
throughout the house. Soon they
heard the sounds when they were wide
awake, sometimes accompanied by a chill
draft on the stairs, or an unmistakable
scent of mimosa. There could be no
doubt their house was haunted. But why?

Was there a connection with the
violent death of the former owner? And
most important to Roderick, was the ghost
a menace to the dead woman's daughter
Stella, a winsome girl Roderick
cared more about with each day?

Dorothy Macardle has written a
delightful twentieth century ghost story,
its spookiness heightened by the high
spirits and wit of her characters.

Chapter One

THE CAR SEEMED to share the buoyancy of the April morning, humming along over the moorland roads. I was glad we had taken the top down. There was a heady exuberance in the air. The sky was a light haze; the trees and hedges were sprayed with young color. Pamela pulled her hat off; otherwise the breeze would have sent it flying. It was her doing that we were on the road before nine in the morning and heading for the sea.

We were two hundred miles from London already, and I had to be at my desk by twelve the next day. Even on a paper as smoothly run as *Tomorrow*, and with a chief as easygoing as mine, you cannot stretch a weekend further than from four o'clock on Friday to Tuesday at noon. But I was not going back to town without saluting the Atlantic from those famous North Devon cliffs, and my sister Pamela had insisted on seeing a house she had heard praised.

She was a little delirious with enjoyment of the spring morning, and talkative. "Roddy, look at that blackthorn; it's dazzling! I feel lucky this morning—do you? Isn't Marathon a gorgeous name?"

"And that," I replied, "is your reason for wanting to see it! You

143

ought to have discovered by this time how much innkeepers' recommendations are worth!"

"This must be the village. Turn to the right."

I turned off the paved road onto a steep byroad. The car topped the rise easily, and we came in sight at the same moment of the house and the sea. I drew up because MARATHON was written on the gateposts, but I did not stir from the wheel: the house was a drab barrack with its face to the northeast and a blind back to that superb view.

Pamela's first "Oh!" was a cry of elation, her second a groan of disgust. She sat glowering. "The man who built a house like that in a place like this should be condemned to haunt it for all eternity."

I said bitterly, "If only there had been no house here!"

The ocean below seemed to laugh at us. The water glittered and danced in the windy light. To the right and left, the coast swept in broken arcs, its rocks hewn into caves, arches and islets, its cliffs topped with yellow gorse. There were green headlands near, silvery and hazy headlands beyond. I felt that I would hunger for that view for the rest of my life.

We drove back down to the main road, studied the map and set a course for the shortest route to London, the golden mood of the morning dead. Silently, we came to the same dismal conclusion: our hopes had been preposterous.

At length I spoke. "We have just got to make up our minds that what we want doesn't exist."

Pamela caught her lower lip between her teeth—a sure sign, in childhood, that she was going to cry. To my relief, she laughed. She said, "We'll have to advertise for a haunted house."

It was too bad. I had been thankful to see Pamela set her heart on anything, and now this scheme, which had promised escape and adventure to both of us, seemed doomed to fail.

Six years of nursing our father had changed Pamela a great deal. When he died, I had persuaded her to come and live with me in Bloomsbury, thinking she might find new interests and regain her spirits in my lively bachelor flat. The plan had not worked. She started a course in library work, but realized that this would only lead her from one cloistered life to another and gave it up. Finally she told me that she wanted to live in the country and was thinking of buying a cottage and growing raspberries.

I at once realized that I would miss Pamela and that London had also let me down. My book was not progressing. I could now earn as much by free-lance writing of articles and reviews as by working as literary editor at *Tomorrow*. I said, "Why not share a cottage with me?"

Her delight was flattering. Enthusiasm seized us: a complete break with town, a life with air, space and growth in it, were what we needed. And so the search began. This weekend was our fifth defeat.

Now THE SEA was out of sight. The road ran down between pines and up over moorland. At a crossroads we saw a sign reading BIDDLECOMBE and an inn called The Golden Hind.

Pamela began to chatter. "How depressing it is to turn one's back on the sea! Oh, Roddy, do run up that lane! There must be a grand view from the top!"

"It will be the same view," I grumbled. "However, if it will get the sea out of your system!"

To please her, I turned up a gorse-lined smugglers' lane. It coiled up among rocks and budding rhododendrons and came out on a small windy plateau high on the cliffs. The view was the same, but there was more of it, for here a little headland ended and the sea lay out to the south as well as the west.

Pamela was first out of the car. She rounded a clump of trees to the left but, instead of walking forward, stood staring, her back to the view. I joined her and saw an empty house.

Stone-built, plain-faced, two-storied, so beautifully proportioned that one would have halted to gaze at it anywhere, it stood confronting the bay.

"Roddy," Pamela said, "it's a house!"

"So it seems."

I walked around it. It was a solid structure with large windows on either side of the door and three windows above. There was a pillared porch with a fanlight over it, and the ground-floor windows were set in shallow arches that repeated the fanlight's curve. The house faced south. A wooded rise sheltered it on the east, and on the north was the windbreak of trees.

The shape of the house was odd, for its sides were much longer than its frontage, the ground floor projecting at the back with a flat roof. There was a yard and a stable. The place had been neglected for years; the storm shutters that protected the windows were denuded of paint and one of them hung askew. The walls, however, looked sound.

Rough lawns, sloping down on two sides to the cliff's edge, merged with the heather. I walked to the edge of the cliff. Not a building was in sight except a lighthouse. I listened, and heard only the rumble of the sea, a gull's cry and the distant bleating of sheep. The cliff fell steeply to the sea. On the west side, the edge was not a hundred yards from the house; at its brink stood a dead, twisted tree. When I looked down and saw, beyond juts and shelving rocks, the amber gleam of a minute beach, I was seized by covetousness.

"Roddy, Roddy," Pamela was calling, "it's for sale!"

She was in the drive, near the stable. She had found a faded placard, half hidden by shrubs. The name of the place was Cliff End.

"It's worth twice our money, derelict as it is. Forget it!" I said.

" 'Commander Brooke, Wilmcote, Biddlecombe,' " Pamela read. "Roddy, come on!"

AT THE GOLDEN HIND we asked the way to Wilmcote. One could walk through the village and climb a steep path to the right, or else drive along the main road and take a winding course around the hill.

Very trim, very shipshape, Wilmcote appeared. It was on the slope of the hill on the opposite side of the village from Cliff End.

When I had rung the bell, I suddenly felt embarrassed, realizing that it was scarcely ten o'clock. The door was opened quickly by a girl who looked at us with dismayed dark eyes. Her hair was enveloped in a pink towel turban and her cheeks were pink from the heat of a fire. The effect was charming and I smiled. This made her flush more deeply, and she asked us quickly to come in. We murmured apologies for intruding so early, and she accepted them with a grave nod.

"I thought it was our maid; you must please excuse me," she said.

She looked like a child, but her manner would have been appropriate in a hostess of thirty.

"Quite by chance," Pamela told her, "we have seen the house called Cliff End. We would like to look it over, if we may have the key."

"My grandfather is out; I am sorry," the girl answered politely, and then her face came to life with a look of almost incredulous excitement. "Oh," she breathed, looking from me to Pamela and back again, "you are going over the house?"

"If we may," Pamela replied.

"I have no idea where the key is!" she said despairingly, then added, "But I will find it. Won't you wait in here?"

She left us in a small formal dining room but came back very soon with a large rusty key.

"I think this must be it. I expect you may have it. Or could you possibly wait?"

I explained that we had a day's drive ahead of us and were anxious to lose no time.

She handed me the key. "Take it. I will explain to my grandfather." She accompanied us to the door and heaved a sigh of frustration. "I can't possibly come with you because I have just washed my hair. What a misfortune!"

"Don't let us keep you in a draft!" Pamela said.

The girl smiled and looked frankly, yet shyly, into Pamela's eyes. I felt, when the door was closed behind us, that she sent longing thoughts after us.

THE KEY WOULD NOT TURN in the lock of the front door. Walking along the east side of the house, under the hillside that rose close to its windows, we found a small door, and this, with much creaking and sticking, let us in.

We passed through a scullery to a big kitchen. It was dim, for the windows were overshadowed by the rising ground and caked with dust. Every corner, the sink, the faucets and the pipes were festooned with cobwebs cradling dust. But the room was wired for electricity, had a generous sink and, Pamela thought, a tolerable range.

"Not labor-saving," she pronounced, "but spacious: room for Lizzie and her cat."

This was quite a point. Lizzie Flynn had cooked for us from the time I was seventeen and Pamela eleven. She had comforted Pamela when our mother died and trained her to take the mistress's place. Lizzie had sworn when we parted that she would come back to Pamela at any time, to any part of the world, provided her ginger cat might come, too. And Lizzie required space.

"These would appeal to her!" Pamela was looking into larders, pantries and the servant's bedroom, which opened off a passage behind the kitchen.

We went to the front of the house. A wide corridor led us straight to the front door. Standing with our backs to the door, we looked at the hall and stairs with delight. It was a fine entrance, broad, balanced, ample. The stairs had a mahogany banister that curved gracefully at the top and continued along the upstairs corridor to the left.

At the foot of the stairs, on our right, was a door with good, simple lines. One exactly the same faced it across the width of the hall.

"Elegant!" Pamela exclaimed, opening the door on the right.

This would be the dining room. It was almost dark, the shutters only letting in thin blades of light, but one could see that it was a long room, high-ceilinged, with a beautiful marble mantelpiece. The south window looked over the bay, and the window in the east wall had been set forward to escape the shadow of the knoll. What a room to breakfast in!

I crossed the wide hall to the opposite door, opened it and stood silent. I had seen no lovelier room. Though it was in submarine dimness, I could discern its perfect shape, the beauty of the cornices and the mantelpiece; I could imagine it with its windows open, all the lucent charm of sea and moorland flowing in.

The room was a pool of peace; our footsteps, loud on the parquet, violated its ancient quiet. Here, nothing that would disturb the mind's creative impulse would intrude. I suddenly felt that I could beggar myself to live here, but I did not tell Pamela that.

Mute with excitement, Pamela ran upstairs, and I followed. We stood at the hall window looking over the radiant bay. I opened a door on my right. Here, over the drawing room, were two rooms, with a connecting door. Unexpectedly, the front room was the smaller. The other was almost square; from its windows I looked westward over that magnificent broken coast and the open sea. In the foreground the dead tree, all its boughs grown inward, made a black fantastic figure against the blue sheen of the water. I said aloud, without turning, "I want this view."

"You may have it," Pamela called back, exultant. "I want this room!"

I found her in the front room across the hall, which, like the dining room, had windows facing east and south. Sunlight and sea light danced on the ceiling and walls.

" 'Farewell! Thou art too dear for my possessing!' " she sighed.

I looked into the room behind it, which opened near the head of the stairs, and called to her, "Don't despair: here's the snag!"

The east window of this room had been blocked up, and a very large window in the north wall looked over the flat roof to the yard. The brick fireplace was much too small, and the room struck cold. It and was dim, graceless, wholly without charm.

149

"A painter's studio," Pamela said. "The spiders like it, don't they? It would have to be the guest room."

I jeered at her notion of hospitality.

"It's you and me and Lizzie who matter," she contended, "and you must have a study. Lizzie will have to sleep downstairs."

The bedroom accommodations ended here. Other doors in the upstairs hall revealed only a large bathroom and a sort of storage room with a ladder to the attic.

"It is really a small house, isn't it?" Pamela said wistfully. Her face was taut, as if with hunger. She wanted it, and so did I.

Chapter Two

THE COMMANDER was at home. The maid showed us into an officelike room at the back. He stood waiting for us, a man not far from seventy, with white hair and beard, his head erect and blue eyes alight. He motioned us into leather armchairs and, sitting in his swivel desk chair, waited for me to begin.

He listened to my questions studiously and replied with precision. Yes, except for a brief period, the house had been untenanted for some time—for fifteen years, in fact. Yes, the roof and the stable would need repair. It was a well-built house, however; the man who designed it had been an architect and built it for himself.

"Five generations of my family," Commander Brooke said, almost defiantly, "lived there in health and comfort."

It was for sale. The property included the knoll on the east side and part of the grove; also the sandy beach, from which bathing was safe at low tide.

"And the price?"

"In its present condition, fourteen hundred."

I shook my head. I saw Pamela's face change. The old man studied her from under his jutting brows.

"Perhaps the Commander would consider an offer?" she said.

I offered a thousand, pointing out that repairs would certainly cost a good deal. He sat absorbed in thought, then looked up, saying, "I beg your pardon?" I repeated my offer, and he said, impatiently, "Yes, yes, that would do. . . ."

"You would sell for a thousand?" I asked, not certain that he had understood me. He sat motionless for a moment, his face stony. He seemed to be forcing himself to some ordeal. Then he said, "Yes."

Pamela looked incredulous, then relaxed with an immense sigh. I had as much as I could do to keep a businesslike rigidity and remember to say that I would like to examine the place thoroughly with an architect. Still abstracted in his manner, the Commander told me that there was, he believed, a good man at Barnstaple, and called a bank there to secure the number and address. His telephone was at my disposal, if I would like to make arrangements at once.

I telephoned. Mr. Richards could be at Cliff End at three o'clock. No, he was sorry; he could not make it earlier than that. I asked Pamela how she would feel about driving most of the night. She said that she would enjoy it, and the appointment was made.

As I hung up the receiver, I caught the Commander's eyes fixed on me searchingly. His face, narrow and aquiline, stamped with experience and authority, had a look of doubt. Was there some defect in the house that he feared the architect might expose? No, the man had rectitude in every line of him; it was not that. Was he uneasy about what sort of people we were? I returned his stare with a frank regard, perhaps a little amused, and, as though reassured, he turned to Pamela and said with a courteous gesture, "May I invite you to drink a glass of sherry?"

He rang, ordered the sherry and, after a moment's reflection, told the maid to ask Miss Meredith to come in.

While we waited, the Commander talked to Pamela, and I had time to look around the room. It was not interesting: there were filing cabinets and shelves full of old books; no fire, no flowers, no photographs except of ships. There was only one work of art in the room, a large portrait in oils over the fireplace, and that was not very good.

Yet, on second thought, that picture had quality; one would remember it. It was the portrait of a girl. The artist had obviously skimped labor on the hands and hair and white muslin dress, but he had painted a living face.

The girl was beautiful—fair-skinned, fair-haired, with large ice-blue eyes. Her hair was piled high above a noble forehead; her mouth was set in sweet, stern lines; she held her hands like a nun's, crossed on her breast. I could imagine her in a stained-glass window with a halo about her head.

The Commander, catching the direction of my gaze, became silent. I hesitated to speak of the picture, and there was an awkward pause. It was a relief when the girl who had given us the key came in with a decanter and glasses on a tray. The old man introduced us.

"This is my granddaughter, Stella Meredith. Stella, Miss Pamela Fitzgerald and Mr. Roderick Fitzgerald. They are considering purchasing Cliff End. The house," he explained to us, "actually belongs to my granddaughter."

A flash of excitement lighted the girl's face, but she bowed formally and set down the tray. Her hand shook slightly as she gave us our glasses. She looked seriously at Pamela and then at me. "I hope you will be lucky in it," she said.

Now, wearing a brown dress with cream collar and cuffs, her brown hair parted and held as smooth by combs as springy curls would allow, she looked seventeen. Her manner would still have served for a woman of thirty or more, but not all the time. Again she rested that frank yet shy gaze on Pamela's face, transferred it to mine and smiled.

We told her how charmed we were by the house. She listened greedily. "It must be fabulous," she sighed.

The Commander turned to her. "How's the commissariat, Stella? Can we invite our new acquaintances to lunch?"

"Yes! Yes!" she responded eagerly. "That would give us great pleasure," she amended, under her guardian's repressive glance. "If you will excuse a very simple meal."

We accepted, and Pamela was conducted to Stella's room.

The Commander offered me a cigarette. There was something about which he wanted to speak to me alone; that was evident. He began awkwardly.

"Miss Fitzgerald looks a little delicate. The air here should do her good."

That, I conceded, was one of our reasons for leaving London.

"Yes," he went on reflectively, "delicate, hypersensitive."

"Scarcely hypersensitive," I protested.

"I beg your pardon." He was sincerely apologetic.

"The air at Cliff End," I suggested, "must be superb."

"It is, of course, a lonely spot," he said, tapping his blotter with an ivory paper knife.

I waited, thinking I had better let him come out with it. At last, he said abruptly, "A clear duty is imposed on me."

"Yes?"

"Six years ago the house was occupied for some months. I must inform you why the people did not stay very long. They experienced disturbances there."

Experienced! I smiled at his word; most men in his place would have said "fancied" or "imagined."

"As long as the cause was not rats," I replied lightly.

"It was not rats."

I waited. Was he going to tell me any more? Obviously not. His mouth was set in a firm line. "I felt obliged to mention it," he said.

"A story like that will be quite an attraction to my sister," I told him.

"Indeed?" He turned to his desk and wrote down for me the address of the solicitor in London who had charge of all business concerning the house. I admired the integrity that had forced him to warn me about "disturbances" and the delicate consideration that had made him, rather than mention these before Pamela, reluctantly invite us to lunch.

Conversation with him was difficult in this mood, and I rose with too much alacrity when Stella returned to summon us to the table.

We had a delicious meal. Chicken with asparagus and potato croquettes was followed by a trifle on which the custard was still warm. The Commander entertained us with stories of the ways and characters of Devonshire men.

Stella, who was seated at my right, looked at her plate and said little. Her face was firmly molded on delicate bones, with a wide smooth forehead and hollowed temples. Little shadows and contractions, continually in play, betrayed what lips and eyes might conceal—that she had turned her mind on some other track.

We asked her about the neighborhood and its entertainments, whether there were dances sometimes or amateur acting, and where one could hear music. There was a tennis club, she told us, and a cinema, but no music and no theater.

"My granddaughter," the Commander gravely informed us, "has recently returned from a school in Brussels. It is an exceptional school; the pupils attend concerts and visit galleries. I hardly think that the local choral society would interest her after that."

The girl took up her cue and talked appropriately about the amenities of life in Brussels. At one point she nervously crumpled her handkerchief and a strong, flowery perfume came from it; the Commander noticed and frowned. Dismayed, Stella hurriedly put it away. She spoke gently. "I am sorry, Grandfather. I forgot how much you dislike mimosa."

"I supposed that you had forgotten," he replied.

Coffee was served at the table, and then it was time for us to return to Cliff End to meet the architect. Stella had such a look of eagerness held in leash as we prepared to leave that I contrived to ask her privately whether she could not come with us.

She smiled sadly and shook her head. "You ask," she said.

I signaled to Pamela, but she had already had the same notion and was saying, lightly, to the old man, "Would you come with us? Both of you, perhaps?"

"Thank you," he said, "but I dislike motoring, and the walk takes an hour."

"The proprietress, then?"

Surely he could feel the child's eyes, eloquent with pleading, though he did not glance her way.

"I am sorry. I cannot spare Stella this afternoon."

He produced a great bunch of old-fashioned keys and bade us a polite good-by.

Stella's face was set in resigned, sad lines; it was the expression of the face in the painting, and I resented it. Despite the excitement of our enterprise, I could not seem to get it out of my mind.

In the car Pamela dangled the bunch of keys joyously and read out the labels—"Stable," "Studio," and so on. "They make me feel like a landowner," she said.

"We have been a bit precipitate," I warned her. "We didn't stamp on the floors or examine cupboards or look at the woodwork; it's probably full of dry rot."

"Dry rot!" she exclaimed, as though it were a term of abuse. "That's what's the matter with the old man! Does he want us to buy the house or doesn't he?"

"He has to sell it and hates being made to."

"Do him good! I couldn't stand him refusing that enchanting child!"

"Child!" I mocked. "What's the difference between you? Five years?"

"Just about. She is eighteen."

"She doesn't look it."

"She has not been permitted to grow up."

"Did she say so?"

"Heavens, no! She hasn't realized it yet. Something will happen when she does."

"She seems all thrilled about the house," I went on.

"Yes. She left it before she was three and has never been in it since."

"That's odd—I wonder why."

"Her mother died there."

"That's not a reason."

"I know. . . . Her mother was the girl in the picture, and as good as she was beautiful, it appears. Stella's father painted it—Llewellyn Meredith. Do you know his name?"

"I believe I *have* heard his name."

I pulled up outside the stable, which would make a garage for two cars, and we walked around the trees. The house was splendid, standing there in its austerity and steadfastness amid the wildness and freedom of moors and sea.

"Are you sure you will be satisfied," I asked Pamela, "living up here on the edge of the world?"

"Satisfied?" She laughed. It had been love at first sight.

Inside, inspecting more carefully, I found an alcove under the stairs big enough to put a telephone in. Behind it was a cloak-room, and opposite that, a bathroom.

"Glory, have we missed a room?" I heard Pamela say.

She was at a door between the drawing room and the bath-room, trying keys in the lock. She opened it with one that had no label. We looked straight through a bay window filled with sunshine to the twisted tree.

It was a charming, odd little room. On the right was an alcove large enough to take a couch, and opposite it was a fireplace with yellow tiles. The sun-bleached wallpaper showed a faint pattern of small yellow garlands.

"It's a gift!" Pamela said, enchanted. "What do you suppose it was used for?"

She examined the door to the garden, of which the upper half was of glass. She pulled, and the glazed panels opened inward, leaving a half-door locked.

"It's bolted outside!" she exclaimed. "The steps are covered with a board. It's a gangway! Oh, it's a gangway for a pram! It's the nursery—Stella's room! The prettiest room in the house! How she will enjoy spending a night here!"

The bolt was stuck. I swung over the half-door and went across the lawn and stood by the tree, looking down at the bright crescent of sand. To own that would be to own the ocean.

There was wine in the air of Cliff End.

Chapter Three

EXTRICATING MYSELF from London was a long business. My chief had always been so decent to me that when he was ordered abroad for spa treatment, I couldn't let him down: I had to take his place. It was infuriating, but I saw no hope of escaping finally until July.

On the nineteenth of April, Cliff End became ours, equally and jointly. Pamela simply "threw London overboard," as she expressed it, and went. She put up at The Golden Hind. I snatched a few days with her there, engaged workmen and left her in charge. I ran down for three weekends and found that she was managing capitally and enjoying it all no end. No help or interest seemed to be forthcoming from Wilmcote, but that neither surprised nor troubled me. The old man, I thought, was difficult and better left to himself, and I had no doubt that Pamela would make friends with his granddaughter sooner or later.

I saw Lizzie off at Paddington Station with her collection of hampers and her cat.

"That's my Whisky," she said, chuckling, as the porter handed in the basket. "I have to have my Whisky wherever I go, night and day."

She never tired of that joke. This porter was her equal, however. "That's right, ma'am," he replied with a twinkle. "Don't lose your spirits, whatever happens."

How Lizzie laughed! And when Lizzie laughs, she shakes in all her ample being; her eyes run, her cheeks grow crimson and everyone within hearing is forced to smile. She would be talking about this porter for weeks.

"Whisky and gossip are your only vices," I told her as the train pulled out. Still convulsed with laughter, she called back, "Good-by, Mr. Roderick! Take care of yourself!"

July was perversely pleasant, with shade in the parks and sun and breeze in the streets. London, abandoned to honest workers like myself, began to seem my proper home; I was not sure that I wanted to give it up. I was going to miss the theater, and I was going to miss the paper—the office politics, the hasty lunches in pubs with our odd, amusing drift of contributors, and the weekly rush to deadline.

My chief called me in for a cup of tea and a farewell chat. "Your name means a lot to our readers, R.D.F.—quite a lot. You must send us plenty of stuff; don't let us down."

As I drove out of the city, the morning was hot and glaring, but on the uplands a breeze blew and by midafternoon I could feel in it the vigor of the sea. The road kept cheating me of a sight of the water, dodging down into wooded valleys and winding behind high banks, but at last the bay lay before me. I was seized with a crazy elation and sped wildly until I drew up at Cliff End.

For a minute the whole scene quivered, then I saw it clear, in the pure, strong colors of childhood, as if a gap had been torn in the veil that dulls the world to older eyes. The house was alive: new paint shone; polished windows glittered; upstairs, fresh white curtains waved. From inside, I heard Lizzie's welcoming shout.

Pamela came flying out of the house, a rich color in her sunburned cheeks, her gray eyes alight. She wore slacks and a loose white pullover and looked eighteen.

"The girl's rejuvenated!" I exclaimed.

She studied me, laughing and disapproving. Lizzie, too, crushing my hands in the warmth of her welcome, shook a commiserating head. "God help us, you're looking badly," she exclaimed with relish.

"Poor, town-blighted son of a hangman's ghost," Pamela said, "we've got you just in time! Quick, Lizzie—tea! I know you want to swim first, Roddy, but you can't—the tide's too high."

She made me begin my inspection of the rooms at the top, chattering all the time.

To my surprise, the rooms looked larger than when they were empty. Most of them had been painted light green, the halls ivory; I liked the effect. And our old family furniture, which had looked elephantine in London, seemed in proportion here.

I would not have believed that a room could be at once so peaceful and so exhilarating as my bedroom was. I decided to change the position of the bed: I wanted to wake facing that view. In the room opening off it was my flat-topped desk. Sunlight poured over it; a jar of pinks spiced the air; my parcels of papers, each with a label corresponding to its drawer, were set out on top. Ten minutes' work would make this my home.

"You have done pretty well," I said.

"The studio isn't papered yet," Pamela told me. "And for the present, we'll just have to shut off the dining room. It will have to wait till we're rich."

The lovely drawing room had accepted its role as general sitting room with good grace. The colorless birch of our sideboard, dining table and chairs, the faded rose of the armchairs and chesterfield, and my bookcases, painted green, settled pleasantly together. The window seat was piled with cushions. At the opposite end of the room, by the fireplace, my book-reviewing corner was complete, with deep chair, low table and bridge lamp, and the radio within reach. Lizzie came in to bid us to tea.

A lavish tea was set out on the checkered cloth. Lizzie spread jam on our scones, more generously than in schoolroom days, and piled them thick with Devonshire clotted cream.

"Tomorrow," Pamela said while we were eating, "we will hang the sitting room curtains and settle the books and put up the chandelier. Charlie Jessup is coming to help in the afternoon. He's a useful neighbor. There's nothing that he won't undertake to do. 'I be a bit of a tomato grower,' he'll tell you one day, and 'I be a sort of a blacksmith' the next. The trouble is, when he is half through one job, a passion seizes him to begin another. He and his aunt were supposed to take care of the house, I believe, and to clean it up for us, but it was left in rather a mess."

This surprised me; I should have thought that Commander

Brooke would be scrupulous in a matter like that. I asked Pamela whether the Commander had offered her any help at all.

"Very little," she answered. "Just a formal note asking me to let him know whether everything was in order, then a list of local addresses I had requested. Not another word."

"Nothing from his granddaughter?"

"Not a sign of life."

"I thought she would be running up on every pretext."

"It is not that she wouldn't love to, I'm certain of that. It's the Curmudgeon."

I had counted on Stella's companionship for Pamela. And, I began to realize, I had looked forward to taking her on picnics or for swims—in short, to giving her a good time.

"Yes," Pamela said, with her disconcerting habit of reading my thoughts aloud, "a spot of knight-errantry is wanted there."

"Rot!" I replied.

"I'm not going to stand for it," she said.

"You are not proposing to fight the Commander?" I asked. "I wouldn't, my girl! That's a formidable old man."

"I am going to make friends with Stella."

Her tone was one of unshakable resolution.

THE NEXT MORNING, I woke to the crying of gulls and breathed the sea air that was blowing in through my windows.

I ran out in a bathing suit, startling a rabbit who was nibbling on the lawn, sending him scuttling back into the heather. The water was cold. I swam until I was hungry, and even Lizzie was satisfied by the breakfast that I demolished when I came in. I was arranging the papers in my study when Pamela emerged from her room.

She put her head in. "You look a bit more human already."

"Do you want things from the village?" I said. "I'm going for a walk."

"Biddlecombe, please note, does not consider itself a village. It is a market town."

She made me a list and added, in charity, that everything

could wait to be sent except half a dozen eggs, which were wanted for lunch. I was to get those, and the butter and cream, from Mrs. Jessup at the farm.

Jessup's farm, I learned, not only supplied us with milk, butter, cream, eggs and Charlie, but gave Cliff End a right-of-way. I said that I would go by the lane, the highroad and The Golden Hind, and return through the farm.

The village post office yielded the envelopes on Pamela's list. At the tobacconist's I noticed a tray of picture postcards—local views, badly photographed and reproduced. One of them showed a roof and chimneys that I thought must be Cliff End.

"That's Cliff End, isn't it?" I asked the shopkeeper.

"That be it; a fine house, too," he replied. "I'm thankful to hear there be folk in it again."

"Have you a dozen of these?"

"Likely I have. Maybe you are the new owner? Well, well! I hope you and the lady will bring it back to itself. The last lot went away owing eight pounds in the village and making excuses to get out of it by starting ugly stories about the place."

"So that's what started the stories?" I said.

"There's others says different. But that's what I say."

"Such stories could do a house no good," I remarked ruefully.

"The poor Commander," the shopkeeper confided, "things are changed with him indeed. He and his daughter, they used to live there in pride, with the best of everything. I had to import his tobacco from London. Now he takes it ordinary."

At the thought of that downfall the man looked ready to weep.

The village was a busy little place, full of strong, briny smells and cheerful noise. Some very old houses crowded together at the lower end. The marketplace was separated by chains and stanchions from the wharf and jetty, where small boats of all sorts were docked. Some fishermen were spreading their nets to dry in the midday heat, and women came out of the houses and settled to mending them. There was a babble of jocular talk. I caught curious glances, which were quickly followed by nods of greeting as I passed. I wondered whether our friend Max Hilliard would feel that he could paint in this place. It would be grand to get Max down. . . . Well, one could loiter hours away on the quayside, but it was too hot for hurrying and I had a steep road to go.

A stiff climb it certainly was on the cobbles. I was glad to come out on the moorland, where there was a pleasant breeze, and to accept an invitation to "step inside to the cool and take a sup of buttermilk" when I arrived at the farm.

Mrs. Jessup, small and alert, with wrinkles enough for a centenarian but the agility of a young woman, studied me with keen brown eyes as she moved about between her living room and dairy, getting the things for which I had asked.

" 'Tis a real comfort to have neighbors again," she said warmly, "and such a kind, considerate lady as Miss Fitzgerald. Pays me every Saturday, regular, and mentioned the extra pint that I forgot. Not like the others that did let their great dogs chase the sheep and paid ne'er a penny for the three that were scared over the cliff. Unchristian it may be, but I blessed whatever it was chased they out of Cliff End. I do pray, though, that you and Miss Fitzgerald will have peace."

"Thank you, I'm sure we will."

"And so you should. For why would anyone wish to frighten a kind lady like your sister? Certainly not the gentle soul that's gone."

"The Commander's daughter?"

"Aye, his only child. She wouldn't hurt her worst enemy, would Mary Meredith. Threw her life away striving to save that wildcat Carmel—that's what most believe."

This was the first time I had heard this local legend. "Who was Carmel?" I asked.

"God only knows. An artist's model, folks did say. The Merediths brought her back with them from foreign parts. Supposed to be a lady's maid to Mrs. Meredith, she was, but a queer sort of a maid, if you ask me; wild as a gypsy in her ways. She'd dress up in her shawls and ribbons and dance on the lawn, then she'd break out in passions and weep and give out curses in her foreign lingo and threaten she'd throw herself over the cliff."

"Is that what happened?"

Mrs. Jessup gave me a doubtful glance, eager to say more, yet undecided how much to tell. She went to her dairy and came back with butter on a plate. Standing at the table and shaping the butter with wooden pats, she answered at last.

"No living soul knows what happened, Mr. Fitzgerald, or ever will know. Unless," she added, her eyes on her work and her voice lowered, "the nurse knew more than she'd say."

"What did the nurse say?"

"Miss Holloway said she saw them there at the edge of the cliff. Carmel was running, and Mrs. Meredith after her. It was dark night and a gale from the southwest. It was as if the wind took Carmel and flung her into the tree. She could see her, in her black dress, clinging to it, Miss Holloway said. Mrs. Meredith couldn't stop herself on the slope—'tis steep there. She flung herself sideways, making a grasp at the tree, but fell back and went down. That's what the nurse said, but by the way she said it, I thought she could have told more."

"Was Mrs. Meredith killed?"

"You didn't know that?" The brown eyes were startled; she shook her head. "Broke her back, poor lady. Not a scar on her lovely face, but a bruise, they did say, on the side of her head."

"What a terrible tragedy!"

"It broke her father's heart."

"And the girl she was trying to save—Carmel? She was all right?"

"Aye, but not for long. Dead in a week she was; died in her bed up at Cliff End. Ran off, that night, in the storm, no one knew where. My own uncle Jacob found her, two days later, sick with pneumonia and raving, up in Hartley's barn. Old Mrs. Hartley was afraid to take her in, so they put her in a farm cart and brought her home. She died in Miss Holloway's arms."

"And Meredith—what happened to him?"

"Him?" The way Mrs. Jessup slapped up the butter was more eloquent than words. "That man had no heart to break! Finished his picture and took himself off abroad. We saw nor heard no more of him for maybe three years, when the news came he'd been drowned somewhere at sea. There were no tears spilt in Biddlecomb for him."

She packed the things firmly into a basket and then, having kept me all this time waiting for them, said that her nephew, Charlie, was coming to us after his dinner and would bring them along.

"I'll take six of the eggs, please; they are needed for lunch," I said. "Well, I suppose it's fifteen years or more since that tragedy happened, but stories like that linger a long time in a lonely place."

"Aye, they linger," she said. There was something depressing and ominous in her tone. She extracted six eggs and put them in a paper bag.

"Well," she concluded with a sigh, "Lizzie Flynn says there's not a stir in the place. She's a kindly body. 'Tis nice for me and Charlie having her in and out. Good-by, sir, and I hope all will be well."

She stood watching me from her door. I could feel her good-will and her foreboding following me as I walked over the rutted field, perplexed and amused.

Here was a fine mesh of gossip weaving between Cliff End, the village and the farm. I wondered how much of it Commander Brooke took seriously, and how much Stella had heard. And why on earth had my communicative, dramatizing sister kept all this from me? Lizzie could not possibly have failed to collect and relay every word of the tale to Pamela long ago.

I struck across the heath where a beaten track meandered in the direction of the house. This was a grand place to walk in, with the sea crashing against the crags below, the gable of Cliff End ahead and the springy heather underfoot.

The track led me through a gap in our rhododendrons and into the drive, just opposite the yard door. Pamela called to me from the nursery, took the eggs, delivered them to Lizzie and joined me on the lawn.

"It's fun shopping in the village, isn't it," she said. "Did you get everything?"

"I did, and a fine parcel of gossip into the bargain."

She nodded. "I thought you would."

"The whole place is bubbling with it," I told her. "Attempted suicide, suspected murder, haunting and dear knows what! We seem to be at the center of a legend. It explains the Commander's manner. It explains a lot. In the name of goodness, why did you send me out in ignorance among the natives to learn it from them?"

She took my arm and led me to the twisted tree. It was long dead, bent inland, its roots clinging precariously to the cliff's edge, half exposed where turf had fallen away.

"This is where she fell," Pamela said.

"And was caught on that ledge, I suppose?"

"So Charlie says. And lay there, dying . . ."

"Queer kid you are, never mentioning it!"

"Roddy, it is such a dreadful story. At first I couldn't get it out of my head. It seems, somehow, so close."

"But you told me Stella left the place when she was about three, so it must have happened about fifteen years ago. That's not exactly close!"

"I know. It was silly of me. I've got over it now. I didn't want to spoil your first day by blurting it out, and I told Lizzie she mustn't."

"Good heavens, you don't suppose I'm going to mourn for a woman I never knew?"

She sighed and laughed. "Oh, Roddy, you good old buffer, I'm glad you've come!"

"I do believe you've been lonely!"

"I wasn't, really—at least, I don't think so." Pamela smiled, but her face looked a bit pinched; she was brooding over the Meredith story still.

"It is hateful," she said, "to think of the child losing such a mother and growing up with a heartbroken old man. I wonder whether she knows what happiness is?"

Chapter Four

WE HAD NEVER enjoyed ourselves more. On the tenth day after my arrival, suddenly Cliff End was a home. That evening it turned cool enough to justify our first sitting room fire. It was a fire of logs from our own timber, and they filled the room with a fine country smell. With the books in their places, our ancient curtains of pale gold velvet drawn and the lamps lighted, we settled down to an evening of leisurely work. Pamela's sewing table was crammed with cuttings and I had a new book of Walter de la Mare's stories to review. All we lacked was a cat, but we had discovered that nothing would induce Whisky to leave the kitchen at night, even when Lizzie went "Jessuping"—Pamela's word for her frequent visits to the farm.

After half an hour or so, when I paused to relight my pipe, Pamela said absently, "The weekend after next, don't you think?"

"For what?"

"I told you! The housewarming."

"Did you tell me? All right. But who's going to be the party?"

Pamela smiled. She had been thinking all this out. "Wendy, for one."

"Wendy Flower! Where is she?"

"Playing at Bristol."

"And Peter Carey?"

"Of course!"

"With the Argosy Company, I suppose?"

"Yes, I had a card. Wendy says they're exploring pubs and want to try a weekend at The Golden Hind. They are free on Monday nights, and want us to invite them to a meal. It would be rather fun having them here."

The idea was intriguing—those two at Cliff End! I had never quite learned to think of them as ordinary mortals. I saw them first in a revival at the Matinee Club, and they had startled me. They had poetry in their work, and played to one another in a way that made the piece lyrical. I said as much in my review and it brought them luck. They wrote me a joint letter, all rapture and gratitude, and a friendship sprang up. They came a good deal to my London flat. Pamela imagined that they did not have enough to eat and sometimes invited them to supper. Peter had given up performing for stage design—a precarious adventure.

"And who else?" I inquired.

Her answer startled me, as she had meant it to. "Max and Judith," she said.

"We can't ask them to come hundreds of miles."

"Max is always ready to do things. They'd come."

"I believe they would, too!"

"Good! You write to Max. Ask them to come a week from Saturday and stay a few days."

"Well, that ought to warm the house right enough! What about the local gentry? Are you inviting any of them?"

"Dr. Scott," she replied. "He's rather new here. He was kind when Lizzie scalded her hand, and so careful not to seem curious about the house that I promised to invite him sometime."

"Very good. . . . And?"

"And Stella, of course."

Stella, of course. So the housewarming was to be the first engagement in Pamela's campaign! "I'm afraid there's no 'of course' about Stella's accepting," I said.

"I know. I shall have to write very carefully, but I think I see how it can be done."

"I wouldn't put it past you!"

I wrote the letter to Max and went out to post it. The letter box was near the Jessups' house, but there was no finding the short-cut in the dark, so I went around by the drive and the farm road, a good twenty minutes' walk. A fine rain was falling and the air was soft; the sea made a low drowsy sound. I hoped Max would come. He would like this place. It would be grand to show him the house, and walk and talk and swim.

When I returned, Pamela had gone to bed. I sat up late, working, and produced the warmest book review that I had written since my apprentice days. The hour suited the book. The rain had ceased, and the last smoldering log had crumbled and died into white ash. The curious living stillness, with a tremor of the invisible vibrating in it, that de la Mare creates in his stories possessed the place. The sound from the sea was no more than the breathing of nature in her sleep. I shivered, then laughed. I had made myself nervous reading those queer tales. I went to bed.

TWO DAYS LATER, in the middle of the morning, a telegram came from Max: BOTH DELIGHTED. The message was characteristic in its promptness, brevity and warmth. Suddenly we felt excited. It was splendid to be able to gather together friends like this. I telephoned the theater in Bristol while Pamela wrote notes to Stella and Dr. Scott.

Mr. Carey was out, a charming girl's voice told me. Would Mrs. Carey do?

This was startling.

"Hold on a minute, would you?" I called Pamela, covered the mouthpiece and said, "Did you know Peter was married?"

"He can't be! He hasn't a cent!"

"He is so! Do we assume it is Wendy, or what?"

"It *can* only be Wendy. Ask."

It seemed the only way.

"Hullo, are you there? I say, who is Mrs. Carey? Who *was* she, I mean. . . . Oh, yes, do please ask her to come to the phone."

Wendy's light voice was full of laughter. "Yes, darling, we've done it! We were dying to for months. Didn't you know? . . . Yes, we'd simply adore to come."

I relayed all this to Pamela, who was as pleased with the news as I. "Good luck to them," she said. "They really are Siamese souls, you know—almost too twin. Come and vet my letter to Stella!"

She had struck a nice balance between the prerogatives of a grandparent and the emancipation proper to eighteen. "Some rather young friends" were coming from Bristol and we were inviting Dr. Scott. Would Miss Meredith come? We should be so happy if Commander Brooke would entrust her to us for the evening, and she would be escorted home in a car at whatever hour was decreed, though we hoped it would not be before twelve. Our enjoyment of the tranquillity of Cliff End was expressed, and we sent the Commander our kind regards.

The letter was addressed and stamped and I put it in my pocket to post after tea.

Work on the studio had begun. Pamela and I were papering the walls. With new paper and carpet, my favorite old curtains, and new twin beds and covers, the room should look less lugubrious.

"It can be a nice guest room, anyhow," Pamela remarked.

I covered my share of the wall rapidly. I wanted a swim. Pamela showed no intention of quitting, however, so I worked doggedly on beside her.

"You can hardly believe, in here," I grumbled, "that there's bright July weather outside. Someday I'll have that east window knocked out again. Did you know the Jessups told Lizzie that the last tenants locked this room up?"

I saw Pamela pause in her work, a look of trouble on her face. After a moment she asked, rather seriously, "Are you sleeping well?"

"Like a dormouse," I answered. "Aren't you?"

"I haven't wanted to worry you. I thought perhaps it wouldn't come back, but it does. Roddy, there *is* something—at night."

I turned and faced her; her brows were drawn and her gray eyes rested distressfully on mine.

"What do you mean?" My voice sounded rough.

"Haven't you heard anything, Roddy?"

"Of course not!"

"Not last night, or the night before last, when you came upstairs so late? The night we had a fire?"

"I heard the sea—nothing else."

"There was a sound, Roddy. I heard it just before I heard you come up."

"What kind of a sound?"

"A sigh—no, a sharp, shaky breath, a sort of gasping sob."

"That's the wind, Pamela. It makes queer noises between the hill and the house."

"There was no wind those nights."

"That's true. . . . Have you heard it before?"

"Yes."

"Always at night?"

"Yes. But the last two nights it has been much more—sort of *actual*. Roddy, it's a heartbreaking sound."

"You realize, don't you," I said, "that suggestion could account for it? All those stories have been very much on your mind."

"Yes, that's what I said to myself at first, but it isn't that."

"Where do you think the sounds come from?"

"I can't make out."

"Why didn't you come and call me?"

"I made up my mind to, Roddy, and last night I tried. I tried to make myself get out of bed, but I—couldn't move."

"You were dreaming," I declared. "It's a common dream sensation, that kind of paralyzed fright."

She shook her head. "It wasn't a dream. I wish you had heard the sound too."

"Why, Pamela? So that you could be sure there's something wrong?"

"No, Roddy, so that I would know that I wasn't alone with it."

I paused; she was in dead earnest. Then I asked, "Does it go on for long?"

"Only a few minutes."

"It's something in the house, Pamela—birds or mice or a bat."

"Perhaps it is."

Relieved by her acquiescence, I said lightly, "We'll shut Whisky in here! He'll chase your *revenants*," but I was not sorry a few minutes later to hear Lizzie's bell ringing for lunch.

Over lunch, Pamela began making plans for the party with so much zest that I felt reassured. Whatever it was that made strange sounds at night must be harmless, I told myself, since its effect on her could so quickly be shaken off.

Chapter Five

I HAD MADE MYSELF an impressive timetable of work. Jobs in the house and garden were henceforth to be counted as recreation and confined to the hours between lunch and tea. The late afternoon and evening were reserved for articles and reviews, while every morning from ten until one o'clock was stringently allocated to my book.

Very promising, and yet work on the book did not progress. What ailed me?

Pamela's prescription was simple: give the summer mornings to Cliff End, then, in September, go full blast at the book. But I knew that the longer the respite, the more painful would be the labor of a fresh start. I decided on a compromise: I would abandon the book for a couple of weeks and see what happened.

Pamela approved. "There's still plenty of occupation for you," she said.

There was. Just as soon as I could afford it, I was going to have new electrical wiring put in. I wanted more outlets for desk lamps, two-way switches for the halls, wall lights for the stairs. Meanwhile, I did what I could with adapters and yards of electric cord, while Pamela made pink shades for the party.

"It is a scientific fact that people talk better in rose-colored light," she declared.

Stella was coming. In a stately little letter she informed Pamela that her grandfather appreciated our kindness in inviting her and that she gave herself the pleasure of accepting. Dr. Scott had been good enough to promise to bring her and drive her home.

Max wired: REGRET POSTPONE SUNDAY WEATHER, which meant that he was at work on his cloud sketches and must take conditions while they served. In my opinion, there was no one painting in the British Isles whose skies could compare with his. The change meant that our entertaining would start with dinner for our four old friends on Sunday. The house-warming proper was to begin on Monday at nine.

On Saturday, while Pamela and Lizzie did things with prawns and duck and mushrooms, I completed my lighting scheme. Now the sitting room had a lovely little chandelier, every bed had its reading lamp, and each dressing table a flattering strip light. After dark we switched everything on and surveyed the effect. Pamela had filled the house with flowers—roses and stocks in the rooms and gladioli in the upstairs and downstairs halls. The whole place glowed softly.

On Sunday afternoon I drove to the station to meet Max and Judith. Bronzed, lithe and untidy, Max had the air of a man filled with health and content. Judith, who was at least six years older than Max, looked beautiful, serene and composed, with her smooth dark head, controlled movements and quiet voice.

"Max fell in love with a bank of cumulus," she explained apologetically. "I had no influence. When these things happen, I cease to exist for him. Fortunately, the affairs are necessarily brief."

"Has he immortalized his beloved?" I asked.

She replied in a low voice, "He is doing a lovely thing."

Max smiled. "Judith has her prejudices."

"You have no rivals today, at least," I remarked to her. The late afternoon was as calm as Judith's eyes.

Max had been silent as we drove, gazing about him. Suddenly he asked, "Could I get out and walk? Is it far? Will I get to the house in time?"

I dropped him at the crossroads, describing the shortcut to Cliff End, and stopped to pick up the Careys at the inn.

The Careys looked like visitants from some far star: Wendy's head aflame above a skimpy sea-green garment, Peter in white silk shirt and scarlet cummerbund. "We've hiked twenty miles," he told me in sad, musical tones as we drove on, and Wendy said, "It's the tag end of our honeymoon."

As we drew up at the garage, Pamela ran eagerly to welcome her guests. She and Judith, who had not met more than three or four times, greeted each other with warm pleasure, and Pamela

173

gave Wendy the kiss due a bride. When I had put the car away and followed them into the house, I found Peter studying every corner from every angle, while Wendy just breathed, "Oh, Roddy, it's swell, it's swell!"

"Marvelous potentialities," Peter concluded. "I'd do it in silver and geranium, with purples and just a streak of jade."

"I like it just as it is," Judith said, "full of harmony and ease."

Pamela was pleased.

IT WAS WELL THAT the ducklings were fat; our friends were hungry. It was a picturesque group that we had assembled. Pamela, in wine-colored taffeta, looked a stately chatelaine, and Max, with his soft brown beard, was patriarchal and comfortable in a brown velvet jacket. Judith wore filmy black with a raised pattern in gold, and long filigree earrings hung from her delicate ears.

Max engaged Peter in theater talk. The younger couple were in rampageous spirits. Wendy had just been cast for her first professional lead. It was Salomé. Peter was to design the dresses and sets. He called us all into session on the question of what colors Wendy ought to wear to set off what he described as her "orange" hair.

Among us, after dinner, a scheme of seven veils was devised. We cleared the floor and called upon Wendy to rehearse the dance for us. She produced a hilarious caricature, using a jug for John the Baptist's head.

The fun might have gone on until morning, but Max broke it up by saying that Pamela ought to rest. Judith said that she, too, felt a little tired. She smiled very sweetly at Wendy, whose ebullient youth had charmed her. Judith looked thirty and was twelve years or more older; she had beauty, dignity, sweetness, but no longer that vibrant joy.

The night was warm and scented; the bay lay entranced under a high half-moon. Max and I walked with the Careys partway to The Golden Hind, then strolled home across the heather and along the edge of the cliff, talking.

"Don't be surprised," he said, "if this place changes you and your work. It may push you toward something creative. It's exciting. You're glad, aren't you, that you made the break?"

"Thoroughly glad."

He stopped before the dead tree. "That's interesting."

"Interesting in more ways than one," I said, and told him the story of the place.

He had half a memory of Meredith's name. "It will come back to me."

"An ugly character, according to local legend, and the odd thing is that the girl he married is regarded as almost a saint."

We walked back up to the house. Alone in the sitting room, over whiskies and soda, we talked for another half hour. Suddenly Max remembered Meredith's name. "Lyn Meredith! That's he: Llewellyn, and called Lyn. By Jove, that man painted a picture that made him famous for a season—notorious, rather—but not through its merits. It was one of those 'story pictures.' I wish I could remember the subject. I have the volumes of Royal Academy photographs somewhere; I'll look it up."

"You'll be meeting his daughter tomorrow."

It was time for bed. There was so deep a quiet in the house that we took off our shoes and tiptoed upstairs. Before reaching the top, we paused, halted by a sound—a gasping, long-drawn sob. It came from the studio/guest room. In an instant Max had pulled the door open. He exclaimed, "Judith," in amazed distress and went in, shutting the door behind him.

Yes, it was Judith's voice—weeping, babbling, hysterical. What on earth had happened?

I hurried to Pamela's door, but before I reached it she opened it and stood in the doorway, clutching her white dressing gown around her. "Now do you hear it, Roddy?" she whispered.

"Hear it! Good Lord, of course I do! It's Judith!"

Astounded, she listened. The sobbing was rhythmic and desolate now.

"It *is* Judith! Oh, Roddy, thank heaven it isn't . . . But Judith—I must go to her."

"Don't! Max is there."

At this moment Max came out into the hall. "For God's sake, Pamela, take Judith to your room," he implored. He was pale and stupefied.

"There's nothing wrong," he told me when Pamela had gone, "nothing whatever. It's pure hysterics. I've never even seen her cry before." The poor fellow paced up and down the corridor. "I only made her worse," he said despairingly, and drew back as they passed—Judith weeping helplessly and Pamela pulling her into her own room.

Presently there was silence and Pamela came out to us. "Go in to her, Max," she ordered, and Max obeyed.

I gave Pamela a cigarette. "Has she seen a ghost?" I asked.

"No," Pamela replied.

"Heard something?"

"No, nothing at all." She hesitated. "It's very much a woman's trouble. When she sat down to cream her face in front of the mirror, she thought she looked old. It gave her a hideous shock."

"But, good heavens, that's not enough to throw a woman like Judith into such a frantic state!"

"She says it was ghastly: 'stark old age—death's-head old age.' Roddy, it *would* be a shock."

"But it's grotesque! Judith couldn't look like that."

"I know. I made her look in my hand glass, and that did reassure her a little."

"There must be more to it than that. I don't understand."

"Nor do I, Roddy. But you've seen people suffering from shock, haven't you? That's her condition. She can't go back to that room tonight. I'll give them mine and sleep in there."

"You'll take my bed, Pamela. I'll sleep in my study."

Max came out to us, his face dull with misery. He had heard what I said.

"No, Roderick, she'll have to go back and look in that mirror again. She has got to be convinced that it was her own imagination—and perhaps the light."

"It's not the light," I replied.

"And the mirror is a good one," Pamela added. "Max, Judith is really ill. Don't put any more strain on her tonight. Please stay in my room. I'll take Roddy's."

"I'm not ill; it isn't that." Judith was standing in the doorway, blanched to the lips. She leaned her head against the doorjamb and wept.

Desperation made me say the first thing that came into my head, and I said it in a tone of conviction that astonished myself. "Judith, it's not you. There is something wrong with that room. The last tenants kept it shut up. We should never have put you in there."

Judith said pleadingly to Max, "Oh, it *is*, it *is* something outside me! I never felt like that, and I *couldn't* look like that, could I, Max?"

"The sighing—" Pamela said tremulously, "it must have been from that room. Oh, Roddy, it *is* haunted! The house is full of some misery that can't die. What shall we do?"

"We'll shut up that room and forget it," I said. "We were crazy to put them in it. Judith has had a horrible shock, and instead of shouting for us, she tried to fight through it alone. The proper thing to do when you see a ghost," I said to Judith, "is to yell. You plucky women are the dickens to deal with!"

Between diminishing sobs, Judith smiled. "Oh, you are nice, Roddy!"

Pamela had run downstairs for brandy. Judith took a minute sip, then she and Max said good night. For the present, there was nothing more to say. Pamela left a note for Lizzie, telling her not to call us but to start breakfast when she rang, as we had been up very late.

It was nine when I woke—too late for a swim. Pamela came down somewhere about ten, refreshed. Then Max and Judith arrived, declaring that they had slept beautifully and looking only a shade subdued.

After breakfast Pamela whispered to me, "Come and see what I've found in the nursery."

It was a parcel labeled "For Roderick and Pamela for the

party" in Peter's ornate hand. A box of fireworks! Grand! I have a passion for fireworks. When had Peter discovered that? This would be splendid at midnight on the edge of the cliff.

Then, leaving Pamela to her sandwich making, I took Max and Judith down to the rocks. It was a hot, lazy August day, and the sea held a stronger blue than the sky. Max chose a ledge and dove into the deep water again and again, reveling in the vigor he found in himself. Judith was quiet and tired and content to be so. She swam a little, then lay on a smooth rock watching Max with a smile on her face that deepened when their eyes met.

"I suppose I ought to go and give Pamela a hand," I murmured, but nobody heard me.

I clambered back up the rocky path alone.

Chapter Six

THE PARTY SAILED away on a high tide. Dr. Scott came rather late with Stella, who, in her dark hooded cloak, was hurried away by Pamela. Scott was a lanky, loose-jointed man, clean-shaven and tanned by the summer sun, who looked about my own age. He had come from examining a patient and obviously felt out of place in this irresponsible atmosphere. In a few minutes, however, Max had him talking with absorption on the subject of dogs. Judith and Wendy insisted on putting a fox-trot record on the gramophone, which made Peter look pained. Marriage was wearing him out, he complained, as he helped me clear the floor. It seemed that he and his wife, aware of the deadly danger of merging into one soul, had each resolved to go on studiously doing things that the other disliked. "One is forced to *cultivate* differences, and it is so fatiguing," he moaned.

Judith, fascinated by this philosophy of marriage, asked questions, which produced a babel of exposition. But all the chatter in the room died down when Pamela came in with Stella, for Stella was beautiful.

The talk and laughter bubbled up again instantly, but that pause had been a genuine tribute to this dark-eyed girl who moved shyly in her straight, rather stiff ivory frock by Pamela's side. She waited for introductions and, as Pamela and I made them, gazed with candid wonder into each face, as though longing to know everything about everyone all at once.

While the rest danced a fox-trot, I stood with Stella, who said she only knew how to waltz, and told her about my friends.

"Oh, how beautiful they are! Look!"

She was right. Judith's dancing was perfection, and Peter had once studied ballet. Scott steered Pamela along conscientiously, his head bent in earnest talk. Stella chuckled as Wendy went by with Max, who was moving, as so many large men do, with buoyant ease.

"A waltz now. May I have the pleasure of this dance, Miss Meredith?" I asked.

"I promised Dr. Scott," she said, laughing as she danced off with him.

"Roderick," Judith asked as we waltzed together, "why does that girl look so joyous? It isn't just a party look. She is really starry-eyed."

"Would you call her beautiful, Judith?"

"Oh, yes! She startled me."

"She is in love with this house. It has been a dream house to her for years, and now she is here."

"What an engaging child she is!"

"She is nearly nineteen; hardly a child," I heard myself say brusquely.

"Where has she lived?"

"At a prim school in Brussels and a neat little villa near here."

"Ah, now I understand! Roderick, don't let them put her back in a cage!"

Pamela put on another fox-trot and danced with Max, while Judith went around sedately with the doctor and Peter taught Stella the step. When that dance was over, I took control of the gramophone and put on "Invitation to the Waltz."

Stella did not talk while she danced. Her movements were light and precise and her enjoyment was evident. I recognized the scent she was wearing: it was the mimosa that her grand-father so intensely disliked.

When our waltz ended, it was time for supper. A bar and buffet had been set up in the hall, and here Lizzie presided in supreme satisfaction. Mrs. Jessup was in the kitchen, and Char-lie, his face crimson with heat and excitement, acted as runner between the two. The door was open to the moonlit night; glasses and plates were carried out to the porch.

After supper I signaled to Stella from the stairs and she joined me.

"I'll show you the house," I told her. "Is this your first visit since you lived here?"

She nodded. "Grandfather . . ." She hesitated. "You see—it was very natural—he never wanted me to come."

"Do you want to see the kitchen first?"

"No, no—just my mother's room, if nobody minds."

"You'd like to see the studio, too, wouldn't you? This is it."

She stood still in the middle of the room. "I wish I knew more about my father. Grandfather has never talked about him, nor has Miss Holloway. They disliked him, I'm afraid," she said, and explained that Miss Holloway had been her nurse, then her governess.

"Were you fond of her?" I asked.

Stella looked a little perplexed. "She is a fine person and was my mother's devoted friend. I ought to be fond of her, but a gov-erness's business is to make you different from what you are."

"Is it? . . . Your tenants kept this room shut up," I told her.

She nodded. "I heard about it. Our servant told me. Grand-father was very angry with her. It made us both very happy to know that you find the house peaceful," she said. "We were truly afraid of your being disturbed. I know that my grandfather warned you."

Nothing would have induced me to tell her all was not well.

"We appreciated his candor," I assured her. "Tell me, what memories do you have of Cliff End?"

"Nothing fresh," Stella answered. "There is just one memory

I have always had, because it comes again and again in my dreams. You see, I was not quite three when—when I went to live with my grandfather."

"I would like to hear that memory if it isn't a depressing one," I said.

"Only parts of it are depressing. I am in a room alone in the dark. There is a black thing outside, clutching at me—perhaps it is that twisted tree. I am frightened in the dark and I cry. I cry for a long time, and finally somebody comes in. She leans over me and whispers some pretty words—I never know what they are—then she lights a light. It is lovely and I am happy, but someone else comes and puts the light out."

"And you cry again?" I asked.

"Then I am too frightened to cry."

We talked about dreams and I found myself propounding the theory that dreams are an abstraction of a repressed conflict. Stella followed with an intense absorption, less like the average girl's attentiveness, which is often mere personal flattery, than like a small boy's when he is being shown how a clock works.

"Come and see the other rooms," I said at last.

I showed her my room, and my study. She paused beside the bookcases, smiling. "What a nice workmanlike room," she said.

I asked whether she would like to borrow a book, and she asked for the stories by Walter de la Mare. I found the book under a pile of journals, wondering how she had known that I possessed it.

"It was intriguing, what you said in your review," she murmured, glancing at the woodcuts. "That 'he brings us into the world of the unseen, not by enshrouding our senses in veils of fantasy, but by lifting veils away.' "

When had I been so charmingly flattered? Stella had my very syllables, and they sounded musical spoken with such slow pleasure.

"How, please," I asked her, "did you recognize R.D.F.?"

"You mentioned writing for *Tomorrow* to Grandfather, and then I guessed."

I could have enjoyed more of this, but I had my duties to our other guests. I took Stella across to Pamela's room. "This was probably your mother's room."

She stood with downbent head, as if waiting for some quickening of memory or listening for the echo of a voice. Then she looked up at me with a little sigh. "What a pity that one forgets!" she said.

"No," I replied tersely, "you should be living in the future, not in the past."

"The whole house is lovelier than my dreams," she said as we went downstairs, "but the little room where we left our cloaks is the one I love best. Pamela thinks it must have been the nursery."

It was now past eleven, and as Stella had to leave at twelve, I asked her which she would prefer, fireworks or a game of charades. Without hesitation she chose the fireworks, and I hurried to collect them.

"Seriously, Roderick," Peter urged as we prepared our display at the farthest edge of the lawn, "you ought to write a play. The company is famished for new stuff."

"Avaunt, Beelzebub!" I replied to this. "How many honest critics have been thus seduced? How many led up the garden path 'that leads to the eternal bonfire'?"

The night was warm; our audience gathered on the steps of the porch. I could distinguish their silhouettes against the glow in the open doorway.

Our fountains of fire soared into the blue night, saluting the moon, then broke and showered flakes of flame into the sea. The last flung a flaring banner over our heads and, quivering, died away. For a minute the group in the doorway was still; then, with a babble and clapping, it broke up. Pamela called me. Scott and Stella were hurrying toward his car.

"Cinderella's time is up," Judith said.

Stella said good-by to everyone, and for me had a shy "Thank you." I heard her say to Pamela, as she leaned from the car, "I have never been so happy in all my life."

"Don't forget: tea at four o'clock on Monday!" Pamela called.

"Cinderella? No," Judith reflected, "Sleeping Beauty, just waking."

A bonfire was blazing on the edge of the cliff; Peter had robbed my woodpile. He and Wendy were enacting a wild scene about the Devonshire wreckers, who had plundered ships off the coast in the old days. They peered over the cliff, pointing, crouching, dashing about from rock to rock, describing the approach of the victim ship with such vividness that one almost saw it. Wendy's shriek became the death shriek of the doomed crew. Her frenzy as she bashed clambering phantoms on their heads, and her dance of gloating and triumph, made Judith declare that Wendy must have been a wrecker in a previous incarnation.

"I was," she declared, kneeling on the grass, erect and excited, "and gods, what a life! Duping the fools, seducing beautiful ships! Flaring your beacon and watching them change course, watching them head for the rocks—so proud, so near home, so puffed up with their brave voyage! And then, the crash, the yells—and the loot!" She looked like a little demon.

"I can't wait to see your Salomé!" I said.

Before they left, our promise had been given: Pamela and I would go to Bristol for a night and see the play.

I offered to drive them back to the inn, but they wanted to walk. Max went with them, and Pamela and Judith and I returned to the quiet house.

Lizzie had disappeared from the scene. The chaos was too complete to be tackled at night. We bolted the front door and latched the ground-floor windows, leaving the nursery door open for Max to come in by.

"How curious!" Pamela said as she switched off the nursery lights.

"What's curious?"

"I noticed that she was wearing it, but it was faint, and now it is overpowering in here, isn't it?"

"What are you talking about?"

"Don't you notice it—Stella's mimosa scent?"

"I do not."

"But, Roddy, you must!"

"Well, now, of course, you have made me imagine I do."

"The noselessness of men!" she said incredulously as we went upstairs.

The study sofa was comfortable; I liked lying there among my books. The sea made a drowsy sound, and there was a soft warmth in the night, a flowery sweetness. It was a small, secret room. . . . I heard Max come in and then I fell asleep.

I thought it was a sound that had roused me. Pamela had not called. There was only the connecting door between us. I listened; there was no stir in there. Could it be Judith in trouble again?

I was out in the hallway in an instant, listening at their door, but no sound came from that room. There was not a sound from the studio either, or from anywhere: a heavy cloak of silence shrouded the house.

I leaned over the banister, looking down. There was neither sound nor light downstairs—or so I thought for a moment, but then I became aware that there shone, very faintly, through the half-open door of the nursery, a pale, pulsating gleam. It was not moonlight: it moved.

A sense of deep uneasiness held me rigid. Down there, in the nursery, somebody moved and sighed; somebody moaned.

I had been listening in a half-trance, but the shock of astonishment roused me. I had seen a light and heard a voice—a young voice—moaning. Now light and sound were gone. They had not been natural: my own pounding pulses told me that. Someone out of the world of the dead was moving about the house.

My trembling hand groped for the light switch; I turned it on and ran downstairs barefoot. Everything was as we had left it: the nursery was empty, the curtains were closed, the scent of mimosa lingered, potent still.

I leaned against the wall, waiting for my heart to recover its natural beat, but a cold shivering had taken me and I longed for my own room. I turned the lights out and tried to go upstairs.

I could not do it; I trembled at the knees and shuddered convulsively, sick with the chill that seemed to shrink the flesh on my bones. I thought something was coming down the stairs. Nothing came; my eyes lost their power to focus and everything looked blurred.

At last, step by step, hand over hand on the rail, I dragged myself up the stairs. By the time I reached my room I was faint with the deathly weakness that comes when one has lost too much blood. I huddled under the blankets, clammy with sweat. There was no interval for thought—no sooner had the thudding of my pulses stopped and warmth come back to me than I slept.

In the morning, when I woke, I was scarcely able to believe the experience. I stood at my window looking out at the radiant day, telling myself what had happened but unable to credit the tale. Today joined up with yesterday, and the night between was like a dream.

My thoughts were full of our friends and the pleasures we were going to enjoy here and the work that I was going to do. We had made a good beginning at Cliff End. It had been a good party. A pity Stella could not have stayed till the end; she would have reveled in Wendy's acting. Wendy was a bit of a witch.

In my bath an idea came to me that held me enthralled while the warm water grew cold. There was a play in that reincarnated wrecker of Wendy's—a psychological crime play, a melodrama rooted in character, a thriller true to life. . . . Peter, for once, had talked sense. This was what Max had meant when he spoke of my doing something creative. All my avid reading of plays, my dramatic criticism, my devotion since childhood to the theater, pointed to this. The book could wait.

I went to the kitchen and demanded a large and immediate breakfast. Lizzie was in a good humor and she fried potatoes, bacon and sausages for me at once.

"That is what I call a party," she said with satisfaction. "Did you ever see the like of the mess that's in the sitting room? I have been up since seven clearing the kitchen. You eat here while I attack in there. I'll ready it before they come down. You could maybe," she added persuasively, "get Miss Pamela's breakfast when you're done?"

Obediently, when I had eaten, I boiled an egg, made tea and toast, and carried a tray upstairs.

Pamela was splashing in the bathroom. I set the tray on the table by the bed and went to tidy my study. When I returned, Pamela was back in bed, Whisky purring at her elbow and the tray on her knee.

"I had a marvelous sleep. Did you?"

"Part of the night." I sat on the window seat, meditating. No, I hadn't the right to keep this to myself. I said, "I feel it my duty to inform you that I experienced disturbances."

"Roddy!"

"I heard moaning and I saw a light."

"A light! Where?"

"In the nursery."

She spoke slowly. "Did Stella tell you about her dream?"

"Yes. I went down, but there was nothing."

She looked at me hard. "You're keeping something back."

"There was a sickening chill in the place," I confessed.

"I am immensely relieved that you heard . . ."

"I can understand that."

"It's rather dreadful to think . . ."

"Don't think! We'll get used to it: people do. It's a glorious morning. Forget it! Low tide's about midday, and Max and Judith needn't leave till two. What about an early lunch on the beach?"

REGARDING THE FEAST of remnants—salads, sandwiches and cakes—spread on the sand about us, Max sighed and wished loudly that he was about nine. He had been for a walk and now had good news for us: he wanted to come back in the autumn and paint.

186

"Grand!" Pamela said. "I do hope," she added, "that we shall have a peaceful room for you by then."

The sea glistened; the air quivered with heat. Max in his white flannels, Judith in her vivid green wrap, Pamela in a sky-blue bathing suit, and the plates and glasses scattered on the colored cloth made a dazzling picture. Casually I told Judith and Max what I had heard and seen in the small hours of the night.

There was a troubled silence, and then Max spoke perplexedly. "I wonder what on earth can be done?"

"Shut the whole thing out of our minds," I replied.

Pamela shook her head. "I can't shut it out," she said.

"You are getting used to it already. You are learning to sleep through it," I reminded her.

"But it may come again, any night, Roddy, and it is such an inconsolable sound."

"Well," I asked her, "what do you want to do?"

"I would like to understand what the *cause* is. Who is grieving and weeping, and why? What keeps the spirit lingering on? If we could only find out what would give it rest."

Judith had been silent; she spoke thoughtfully now. "Do we need to suppose that there *is* a restless spirit? It may all belong to the past. Isn't there a theory that a violent emotion can impregnate matter, saturate floors and walls, and then, with a sensitive person in a receptive mood, be reproduced? Mightn't something of that sort account for my experience, and for Roderick's, too?"

It might, we all agreed.

"But how would you deal with these violent emotions out of the past?" I asked.

Judith smiled. "Simply by living in the house as you are living in it."

We packed up and climbed the rock path, where a fresh breeze caught us and blew our towels about. Judith was right, I thought. Life was active and rich and free at Cliff End. It would be strange, indeed, if the vigor and contentment of the living could not banish the lingering sorrows of the dead.

Chapter Seven

MY PLAY GALLOPED. In three days it was mapped out. The dark passions of Barbara, my girl wrecker, swept the action along, and I, too, was carried away. Even the grim conviction that the house was haunted, which I could resist no longer, failed to distract me from my work.

I heard the sighing again the next two nights, and I assured myself that it came out of the past and no more told of present sorrow than would a gramophone disc. To my relief, Pamela told me she had heard nothing on either Tuesday or Wednesday night.

I had a fine distraction for her on Thursday. By seven o'clock that evening I had made sure that the plot would hold water, contrived my ending and determined to go on with the play. I came down and found her laying the table for dinner and told her what I was writing.

She was pleased out of all proportion to the cause. "I knew you were at something different," she exclaimed. "You looked so alive. This is the grandest idea!"

I asked her what she would think of a night in Bristol. Since I had Wendy in mind for Barbara, I thought it would be well to see her on the stage again. I also wanted to see the rest of the company at work, for there is no doubt about it: actors' personalities can give a dramatist no end of help in creating characters. They were doing *Death Takes a Holiday* this week—a play Pamela and I both wanted to see.

"I'd love it! Let's go tomorrow," Pamela said.

"I've got two articles to do. What about Saturday?"

"Tennis with Dr. Scott! But I'll put him off."

"It's on Monday, isn't it, that Stella is coming to tea?"

"Yes."

"If we started early, I could see the show twice on Saturday. By the way, will Lizzie mind sleeping here alone?"

Lizzie looked dubious when we put the proposition to her.

"You're going to supper with the Jessups on Sunday, aren't you?" Pamela asked her. "Perhaps you could sleep there Saturday night."

The struggle in Lizzie's mind was visible. It would be a fine boast at the Jessups' table to say that she had slept in the house alone, but she was nervous. "Well," she concluded, "if there were ghosts in it, they would have shown up before this. All right, I'll stay! Go off and enjoy yourselves."

THE DRIVE TO BRISTOL was a delight. It was exciting to be in a big, busy town again, with its steep streets and wide vistas over the valley. Pamela had no end of purchases to make for the house, and I needed books. At a flower shop with the inauspicious name of Withers we ordered roses to be sent to Wendy on the first night of *Salomé*. Then we went to the theater.

It was a curious experience to watch the actors and try to cast them in imagination for my play. Fortunately we thought Wendy good and liked Peter's sets immensely. Over tea at a café I lured Wendy and Peter into talking about the members of the company, their best and weakest points.

It was a profitable excursion. We both enjoyed the evening's performance, which had more pace and atmosphere than the matinee, and when we set out homeward on Sunday, I had a packet of useful notes.

We reached Cliff End late in the afternoon. As we walked to the door, we saw Mrs. Jessup and Charlie going home by the shortcut. Pamela laughed. "Lizzie hasn't been too much alone." She turned her key in the lock and went straight to the kitchen. After a moment I heard her calling me and went in.

"Roddy," Pamela said, "Lizzie has seen a ghost."

They were sitting at the table, both of them rather pale. Lizzie was changed. She was sagging over the table, her face dull with shock. She looked up at me in deep distress. "Oh, Mr. Roddy, you and Miss Pamela daren't go on living in it—you daren't!"

"Lizzie dear," Pamela pleaded, "do try to tell us quite clearly what you saw."

"I ought to be able to tell it, Miss Pamela, for 'twill be carved on my heart till my dying day. In the hall I was, locking the door. That top bolt's a bit high for me; I had to get up on a chair. I had only the downstairs hall light on; it was dark upstairs. 'Twas Whisky I noticed first. I heard a fierce snarl from him, and, heaven shield us, there he was under the chest, flattened to the floor with terror, his two eyes glaring like lamps and his teeth savage. It was a lady, Miss Pamela. I screamed like mad, because it gave me such a fright. She was standing there, leaning over the banister, just as you might yourself, and staring down into the hall. All in white she was, with long fair hair. But oh, pitiful saints, the awful look in her eyes!"

"What kind of a look was it?" Pamela asked.

Lizzie began to cry. "Don't ask me, miss! I wish I might forget it. Blue her eyes were, and terrible, as if she was looking down into hell. It went through me like a blast of ice. And then, in a wink, she was gone. I near fainted; my heart was beating fit to break my side. I could hardly get to my room."

"Poor Lizzie," I said mechanically, "you've had a shock."

"I couldn't sleep a wink, believe me, Mr. Roddy. In the morning I got up and went to early mass and I had a lovely talk with the priest after. He is a grand, wise man, is Father Anson—he says I'm not to stay alone here again."

"We wouldn't ask you to, Lizzie," Pamela said.

"And what did Mrs. Jessup say?" I inquired.

"She says the next time you go away, I'm to sleep at the farm. And she says there's no doubt by the blue eyes—it is the lady who was killed on the cliff."

We left poor Lizzie to quiet her nerves and walked around the knoll. The heat was intense and the light from sea and sky glaring.

"I am not inclined to believe it," I told Pamela. "It is too like the conventional apparition—a lady in white with long fair hair."

Pamela shook her head. "But the condition Lizzie was in, Roddy! Imagination wouldn't do that."

"Autosuggestion can do anything."

"Her description is very like the portrait."

"Exactly! She has heard Mary Meredith described."

"I wonder why you are so skeptical, Roddy. It doesn't help."

"Will it help to let hysteria run amok?"

"Listen, Roddy," Pamela said gravely, "I believe that Lizzie did see Mary, and I'm glad, because now we know one thing: who haunts the house. What we have to find out is *why*. I have the strongest feeling that if we could discover that, we would be able to put everything right. And you've got just the sort of mind to investigate a problem like this."

"I'll think about it," was all I would say.

But I scarcely gave it another thought all day. A gallery of lively characters occupied my mind. I had a fascinating job on hand, the weather was glorious and tomorrow Stella was coming to tea.

The pleasure that thought gave me was disturbing, and I did not want to be disturbed. I had found my work and I wanted to get on with it. This "engaging child," as Judith had called her, was a charming friend for Pamela. . . . Charming, yes . . . but I must keep my balance.

But I was not so equable when on Monday at lunchtime a telegram came: I AM DESOLATED UNABLE TO COME.

"Why a telegram?" I demanded. "Why not a telephone call?"

"There must be something that Stella didn't want to discuss," Pamela said, her voice depressed. "Do you think the Commander is going to cut her off from us? Never allow her to come here again?"

I saw it in a flash. "I do. The Commander has heard that his daughter's spirit is haunting this house."

"Oh, Roddy!" Pamela's eyes filled with tears.

WE DID HAVE a caller after all that afternoon.

At about three o'clock Lizzie announced Father Anson. The man came in a little diffidently, but was quickly at ease. He sat looking about the room and talked with lively appreciation about the pleasures of settling into such a home.

He was taking our measure, sensing the atmosphere and approving what he found. We took an instant liking to him, both of us. He looked not far from seventy, though hardy. He was not a tall man; his weathered face was creased with lines of experience and humor; he had a slow, comprehending smile and a direct, steady blue regard from deep-set eyes.

When Lizzie brought in the tea, he smiled at her and asked whether she would come and teach his housekeeper to make soda bread. "But it needs the air of Ireland to take the true flavor, I am afraid," he said.

"Let's see what you think of this, Father," Lizzie rejoined, delighted, "and if you give the word, I'll come."

He praised the soda bread and enjoyed a substantial tea.

"Lizzie told you about the ghost, Father Anson?" Pamela said.

He nodded. "I am very sorry, Miss Fitzgerald. It is grievous for you all."

I told him that if he could spare the time, we would like to consult him about it, and he looked up with a smile. "I would feel grateful for your confidence."

We told him everything—more than we had told each other. Pamela learned for the first time about the sickening sense of cold and fear that had come over me on the stairs, and I for the first time heard that while she and Lizzie had been alone here, the sound of sighing had often roused her at night and kept her wandering about the house. We told him of the Commander's warning and spoke of the portrait of Mary Meredith and how closely Lizzie's description of the apparition resembled it.

Father Anson cross-examined us on the details of our experiences, and discounted a good deal. Finally, however, he shook his head slowly, and there was compassion in his tone when he said, "Undoubtedly a residue of the inexplicable remains. I fear you may find that you cannot live in this house."

Pamela's voice trembled. "Father, can nothing be done?"

"My daughter, we can all pray."

"But mustn't we," she persisted, "try to understand—to do something?"

"Keep your own spirits calm." He paused. "In the last resort, there is exorcism."

The idea was abhorrent to me, redolent of superstition.

"Don't you think, Father," Pamela urged, "that it might be possible to do something that would give the troubled spirit rest?"

He smiled. "If there is, indeed, a troubled spirit—and if you have the faith and the courage."

"And the knowledge," I put in. "We know very little about the Merediths. The Commander will not even allow his grand-daughter to visit us, and village gossip is not a reliable guide."

"Ask me whatever you wish," the priest volunteered. "I may have to use a little discretion in answering, but you will under-stand that."

Pamela's first question was very direct. "Did Mary Meredith die by an accident?"

"As far as I know, her death was accidental," Father Anson replied. "As far as I know. . . ."

"There was some doubt?" Pamela went on.

"I understood that there was a doubt in Miss Holloway's mind."

"Do *you* think it possible that the girl—Carmel—struck her?"

"It is not likely, but at such a moment of terror, it is not impossible."

I asked him whether he had known Carmel.

He bent his head. "She was one of my parishioners."

That surprised me: I had thought of the girl as a gypsy.

When I asked him whether Carmel had been very attractive, Father Anson hesitated, then said, "I believe some admire the type. She had bright eyes, a fresh color, a pretty smile."

"Is it true that she was Meredith's model?"

"Yes. She was a dancer, I understand, but posed for him a great deal in Spain."

"That was before his marriage, of course?" I asked.

"Just before he and Mary Meredith met. She was wintering for her health in Seville and studying art. After the marriage she insisted on returning to England. The Commander gave them this house."

"And they brought Carmel with them? That seems extraordinary!" I exclaimed.

"It seems that Meredith insisted that he could not lose his model, and Mary"—the priest shook his head—"well, great magnanimity is seldom accompanied by worldly wisdom, and Mary loved to do a generous thing."

"I have wondered whether she was unhappy," Pamela said.

"Meredith was not a man to keep his wife happy."

Pamela sat thoughtful. I felt depressed. Was the house impregnated with the anguish of a woman who had been betrayed?

Pamela asked, "Was Carmel here for long?"

"She came twice. Her first stay lasted perhaps six months. Then, in the winter, they all went abroad. Mary was delicate and our winters are harsh. In the spring they returned—Meredith, that is, and Mary and their baby, who had been born in France."

"Stella?"

"Little Stella. I was told that Meredith was devoted to her— his saving grace. They had no other child."

"What had become of Carmel?" I asked.

"Mary had found a post for her in Paris. Carmel remained there for two years. But a hard time followed; she was poor— even, I fear, destitute. She became ill. When she came back, I was shocked: she was pitifully changed."

"She returned to Cliff End?" I said.

"Yes, she came to this house almost a beggar, you might say. Mary took her in. She nursed the girl, gave her clothes, tried her best to restore her to health of body and mind."

"She had become unbalanced?" Pamela asked.

"Overemotional. Sick people sometimes do."

He was silent for a time, then said, "I am afraid that is all I can tell you. How it ended, you already know."

"But, Father, we don't know how it ended," Pamela protested. "Was Mary murdered? Is it the old story of the spirit of a murdered victim 'ranging for revenge'?"

The priest looked shocked. "My daughter, Mary Meredith was not a heroine of melodrama. Mary was almost a saint. Revenge is unthinkable in connection with her."

"Either it was an accident, and that suggests no cause of haunting," Pamela said, "or she was struck, and that doesn't guide us to a motive either, since you say revenge could not be one."

Father Anson spoke very gravely. "You must not ask me to believe that the spirit of Mary Meredith is not at rest—"

I broke in. "Were you with Carmel when she was dying?"

An expression of stern anger hardened the priest's face. "Unhappily, I was not with Carmel when she died," he said in a low tone. "As her confessor, I ought to have been. But I was not sent for. I saw her twice while she was delirious, and I did not see her again."

Pamela asked, "Who nursed her?"

"Nurse Holloway was in charge. Carmel died of pneumonia."

"Miss Holloway!" Pamela exclaimed. "She lived with them all. Do you think we could find her and talk to her?"

Father Anson hesitated, then replied, "She lives near Bristol now. She is not a very approachable woman, I fear, but if you should decide to approach her, I could obtain her address."

I was remembering Mrs. Jessup's story of Carmel, dying from exposure, sent home in a farm cart. I said, "There was a good deal of prejudice against Carmel in the village, it seems."

"I suppose they thought her a sinful woman," Pamela said.

The priest had risen. "We are all poor sinful creatures, and the wiser we grow, the harder it is for us to avoid falling into sin. I sometimes envy the very simple." He smiled at Pamela and pressed her hand. "You may become accustomed to these little disturbances, my child, or they may cease. I will pray for you. If you need my help, send for me. At any hour, day or night, I will come. And now I will talk to Lizzie, if you please."

We thanked him, inadequately, it seemed to me, and I went up to my study to work. An hour later I saw him walking across the fields, his head bent against the rising wind.

Chapter Eight

"YOU'LL SEE, NOW THE house will be quiet," Lizzie said confidently after Father Anson's visit, and it was: night after night went by without trouble of any kind.

One breezy morning Pamela and I were working in the garden. "Look here," I demanded, "all this peace and quiet is beginning to seem too good to be true. Are you keeping things back?"

"Cross my heart, I wouldn't keep anything of that sort from you, Roddy," she replied. "Because if there is haunting, it has to be fought. I've not heard a sound since we came back from Bristol: eleven quiet nights. I'd like to run up a flag."

"Yes, I wish we could tell the world."

Actually, I wished that we could tell the Commander. A few days after the arrival of the telegram, Pamela had written Stella a note, but it remained unanswered. He must have forbidden Stella to write—selfish, tyrannical old man!

"Come for a walk to the village?" I suggested.

Pamela shook her head. "Don't want to leave this. Oh," she added, "it's Thursday—market day. Could you bring back some cream cheese?"

Biddlecombe market was quite an important affair, to judge by the carts, piled with produce, that thronged the roads. The stalls had been set up in the cobbled square by the wharf. Women chattered, poultry squawked, children dodged in and out, and fishermen strolled around, carrying strings of glittering mackerel and gossiping with their friends. I bought the cream cheese and paused at a flower stall. The house demanded flowers, and I really owed Pamela some attention, but these particular flowers were drooping.

While I contemplated them, I heard a soft, excited voice say, "Mr. Fitzgerald," and turned to see Stella looking up at me with flushed cheeks and troubled eyes.

"Tell me," I asked, "are these fresh? Would they last?"

She examined the cut ends of the stalks. "They'll revive in water," she said. "They might like an aspirin."

"I have to buy aspirin for them?"

She chuckled at my astonishment. "I am quite sure Miss Fitzgerald has aspirin."

I bought the flowers and feebly began to make conversation, intent on keeping Stella from vanishing again into the blue. "What would you think of an ice at the Lavender Café?"

She hesitated, then nodded. "Yes, thank you. I would like it very much."

We went into the dark little shop with its awkward steps and ostentatious oak beams. Stella settled into a corner seat.

"You disappointed us," I said.

She nodded. "Yes. And I was rude. I would have written to explain, but I couldn't think what to say . . ."

"Don't bother about explanations. When will you come?"

She flushed painfully. "That is what makes me so unhappy: my grandfather doesn't wish me to come."

"Do you mean—ever?"

She nodded and bent her head; she was upset. "I give you my word of honor that it is not because Grandfather feels . . . unfriendly or anything toward you or Pamela."

"No," I replied, "I am aware of that. It's the house."

She looked immensely relieved but said nothing.

"Somebody has told the Commander that the house is haunted, and he believes it. Isn't that so?"

"Exactly!"

"Tell me what is being said."

"I haven't heard very much," she replied, "but someone said your maid saw a white nun walking up and down the stairs, wringing her hands; that then your maid fainted and you found her in a swoon on the floor."

"Some strange things have happened at Cliff End and we believe that there is some kind of psychic atmosphere there, although, probably, there is no ghost. I can assure you nobody has seen a white nun."

"Oh, I am glad!"

"Did your grandfather speak of this to you?"

"He said the whole subject was morbid and abominable and he forbade me to mention it to him. Then he said, 'If you go to Cliff End, it will be against my wishes and against my judgment.' He told me that I must decide for myself. He said, 'You are eighteen, and I have never been a tyrant.' So I said that I would think about it, and I have been thinking ever since."

"Tell me," I asked her, "would you be afraid to come?"

"Oh, no!"

I hesitated. She was clearly longing for me to offer her some advice, but what could I say? It seemed atrocious that an old man's morbid fears should deprive Stella of friendship and pleasure, but dared I counsel a course that might destroy the relationship between the two? "You don't feel that you could come and say nothing?" I asked finally.

Stella flushed and shook her head.

"I myself prefer a fight to a lie anytime," I said.

"I believe you think I ought to come and tell him I'm coming," she said.

"I believe I do."

Stella looked into the distance, her eyes, with their long dark lashes, large and sad, her sensitive profile set. I saw that she would be a beautiful woman even in old age. I saw, too, how easily that gentle expression might become one of resignation. But she lifted her head, saying, "I will decide tonight."

"Fine! And if the decision is favorable, will you come to tea tomorrow?"

"But that would leave you and Pamela not sure whether I am coming or not."

"If you don't mind finding Pamela in dungarees and gardening with her, that doesn't matter a bit."

She smiled. "Oh, I should like that. . . . And now I will go home. Thank you for everything."

"I'll explain to Pamela," I promised, and then I took the steep road home.

On Friday I was lost in *Barbara*—the working title of my play. I lunched in my study on coffee and a sandwich, and when I began to feel hungry again, I rang my bell as a signal to Lizzie that I would have my tea upstairs.

I was convinced that Stella would come and was a great deal too much aware of that simple fact. But must I break off the most critical day's work I had ever attempted, lose my way, waste an impulse that might not be capturable again? The play was winding up in a fine flare of action and passion; I would not slack it down.

The battle it cost me to make this decision and stick to it added tension to the play. Once I wavered; I heard the sound of Stella's laugh from the garden. She had come! I put down my pen and looked out the window. They were building a weed-fire at the foot of the knoll. I ought to go down . . .

I picked up my pen again.

At last it was done. I wrote "Curtain," stretched like a cat and went out. It was nearly six o'clock.

Stella was absorbed in her weeding, kneeling on a sack on the grass. When I greeted her she looked at me over her shoulder, smiling, and then stooped to her work again.

"So the battle's fought and won?" I inquired facetiously.

"There was no battle," Stella replied.

Pamela pushed up a barrow full of weeds and tipped it over into the fire. "What have you to say for yourself?" she asked me, and then remarked to Stella, "I can always tell whether he has done an honest afternoon's work if his hair is less than tidy."

I grinned. "Well? Does it give me an excuse?"

Stella studied my appearance and nodded. "I think so."

"That's really nice of you," I said. "I was well punished up there. I'd rather make a weed-fire than anything, but I was finishing a play."

Stella sprang to her feet and opened her eyes wide. "Do you mean you have really just finished a play?"

Pamela, too, swung around. "Properly finished? The whole first draft, Roddy? Oh, good work!"

"What is it called?" Stella asked eagerly.

"For the present it's called *Barbara*. Honestly, its winding up this afternoon was bad luck. I didn't dare leave it."

"Of course! Oh, but of course!"

Stella understood; I was forgiven.

"What happens next?" Pamela asked.

"I'll read it to Milroy, the Careys' director, and see what he thinks of it. When could we go to Bristol? When does *Salomé* come on?"

"It starts on Tuesday. Would Friday do?"

"Fine. That gives me a week to trim it up."

"When are you going to read it to me?" Pamela went on.

"Whenever you like."

"This evening?"

"All right!"

Stella's sigh made me smile. There was a war going on between her interest in the play and the demands of social behavior.

Pamela, who was stacking up the tools, asked me with her eyebrows whether we should invite Stella to stay on. I assented.

"Stella," Pamela said, "would it make difficulties for you to stay to dinner with us and hear the play?"

Stella looked from one to the other of us, as if we had dangled the keys of Paradise before her eyes. "How I should love it! And it *is* possible. Grandfather never comes in on Fridays until after half past ten. He goes to supper with Captain Pascoe, who is an invalid, and they play chess."

"I suggest a quick dinner, then," I said. "I'll read immediately afterward and drive you home before ten."

Pamela hurried inside with Stella to wash. I followed and lighted the sitting room fire.

Stella came down presently, all tidy and proper, and sat in Pamela's chair.

"I am glad there was no battle," I said, standing by the mantelpiece.

For a moment she did not reply. Her face was turned away. At length she said, a little sorrowfully, "All the same, it is as if something has gone. He looked at me for such a long time, then he said, 'So you have passed out of my control.' For a minute I very nearly gave in."

It was half past seven when we sat down to dinner, and after eight before Lizzie cleared it away. Then, with coffee bubbling beside us on the low table, Pamela in her chair and Stella on the footstool near her, I switched on my lamp and the reading began.

The wind was whining on a low note outside and the logs crackled; to the accompaniment of those sounds, I read the first act.

Pamela exclaimed, "Roddy, it's masterly! And only three weeks' work. You're a dramatist! Why have you been hiding your talent? What a character! Where on earth did she come from?"

"Wendy and her charade, of course. Anything you think should be changed?"

"There's one stage direction," she said. "That moment when the devilish idea first comes into Barbara's head. I think she's got to have words or a gesture there, or it may not get across."

We had both been ignoring Stella, who was sitting there, rapt. "Oh," she murmured now, "I saw her standing still, like stone."

"That will do it," Pamela said.

"Right! She must suggest implacable coldness," I said.

Stella repeated "implacable coldness" with a sigh, and said, "Oh, please go on."

For the opening of the second act I wanted a song. It was to be sung offstage in the half-dark by the Welsh lad who is in love with Barbara's maid and has given up all hope of winning her. I explained what I wanted—something grave and tender—and asked Stella whether she happened to know such a song.

She pondered deeply for a moment, then said, "I think perhaps 'All Through the Night.' "

I remembered it vaguely and asked her whether she could sing it or hum the tune.

"I did learn it once, and it doesn't matter, does it, how badly I sing?" Then, looking into the fire, oblivious of everything but the words and their feeling, she sang. I remembered the old song now, with its wistful, moving cadence. Stella's true, very sweet contralto suited it perfectly.

I thanked her rather absently when she ended, Pamela murmured something, and then there was silence. I did not want to break that silence; I did not want to go on reading my play. I wanted to rest and look at Stella, sitting so still, not lifting her eyes from the fire, but flooded, as I was, by an overwhelming apprehension of the dangers and the sweetness of love.

I rose and crossed the room to the window. The sky was quite overcast. I drew the curtains, went back to my place, took up the play again and read to the end. I looked up and met Stella's eyes fixed on me.

"I'll just put my things on," she said a little anxiously, and slipped from the room.

"Hurry!" I called after her, dismayed to see that it was past ten o'clock. Not for the world would I have made her late. I threw down the script and ran to the garage. I backed the car up near the house. There was rain in the west wind.

"Better get a coat," Pamela said as I came in again. She called to Stella upstairs, then turned back to me to say, "Roddy, I'm thrilled to the marrow of my bones about the play."

"You think it will go?"

"Bound to! It's got everything: original characters, nice, dry humor, juicy dialogue, and plot."

I was really delighted. The world was mine oyster, which I was going to open with this play. And then . . .

A sharp cry sent us racing up the stairs. Stella was lying in the hallway unconscious.

I carried her down and laid her on the couch. Her face was as pale as wax, her breathing so faint that, for one agonized moment, I thought she was not breathing at all. My heart was constricted with fear while we worked to restore her, but there was no trace of terror on Stella's face. I asked Pamela whether she had seen or felt anything wrong upstairs, and she shook her head.

It was a profound faint. For a long time there was no sign of recovery, then, just as I was panicking, thinking that we must call Dr. Scott, Stella's breathing deepened and color began to appear in her lips. She opened her eyes. I felt as though my own spirit had come back from the edge of death.

"What is it?" she whispered. "What is wrong?"

"Nothing, darling," Pamela answered. "You fainted. Lie still for a little." Pamela poured out brandy, but Stella was so shaken by tremors that at first she could not drink. She tried patiently and swallowed a little at last. For a moment she shut her eyes, then opened them and looked at us, and a smile deepened the shadows in her cheeks. "Don't be worried; I didn't see anything," she said faintly.

My relief was immeasurable, and Pamela drew a long breath. She busied herself settling cushions under Stella's head, stoking the fire and lighting the flame under the coffeepot.

It was now twenty to eleven. "Is she fit to go home?" I asked.

"I don't think she should go out," Pamela replied anxiously. "She might faint again. I would like to put you straight to bed here, Stella," she said.

"Yes," Stella pleaded, "do please let me sleep here."

She was very pale and still trembling. It would certainly be better for her to keep warm and go to sleep as soon as possible, but was this house fit for her? Was it safe?

Her dark eyes met mine, troubled and shy. "Please, please, don't look so worried," she said.

"Are you sure you would prefer to sleep here?" I asked her. "Oh, yes!"

"You are quite sure you didn't see anything that frightened you up there?"

"Quite sure. Please telephone my grandfather and tell him I have one of my chills."

Commander Brooke answered the telephone. When I mentioned my name, he repeated it, his surprise undisguised. He probably supposed that Stella had returned and was in her own room.

"Stella dined with us," I told him, trying to sound as if that was something of which he would naturally approve, "and I am sorry to say she is not feeling well. It seems to be a chill. She is resting now. My sister would like her to stay the night, if you agree."

There was silence; then, in a constrained voice, he said, "Stella is subject to chills; they are said to be a nervous affliction. Has she—has she had a shock?"

"No."

"Are you sure of that?"

"She assures us that there was nothing of the sort, and we have no reason to think there was."

"Stella must come home," he said slowly.

I hesitated, recalling Stella's pale, exhausted little face. "You wish me to rouse her and bring her home instead of letting her sleep?"

I felt the anger in his silence, but knew that he would not unleash it over the telephone. Finally he asked in a stiff voice, "I should like to speak to Miss Fitzgerald."

I called Pamela. She spoke to him gently. "Commander Brooke, Stella asks me to tell you that there is nothing wrong— just one of her chills and a little fainting fit—but she feels too tired to come to the telephone. She asks your permission to stay with us tonight. I will take great care of her."

There were more assurances, and at last Pamela won his consent.

Stella sighed with relief when we told her, but inquired anxiously whether her grandfather had seemed displeased. We were forced to confess that he had.

When Pamela asked her whether she thought she could walk upstairs, Stella hesitated. "Please," she whispered, "not up there."

"You told us you didn't see anything!" I exclaimed.

She looked unhappy. "It's true I didn't see anything, and I

was not frightened, exactly. But something did sort of overpower me. I don't know what it was. Please don't go up there! What I would love is to sleep in the little room."

"The nursery? Your own room! Why, yes," Pamela consented, smiling.

I was not easy about this—it was in the nursery that I had heard sighing and seen the light—but Stella's eyes were wide with joy and warm color had come into her cheeks.

"You are both very, very good to me," she said and smiled at me, but I could not respond. I was filled with foreboding. An hour ago all had been well, but now a dark and chilling shadow had fallen between us.

"Please, try not to worry so much," she pleaded again, laying a gentle hand on my arm.

I was glad when Pamela took her to the nursery and I could go out in the rain and put the car back in the garage.

I was pacing up and down in the sitting room, my mind a turmoil of hopes and impulses and fears, when Pamela returned.

"She's all right now," she told me quickly. "I've lighted a fire so she won't be in the dark. I'm going to sleep here on the couch."

I told her that I would patrol now and then during the night. We promised to call each other if we heard the least sound.

There was nothing. I kept my bedroom door open, slept only in snatches and went downstairs several times. The lights stayed on in the hall all night. The wind subsided gradually. The house was quiet; through the half-open door of the nursery came the flickering glow of the fire Pamela had made, and I heard, now and then, a small, easeful sigh and the murmur of drowsy words. No wonder, I thought, if Stella slept lightly and had restless dreams. My heart grew lighter: if there was some obscure menace in this house, it was in abeyance now. Perhaps there was no menace at all. It was possible that the mere excitement of her evening with us, the play, and then her agitation about getting home before her grandfather had caused Stella to faint.

At last the thinning of the darkness in the east relieved my guard. I fell asleep then and slept heavily for two or three hours.

When Lizzie called me, I told her that Miss Meredith had been taken ill and had stayed the night in the nursery. She promised to be very quiet downstairs and to go in, as soon as she heard Stella stirring, with a cup of tea.

I had my bath, shaved and dressed. As I left my room, I met Pamela on her way from her bath. She said she had slept well. "I have never seen anyone sleep so contentedly as Stella," she continued.

We stood at the banister, listening. Lizzie and Stella were chatting in the nursery. Stella's voice had a joyous lilt in it.

The telephone rang. It was Commander Brooke. I reported all well and promised to bring Stella back within an hour.

"Quick with breakfast, Lizzie!" I called.

The sun was shining on a wet, glittering world. Stella had not appeared at breakfast and did not answer when we knocked at the nursery door. Pamela and I went out into the garden to look for her. She was standing motionless beside the dead tree. She heard us and turned her head slowly. There was no need to ask whether she was well. She was brimming over with joy; tears of happiness shone in her eyes.

"Oh, why didn't you tell me?" she said tremulously. "Didn't you know? She came to me in the night: she was with me in the nursery. I was afraid that it must be a dream, but Lizzie has seen her. It was she who was on the stairs. It is my mother."

Chapter Nine

No one spoke until we were seated at the breakfast table. None of us could eat—Stella was lost in a state of dreamy exaltation; Pamela and I, in our distress.

"Lizzie did wrong to say anything to you at all," Pamela finally said.

"No!" Stella protested. "I simply told her how I had fainted, and she said she had nearly done the same thing. She said that in another moment I would have seen her, as clear as life!"

"I am convinced," I told her, "that Lizzie only imagined that apparition."

Stella shook her head. "I know it is true."

"And you want it to be true?" Pamela asked her.

"But of course! Could anything be more wonderful?"

"But," I burst out, "it's unnatural!"

Stella paused, meditating. Her face was very serious. "I am going to tell you something," she said at last. "It was not upstairs that I felt her presence, but all night, in the nursery."

"Stella," Pamela said, "you were asleep!"

"I was too happy to sleep. I was happier than I have ever been in my life. I just lay, warm and quiet, watching the light, and knowing that she was there."

"What light?" I asked sharply.

"The firelight at first, and when I woke later and that was gone, the night-light on the table."

I turned to Pamela and asked whether she had left a night-light in the room. No, she had not.

"Didn't you?" Stella exclaimed. "A baby's night-light with a tiny flame? Didn't you, Pamela? Isn't that strange!"

"And isn't that proof that you were dreaming?" I reminded her that she had told me how often she dreamed of the nursery and the light, and I tried to make her see how probable it was that, when she slept in the same room, the dream had returned.

She smiled and said, "But there was another curious thing. The room was full of the scent I love best of all—mimosa—and I was wearing no scent."

Pamela glanced at me, startled. Neither of us spoke.

Stella went on. "Once I heard a soft, whispering voice. I couldn't make out what the words were, but they made me feel safe and cherished."

It was ruthless to try to tear down this illusion, but to let Stella live in it would be worse.

"You are obstinate," I declared.

She looked into my face searchingly, disappointed and distressed. "I don't understand you, Roderick! Why should you try to prove that it was not my mother? Surely you understand that for me it is an unimaginably happy thing?"

I did not know what to say, nor did Pamela. It was what Stella said next that fixed my wavering decision. She said, "Another time I shall see her, perhaps."

"You are not coming here again, Stella," I said.

Stella sprang to her feet and stood by Pamela, clutching her shoulder and staring at me. "You can't mean it!"

Pamela put a hand over hers, compassionately, but upheld me. "I am afraid Roddy is right." She looked very unhappy.

Stella stared at her incredulously. "But my own mother!" she said.

"I mean it," I told her. "Now listen, Stella: either there is no ghost there and your imagination is running to dangerous lengths, or there is one, and you were in its presence last night at the top of the stairs and it made you ill. You were in such a ghastly faint, Stella, that for a moment I thought you had died—" I broke off. The memory of that instant overwhelmed me.

Stella said gently, "I am so sorry."

"This house is no place for you. The Commander is right. I have been a fool."

I went to the garage to get the car, leaving Stella sobbing in Pamela's arms.

Pamela did not come with us, and we were silent until Wilmcote came in sight. Then I slowed down.

"You have to forgive me, Stella, but I am not being selfish," I said.

She answered in a faint voice, "I know."

"You think I am cruel?"

"I have been longing all my life for my mother, and she came to me, and you are separating us."

"Stella—this is terrible."

"But that's not the worst part of it," she went on tensely. "My mother isn't happy; she can't rest. There is something that she wants, and it may be something that I could do. I must find out— I must! I would face anything to give her rest."

My heart sank listening to her: a child's wild romantic ideas and devotion—and for a ghost!

We had reached Wilmcote. I drew up.

"Listen," I said. "I want to make Cliff End safe for you. Can you understand that? Try to be patient; give me time. Meanwhile I'll do everything possible. Don't desert us. You'll come and swim with Pamela, won't you?"

She shook her head. "I'll wait until I may come to the house."

I was hurt. "Is your friendship for the house, Stella," I asked, "not for us?"

Her lips trembled. "Don't make me cry," she whispered, and ran to the door.

The Commander opened it. He looked keenly at Stella and said something to her in a low tone. Then she hurried upstairs and he waited for me to come in.

He had aged. As he stood before the fireplace in his study, I saw the face of a very tired man. I told him that Stella was well again and had spent a peaceful night, and I gave him a fuller account of how we had found her unconscious at the top of the stairs.

"Where your servant believes she saw an apparition?" His voice was like frost.

"She is a superstitious old woman," I told him.

"You will remember," he said coldly, "that I gave you an indication of this."

"I appreciate that."

"I regret that you have been disturbed."

"If we could discover something about the cause of the disturbance, we might find some way to bring it to an end—"

His eyes flashed. "You would do well not to meddle."

His "meddle" infuriated me; the house was supposed to be ours, after all. "I think you owe it to us to give us any help that you can."

"I can give you no help."

I protested vehemently. "One room is uninhabitable—a friend of ours was made ill by depression there. Our servant has had a shock, and I myself experienced the most sickening sensation on the stairs—"

I broke off; I knew what was coming, and I deserved it. His voice shook with anger. "And yet, knowing all this, you and your sister have undermined my authority, flouted my judgment and induced Stella to visit Cliff End!"

I had no defense. "We supposed it was all over," I answered weakly. "We have told her that until this has been cleared up, she must not come again."

"There will be no question of her going to Cliff End ever again," he informed me in a stony voice. "My granddaughter is going abroad."

I was dismissed. We exchanged formal good mornings and I left.

When I reached home, I left the car in the drive and walked up the knoll. The wide view from there, the unbroken vista of sea and sky and moorland, should have had power to quiet storming thoughts, but now it brought no relief. I loved Stella, yet I had done her harm that might be irreparable: I had destroyed her peace. Yesterday I had felt confidence in my power to make Stella love me, to open to her a world of happiness. Today she thought of me as an enemy, and soon she would be out of my reach.

I found Pamela in the sitting room and told her what the Commander had said. She was dismayed.

"He'll send her back to that school. They wanted her to stay as a teacher. . . . Roddy, we can't let her go," she declared. "It will break her down."

"Scarcely more than we have done," I replied bitterly. "He's right to send her away. He has been right all the time."

Pamela shook her head. "Do you believe that Mary was with Stella in the nursery?" she asked me.

"I do not: it was wish-thinking," I replied.

"But one could understand it so well, Roddy, and if it *is* true, don't you see, that may be what Mary wants—the thing that has kept her spirit restless and haunting—longing for her child."

"I don't think you are right. I don't believe Stella was near any ghost."

"Don't you? But why?"

"She didn't feel that horrible cold."

"Yes, that's true. She felt warm, she said, safe and warm."

"I felt the cold. So did Lizzie."

"Roddy"—Pamela's voice was changed—"could there be *two* ghosts?"

Her face was alight with excitement. "There is Mary," she said, "Mary, who sighs and weeps, suffers a nightmare of misery in the studio, looks down in anguish over the stairs, and comforts her daughter and gives her a light. And there is the other— terrifying, unmerciful, cold."

"It's possible," I said. "Stella's father was as cold as a stone."

"As cold as a snake," Pamela corrected me. "But Meredith didn't die here. *Carmel* died here, and without a doctor or a priest. Father Anson must have said masses for her, of course. . . ."

"Didn't Father Anson promise to send you the address of that nurse?"

"Why, yes!" Pamela exclaimed. "And he said she lives near Bristol. Let's try to see her on Friday!"

"I think we should."

"I'll send Lizzie to Father Anson with a note."

Lizzie brought back a kindly reply from Father Anson, expressing his deep concern, and a letter of introduction to Miss Holloway, who now ran a "Center of Healing Through Harmony." He asked her to see us on Friday afternoon, telling her that we were "anxious about certain matters concerning Cliff End" and desired information that she alone could give. "It would be helpful," he concluded, "if you would treat my friends with the utmost confidence and give them particulars of the events preceding Mary Meredith's death."

We observed that Father Anson did not ask her to tell us about Carmel's death. Did he think the request would scare her off? We sent his letter, with a covering note, to Miss Holloway, feeling very doubtful that she would reply.

Chapter Ten

MISS HOLLOWAY wrote briefly that she would see us on Friday at six o'clock. I arranged by telephone with the Careys' director to come to the theater at about three to read my play to him. Milroy's eagerness would have pleased me if I had been capable of taking pleasure in anything.

The nights were detestable: the house was a cavern of mournful sound. To my ears, it was not sound so much as a kind of vibration. Lizzie, fortunately, appeared to hear nothing at all. But Pamela told me that to her it was a moaning human voice. On Sunday night and again on Tuesday we were both out of bed, exploring and listening. We had begun to distrust the evidence of our senses, to feel our hearts lurch at shadows, and to take every murmur of winds and waves for a supernatural sound.

On Wednesday Pamela received a letter from Stella that upset her a good deal.

I have told him that I will not go abroad. How could I go when he is obviously not well? But it would be dishonest of me to pretend that this is my chief reason, and indeed, as he says, my obduracy is making him worse. But, Pamela, I cannot go. For all of my life I have so longed for my mother. You would not believe how intensely I have imagined, sometimes, that she came to me at night. That was only make-believe, but in the nursery she really did come. I think she is lonely, and wants me as I want her. So you must let me come. Dear, dear Pamela, please try to persuade Roderick, and write to say that I may. You are my friend; you don't want my heart to break.

Pamela put down the letter and spoke shakily. "She is being torn in pieces."

I was moved, but not ready to give way. "All we can do for Stella," I said, "is to get rid of the danger, wherever it comes from. Tell her we are doing our best."

Pamela wrote Stella, telling her of our appointment with Miss

Holloway and promising to leave nothing undone. She said, too, that we both thought, grievously as we would miss her, that Stella would be wise to yield to her grandfather and go abroad for a time.

We would all be better for a night away from Cliff End. Lizzie was delighted to be spending a night with the Jessups, and Charlie had promised to come and carry Whisky's basket across the fields. I hoped that the visit to Bristol would give me a fresh start with the play. If Milroy liked it, he would make useful suggestions. I ought, then, to be able to break through my deadly inertia and complete the revision for final approval by the company producer, Adrian Ballaster, within a couple of months.

In spite of her fatigue after a week of broken nights, Pamela was in good spirits on Friday when we set out for Bristol.

Claude Milroy received us in his private office at the theater with delight. He beamed at Pamela through the rimless glasses that gave him the look of a solemn cherub. He adjusted the angle of my chair, fussed with the blinds to give me the best light and placed a carafe of water at my right hand.

"To think that you should give us the first offer of your play," he murmured, making me wretchedly nervous.

"Isn't it a truism," I said, "that critics can't write plays?"

"Shaw was a critic once," said a crisp voice at the door.

This was alarming: Ballaster had come. I read skepticism in every inch of his trim, disciplined figure and every line of his vigorous face. I had not wanted him to hear my rough draft.

There was nothing to be done, however. Milroy was as pleased as Punch at having secured the personal attendance of the great Adrian, and I had to pretend that I felt honored.

I read to this audience of three stumblingly, detesting the men and my play. When my voice grew husky, Milroy leaped to his feet and poured water for me. Neither of them spoke a word, even between the acts, and Pamela sat silent, too.

At the end there was a pause. Milroy opened his mouth and closed it again without speaking, his gleaming glasses turned on Ballaster's face. Pamela looked pale.

"Contemporary, meaty, good theater," Ballaster pronounced at last.

Milroy exploded. "Boy!" he cried, his pink face damp with excitement. "Oh, boy, it's a play!"

They plunged at once into questions of casting. There was a contention over Wendy. Milroy did not believe she could do it; Ballaster said, "Let her try."

I was relieved. I would have hated to intervene, but I felt I owed something to Wendy for inspiring my Barbara. Their views on casting the other parts were the same as my own.

"When can we have the final version?" Ballaster asked.

I held out for a month.

"First week of October? Good!"

Hospitality was pressed upon us, but I wanted to collect my wits before facing Miss Holloway, and made excuses to get away.

MISS HOLLOWAY lived on a height in Bristol's Clifton suburb. Her Center of Healing Through Harmony was a considerable stone villa on the side of the hill overlooking the wooded downs. Sad-looking women with thin hair hanging loose paced up and down the graveled drive in sandals. We waited in a chaste parlor decorated with reproductions of Botticelli, and as six o'clock struck, Miss Holloway came in. She was a tall woman whose impressiveness was increased by the starched cap she wore and the long full skirt of her dark green dress. Her eyes were deep-set in a sallow symmetrical face—dark eyes, which she used effectively, seldom blinking, and focusing on one's own. Her voice was strong, but gently and smoothly modulated.

"How is dear Father Anson?" She sat down. Her large hands lay still on the polished table.

"He is well," I replied.

She inclined her head slightly; it was the gesture of a distinguished person giving audience. "I am free for forty minutes. You are in trouble. Can I help you in some way?"

I let Pamela tell our story. She did it well and fully.

"My poor little Stella!" Miss Holloway said. "Deprived of such a mother, so young."

"You lived with Stella for some years, didn't you?" Pamela asked.

"For ten years," the musical voice replied. "I sacrificed ten years of my career to complete the work that Mary had begun. That was my tribute to my martyred friend."

We were silenced.

"I have not regretted it," she said.

Pamela recovered first. "We thought you would, perhaps, tell us whether Mary Meredith—whether she went through some great sorrow at Cliff End. We hear so much weeping."

"Sorrow was Mary's portion," Miss Holloway answered, "but she did not weep."

Pamela looked at me, disconcerted. Our hypothesis was thrown out.

"You may satisfy yourselves," Miss Holloway said firmly, "that if any uneasy spirit haunts Cliff End, it is not Mary's."

"It is a woman's voice we hear," Pamela said.

Miss Holloway said "Yes?" gently.

It was curiously difficult to ask questions of this woman. Our mission was, after all, intrusive. This had been an intimate friendship.

I said, "I believe you knew Mary Meredith very well?"

Miss Holloway bowed her head in assent. "I knew Mary as no one else ever knew her."

Pamela said in her gentlest voice, "We have no right to ask, but we think that possibly her grief, her emotions, may have left some influence in the house. If we could understand it, it would not be quite so tormenting for us. You would be doing us a great kindness if you would tell us something of her life at Cliff End."

"I understand," Miss Holloway said. "I will try."

Her voice became yet more quiet as she began her narration. "Our first meeting took place here, in this very room. This was an ordinary nursing home at that time, and my duties were those of an ordinary nurse. Mary had been sent here to recuperate from influenza. We recognized one another at once. My life's purpose—to create a center of healing which would use means beyond the physical—found a deep response in her spirit. 'Let us do this together,' she said. Mary had inherited a little money from her mother, and she was eager to use it in doing good.

"Alas, there followed the journey to Spain, that disastrous marriage and the entrance of her evil genius into Mary's beautiful life."

"Carmel!" Pamela exclaimed.

"Carmel. They were together at Cliff End when I was asked to come to Mary as a private nurse. Her illness was called jaundice, but to me it was apparent that it was due to grief and shock. The illness passed, but Mary's heart was broken. 'I felt it breaking,' she told me, 'like a bell of glass.' It never gave out the sound of gladness again."

Miss Holloway was telling us nothing. This was deliberate, I felt sure. There was antagonism here, either toward Father Anson or us. I was determined to have facts.

"Meredith had had an affair with Carmel," I broke in.

Miss Holloway assented with a gesture.

"But, good heavens," I exclaimed, "Mary knew it—you say she knew it—and yet she allowed the girl to stay on!"

The voice was soft and even, rebuking my outburst. "Mary was unique: a woman of infinite magnanimity."

"Carmel remained in the house," I pursued. "Then she accompanied Mary and Meredith to France!"

"You do not help the weak to overcome their sin by removing them from temptation," Miss Holloway explained patiently. "With anyone less depraved than those two, Mary's shining trust, her tender, watchful guidance, would have prevailed."

"You mean," I said, staggered, "that she deliberately . . ."

The word betrayed me: I was daring to disapprove. Miss Holloway's sallow face grew dark with anger; the hands on the table clenched as she answered, with tightened throat, "Mary refrained, Mr. Fitzgerald, from driving a young, passionate, reckless girl out into the sinful world."

"It is incomprehensible to me—"

"Mary," she broke in, her voice trembling with contempt, "*would* be incomprehensible to you."

I had blundered. We would get nowhere now. Deftly, Pamela diverted the current of anger from me. She said, "Mary even trusted Carmel with her baby, didn't she? She must have been terribly deceived."

"Deceived," Miss Holloway echoed. "Yes, but not for long. Mary had sacrificed herself for Carmel out of charity, but she would not sacrifice her child. She sent to England for me."

"To save the baby from Carmel?" Pamela suggested. "Was Carmel doing Stella harm?"

"When I arrived in Paris, I feared it was already too late. The child had been weaned; she was sickly; she did nothing but cry. She had only to cry and Carmel would rush to rock her, put a pacifier in her mouth, cover her with kisses—these peasant girls never learn." Miss Holloway stopped in disgust.

Pamela spoke quickly. "Did Carmel resent your replacing her in caring for Stella?"

A tight-lipped smile answered this. "She was furious; she made outrageous scenes."

"Then Carmel," I prompted, "was left in Paris and you returned to England, where, free from Carmel, I expect you had peace—you and Mary and the child?"

"Yes."

There was a pause. The calm, lofty expression stole back to Miss Holloway's face; her hands relaxed; her voice grew reminiscent. "Yes, peace. Peace for two perfect years. Mary created an atmosphere of heavenly serenity. Her father came sometimes, but only when Mr. Meredith was away."

"Did he go away a good deal?" I asked.

"He went abroad."

"To Paris?"

"Probably."

Pamela asked then, "Was Mary very fond of the child?"

"She was a devoted mother."

"Where did Stella sleep?"

"In the small room beside the drawing room on the ground floor."

"And at night—did she sleep alone?"

"Naturally. You know what psychologists think of parents who keep children in an adult's room!"

"Then Carmel returned?" I said.

"Yes." The voice was stern.

"How was she received?" Pamela asked. "Was Meredith there at the time?"

"It was he who opened the door to her knock. I shall never forget the look on his face. Carmel was a bedraggled, hollow-cheeked slut. His face became a mask of distaste. He stared at her, called for Mary and went up to his studio and locked himself in."

"Did Mary come down to Carmel?" Pamela asked. "Did you see it all? Were you there?"

"I was there. I saw Mary come out of the studio—she had been posing there for her husband—and lean over the banister and look down. If she had ordered the girl straight out of the house, I would have thought it justified. But Mary did not do that. She looked into Carmel's face for a long time, then she went quietly downstairs."

"And took Carmel in?"

"Took her in, lit a fire for her in the guest room, ran a bath for her, laid out clothes of her own. The girl coughed and sobbed and called out abuse of Mr. Meredith. Since she had never troubled to learn English, her vulgar patois passed over my head."

"So she stayed," Pamela said, and added, "In which room?"

"The small front room, opposite Mary's. But her coughing disturbed the whole house, so we had a bed made up for her downstairs in the dining room."

"But Meredith," I broke in, "what did he propose to do?"

"He proposed to paint her," Miss Holloway replied.

"Good Lord!"

"I heard him talking about it to Mary. 'If you can put up with her,' he said, 'let her stay. I can use her.' He had this idea for what he called an old-style story picture."

"Did Carmel pose for him—in that state?"

"No, she knew nothing about his idea. He did not invite her into the studio; he kept that door locked. No, he would merely stare at her during meals. It made the girl cry—she was madly in love with him still. He would sit and stare, then he would run up the stairs to the studio to paint."

"How long did this go on?"

"Nearly two weeks. If I had had my way, the end would have come sooner. And," she continued in a low, tragic tone, "it would have been a different end. After a very few days I told Mary that Carmel must go. She was destroying the child."

"You mean spoiling?" Pamela asked.

"In the most pernicious sense. She broke all discipline, ignored all rules. Naturally I forbade her to go into the nursery, but she would sneak in at night."

Pamela's eyes stretched wide. "Was it she . . . ? Was it against your rules to have a light in the nursery?" she asked.

"Certainly."

"And did Mrs. Meredith agree?"

"Our minds were as one."

"I see."

Miss Holloway looked at Pamela searchingly, as though wondering whether she had seen too much. This woman was telling us precisely what she wished us to believe, no less and no more.

"Nevertheless," I remarked, "Mary did not send Carmel away."

"Mr. Meredith objected. He told Mary, 'Keep her here three more days and, I promise you, she'll never come back.' His obstinacy was directly responsible for Mary's death."

"Tell us," I requested bluntly, "about the last day."

"I was about to do so." Her even, repressive tone was in itself a reprimand. It sickened me to think of Stella's childhood spent under this cold control.

"He drove the girl into a frenzy, and he did it deliberately. A storm had been raging all day, and the wind at Cliff End always made him insufferable. He came out of his study that evening and told Mary that Carmel could go now. He was laughing. 'Come and look at it,' he said.

"Mary went with him to the studio, and I remained in her room reading. I had put Stella to bed. In a few minutes I heard Mary calling Carmel to the studio. Then there came a wild outcry and Carmel burst out of the studio and fled downstairs, crying as though she had gone out of her mind. Mary came back to me, looking pale."

Miss Holloway paused; tears shone in her eyes, but they did not fall. A gong was now sounding through the house. She looked significantly at the clock. It was twenty minutes to seven; our time was up. The chiming was prolonged. At length it died away and Miss Holloway unhurriedly resumed her story.

"I supposed that Carmel had gone to the dining room. It was Mary who realized that she was in the nursery. It was Mary," she said tragically, "who went down. I heard the frenzied voice and followed. Carmel was standing beside Stella's cot. She had turned on Mary like a tigress—on Mary, who had been her angel! They spoke Spanish; I could only guess what vile abuse Carmel was hurling out. Mary looked like an avenging angel, tall and shining, her eyes filled with blue fire. She never once raised her voice, but her words fell like a sword. Carmel cowered then, screaming madly, burst open the garden door and ran straight for the cliff—and Mary ran after her.

"The child was clinging to me, frightened, but I loosened her hold and ran after them. I saw Carmel make a clutch at the tree and check herself just at the edge. The black tree and that girl in her black dress—I can see them now, swaying together over the brink. I saw Mary fling herself toward Carmel. She cried out and reached for a bough, and then—"

She broke off. Her eyes rested, doubtfully, on Pamela's and then on mine. When she spoke again, it was with every sign of reluctance. "Since Father Anson has requested it," she said slowly, "I will say to you what I have never said before to anyone except him. As Mary swayed there, on the edge of death, I saw a black arm swing out and strike her on the head. She went over without a cry."

Miss Holloway closed her eyes. She remained silent, tense with emotion, for a moment, then she looked at us and rose. We stood up.

"And Carmel?" I asked.

"Carmel died a few days later in my arms. I had nursed her night and day, but she was almost gone when they brought her to me. The end was sudden, but I had never had any hope. . . . I trust," she concluded impressively, "that I have made you both realize that if some unhallowed spirit haunts Cliff End, it is not Mary's. And now I must bid you good-by."

We thanked her; she rang a bell and left the room. A maid appeared and showed us out.

"Curtain!" I said as I started the car. "I have a feeling that one ought to applaud. What do you make of all that?"

"Just what she meant us to make of it," Pamela answered in a tired voice. "It is Carmel who weeps."

Chapter Eleven

"I AM SO TIRED," Pamela said as we wound down the hill again.

I, too, felt exhausted. Miss Holloway's histrionic performance had left me feeling as if I had been beaten on the brain. Pamela and I talked little until we had had a martini each and were eating a hurried meal at the hotel.

A spray of carnations and a note from Peter had greeted us. We were to go straight to their digs for drinks after *Salomé*. It would be fun telling the Careys about my play.

"Feeling better?" I asked Pamela.

"A bit. . . . The whole story's hideous, isn't it, Roddy?"

I agreed. "What a household! Meredith a cynic, Carmel a vixen, Holloway a hypocrite, and Mary a—"

"Prig?" Pamela offered.

"Well, say 'a creature' much 'too bright and good for human nature's daily food.' "

"Yes, I'm out of sympathy with Mary. Think of leaving the baby in those great cold hands! Gosh, how that woman hates Carmel! She probably strangled her."

"She didn't have to. In pneumonia, a little neglect goes quite a long way."

We sat at the table smoking cigarettes until it was time to go to the theater.

If the production had not been really brilliant, it could not have gripped us both as it did. Peter's set was superb; Wendy's dress sent a buzz around the house, and I liked her performance. She looked as pretty and dangerous as a tongue of flame. The Careys would do my *Barbara* proud.

When the curtain fell, I said to Pamela, "I'm feeling more human, aren't you?"

"Loads better," she answered. "But I want coffee before we go. I liked Wendy, didn't you? I'm beginning to see her as Barbara."

It was in the foyer, as I was being crushed and pushed by laughing, lighthearted people, that a desperate compulsion seized me to get back to the car and tear home.

It was Stella: danger was closing in on Stella, and she was a hundred miles away.

For a moment I was crippled by apprehension, then I elbowed my way brutally through the crowd, gave a message for the Careys to a program seller, extricated Pamela and hurried her to the car.

"Sorry, but I have to get home," I told her. "I've an overpowering feeling that something's wrong."

I thought she would protest—such a thing had never happened before—but she glanced at my face and simply did as I wished. I drove straight out of town.

"Have you got your script?" was all she asked.

"Yes. Heavens, I forgot the hotel!"

"There's nothing there that matters. We can phone tomorrow."

I seldom drive recklessly, but tonight I took risks. We scarcely spoke. Once Pamela asked, "Have you any feeling of *what* is wrong? Anything might be, mightn't it?"

"That's it. Anything might be."

Yes, there were plenty of things one could think of: burglars, fire . . . But it was not for the house that I was afraid.

The moon, a crazy fugitive, was flying about, seeking sanctuary among torn clouds in vain. Terror seemed to infest the night, but the wind was behind us and the car raced. It was not long after midnight when I was first able to hear the booming of the sea.

I shot over the crossroads and up the lane. Pamela, infected by my panic, cried, "Quick, quick!" I wondered why I had not gone to Wilmcote, since it was Stella who needed help. I did not know why; I was obeying a blind impulse.

There stood the house, square-set and steadfast. There was the tree, lashing itself demoniacally. Pamela was out of the car and around the corner of the house before the hand brake clicked. The thundering of the breakers on the rocks filled the night with noise. As I got out, the wind attacked me like a pack of hounds. Someone screamed.

I wheeled and saw the bay of the nursery lit up by a bluish gleam, then its door burst open and someone ran out—ran frantically, straight for the edge of the cliff.

I could not have been in time but for the tree. She caught and clung to it and swung out over the brink. It was Stella. As she swung there, she screamed, and I shouted, "Hold on!"

I could not stop and would have gone over myself except that, lurching sideways, I gripped a bough. A twig whipped my face, half blinding me, and I groped. At last I had a grip on the trunk and clung there, Stella within the clasp of my right arm.

I heard Pamela calling, "Roddy, Roddy, where are you?" I shouted, and saw her starting to run. I yelled to her over the howl of the wind, telling her to go slow, that we could hold on. She ran down to within arm's length of the tree, where outcropping rocks gave her a foothold, and, braced there, dragged

224

Stella up. A leap sent me sprawling on the ground beside them, and then we all stumbled up to the house.

When we were inside the lighted hall, I stood still, confused and dizzy, with blood trickling into my eyes, knowing nothing except that Stella was safe. I heard Pamela saying, "Oh, your eyes, your eyes!"

I told her that my eyes were not hurt. She put her coat over Stella, who was sitting, half-dressed, trembling and deathly pale, on the chest, then went upstairs and turned on the hall light.

"Bring her up, Roddy," she called.

Stella could not speak; she was fighting to keep back tears. When I drew her to the foot of the stairs, I felt her shrinking, but she made a strong effort and went up. She did not cry until she was sitting on the couch in Pamela's room. Then, her hands over her face, she let tears come, and choking sobs. Pamela tried to console her, but Stella was oblivious to everything. Pamela looked at me, then took bandages from her cupboard and went for warm water to bathe my forehead.

I was standing by the mantelpiece, gripping it, when Stella took her hands from her face and stared at me with dark, dilated eyes, gasping, "You might have been killed—oh, you might have been killed!" Then she buried her face in the cushions and shook with smothered sobs.

She needed comfort, but I was rigid with misery. In her crazy infatuation, Stella had almost thrown herself to her death. Oblivious of me, of her own life, of all human needs, she had given her heart to this myth. She was no longer the Stella I understood. I could say nothing to comfort her. I would not try to compete with this mad obsession; I would batten my love for her down under hatches until Stella was herself again.

Pamela came back and bandaged my head. Then she asked me to bring in the oil stove from my study. I did so and lighted it; the room was cold. I brought up drinks. It was nearly half past one. Pamela made Stella drink some brandy and water.

"I think you must hate me," Stella said.

"No," Pamela answered, "because we understand."

"Nobody could possibly understand." Stella's voice sounded hopeless.

"What happened?" Pamela asked.

"I saw her."

"You saw her?" I cried, startled.

Stella said despairingly, "I saw her, and I ran away."

"Of course you ran away," I exclaimed.

"But she is my mother! Don't you understand? She is my mother and she wanted me. I came because I knew she wanted me, but when I saw her, I couldn't, I couldn't . . ." She was tense with bitterness now, sitting with her hands clenched.

"Fifteen years," she went on, her self-contempt needing to find vent, "think of it! Wandering about alone in the empty house, waiting for someone to see her and listen to her. And then, at last, her own daughter, that she loved . . ."

Her thoughts appalled her, but we could not make her stop.

"I meant to be brave. I thought, Presently I shall see her and we'll speak to one another. I must have fallen asleep. I woke with my heart jumping, and it was cold—it was the deadliest cold I have ever known. And then"—Stella's voice faltered— "then she began to come through the door—she came right through the locked door, like a mist. It was there, beside the bed, a tall, shining cloud that was almost a woman. It moved. It had eyes—and I ran."

She drooped forward, half fainting, and Pamela caught her.

"Oh, heavens, Roddy," Pamela gasped, "what can we do? She'll go out of her mind."

"I am going to take her home," I said.

Stella lay on the couch now, too exhausted even to cry.

"Better make hot drinks, Roddy," Pamela begged. "She can't go home like this."

Thankful to escape, I went down to the kitchen and assembled things on a noisy tin tray. My nerves were a peal of bells that the devil was jangling and this house was hell. What could you do for a girl who forced her way into a haunted house, to be terrified half out of her mind by a ghost? I groaned and put my hand to my head. That cut was burning. I saw her again, swinging over space, clinging for her life to the swaying bough of the tree.

Then my misery left me. I finished making the hot drinks. Stella was not dead—she was upstairs, here in my house, the proper place for her to be. She was my darling and I loved her, and all would be well.

When I brought the tray up, Pamela looked it over. "No spoons!" She went downstairs for them.

Stella lay on the couch, propped with pillows and wrapped in an eiderdown. She glanced up at me as I stood by the fire, and I saw that she was afraid of me. I asked as gently as I could, "Are you feeling better?"

"Yes, thank you," she said softly, and added, "You despise me, don't you, Roddy?"

"On the contrary," I answered, "I think you were heroic. But I don't want you to be heroic. I want you to be safe."

Her eyes looked immense in her blanched face, the long lashes wet. The defiant, tense look was gone; her lips, half open, had a childlike softness. "You saved my life," she whispered.

"It would be a pity," I replied, "to throw it away."

Her eyes met mine, and she flushed. Shyness overcame her and she did not speak again until Pamela returned with the spoons.

Sipping her drink, she smiled at Pamela and said, "I broke into your house like a thief, and you are still my friends."

"What about the Commander?" I exclaimed, remembering him for the first time.

She replied in a subdued voice, "He thinks I'm at home in my bed."

"I'd better take you home at once."

Pamela protested. "Stella ought to have some sleep first, and an hour or two can't make much difference now. Would you feel afraid," she asked Stella, "to stay here, sharing my big bed?"

"Oh, no! Not if I'm not alone!"

"In a couple of hours, then," I agreed, and went downstairs.

I tried to put the events of the night together. How had Stella deceived her grandfather? Was this the night on which he regularly went out? Friday: yes! And we had to choose tonight to leave the house empty! How had Stella known? Had she been present when we were making our plans? Was this devilry, or was it chance? And what was it that had summoned me back from Bristol?

Stella's coat and dress lay on a chair in the nursery. I gathered them up and carried them to my study. The light burden filled me with happiness: Stella was safe. I sat there at the window where I could watch Pamela's door.

Stormy though the night was, it was warm. The wind was not screaming now; in those open spaces it rioted, strong and free. The veiled moon was ringed with a circle of gold. For a moment it shone out in brilliance and the war of wind and water was visible. Even if the powers of evil were loose in it, this was a glorious night.

Pamela's door opened. She closed it and came across the hall quickly, glancing nervously to her right. "Roddy," she asked, "has the night turned cold?"

"No," I said sharply. "What is it?"

"That ghastly cold is seeping into my room."

I thrust Stella's clothes into her arms. "Get her out of the house!"

While I waited in the hall, I watched the studio door. I did not know whether the hall light was reflected on it in some curious way or whether what I saw was a wreath of luminous mist; but it moved; it crawled and spread over the door. A chill nausea seized me and I called to Pamela. She and Stella appeared in a moment and we ran downstairs. Stella had a coat on, but Pamela wore only her dressing gown.

"Fetch a coat from the closet," I said, and she ran to do so.

Suddenly Stella gasped and flung herself against me. I pulled her head down, so that she should not see what I saw now. I shouted to Pamela, "Go out the back way," but she rushed to the front door, pulled it open and shut it behind us. We stood on the lawn, holding together against the gale. Even here I had to fight down panic. One minute more, and the form at the head of the stairs would have been a woman—a tall woman, with ice-cold eyes.

In the car Stella sat between us, trembling. I drove fast down the lane; we were at the crossroads before I had recovered sufficiently to go slower. Here, in sight of houses, under the shelter of the oak trees, I drew up.

"What did you see?" Stella asked shakily.

"A whitish wreath of mist," I replied. I asked her what would happen when she went into her house.

"I think I can get to my room without waking Grandfather," she answered. Ashamed, but determined, she told us what she had done. "I lied to him. I told him I had a headache and was going to bed. I asked him not to wake me when he came in. I was treacherous and horrible."

She was silent as we drove on.

Pamela said that I had better pull up a few doors before Wilmcote. "He may be patrolling," she said. I pulled up and she slipped out of the car.

Stella was crying again, very quietly. "Roderick," she said, "you have forgiven me, haven't you? I promise solemnly that I won't trouble you and Pamela anymore. As soon as Grand-father's better, I'll go away."

"Don't do that, Stella! Don't go! God knows when I'd see you again!"

"But I thought you wished me to!" There was a lilt of surprise in her voice—almost, I imagined, of joy.

What had I said? The last thing I had meant to say. "No, I didn't mean that, Stella. You must get away for a time. But don't take risks anymore—I can't stand it. Promise?"

"I promise, Roderick," she said.

Pamela returned to tell us that there was no one about.

Stella tiptoed up the garden and put her key carefully into the lock. I remembered vividly how she had opened that door to us five months ago. She looked back to smile at us before she slipped in and gently closed the door.

Chapter Twelve

THE HOUSE WOULD have to go. Let it go. What did it matter? It was wrecking our lives—Stella's and Pamela's and mine.

Up on the knoll, in the gray, gusty morning, I came to my senses. The rain had blown over but the bracken was wet. I had come up with an axe and a saw to cut timber for a fence. For a man who has got to make order out of emotional chaos, no activity is better than sawing wood.

I chose a tall sapling and set to work. I enjoyed the clean strokes of the axe, and felling the tree. It cut through my problems, too. I knew I needed Stella's love and sweetness as I needed air, and that she was not a child. Stella had her own maturity, a maturity wrought out of stern discipline imposed on a nature intrinsically wild and free. What did she see when she looked at me? A man of the world, a sensible elder brother, helpful in trouble, ready with advice? If that was how she saw me, it was my own fault, and I was going to remedy it.

Pamela was climbing up through the bracken. She had heard me bringing the sapling down. Yes—there was the question of Pamela and her share of the house. She wanted to fight for Cliff End, to cling to it. So did I, but not at all costs.

She came and stood beside me.

"I have a proposition to make to you," I said. "Supposing that my play is a success—I mean, has a run in London. If I were in a position to offer you your half of the price of the house, plus what you contributed to improvements, would you accept?"

She was astonished and a little distressed, but nodded. "If you want to live in it, yes."

"My notion might be to shut it up."

"Just throw your capital into the ocean?"

"Exactly." I continued to saw boughs off my tree.

"It isn't as desperate as that. We won't have to give it up."

I hesitated, then said, "You can't stand this indefinitely, nor can I. It ruins my work."

"For a few more weeks I can."

"Weeks, but not months. We are not going to spend the winter in Cliff End with ghosts. Would you accept my offer?"

"I don't think so. We can't just quit without a fight." She thought in silence for a minute. "If the trouble is hallucinations, then we're beaten and I'll go. But I think there is a spirit who comes for a purpose and who would rest if it were achieved. . . . I'm making a chronicle of everything that has happened, and I want your help. Then we can go through the whole story and try different theories. A rather awful idea came into my head just as I was falling asleep: that there were two spirits fighting—contending for Stella—last night."

"Lord," I exclaimed, "I hope that isn't so!" I thought it over. "But it's conceivable, all the same."

"We haven't really given our minds to the question of Carmel yet."

That was true. Back in the house, I racked my brains to discover what clue it was, connected with Carmel, that I had left untouched. Then I recalled the picture of which Max had spoken and the photograph that he had promised to let me see. I put a call through to him, and he answered, his voice full of pleasure and warmth.

"I didn't forget those Academy photographs. Judith has unearthed them and she'll post them at once. You'll be interested; we were! How are things at Cliff End? You don't sound too fit."

"A bit short of sleep," I confessed.

"Not still? How's Pamela?"

"Not too fit, either."

There was a pause. "I was thinking of coming down. Judith's sister's going to be in town for a couple of days, and she'll be occupied. Could you put me up from Thursday to Saturday?"

I hesitated. "That's a long journey for two nights—"

"It's settled, then! Thursday evening. So long!"

Max had rung off before I could either thank him or protest.

Lizzie arrived at noon, astonished to find us at home; she had not expected us until teatime.

"But, sure, the weather wouldn't tempt you to be dilly-dawdling. 'Tis good-by to summer," she said.

Pamela wanted me to work with her on the journal, but I had to give the afternoon to my play. I set out the blue paper on which my second draft was to be written and sat down. Then I heard a sound out of childhood—a horse's hooves and cab wheels outside.

I went to the front door, and sure enough, there was an old horse cab. Commander Brooke stepped out. He stood surveying the house, his face stamped with age-old pain.

"Roddy, we're in for it! Poor Stella!" Pamela said, and she added sadly, "The poor old man!"

What had Stella been through with her grandfather? And what would he have to say to us? I had a keen recollection of the sword flash of those blue eyes, but the eyes were dull with bewilderment when they met mine.

"I have called to ask you for an explanation," he said.

I told him that I was glad to have the opportunity to offer it and asked him to sit down. He chose a dining chair. We waited, not knowing how much Stella had said to him. The man looked too ill to be out of his bed.

He spoke heavily. "My granddaughter has given me her version of what happened here last night. You brought her home after two o'clock, encouraging her to creep in like a—like a thief." He was controlling his agitation by an immense effort. "I have a right to ask for your version, I think."

I replied, "You most certainly have."

Pamela said gently, "I hope Stella is well?"

"She is very far from well," he replied. "Her penitence and shame are overwhelming, as one would expect."

"She has told you what happened?" Pamela asked.

"I believe," he answered bitterly, "that this time she has told me the truth."

"I feel quite sure she has. She was so unhappy over having deceived you."

He turned to me. "What happened?"

I told him. I told him of our leaving the house empty and of our sudden return because of my feeling that something was wrong. I told him about Stella's dash from the house, of her exhaustion, of the malignant coldness that had gathered while she was resting and the figure that I had seen at the head of the stairs.

He stared at me, appalled. "This is worse than anything I had supposed."

"Fortunately," Pamela said, "Stella thinks that the presence is a gentle, loving one. That saved her from a much worse shock."

"Don't you think," I asked him, "that the time has come when you would do well to help us with any information you may have?"

"I can give you no help whatever! I refuse, absolutely, to discuss my private memories with unscrupulous intruders." He paused, and said, "I beg your pardon," stiffly.

"You have had a distressing night," Pamela said, offering for him the excuse he had failed to offer for himself. "You see," she went on, "my brother and I have thought that there may be two spirits haunting this house: Stella's mother and another. We thought—"

He turned on her, his face suffused with anger. "Are you so superstitious as to credit these stories? So cynical as to imagine that a saintly soul like my daughter is doomed to a fate so horrible? That she walks the night, terrifying harmless people, including her own child? That she is not at rest? No!"

Now the blue light in his eyes shone, fanatical. "My daughter—" His voice broke; he bowed his head and ended weakly, "My daughter is at rest."

I sat silent. Pamela said quietly, "May she rest in peace!"

She had tears in her eyes. I, too, felt sorry for the tormented man.

"I have never heard a woman praised and remembered as your daughter is," I said.

"And *her* daughter," he groaned, not lifting his head, "is secretive, cunning, disobedient, a trickster—" He raised eyes almost blank with pain and spoke without knowing to whom. "Mary was as clear as spring water; she never lied to me in her life. Stella is her father's daughter. She remembers him—that is the trouble—and she resembles him physically. The influence of that strain in her is so potent that it has been my aim to break it down. When Mary died, I retired from the navy and dedicated myself to that purpose—to making Mary's child the woman Mary would have wished her to be. I paid an exorbitant salary to Mary's nurse. I surrounded Stella with Mary's pictures, gave her Mary's books, sent her to the same school. It was a sacrifice: I missed her. When she returned home a year ago, I was pleased."

"I think," Pamela said, "that you have every reason to be content. These little deceptions—"

"Little deceptions! That is how you speak of them! Such is your influence over Stella! The change in her was sudden: I begin to comprehend it now."

"You can scarcely mean to be so insulting," I said.

"My intention was to hold no discussion with you or Miss Fitzgerald," he replied brusquely. "I was carried away. My purpose was to receive your explanation and to make you an offer." He spoke exclusively to me now. "You are uncomfortable in this house. You doubtless regret purchasing it. You have not found the change beneficial to your sister's health, as you hoped. I offer to repurchase the house from you at the price you paid."

Pamela threw me a warning glance. I hesitated, then I answered the Commander in the most noncommittal manner I could assume. "I would think this the offer of a very fair-minded man, Commander, if you had not spoken to us as you did just now."

"I may have expressed myself too strongly," he replied unyieldingly, "but my feelings on the subject of honor are strong."

I was tempted by his offer. It would free me from the house without a financial loss that might take years to retrieve.

"If my sister agrees, and if your offer is unconditional, I should like to think it over," I told him.

Pamela said, "I would want a few weeks to decide, Roddy."

"Naturally," I replied.

There was a pause. The Commander shook his head. "My purpose in making this offer was to enable you to leave the neighborhood at once."

A slow fury began to consume me. I said, "It is not unconditional, then?"

"No."

"And what further condition had you in mind?"

"All association between either of you and my granddaughter must cease. It has been calamitous for her. Nothing connected with it must remain!"

Pamela spoke quietly. "Commander Brooke, Stella is not a child. We have insisted that she is not to come to the house as long as these manifestations go on. But if she wants my friendship, it is hers. It is not for sale."

We were all standing. The Commander looked utterly taken aback. He had steeled himself to face this scene and make this offer—and his offer had failed.

He turned to me, almost in appeal. "Do you endorse this—this exaggerated attitude?"

"Certainly I do."

He looked around the room as though expecting help from it. His eyes dwelt on the fireplace, the door, the windows, as if unable to believe that the solace he had once found here awaited him no more. Then he moved across the hall and we accompanied him out to the porch. He said, "You force me to send Stella away from home."

He climbed into the cab and was driven away without another word or glance for us, absorbed in his bitter thoughts.

"Lord," I exclaimed, "I'm sorry for him! He's a sick man. If he sends her away, it will kill him. He'll never see her again."

"There are too many people to be sorry for," Pamela said brokenly. "I'm sorry for all of them. I'm sorry for myself."

She caught her lower lip between her teeth and hurried back into the house.

Chapter Thirteen

SUNDAY WAS WET, our wide world one blur of rain.

"We have been on the wrong track." That was all that I had to say. I was convinced of it, after working on Pamela's chronicle, but my thoughts had led me no further. I could say nothing more definite than that.

Pamela had started her record in the form of a journal, reporting each event under its date: her own experiences, Judith's, Lizzie's and mine. There were also the several accounts that we had heard of the Meredith story—even scraps of gossip—each with its narrator's name. This was important, because we were being forced to look at Meredith and Mary and Carmel through the memories of others. We realized that we must allow for charity and prejudice, devotion and jealousy and hate.

We went through the record from beginning to end, tried to make a pattern of the fragments, and failed. At last I said, "The Commander was right: there is no ghost."

Pamela looked discouraged, reluctant as ever to believe in the hallucination theory. "I *feel* that there are spirits in the place, Roddy. I can't put up a case against you, but that is what I believe."

"Well, what *I* believe is that the place is saturated with passions and emotions, inexpungeable misery and despair, so that no sensitive person can be in it and not be overcome by hallucinations or depression or both."

"If that's so, it's hopeless."

"The subjective element in the whole thing is so strong. All of us are reacting in a way that is obviously attuned to our own temperament or expectations. Take each of us in turn. First, Judith. Judith, naturally, is concerned for her appearance, anxious to keep her youth and looks. How does the studio affect her? She thinks her beauty is gone. Take Lizzie: her head is chock-full of stories and descriptions of Mary Meredith, and she sees a tall, fair lady with blue eyes. You hear heartbroken weeping, but you are too much inclined to imagine that other people are having a hard time. Lizzie hears none of that weeping, and I, very little."

"And," asked Pamela, "what made *you* feel that horror on the stairs?"

"I was brewing my play. It boiled up a few hours later. Wendy's wrecker had already planted the germ. My imagination was full of ideas of danger and malignancy."

"That's very ingenious," she replied, sobered. "Go on!"

"Stella is obsessed by thoughts of her mother and craving for her mother's love. She had imagined her mother coming to her at night, remembered it, dreamed of it. Then, when she was sleeping in the nursery for the first time since her childhood, the hallucination was almost bound to come. It began, I should think, with remembering the scent. Nothing has such powerful associations as a smell. Mary had used it, or perhaps often had mimosa in her rooms. That scent is Mary's motif. Stella remembers it so vividly that, I suppose by some kind of telepathy, she causes us to smell it, too. Very soon Stella begins to see Mary—a tall, shining figure. To me, remember, the apparition seemed a slimy fog."

Pamela sighed. "Oh, Roddy, my mind does nothing but run around in circles when I try to see straight myself."

We were still lost in the labyrinth when Dr. Scott turned up unexpectedly at our door. Poor Scott! Pamela had accepted only one of his repeated invitations to tennis, and then she had broken the date to go to Bristol. He looked at her keenly now; she had lost her summer color and had dark shadows under her eyes, but he was too tactful to offer either sympathy or advice.

I liked Scott a good deal more than I had expected to when I first met him. His awkwardness of manner concealed a sensitive nature, and he had serious, honest eyes. He must have heard as much as anyone in the village about our troubles, but he would not encroach on our privacy.

If the Commander was as ill as he looked, Scott was probably attending him. In that case, the doctor was the one link left with

Stella. I decided to tell him something about our situation and enlist his support.

"We're having rotten nights," I said. "There are all sorts of unpleasant disturbances in the house. I expect you've heard about them?"

"People say this house is haunted, that the ghost of Stella's mother walks. I suppose that's absolute rot?"

"We can't make out. But it affects Stella: the Commander forbids her to come here."

"That's like him." Scott hesitated.

"I have a feeling you know something," Pamela said.

"It's something my predecessor, Dr. Rudd, used to talk about. He had a patient in this house—the girl who lived with the Merediths."

"Carmel?"

"Yes. She died here, you know, of pneumonia. Only Rudd swore that she needn't have died. He used to get fairly worked up about it—said the woman who looked after her ought to be drummed out of the nursing profession."

I saw Pamela go greenish-looking. After a minute she said, "It was nice of you not to want to tell us, and to tell us anyway."

After Scott left, since Lizzie was out on her Sunday "Jessuping," we made our own supper. We did not eat much: baked eggs, toast and coffee, on the low table by the fire, were all we wanted. We finished quickly and pushed the table away.

It was a relief when Lizzie came in and sat down by the fire. This Sunday evening chat was a ritual. We heard all about who had been at the farm, what they had eaten for supper, what they had heard on the radio. Pamela was less responsive than usual, and Lizzie cut her chatter short.

"Miss Pamela," she said, rising, "you get to bed with you, you are tired. Go on now and get your beauty sleep for a change!"

It was a sound idea; I supported it. Pamela went, and I took up a book. It was not long before Lizzie reappeared, hovering in the doorway. "Could I speak to you, Mr. Roderick?"

She closed the door behind her with conspiratorial caution.

"What's the trouble, Lizzie?" I asked.

" 'Tis Miss Pamela," she answered. "For the dear's sake, get her away out of this!"

"What is it?"

"I heard her last night, crying fit to break her heart. Walking about the house she must have been. I got up, but by the time I had my things on, she was gone."

"That wasn't Miss Pamela."

"Dear sakes, Mr. Roderick, you're not telling me 'tis ghosts?"

"Not ghosts exactly, Lizzie," I said, "but a sort of mournful memory that is hanging about the house."

This sophistry had no appeal for Lizzie. She shook her head. "If it wasn't Miss Pamela, 'twas a ghost."

I tried to convince her that ghosts might be harmless. "You have heard that Mrs. Meredith was a saintly woman. Why should you be afraid of her spirit, even if it is haunting the house?"

"No good spirit spends eternity that way," she said firmly. "Mr. Roderick, for the love of heaven, won't you send for the priest? Exorcism's a fearful thing, God help us. They say any priest that does it three times will die of it. But Father Anson would do it for you if you asked him, I haven't a doubt."

I promised to have another talk with Father Anson but still Lizzie delayed. I asked her if there was anything I could do for her.

She nodded. "I'm afeared of hearing it again. Could I sleep, maybe, in the kitchen? Would you give me a hand with my bed?"

That was quickly done. We were forever hauling beds about in this house. I wished Lizzie sound sleep but felt that there was little hope of it for any of us.

Burdened with anxiety and more than ever thankful that Max was coming, I went upstairs, prepared for an uneasy night. After a restless half hour or so I slept.

Pamela woke me. She had never done this before, and I was startled when I saw her standing in my doorway in her white dressing gown, but she did not seem agitated. She said quietly, "Please come out here."

She made me stand by the banister; there was nothing to be seen and no sound. Pamela did not explain, but after a moment I realized what had excited her—it was the scent: the perfume of mimosa was wafting up through the house, wave upon wave, as if on a warm, soft breeze.

"Let's see if we can trace it," she whispered.

We went downstairs. The scent was a great deal stronger in the hall, but was faint in the nursery, to my surprise. I unlocked the door of the still unfurnished dining room and stood astonished. The room was as we had left it: bare except for a corner cupboard, packing cases, pictures stacked with their faces to the wall, and rolled-up rugs. There were no electric lights in this room; in the moonlight it looked unnaturally still, dead, but the air was fragrant with that golden mimosa scent.

"It makes me dizzy," Pamela whispered. She was moving among the packing cases. Leaning over one, she breathed deeply and beckoned to me. When I stood beside her I was sure, as she was, that the scent was strongest here. A feeling of mystery made us both talk with hushed voices and move as if in the presence of someone who must not be disturbed. Pamela lifted the loose lid of the case and laid it down quietly.

I heard her gasp and saw her lean on the sides of the box as if she were faint.

"What on earth is it?" I whispered, standing beside her.

"Don't you see?" she replied. "It's not ours. It's the old stuff that was in the studio cupboards."

We lifted the packing case and set it on the floor between the windows, where there was a faint beam of moonlight. I pulled out, one by one, all sorts of oddments, which Pamela, kneeling, laid out on the floor.

It was an assortment of the kind of rubbish that people hoard because it may come in useful someday. There were rolls of wallpaper, lengths of stained old silk and brocade, probably used for draping the artist's models, a teddy bear, a headless doll and a large chocolate box with the picture on its cover unstuck.

I said to Pamela, "Are you sure we're not imagining the mimosa? Do you smell it still?"

"Indeed I do! It seems to be coming in waves, as if the air were being fanned. It is making me a little faint."

She sat with her head drooping. I was in a daze.

"Shall we leave it?" I said. "There's nothing else."

"No," she answered weakly. "Open the chocolate box."

I felt a curious reluctance to touch it. Mary might be all that was gracious and lovely, but I did not want her to appear in this moonlit room. I said, "Leave it till tomorrow," but Pamela shook off her faintness and lifted the lid of the box. On top, carefully rolled, was a piece of gaudy striped silk—a small shawl with a tangled fringe. Next Pamela took out a sequined fan, a high tortoise-shell comb, a pair of castanets, an artificial red carnation, a small empty heart-shaped flask with a faded label. "Carmel's treasures," she whispered.

A shiver passed through me. I felt a ghostly presence too close. I scarcely heard what Pamela was saying; she repeated it: "What's on the label? Have you a match?"

There were matches in my dressing gown pocket. I struck one and held it to the printing. *Parfum Mimosa,* I read.

Pamela caught my arm and stood up dizzily. We left the room. I locked the door behind me and put the key in my pocket.

Pamela sat down in the hall while I opened the front door and let in the night air to blow the fragrance away. When I shut it again, the scent was gone, but the hall was sickeningly cold.

"Did you see anything?" Pamela whispered.

"No," I replied, "and I don't want to. Hurry up to your room!"

She hesitated, very white, but there was nothing to be seen on the stairs, so we ran up. We lighted the oil stove in the fireplace in Pamela's room.

Pamela was shivering; the small flask was still in her hand. "There is no scent from it now," she said.

It was true; not the faintest trace of the perfume remained.

"Those things were Carmel's, weren't they?" she said.

"I'm afraid there's no doubt of that," I replied. "They're the insignia of a Spanish dancer; she must have posed as a dancer for Meredith. Yes, they are Carmel's."

Pamela looked at me with a rather awed excitement in her face. "Do you remember saying that the mimosa scent was Mary's motif?"

"I do."

"Do you think it is possible that she heard you?"

"Who? Mary? Good heavens!"

"Don't you see, Roddy, somehow she made the scent come, to show us that she was there. I feel sure that she made us find that box." I nodded my agreement. Pamela was elated. "It means," she went on joyously, "that Mary wants to tell us what is wrong, and that she can reach us."

"Don't forget the other," I said.

"Do you think the other may—try to interfere?"

"Didn't you speak of two spirits contending for Stella? That's probable enough, I'm afraid."

Pamela restrained a shudder. "I have been wondering," she said slowly, "what Carmel meant to do in the nursery that last evening when she rushed down from the studio in such a frantic state."

"Kidnap the baby," I suggested. "Kill her, perhaps, by way of revenge."

"What a ghastly idea, Roddy! If she had that in her mind—if she died wishing that she could have done it . . ."

"The impulse may go on?"

"Exactly."

"I'm afraid it's possible. On Friday, remember, Stella was very near death."

Pamela grew pale, then she spoke hopefully. "I suppose Meredith bought the perfume. Mimosa scent is very rare. I expect he bought it for Mary in Paris. I wonder whether Mary gave it to Carmel—or did Carmel steal it? Or had Meredith given it to her when they were in Spain? And how did Stella come by hers? Did Meredith send her some later on?"

"That would be an odd present," I remarked, "for a kid of six, which was her age when he died."

"Oh, Roddy," she replied, "our theories are skating about in figure eights. And isn't it infuriating, if Mary is trying to make us understand something and can't? Why *did* she want us to find Carmel's box? I can't imagine any reason."

"Imagining won't get us very far, I'm afraid."

"There must be something we can do."

Yes, there *was* something that we could do; we could leave the house. I changed the subject, telling Pamela for the first time of my talk with Lizzie the night before.

"That settles it," Pamela decreed. "Her heart is not strong, and anybody living in this house is liable to get a frightful shock. In future, Lizzie must sleep at the farm."

I agreed.

"Well, I'm going to bed," Pamela said. "I'll leave you in peace. Good night."

She left me, but not in peace.

ON TUESDAY THE POSTMAN delivered a package from Max. There were two volumes, with a marker in each. Pamela looked at one; I opened the other, and sat stupefied.

This could not be Carmel! Even in early girlhood Carmel would have had a dark, hard, audacious face. The name under the picture was Llewellyn Meredith. He had painted other models, of course, but this girl wore a fringed shawl and had a tall comb in her hair, and she held a carnation against her throat. The title was *Dawn*. She was very young, soft-eyed and joyous, with dimpled cheeks and lips half open in a shy, wondering smile. It was a picture of the dawn of love.

Father Anson had said that Carmel was pretty, that she had bright eyes and a sweet smile. This girl was lovely: it *must* be Carmel.

Pamela sat silent over her volume, a look of sick revulsion on her face. "Meredith was a devil," she said, and she passed the book to me.

This picture was called *The Artist's Model*. His *Dawn* was reproduced in it as a framed portrait hanging on a wall. Turning away from it, with an expression of anguish, was a woman—just the head and shoulders, filling most of the canvas. At first glance one was shocked simply by the contrast between youth and age, for the face of the agonized woman and the face of the girl were depicted at the same angle. Then one saw that the woman had the same face as the portrait, and it had not really aged; it was young still, but gaunt, haggard and hungry, the pallid skin stretched tight over the bones, a hideous caricature. The stricken woman wore the same shawl as the young girl; her hand lay at her breast in the same position. It was an unmerciful study of decay.

Pamela's voice was appalled. "She was madly in love with him still. She came back because she couldn't bear life without him, and he did that. He painted that when she was sick in his house. He showed it to Carmel that last day and he watched her face when she looked at it." Pamela looked shriveled with horror. "No wonder she rushed out to throw herself over the cliff! No wonder she died so full of hatred and vengeance that her spirit can't rest!"

"I can see why he said to Mary, 'I promise you she won't come back.'"

"He was wrong," Pamela said. "What do you suppose Judith saw in the glass? 'Death's-head old age' was her phrase. She thought it was herself. Did she see Carmel, like this?"

"I don't know what she saw, but I think that she felt as Carmel felt at that moment—struck by decay."

Pamela sighed and said, "If we could only communicate with Mary . . ."

"We can hardly hope for Mary to give us a sign."

"Roddy, we must make her communicate! We must hold a séance!"

I hedged. "It's a dangerous game."

"We've got to try it. This has all become so dangerous for Stella—and the danger may not be confined to this house."

Pamela had found a conclusive argument. I said, "Very well."

Neither of us knew what to do next. Except for frivolous table turning with friends in Chelsea, we had no experience of this sort of thing. In the end, we sent Max a long telegram asking him to try to find somebody, not a professional medium, who would help us to conduct a séance. I drove six miles to a telegraph office to send it, not wishing to start all Biddlecombe chattering about the devil raising at Cliff End.

Then I called Dr. Scott's lodgings to find out what was happening at Wilmcote. His landlady told me that he was out on an urgent call; the telephone number was three seven, but I was not to say she had given it to me. I left a message asking Scott to phone.

Three seven was the Wilmcote number. Pamela and I were both strained and restless waiting for Scott's call. Finally, at about nine o'clock, he came in person, on foot.

"We felt anxious about Stella," Pamela told him frankly, "and hoped you would let us know whether she is all right."

"She's a long way from all right," he replied. "The Commander sent for me, and he would not like my speaking of it, but Stella begged me to come here."

"What's wrong with her?"

"Insomnia. This is Tuesday. Stella has had about four hours' sleep since Friday night, and last night none at all."

"What are you doing?"

"I got her asleep under drugs."

"Good Lord!"

"What else can I do?"

"Get her away from her grandfather!" Pamela exclaimed angrily. "He puts an impossible strain on her. Heaven knows what he has been saying to her!"

"That's arranged: she's going away."

"When?" and "Where to?" we asked, both speaking at once.

"On Saturday. The nurse or matron or whoever she is won't come for her sooner, and of course the old man can't travel. She's going to Bristol to a rest-cure place of sorts."

"Not Miss Holloway's?" Pamela was appalled.

"That's the name. The matron is Stella's old governess."

There was a shocked silence. Scott looked puzzled by our dismay.

I enlightened him. "Miss Holloway is the woman who was nursing Carmel when she died."

He was dumbfounded. "Do you mean to say the Commander knows that, and . . ."

"And trusts her, because she was his daughter's friend."

"Dr. Scott," Pamela pleaded, "the strain on Stella will be worse there! Miss Holloway is a dreadful person—as cold as a stone. Can't you stop this?"

He shook his head. "Impossible! The Commander's completely satisfied with this plan and nothing will induce him to change it. She will have a complete and prolonged rest, and after that go abroad."

"What was Stella's message?" I asked.

"It's an extraordinary message and there's no sense in delivering it, but she made me promise. She wants to come here for a night. She declares that if she were here, she could sleep."

"No!" I shouted, leaping to my feet. "Has she not had lessons enough? Is she crazy? Has she forgotten last Friday night?"

"It is unthinkable," Pamela said.

Scott looked from her to me, bewildered. His eyes searched Pamela's face. "You're not sleeping properly yourself."

"No one sleeps in this house," I told him angrily. "You know what's going on here! Why didn't you tell Stella to put it out of her mind at once?"

"I did," he replied, "and the result was incredible. When I was called in this morning, she was all obedience, all good manners, ready to do anything that was advised, much more anxious about her grandfather than about herself. Then, this afternoon, when she came out of the drug, she was in a curious state. I suppose she'd been having nightmares; she was moaning to herself. She kept on saying in a desperate sort of way, 'He might have been killed! He might have been killed!' "

"And then?" I prompted, my voice steadier than my heart.

"She started to cry bitterly and said, 'I can't bear it here anymore.' It was then that she came out with this notion about sleeping here. When I said the Commander wouldn't think of allowing it, she sobbed and pleaded and carried on—it simply wasn't Stella at all. She seemed to have no control of herself. She seemed frightened of me, of her room, of her grandfather. When he came in, she turned on him. The poor man was utterly taken aback; I am sure she had never before in her life been rude to him. In the end, to quiet her, I had to swear to her privately that I'd come here and put it to you."

"Did she tell you what had upset her?" I asked.

"Everything has upset her! She's in a state of rebellion against everybody. She is simply not herself. Can you imagine Stella violently snatching up an ornament and deliberately smashing it on the floor?"

This was appalling. "What ornament?"

"A white plaster statuette of her mother," Scott said.

Pamela looked at me aghast. I said, "I'm afraid this is serious, Scott."

"Haven't I been trying to make you see that it's serious?" he answered angrily. "There's a tug-of-war going on in the girl—on one side, the Commander and all her training; and on the other, you two and whatever this house stands for in her life. If you'd tell me what is on her mind, it might help."

Pamela looked at me. "We'd better tell Dr. Scott everything, hadn't we?"

I nodded.

Scott listened to Pamela's story, enthralled. At the end, he exclaimed, "Good heavens, there's only one logical end to these ghastly psychic experiences!"

"What end?" I demanded.

"Schizophrenia," he said.

"Split personality?"

"Yes."

"What's the treatment for schizophrenia?"

His answer was evasive. "These things aren't tackled by general practitioners."

That told me enough.

"She'll be all right," Pamela said shakily. "She'll pull herself through."

"That's the best we can hope for," Scott replied. "I appealed to her on her grandfather's account. I told her he was seriously ill, and it did produce an effect: she made an effort to quiet down. She cried passionately over the statuette and begged me to tell him it was an accident."

"Did you tell him that?" I asked.

"Yes. Good heavens, I couldn't tell him the truth!" His brow contracted in a worried frown. "I have done an awfully irregular thing in telling you so much. Only this tug-of-war can't go on. It's destroying Stella."

Pamela said, "Stella has no end of willpower. I think she'll get over this. She'll probably be herself again in the morning."

"And who," Scott said bitterly, "in the afternoon? It was the alternation that scared me. A stained-glass saint in the morning and a crazy little gypsy in the afternoon."

"A saint and a little gypsy," Pamela repeated weakly. She leaned on the table. I thought she was going to faint.

"I'll phone you in the morning," Scott said, and rose to go. He looked exhausted. I drove him to his lodgings. Pamela came, too. I would not leave her alone in the house. As we drove home, she began to cry quietly. I could say nothing to console her. I was in the grip of deadly apprehension myself.

A TELEGRAM from Max came the next afternoon: BRINGING INGRAM DUBLIN WRITERS' WHO'S WHO LAST TRAIN TOMORROW.

We looked him up: Garrett Ingram, member of the Irish bar. He was a man of thirty with a curious variety of achievements to his credit. He had written plays for the Abbey Theatre and published verse; he was the author of a monograph on Waterford glass, which he collected, and of a book called *Parapsychic Phenomena: An Analysis.*

It was exhilarating to be preparing a frontal attack rather than waiting passively for chance, occasional manifestations. I had sworn to Stella that I would try everything, and if our séance did nothing else, it would probably stir up whatever psychic influences were around. Watching all night, together or in pairs, we would almost certainly see something that would help, and as Pamela said, "the worse, the better."

Chapter Fourteen

ALL MORNING Thursday there was bustle in the house. It had been neglected, with Pamela preoccupied and Lizzie with no heart, as she expressed it, for "beautifications" when we would likely be leaving soon. But guests were guests.

The studio was not to be slept in, nor was the nursery. Fires were lighted, nevertheless, in both rooms. A bed was put in the study for Mr. Ingram, and Max would have mine; I was going to sleep on the sitting room couch.

While Lizzie readied the rooms, Pamela prepared food for a late supper. She was quiet and tense with anxiety about Stella. I telephoned Scott. His hurried words brought supreme relief: "Pamela was right. Stella's pulling herself out of it."

Stella was pulling through. The horror that had weighed down like a roof, cramping us into a dark cell of dread, was gone, and the wide spaces of life lay around with clear skies overhead.

Pamela ran about the house as if trouble did not exist. It was too stormy to swim, but we got into the car and drove southward to the high cliffs at Hartland Point. She had wanted to see the Atlantic racing and breaking here, and this was the day for it— strong wind, moving clouds and clear spells of sun. The long ocean breakers rolled in with a tremendous roaring, throwing cataracts of dazzling spray onto the rocks. The power and the noise were glorious; they swept one's spirit clear of nightmare. Color came into Pamela's face. She would be fresh and steady now for the evening's work.

We came back for tea, idled over it, listening to music, and then rested in silence by the fire. I came out of a drowse to find the room filled with champagne-colored light from a windy sunset. It seemed the color of peace.

But as the dusk closed down and the curtains were drawn, and the time for our guests' arrival drew near, tension grew. Pamela became restless. The house could not be left empty with all these fires blazing, and I would not leave Pamela alone in it, so I asked her to drive to the station to meet Max and Ingram. She set off at half past nine. Lizzie had already gone to the farm.

I cleared my book table; it was a low round table and would probably serve for the séance. I stoked the fires and filled the baskets with logs.

At last I heard the car.

Never were men more welcome. They came in like two boys on a holiday, Max delighted with himself for having captured Ingram, and Ingram brimming with interest, which he made no effort to conceal. He was a man of my own age, slight and compact, and in fine training after a month climbing the Alps at Zermatt. His keen hazel eyes, mobile brows and mouth, crisp hair and vigorous movements gave him an air of well-being and confidence in whose presence depression could not survive.

As we sat at supper, Pamela's vivacity, eclipsed for weeks, came back. Her dark red frock gave her color. She wore, on a thin silver chain, a fish of white jade, a gift from Judith. "It is Chinese. It wards off evil spirits," Max explained smilingly.

"A fine wild-goose chase you set me!" he said as we drank coffee beside the fire. "What sort of reputation I'll go back to I can't imagine, after ringing up eleven people to ask if they knew a ghost hunter! I caught Mr. Ingram by such a fluke that I think the stars must be on our side."

I asked Ingram, "How did you chance to be free?"

"I wasn't." He grinned. "But who could resist such an adventure as this?"

He began to talk, telling us a good deal about himself with

humor and discretion. As usually happens when Irish meet Irish, we discovered that we had common friends. And his mother, with whom he lived when not in his rooms in Dublin, and our aunt Kathleen were old friends and rival horticulturalists.

"What started you studying occultism?" Pamela wanted to know.

"A client of mine bought a house in Donegal. He found it infested with poltergeists. Bells were jangled; there was incessant knocking; things were flung downstairs; beds were dragged about. I spent a night in the house. It was unholy."

I told Ingram that I was sorry I had not read his book.

"My book wouldn't have helped you," he said. "I hope sincerely that I shall be able to. I can only help as any stranger might—by bringing an unprejudiced mind to interpreting any communications we may get."

Pamela asked him, "Shall we tell you about the tragedy connected with the house and our experiences, or ought that to come afterward?"

"Afterward, please—it will be so much easier for me to avoid suggestion. That's the very devil in these séances: what you expect is what you get. Have you thought about which method you'd like to use?"

I told him we would leave that to him.

"Then, as there are four of us, I suggest the spelling glass. I brought a pack of alphabet cards. Excuse me; they are in my room."

"Interesting fellow!" I remarked to Max when Ingram had gone. "He has such a sane approach to the whole thing. You were grand to hunt him down for us."

Max beamed. "I thought you'd like him. Can't you just see him, in wig and gown, addressing a jury? He warned me at the first possible minute not to give him any hint of the story. I think that's wise."

Ingram returned with his cards and laid them in a circle on the table in order; the alphabet was broken at opposite points by cards marked "Yes" and "No." He inverted a wine glass in the center and said that our preparations were complete.

I looked at the clock; it was past midnight. The house was quiet. From outside came the dull, rhythmic rumble of the sea and the higher and steadier note of the wind.

We sat around the table with fingers laid lightly on the rim of the upturned base of the glass. Nothing happened. We rested without talking, then tried again. First Max took his fingers off the glass, thinking that he might be an impeding influence, then they tried without mine.

"It is seldom so slow," Ingram said, depressed.

"Shall we try in the studio?" Pamela suggested.

"I think that's the idea," Max agreed, and we carried the cards and the table up there.

The room held a damp but not unnatural chill. We laid our fingers on the glass and at once it tilted a little to one side. It was still again for some time. Ingram spoke quietly. "We are waiting," he said.

A slow sliding movement began. The glass traveled uncertainly around the circle of letters, pausing now and then. It completed the circle and came to rest. It gave one the queerest sensation of watching some groping intelligence that was trying to understand our layout. It tilted again, and Ingram spoke, using the lower register of his expressive voice. "Is there someone who wants to communicate with us?"

The glass rocked, then steadied and began to slide with a smooth, even movement in the reverse direction from the *A*, where it had settled, to *Y*. It paused there, but then glided straight across the table and pushed the card marked "Yes."

INGRAM'S FACE HAD changed: it was hard and concentrated, no longer lively, except for the eyes. He sat with his back to the door, at my left, with a notebook on the stool beside him and a pencil in his right hand. Three fingers of his left hand were on the glass, touching Pamela's fingers and mine. I had taken the chair opposite Pamela, in order to watch her. She looked strained. Max was taking the thing calmly and gave me a pleased glance when the glass moved.

Ingram said gently, "What is your name?"

The glass traveled steadily as far as M and then, after a little groping and hesitation, glided across the table and paused at A; it slid quickly to R, then to Y, and stopped.

Pamela, Max and I exchanged excited glances.

Ingram went on. "Did you die at Cliff End?"

The glass paused at "Yes."

"Did you die a natural death?"

"No."

"A violent death?"

"Yes."

"Was it an accident?"

After a brief pause the glass crossed to "No."

"Do you blame someone for your death?"

I thought the glass was going to stop at the "Yes," but it passed and went on to C. "Carmel" was steadily spelled out. Pamela drew a sharp breath and Ingram took his fingers from the glass. We all rested.

"Do these names mean anything to you?" Ingram asked me.

I told him that they did.

"Will you take over the questioning?" he said.

I agreed, but found myself unable to think of what I wanted to ask. The idea that we were in the presence of Mary Meredith, conscious and intelligent, was stupefying. I nodded to Pamela. "You go ahead."

"Did Carmel strike you?" she asked.

"Yes."

"Do you know that Carmel is dead?"

"Yes."

"Do you want her punished?"

The glass traveled smoothly to "No," paused, began to make the circle, and stopped at F. I guessed what was coming. The word spelled out was "Forgive."

"Characteristic," I said, and Ingram looked at me dubiously.

"Try not to anticipate answers," he warned me. "The power in your fingers responds to a thought."

"Why, the glass *drags* my fingers; I'm certainly not pushing it!" I replied, and Pamela said, "I feel the drag, too."

I asked a question now. "Have you a purpose in remaining?"

"Yes."

"Can you tell us what it is?"

I was becoming extraordinarily tired; this was a strain. I could scarcely believe that my question would be answered, but the glass moved. It slid to the letter *I*. There was a little confusion then. It moved across the table and paused just between two letters—*F* and *G*—and again between *U* and *V*; but it ran smoothly then to *A* and *R* and *D*. Pamela said, " 'I guard.' "

Ingram took over the questioning. "Do you mean that you guard this house against some danger?"

"Yes."

"From where does the danger come?"

"Carmel."

"Whom is she trying to injure?"

We had our first surprise now. The glass was almost wrenched from under our fingers. It rushed at the letters *L* and *I* and then at *L* again. There it stopped, rocking violently.

" 'Lil!' " Ingram cried. "She threatens someone called Lil!"

The tips of Pamela's two fingers resting on the glass were white and the skin of her face had a shriveled look. I asked her whether she felt cold. She said impatiently, "Never mind!"

Steadily the glass moved again, traveling straight across to *S*. It spelled "Stella."

"Do you mean that Carmel would harm Stella?" I asked.

At this point something went wrong. The glass rocked, and then, with agitated, zigzagging movements, careered around the table. It fell over, but as soon as it was set up again, it darted straight to the "Yes" with such force that it pushed the card over the edge. Pamela clenched her teeth to keep them from chattering. Max rearranged things and put the next question: "Was *L–I–L* a mistake, then?"

At once the glass moved to "Yes."

"Is Stella still in danger?"

Again the agitation, the rocking and the dash to "Yes."

Pamela's breath was coming unevenly now. She removed her numbed fingers from the glass and used her left hand. She was very white, and Ingram looked at her anxiously. He took his hands from the glass.

"Shall we try to warm up?" he said. We crowded around the fire. It had sunk low, the logs burned out, the coals black. I labored with the bellows, but nothing would make it burn well. I gave up.

"Better go downstairs for a bit, hadn't we?" Max suggested, but Pamela shook her head. "I'm all right now, and the most important question hasn't been asked." She went back to the table and put her fingers on the glass. At once, before anyone else had touched it, the glass ran backward and forward between two letters: *L–I–L–I*.

" 'Lili,' again 'Lili,' " Ingram said.

Still with only Pamela's fingers on it, the glass raced around and around on the table, flinging the cards off. Then it rushed over the edge itself and rolled onto the floor.

Pamela was shivering violently, so we took her down to the sitting room.

"The cold is horrible," Max said.

Ingram smiled. "The cold is extremely interesting."

Max heated chocolate in a saucepan over the sitting room fire, poured it out and piled on whipped cream. Ingram drank his absently, plunged in thought. Pamela, lying in her deep chair, gradually came back to normal. "The results couldn't have been better, could they?" she said happily.

"They are infinitely better than anything I expected," I said to Ingram gratefully.

He shook his head slowly. "I'm not so sure." He turned to Pamela and said dryly, "Almost every syllable was what you expected, wasn't it?"

Pamela gazed at him bewildered. "It went well, didn't it?"

"Too well."

Our elation damped, we waited for Ingram to explain.

"Tell me," he said, "have you thought and talked a great deal about these women, Mary and Carmel?"

I told him that we were obsessed with them.

"And you are strongly prejudiced against Carmel?"

"Well, yes, I suppose so," I admitted, but to my astonishment Pamela said, "No—I was, for a time, but I'm changing my mind."

"Since when? For what reason?" I asked severely.

She sighed. "For no reason at all. That's the trouble. I'm crammed with feelings that I can't account for."

Ingram handed me his notes. "Look at the answers, please. Tell me—is there one word, one syllable, or even one letter which is not precisely what you expected it to be?"

"Certainly there is," I replied. " 'Lili' means nothing to me."

"Was there anything else that you did not expect?"

"There's the word 'guard.' I expected 'protect.' "

"But the glass paused near *G* and then near *U*—not precisely at either, I think. Given *G–U*, what word *would* you—*did* you, in fact—expect?"

Max intervened. " 'Guide' leaped to my mind."

" 'Guard,' " I confessed, "did come into mine."

"And mine," Pamela admitted.

With the shrug of a satisfied prosecuting attorney, Ingram said to me, "You see!"

"Do you mean the whole thing is invalid?"

"No, no!" Ingram replied. "I only mean that we mustn't accept it, blindly, as evidence."

"Doesn't the cold convince you?"

"It convinces me that your studio is haunted."

"But not that we were in touch with the ghost?"

"Just so. The most interesting parts of the séance, to my mind," he went on, "were the repetition of 'Lili' and the agitated movements which flung the cards about. There, I think, a ghost may have taken a hand."

"And all the rest was mere autosuggestion?"

He looked distressed. "I don't insist on that. I only ask you to consider the possibility."

Ingram entered his notes of the séance on blank leaves in Pamela's journal, which he would not read yet. "I'll take it to my room, if I may, and study it in the morning," he said.

Max was pondering over the word "Lili," saying, "I feel that's the key."

Pamela had grown sleepy and closed her eyes; she opened them to murmur, "Perhaps some other spirit was trying to break in with a word."

I was about to say that I could think of no word beginning with "lili" when a sighing sound made us all hold our breaths to listen. It was a long, sad, despairing sigh. Max glanced from me to Pamela; we said nothing. Ingram listened, then said with a good deal of excitement, "I don't think that was wind."

"No," I told him, "that is a sound which we hear night after night."

"The sound of weeping lingers sometimes where there is no other evidence of haunting," he said. "I heard it myself in a house in Edinburgh, but that was a nightmarish sound—not like this."

Pamela stood up. "We'd best go upstairs."

We hurried past the studio door, shuddering, and crowded together in the upstairs hall.

"Listen," Ingram whispered, looking down over the banister. I expected to hear the moaning again, but what I heard was a murmur of soft, sibilant words. It came from the nursery, and there gleamed from the nursery doorway a faint, flickering light. On the night when Stella slept there I had seen it, and I had heard that sound and thought it was Stella talking in her sleep.

"Good heavens," Max whispered beside me, "who is down there?"

Pamela had not moved. She said urgently, "Don't go down."

But Ingram ran down. After a moment the light vanished and the whispering ceased. He came back, pulling himself up the stairs slowly. When he reached us, his face was pale and clammy.

"It's queer," he said, "on the stairs."

"I know," I replied.

"I saw nothing," he said in a low voice. "We should hold a séance in there."

"Look at the studio door," Max exclaimed under his breath.

I put a hand on Pamela's shoulder, but my hand shook and I took it away. My knees were trembling, too. I could not stand it.

It was not uncoiling from the floor this time, but emerging through the closed studio door—a phosphorescent figure in a white gown that drew out and grew slowly and rounded, and at last was free. It hovered in the hallway, growing tall.

Pamela trembled convulsively. Max was stone-still, his eyes dilated, his hand on her wrist. Ingram was standing against the window curtains, drawing hard, steady breaths. Downstairs a forlorn moaning went on. Ingram turned his head very slowly and looked at me: he had heard it too. Then his eyes were fixed again on that luminous shape.

It moved smoothly forward. I saw hands rest on the banister. I saw a long throat and a head—a head with hair hanging down. As though the mist were crystallizing, the outlines were defined gradually and the features became clear, shining in their own pale light. I saw the classic brow; the lips, fine and stern; smooth eyelids veiling the eyes. Her head was bent, listening to those piteous moans. My heart was clenching with dread. I could not hear anyone breathe.

She lifted her head slowly, the eyelids lowered still, in a strange gesture of pride, and the lips parted in a smile. She opened her eyes—great ice-blue eyes, alight with so fierce a flash of power and purpose that I closed my own.

When I opened them, she was sweeping down the stairs. A cry, so low that I doubted I had heard it, shivered up through the house, and then that dead, timeless stillness fell.

Ingram did something that I could not have done: he walked downstairs steadily, like an automaton. When he came upstairs again, his face was grayish, but his eyes danced.

"Nothing there now," he said, his teeth chattering slightly, "but that was absolutely the most perfect manifestation I have ever seen! Magnificent! I wouldn't have missed this!"

He looked at Pamela. We were all at the doorway of my room. "'It is well to take counsel of one's pillow,'" he quoted gravely.

She nodded. "Yes, I'm going to bed."

We all decided to turn in. I went into my study to see that Ingram was all right. He had put the journal on the night table and was sitting on the edge of the bed, still shivering slightly. His eyes met mine, glowing with excitement and delight. "It's the first time that I have seen a veritable, complete apparition. Shall I read about her in this? Who is she?"

"You will. She is Mary," I said.

Chapter Fifteen

THE MORNING WAS brilliant, but a rough wind was blowing and bundling puffy clouds up from the west; the sunshine would not last long. When I came down, I found Ingram outside, walking on the heather by the cliff's edge, avidly enjoying the air and the view.

"You certainly live on the top of the world!" he greeted me. "What a coast! Look at that water!"

Great waves were seething, flinging their crests onto the rocks to riot there and pour out again as satiny waterfalls.

"Doesn't your sister love it?"

"She does."

"We have certainly got to lay those ghosts to rest!"

"Do you think we have any hope?"

"Why not? I say, this journal, this story"—he had the book in his pocket—"it is the most enthralling thing of the sort that I have ever encountered." He had waked early and read the whole chronicle through.

Ten was the time scheduled for breakfast. Max appeared punctually, looking as though he had not had much sleep.

Pamela seemed thoroughly recovered. She had slept like a dormouse, she told us, in spite of seeing Carmel's face.

"What?" I cried.

"It was floating in the darkness," she said, "in the far corner of my room, just as I was falling asleep. It was vague, like an image in water, but it was the face in the picture—*Dawn*."

"The young face?" Ingram asked eagerly.

"Yes."

"And was there any sense of fear—any cold?"

"No. I went straight to sleep."

"Interesting . . ."

The comings and goings of Lizzie with relays of waffles held up discussion, but as soon as she had cleared the breakfast things away, we set to work.

Ingram, brimming with energy, took the lead.

"And now I will cross-examine, if you agree."

I told him to go ahead.

He looked around the table and smiled. "I would like to dispense entirely with *politesse*. You are all hostile witnesses and I shall endeavor to discredit everything you say. Let us see whether there is sufficient evidence to permit us to connect the hauntings with the Meredith story at all."

"Heavens, yes," I protested, "there's everything!"

"The face of Mary—the face of Carmel!" Pamela exclaimed.

"Remember those portraits," Ingram countered. "A strong element of suggestion comes in."

"The séance," I said.

"Will you be offended if, for the present, I discount the séance? It may prove acceptable, but I want to be certain we are on solid ground first."

"Of course!" Pamela consented. "But," she insisted, "there *is* evidence: there's the scent."

Ingram nodded. "Yes, here we have a definite link. Stella possesses some of the same perfume; she connects it with memories of her mother. If we had smelled mimosa last night, I would agree that we saw Mary and that the scent is her motif."

"It never comes with the cold," I told him.

"That," he declared, "is the most curious factor of all."

"And the box?" Pamela asked eagerly. "Why did Mary guide us to Carmel's box?"

"One possibility," he replied, "is that Mary wished to indicate to you that Carmel is the source of the danger."

"It strikes me as excellent reasoning," I told him. "But what do you make of the empty scent bottle?"

"That would give Mary her link. We don't fully understand the phenomenon of materialization yet. But it is probable that Mary needed some link with Carmel and with you before she could produce a guiding manifestation."

"I see!" Pamela said, impressed.

"So you are satisfied to admit a connection with the Meredith story?" I asked.

Ingram replied definitely, "Yes."

"And you let us assume," Pamela said, "that it was Mary whom we saw last night?"

"I think we may assume it," he agreed.

"Thank you," said Pamela a little dryly, and Ingram grinned.

Max had been looking through the journal; he frowned. "I want to know," he said, "why Mary Meredith, who was a woman of fabulous gentleness, brings that malignant cold."

"Exactly!" I said. Max had formulated the problem that had frustrated us at every turn.

"I think I can explain," Ingram said. "In order to materialize, a spirit is thought to draw something from the human bodies within reach."

"I certainly felt depleted," Max said.

"That sensation," Ingram continued, "produces the physical symptoms of fear, and something like terror overwhelms one. But I do not believe that we should take this as evidence of any malice in the ghost."

Pamela shook her head. "But—I can't help it, Mr. Ingram— that cold seems to me evil."

"And look here," Max demanded, "why is no cold felt with

the other manifestations? For instance, when Mary visited Stella in the nursery that first time?"

"I am afraid Stella's reaction must be eliminated; the suggestive power of that room would be very strong."

"You're eliminating quite a lot!" I commented lightly.

"Never mind," Max said, chuckling, "as long as he eliminates the ghost."

Ingram sat silent. Had he taken offense? No! He looked with a rather troubled expression at Pamela and said gently, "I do hope you understand that I can't possibly promise to do that?"

"Why, of course," she responded warmly. "You are helping us to understand it; that is what we hoped for. We must do the rest for ourselves."

"That is understood, isn't it, Ingram?" Max said. "But to come back to this problem: why was no cold felt that night in the dining room when Mary led them to the box?"

"Don't you see," Ingram replied eagerly, "she was not trying to materialize. As long as Mary remains invisible, she causes no sensation of fear or cold, but as soon as she tries to materialize, she becomes dreadful and dangerous."

"Well," Max exclaimed, delighted, "I never heard anything so ingenious."

"It's *too* ingenious," Pamela murmured.

"There are not two spirits, then," I conjectured. "It is Mary all the time. Carmel is eliminated—or is she?"

Ingram laughed. "Look here, I've only just arrived at this notion about the cold myself. I haven't digested it. I would really, if you don't mind, like to do some thinking before I say any more."

I endorsed this. "Let's leave it," I said. "We'll come back to it this evening. The sun will be out for another hour or so. Let's go outdoors."

Pamela and I spent an hour showing Max and Ingram our wilderness and collecting fallen branches for the woodpile, then we were ready for lunch. By tacit consent, our troubles were not discussed at the table. After lunch I suggested a run in the car or a walk, but Pamela said that she thought she would idle in the garden and Ingram wanted to do some writing.

"I never know what I think," he explained, "until I have written it down."

Max and I set out by ourselves for "the Ghouls," Pamela's private name for curious rock formations on the southward coast. The sun was fighting a losing battle with the clouds, and a gusty wind hurried us along. We had a good three-mile walk over the moors southward.

By the time we reached the Ghouls, the sun was buried and the queer-shaped rocks and islets were not showing up at their best. Nevertheless Max prowled among them, excited. "By Jove," he exclaimed, "imagine that one in a low light from the east! And that one up there! A stormy sunrise. . . . Gods, yes, I must paint them!"

"Good! I hope we'll still be here."

Returning, we were in time to see a gleam on the knoll—the last salute of the defeated sun, blazoning the heather and gorse. We climbed to the top and looked down at the house. It, too, was washed in the flying light, but only for a moment. We could see Ingram down on the lawn, striding from rock to rock and gesticulating. Pamela followed him, vividly interested. She drew me along eagerly when we came down. "Look! Mr. Ingram believes we could grow gentians here—the kind you find in Galway. He says we could have a lot of alpine plants and a real sea garden, with things spilling down the cliff."

"You might have something unique," he responded, "but it would be pretty hard work."

A fine time Ingram had chosen, I thought, to make Pamela more than ever in love with Cliff End.

Pamela decreed a light supper, which we would clear away ourselves, and after that the adjourned conference. There were no dissenters, but Lizzie, when told that she might leave early, looked suspicious. And what sort of goings-on will you be up to, her glance plainly asked, when you have me out of the way?

During supper Ingram failed to persuade Pamela to forgo her

conviction that she had seen Carmel and heard Carmel weep. Pamela, challenged, could still give no reason for her tenacity. "I am afraid I've gone all feminine and intuitive," she confessed.

Max teased Ingram. "Actually, it's you and Roderick who should be barred as investigators. You both write plays. Pamela and I are the ones with honest, undramatizing minds."

"Bless you, Max!" Pamela said.

As soon as we had settled around the fire, Ingram took up the notes that he had written and prepared to tell us his conclusions.

"I am afraid I am going to worry you a little," he began, "about Miss Meredith—Stella. Did you observe that the hauntings became intensified after her visits to this house?"

"I think we realized that," Pamela said. It was certainly true.

"You think there is a direct connection with Stella?" Max asked Ingram.

He replied gravely, "I am afraid there is."

"You have worked out a theory, I expect?" Max said.

Ingram answered, "Yes. I make the assumption which you wished to make—that it is Mary Meredith whom we saw. But I reject 'Lili' as a meaningless intrusion from outside or a mere chance movement of the glass."

Pamela looked as if she were about to oppose this, but she refrained.

"I imagine that Mary died as gentle as she lived. She grieves about Stella, imagining that she is lonely, and desires to comfort her. She visited Stella in the nursery and made her feel cherished. She carried a ghostly light. She created the delicious perfume of mimosa. She led you to Carmel's box because she wanted you to find the scent bottle, to realize that she is here, a conscious presence, and to tell Stella this. She is aware of Stella's eagerness to see her and longs for contact with her child. She comes when Stella is here and returns seeking her, and when she cannot find her, she weeps. But this is Mary's tragedy—"

Ingram broke off when he looked at Pamela: her face was a

little resistant. Max sat as if spellbound by the story, and I was feeling convinced.

Ingram went on in a tense, compassionate tone. "Her fate is tragic, even after death. When she tries to appear, tries to make herself visible, she becomes a thing of horror and nearly frightens Stella to death. And that will always be so: Mary, materialized, visible, will always appall."

There was silence, and then I said, "I believe you are right."

Ingram smiled. "Mary," he continued, "protects Stella, and she forgives the girl who killed her. She wants to save all in Cliff End from harm. There is danger from Carmel."

He paused. Our absorption stimulated him; consciously or otherwise, he was making the most of his effects.

"Carmel," he went on, "as one sees from the story, was madly in love with Meredith. Then Mary came and took him away. Carmel is a southern woman, with whom love goes deep. She resolves to destroy that marriage. She trades on Mary's pleasure in making magnanimous gestures and secures a position as her maid. Meredith becomes her lover again, and Mary, discovering it, falls ill. When the household breaks up, Carmel is clever—it is to Mary that she clings. She has not done with Mary yet. When Stella is born, Carmel proceeds to undermine her influence with the child. Now, at last, Mary stands firm. She leaves Carmel in Paris and brings Stella home. We know what happened. Carmel returned, perhaps out of longing for her lover, perhaps to beg or blackmail—we can't tell. But we know what Meredith did to her. It would fill any woman with hatred. Carmel's passion for revenge becomes a madness: she weeps, she rages, she desires to die. But, in dying, she will perfect her vengeance against both of them. She will destroy their child. She failed to do that—Mary stopped her—but she killed Mary. Carmel, when she was dying, was still in a frenzy of unsatisfied revenge. She is probably in an endless delirium, trying to kill Stella still."

Pamela turned white in her chair. She looked as if she would cry in a moment. "I'm going to phone Wilmcote," she said.

"You know you mustn't do that," I told her.

"Yes, I know, but I can't stand it."

"Scott would telephone if she were worse."

Ingram's face was utterly miserable. "I don't know how to ask you to forgive me," he said.

There was a pause. Max poured out drinks and handed them around. "Look here, Ingram," he said, "your theory makes this house seem quite uninhabitable. It leaves no way out."

"Exactly—that is what troubles me so much," Ingram replied. "If Carmel is haunting, it is for an evil purpose, and Mary, in her very desire to help and protect, becomes a terribly dangerous presence. It's a deadlock, I'm afraid."

"You certainly suggest no way of doing what we had hoped to do," I told him. "Find a means of giving the spirits rest."

"I see no hope now," Pamela said sadly, "unless it comes in tonight's séance."

There was a pause. She was looking unlike herself, forlorn and dispirited.

"It is getting late," she said. "Let us begin."

Chapter Sixteen

THE CARDS WERE set out in the nursery. I told Ingram that I thought it would be better for one of us—Pamela or me—not to take part. He agreed.

"We'll try without Pamela, then," I said, and put my fingers with Ingram's and Max's on the glass, while she lay back in her chair with a vacant look on her face, seeming to have lost interest in the séance.

There was a long wait and then, suddenly, the glass moved. The circle of letters was explored, as before. The glass rested and rocked and Ingram signed to me to begin.

"Who are you?" I asked.

"Mary" was spelled out at once.

"Was it you we saw last night?"

"Yes."

"Did you wish to frighten us?"

The glass moved to *N* and then to *O*. It spelled out "Not you."

"Did you wish to frighten someone?"

"Yes."

"Who was it?"

"Carmel."

The movement was even and unhurried.

I went on. "Do you want her to leave Cliff End?"

"Yes."

"Can we do something to make her go?"

"No."

Max said, "Mary, try to tell us what we should do."

The answer was "Go."

I asked, "Do you mean that we must leave Cliff End?"

Three times the glass moved between *G* and *O*.

"Why must we go?"

"Danger" was spelled.

"From what? From whom is there danger?"

The glass moved quickly to *C–A–R* and *M*, but before it had reached *E*, it fell over and lay swiveling on its side. When we began again, it ran, exactly as it had done on the previous evening, backward and forward between *L* and *I*. The glass slid wildly about among the letters, flinging every one of them off the table. Then it was thrown on the floor and it broke.

Max stooped to retrieve the fallen letters, while Ingram and I collected fragments of glass. Pamela had taken no notice of the confusion; she was limp in her chair, asleep.

"Pamela," I cried sharply, "wake up!"

Ingram gripped my arm, saying urgently, "Don't!"

Max put an arm around Pamela and raised her shoulders, but she did not wake. He looked in alarm at Ingram. I was shaking.

"For God's sake, Ingram," I said, "wake her up!"

Ingram had turned pale, but he replied quietly, "Much better not: it might shock her. This is a trance. It won't do any harm."

Pamela sighed; she breathed slowly and deeply, as if in uneasy sleep; her face was not paler than usual. Max put his finger on her pulse. He nodded to me, saying, "She'll be all right."

Her breathing grew deeper and her lips parted; she seemed to smile. After a little while she half opened her eyes and spoke.

The syllables that Pamela uttered were as strange to me as the voice in which she was speaking—a light, joyous voice, soft and lilting, altogether different from her own.

"I think it's Spanish," Ingram whispered. He snatched my notebook and began to write.

I heard tender little sounds repeated over and over again. Pamela smiled.

It is Carmel, I thought—Carmel's love talk with Meredith; Carmel living her youth over again.

I turned on Ingram. "You've got to wake her! You can't do your damned researches at Pamela's expense! Remember that Carmel was a suicide, a maniac, a murderess—"

Pamela cried out—it was a dreadful cry—then she began to moan and weep with abandonment. This was the helpless sobbing that we had so often heard. It chilled me to the heart to listen to it. I was shuddering with cold, and I saw fear on Ingram's face.

Suddenly Max opened the door into the hall. He looked out and shut the door again at once. "Take her out by the garden door. Be quick."

While I unbolted the half-door, Max and Ingram lifted Pamela between them. They carried her out, around the house and in through the front door, and laid her on the sitting room couch. She had stopped moaning. She opened her eyes.

"Are you all right?" Ingram's voice shook.

She replied, "Yes, of course! Roddy, what's wrong? Why are you so white? What happened? Surely I didn't faint?"

Her voice was her own; she was herself. Almost sick with relief, I sank into a chair.

Ingram said, "Thank God!" and went out of the room.

Max answered her. "No, you went into a trance."

She was intensely interested. He told her what had happened. She said at once, "It was Carmel speaking through me!"

"But Mary was coming," I told her. "We got you out just in time."

She took hold of my arm. "Where's Mr. Ingram? Oh, Max, please!"

Max went to the hall and came back with him. Both had lost color, and Ingram was trembling. He sat on the footstool, too cold to speak.

Max said, "She disappeared into the nursery—a sort of wraith, shrouded. There's a fog in there now, savagely cold."

"It's very dangerous," Ingram added.

Of the four of us, Pamela was the calmest. She remembered nothing that had happened after the glass had spelled "Lili" again. "Was it a real trance?" she asked Ingram.

"Yes," he replied, "a deep, mediumistic trance. . . . Is your head aching?"

"It is, rather, but never mind. Tell me what I said."

He read from his notes, trying to reproduce the syllables she had spoken.

"It must be Spanish, and I don't know a word of it!" she exclaimed. "It was Carmel, of course."

None of us could make anything of the syllables, and there was no Spanish dictionary in the house.

Ingram said, "I did not have the impression that this was intended as a communication." I agreed and told him how I had felt that it was Carmel reliving some moment with her lover.

"The voice was very happy," Max said. "It doesn't seem to affect your theories one way or the other, does it, though?"

No one replied. We were all rather appalled at what we had done.

"I'll keep these and make you a copy," Pamela said finally, putting Ingram's notes into her journal. Then she smiled. "Well, here ends our investigation! I don't suppose we shall ever know the truth, but at least we know what we have to do."

"Come to London with me, both of you, tomorrow," Max begged. "Don't spend another night here."

"It won't be London, Max," I replied. "Bristol for me, as soon as we've wound up here. On account of my play," I added.

"Oh, yes—I forgot your play."

"But definitely," I said to Pamela, "this is your last night at Cliff End."

She stood up, ready to go to bed. Ingram, saying, "Please wait," went out to explore the hall and stairs. He called from upstairs, "It is all right."

"This is all rather horrid for Mr. Ingram," Pamela said as she left us. "Do try to cheer him up."

She must have found something consoling to say to him, for he looked much happier when he returned. He looked at me penitently, saying, "You have a right to be very angry with me."

"Not with you," I replied, "and I beg your pardon for bursting out so absurdly before."

He shook his head. "I ought to have warned Miss Fitzgerald."

"We were warned. Pamela knew what she was risking."

"So she told me. She says it was interesting! She is the most intrepid woman . . ."

He stopped, inarticulate for once.

Max intervened firmly. "Why worry? Pamela's all right."

But Ingram persisted. "It all means so much more to you than I realized," he said remorsefully. "Your friend, Miss Meredith, involved so horribly, and this lovely place, and the frightful danger of possession—and I treated it all as an abstract problem, quite heartlessly. I can't say how I regret—"

Before I could find an answer, Max broke in. "That was my doing, Ingram! I deceived you as completely as I could. Roderick and Pamela had been stifling here among ghosts. I knew that your alpine breezes were just what would do them good. If you had guessed they were in real trouble, you couldn't have been nearly such a tonic. Isn't that so, Roderick?"

"Of course it is!" I realized just how refreshing Ingram's zest had been. "You have done what we wanted: helped us to make our decision."

He was looking into the fire, his elbow on the mantelpiece. He sighed. "I wish it could have been a different one." Then he said good night and left us. He was distressed.

"I am sorry about Ingram," I told Max.

"Don't be," he replied. "He's a charming fellow, but he needed this plunge into deep waters, I think. He has splashed about a bit too merrily in the shallows, I imagine. Do him good to find he has floundered out of his depth. I like him."

"So do I."

"Does Pamela?"

"It's hard to know."

We sat on until Max had finished smoking his pipe and then went to bed.

I SLEPT LIKE A drunkard. When I woke, reluctantly, it was to find the sitting room full of sunlight and Lizzie looming over me, big with reproach. She said, "Miss Pamela's not well."

I got my wits into gear gradually. I recollected that this was Saturday—today Stella was going to Miss Holloway's Center of Healing Through Harmony, and we were leaving Cliff End.

"What is it, Lizzie?"

"I'm telling you she's not well."

"What's the matter with her?" I asked abruptly. I was scared.

"Her orders is to say it's an ordinary headache and she's afraid she'll have to rest and you're to tell the gentlemen she's sorry, and it isn't a case of the morning-after-the-night-before."

This was authentic Pamela! I laughed with relief. Lizzie demanded, "What were you doing in the nursery last night?"

"Good heavens," I groaned, "did nobody tidy up?"

"Table turning, wasn't it?" Lizzie went on. "Heathen practices, enough to call devils out of hell! I know what the priest thinks of such conjurings, and I know what he'd say to me about staying in a house where people are after doing it, too."

"I can tell you truthfully, Lizzie, that we saw no devils."

"You saw or heard something," she declared, "or why is Miss Pamela's eyes sunk like two stones in her head? No, Mr. Roderick, I suspicioned it and now I know. And I won't stand for it."

"Which means, Lizzie?"

She turned to me, her face crumpled with sorrow and perplexity. "Won't you give Father Anson a chance?"

"No more talk about exorcism, Lizzie."

"But he's willing—"

"I'm not."

Dubiously she accepted this.

It was a gray, windy morning. No one else was down yet. I went out. There was a glint of light over the headlands northward. You would never look out from here on two days running and see the same scenes. The variations played by the weather and the seasons, the time of day, the tides and the winds, over sea and land and sky were infinite. All day long the excitement of changeful beauty quickened one's nerves. "It is magical," Stella had said.

The thought reminded me of her. I went in and rang Scott's lodgings. He had gone out, but his landlady said that if I was Mr. Fitzgerald, she was to tell me that my friend was better and was leaving this afternoon.

How would Stella react to a hygienic little bedroom in Miss Holloway's home? Would she feel a prisoner, without friends? Surely we might remind her that she had friends! What was the name of that flower shop in Bristol where we had bought roses for Wendy? It could not possibly do any harm—a gift of flowers sent without a name. She would guess but would not write. It might avert a flood of desolation.

Withers—the name was Withers.

I found the number in Bristol and telephoned. A woman's voice answered. She accepted my commission and promised to send roses without a name or message of any sort.

Max came downstairs and we stood on the porch. I told him what I had done and poured out my fears about Stella. He listened thoughtfully.

"She won't put up with it for long, Roderick," he declared. "The girl's full of spirit; she'll rebel!"

"Even if she wants to, what can she do?"

"She'll write to Pamela."

"They'll stop her letters going out."

"It's not a prison!"

"A 'rest-cure' will be the excuse."

"She'll do something. She'll run away."

"Where to? We have forbidden her to come here, and she won't upset her grandfather: he's ill."

"Roderick, the girl's eighteen! There are hotels. I'll send her our address."

"She'll never receive it."

"She must have friends somewhere."

"I doubt it. Besides, they'll take her money away."

Max looked startled. "It's a pretty bad jam."

Ingram's arrival on the porch was a relief. He came running downstairs, as airy as the morning, with some pleasant excitement alight in his eyes. The news that Pamela was still resting disconcerted him, but he enjoyed the way in which she had assured us that she was none the worse for the séance. Over breakfast his project came out.

"If your sister thought of going to her cousin in Dublin—and it would be a splendid change, wouldn't it?—do you think she might like to travel by air? You can do it, you know, from Bristol in under two hours. I've been wanting a pretext to do it, and I could go that way perfectly well. I might have the pleasure of traveling with her, perhaps? That is, if, by any chance, she could do it about eight days from now?"

He was so delighted with his notion that I felt sorry to have to tell him that I knew Pamela had no intention of going to Ireland yet. When Lizzie came to clear away, she reported that Pamela was still asleep. At eleven, when it was time to drive Ingram to his train, she had not waked.

Ingram could not recover his spirits. He sat in the car, looking at the house with the wistful gaze of a boy being sent back to school. Max, too, was depressed.

Ingram's train for Bristol was to leave at eleven thirty-five. Max, who was returning to London, said that he did not want to waste the morning in a train; he decided to walk by a round-about route to the station, lunch at a pub and leave by the three fifteen. "Good luck, Roderick!" he said in parting.

Ingram was rather silent during the drive to the station. When he spoke, it was about the house.

"So often haunting does little or no harm—only scares a servant now and then—but this is so acute, and Miss Fitzgerald is so sensitive. I am sure you are doing the only possible thing."

When we topped the hill, I pulled up for a moment, the view was so fine. The leaden sea blazed with silver streaks. The sun was covered by a vast cloud, almost black, with an underedge of brilliant white.

"Gosh!" I exclaimed. "Max is enjoying this!"

Ingram paused before he said, "This place must be magnificent in midwinter."

"I wish I could invite you to Cliff End for Christmas," I replied. He looked at me gratefully.

"If you are in any place where I might join you for a few days, will you let me? That is, if we don't meet in Ireland," he said.

He showed his first sign of diffidence in asking this, and I was able to respond cordially.

For the few minutes that remained he talked in his liveliest manner about the odd places and people he had met in the course of his researches. "I never imagined," he said, "that ghosts would bring me such a great pleasure as this visit has been. Please give my warm regards and wishes to your sister. She has promised to let me know how things turn out. Give her my thanks. Tell her I would sin again to be forgiven so graciously."

When his train had gone, I found that I missed him; his vitality had been stimulating. Max would be gone, too, when I reached home, and tonight Pamela and I would sleep at the inn. Stella would be a hundred miles away.

I studied the timetable in the station. The afternoon train to Bristol left at five fifty. I must not come to the station. I must not drive over and look at Wilmcote. I drove straight home. Passing The Golden Hind, I hesitated—ought I to book our rooms for tonight? Pamela might not feel well enough to come out; we could fix it by telephone.

Pamela was much better. She lay propped up on pillows in

the half-darkened room, her headache almost gone. "It was a splitter," she told me. "I was awake until five. I'm sorry about not saying good-by to Mr. Ingram and Max. . . . Roddy, I want one night's reprieve!"

"Granted," I replied, "on condition that you stay in this room."

"I'm too busy to move. I want to do nothing but think. We've been wildly, crazily wrong."

"I won't have it, Pamela. You're not going to start all over again!"

"But, Roddy, I am! There's hope—"

"Don't addle your brains with it, Pamela! Nothing will do any good, and you'll wear both of us out."

"Very well, I won't talk till I'm sure."

I relayed Ingram's messages to the best of my ability, saying that I was afraid they had lost some of their elegance on the road. "What was he talking about—sin and forgiveness?" I wanted to know.

"Oh, I suppose, when he was upset last night. It really is hard luck on him, and you weren't as civil as you might have been."

"Well, I like that! And my teeth seething with irritation and I keeping it all back!"

"You didn't! Go along, Roddy. You're making my head ache!"

"Oh, all right. Send for me when you want something to sharpen your claws on."

Pamela regarded me with dignity. "When I send for you, it will be to announce something of the utmost importance."

Chapter Seventeen

I SPENT A GRIM afternoon packing up my manuscript, writing business letters and making lists of things to be done in connection with shutting up the house. Where were we going to live? For a few weeks, rooms in Bristol. But where after that?

When Lizzie brought up my tea she said, "Miss Pamela will take only an omelet for dinner. Will a cutlet do you?"

"No, Lizzie," I answered. "I'll have an omelet, too, and I'll make it myself: a cheese omelet. I'll make hers as well. I wouldn't trust you to cook for her when she's in delicate health."

I angled in vain for Lizzie's rich laugh. She stood grave as a Buddha. "I'm not going to the Jessups' tonight," she announced.

"Oh, but, Lizzie, you must! You'll be nervous here."

"I'll be found dead in my bed, stiff with fright, in the morning, maybe, and my death will be on you."

"Good heavens, why won't you go?"

"Because I can't trust you when my back is turned."

"Lizzie," I said, "you have me beat. If I give you my solemn word of honor that we'll do nothing tonight that the priest wouldn't approve of, will you go?"

She heaved an immense sigh of relief. "God bless you, Mr. Roderick, I will!"

I wished Pamela would not begin playing with indecision again. It was useless; my mind was irrevocably made up. I went down to the sitting room and set to work on a review, which I finished just as daylight failed.

Rain was falling in a deluge, and the sound of footsteps outside surprised me. It was Father Anson, struggling under a huge umbrella to which he clung with both hands against the wrenching wind. I hurried to open the door, and he was blown in.

"Are you free?" he asked, out of breath and anxious.

I was able to tell him in all sincerity that I was delighted to see him. His deep-set eyes searched my face as he said gravely, "I hope Miss Fitzgerald is well?"

I told him that she had stayed in bed with a headache but was better. He sat down, looking relieved.

"I am very happy to hear that she is not ill, and"—he smiled—"if I am going to be told that I am impertinent, I would rather hear it from you alone."

"You are not going to be told that."

"Were you of the Faith, it would have been my duty as a priest to come. But as it is, my visit will be an intrusion unless you can accept it as from a friend."

"Thank you, Father Anson. We need friends just now."

"So I fear, so I fear."

I could not help smiling; it was so obvious that rumors of our "wicked practices" had reached him. "Things are not as serious as you imagine," I told him. "I would like to explain—but first let me work it out! Lizzie told Charlie. Charlie told Mrs. Jessup, who repeated it to—let me see—"

"The grocer's boy," Father Anson contributed with a smile, "who told my housekeeper, who spoke to me." He was suddenly grave again. "You felt driven to hold séances?"

"It was a last resort."

"And has it shown you how to give the spirits rest?"

"No. We have decided to give up the house."

"That is a hard decision."

"We have no alternative." I explained Stella's condition, repeating what Scott had said about schizophrenia.

Father Anson was overcome; he bowed his head and his lips moved in prayer. "May God forgive me," he said brokenly.

"Surely," I protested, "you had no responsibility in all this."

He did not reply. To distract him, I began to talk about the séance and to describe Pamela's trance, but Lizzie came in to say that Pamela hoped Father Anson would visit her in her room before he left. We went upstairs at once.

Pamela was sitting up in her elegant lace jacket. Her room looked cozy, with lamps lighted and the curtains drawn against the gloom outside. She welcomed Father Anson warmly. "Do you know Spanish, Father?" she asked.

"I used to," he replied.

She passed Ingram's notes to him, explaining, "These are words which I spoke last night, in a trance."

He shook his head reproachfully. His eyes lit with interest, nevertheless, as he read aloud *niña mía, chica, guapa* and the rest.

"Those are simply words of endearment—diminutives such as 'my darling,' 'my baby,' 'my darling little girl.' The words of a mother to her child."

Pamela's eyes danced. "So I imagined!" She looked straight in the priest's face and asked him, "Did Carmel have a child?"

He studied the paper as if he had not heard and, after a moment, replied vaguely, "Carmel came from Spain. I only knew her for a few months. Many things may have happened in her own country of which she never told me."

"When you first knew Carmel, was she a gentle, warm-natured girl?"

"So indeed I believed."

"Her tempers, her passions—were they as outrageous as people say?"

The priest smiled. "I saw Carmel lose her temper once. She was like an angry, unhappy, tearful child."

I heard Lizzie lumbering up the stairs and went to help with her tray. This chatter of Pamela's was annoying me a good deal. What did I care if Carmel had deserted a baby in Spain? It was not Carmel and her weeping that were driving us out.

Lizzie had brought Father Anson tea, sandwiches and a dish of buttery potato cakes. There was unconcealed pleasure in his face when she set the tray in front of him. "Well, Lizzie," he said, his eyes twinkling, "I was just thinking out a terrible new penance for gossip, but, do you know, I believe I'll let you off."

She chuckled. "That Charlie! . . . Well, Father, I can't say in conscience I'm sorry for whatever brought you to the house!"

While Father Anson enjoyed his meal, Pamela was in the highest excitement and expressed herself without restraint.

"Roddy, we have been as blind as bats! Carmel was a simple, warm-hearted, loving girl, and Mary"—her voice took on an edge of detestation—"Mary was a cold, hard, self-righteous prig!"

Father Anson glanced at her warningly. "My daughter—*de mortuis*—"

"Good heavens, Pamela, what are you getting at?" I interjected. "Everybody's admiration for Mary is scarcely 'this side idolatry'!"

The priest nodded. "Mary Meredith inspired strong feelings."

Pamela's face hardened. "Mary Meredith," she said, "was an overweening, hypocritical egoist."

Father Anson was startled. "What can have made you think so hardly of her?"

"What do *you* think, Father, of a woman who could leave a child in the dark, crying with terror, and refuse it a light?"

"She had her own system of discipline."

"Just so: a system of discipline! She had *her* method of training, *her* scheme for saving souls! A fine system—to subject a baby to terror, and a young hot-blooded girl to temptation, in order that *she* might play the redeeming angel!"

"I begin to fear," Father Anson said seriously, "that you have not quite recovered from the trance. Oh, my child, I cannot sit here and listen to such bitter talk."

"Very well, I won't go on. But I believe you agree with me in your heart."

Father Anson spoke deliberately. "I agree with you to this extent—I think that Mary, like many virtuous and noble women, put an undue strain upon human nature at times."

"That will do nicely," Pamela said.

When the priest had finished his meal, he rose, saying, "I am afraid I must play the beggar—eat and leave you." He stood by Pamela's bed and implored her to take part in no more séances.

She thanked him warmly for his visit and his concern.

Lizzie was sitting in the downstairs hall, waiting to set out for the Jessups' farm. I watched them go out into the heavy rain and darkness together, Father Anson's immense umbrella protecting them both. Then I ran upstairs.

Pamela's door was shut. I knocked on it.

"What *is* all this?" I said.

"I'll tell you at supper," she answered. "I'm getting up! Run the bath for me, like a nice buffer. Start the omelet when I ring!"

My OMELET LAY between us on its blue dish, puffed up and shapely. I cut into it carefully and it did not subside.

"Delicious, Roddy!" Pamela said.

In her red dress, with rose-shaded lights giving her face color, Pamela did not look ill, but I was still at a loss to interpret the joyous excitement that shone in her eyes.

"I hope," I said, "that you have some rational excuse for looking so pleased with yourself."

"Roddy, I don't know how to tell you this. I so desperately want you to believe it. If you do, it will change everything."

"Pamela, have sense! What can it change? Even if you have accounted for Carmel and her weeping—and I doubt it—it is not Carmel who matters. It is Mary."

"I wish you could think it out for yourself!"

"Think what out?"

"That all the prejudice against Carmel is utterly unfair."

"Does it matter?"

"It matters enormously. Oh, Roddy, she has been so maligned by everyone! Just because she was vivacious and foreign and they knew she had once been seduced! She *was* seduced, but she was faithful: she loved Meredith right to the end."

"But, good Lord, Carmel killed Mary—or didn't she?"

"She didn't, Roddy! That was the tree! The tree struck Mary, just as it struck you when you were trying to grab hold of Stella."

"Gosh! Why didn't I think of that? It, so to speak, hit me in the eye."

"Miss Holloway knew it. She knows it, and she lies. She lies to herself, to salve her crooked conscience for Carmel's death. And Mary knows it, and she lies, even now."

"Are you telling me that ghosts tell lies?"

" '*L–I, L–I.*' That was Carmel trying to tell us, trying to break through. She couldn't spell English."

"My word, that's ingenious!"

"It's simple. Both times that came immediately after Mary said that Carmel was trying to harm Stella. No one is trying to harm Stella."

I got up and walked about the room. Now I was interested.

"Roddy, try to clear your mind of all these prejudices about Carmel. Father Anson knew her, and he was fond of her."

"Yes, I imagine he was."

"And that lonely weeping: the voice is gentle and pitiful."

Yes, I reflected, that was perfectly true. Moreover, the voice in which Pamela, in trance, had spoken those words of endearment was the softest and tenderest voice I had ever heard.

"And think how she suffered! Think of her in Spain, a girl who was young and joyously in love. Meredith made her happy there. Then Mary comes, all cool and English and exquisite—with some money, too, and a home. I expect he was growing tired of a vagabond life. And they marry. Was Carmel heart-broken, I wonder? Anyhow, she forgave him. Rather than lose sight of him, she became Mary's servant. I believe she meant to be good—meant to be only his model after that. But he seduces her again. And then her baby, whom she adored, is taken away from her. And when she comes back—"

"Steady, Pamela!" I stood still. The world was revolving backward. "What, in heaven's name, are you trying to tell me? Her baby? Stella? Is Stella Carmel's child?"

"Yes, Roddy. Don't you see?"

I could see nothing—nothing about Stella or Carmel or Mary anymore. All logic was fallen into chaos. I only knew that the wind was moaning dismally and that rain was thrashing the roof and that Stella was a hundred miles away. I put logs on the sitting room fire and sat on the footstool, trying to see into all this.

"Miss Holloway would have found out," I argued, "and she would never have stayed ten years with Carmel's child."

"She might, for the 'exorbitant salary'! But I don't think she knows."

"But in Paris!"

"The baby was weaned before she came."

"Good Lord! What about Father Anson?"

"Carmel may have confessed that she had a baby but never told him that it was Meredith's. I don't know. I don't believe he has known all these years, but I think he has guessed now."

"That would account for his sudden concern about Stella."

"Yes."

I sat thinking about this for a long time. Pamela lighted a flame under the coffee, then said, "If things are all right on the stairs, I want to try something. Put the oil stove in the upstairs hallway and see whether its heat will keep that cold away."

I moved the oil stove. There was no cold, no mist. A faint moaning sounded through the house: it could easily be the wind. I came down and told Pamela all was well.

I wanted to believe the explanation she had worked out. But I was not going to give in just like that. I walked up and down.

"A woman doesn't adopt her husband's child by another woman," I said. "It's all too far-fetched."

"It's exactly the sort of thing Mary would do."

"I don't see a motive."

"To keep Meredith, of course! He got bored. Spain was calling, Carmel adored him and he was fond of the child."

"And Mary did it to turn the scale?"

"Just!"

"But would Carmel give her baby up?"

"What future had she if they discarded her? An artist's model with a baby to keep! Can't you imagine the great persuasion scene? 'What can you do for the child, you poor outcast? And we can give her such a beautiful life!' "

"It's sheer melodrama."

"That doesn't mean it's not true."

"Aren't you inventing rather a lot?"

"I'm not, Roddy! Think of the things we *know* about Mary. Keeping Carmel in the house after she discovered . . . She must have *wanted* it to go on. Think of what she did when Carmel came back, desperate! Can't you see her leaning over the banister, staring into that ravaged face, and then smiling, realizing what she could do? Not drive Carmel out. No—keep her! Let Meredith paint her; let him stare and stare at that death's-head! And then—do you remember?—it was Mary who called Carmel to the studio that last evening to show her what he had done . . . "

Pamela's voice trailed off.

"You make her a fiend."

"A wrecker; rather like your Barbara."

"How astounding!"

The coffee had got pretty strong, bubbling unnoticed. I poured myself a cup and raised it to Pamela. "You're a better sleuth than Ingram," I said.

"He didn't know Carmel, he hadn't seen Carmel, *been* Carmel, as I was last night."

I said, "I hope the Commander has never suspected this."

"Oh, Roddy," Pamela said, "heaven forbid!"

"It would be cruel."

"Think of the cruelty to Stella ever since she was born! You can see Carmel's nature in her, can't you? The impulsive joyousness, the affection and warmth? And all that cramped and repressed! I think, when she knows, there'll be an amazing release."

"We can't tell Stella!" I exclaimed.

Pamela stared at me, wide-eyed. "Not tell her?"

"After all these years of idolizing Mary—it would be a frightful shock."

"Could you face Stella and keep up that sickening lie, Roddy?"

I heard no more of Pamela's argument because I was listening to that moan, rising and falling, now muffled, now a long, low wail. It was not the wind.

I sprang up. "Listen to that!" I said sharply. "We know all this! And what use is it? Where does it get us? What can we do?"

Pamela stood up too, trembling slightly. "We must tell Stella," she said. "Carmel wants her to know. She can't bear her own child believing all these slanders and lies, not knowing that she *is* her child! I'm quite sure that's why she stays."

"No!" I said violently. "We will not tell Stella!"

"Oh, Roddy, don't you see, Mary is haunting only because of Carmel—for fear of her telling the truth? I am quite sure of that. If we can satisfy Carmel, and she goes, Mary will disappear too."

Did the key to the whole thing really lie in our hands? I was trying to unravel this new tangle when the telephone rang.

It was Max. "I've just got home this minute. How's Pamela?" he said.

"Fine," I replied. "I'm delighted you rang. She has just sprung an amazing theory—but, I say, you should have been home long before this. What held you up?"

A short, embarrassed laugh came over the phone. "I missed the train. But I meant to. I had Stella a good deal on my mind."

"Stella!"

"Yes. Roddy, I've done a rather outrageous thing. I don't know what you'll say."

I relayed this to Pamela, who was standing by, looking anxious. She nodded. "I can hear."

"Well," Max went on, "I thought it might be a good notion to see Stella off, and I found that I could wait for the later train and get this connection at Taunton, so I did. She came into the station with this matron person. Stella looked pretty bad."

"Ill?"

"More sort of scared—helpless and desperate."

"You spoke to her?"

"Yes; she flew to me. The woman rushed between us, but I had time to stick some money in the pocket of Stella's coat."

"Max! Money?"

"Yes, and Judith's and my address. I had it ready."

"It's the brightest idea you ever had in all your bright life!"

"I'm glad you approve! I just had time to whisper, 'There's three pounds,' when the woman intervened. I was terrified that Stella would cry, but she didn't. She introduced us, all correct."

"She would!"

"She told me that her grandfather was in the hospital—had an operation early this morning. She seemed awfully anxious about him. We hadn't time for any more. The woman got a 'ladies only' ticket stuck on their compartment. I thought I'd see Stella in the corridor later, but I didn't. Roddy, she hopped it! She got out of the train before it started!"

I laughed in relief. I couldn't help it. The thought that Stella was still at Wilmcote, the spectacle of Max playing the part of instigator, and the picture of Miss Holloway's consternation were too much for me.

"What happened?" I asked, choking.

"Well, when the matron missed her, she came looking for me. She made me help her search the train. She had the guards crawling on their knees. It was as much as I could do to elude her clutches at Taunton."

"It was a genuine rescue, Max. . . . Here's Pamela. She wants to talk to you."

I handed the receiver to Pamela and ran upstairs. The windows were open in my bedroom and things were blowing about. I shut them. I had a feeling that Mary would come tonight. Let her come! Stella was not in that prison; she was at Wilmcote. Somehow, somewhere, very soon, I would see her.

I had not heard the doorbell ringing, but I heard the loud bang on the knocker. Pamela ran to the door and opened it.

Stella came in.

Chapter Eighteen

FOR AN INSTANT I was transfixed on the stairs, too astonished to move. Stella stood in the hall, breathless from the blast that had blown her in, looking at me with anxious eyes. She spoke shakily. "My grandfather is dying. . . . I thought if I might talk to you, just for a little . . . But I am afraid that it is later than I imagined. . . . I . . . I'll go."

"You won't go. You shan't disappear again!" I shouted. I had no thought for any danger except the danger of losing Stella once more. I saw Pamela lead her into the sitting room.

When I ran into the room after them, Pamela said, "Stella wants you to ring the hospital."

I went to the hall alcove and telephoned the hospital. The night nurse told me that the Commander was in a coma but might linger for a day or two.

"My sister or I will drive his granddaughter over at once if he asks for her," I said.

The nurse replied, "He is unlikely to ask for anyone, I am afraid, and it might be better for Miss Meredith not to see him. But I will telephone you if there is any change."

She sounded like a sensible woman: that was good.

When I got back to the sitting room, Pamela hurried off to the kitchen, saying, "I'll heat up some soup."

Stella was sitting in a small chair close to the fire. She was paler, thinner, and her hands trembled a little as she held them to the blaze. She gave me a quick, timid glance and then looked away.

I said tensely, "I didn't know whether I should ever see you again."

She did not turn her head. "Thank you for telephoning. Is there any change?"

"No. They will let us know if there is."

"They would have let me sleep in the hospital, but there was no room."

"I am glad there was no room."

"But you didn't wish me to come here."

"I have never wished for anything so much in my life."

She turned her head slowly and rested astonished eyes on mine.

"Oh, Stella, Stella," I cried, "have you not discovered yet that wishes and wisdom have nothing to do with one another at all? I was trying to be wise for you, and it half killed me."

She said in a low voice, "It nearly killed me too."

I caught her cold little hands in mine. "Shall we give up trying to be wise, Stella?"

She did not answer, but gave me a fleeting smile, so sweet and happy that it took my breath away. Still, there was a tiny gesture of shyness and withdrawal, which sent me back to my chair and kept me silent until Pamela returned.

Putting the soup down beside Stella, Pamela asked lightly, "What have you done with poor Miss Holloway?"

"Miss Holloway," Stella answered with energy, "is a heartless woman. I hope that I shall never see her again."

I responded fervently, "I hope so, too."

"She made me leave, even though Grandfather was in a coma. Miss Holloway said that she had received a letter from Grandfather to take me on Saturday, whether he lived or died, and she refused to wait for the later train. I meant to slip away from her at the station, but she took my handbag, so that I had no money. I was helpless, but then the most miraculous thing . . . "

Her eyes opened wide; they stretched wider still when Pamela said, laughing, "Max *is* miraculous sometimes."

"But how did you know what happened?" Stella asked.

She laughed over the story of Max's search for her and his scared escape from Miss Holloway, but then, rather near to tears, told us how she had taken a cab straight back to the hospital, only to hear that her grandfather's coma had grown deeper and he was unlikely to become conscious again. The nurse had finally persuaded her to go home.

Pamela said unhappily, "Stella dearest, if only I had known! Why didn't you telephone?"

"The telephone at Wilmcote had been cut off. I think he had arranged"—her voice faltered—"not to come back. In the end I just ran out of the house."

"In all that rain?" I exclaimed.

"It had nearly stopped. I went into Mrs. Dendle's house and she had her son drive me here."

"You have had a terrible day," Pamela said.

Stella shook her head. "Today has not been so terrible as last night. The unbearable time was when Dr. Scott told me that Grandfather was likely to die. For some reason, I think I can bear that now. Life couldn't be happy for him much longer, could it? He isn't suffering today. Last night he was in such pain. His mind was wandering and he thought that I was my mother and that she had told him a lie."

Pamela glanced at me, startled.

"Do you know what he thought the lie was about?" I asked.

"No. He just kept repeating, 'Mary, you didn't lie to me? Tell me you didn't.' And I kept saying, 'Never, Papa darling—never in all my life.' Then he would be peaceful again and rest a bit."

I was relieved. The Commander had revealed nothing. It would have been a ghastly way for Stella to learn the truth.

"There is something I ought to tell you," she said now. "You were right, Roddy. It was not my mother in the nursery. I imagined it."

"What makes you think that?"

She replied with difficulty, "My grandfather told me. I tried to tell him what it was like in the nursery. I told him about the scent, and the comfort, and the lovely little words. I hoped that he might be glad, but he was angrier than I have ever seen him. He made me see that I had been imagining it, because, it seems"—she steeled herself to go on—"it seems that my mother was not that sort of person. He said, 'She was not sentimental about you. She was never a baby worshiper.'" Her hands covered her face suddenly, and tears trickled through.

I said quickly, "Stella, he was wrong. He has been wrong about everything. She did lie to him, and he believed the lie."

Stella looked at me, her face incredulous, then looked into Pamela's smiling eyes.

Kneeling by Stella, Pamela said, "Darling, it was not your imagination. We have found out the truth. I want to tell you, if you can be calm."

Stella drew a long breath and said steadily, "Tell me, please."

"Your mother did love you. She adored you; she petted and caressed you and stole into your room with a light. No baby was ever more loved. She has never stopped loving you. But everyone has made an extraordinary mistake."

Stella gazed at Pamela's face intently. "I knew something was wrong," she said slowly.

Pamela went on. "It was your mother who was with you in the nursery and who made you happy, but, Stella, it was not Mary Meredith. That was a lie. You are not Mary Meredith's child."

Stella stared into the fire for a moment. She spoke in a low voice. "I did wonder sometimes. I am so unlike her. Do you know who my mother was?"

Pamela hesitated and I felt uneasy, but Stella read our faces. "You do know! Can it have been Carmel?" she said.

I found the volume of photographs and handed it to her, open at *Dawn*. She looked at the portrait for a long time, with a tender smile. "I have seen her face in my father's sketches and I always loved it," she murmured. "Her face is as loving and kind as the voice in the nursery."

Pamela began to talk to her about Carmel as she had talked to me, only softening Mary's and Meredith's part. Stella's face had a grave and compassionate look as she listened.

"But think of Grandfather," she said when Pamela finished, "cheated all these years. I'm the child of that girl he despised and that man he detested, and he has given me everything."

I said, "He was lucky. He has had a loving companion who was attentive and loyal to him. That's more than a daughter of Mary and Meredith would have been. And he'll never know."

"No," Stella said resolutely, "he will never know. If he recovers, I'll be so good to him. . . . But I'm afraid it's foolish to think of that. . . . The storm is growing fierce, isn't it? It sounds as if it were angry with the trees."

The wind had shifted and was charging over the moors like a horde of demons now. Nobody would be able to sleep while that clamor lasted.

Pamela, moving about the room uneasily, said, "It seems to me that we've had mighty little to eat."

"Now that you mention it, I'm famished," I declared.

"I wonder what happens to people who eat at midnight?"

"They bless the cook and sleep sweetly."

"I'm going to the kitchen." Pamela glanced at me and left the room.

"I have been thinking about poor Carmel," Stella said. "How she was hurt and wronged! Her lover and her baby both taken away from her, and her own child not even knowing that she *was* her child and giving all her love to somebody else!"

I said abruptly, "Stella, I am going to give up Cliff End. I'll be living in a mean little flat or an ugly bungalow soon."

She gave me a quick glance and looked away for a minute. My heart beat rapidly while I waited for her to speak.

"I am sorry for you about the house, Roderick, but it isn't *necessary* to you, is it? You'll be happy. You and your sister have each other, and it is people who matter most."

"You loved this house so much."

"I was childish about it, wasn't I?"

"Could you be happy in a mean little place?"

She answered in a level voice, very deliberately, still without looking at me, "Certainly I could."

"Are you wearing mimosa scent?"

It was not what I had intended to say. I had been going to say something much more important, but the rush of perfume took me by surprise, it was so strong.

"Why, no. Where is it coming from?" Stella started to her feet, breathless with expectation. "What does it mean?"

"Stella, try not to be upset. I think it means that Carmel is about."

Stella stood by my side, listening, a hand on my arm. "Is that Carmel weeping?" she asked.

It was: there was no mistaking this for the wind. No human voice could have been clearer.

Stella said in a low voice, "I think, perhaps, she could hear me. I think, perhaps, she would understand."

She moved to the door, just as if she were hurrying to console some human woe. I said, "Wait," and went out into the hall.

There was no cold and no snaking vapor. I switched the lights out in the hall and the nursery in order to see whether there was any trace of that evil, luminous mist. I saw none. Still, from the nursery, came the mournful sound and the flowery scent.

"She is in the nursery now," Stella said.

She stood in the light from the sitting room doorway and looked at me. My fear was subdued by the beauty in her face, her glowing and calm conviction of her own power to help. She said, "Roderick, I think I will be happier all my life if I go into the nursery now, alone. But I will do whatever you wish."

"If you will leave the door open," I said, "you may go."

She slipped quietly into the dark room and I stood outside. I could hear her quick, eager breathing and Carmel's sobbing breath, as if there were two women in that room. Then Stella began to speak. She began with fragments of Spanish, little words, broken phrases; then phrases of English came. But neither the words nor the language mattered, there was such tenderness in her voice. It rose and fell, soft, persuasive, a little lyric of pity and love, as if a mother were comforting a child. "*Madre mía, madre carissima,*" I heard. When she ended, there was quiet in the nursery. I could hear no sound but the wind; the sighing had ceased. The scent, too, had faded away.

"Rest in peace," I heard Stella say gently, and then, after a moment, she whispered my name.

"She has gone! Oh, Roddy, I believe she has gone—in peace."

She was trembling. I held her in my arms. I told her it was the bravest and sweetest thing I had ever seen done, and that no one else in the world would have done just this, and that there was nobody like her in all the world. I told her that if she could not love me, I would not know how to live.

"But you know—you must have known," she whispered. "Oh, my darling, I would have died . . ."

PAMELA HAD CALLED more than once before I realized why she was calling and opened the door.

The sudden cold made me gasp. I thrust Pamela into the nursery with Stella and switched off the hall light, which Pamela had turned on. I wanted to see what I had to fight. Mary was coming. Well, let her do her worst!

I forced my way against an impalpable pressure to the foot of the stairs and looked up at her. She stood, taller than I had seen her before, palely luminous. She began to float down toward me with a slow, sweeping movement. The eyes were intensifying their light. I did not want Stella to see those eyes.

I stood on the second step, with my hands behind me gripping the rail. In that way I could hold myself up despite the trembling

of my knees. I shook all over. My skeleton was of ice and my flesh shrank from it. I could not get my voice out of my throat; the words that I spoke were whispered and my laugh hoarse.

She loomed there, wavering, while, step by step, I mounted up against her, pouring out my derision. "You pitiful trickster, you are finished! You are shown up! Your mummery and your poses are done with, you shallow fraud!"

The form shrank and dwindled, losing outline and light; it became a grayish column of fog with a luminous nucleus. As I pressed upward, it doubled back. I saw it cowering, wreathing and writhing like smoke under a downward wind.

"There is nothing left of you, Mary," I mocked, "but a story to laugh over, a tale for maids to giggle at in the kitchen—go and scare crows!"

I was fainting now. The cloud was cold. But its incandescent center was dead. It thinned, dissolved and lifted, and seemed to ooze away through the roof. I could not have fought anymore; I had no strength left. In the upstairs hall I staggered and leaned against the studio door. It gave, and I stumbled into the room. Darkness and cold overwhelmed me and I fell.

Chapter Nineteen

IT CAN ONLY have been for an instant that I was unconscious. The glare of flames acted like magic to bring me to myself. Stella and I were beating the door with pillows before more than its surface had caught, while Pamela, in the hallway, wielded the fire extinguisher, making a hissing steam.

The carpet was ablaze and the doorsill had caught. I hauled a mattress from one bed and covered it; Stella dragged the other over and we threw it down on the big patch of flaming oil. The blaze was smothered: now there were only impudent tongues and spittings to be dealt with. Pamela tossed wet towels and blankets across to me, and with these I fell on each flame as it spurted up. We were like lunatics, stamping and dancing on those mattresses in the thick of the smoke.

Stella was coughing and choking. The window stuck, but I got it open at last and we leaned out, gulping the fresh air.

The wind had blown a corner of the smoldering mattress into flames. Pamela doused them with water; they hissed venomously and died.

"It's out!" she shouted.

"Are you all right?"

"Yes. Don't try to come out this way; it may be burned through. Go out on the roof! I'll get a ladder."

I heard her running downstairs.

Stella was crying out to me wildly. We could not see one another in the smoke-filled room, but I caught her arm and scrambled out with her onto the flat roof. She clung to me, choking and coughing and frightened.

"Oh, how could you, how could you?" she gasped. "She was so dreadful, and you went up and up! I couldn't even scream! Oh, you were lying on the floor and I couldn't rouse you, and the flames . . . the flames . . ."

I had all that I could do to calm her. I do not know how long we crouched there before I heard Pamela's voice.

"It's too heavy," she was shouting. "I can't."

Back in the room the smoke was thinner now; we went in. The damage was not much. The door was blackened and blistered halfway up. The doorsill and part of the floorboards in the hallway were burned through, but it was easy to jump over the hole. We ran down to the kitchen and met Pamela, as black as a chimney sweep. She laughed when she saw us also covered with soot. That ended Stella's panic: she looked at me and laughed too. We washed in turns at the scullery sink.

"Will somebody tell me what happened?" I demanded. "I suppose I stumbled against the stove?"

"You did mad things tonight, Roddy, but not that," Pamela declared. "It was horrifying to watch, but the incredible thing is that it worked! I know it did: she won't come back. Tomorrow we won't believe any of this! I wish we had some champagne! Our supper is spoiled; I'll have to scramble some eggs."

Whisky welcomed this small-hours' invasion gracefully, visiting each of us in turn with excited purring and affectionate rubs. He settled in Stella's lap and began licking her hand. Stella contrived to stroke him and to eat from a tray at the same time.

"Lizzie will think the devil was in it this time and no mistake!" Pamela said. "Your blankets are burned, Roddy, and our beautiful carpet."

"Doesn't matter," I told her. "They were insured."

She chuckled. "The insurance doesn't cover malicious damage, and this was malicious, I swear!"

"Mary's parting gesture? I'd like to see them try to prove that."

"As long as they don't seek Mr. Ingram's advice."

"By the same token," I reflected, pushing my cup across the table for some more tea, "Ingram can come for Christmas now."

The jet of tea swerved into the saucer. Pamela set the pot down and stared at me.

"Mr. Ingram? Christmas? What on earth are you talking about?"

"Didn't I tell you? How he got himself invited to come at midwinter if we were here? It was neat!"

"This is the first I've heard of it!"

"Glory! And I don't believe I mentioned that he proposed that you should fly to Ireland with him!"

"He didn't!"

"Cross my heart!"

"I? To Ireland? With him? Well, upon my word, you old wooden-head, you might at least give a message!"

"It wasn't a message!" I tried, in self-defense, to explain that I had not thought his notion of any importance, as she would obviously not want to go.

"Oh, it's not of the slightest importance," she admitted. "Do you want some more toast?" She got up and scribbled a note for Lizzie: *All's well, but don't disturb anybody until somebody rings.* "That's the only thing of real importance," she said. She looked inordinately amused.

I turned to Stella and found that she was asleep in her chair.

The upstairs rooms were still full of smoke. We took bed-clothes down, made up the sitting room couch for Stella and fixed a cot there for Pamela. I slept in the nursery.

THE CAT WOKE ME: I felt his soft weight as he padded over the bedclothes on my chest. His great eyes met mine complacently; he purred and waved his golden tail. I stared at him, wondering whether the things that I was remembering could possibly have happened. But here I lay in the nursery, and there were my clothes, smudged with soot. It was true, all of it: Carmel and Mary and the fire, and Stella in my arms.

While I was dressing, incredulity took hold of me once more and I looked out on the sparkling rain-washed world. I opened the window. The air was scented with heather and alive with the singing of larks.

Pamela tapped at my door and came in. "Are you all right, Roddy? Stella has had her bath. Have you? I've put her to bed properly in my room. Ring the hospital, will you? Unless she wants to go to her grandfather, she'd better stay in bed all day. She is really terribly tired."

"Do you know what Stella did last night?"

"I know she made one bound through the flames into the studio after you! Oh, Roddy, you scared us."

I told her what had happened in the nursery.

"So she sent her mother away," she murmured. "She doesn't need to love a ghost anymore."

"No, Stella doesn't need to love a ghost anymore."

"Oh, I am glad!"

"Are you glad, really?" I asked her.

"Entirely. I am happier than I have been for years. Now I'm going to have my bath."

Nature can be cruel to the old, I thought as I telephoned the hospital. The Commander could have no share in our present happiness. The dark web that Mary had woven had made him its final victim. I pitied him.

He was failing slowly, they told me, and there had been no

return of consciousness. They were expecting Dr. Scott and would ask him to ring me up.

I was as hungry as a Viking. "Lizzie," I called, "breakfast in Miss Pamela's room for three."

I ran up and knocked at the door, and Stella said, "Come in."

She looked very small sitting up in Pamela's big bed, and pale in Pamela's creamy lace jacket. When I told her the news from the hospital, her eyes filled with tears.

"If only he could have had a little longer," she said wistfully, "now that I understand! But I would have had to deceive him all the time, and he would rather die than be lied to, I believe."

A few tears fell. I comforted her as best I could and claimed a good-morning kiss. She smiled at me and sighed. "I am happy. Is it heartless to be as happy as I am?"

When Pamela came in and I told her what the report was, she promised Stella that we would drive her to the hospital unless Scott forbade it.

Lizzie arrived with her tray, planted it on the table and herself in the middle of the room, visiting each of us in turn with a bewildered and accusing gaze.

"I come in," she said, "and I find the house half burnt down. I come upstairs and I find Miss Meredith like a picture in a prayerbook and Miss Pamela with a smile on her face and Mr. Roderick on top of the world. What in the name of Creation does it mean?"

"Can you keep a secret, Lizzie?" I asked.

Pamela chuckled, and Lizzie, with a shamefaced gurgle, replied, "I won't put my soul in jeopardy with a promise."

Stella's hand slipped into Pamela's and she smiled. "Tell her, Roddy! I want Lizzie to know."

"It means, Lizzie," I said, "that Miss Meredith has promised to marry me, and we are staying at Cliff End. The ghosts are gone."

Tears came to Lizzie's eyes. "Well, if I had three wishes," she murmured brokenly. "Miss Pamela, darling ... Miss Meredith ... Oh, Mr. Roddy!" Her face cleared and shone upon us, aglow with loving-kindness. "May God bless us all," she said.

The Strange Case of
Dr. Jekyll and Mr. Hyde

The Strange Case of Dr. Jekyll and Mr. Hyde

BY

**Robert
Louis
Stevenson**

ILLUSTRATED BY GUY DEAL

Dr. Henry Jekyll was a London
physician widely known and respected.
Only his closest friends knew of
his research in an area of medicine that
most called "unscientific balderdash."
Still there seemed no cause for alarm, until
the man Edward Hyde began to visit
Jekyll's house — a man as evil as the physician
was upright. One dreadful night there
came a cry for help from the depths of Jekyll's
being, and the full horror of his plight
was revealed.

The classic tale, published in 1886,
places Robert Louis Stevenson years ahead
of his time in psychological insight,
and among fiction's true masters
of the eerie and macabre.

1. Story of the Door

MR. UTTERSON, the lawyer, was a man of a rugged countenance never lighted by a smile; cold, scanty and embarrassed in discourse; backward in sentiment; lean, long, dusty, dreary, and yet somehow lovable. At friendly meetings, and when the wine was to his taste, something eminently human beaconed from his eye; something, indeed, which never found its way into his talk, but which spoke not only in the silent symbols of the after-dinner face, but more often and loudly in the acts of his life. He was austere with himself, drank gin when he was alone to mortify a taste for vintages, and though he enjoyed the theater, had not crossed the doors of one for twenty years. But he had an approved tolerance for others—sometimes wondering, almost with envy, at the high pressure of spirits involved in their misdeeds—and in any extremity was inclined to help rather than to reprove. "I incline to Cain's heresy," he used to say quaintly. "I let my brother go to the devil in his own way." In this character it was frequently his fortune to be the last reputable acquaintance and the last good influence in the lives of down-going men. And to these, so long as they came to his chambers, he never marked a shade of change in his demeanor.

No doubt the feat was easy to Mr. Utterson, for he was unde-monstrative at best, and even his friendships seemed to be founded in good nature. It is the mark of a modest man to accept his friendly circle ready-made from the hands of opportunity, and that was the lawyer's way. His friends were those of his own blood or those whom he had known the longest. His affections, like ivy, were the growth of time; they implied no aptness in the object. Hence, no doubt, the bond that united him to his distant kinsman, Mr. Richard Enfield, a well-known young man-about-town. It was a nut to crack for many what these two could see in each other, or what subject they could find in common. It was reported by those who encountered them in their Sunday walks that they said nothing, looked singularly dull, and would hail with obvious relief the appearance of a friend. For all that, the two men put the greatest store by these excursions, counted them the chief jewel of each week, and not only set aside occasions of pleasure but even resisted the calls of business so that they might enjoy them uninterrupted.

It chanced on one of these rambles that their way led them down a bystreet in a busy quarter of London. The street was small and what is called quiet, but it did a thriving trade on the weekdays. The inhabitants were all doing well, it seemed, and all eagerly hoping to do better still. They laid out the surplus of their gains in coquetry, so that the shop fronts stood along that thoroughfare with an air of invitation, like rows of smiling sales-women. Even on Sunday, when it veiled its more florid charms and lay comparatively empty of passage, the street shone out in contrast to its dingy neighborhood. With its freshly painted shutters, well-polished brasses, and general cleanliness and gaiety of note, it instantly caught and pleased the eye of the passerby.

Two doors from one corner, on the left hand going east, the line of buildings was broken by the entry of a courtyard. Just at that point, a certain sinister structure thrust forward its gable on the street. It was two stories high; showed no window, nothing but a door on the lower story and a blind forehead of discolored wall on the upper. It bore in every feature the marks of prolonged and sordid negligence. The door, which was equipped with neither bell nor knocker, was blistered and discolored. Tramps slouched in the recess and struck matches on the panels; children kept shop upon the steps; the schoolboy had tried his knife on the moldings; and for close to a generation, no one had appeared to drive away these random visitors or to repair their ravages.

Mr. Enfield and the lawyer were on the other side of the bystreet, but when they came abreast of the door, Mr. Enfield lifted his cane and pointed. "Did you ever remark that door?" he asked, and when his companion had replied in the affirmative, he added, "It is connected in my mind with a very odd story."

"Indeed?" said Mr. Utterson, with a slight change of voice. "And what was that?"

"Well, it was this way," returned Mr. Enfield: "I was coming home from some place at the end of the world, about three o'clock of a black winter morning, and my way lay through a part of town where there was literally nothing to be seen but lamps. Street after street, and all the folks asleep—street after street, all lighted up as if for a procession and all as empty as a church—till at last I got into that state of mind when a man listens and listens and begins to long for the sight of a policeman. All at once I saw two figures: one a little man who was stumping along eastward at a good walk, and the other a girl of maybe eight or ten who was running as hard as she was able down a cross street. Well, sir, the two ran into one another naturally enough at the corner. Then came the horrible part of the thing: the man trampled calmly over the child's body and left her screaming on the ground. It sounds nothing to hear, but it was hellish to see. It wasn't like a man; it was like some damned juggernaut.

"I gave a loud cry, ran and collared my gentleman and brought him back to where there was already quite a group about the screaming child. He was perfectly cool and made no resistance, but gave me one look, so ugly that it brought out the sweat on me. The people who had turned out were the girl's own family,

and shortly, a doctor. Well, the child was not much the worse—
more frightened, according to the sawbones. There you might
have supposed would be an end to it.

"But there was one curious circumstance. I had taken a loathing to my gentleman at first sight. So had the child's family,
which was only natural. But the doctor's case was what struck
me. He had a strong Edinburgh accent, and was about as emotional as a bagpipe. Well, sir, he was like the rest of us: every
time he looked at my prisoner, I saw that sawbones turn sick and
white with the desire to kill him. I knew what was in his mind,
just as he knew what was in mine; and killing being out of the
question, we did the next best. We told the man we could and
would make such a scandal out of this as should make his name
stink from one end of London to the other. If he had any friends
or any credit, we undertook that he should lose them. And all the
time as we men were pitching it in red hot, we were keeping
the women off him as best we could, for they were as wild as
harpies. I never saw a circle of such hateful faces. And there was
the man in the middle, with a kind of black, sneering coolness—
frightened too, I could see that—but carrying it off, sir, really
like Satan. 'If you choose to make capital out of this accident,'
said he, 'I am naturally helpless. No gentleman but wishes to
avoid a scene,' says he. 'Name your figure.'

"Well, we screwed him up to a hundred pounds for the child's
family. He would have clearly liked to balk, but there was
something about the lot of us that meant mischief, and at last he
agreed. The next thing was to get the money, and where do you
think he led us but to that door? Whipped out a key, went in, and
presently came back with ten pounds in gold and a check for the
balance on Coutts's, drawn payable to bearer and signed with a
name that I can't mention—though it's one of the points of my
story—but it was a name at least very well known and often
printed. The figure was stiff, but the signature was good for more
than that, if it was genuine.

"I took the liberty of pointing out to my gentleman that the
whole business looked unbelievable, and that a man does not, in

real life, walk into a door at four in the morning and come out of it with another man's check for close to a hundred pounds. But he was quite easy and sneering. 'Set your mind at rest,' says he. 'I will stay with you till the banks open and cash the check myself.'

"So we all set off—the doctor, the child's father, our fiend and myself—to pass the rest of the night in my chambers; and the next day, when we had breakfasted, we went in a body to the bank. I gave in the check myself, and said I had every reason to believe it was a forgery. Not a bit of it. The check was genuine."

"Tut-tut," said Mr. Utterson.

"I see you feel as I do," said Mr. Enfield. "Yes, it's a bad story. For my man was a fellow that nobody could have to do with, a really damnable man, and the person that drew the check is the very model of propriety. Celebrated too, and (what makes it worse) one of your fellows who do what they call good. Blackmail, I suppose—an honest man paying through the nose for some of the capers of his youth. Blackmail House is what I call that place with the door in consequence. Though even that, you know, is far from explaining all," he added, and with the words fell into a vein of musing.

From this he was recalled by Mr. Utterson's asking rather suddenly, "And you don't know if the signer of the check lives there?"

"A likely place, isn't it?" returned Mr. Enfield. "But I happen to have noticed his address. He lives in some square or other."

"And you never asked about the—place with the door?" said Mr. Utterson.

"No, sir, I had a delicacy," was the reply. "I feel very strongly about putting questions; it partakes too much of the style of the day of judgment. You start a question, and it's like starting a stone. You sit quietly on the top of a hill, and away the stone goes, starting others; and presently some bland old bird (the last you would have thought of) is knocked on the head in his own back garden and the family have to change their name. No, sir, I make it a rule of mine: The more it looks queer, the less I ask."

"A very good rule, too," said the lawyer.

"But I have studied the place for myself," continued Mr. Enfield. "It seems scarcely a house. There is no other door, and nobody goes in or out of that one but, once in a great while, the gentleman of my adventure. There are three windows looking out on the courtyard on the first floor; none below. The windows are always shut, but they're clean. And then there is a chimney which is generally smoking, so somebody must live there. And yet it's not so sure, for the buildings are so packed together about that court that it's hard to say where one ends and another begins."

The pair walked on again for a while in silence; and then said Mr. Utterson, "Enfield, that's a good rule of yours."

"Yes, I think it is," returned Enfield.

"But for all that," continued the lawyer, "there's one point I want to ask: I want to ask the name of that man who trampled the child."

"Well," said Mr. Enfield, "I can't see what harm it would do. It was a man by the name of Hyde."

"Hm," said Mr. Utterson. "What sort of man is he to look at?"

"He is not easy to describe. There is something wrong with his appearance—something displeasing, something downright detestable. I never saw a man I so disliked, and yet I scarcely know why. He must be deformed somewhere; he gives a strong feeling of deformity, although I couldn't specify the point. He's an extraordinary-looking man, and yet I really can name nothing out of the way. No, sir, I can make no sense of it; I can't describe him. And it's not want of memory, for I declare I can see him this moment."

Mr. Utterson again walked some way in silence, obviously under a weight of consideration. "You are sure he used a key?" he inquired at last.

"My dear sir . . ." began Enfield, surprised.

"Yes, I know," said Utterson, "I know it must seem strange. The fact is, if I do not ask you the name of the other party, it is because I know it already. You see, Richard, your tale has struck home. If you have been inexact in any point, you had better correct it."

"I think you might have warned me," returned the other with a touch of sullenness. "But I have been pedantically exact, as you call it. The fellow had a key, and what's more, he has it still. I saw him use it not a week ago."

Mr. Utterson sighed deeply but said never a word. The young man presently resumed. "Here is another lesson to say nothing," said he. "I am ashamed of my long tongue. Let us make a bargain never to refer to this again."

"With all my heart," said the lawyer. "I shake hands on that, Richard."

2. Search for Mr. Hyde

THAT EVENING Mr. Utterson came home to his bachelor house in somber spirits and sat down to dinner without relish. It was his custom of a Sunday, when this meal was over, to sit by the fire, a volume of some dry divinity on his reading desk, until the clock in the neighboring church rang out the hour of twelve, when he would go soberly and gratefully to bed. On this night, however, as soon as the tablecloth was taken away, he took up a candle and went into his business room. There he opened his safe, took from the most private part of it a document labeled on the envelope as Dr. Jekyll's will, and sat down with a clouded brow to study its contents. The will was in the doctor's own handwriting, for Mr. Utterson, though he took charge of it now that it was made, had refused to lend the least assistance in the making of it. It provided not only that, in case of the decease of Henry Jekyll, M.D., D.C.L., L.L.D., F.R.S., etc., all his possessions were to pass into the hands of his "friend and benefactor Edward Hyde," but that in case of Dr. Jekyll's "disappearance or unexplained absence for any period exceeding three calendar months," the said Edward Hyde should step into the said Henry Jekyll's shoes without further delay and free from any burden or obligation, beyond the payment of a few small sums to the members of the doctor's household. This document had long offended Mr. Utterson—both as a lawyer and as a lover of the sane and customary sides of life, to whom the fanciful was the immodest. Hitherto it was his ignorance of Mr. Hyde that had swelled his indignation; now, by a sudden turn, it was his knowledge. It was already bad enough when the name was but a name of which he could learn no more. It was worse when it began to be clothed with detestable attributes. Out of the shifting, insubstantial mists that had so long baffled his eye, there leaped up the sudden, definite presentiment of a fiend.

"I thought it was madness," he said as he replaced the obnoxious paper in the safe, "and now I begin to fear it is disgrace."

With that he blew out his candle, put on a greatcoat and set forth in the direction of Cavendish Square, that citadel of medicine where his friend, the great Dr. Lanyon, had his house and received his crowding patients. If anyone knows, it will be Lanyon, he thought.

The solemn butler knew and welcomed him; he was subjected to no stage of delay, but ushered directly from the door to the dining room, where Dr. Lanyon sat alone over his wine. This was a hearty, healthy, dapper, red-faced gentleman, with a shock of hair prematurely white and a boisterous and decided manner. At the sight of Mr. Utterson, he sprang up from his chair and welcomed him with both hands. The geniality, as was the way of the man, was somewhat theatrical to the eye, but it reposed on genuine feeling. For these two were old friends, old mates both at school and college, thorough respecters of themselves and of each other, and men who thoroughly enjoyed each other's company.

After a little rambling talk the lawyer led up to the subject which so disagreeably preoccupied his mind. "I suppose, Lanyon," said he, "you and I must be the two oldest friends that Henry Jekyll has?"

"I wish the friends were younger," said Dr. Lanyon, chuckling. "But I suppose we are. And what of that? I see little of him now."

"Indeed?" said Utterson. "I thought you had a bond of common interest."

"We had," was the reply. "But it is more than ten years since Henry Jekyll became too fanciful for me. He began to go wrong, wrong in mind. And though of course I continue to take an interest in him for old time's sake, as they say, I see and I have seen devilish little of the man. Such unscientific balderdash," added the doctor, flushing suddenly purple, "would have estranged Damon and Pythias."

This little spirit of temper was somewhat of a relief to Mr. Utterson. They have only differed on some point of science, he thought, and being a man of no scientific passions (except in matters of property deeds), he even added, It is nothing worse than that! He gave his friend a few seconds to recover his composure, and then approached the question he had come to put. "Did you ever come across a protégé of his—one Hyde?" he asked.

"Hyde?" repeated Lanyon. "No. Never heard of him. Since my time."

That was the amount of information that the lawyer carried back with him to the great dark bed on which he tossed to and fro until the small hours of the morning began to grow large. It was a night of little ease to his toiling mind, toiling in darkness and besieged by questions.

Six o'clock struck on the bells of the church that was so conveniently near to Mr. Utterson's dwelling, and still he was digging at the problem. Hitherto it had touched him on the intellectual side alone, but now his imagination also was engaged, or rather enslaved. As he lay and tossed in the gross darkness of the night and the curtained room, Mr. Enfield's tale went by before his mind in a scroll of lighted pictures. He would be aware of the great field of lamps of a nocturnal city; then of the figure of a man walking swiftly; then of a child running; and then these met, and that human juggernaut trod the child down and passed on regardless of her screams. Or else he would see a room in a rich house, where his friend lay asleep, dreaming and smiling at his dreams; and then the door of that room would be opened, the curtains of the bed plucked apart, the sleeper recalled, and lo! there would stand by his side a figure to whom power was given, so that even at that dead hour he must rise and do its bidding. The figure haunted the lawyer all night. If at any time he dozed, it was but to see it glide more stealthily through sleeping houses; or move the more swiftly and still the more swiftly, even to dizziness, through wider labyrinths of lamplit city, and at every street corner crush a child and leave her screaming.

And still the figure had no face by which he might know it; even in his dreams it had none, or one that baffled him and melted before his eyes. Thus it was that there sprang up and grew apace in the lawyer's mind a singularly strong, almost an inordinate, curiosity to behold the features of the real Mr. Hyde. If he could but once set eyes on him, he thought, the mystery would lighten and perhaps roll altogether away, as was the habit of mysterious things when well examined. He might see a reason for his friend's strange preference or bondage (call it which you please), and even for the startling clauses of the will. At least it would be a face worth seeing: the face of a man who was without bowels of mercy, a face which had but to show itself to raise up, in the mind of the unimpressionable Enfield, a spirit of enduring hatred.

From that time forward, Mr. Utterson began to haunt the door in the bystreet of shops. In the morning before office hours; at noon, when business was plenty and time scarce; at night under the face of the fogged city moon—by all lights and at all hours of solitude or concourse, the lawyer was to be found at his chosen post. If he be Mr. Hyde, he thought, I shall be Mr. Seek.

At last his patience was rewarded. It was a fine dry night: frost in the air; the streets as clean as a ballroom floor; the lamps, unshaken by any wind, drawing a regular pattern of light and shadow. By ten o'clock, when the shops were closed, the bystreet was very solitary and, in spite of the low growl of London from all around, very silent. Small sounds carried far, domestic sounds out of the houses were clearly audible on either side of the roadway, and the rumor of the approach of any passerby preceded him by a long time. Mr. Utterson had been some minutes at his post when he was aware of an odd, light footstep drawing near. In the course of his nightly patrols he had long grown accustomed to the quaint effect with which the footfalls of a single person, while he is still a great way off, suddenly spring out distinct from the vast hum and clatter of the city. Yet his attention had never before been so sharply and decisively arrested, and it was with a strong, superstitious prevision of success that he withdrew into the entry of the court.

The steps drew swiftly nearer, and swelled out suddenly louder as they turned the end of the street. The lawyer could soon see what manner of man he had to deal with. He was small and very plainly dressed, and the look of him, even at that distance, went somehow strongly against the watcher's inclination. The man made straight for the door, crossing the roadway to save time. As he came, he drew a key from his pocket, like one approaching home.

Mr. Utterson stepped out and touched him on the shoulder as he passed. "Mr. Hyde, I think?"

Mr. Hyde shrank back with a hissing intake of breath. But his fear was only momentary, and though he did not look the lawyer in the face, he answered coolly enough, "That is my name. What do you want?"

"I see you are going in," returned the lawyer. "I am an old friend of Dr. Jekyll's—Mr. Utterson of Gaunt Street, you must have heard my name—and meeting you so conveniently, I thought you might admit me."

"You will not find Dr. Jekyll; he is from home," replied Mr. Hyde, inserting the key. And then suddenly, but still without looking up, "How did you know me?" he asked.

"On your side," said Mr. Utterson, "will you do me a favor?"

"With pleasure," replied the other. "What shall it be?"

"Will you let me see your face?" asked the lawyer.

Mr. Hyde appeared to hesitate, and then, as if upon some

sudden reflection, fronted about with an air of defiance. The pair stared at each other pretty fixedly for a few seconds.

"Now I shall know you again," said Mr. Utterson. "It may be useful."

"Yes," returned Mr. Hyde, "it is as well we have met. And apropos, you should have my address." He gave a number on a street in Soho.

Good God! thought Mr. Utterson, can he, too, have been thinking of the will? But he kept his feelings to himself and only grunted in acknowledgment of the address.

"And now," said the other, "how did you know me?"

"By description," was the reply.

"Whose description?"

"We have common friends," said Mr. Utterson.

"Common friends?" echoed Mr. Hyde, a little hoarsely. "Who are they?"

"Jekyll, for instance," said the lawyer.

"He never told you," cried Mr. Hyde with a flush of anger. "I did not think you would have lied."

"Come," said Mr. Utterson, "that is not fitting language."

The other snarled aloud, gave a savage laugh, and the next moment, with extraordinary quickness, he had unlocked the door and disappeared into the house.

The lawyer stood awhile when Mr. Hyde had left him, the picture of disquietude. Then he began slowly to walk, pausing every step or two and putting his hand to his brow like a man in mental perplexity. The problem he was thus debating was one of a class that is rarely solved. Mr. Hyde was pale and dwarfish; he gave an impression of deformity without any nameable malformation; he had a displeasing smile; he had borne himself toward the lawyer with a sort of murderous mixture of timidity and boldness; and he spoke with a husky, whispering and somewhat broken voice. All these were points against him, but not all of these together could explain the hitherto unknown disgust, loathing and fear with which Mr. Utterson regarded him. "There must be something else," said the perplexed gentleman. "There is something more, if I could find a name for it. God bless me, the man seems hardly human! Something troglodytic, shall we say? Or can it be the old story of Dr. Fell? Or is it the mere radiance of a foul soul that thus transpires through, and transfigures, its clay container? The last, I think, for oh, my poor old Harry Jekyll, if ever I read Satan's signature upon a face, it is on that of your new friend."

Around the corner from the bystreet there was a square of ancient handsome houses, now for the most part decayed from their high estate and rented in apartments and rooms to all sorts and conditions of men: map engravers, architects, shady lawyers and the agents of obscure enterprises. One house, however—second from the corner—was still occupied entire; and at the door of this, which wore a great air of wealth and comfort, though it was now plunged in darkness except for the fanlight, Mr. Utterson stopped and knocked. A well-dressed elderly servant opened the door.

"Is Dr. Jekyll at home, Poole?" asked the lawyer.

"I will see, Mr. Utterson," said Poole, admitting the visitor, as he spoke, into a large low-roofed, comfortable hall paved with flagstones, warmed (after the fashion of a country house) by a bright open fire and furnished with costly cabinets of oak. "Will you wait here by the fire, sir? Or shall I give you a light in the dining room?"

"Here, thank you," said the lawyer, and he drew near and leaned on the tall fender. This hall, in which he was now left alone, was a pet fancy of his friend the doctor's, and Utterson himself was wont to speak of it as the pleasantest room in London. But tonight there was a shudder in his blood; the face of Hyde sat heavy on his memory; he felt (what was rare with him) a nausea and distaste for life; and in the gloom of his spirits, he seemed to read menace in the flickering of the firelight on the polished cabinets and the uneasy starting of the shadow on the roof. He was ashamed of his relief when Poole presently returned to announce that Dr. Jekyll had gone out.

"I saw Mr. Hyde go in by the old dissecting room door,

Poole," he said. "Is that right when Dr. Jekyll is from home?"

"Quite right, Mr. Utterson, sir," replied the servant. "Mr. Hyde has a key."

"Your master seems to repose a great deal of trust in that young man, Poole," resumed the other musingly.

"Yes, sir, he do indeed," said Poole. "We all have orders to obey him."

"I do not think I ever met Mr. Hyde?" asked Utterson.

"Oh, dear no, sir. He never *dines* here," replied the butler. "Indeed, we see very little of him on this side of the house. He mostly comes and goes by the laboratory."

"Well, good night, Poole."

"Good night, Mr. Utterson."

And the lawyer set out homeward with a very heavy heart. Poor Harry Jekyll, he thought, my mind misgives me he is in deep waters! He was wild when he was young—a long while ago, to be sure, but in the law of God there is no statute of limitations. Aye, it must be that: the ghost of some old sin, the cancer of some concealed disgrace, punishment coming, on laggard feet, years after memory has forgotten and self-love condoned the fault.

And the lawyer, scared by the thought, brooded awhile on his own past, groping in all the corners of memory, lest by chance some jack-in-the-box of an old iniquity should leap to light there. His past was fairly blameless; few men could read the rolls of their life with less apprehension. Yet he was humbled to the dust by the many ill things he had done, and raised up again into a sober and fearful gratitude by the many he had come so near to doing, yet avoided.

Then, returning to his former subject, he conceived a spark of hope. This Master Hyde, if he were studied, thought he, must have secrets of his own—black secrets, by the look of him; secrets compared to which poor Jekyll's worst would be like sunshine. Things cannot continue as they are. It turns me cold to think of this creature stealing like a thief to Harry's bedside. Poor Harry, what a wakening! And the danger of it—for if this

Hyde suspects the existence of the will, he may grow impatient to inherit. Aye, I must put my shoulder to the wheel. If Jekyll will but let me, he added, if Jekyll will only let me. For once more he saw before his mind's eye, as clear as transparency, the strange clauses of the will.

3. Dr. Jekyll Was Quite at Ease

A FORTNIGHT later, by excellent good fortune, Dr. Jekyll gave one of his pleasant dinners for some five or six old cronies, all intelligent, reputable men and all judges of good wine. Mr. Utterson so contrived that he remained behind after the others had departed. This was not a new arrangement, but a thing that had befallen many scores of times. Where Utterson was liked, he was liked well. Hosts loved to detain the dry lawyer when the lighthearted and loose-tongued had their foot already on the threshold. They liked to sit awhile in his unobtrusive company, practicing for solitude, sobering their minds in the man's rich silence after the expense and strain of gaiety. To this rule, Dr. Jekyll was no exception. As he now sat on the opposite side of the fire—a large, well-made, smooth-faced man of fifty, with something of a slyish cast perhaps, but with every mark of capacity and kindness—you could see by his looks that he cherished for Mr. Utterson a sincere and warm affection.

"I have been wanting to speak to you, Jekyll," began the latter. "You know that will of yours?"

A close observer might have gathered that the topic was distasteful, but the doctor carried it off gaily. "My poor Utterson," said he, "you are unfortunate in such a client. I never saw a man so distressed as you were by my will, unless it were that hidebound pedant Lanyon at what he called my scientific heresies. Oh, I know he's a good fellow—you needn't frown—an excellent fellow, and I always mean to see more of him. But he's a hidebound pedant for all that; an ignorant, blatant pedant. I was never more disappointed in any man than Lanyon."

"You know I never approved of it," pursued Utterson, ruthlessly disregarding the fresh topic the doctor had introduced.

"My will? Yes, certainly, I know that," said the doctor, a trifle sharply. "You have told me so."

"Well, I tell you so again," continued the lawyer. "I have been learning something of young Hyde."

The large handsome face of Dr. Jekyll grew pale to the very lips, and there came a blackness about his eyes. "I do not care to hear more about it," said he. "This is a matter I thought we had agreed to drop."

"What I heard was abominable," said Utterson.

"It can make no change. You do not understand my position," returned the doctor with a certain incoherency of manner. "I am painfully situated, Utterson. My position is a very strange—a very strange one. It is one of those affairs that cannot be mended by talking."

"Jekyll," said Utterson, "you know me: I am a man to be trusted. Make a clean breast of this in confidence, and I have no doubt I can get you out of it."

"My good Utterson," said the doctor, "this is very good of you, this is downright good of you, and I cannot find words to thank you. I believe you fully. I would trust you before any man alive—aye, before myself, if I could make the choice—but indeed, it isn't what you fancy; it is not as bad as that. And just to put your good heart at rest, I will tell you one thing: the moment I choose, I can be rid of Mr. Hyde. I give you my hand upon that, and I thank you again and again. I will just add one little word, Utterson, that I'm sure you'll take in good part: this is a private matter, and I beg of you to let it sleep."

Utterson reflected a little, looking in the fire. "I have no doubt you are perfectly right," he said at last, getting to his feet.

"Well, but since we have touched upon this business, and for the last time I hope," continued the doctor, "there is one point I should like you to understand. I have really a very great interest in poor Hyde. I know you have seen him—he told me so—and I fear he was rude. But I do sincerely take a great, a very great interest in that young man, and if I am taken away, Utterson, I

wish you to promise me that you will bear with him and get his rights for him. I think you would if you knew all, and it would be a weight off my mind if you would promise."

"I can't pretend that I shall ever like him," said the lawyer.

"I don't ask that," pleaded Jekyll, laying his hand upon the other's arm. "I only ask for justice. I only ask you to help him for my sake when I am no longer here."

Utterson heaved an irrepressible sigh. "Well," said he, "I promise."

4. The Carew Murder Case

NEARLY A YEAR later, in the month of October 18—, London was startled by a crime of singular ferocity, which was rendered all the more notable by the high position of the victim. The details were few and startling. A maidservant living alone in a house not far from the river had gone upstairs to bed about eleven. Although a fog rolled over the city in the small hours, the early part of the night was cloudless, and the lane, which the maid's window overlooked, was brilliantly lit by the full moon. It seems she was romantically inclined, for she sat down by the window, and fell into a dream of musing. Never (she used to say, with streaming tears, when she narrated that experience), never had she felt more at peace with all men or thought more kindly of the world. And as she so sat, she became aware of an aged beautiful gentleman with white hair drawing near along the lane; and advancing to meet him, another and very small gentleman, to whom at first she paid less attention. When they had come within speech (which was just under the maid's eyes), the older man bowed and accosted the other with a very pretty manner of politeness. It did not seem as if the subject of his address were of great importance—indeed, from his pointing, it appeared as if he were only inquiring his way—but the moon shone on his face as he spoke, and the girl was pleased to watch it, for it seemed to breathe such an innocent and Old World kindness of disposition, yet with something high too, as of a well-founded self-content. Presently her eye wandered to the other, and she was surprised to recognize in him a certain Mr. Hyde, who had once visited her master's house, and for whom she had conceived a dislike. He had in his hand a heavy cane, with which he was trifling. He answered never a word, and seemed to listen with an ill-contained impatience. And then all of a sudden he broke out in a great flame of anger, stamping with his foot, brandishing the cane and carrying on (as the maid described it) like a madman. The old gentleman took a step back, with the air of one very much surprised and a trifle hurt. At that, Mr. Hyde broke out of all bounds and clubbed him to the earth. The next moment, with apelike fury, he was trampling his victim underfoot and hailing down a storm of blows, under which the bones were audibly shattered and the body jumped upon the pavement. At the horror of these sights and sounds, the maid fainted.

It was two o'clock when she came to herself and called for the police. The murderer was gone long ago, but there lay his victim in the middle of the lane, incredibly mangled. The stick with which the deed had been done, although it was of some rare and very tough and heavy wood, had broken in the middle under the stress of this insensate cruelty. One splintered half had rolled in the neighboring gutter; the other, without doubt, had been carried away by the murderer. A purse and a gold watch were found upon the victim, but no cards or papers, except a sealed and stamped envelope, which he had probably been carrying to the post and which bore the name and address of Mr. Utterson.

This was brought to the lawyer the next morning, before he was out of bed. He had no sooner seen it, and been told the circumstances, than he shot out a solemn lip. "I shall say nothing till I have seen the body," said he. "Have the kindness to wait while I dress."

With the same grave countenance he hurried through his breakfast and drove to the police station, whither the body had been carried. As soon as he came into the cell, he nodded. "Yes," said he, "I recognize him. I am sorry to say that this is Sir Danvers Carew."

"Good God, sir," exclaimed the officer, "is it possible?" The next moment his eye lighted up with professional ambition. "This will make a deal of noise," he said. "Perhaps you can help us to the murderer." And he briefly narrated what the maid had seen and showed the broken stick.

Mr. Utterson had already quailed at the name of Hyde, but when the stick was laid before him, he could doubt no longer. Broken and battered as it was, he recognized it as one that he had himself presented many years before to Henry Jekyll.

"Is this Mr. Hyde a person of small stature?" he inquired.

"Particularly small and particularly wicked-looking is what the maid calls him," said the officer.

Mr. Utterson reflected, and then, raising his head, "If you will come with me in my cab," he said, "I think I can take you to his house."

It was by this time about nine in the morning, and the first fog of the season—a great chocolate-colored pall—lowered over heaven. But the wind was continually charging and routing these embattled vapors, so that as the cab crawled from street to street, Mr. Utterson beheld a marvelous number of degrees and hues of twilight. Here it would be dark like the back end of evening; and there would be a glow of a rich, lurid brown, like the light of some strange conflagration; and here, for a moment, the fog would be quite broken up, and a haggard shaft of daylight would glance in between the swirling wreaths. The dismal quarter of Soho seen under these changing glimpses— with its muddy ways and slatternly inhabitants, and its lamps, which had never been extinguished or had been kindled afresh to combat this mournful reinvasion of darkness—seemed, in the lawyer's eyes, like a district of some city in a nightmare. The thoughts of his mind, besides, were of the gloomiest dye. When he glanced at the companion of his drive, he was conscious of some touch of that terror of the law and the law's officers which may at times assail the most honest.

As the cab drew up before the address indicated, the fog lifted a little and showed him a dingy street with a gin palace, a low

French eating house, many ragged children huddled in the doorways, and many women of many different nationalities setting out, key in hand, to have a morning glass. The next moment the fog settled down again upon the street, as brown as umber, and cut him off from his blackguardly surroundings. This was the address given Mr. Utterson by Henry Jekyll's favorite—the man who was heir to a quarter of a million pounds sterling.

An ivory-faced and silvery-haired old woman opened the door. She had an evil face, smoothed by hypocrisy, but her manners were excellent. Yes, she said, this was Mr. Hyde's, but he was not at home. He had come in that night very late, but he had gone away again in less than an hour. There was nothing strange in that; his habits were very irregular, and he was often absent. For instance, she had not seen him for nearly two months till yesterday.

"Very well then, we wish to see his rooms," said the lawyer. When the woman began to declare it was impossible, he added, "I had better tell you who this person is. This is Inspector Newcomen of Scotland Yard."

A flash of odious joy appeared upon the woman's face. "Ah," said she, "he is in trouble! What has he done?"

Mr. Utterson and the inspector exchanged glances. "He don't seem a very popular character," observed the latter. "And now, my good woman, just let me and this gentleman have a look about us."

In the whole extent of the house, which but for the old woman remained empty, Mr. Hyde had used only a couple of rooms, but these were furnished with luxury and good taste. A closet was filled with wine; the plate was of silver, the table linens elegant; a good picture hung upon the walls, a gift (Utterson supposed) from Henry Jekyll, who was a connoisseur; and the carpets were thick and agreeable in color. At this moment, however, the rooms bore every mark of having been recently and hurriedly ransacked. Clothes lay about the floor with their pockets inside out; lock-fast drawers stood open; and on the hearth there lay a pile of gray ashes, as though many papers had been burned.

From these embers the inspector disinterred the butt end of a green checkbook, which had resisted the action of the fire. The other half of the murderer's stick was found behind the door, and as this clinched his suspicions, the officer declared himself delighted. A visit to the bank, where several thousand pounds were found to be credited to the murderer's account, completed his gratification.

"You may depend upon it, sir," he told Mr. Utterson, "I have him in my hand. He must have lost his head or he never would have left the stick or, above all, burned the checkbook. Why, money's life to the man. We have only to wait for him at the bank and get out the notices."

This last, however, was not so easy to accomplish, for Mr. Hyde had numbered few familiars. Even the master of the servant maid who had witnessed Carew's murder had only seen him twice; his family could nowhere be traced; he had never been photographed; and the few who could describe him differed widely, as common observers will. Only on one point were they agreed, and that was the haunting sense of unexpressed deformity with which the fugitive impressed his beholders.

5. Incident of the Letter

IT WAS LATE in the afternoon when Mr. Utterson found his way to Dr. Jekyll's door. He was at once admitted by Poole and conducted by the kitchen offices and across a yard, which had once been a garden, to the building which was indifferently known as the laboratory or dissecting room. The doctor had bought the house from the heirs of a celebrated surgeon, and his own tastes being chemical rather than anatomical, had changed the designation of the building at the bottom of the garden. It was the first time that the lawyer had been received in that part of his friend's quarters.

He eyed the dingy structure with curiosity and gazed around with a distasteful sense of strangeness as he crossed the operating theater, once crowded with eager students and now lying silent, the tables laden with chemical apparatus, the floor strewn with crates and littered with packing straw, and the light falling dimly through the foggy cupola. At the farther end a flight of stairs mounted to a door covered with red baize, and through this Mr. Utterson was at last received into the doctor's chamber. It was a large room furnished with, among other things, glass cabinets, a cheval glass and a desk; and looking out upon the court by three windows barred with iron. A fire burned in the grate; a lamp was set lighted on the chimney shelf, for even in the houses the fog began to lie thickly; and there, close up to the warmth, sat Dr. Jekyll, looking deadly sick. He did not rise to meet his visitor, but held out a cold hand and bade him welcome in a changed voice.

"And now," said Mr. Utterson, as soon as Poole had left them, "you have heard the news?"

The doctor shuddered. "They were crying it in the square," he said. "I heard them in my dining room."

"One word," said the lawyer. "Carew was my client, but so are you, and I want to know what I am doing. You have not been mad enough to hide this fellow?"

"Utterson, I swear to God," cried the doctor, "I swear to God I will never set eyes on him again. I pledge my honor to you that I am done with him in this world. It is all at an end. And indeed he does not want my help. You do not know him as I do; he is safe, he is quite safe. Mark my words, he will never more be heard of."

The lawyer listened gloomily; he did not like his friend's feverish manner. "You seem pretty sure of him," said he, "and for your sake, I hope you may be right. If it came to a trial, your name might appear."

"I am quite sure of him," replied Jekyll. "I have grounds for certainty that I cannot share with anyone. But there is one thing on which you may advise me. I have—I have received a letter, and I am at a loss whether I should show it to the police. I should like to leave it in your hands, Utterson. You would judge wisely, I am sure—I have so great a trust in you."

"You fear, I suppose, that it might lead to his detection?" asked the lawyer.

"No," said the other. "I cannot say that I care what becomes of Hyde; I am quite done with him. I was thinking of my own character, which this hateful business has rather exposed."

Utterson ruminated awhile. He was surprised at his friend's selfishness, and yet relieved by it. "Well," said he at last, "let me see the letter."

The letter was written in an odd, upright hand and signed "Edward Hyde." It signified, briefly enough, that the writer's benefactor, Dr. Jekyll, whom he had long so unworthily repaid for a thousand generosities, need labor under no alarm for his safety, as he had a means of escape on which he placed a sure dependence. The lawyer liked this letter well enough; it put a better color on the intimacy than he had looked for, and he blamed himself for some of his past suspicions.

"Have you the envelope?" he asked.

"I burned it," replied Jekyll, "before I thought what I was about. But it bore no postmark. The note was handed in."

"Shall I keep this and sleep upon it?" asked Utterson.

"I wish you to judge for me entirely," was the reply. "I have lost confidence in myself."

"Well, I shall consider," returned the lawyer. "And now one word more: it was Hyde who dictated the terms in your will about disappearance?"

The doctor seemed seized with a qualm of faintness; he shut his mouth tight and nodded.

"I knew it," said Utterson. "He meant to murder you. You had a fine escape."

"I have had what is far more to the purpose," returned the doctor solemnly, "I have had a lesson. Oh, God, Utterson, what a lesson I have had!" And he covered his face for a moment with his hands.

On his way out, the lawyer stopped and had a word or two with Poole. "By the by," said he, "there was a letter handed in today. What was the messenger like?"

But Poole was positive nothing had come except by post—"and only circulars by that," he added.

This news sent off the visitor with his fears renewed. Plainly the letter had come by the laboratory door. Possibly, indeed, it had been written in the chamber, and if that was so, it must be differently judged and handled with more caution. The newsboys, as he went, were crying themselves hoarse along the footways:

SPECIAL EDITION. SHOCKING MURDER MEMBER OF PARLIAMENT.

That was the funeral oration of one friend and client, and he could not help a certain apprehension lest the good name of another should be sucked down in the eddy of the scandal. It was, at least, a ticklish decision that he had to make; and self-reliant as he was by habit, he began to cherish a longing for advice. It was not to be had directly, but perhaps, he thought, it might be fished for.

Presently he sat on one side of his own hearth, with Mr. Guest, his head clerk, on the other, and midway between, at a nicely calculated distance from the fire, a bottle of a particular old wine that had long dwelt in the cellar of his house. The fog still slept on the wing above the drowned city, but the room was gay with firelight. In the bottle the imperial dye had softened with time, as the color grows richer in stained-glass windows; and the glow of hot autumn afternoons on hillside vineyards in a warmer climate was ready to be set free and to disperse the fog of London.

Insensibly the lawyer melted. There was no man from whom he kept fewer secrets than Mr. Guest, and he was not always sure that he kept as many as he meant. Guest had often been on business to the doctor's; he knew Poole; he could scarcely have failed to hear of Mr. Hyde's familiarity about the house; he might have drawn conclusions. Was it not as well, then, that he should see a letter which put that mystery to rights? Above all, since Guest, being a great student and critic of handwriting, would consider the step natural and obliging? The clerk, besides, was a man of counsel; he could scarcely read so strange a document without dropping a remark, and by that remark Mr. Utterson might shape his future course.

"This is a sad business about Sir Danvers," the lawyer said.

"Yes, sir, indeed. It has elicited a great deal of public feeling," returned Guest. "The man, of course, was mad."

"I should like to hear your views on that," replied Utterson. "I have a document here in his handwriting. It is between ourselves, for I scarcely know what to do about it—it is an ugly business at best. But there it is, quite in your line: a murderer's autograph."

Guest's eyes brightened and he studied it with passion. "No, sir," he said, "not mad, but it is an odd hand."

"And by all accounts a very odd writer," added the lawyer, looking at Guest expectantly.

Just then the servant entered with a note.

"Is that from Dr. Jekyll, sir?" inquired the clerk. "I thought I knew the writing. Anything private, Mr. Utterson?"

"Only an invitation to dinner. Why? Do you want to see it?"

"For a moment. I thank you, sir." And the clerk laid the two sheets of paper alongside and sedulously compared their contents. "Thank you, sir," he said at last, returning both. "It's a very interesting autograph."

There was a pause, during which Mr. Utterson struggled with himself. "Why did you compare them, Guest?" he inquired suddenly.

"Well, sir," returned the clerk, "there's a rather singular resemblance: the two hands are in many points identical, only differently sloped."

"Rather quaint," said Utterson.

"It is, as you say, rather quaint," returned Guest.

"I wouldn't speak of this note, you know," said the master.

"No, sir," said the clerk. "I understand."

No sooner was Mr. Utterson alone that night than he locked the note in his safe, where it reposed from that time forward. What! he thought. Henry Jekyll forge for a murderer! And his blood ran cold in his veins.

6. Remarkable Incident of Dr. Lanyon

TIME RAN ON. Thousands of pounds were offered in reward, for the death of Sir Danvers was resented as a public injury, but Mr. Hyde had disappeared from the purview of the police as though he had never existed. Much of his past was unearthed, indeed, and all disreputable. Tales came out of the man's cruelty, at once so callous and violent; of his vile life; of his strange associates; of the hatred that seemed to have surrounded his career—but of his present whereabouts, not a whisper. From the time he had left the house in Soho on the morning of the murder, he was simply blotted out. Gradually Mr. Utterson began to recover from the hotness of his alarm and to grow more at ease with himself. The death of Sir Danvers was, to his way of thinking, more than paid for by the disappearance of Mr. Hyde. Now that that evil influence had been withdrawn, a new life began for Dr. Jekyll. He came out of his seclusion, renewed relations with his friends and became once more their familiar guest and entertainer. Whilst he had always been known for charities, he was now no less distinguished for religion. He was busy, he was much in the open air, he did good. His face seemed to open and brighten, as if with an inward consciousness of service, and for more than two months the doctor was at peace.

On the eighth of January, Utterson had dined at the doctor's with a small party. Lanyon had been there, and the face of the host had looked from one to the other as in the old days when the trio were inseparable friends. On the twelfth, and again on the fourteenth, the door was shut against the lawyer. "The doctor is confined to the house," Poole said, "and will see no one." On the fifteenth Utterson tried again, and was again refused. Having been used for the last two months to see his friend almost daily, he found this return to solitude to weigh on his spirits. On the fifth night he had Guest in to dine with him, and on the sixth he betook himself to Dr. Lanyon's.

There at least he was not denied admittance, but when he

came in, he was shocked at the change which had taken place in the doctor's appearance. He had his death warrant written legibly upon his face. The rosy man had grown pale, his flesh had fallen away, he was visibly balder and older. And yet it was not so much these tokens of swift physical decay that arrested the lawyer's notice as a look in the eye and a quality of manner that seemed to testify to some deep-seated terror of the mind. It was unlikely that the doctor should fear death, and yet that was what Utterson was tempted to suspect. Yes, he thought, he is a doctor, he must know his own state and that his days are counted, and the knowledge is more than he can bear. When Utterson remarked on his ill looks, it was with an air of great firmness that Lanyon declared himself a doomed man.

"I have had a shock," he said, "and I shall never recover. It is a question of weeks. Well, life has been pleasant. I liked it—yes, sir, I used to like it. I sometimes think if we knew all, we should be more glad to get away."

"Jekyll is ill, too," observed Utterson. "Have you seen him?"

Lanyon's face changed, and he held up a trembling hand. "I wish to see or hear no more of Dr. Jekyll," he said in a loud, unsteady voice. "I am quite done with that person, and I beg that you will spare me any allusion to one whom I regard as dead."

"Tut-tut," said Mr. Utterson. Then, after a considerable pause, "Can't I do anything?" he inquired. "We are three very old friends, Lanyon. We shall not live to make others."

"Nothing can be done," returned Lanyon. "Ask Jekyll."

"He will not see me," said the lawyer.

"I am not surprised at that," was the reply. "Someday, Utterson, after I am dead, you may perhaps come to learn the right and wrong of this. I cannot tell you. And in the meantime, if you can sit and talk with me of other things, for God's sake, stay and do so. But if you cannot keep clear of this accursed topic, then in God's name, go, for I cannot bear it."

As soon as he got home, Utterson sat down and wrote to Jekyll, complaining of his exclusion from the house and asking the cause of this unhappy break with Lanyon. The next day brought him a long answer, often very pathetically worded, and sometimes darkly mysterious in drift. The quarrel with Lanyon was incurable. "I do not blame our old friend," Jekyll wrote, "but I share his view that we must never meet. I mean from henceforth to lead a life of extreme seclusion. You must not be surprised, nor must you doubt my friendship, if my door is often shut even to you. You must suffer me to go my own dark way. I have brought on myself a punishment and a danger that I cannot name. If I am the chief of sinners, I am the chief of sufferers also. I could not think that this earth contained a place for sufferings and terrors so unmanning. You can do but one thing, Utterson, to lighten this destiny, and that is to respect my silence."

Utterson was amazed. The dark influence of Hyde had been withdrawn; the doctor had returned to his old tasks and friendships. A week ago, the prospect had smiled with every promise of a cheerful and an honored age. Now, in a moment, friendship, peace of mind and the whole tenor of his life were wrecked. So great and unprepared a change pointed to madness, but in view of Lanyon's manner and words, there must be for it some deeper ground.

A week afterward Dr. Lanyon took to his bed, and in something less than a fortnight he was dead. The night after the funeral, at which he had been sadly affected, Utterson locked the door of his business room and, sitting there by the light of a melancholy candle, drew out and set before him an envelope addressed by the hand and sealed with the seal of his dead friend. "PRIVATE: for the hands of G. J. Utterson ALONE, and in case of his predecease *to be destroyed unread*"—so it was emphatically inscribed, and the lawyer dreaded to behold the contents.

I have buried one friend today, he thought. What if this should cost me another? And then he condemned the fear as a disloyalty and broke the seal. Within there was another enclosure, likewise sealed, and marked upon the cover as "Not to be opened till the death or disappearance of Dr. Henry Jekyll."

Utterson could not trust his eyes: yes, it was *disappearance*. Here again, as in the mad will which he had long ago restored to its author, here again the idea of a disappearance and the name of Henry Jekyll were bracketed. But in the will that idea had sprung from the sinister suggestion of the man Hyde; it was set there with a purpose all too plain and horrible. Written by the hand of Lanyon, what should it mean? A great curiosity came on the trustee to disregard the prohibition and dive at once to the bottom of these mysteries, but professional honor and faithfulness to his dead friend were stringent obligations, so the packet slept in the inmost corner of his private safe.

It is one thing to mortify curiosity, another to conquer it. It may be doubted if, from that day forth, Utterson desired the society of his surviving friend with the same eagerness. He thought of him kindly, but his thoughts were disquieted and fearful. He went to call, indeed, but he was perhaps relieved to be denied admittance. Perhaps, in his heart, he preferred to speak with Poole upon the doorstep, surrounded by the air and sounds of the open city, rather than to be admitted into that house of voluntary bondage and to sit and speak with its inscrutable recluse. Poole had, indeed, no very pleasant news to communicate. The doctor, it appeared, now more than ever confined himself to the chamber over the laboratory, where he would sometimes even sleep. He was out of spirits, he had grown very silent, he did not read; it seemed he had something on his mind. Utterson became so used to the unvarying character of these reports that he fell off little by little in the frequency of his visits.

7. Incident at the Window

IT CHANCED ON SUNDAY, when Mr. Utterson was on his usual walk with Mr. Enfield, that their way lay once again through the bystreet, and that when they came in front of the door, both stopped to gaze on it.

"Well," said Enfield, "that story's at an end at least. We shall never see more of Mr. Hyde."

"I hope not," said Utterson. "Did I ever tell you that I once saw him, and shared your feeling of repulsion?"

"It was impossible to do the one without the other," returned Enfield. "And by the way, what an ass you must have thought me not to know that this was a back way to Dr. Jekyll's! It was partly your own fault that I found it out even when I did."

"So you found it out, did you?" said Utterson. "But if that be so, we may step into the court and take a look at the windows. To tell you the truth, I am uneasy about poor Jekyll, and even outside, I feel as if the presence of a friend might do him good."

The court was very cool and a little damp, and full of premature twilight, although the sky, high up overhead, was still bright with sunset. The middle one of the three windows was halfway open, and sitting close beside it, taking the air with an infinite sadness of mien, like some disconsolate prisoner, Utterson saw Dr. Jekyll.

"What! Jekyll!" he cried. "I trust you are better."

"I am very low, Utterson," replied the doctor drearily, "very low. It will not last long, thank God."

"You stay too much indoors," said the lawyer. "You should be out, whipping up the circulation, like Mr. Enfield and me. (This is my cousin—Mr. Enfield—Dr. Jekyll.) Come now; get your hat and take a quick turn with us."

"You are very good," sighed the other. "I should like to very much, but no, no, no, it is quite impossible; I dare not. But indeed, Utterson, I am very glad to see you. This is really a great pleasure. I would ask you and Mr. Enfield up, but the place is really not fit."

"Why then," said the lawyer good-naturedly, "the best thing we can do is to stay down here and speak with you from where we are."

"That is just what I was about to venture to propose," returned the doctor with a smile. But the words were hardly uttered before the smile was struck out of his face and succeeded by an expression of such abject terror and despair as froze the very blood of the two gentlemen below. They saw it but for a glimpse—for the window was instantly thrust down—but that glimpse had been sufficient, and they turned and left the court without a word. In silence, too, they traversed the bystreet; and it was not until they had come into a neighboring thoroughfare, where even upon a Sunday there were still some stirrings of life, that Mr. Utterson at last turned and looked at his companion. They were both pale, and there was an answering horror in their eyes.

"God forgive us, God forgive us," said Mr. Utterson.

But Mr. Enfield only nodded his head very seriously, and walked on once more in silence.

8. The Last Night

MR. UTTERSON was sitting by his fireside one evening after dinner when he was surprised to receive a visit from Dr. Jekyll's butler.

"Bless me, Poole, what brings you here?" he cried. Then, taking a second look at him, "What ails you?" he added. "Is the doctor ill?"

"Mr. Utterson," said the man, "there is something wrong."

"Take a seat, and here is a glass of wine for you," said the lawyer. "Now, take your time, and tell me plainly what you want."

"You know the doctor's ways, sir," replied Poole, "and how he shuts himself up. Well, he's shut up again in the chamber, and I don't like it, sir—I wish I may die if I like it. Mr. Utterson, sir, I'm afraid."

"Now, my good man," said the lawyer, "be explicit. What are you afraid of?"

"I've been afraid for about a week," returned Poole, doggedly disregarding the question, "and I can bear it no more."

The man's appearance amply bore out his words. His manner was altered for the worse, and except for the moment when he had first announced his terror, he had not once looked the lawyer in the face. Even now, he sat with the glass of wine

untasted on his knee, and his eyes directed to a corner of the floor. "I can bear it no more," he repeated.

"Come," said the lawyer, "I see you have some good reason, Poole. I see there is something seriously amiss. Try to tell me what it is."

"I think there's been foul play," said Poole hoarsely.

"Foul play!" cried the lawyer, a good deal frightened and rather inclined to be irritated in consequence. "What foul play! What does the man mean?"

"I daren't say, sir," was the answer. "But will you come along with me and see for yourself?"

Mr. Utterson's only answer was to rise and get his hat and greatcoat. But he observed with wonder the greatness of the relief that appeared upon the butler's face, and that the wine was still untasted when Poole set it down to follow him.

It was a wild, cold, seasonable night in March, with a pale moon lying on her back as though the wind had tilted her, and flying clouds of the most diaphanous texture. The wind made talking difficult, and flecked the blood into the face. It seemed to have swept the streets unusually bare of pedestrians besides, for Mr. Utterson thought he had never seen that part of London so deserted. He could have wished it otherwise; never in his life had he been conscious of so sharp a wish to see and touch his fellow creatures. For struggle as he might, there was borne in upon his mind a crushing anticipation of calamity.

The square, when they got there, was full of wind and dust. Poole, who had kept all the way a pace or two ahead, now pulled up in the middle of the pavement, and in spite of the biting weather took off his hat and mopped his brow with a red pocket handkerchief. But for all the hurry of his coming, these were not the dews of exertion that he wiped away, but the moisture of some strangling anguish, for his face was white and his voice, when he spoke, harsh and broken.

"Well, sir," he said, "here we are, and God grant there be nothing wrong."

"Amen, Poole," said the lawyer.

Thereupon the servant knocked in a very guarded manner. The door was opened on the chain and a voice asked from within, "Is that you, Poole?"

"It's all right," said Poole. "Open the door."

The hall, when they entered it, was brightly lighted up. The fire was built high, and about the hearth the whole of the servants, men and women, stood huddled together like a flock of sheep. At the sight of Mr. Utterson, the housemaid broke into hysterical whimpering; and the cook, crying out "Bless God! It's Mr. Utterson," ran forward as if to take him in her arms.

"What, what? Are you all here?" said the lawyer peevishly. "Very irregular, very unseemly. Your master would be far from pleased."

"They're all afraid," said Poole.

Blank silence followed, no one protesting. Only the maid lifted up her voice and now wept loudly.

"Hold your tongue!" Poole said to her with a ferocity of accent that testified to his own jangled nerves. Indeed, when the girl had so suddenly raised the note of her lamentation, they had all started and turned toward the inner door with faces of dreadful expectation. "Now," said the butler, addressing the kitchen boy, "reach me a candle, and we'll get this done at once." And then he begged Mr. Utterson to follow him, and led the way to the back garden.

"Now, sir," said he, "you come as gently as you can. I want you to hear, and I don't want you to be heard. And see here, sir, if by any chance he was to ask you in, don't go."

Mr. Utterson's nerves, at this unlooked-for termination, gave a jerk that nearly threw him from his balance, but he summoned up his courage and followed the butler into the laboratory building and through the surgical theater, with its crates and bottles, to the foot of the stairs. Here Poole motioned him to stand on one side and listen; while he himself, setting down the candle and making a great and obvious call on his resolution, mounted the steps and knocked with a somewhat uncertain hand on the red baize of the chamber door.

"Mr. Utterson, sir, asking to see you," he called, and even as he did so, once more violently signed to the lawyer to give ear.

A voice answered from within. "Tell him I cannot see anyone," it said complainingly.

"Thank you, sir," said Poole with a note of something like triumph in his voice. Taking up his candle, he led Mr. Utterson back across the yard and into the great kitchen, where the fire was out and the beetles were leaping on the floor.

"Sir," he said, looking Mr. Utterson in the eyes, "was that my master's voice?"

"It seems much changed," replied the lawyer, very pale, but giving look for look.

"Changed? Well, yes, I think so," said the butler. "Have I been twenty years in this man's house to be deceived about his voice? No, sir. The master's been made away with; he was made away with eight days ago, when we heard him cry out upon the name of God. And who's in there instead of him, and why it stays there, is a thing that cries to heaven, Mr. Utterson!"

"This is a very strange tale, Poole. This is rather a wild tale, my man," said Mr. Utterson, biting his finger. "Suppose it were as you suppose, supposing Dr. Jekyll to have been—well, murdered—what could induce the murderer to stay? That won't hold water; it doesn't commend itself to reason."

"Well, Mr. Utterson, you are a hard man to satisfy, but I'll do it yet," said Poole. "All this last week (you must know) him, or it— whatever it is that lives in that chamber—has been crying night and day for some sort of medicine and cannot get it to his liking. It was sometimes his way—the master's, that is—to write his orders on a sheet of paper and throw it on the stair. We've had nothing else this week back—nothing but papers and a closed door and the very meals left there to be smuggled in when nobody was looking. Well, sir, every day—aye, and twice and thrice in the same day—there have been orders and complaints, and I have been sent flying to all the wholesale chemists in town. Every time I brought the stuff back, there would be another paper telling me to return it because it was not pure, and another order to a different firm. This drug is wanted bitter bad, sir, whatever for."

"Have you any of these papers?" asked Mr. Utterson.

Poole felt in his pocket and handed out a crumpled note, which the lawyer, bending nearer to the candle, carefully examined. Its contents ran thus:

"Dr. Jekyll presents his compliments to Messrs. Maw. He assures them that their last sample is impure and quite useless for his present purpose. In the year 18— Dr. Jekyll purchased a somewhat large quantity from Messrs. M. He now begs them to search with most sedulous care, and should any of the same quality be left, to forward it to him at once. Expense is no consideration. The importance of this to Dr. Jekyll can hardly be exaggerated."

So far the letter had run composedly enough, but here with a sudden splutter of the pen the writer's emotions had broken loose. "For God's sake," he added, "find me some of the old."

"This is a strange note," said Mr. Utterson, and then sharply, "How do you come to have it open?"

"The man at Maw's was that angry, sir, he threw it back to me like so much dirt," returned Poole.

"This is unquestionably the doctor's hand, do you know," resumed the lawyer.

"I thought it looked like it," said the servant rather sulkily; and then, with another voice, "But what matters handwriting?" he said. "I've seen him!"

"Seen him?" repeated Mr. Utterson. "Well?"

"That's it!" said Poole. "It was this way. I came suddenly into the theater from the garden. It seems he had slipped out to look for this drug or whatever it is, for the chamber door was open, and there he was at the far end of the room digging among the crates. He looked up when I came in, gave a kind of cry and whipped upstairs into the chamber. It was but for one minute that I saw him, but the hair stood upon my head like quills. Sir, if that was my master, why had he a mask upon his face? If it was my master, why did he cry out like a rat and run from me?

I have served him long enough. And then . . ." The man paused and passed his hand over his face.

"These are all very strange circumstances," said Mr. Utterson, "but I think I begin to see daylight. Your master, Poole, is plainly seized with one of those maladies that both torture and deform the sufferer. Hence, for aught I know, the alteration of his voice; hence the mask and the avoidance of his friends; hence his eagerness to find this drug, by means of which the poor soul retains some hope of ultimate recovery—God grant that he be not deceived! There is my explanation. It is sad enough, Poole, aye, and appalling to consider, but it is plain and natural, hangs well together and delivers us from all exorbitant alarms."

"Sir," said the butler, his face turning to a sort of mottled pallor, "that thing was not my master, and there's the truth. My master"—here he looked around him and began to whisper—"is a tall, fine build of a man, and this was more of a dwarf." Utterson attempted to protest. "Oh, sir," cried Poole, "do you think I do not know my master after twenty years? Do you think I do not know where his head comes to in the chamber door, where I saw him every morning of my life? No, sir, that thing in the mask was never Dr. Jekyll—God knows what it was, but it was never Dr. Jekyll—and it is the belief of my heart that there was murder done."

"Poole," replied the lawyer, "if you say that, it will become my duty to make certain. Much as I desire to spare your master's feelings, much as I am puzzled by this note—which seems to prove him to be still alive—I shall consider it my duty to break in that door."

"Ah, Mr. Utterson, that's talking!" cried the butler.

"And now comes the second question," resumed Utterson. "Who is going to do it?"

"Why, you and me, sir," was the undaunted reply.

"That's very well said," returned the lawyer, "and whatever comes of it, I shall make it my business to see you are no loser."

"There is an axe in the theater," continued Poole, "and you

might take the kitchen poker for yourself." He pointed it out.

The lawyer took that rude but weighty instrument into his hand and balanced it. "Do you know, Poole," he said, looking up, "that you and I are about to place ourselves in a position of some peril?"

"You may say so, sir, indeed," returned the butler.

"It is well, then, that we should be frank," said the other. "We both think more than we have said; let us make a clean breast. This masked figure that you saw, did you recognize it?"

"Well, sir, it went so quick, and the creature was so doubled up, that I could hardly swear to that," was the answer. "But if you mean, was it Mr. Hyde, why, yes, I think it was! You see, it was much of the same size, and it had the same quick, light way with it. And then, who else could have got in by the laboratory door? You have not forgot, sir, that at the time of the murder of Sir Danvers Carew he had still the key with him? But that's not all. I don't know, Mr. Utterson, if you ever met this Mr. Hyde?"

"Yes," said the lawyer, "I once spoke with him."

"Then you must know as well as the rest of us that there was something queer about that gentleman—something that gave a man a turn. I don't know rightly how to say it, sir, beyond this: that you felt in your marrow kind of cold and thin."

"I own I felt something of what you describe," said Mr. Utterson.

"Quite so, sir," returned Poole. "Well, when that masked thing like a monkey jumped from among the chemicals and whipped into the chamber, a chill went down my spine like ice. Oh, I know it's not evidence, Mr. Utterson—I'm book-learned enough for that—but a man has his feelings, and I give you my Bible-word it was Mr. Hyde!"

"Aye, aye," said the lawyer. "My fears incline to the same point. Evil was sure to come of that connection. Aye, truly, I believe you. I believe poor Harry is killed, and I believe his murderer (for what purpose, God alone can tell) is still lurking in his victim's room. Well, let our name be vengeance. Call Bradshaw."

The footman came at the summons, very white and nervous.

"Pull yourself together, Bradshaw," said the lawyer. "This suspense, I know, is telling upon all of you, but it is now our intention to make an end of it. Poole here and I are going to force our way into the chamber. If all is well, my shoulders are broad enough to bear the blame. Meanwhile, lest anything should really be amiss, or any malefactor seek to escape by the back, you and the kitchen boy must go around the corner to the bystreet with a pair of good sticks and take your post at the door there. We'll give you ten minutes to get to your station."

As Bradshaw left, the lawyer looked at his watch. "And now, Poole, let us get to our station," he said, and taking the poker under his arm, he led the way into the yard.

The clouds had banked over the moon, and it was now quite dark. The wind, which only broke in puffs and drafts into that deep well of buildings, tossed the light of the candle to and fro about their steps until they came into the shelter of the theater, where they sat down silently to wait. London hummed solemnly all around; but nearer at hand, the stillness was broken only by the sounds of a footfall moving to and fro along the chamber floor.

"So it will walk all day, sir," whispered Poole. "Aye, and the better part of the night. Only when a new sample comes from the chemist, there's a bit of a break. Ah, it's an ill conscience that's such an enemy to rest! Ah, sir, there's blood foully shed in every step of it! But hark again, a little closer. Put your heart in your ears, Mr. Utterson, and tell me, is that the doctor's foot?"

The steps fell lightly and oddly, with a certain swing, for all they went so slowly. They were different indeed from the heavy creaking tread of Henry Jekyll. Utterson sighed. "Is there never anything else?" he asked.

Poole nodded. "Once," he said. "Once I heard it weeping!"

"Weeping? How's that?" said the lawyer, conscious of a sudden chill of horror.

"Weeping like a woman or a lost soul," said the butler. "I came away with that upon my heart, and I could have wept too."

346

The ten minutes drew to an end. Poole disinterred the axe from under a stack of packing straw, the candle was set upon the nearest table to light them to the attack, and they drew near with bated breath to where that patient foot was still going up and down, up and down, in the quiet of the night.

"Jekyll," cried Utterson, in a loud voice, "I demand to see you." He paused a moment, but there came no reply. "I give you fair warning, our suspicions are aroused, and I must and shall see you," he resumed. "If not by fair means, then by foul—if not of your consent, then by brute force!"

"Utterson," said the voice, "for God's sake, have mercy!"

"Ah, that's not Jekyll's voice—it's Hyde's!" cried Utterson. "Down with the door, Poole!"

Poole swung the axe over his shoulder. The blow shook the building, and the red baize door leaped against the lock and hinges. A dismal screech, as of animal terror, rang from the chamber.

Up went the axe again, and again the panels crashed and the frame shook. Four times the blow fell, but the wood was tough and the fittings were of excellent workmanship. It was not until the fifth blow that the lock burst and the wreck of the door fell inward on the carpet.

The besiegers, appalled by their own riot and the stillness that had succeeded, stood back a little and peered in. There lay the chamber before their eyes in the quiet lamplight—a good fire glowing and chattering on the hearth, the kettle singing its thin strain, a drawer or two open, papers neatly set forth on the desk and, nearer the fire, the things laid out for tea. The quietest room, you would have said, and, but for the glass cabinets full of chemicals, the most commonplace that night in London.

Right in the midst there lay the body of a man sorely contorted and still twitching. They drew near on tiptoe, turned it on its back and beheld the face of Edward Hyde. He was dressed in clothes far too large for him, clothes of the doctor's bigness. The cords of his face still moved with a semblance of life, but life was quite gone; and by the crushed vial in the hand and the strong smell that hung upon the air, Utterson knew that he was looking on the body of a self-destroyer.

"We have come too late," he said sternly, "whether to save or punish. Hyde is gone to his account, and it only remains for us to find the body of your master." .

The far greater proportion of the building was occupied by the theater, which filled almost the whole ground floor and was lighted from above; and by the chamber, which formed an upper story at one end and looked out upon the courtyard. A corridor joined the theater to the door opening onto the bystreet; the chamber was accessible from this corridor by a second flight of stairs. There were besides a few dark closets and a spacious cellar. All these they now thoroughly examined. Each closet needed but a glance, for all were empty, and all, by the dust that fell from their doors, had stood long unopened. As they opened the cellar door they were convinced at once of the uselessness of further search by the fall of a perfect mat of cobweb which had for years sealed up the entrance. Nowhere was there any trace of Henry Jekyll, dead or alive.

Poole stamped on the flagstones of the corridor. "He must be buried here," he said, hearkening to the sound.

"Or he may have fled," said Utterson, and he turned to examine the door to the bystreet. It was locked, and lying nearby on the flagstones they found the key, already stained with rust.

"This does not look usable," observed the lawyer.

"Usable!" echoed Poole. "Do you not see, sir, it is broken? Much as if a man had stamped on it."

"Aye," continued Utterson, "and the fractures, too, are rusty." The two men looked at each other with a scare. "This is beyond me, Poole," said the lawyer. "Let us go back to the chamber."

They mounted the stairs in silence and, with an occasional awestruck glance at the dead body, proceeded to examine the contents of the chamber more thoroughly. At one table there were traces of chemical work: various measured heaps of some white salt laid on glass saucers, as though for an experiment from which the unhappy man had been prevented.

"That is the same drug that I was always bringing him," said Poole, and even as he spoke, the kettle with a startling noise boiled over.

This brought them to the fireside, where the easy chair was drawn cosily up and the tea things stood ready to the sitter's elbow, the very sugar in the cup. There were several books on a shelf. One lay open beside the tea things, and Utterson was amazed to find it a copy of a pious work for which Jekyll had several times expressed great esteem, annotated, in his own hand, with startling blasphemies.

Next, in the course of their review of the chamber, the searchers came to the cheval glass, into whose depths they looked with an involuntary horror. But it was so turned as to show them nothing but the rosy glow playing on the roof, the fire sparkling in a hundred repetitions along the glass doors of the cabinets, and their own pale and fearful countenances stooping to look in.

"This glass has seen some strange things, sir," whispered Poole.

"And surely none stranger than itself," echoed the lawyer in the same tones. "For what did Jekyll"—he caught himself up at the word with a start, and then, conquering the weakness—"what could Jekyll want with it?" he said.

"You may say that!" said Poole.

Next they turned to the desk. Among the neat array of papers, a large envelope was uppermost, and bore, in the doctor's hand, the name of Mr. Utterson. The lawyer unsealed it, and several enclosures fell to the floor. The first was a will, drawn in the same eccentric terms as the one which he had returned six months before, to serve as a testament in case of death and as a deed of gift in case of disappearance; but in place of the name of Edward Hyde, the lawyer, with indescribable amazement, read the name of Gabriel John Utterson. He looked at Poole, and then back at the paper, and last of all at the dead malefactor stretched upon the carpet.

"My head goes around," he said. "He has been all these days in possession of this chamber; he had no cause to like me; he must have raged to see himself displaced; and he has not destroyed this document."

He caught up the next paper; it was a brief note in the doctor's hand and dated at the top. "Oh, Poole!" the lawyer cried, "he was alive and here this day! He cannot have been disposed of in so short a space; he must be still alive, he must have fled! But why fled? And how? And in that case, can we venture to declare this suicide? Oh, we must be careful. I foresee that we may yet involve your master in some dire catastrophe."

"Why don't you read it, sir?" asked Poole.

"Because of fear," replied the lawyer solemnly. "God grant I have no cause for it!" And with that he brought the paper to his eyes and read as follows:

"My Dear Utterson, When this shall fall into your hands, I shall have disappeared, under what circumstances I have not the penetration to foresee, but my instinct and all the circumstances of my nameless situation tell me that the end is sure and must be early. Go then, and first read the narrative that Lanyon warned me he was to place in your hands; and if you care to hear more, turn to the confession of

"Your unworthy and unhappy friend,

"HENRY JEKYLL"

"There was a third enclosure?" asked Utterson.

"Here, sir," said Poole, and gave into his hands a considerable packet sealed in several places.

The lawyer put it in his pocket. "I would say nothing of this paper. If your master has fled or is dead, we may at least save his reputation. It is now ten. I must go home and read these documents in quiet, but I shall be back before midnight, when we shall send for the police."

They went out, locking the door of the theater behind them. And Utterson, once more leaving the servants gathered about the fire in the hall, trudged back to his office to read the two narratives in which this mystery was now to be explained.

9. Dr. Lanyon's Narrative

ON THE NINTH of January, now four days ago, I received by the evening delivery a registered envelope, addressed in the hand of my colleague and old school companion Henry Jekyll. I was a good deal surprised by this, for we were by no means in the habit of correspondence. I had seen the man—dined with him, indeed—the night before, and I could imagine nothing in our intercourse that should justify the formality of a registered letter. The contents increased my wonder, for this is how the letter ran:

> "*9th January, 18—*
>
> "Dear Lanyon, You are one of my oldest friends, and although we may have differed at times on scientific questions, I cannot remember, at least on my side, any break in our affection. There was never a day when, if you had said to me, 'Jekyll, my life, my honor, my reason, depend upon you,' I would not have sacrificed my left hand to help you. Lanyon, my life, my honor, my reason, are all at your mercy; if you fail me tonight, I am lost. You might suppose, after this preface, that I am going to ask you for something dishonorable. Judge for yourself.
>
> "I want you to postpone all other engagements for tonight—aye, even if you were summoned to the bedside of an emperor—to take a cab, unless your carriage should be actually at the door; and, with this letter in your hand for consultation, drive straight to my house.
>
> "Poole, my butler, has his orders; you will find him awaiting your arrival with a locksmith. The door of my chamber in the laboratory building is then to be forced and you are to go in alone; to open the glass cabinet on the left side, breaking the lock if it be shut; and to draw out, *with all its contents as they stand*, the fourth drawer from the top or (which is the same thing) the third from the bottom. In my extreme distress of mind, I have a morbid fear of misdirecting you, but even if I am in error, you may know the right drawer by its contents: some

powders, a vial and a notebook. This drawer I beg you to carry back with you exactly as it stands.

"That is the first part of the service. Now for the second. You should be back, if you set out at once on the receipt of this letter, long before midnight; but I will leave you that amount of margin, not only in the fear of one of those obstacles that can neither be prevented nor foreseen, but also because an hour when your servants are in bed is to be preferred for what will then remain to do. At midnight, then, I have to ask you to be alone in your consulting room, to admit with your own hand into the house a man who will present himself in my name, and to place in his hands the drawer that you will have brought with you from my chamber. Then you will have played your part and earned my gratitude completely.

"Five minutes afterward, if you insist upon an explanation, you will have understood that these arrangements are of capital importance; and that by the neglect of one of them, fantastic as they must appear, you might have charged your conscience with my death or the shipwreck of my reason.

"Confident as I am that you will not trifle with this appeal, my heart sinks and my hand trembles at the bare thought of such a possibility. Think of me at this hour, in a strange place, laboring under a blackness of distress that no imagining can exaggerate, and yet well aware that, if you will but punctually serve me, my troubles will roll away like a story that is told. Serve me, my dear Lanyon, and save

"Your friend, H. J.

"P.S.—I had already sealed this up when a fresh terror struck my soul. It is possible that the post office may fail me and this letter not come into your hands until tomorrow morning. In that case, dear Lanyon, do my errand when it shall be most convenient for you in the course of the day, and once more expect my messenger at midnight. It may already be too late. If that night passes without event, you will know that you have seen the last of Henry Jekyll."

Upon reading this letter, I was sure my colleague was insane; but till that was proved beyond the possibility of a doubt, I felt bound to do as he requested. The less I understood of this farrago, the less I was in a position to judge of its importance; and an appeal so worded could not be set aside without grave responsibility. I rose accordingly from my table, got into a hansom cab, and drove straight to Jekyll's house.

The butler was awaiting my arrival. He had received by the same post as mine a registered letter of instruction, and had sent at once for a locksmith and a carpenter. The tradesmen came while we were yet speaking, and we went in a body to old Dr. Denman's surgical theater, from which (as you are doubtless aware) Jekyll's private chamber is most conveniently entered. The door was very strong, the lock excellent. The carpenter avowed he would have great trouble and have to do much damage if force were to be used; and the locksmith was near despair. But the latter was a handy fellow, and after two hours' work, the door stood open. The cabinet was unlocked. I took out the drawer, had it filled up with straw and tied in a sheet, and returned with it to my house.

Here I proceeded to examine its contents. The powders were neatly enough made up, but not with the nicety of the dispensing chemist; so that it was plain they were of Jekyll's private manufacture. When I opened one of the packages, I found what seemed to me a simple crystalline salt of a white color. The vial, to which I next turned my attention, was about half full of a blood-red liquor, which was highly pungent to the sense of smell and seemed to me to contain phosphorus in some form and some volatile ether. At the other ingredients I could make no guess.

The book was an ordinary notebook and contained little but a series of dates. These covered a period of many years, but I observed that the entries ceased nearly a year ago, and quite abruptly. Here and there a brief remark was appended to a date, usually no more than a single word: "double" occurring perhaps six times in a total of several hundred entries; and once, very early in the list and followed by several marks of exclamation, "total failure!!!"

All this, though it whetted my curiosity, told me little that was definite. Here were a vial of some tincture, a package of some salt and the record of a series of experiments that had led (like too many of Jekyll's investigations) to no end of practical usefulness. How could the presence of these articles in my house affect either the honor, the sanity or the life of my flighty colleague? If his messenger could go to one place, why could he not go to another? And even granting some impediment, why was this gentleman to be received by me in secret? The more I reflected, the more convinced I grew that I was dealing with a case of cerebral disease; and though I dismissed my servants to bed, I loaded an old revolver so that I might be found in some posture of self-defense.

Twelve o'clock had scarcely rung out over London ere the knocker sounded very gently on the door. I went myself at the summons, and found a small man crouching against the pillars of the portico.

"Have you come from Dr. Jekyll?" I asked.

He told me yes by a constrained gesture, and when I had bidden him enter, he did not obey me without a searching backward glance into the darkness of the square. There was a policeman not far off, advancing with his bull's eye open; and at the sight, I thought my visitor started and made greater haste to come inside.

These particulars struck me, I confess, disagreeably, and as I followed him into the bright light of the consulting room, I kept my hand ready on my weapon. Here, at last, I had a chance of seeing him clearly. I had never set eyes on him before, so much was certain. He was small, as I have said. I was struck besides by the shocking expression of his face, with its remarkable combination of great muscular activity and great apparent debility of constitution. I was also struck by the odd, subjective disturbance caused by his nearness. Its effect on me bore some resemblance to incipient rigor, and was accompanied by a marked sinking of the pulse. At the time, I set it down to some idiosyncratic personal distaste, and merely wondered at the acuteness of the symptoms. But I have since had reason to believe the cause lay much deeper in the nature of man, and to turn on some nobler hinge than the principle of hatred.

This person (who had thus, from the first moment of his entrance, struck in me what I can only describe as a disgustful curiosity) was dressed in a fashion that would have made an ordinary person laughable. His clothes, that is to say, although they were of rich and sober fabric, were enormously too large for him in every measurement—the trousers hanging on his legs and rolled up to keep them from the ground, the waist of the coat below his haunches, and the collar sprawling wide upon his shoulders. Strange to relate, this ludicrous accoutrement was far from moving me to laughter. Rather, as there was something abnormal and misbegotten in the very essence of the creature that now faced me—something seizing, surprising and revolting—this fresh disparity seemed but to fit in with and to reinforce the abnormality. Thus, to my interest in the man's nature and character, there was added a curiosity as to his origin, his life, his fortune and status in the world.

These observations, though they have taken so great a space to set down, were yet the work of a few seconds. My visitor was, indeed, on fire with somber excitement.

"Have you got it?" he cried. "Have you got it?" And so lively was his impatience that he even laid his hand upon my arm and sought to shake me.

I put him back, conscious at his touch of a certain icy pang along my blood. "Come, sir," said I. "You forget that I have not yet the pleasure of your acquaintance. Be seated, if you please." And I showed him an example by sitting down myself in my customary seat with as fair an imitation of my ordinary manner toward a patient as the lateness of the hour, the nature of my preoccupations and the horror I had of my visitor would suffer me to muster.

"I beg your pardon, Dr. Lanyon," he replied civilly enough.

"What you say is very well founded; my impatience has shown its heels to my politeness. I came here at the request of your colleague Dr. Henry Jekyll on a piece of business of some moment, and I understood . . ." He paused and put his hand to his throat, and I could see, in spite of his collected manner, that he was wrestling against the approaches of hysteria. "I understood, a drawer . . ."

But here I took pity on my visitor's suspense, and some perhaps on my own growing curiosity.

"There it is, sir," said I, pointing to the drawer where it lay on the floor behind a table, and still covered with the sheet Jekyll's servant had tied around it.

He sprang to it, and then paused and laid his hand upon his heart. I could hear his teeth grate with the convulsive action of his jaws, and his face was so ghastly to see that I grew alarmed for both his life and reason.

"Compose yourself," said I.

He turned a dreadful smile to me and, as if with the decision of despair, plucked away the sheet. At sight of the contents, he uttered one loud sob of such immense relief that I sat petrified. He thanked me with a smiling nod, measured out a bit of the red tincture and added one of the powders. The mixture, which was at first of a reddish hue, began, in proportion as the crystals melted, to brighten in color, to effervesce audibly and to throw off small fumes of vapor. Suddenly the bubbling ceased and the compound changed to a dark purple, which faded again more slowly to a watery green. My visitor, who had watched these metamorphoses with a keen eye, smiled, set down the glass upon the table, and then turned and looked upon me with an air of scrutiny.

"And now," said he, "to settle what remains. Will you be wise? Will you be guided? Will you suffer me to take this glass in my hand and to go forth from your house without further explanation? Or has the greed of curiosity too much command of you? Think before you answer, for it shall be done as you decide. As you decide, you shall be left as you were before—

neither richer nor wiser, unless the sense of service rendered to a man in mortal distress may be counted as a kind of riches of the soul. Or, if you prefer to choose so, a new province of knowledge and new avenues to fame and power shall be laid open to you, here in this room, upon the instant; and your sight shall be dazzled by a prodigy that would stagger even the unbelief of Satan."

"Sir," said I, affecting a coolness that I was far from truly possessing, "you speak enigmas, and you will perhaps not wonder that I hear you with no very strong impression of belief. But I have gone too far in the way of inexplicable services to pause before I see the end."

"It is well," replied my visitor. "Lanyon, you remember your vows: what follows is under the seal of our profession. And now, you who have so long been bound to the most narrow and material views, you who have denied the virtue of transcendental medicine, you who have derided your superiors—behold!"

He put the glass to his lips and drank at one gulp. A cry followed; he reeled, staggered, clutched at the table and held on, staring, gasping with open mouth. And as I looked, there came, I thought, a change—he seemed to swell, his face became suddenly black and the features seemed to melt and alter. The next moment I had sprung to my feet and leaped back against the wall, my arm raised to shield me from that prodigy, my mind submerged in terror.

"Oh, God!" I screamed, and "Oh, God!" again and again, for there before my eyes—pale and shaken, and half fainting and groping before him with his hands, like a man restored from death—there stood Henry Jekyll!

What he told me in the next hour, I cannot bring my mind to set on paper. I saw what I saw, I heard what I heard, and my soul sickened at it; and yet now when that sight has faded from my eyes, I ask myself if I believe it, and I cannot answer. My life is shaken to its roots; sleep has left me; the deadliest terror sits by me at all hours of the day and night; and I feel that my days are numbered, and that I must die; and yet I shall die incredulous.

As for the moral turpitude that man unveiled to me, even with tears of penitence, I cannot, even in memory, dwell on it without a start of horror. I will say but one thing, Utterson, and that (if you can bring your mind to credit it) will be more than enough. The creature who crept into my house that night was, on Jekyll's own confession, known by the name of Hyde and hunted for in every corner of the land as the murderer of Carew.

HASTIE LANYON

10. Henry Jekyll's Full Statement of the Case

I WAS BORN in the year 18— to a large fortune, endowed besides with excellent talents, inclined by nature to industry, fond of the respect of the wise and good among my fellowmen, and thus, as might have been supposed, with every guarantee of an honorable and distinguished future. And indeed the worst of my faults was a certain impatient gaiety of disposition, such as has made the happiness of many, but such as I found it hard to reconcile with my imperious desire to carry my head high and wear a more than commonly grave countenance before the public. Hence it came about that I concealed my pleasures, and that when I reached years of reflection and began to look around me and take stock of my progress and position in the world, I stood already committed to a profound duplicity of life.

Many a man would have bragged of such irregularities as I was guilty of, but from the high views that I had set before me, I regarded and hid them with an almost morbid sense of shame. It was thus the exacting nature of my aspirations rather than any particular degradation in my faults that made me what I was, and, with an even deeper trench than in the majority of men, severed in me those provinces of good and ill which divide and compound man's dual nature. In this case, I was driven to reflect deeply and inveterately on that hard law of life which lies at the root of religion and is one of the most plentiful springs of distress. Though so profound a double-dealer, I was in no sense a hypocrite; both sides of me were in dead earnest. I was no more myself when I laid aside restraint and plunged into shame, than when as a man of science I labored, in the eye of day, at the furtherance of knowledge or the relief of sorrow and suffering.

And it chanced that the direction of my scientific studies, which led wholly toward the mystic and the transcendental, reacted to and shed a strong light on this consciousness of the perennial war inside me. With every day, and from both sides of my intelligence—the moral and the intellectual—I thus drew steadily nearer to that truth by whose partial discovery I have been doomed to such a dreadful shipwreck: that man is not truly one, but truly two. I say two because the state of my own knowledge does not pass beyond that point. Others will follow, others will outstrip me on the same lines in the future; and I hazard the guess that man will be ultimately known for a mere polity of multifarious, incongruous and independent denizens. I, for my part, from the nature of my life, advanced infallibly in one direction and in one direction only. It was on the moral side, and in my own person, that I learned to recognize the thorough and primitive duality of man. I saw that, of the two natures that contended in the field of my consciousness, even if I could rightly be said to be either, it was only because I was radically both.

From an early date, even before the course of my scientific discoveries had begun to suggest the most naked possibility of such a miracle, I had learned to dwell with pleasure, as a beloved daydream, on the thought of the separation of these elements. If each, I told myself, could be housed in separate identities, life would be relieved of all that was unbearable: the unjust might go his way, delivered from the aspirations and remorse of his more upright twin; and the just could walk steadfastly and securely on his upward path, doing the good things in which he found his pleasure, and no longer exposed to disgrace and penitence by the hands of this extraneous evil. It was the curse of mankind that these incongruous faggots were thus bound together—that in the agonized womb of consciousness these polar twins should be continuously struggling. How, then, were they dissociated?

I was so far in my reflection when, as I have said, a side light began to shine upon the subject from the laboratory table. I began to perceive more deeply than it has ever yet been stated the trembling immateriality, the mistlike transience, of this seemingly so solid body in which we walk attired. Certain agents I found to have the power to shake and pluck back that fleshly vestment, even as a wind might toss the curtains of a pavilion.

For two good reasons I will not enter deeply into this scientific branch of my confession. First, because I have been made to learn that the doom and burden of our life is bound forever on man's shoulders, and when the attempt is made to cast it off, it but returns upon us with more unfamiliar and more awful pressure. Second, because, as my narrative will make, alas! too evident, my discoveries were incomplete. Enough, then, that I not only recognized my natural body from the mere aura and effulgence of certain of the powers that made up my spirit, but also managed to compound a drug by which these powers should be dethroned from their supremacy and a second form and countenance substituted—no less natural to me because they were the expression, and bore the stamp, of lower elements in my soul.

I hesitated long before I put this theory to the test of practice. I knew well that I risked death, for any drug that so potently controlled and shook the very fortress of identity might, by the least scruple of an overdose or at the least mishap, utterly blot out that immaterial tabernacle which I looked to it to change. But the temptation of a discovery so singular and profound at last overcame the suggestions of alarm.

I had long since prepared my tincture. I purchased at once, from a firm of wholesale chemists, a large quantity of a particular salt which I knew, from my experiments, to be the last ingredient required. Late one accursed night I compounded the elements, watched them boil and smoke together in the glass, and when the bubbling had subsided, with a strong glow of courage, I drank off the potion.

The most racking pangs succeeded: a grinding in the bones, deadly nausea and a horror of the spirit that cannot be exceeded at the hour of birth or death. Then these agonies began swiftly to subside, and I came to myself as if out of a great sickness. There was something strange in my sensations, something indescribably new and, from its very novelty, incredibly sweet. I felt younger, lighter, happier in body. Within I was conscious of a heady recklessness, a current of disordered sensual images running like a millrace in my fancy, a melting of the bonds of obligation, an unknown but not an innocent freedom of the soul. I knew myself, at the first breath of this new life, to be more wicked, tenfold more wicked, sold a slave to my original evil; and the thought, in that moment, braced and delighted me like wine. I stretched out my hands, exulting in the freshness of these sensations, and in the act I was suddenly aware that I had lost some inches of stature.

There was no mirror, at that date, in my room. That which stands beside me as I write was brought here later on, and for the very purpose of these transformations. The night, however, was far gone into the morning—the morning, black as it was, was nearly ripe for the conception of the day. The inmates of my house were locked in the most rigorous hours of slumber, and I determined, flushed as I was with hope and triumph, to venture in my new shape as far as to my bedroom. I crossed the yard, wherein the constellations looked down upon me, I could have thought, with wonder—the first creature of that sort that their unsleeping vigilance had yet disclosed to them. I stole through the corridors, a stranger in my own house, and coming to my room, I saw for the first time the appearance of Edward Hyde.

I must here speak by theory alone, saying not that which I know, but that which I suppose to be most probable. The evil side of my nature was less robust and less developed than the good. In the course of my life—which had been, after all, nine tenths a life of effort, virtue and control—it had been much less exercised. Hence, I think, it came about that Edward Hyde was so much smaller, slighter and younger than Henry Jekyll. Even as good shone upon the countenance of the one, evil was written broadly and plainly on the face of the other. Evil (which I must still believe to be the lethal side of man) had left on that body an imprint of deformity and decay. And yet when I looked upon that ugly idol in the glass, I was conscious of no repugnance, but rather of a leap of welcome. This, too, was myself. It seemed natural and human. In my eyes it bore a livelier image of the spirit, it seemed more express and single, than the imperfect and divided countenance I had been hitherto accustomed to call mine. And in that I was doubtless right. I have observed that when I wore the semblance of Edward Hyde, none could come near to me at first without a visible misgiving of the flesh. This, I take it, was because all human beings, as we meet them, are commingled of good and evil. Edward Hyde, alone in the ranks of mankind, was pure evil.

I lingered but a moment at the mirror. The second and conclusive experiment had yet to be attempted: it remained to be seen if I had lost my identity beyond redemption and must flee before daylight from a house that was no longer mine. I hurried back to my chamber and once more prepared and drank the cup, once more suffered the pangs of dissolution, and came to myself once more with the character, the stature and the face of Henry Jekyll.

That night I had come to the fatal crossroad. Had I approached my discovery in a more noble spirit, had I risked the experiment while under the empire of generous or pious aspirations, all must have been otherwise, and from these agonies of death and birth I might have come forth an angel instead of a fiend. The drug had no discriminating action; it was neither diabolical nor divine. It but shook the doors of the prisonhouse of my disposition, and like the captives of Philippi, that which stood within ran forth. At that time my virtue slumbered. My evil, kept awake by ambition, was alert and swift to seize the occasion, and the thing that was projected was Edward Hyde. Hence, although I had now two characters as well as two appearances, one was wholly evil, and the other was still the old Henry Jekyll, that incongruous compound of whose reformation and improvement I had already learned to despair. The movement was thus wholly toward the worse.

Even at that time I had not conquered my aversion to the dryness of a life of study. I would still be merrily disposed at times; and as my pleasures were (to say the least) undignified, and I was not only well known and highly considered but also growing toward elderly, this incoherency of my life was daily growing more unwelcome. It was on this side that my new power tempted me until I fell into slavery. I had but to drink the cup to doff at once the body of the noted professor and to assume, like a thick cloak, that of Edward Hyde. I smiled at the notion—it seemed to me at the time to be humorous—and I made my preparations with the most studious care.

I took a lease on and furnished that house in Soho to which Hyde was tracked by the police, and engaged as a housekeeper a creature whom I knew well to be silent and unscrupulous. On the other side, I announced to my servants that a Mr. Hyde (whom I described) was to have full liberty and power about my house in the square. To parry mishaps, I even called and made myself a familiar object in my second character. I next drew up that will to which you so much objected, so that if anything befell me in the person of Dr. Jekyll, I could enter on that of Edward Hyde without pecuniary loss. Thus fortified, as I supposed, on every side, I began to profit by the strange immunities of my position.

Men have before hired others to transact their crimes while their own person and reputation sat under shelter. I was the first that ever did so for his pleasures. I was the first that could plod in the public eye with a load of genial respectability, and in a moment, like a schoolboy, strip that off and spring headlong into the sea of liberty. But for me, in my impenetrable mantle, the safety was complete. Think of it—I did not even exist! Let me but escape into my laboratory, give me but a second or two to mix and swallow the draft that I had always standing ready, and whatever he had done, Edward Hyde would pass away like the stain of breath upon a mirror; and there in his stead, quietly at home, trimming the midnight lamp in his study, a man who could afford to laugh at suspicion, would be Henry Jekyll.

The pleasures which I made haste to seek in my disguise were, as I have said, undignified; I would scarcely use a harder term. But in the hands of Edward Hyde, they soon began to turn toward the monstrous. When I would come back from these excursions, I was often plunged into a kind of wonder at my vicarious depravity. This familiar spirit that I called forth out of my own soul, and sent forth alone to do his good pleasure, was a being inherently malign and villainous. His every act and thought centered on self; he drank pleasure with bestial avidity from any degree of torture to another; he was as relentless as a man of stone. Henry Jekyll stood at times aghast before the acts of Edward Hyde, but the situation was apart from ordinary laws and insidiously relaxed the grasp of conscience. It was Hyde, after all, and Hyde alone, that was guilty. Jekyll was no worse; he woke again to find his good qualities seemingly unimpaired; he would even make haste, where it was possible, to undo the evil that had been done by Hyde. And thus his conscience slumbered.

Into the details of the infamy at which I thus connived (for even now I can scarcely grant that I committed it) I have no intention of entering; I mean but to point out the warnings and the successive steps with which my chastisement approached. I met with one accident which, as it brought on no consequence, I shall no more than mention. An act of cruelty to a child aroused against me the anger of a passerby, whom I recognized the other day in the person of your kinsman. The doctor and the child's family joined him, and there were moments when I feared for my life. At last, in order to pacify their too just resentment, Edward Hyde had to bring them to the door of this house and pay them in a check drawn in the name of Henry Jekyll. But this danger of discovery was easily eliminated from the future by opening an account at another bank in the name of Edward Hyde himself; and when, by sloping my own hand backward, I had supplied my double with a signature, I thought I sat beyond the reach of fate.

Some two months before the murder of Sir Danvers, I had been out for one of my adventures, had returned at a late hour and woke the next day in bed with somewhat odd sensations. It was in vain that I looked about me; in vain that I saw the decent furniture and tall proportions of my room in the square; in vain that I recognized the pattern of the bed curtains and the design of the mahogany frame. Something still kept insisting that I was not where I was, that I had not wakened where I seemed to be, but in the little room in Soho where I was accustomed to sleep in the body of Edward Hyde. I smiled to myself, and, in my psychological way, began lazily to inquire into the elements of this illusion, occasionally, even as I did so, dropping back into a comfortable morning doze. I was still so engaged when, in one of my more wakeful moments, my eyes fell upon my hand. Now the hand of Henry Jekyll (as you have often remarked) was professional in shape and size: it was large, firm, white and comely. But the hand which I now saw, clearly enough in the yellow light of a mid-London morning, lying half shut on the bedclothes, was lean, corded, knuckly, of a dusky pallor and thickly shaded with a swart growth of hair. It was, in sum, the hand of Edward Hyde.

I must have stared upon it for nearly half a minute, sunk as I was in the mere stupidity of wonder, before terror woke in my breast as sudden and startling as the crash of cymbals. Bounding from my bed, I rushed to the mirror. At the sight that met my eyes, my blood was changed into something exquisitely thin and icy. Yes, I had gone to bed Henry Jekyll; I had awakened Edward Hyde. How was this to be explained? I asked myself. And then, with another bound of terror: How was it to be remedied? It was well on in the morning; the servants were up; all my drugs were in the chamber—a long journey, down two pairs of stairs, through the back passage, across the open court and through the surgical theater, from where I was then standing horror-struck. It might indeed be possible to cover my face, but of what use was that when I was unable to conceal the alteration in my stature?

And then with an overpowering sweetness of relief, it came to my mind that the servants were already used to the coming and going of my second self. I had soon dressed, as well as I was able, in clothes of my own size; had soon passed through the house, where Bradshaw stared and drew back at seeing Mr. Hyde at such an hour and in such a strange array; and ten minutes later Dr. Jekyll had returned to his own shape and was sitting down at his table, with a darkened brow, to make a feint of breakfasting.

Small, indeed, was my appetite. This inexplicable incident, this reversal of my previous experience, seemed, like the Babylonian finger on the wall, to be spelling out the letters of my judgment. I began to reflect more seriously than ever before on the issues and possibilities of my double existence. That part of me which I had the power of projecting had lately been much exercised and nourished. It had seemed to me of late that the body of Edward Hyde had grown in stature—that when I wore that form, I was conscious of a more generous tide of blood. I began to spy a danger that if this were much prolonged, the balance of my nature might be permanently overthrown, the power of voluntary change be forfeited, and the character of Edward Hyde become irrevocably mine. The power of the drug had not always been equally displayed. Once, very early in my career, it had totally failed me. Since then, I had been obliged on more than one occasion to double—and once, with infinite risk of death, to treble—the amount of the dose. Hitherto these rare uncertainties had cast the sole shadow on my contentment. Now, however, and in the light of that morning's accident, I was led to remark that whereas, in the beginning, the difficulty had been to throw off the body of Jekyll, it had of late gradually but decidedly transferred itself to the other side. All things therefore seemed to point to this: I was slowly losing hold of my original and better self, and becoming slowly incorporated with my second and worse self.

Between these two, I now felt I had to choose. My two natures had memory in common, but all other faculties were most unequally shared between them. Jekyll, who was the composite—now with the most sensitive apprehensions, now with a greedy gusto—projected and shared in the pleasures and adventures of Hyde. But Hyde was indifferent to Jekyll, or but remembered him as the mountain bandit remembers the cavern in which he conceals himself from pursuit. Jekyll had more than a father's interest; Hyde had more than a son's indifference. To cast in my lot with Jekyll was to die to those appetites which I had long secretly indulged and had of late begun to pamper. To cast it in with Hyde was to die to a thousand interests and aspirations, and to become, at a blow and forever, despised and friendless. The bargain might appear unequal, but there was still another consideration in the scales: while Jekyll would suffer smartingly in the fires of abstinence, Hyde would not even be conscious of all that he had lost.

Strange as my circumstances were, the terms of this debate are as old and commonplace as man; much the same inducements and alarms cast the die for any tempted and trembling sinner; it fell out with me, as it falls out with so vast a majority of my fellows, that I chose the better part and was found wanting in the strength to keep to it.

Yes, I preferred the elderly and discontented doctor, surrounded by friends and cherishing honest hopes. I bade then a resolute farewell to the liberty, the comparative youth, the light step, leaping impulses and secret pleasures that I had enjoyed in the disguise of Hyde. I made this choice perhaps with some unconscious reservation, for I neither gave up the house in Soho nor destroyed the clothes of Edward Hyde, which still lay ready in my chamber. For two months, however, I was true to my determination. For two months I led a life of such severity as I had never before attained to, and enjoyed the compensations of an approving conscience. But time began at last to obliterate the

freshness of my alarm; the praises of conscience began to grow
into a thing of course; I began to be tortured with throes and
longings, as of Hyde struggling after freedom; and at last, in an
hour of moral weakness, I once again compounded and swallowed the transforming draft.

I do not suppose that when a drunkard reasons with himself
upon his vice, he is once out of five hundred times affected by
the dangers that he runs through his brutish physical insensibility. Neither had I, long as I had considered my position, made
enough allowance for the complete moral insensibility and insensate readiness to evil which were the leading characteristics
of Edward Hyde. Yet it was by these that I was punished. My
devil had been long caged; he came out roaring.

I was conscious, even when I took the draft, of a more unbri-
dled, a more furious propensity to ill. It must have been this, I
suppose, that stirred in my soul that tempest of impatience with
which I listened to the civilities of my unhappy victim, Sir
Danvers Carew. I declare, at least, before God that no man
morally sane could have been guilty of that crime upon so pitiful
a provocation, and that I struck in no more reasonable spirit than
that in which a sick child may break a plaything. But I had
voluntarily stripped myself of all those balancing instincts by
which even the worst of us continues to walk with some degree
of steadiness among temptations. In my case, to be tempted,
however slightly, was to fall.

Instantly the spirit of hell awoke in me and raged. With a
transport of glee, I mauled the unresisting body of Sir Danvers,
tasting delight from every blow. It was not till weariness had
begun to succeed that I was suddenly, in the top fit of my
delirium, struck through the heart by a cold thrill of terror. A
mist dispersed; I saw my life to be forfeit, and fled from the
scene of these excesses, at once glorying and trembling, my lust
of evil gratified and stimulated, my love of life screwed to
the topmost peg.

I ran to the house in Soho and (to make assurance doubly sure)
destroyed my papers. Thence I set out through the lamplit

streets in the same divided ecstasy of mind, gloating on my crime, light-headedly devising others in the future, and yet still hastening and listening in my wake for the steps of the avenger. Hyde had a song upon his lips as he compounded the draft, and as he drank it, pledged the dead man. The pangs of transformation had not done tearing him before Henry Jekyll, with streaming tears of gratitude and remorse, had fallen upon his knees and lifted his clasped hands to God. The veil of self-indulgence was rent from head to foot. I saw my life as a whole. I followed it up . from the days of childhood, when I had walked holding my father's hand, and through the self-denying toils of my professional life, to arrive again and again, with the same sense of unreality, at the damned horrors of the evening. I could have screamed aloud; I sought with tears and prayers to smother the crowd of hideous images and sounds with which my memory swarmed against me; and still, between the petitions, the ugly face of my iniquity stared into my soul. As the acuteness of this remorse began to die away, it was succeeded by a sense of joy. The problem of my conduct was solved. Hyde was thenceforth impossible; whether I wanted to be or not, I was now confined to the better part of my existence, and oh, how I rejoiced to think of it! With what willing humility I embraced anew the restrictions of natural life! With what sincere renunciation I locked the door by which I had so often gone and come, and ground the key under my heel!

The next day came the news that the murder had been witnessed, that the guilt of Hyde was patent to the world, and that the victim was a man high in public estimation. It had not only been a crime, it had been a tragic folly. I think I was glad to know it; I think I was glad to have my better impulses thus buttressed and guarded by the terrors of the scaffold. Jekyll was now my city of refuge. Let Hyde but peep out an instant, and the hands of all men would be raised to take and slay him.

I resolved in my future conduct to redeem the past, and I can say with honesty that my resolve was fruitful of some good. You know yourself how earnestly, in the last months of the last year,

I labored to relieve suffering. You know that much was done for others, and that the days passed quietly, almost happily, for myself. Nor can I truly say that I wearied of this beneficent and innocent life; I think instead that I daily enjoyed it more completely. But I was still cursed with my duality of purpose. As the first edge of my penitence wore off, the lower side of me—so long indulged, so recently chained down—began to growl for license. Not that I dreamed of resuscitating Hyde: the bare idea of that would startle me to frenzy. No, it was in my own person that I was once more tempted to trifle with my conscience, and it was as an ordinary secret sinner that I at last fell before the assaults of temptation.

There comes an end to all things; the most capacious measure is filled at last; and this brief condescension to my evil finally destroyed the balance of my soul. And yet I was not alarmed; the fall seemed natural, like a return to the old days before I had made my discovery.

It was a fine, clear January day, wet underfoot where the frost had melted, but cloudless overhead. Regent's Park was full of winter chirrupings and sweet with spring odors. I sat in the sun on a bench, the animal within me licking the chops of memory, the spiritual side a little drowsed, promising subsequent penitence, but not yet moved to begin. After all, I reflected, I was like my neighbors. And then I smiled, comparing myself with other men, comparing my active goodwill with the lazy cruelty of their neglect. At the very moment of that vainglorious thought a qualm came over me, a horrid nausea and the most deadly shuddering. These passed away and left me faint. Then, as in turn the faintness subsided, I began to be aware of a change in the temper of my thoughts, a greater boldness, a contempt of danger, a dissolution of the bonds of obligation. I looked down. My clothes hung formlessly on my shrunken limbs, the hand that lay on my knee was corded and hairy: I was once more Edward Hyde. A moment before I had been sure of all men's respect—wealthy, beloved, the cloth laid for me in the dining room at home. Now I was the common quarry of mankind—

hunted, houseless, a known murderer, thrall to the gallows.

My reason wavered, but it did not fail me utterly. I have more than once observed that in my second character my faculties seemed sharpened to a point and my spirits more tensely elastic. Thus it came about that where Jekyll perhaps might have succumbed, Hyde rose to the importance of the moment. My drugs were in one of the cabinets in my chamber. How was I to reach them? That was the problem that (crushing my temples in my hands) I set myself to solve. The laboratory door I had closed permanently. If I sought to enter by the house, my own servants would consign me to the gallows. I saw I must employ another hand, and thought of Lanyon. How was he to be reached? How persuaded? Supposing that I escaped capture on the streets, how was I to make my way into his presence? And how should I, an unknown and displeasing visitor, prevail on the famous physician to rifle the study of his colleague Dr. Jekyll? Then I remembered that of my original character, one part remained to me: I could write my own hand. Once I had conceived that kindling spark, the way that I must follow became lighted up from end to end.

Thereupon I arranged my clothes as best I could, summoned a passing hansom cab and drove to a hotel in Portland Street, the name of which I chanced to remember. At my appearance (which was indeed comical enough, however tragic a fate these garments covered) the driver could not conceal his mirth. I gnashed my teeth at him in a gust of devilish fury, and the smile withered from his face—happily for him, yet more happily for myself, for in another instant I would certainly have dragged him from his perch.

As I entered the hotel, I looked about me with so black a countenance as made the attendants tremble. Not a look did they exchange in my presence, but obsequiously took my orders, led me to a private room and brought me the wherewithal to write. Hyde in danger of his life was a creature new to me: shaken with inordinate anger, strung to the pitch of murder, lusting to inflict pain. Yet the creature was astute. He mastered his fury with a great effort of will; composed his two important letters, one to Lanyon and one to Poole; and that he might receive actual evidence of their being posted, sent them out with directions that they should be registered. Thenceforward, he sat all day in front of the fire in the private room, gnawing his nails.

There he dined, sitting alone with his fears, the waiter visibly quailing before his eye; and thence, when the night was fully come, he set forth in the corner of a closed cab and was driven to and fro about the streets of the city. *He*, I say—I cannot say *I*. That child of hell had nothing human; nothing lived in him but fear and hatred. And when at last, thinking the driver had begun to grow suspicious, he discharged the cab and ventured on foot—attired in his misfitting clothes, an object marked out for observation—into the midst of the nocturnal crowd, these two base passions raged within him like a tempest. He walked fast, hunted by his fears, chattering to himself, skulking through the less frequented thoroughfares, counting the minutes that still divided him from midnight. Once a woman spoke to him, offering, I think, to sell him a box of lights. He smote her in the face, and she fled.

When I came to myself at Lanyon's, the horror of my old friend perhaps affected me somewhat: I do not know; it was but a drop in the sea to the abhorrence with which I looked back upon those recent hours. A change had come over me. It was no longer the fear of the gallows, it was the horror of being Hyde that racked me. I received Lanyon's condemnation partly in a dream; it was partly in a dream that I came home to my own house and got into bed. I slept after the exhaustion of the day, with a stringent and profound slumber which not even the nightmares that wrung me could avail to break. I awoke in the morning shaken, weakened, but refreshed. I still hated and feared the thought of the brute that slept within me, and I had not of course forgotten the appalling dangers of the day before. But I was once more at home, in my own house and close to my drugs, and gratitude for my escape shone so strongly in my soul that it almost rivaled the brightness of hope.

I was stepping leisurely across the court after breakfast, drinking the chill of the air with pleasure, when I was seized again with those indescribable sensations that heralded the change. I had just time to gain the shelter of my chamber before I was once again raging and freezing with the passions of Hyde. It took on this occasion a double dose to recall me to myself. Alas, six hours after, as I sat looking sadly into the fire, the pangs returned, and the drug had to be readministered. In short, from that day forth it seemed only by a great effort as of gymnastics, and only under the immediate stimulation of the drug, that I was able to wear the countenance of Jekyll. At all hours of the day and night I would be taken with the dread premonitory shudder.

Above all, if I slept, or even dozed for a moment in my chair, it was always as Hyde that I awakened. Under the strain of this continually impending doom and the sleeplessness to which I now condemned myself, I became—aye, even beyond what I had thought possible to man—I became, in my own person, a creature eaten up and emptied by fever, languidly weak in both body and mind, and solely occupied by one thought: the horror of my other self. But when I slept, or when the effects of the medicine wore off, I would leap almost without transition (for the pangs of transformation grew daily less marked) into the possession of an imagination brimming with images of terror, a soul boiling with causeless hatreds, and a body that seemed not strong enough to contain the raging energies of life. The powers of Hyde seemed to have grown with the sickliness of Jekyll. And certainly the hate that now divided them was equal on each side.

With Jekyll, it was a thing of vital instinct. He had now seen the full deformity of that creature that shared with him some of the phenomena of consciousness, and was coheir with him to death. Beyond these links of community, which in themselves made the most poignant part of his distress, he thought of Hyde, for all his energy of life, as something not only hellish but inorganic. This was the shocking thing: that the slime of the pit seemed to utter cries and voices; that the amorphous dust gesticulated and sinned; that what was dead, and had no shape, should usurp the offices of life. And this also: that that insurgent horror was knit to him closer than a wife, closer than an eye; lay caged in his flesh, where he heard it mutter and felt it struggle to be born; and at every hour of weakness, and in the confidence of slumber, prevailed against him and deposed him out of life.

The hatred of Hyde for Jekyll was of a different order. His terror of the gallows drove him continually to commit temporary suicide and return to his subordinate station of a part instead of a person; but he loathed the necessity, he loathed the despondency into which Jekyll had now fallen, and he resented the dislike with which he was himself regarded. Hence the apelike tricks that he would play me, scrawling in my own hand blasphemies on the pages of my books, burning the letters and destroying the portrait of my father. Indeed, had it not been for his fear of death, he would long ago have ruined himself in order to involve me in the ruin. But his love of life is wonderful. I go further: I, who sicken and freeze at the mere thought of him, when I recall the abjection and passion of his attachment to life, and when I know how he fears my power to cut him off by suicide, I find it in my heart to pity him.

It is useless, and the time awfully fails me, to prolong this description. No one has ever suffered such torments; let that suffice. And yet, even to these, habit brought—no, not alleviation— but a certain callousness of soul, a certain acquiescence of despair. My punishment might have gone on for years but for the last calamity which has now fallen, and which has finally severed me from my own nature. My provision of the salt, which had never been renewed since the first experiment, began to run low. I sent out for a fresh supply and mixed the draft. The effervescence followed, and then the first change of color, but not the second. I drank it and it was without efficacy. You will learn from Poole how I have had London ransacked. It was in vain; and I am now persuaded that my first supply was impure, and that it was that unknown impurity which lent efficacy to the draft.

About a week has passed, and I am now finishing this statement under the influence of the last of the old salt. This, then, is the last time, short of a miracle, that Henry Jekyll can think his own thoughts or see his own face (now how sadly altered!) in the glass. Nor must I delay too long in bringing my writing to an end, for if my narrative has hitherto escaped destruction, it has been by a combination of great prudence and great good luck. Should the throes of change take me in the act of writing it, Hyde will tear it in pieces. But if some time shall have elapsed after I have laid it by, his wonderful selfishness and stayed attention to the moment will probably save it once again from the action of his apelike spite. Indeed, the doom that is closing in on us both has already changed and crushed him. Half an hour from now, when I shall again and forever put on that hated personality, I know how I shall sit shuddering and weeping in my chair, or continue, with the most strained and fearstruck ecstasy of listening, to pace up and down this room (my last earthly refuge) and give ear to every sound of menace. Will Hyde die upon the scaffold? Or will he find the courage to release himself at the last moment? God knows.

I am careless; this is my true hour of death, and what is to follow concerns another than myself. Here then, as I lay down the pen and proceed to seal up my confession, I bring the life of that unhappy Henry Jekyll to an end.

The
Laughing Policeman

The
Laughing Policeman

A CONDENSATION OF
THE BOOK BY

Maj Sjöwall
and
Per Wahlöö

ILLUSTRATED BY TOM HALL

The scene is Stockholm on a raw, rainy
night in November. A large red bus drones
along a deserted street, its wheels
flinging up cascades of water. It starts to turn,
hesitates, then careens across the
street and comes to a stop against a wire
fence. The engine stops, but the lights stay on.
Only one person gets out . . . for
all the other people aboard are dead or dying
from two blasts of machinegun fire.

One of the victims is a young policeman,
whose presence on the bus that night
is as much a mystery as the mass murder itself.
As Superintendent Martin Beck
and the entire homicide squad begin
to probe their dead colleague's recent behavior,
they pick up a faint, twisting series
of clues that ultimately guide them to the killer.

The Laughing Policeman was written
by the distinguished Swedish husband and
wife team of Maj Sjöwall and Per Wahlöö.
Their creation, Martin Beck, appears in ten
of their mystery novels. *The Laughing
Policeman* became a film in 1973.

Chapter One

ON THE EVENING of the thirteenth of November it was pouring in Stockholm. Martin Beck and Lennart Kollberg sat over a game of chess in the latter's apartment not far from the subway station of Skärmarbrink in the southern suburbs. Both were off duty since nothing special had happened in the city during the last few days.

Martin Beck was very bad at chess but played all the same. Kollberg had a daughter who was just over two months old. On this particular evening he was forced to baby-sit, and Martin Beck had no wish to go home before it was absolutely necessary. Driving curtains of rain swept over the rooftops, and the streets lay almost deserted.

Outside the American embassy on Strandvägen, in the center of Stockholm, 412 policemen were struggling with about twice that many demonstrators. The police were equipped with teargas bombs, pistols, whips, batons, cars, motorcycles, shortwave radios, battery-powered megaphones, riot dogs and hysterical horses. The demonstrators were armed with a letter and with cardboard signs, which grew more and more sodden in the pelting rain. The crowd comprised every possible kind of person, from thirteen-year-old schoolgirls and dead-serious political students to professional troublemakers, and one eighty-five-year-old woman artist with a beret and a blue silk umbrella.

The horses reared, and the police fingered their holsters and made charge after charge with their batons. Altogether more than fifty demonstrators were seized. The operation was directed by a high-ranking police officer trained at a military school. He was considered an expert on keeping order, and he regarded with satisfaction the utter chaos he had managed to achieve.

In the apartment at Skärmarbrink Kollberg gathered up the chessmen, jumbled them into the wooden box and shut its sliding lid with a smack. His wife had come home from her evening course and gone straight to bed.

"You'll never learn this," Kollberg said plaintively.

"They say you need a special gift for it," Martin Beck replied gloomily. "Chess sense I think it's called."

Kollberg changed the subject. "I bet there's a helluva to-do on Strandvägen this evening," he said.

"I expect so. What's it all about?"

"They were going to hand a letter over to the American ambassador," Kollberg said. "Why don't they send it by mail?"

"It wouldn't cause so much fuss," Martin Beck said. He had put on his hat and coat and was about to go.

Kollberg got up quickly. "I'll come with you," he said.

"Whatever for?"

"Oh, to stroll around a little."

"In this weather?"

"I like rain." Kollberg put on his dark blue poplin coat.

Superintendent Martin Beck and Detective Inspector Lennart Kollberg were policemen. They belonged to the homicide squad and for the moment they had nothing special to do.

Downtown no policemen were to be seen in the streets. A person who had just smashed the glass of a showcase with a brick had no need to worry that the rising and falling wail from a patrol car would suddenly interrupt his doings.

The police were busy elsewhere.

A week earlier the commissioner had said in a public statement that many of the regular duties of the police would have to be neglected because they were obliged to protect the American ambassador against letters and other things from people who disliked the war in Vietnam.

By eleven o'clock on this evening it was still raining and the demonstration could be regarded as broken up.

During the same period eight murders and one attempted murder were committed in Stockholm.

RAIN, HE THOUGHT, looking out of the bus window dejectedly. November darkness and rain, cold and pelting. He had trudged about so long in the rain that his hair and the dark blue poplin raincoat were sopping wet, and now he felt the moisture travel down his neck to the shoulder blades, cold and trickling.

He undid the two top buttons of his raincoat, stuck his right hand inside his jacket and fingered the butt of the pistol. It, too, felt cold and clammy. An involuntary shudder passed through him.

He tried to think of something else. For instance, of the hotel balcony on Majorca, where he had spent his vacation five months earlier. Of the heavy, motionless heat and of the bright sunshine over the quayside and of the limitless, deep blue sky above the mountain ridge on the other side of the bay. Then he thought that it was probably raining there too at this time of year. He heard someone coming down the bus stairs and knew that it was a passenger who had got on outside Åhléns department store in the center of the city twelve stops before.

Rain, he thought. I don't like it. What am I doing here anyway? Why am I not at home in bed with—

And that was the last he thought.

The bus was a red double-decker with cream-colored top and gray roof. On this particular evening it was plying route 47 in Stockholm; now it was heading northwest and approaching the terminus on Norra Stationsgatan, situated only a few yards from the city limits between Stockholm and the suburb of Solna.

It was big, this red bus; over thirty-six feet long and nearly fifteen feet high. The headlights were on and it looked warm and cozy with its misty windows as it droned along the deserted street between the lines of leafless trees. Then it turned right onto the long slope down to Norra Stationsgatan. The wheels flung up hissing cascades of water as it glided downward, heavily and implacably.

The hill ended where the street did. The bus was to turn at an angle of thirty degrees, onto Norra Stationsgatan, and then it had only some three hundred yards left to the end of the line.

The turn was never completed. The red double-decker bus seemed to stop for a moment in the middle of the turn. Then it went straight across the street, climbed the sidewalk and burrowed halfway through the wire fence separating Norra Stationsgatan from the desolate freight yard on the other side.

The engine died but the headlights were still on, and so was the lighting inside.

The misty windows went on gleaming cozily in the dark and cold.

The time was three minutes past eleven on the evening of the thirteenth of November, 1967.

In Stockholm.

KRISTIANSSON AND KVANT were radio patrol policemen in Solna.

During their not-very-eventful careers they had picked up thousands of drunks and dozens of thieves, but on this particular evening they had not picked up anything at all, apart from a glass of beer each; as this was perhaps against the rules, it had better be ignored.

Kristiansson was lazy.

No one knew this better than Kvant. While they were still serving as ordinary patrolmen on the beat, he had many a time seen Kristiansson lead drunks along the street and even across bridges in order to get them into the next precinct.

"Why should I get puked on for nothing?" he would say philosophically.

Kristiansson and Kvant were similar in appearance: tall, fair, broad-shouldered and blue-eyed. But they had widely different temperaments and didn't always see eye to eye.

Kvant was incorruptible. He never compromised over things he saw, but on the other hand he was an expert at seeing as little as possible.

Now he drove slowly, in glum silence, following a twisting route that led past the Police Training College, then through an area of communal garden plots, and then zigzag through the extensive university district. It was a brilliantly thought-out course, leading through areas that were almost guaranteed to be empty of people. The whole way they saw only two living creatures, first a cat and then another cat.

Kvant stopped the car one yard from the Stockholm city limits and let the engine idle while he considered how to arrange the rest of their shift.

I wonder if you've got the cheek to turn around and drive back the same way, Kristiansson thought. Aloud he said, "Can you lend me ten kronor?"

Kvant nodded and handed the note to his colleague without even a glance at him. At the same instant he made a quick decision. If he crossed into the city and followed Norra Stationsgatan for some five hundred yards in a northeasterly direction, they would only need to be in Stockholm for two minutes. Then he could turn into the hospital area and continue through the park and along by the cemetery, finishing up finally at the Solna police headquarters. By that time their shift would be over and the chance of seeing anything troublesome on the way should be infinitesimal.

The car turned left onto Norra Stationsgatan in Stockholm.

Kristiansson tucked the ten kronor into his pocket and yawned. Then he peered out into the pouring rain and said, "Over there's a man running this way. He has a dog . . . and he's waving at us."

"It's not my table," Kvant said.

The man, dragging the dog after him through the puddles,

rushed out into the road and planted himself right in front of the car.

"Damn!" Kvant swore, jamming on the brakes.

He wound the side window down and roared, "What do you mean by running out into the road like that?"

"There's . . . there's a bus over there," the man gasped out, pointing along the street.

"So what?" Kvant said rudely. "And how can you treat the dog like that? A poor dumb animal?"

"There's . . . there's been an accident."

"All right, we'll look into it," Kvant said impatiently. "Move aside." He drove on. "And don't do that again!" he shouted over his shoulder.

Kristiansson looked ahead through the rain.

"Yes," he said resignedly. "A bus has driven off the road. One of those double-deckers."

"And the lights are on," Kvant said. "And the door in front is open. Hop out and take a look, Kalle."

He pulled up at an angle behind the bus. Kristiansson opened the door, straightened his shoulder belt automatically and said to himself, "A-ha, and what's all this?"

Like Kvant, he was dressed in boots and leather jacket and carried a baton and pistol at his belt.

Kvant remained sitting in the car, watching Kristiansson, who moved leisurely toward the open front door of the bus.

Kvant saw him lazily heave himself up onto the step to peer into the bus. Then Kristiansson gave a start and crouched down quickly, while his right hand flew to his pistol holster.

Kvant reacted swiftly. It took him only a second to switch on the red lamps, the searchlight and the orange-colored flashing light of the patrol car.

Kristiansson was still crouching down beside the bus when Kvant flung open the car door and rushed out into the downpour. All in the same instant, Kvant had drawn and cocked his 7.65 mm Walther and had even cast a glance at his watch.

It showed exactly thirteen minutes past eleven.

THE FIRST SENIOR POLICEMAN to arrive at Norra Stationsgatan was Gunvald Larsson.

He had been sitting at his desk in Police Headquarters on Kungsholmen, thumbing listlessly through a dull and wordy report while he wondered why on earth people didn't go home.

In the category of "people" he included the police commissioner, a deputy commissioner and several different superintendents and inspectors who, on account of the happily concluded riots, were still trotting about the staircases and corridors. As soon as these persons thought fit to call it a day, he would do so himself, as fast as possible.

The phone rang. He grunted and picked up the receiver.

"Hello. Larsson."

"Radio Central here. A Solna radio patrol has found a whole bus full of dead bodies on Norra Stationsgatan."

Gunvald Larsson glanced at the electric wall clock, which showed eighteen minutes past eleven, and said, "How can a Solna radio patrol find a bus full of dead bodies in Stockholm?"

Gunvald Larsson was a detective inspector in the Stockholm homicide squad. He had a rigid disposition and was not one of the most popular members of the force. But he never wasted any time and so he was the first one there.

In the cone of the police-car searchlight stood two uniformed patrolmen with pistols in their hands. Both looked unnaturally pale. One of them had vomited down the front of his leather jacket and was wiping himself in embarrassment with a sodden handkerchief.

"What's the trouble?" Gunvald Larsson asked.

"There . . . there are a lot of corpses in there," said one of the policemen, indicating the bus.

"Yes," said the other. "And a lot of cartridges."

"And a man who shows signs of life."

"And a policeman."

"A policeman?" Gunvald Larsson asked.

"We recognize him. He's on the homicide squad."

"But we don't know his name. And he's dead."

The two patrolmen both talked at once, uncertainly and quietly. They were anything but small, but beside Gunvald Larsson they did not look very impressive.

Gunvald Larsson was 6 feet 5 inches tall and weighed nearly 220 pounds. His shoulders were as broad as those of a professional heavyweight boxer and he had huge, hairy hands. His fair hair, brushed backward, was already dripping wet.

The sound of many wailing sirens cut through the splashing of the rain. Police cars seemed to be coming from all directions. Gunvald Larsson pricked up his ears and said, "Is this Solna?"

"Right on the city limits," Kvant replied slyly.

Gunvald Larsson cast an expressionless blue glance from Kristiansson to Kvant. Then he strode over to the bus.

"It looks like . . . like a shambles in there," Kristiansson said.

Gunvald Larsson didn't touch the bus. He stuck his head in through the open door and looked around.

"Yes," he said calmly. "So it does."

IT WAS DARK in the hall of his apartment but Martin Beck didn't bother to switch on the light. He heard the record player going inside his daughter's room. He knocked and went in.

His daughter, Ingrid, was sixteen. She had matured somewhat of late, and Martin Beck got on with her much better than before. She was calm, matter-of-fact and fairly intelligent, and he liked talking to her. She was lying on her back in bed, reading. The record player on the bedside table was playing. Not pop music but something classical. Beethoven, he guessed.

"Hello," he said. "Not asleep yet?"

He stopped, almost paralyzed by the utter futility of his words. For a moment he thought of all the trivialities that had been spoken between these walls during the last ten years.

Ingrid put down her book and shut off the record player.

"Hi, Dad. What did you say?"

He shook his head.

"Lord, how wet your legs are. Is it raining so hard?"

"Cats and dogs. Are Mom and Rolf asleep?"

"I think so. Mom bundled Rolf off to bed right after dinner. She said he had a cold."

Martin Beck sat down on the bed.

"You seem hard at work, anyway. What are you studying?"

"French. We have a test tomorrow. Like to quiz me?"

"Wouldn't be much use. French isn't my strong point. Go to sleep now instead."

He stood up and the girl snuggled down obediently under the quilt. He tucked her in and before he shut the door behind him he heard her whisper, "Keep your fingers crossed tomorrow."

"Good night."

Martin Beck went into the living room, listened at the door of his wife's bedroom and heard her light snoring. Cautiously he switched on the wall lamp, let down the sofa bed and drew the curtains closed. He had bought the sofa recently and moved out of the bedroom, on the pretext that he didn't want to disturb his wife when he came home late at night. She had pointed out that sometimes he worked all night and therefore must sleep in the daytime, and she didn't want him lying there making a mess of the living room. He had promised on these occasions to lie and make a mess in the bedroom. Now he had been sleeping in the living room for the past month and liked it.

His wife's name was Inga.

Contact between them had worsened with the years. After seventeen years of marriage there didn't seem to be much he could do about it, and he had long since given up worrying over whose fault it might be.

Martin Beck took off his wet pants and hung them over a chair near the radiator. As he sat on the sofa pulling off his socks it crossed his mind that Kollberg's nocturnal walks in the rain might be due to the fact that his marriage, too, was slipping into boredom and routine.

Already? Kollberg had been married only eighteen months.

Before the first sock was off he had dismissed the thought. Lennart and Gun were happy together, not a doubt of that. Besides, what business was it of his?

He had one leg in bed when the telephone rang. He strode quickly across the floor and lifted the receiver before the second ring had finished.

"Superintendent Beck?" He didn't recognize the voice at the other end.

"Yes, speaking."

"This is Radio Central. Several passengers have been found shot dead in a bus on route 47 near the end of the line on Norra Stationsgatan. You're asked to go there at once."

Martin Beck's first thought was that he was a victim of a practical joke.

"Who gave you the message?" he asked.

"Hansson from the Fifth. Superintendent Hammar has already been notified."

"How many dead?"

"They're not sure yet. Six at least."

Martin Beck thought: I'll pick up Kollberg on the way. Hope there's a taxi. And said, "Okay. I'll come at once."

"Oh, Superintendent . . ."

"Yes?"

"One of the dead . . . he seems to be one of your men."

Martin Beck gripped the receiver hard.

"Who?"

"I don't know. They didn't say a name."

Martin Beck flung down the receiver and leaned his head against the wall. Lennart! It must be him. What the hell was he doing on a 47 bus? No, it must be a mistake.

He dialed Lennart's number and heard Gun's sleepy voice. He tried to sound calm and natural. "Hello. Is Lennart there?"

He thought he heard the bed creak as she sat up.

"No, not in bed at any rate. I thought he was with you. Or rather that you were here."

"He left when I did. To take a walk. Are you sure he's not at home?"

"He may be in the kitchen. Hang on and I'll have a look."

It was an eternity before she came back.

"No, Martin, he's not at home." Now her voice was anxious. "Wherever can he be?" she said. "In this weather?"

"Getting a breath of air. I just got home, so he can't have been out long. Don't worry."

He put down the receiver. Suddenly he felt so cold that his teeth were chattering. He picked up the receiver again and stood with it in his hand, thinking that he must call up someone and find out exactly what had happened. Then he decided the best way was to get to the place himself as fast as he could. He dialed the number of the nearest taxi stand and got a reply immediately.

Martin Beck had been a policeman for twenty-three years. During that time several of his colleagues had been killed in the course of duty. It had hit him hard every time it happened. But when it came to Lennart Kollberg, his feelings were not merely those of a colleague. Over the years they had become more and more dependent on each other in their work. They had learned to understand each other's thoughts and feelings without wasting words. In the last year or two they had also taken to meeting in their spare time.

Quite recently Kollberg had said, in one of his rare moments of depression, "If you weren't there, God only knows whether I'd stay on the force."

Martin Beck thought of this as he pulled on his wet raincoat and ran down the stairs to the waiting taxi.

DESPITE THE RAIN and the late hour a cluster of people had collected outside the police cordon surrounding the lighted bus. They stared curiously at Martin Beck as he got out of the taxi. He accepted a policeman's salute and swung his legs over the rope. The roped-off area was swarming with black-and-white police cars and figures in shiny raincoats.

The ambulance from the State Forensic Laboratory stood at the rear of the bus. The medicolegal expert's car was also on the scene. Behind the broken wire fence where the bus had stopped, some men were busy setting up floodlights. All these details showed that something far out of the ordinary had happened.

Martin Beck glanced up at the dismal apartment houses on the other side of the street. Figures were silhouetted in several of the lighted windows. Behind rain-streaked panes, like blurred white patches, he saw faces pressed against the glass. A bare-legged woman with a raincoat over her nightgown came out of an entrance opposite the scene of the accident. She got halfway across the street before being stopped by a policeman, who took her by the arm and led her back to the doorway while the wet white nightgown twisted itself around her legs.

Martin Beck could see people moving about inside the bus and presumed that men from the forensic laboratory were already at work. He guessed that his colleagues from the homicide squad were somewhere on the other side of the vehicle.

Involuntarily he slowed his steps. He thought of what he was soon to see and clenched his hands in his coat pockets as he gave the forensic technicians' gray vehicle a wide berth.

In the glow from the double-decker's open middle doors stood Hammar, who had been his boss for many years and was now a chief superintendent.

"There you are. I was beginning to think they'd forgotten to call you."

Martin Beck made no answer but went over to the doors and looked in. He felt his stomach muscles knotting. It was worse than he had expected. The whole bus seemed to be full of twisted, lifeless bodies covered with blood.

He would have liked to walk away and not have to look. Instead, he forced himself to make a systematic mental note of all the details, regarding the bodies one by one. He didn't recognize any of them. At least not in their present state.

"The one up there," he said suddenly, "has he—"

He turned to Hammar and broke off short.

Behind Hammar, Kollberg appeared out of the dark, bare-headed and with his hair stuck to his forehead.

Martin Beck stared at him.

"Hi," said Kollberg. "I was beginning to wonder what had happened to you. I was about to tell them to call you again."

He stopped in front of Martin Beck and gave him a searching look. Then he gave a swift, nauseated glance at the interior of the bus and went on, "You need a cup of coffee. I'll get you one."

He squished off. Martin Beck stared after him, then went to the front doors and looked in. Hammar followed.

The bus driver lay slumped over the wheel. He had evidently been shot through the head. Martin Beck turned to Hammar, who was staring expressionlessly out into the rain.

"What on earth was he doing here?" Hammar said tonelessly. "On this bus?"

And at that instant Martin Beck knew to whom the man on the phone had been referring.

Nearest the window behind the stairs leading to the top deck sat Åke Stenström, detective subinspector on the homicide squad and one of Martin Beck's youngest colleagues.

"Sat" was perhaps not the right word. Stenström's dark blue poplin raincoat was soaked with blood and he sprawled on the seat, his right shoulder against the back of a young woman who was sitting next to him, bent double.

He was dead. Like the young woman and the six other people in the bus.

In his right hand he held his service pistol.

Chapter Two

THE RAIN KEPT ON all night and it was nearly nine in the morning before the sun was strong enough to penetrate the clouds with an uncertain, hazy light. Across the sidewalk on Norra Stationsgatan stood the red double-decker bus, just as it had stopped ten hours previously.

By now about fifty men were inside the extensive police cordon, and outside the cordon the crowd of curious onlookers got bigger and bigger. Many had been standing there ever since midnight, and all they had seen was police and ambulance men and wailing emergency vehicles of every conceivable kind.

Two words were whispered from person to person and soon spread in concentric circles through the crowd and the surrounding houses and city, finally taking more definite shape and being flung out across the country as a whole. By now the words had reached far beyond the frontiers of Sweden.

Mass murder.

Mass murder on a bus in Stockholm.

Everybody thought they knew this much at least.

Very little more was known at Police Headquarters. It wasn't even known for certain who was in charge of the investigation. The confusion was complete. Telephones rang incessantly, people came and went, irritable and clammy with sweat and rain.

"Who's working on the list of names?" Martin Beck asked.

"Rönn, I should think," said Kollberg without turning around. He was busy taping a sketch to the wall. It was over 3 yards long and was awkward to handle.

"Can't someone give me a hand?" he said.

"Sure," said Melander calmly, putting down his pipe and standing up.

Fredrik Melander was a tall, lean man of grave appearance and methodical disposition. Kollberg had worked together with him on the homicide squad for many years. He had forgotten how many. Melander, on the other hand, had not. He was known never to forget anything.

An almost white-haired man of about fifty opened the door cautiously and stopped doubtfully on the threshold.

"Well, Ek, what do you want?" Martin Beck asked.

"About the bus . . ." the white-haired man said.

"Well, what about the bus?"

Ek shut the door behind him and studied his notes.

"It's built by the Leyland factories in England," he said. "It holds seventy-five seated passengers. The odd thing is—"

The door was flung open. Gunvald Larsson stared incredulously into his untidy office. His light raincoat was sopping wet, like his pants and his fair hair. His shoes were muddy.

"What a helluva mess in here," he grumbled.

"What was the odd thing about the bus?" Melander asked.

"Well, that particular type isn't used on route 47. They usually put German double-deckers on. This was an exception."

"A brilliant clue," Gunvald Larsson said. "The madman who did this only murders people on English buses. Is that what you mean?"

Ek looked at him resignedly. Gunvald Larsson shook himself and said, "By the way, what's the horde of apes doing down in the vestibule? Who are they?"

"Journalists," Ek said. "Someone ought to talk to them."

"Isn't Hammar or some other higher-up going to issue a communiqué?" Gunvald Larsson said.

"It probably hasn't been worded yet," said Martin Beck. "Ek is right. Someone ought to talk to them."

"Gunvald," Kollberg said. "You were the one who got there first. You can hold the press conference."

Gunvald Larsson stared into the room and pushed a wet tuft of hair off his forehead with the back of his big hairy hand. "Okay. Get them herded in somewhere. I'll talk to them. There's just one thing I must know first."

"What?" Martin Beck asked.

"Has anyone told Åke Stenström's mother?"

Dead silence fell, as though the words had robbed everyone in the room of the power of speech.

At last Melander turned his head and said, "She's been told."

"Good," Gunvald Larsson said and banged the door.

"Was that wise?" Kollberg asked Martin Beck.

"What?"

"Letting Gunvald . . . Don't you think we'll get bawled out enough in the press as it is?"

Martin Beck looked at him but said nothing. Kollberg shrugged. "Oh well," he said. "It doesn't matter."

Melander picked up his pipe and lighted it. "No," he said. "It couldn't matter less."

He and Kollberg had got the sketch up now. An enlarged

drawing of the lower deck of the bus. Some figures were sketched in. They were numbered from one to nine.

"Where's Rönn with that list?" Martin Beck mumbled.

"Another thing about the bus—" Ek said obstinately.

And the telephones rang.

THE OFFICE where the first improvised confrontation with the press took place contained nothing but a table, a few cupboards and four chairs, and when Gunvald Larsson entered the room, it was already stuffy with cigarette smoke and the smell of wet overcoats. He stopped just inside the door, looked around at the assembled journalists and photographers and said tonelessly, "Well, what do you want to know?"

They all began to talk at once. Gunvald Larsson held up his hand and said, "One at a time, please. You, there, can start. Then we'll go from left to right."

Thereafter the press conference proceeded as follows:

Q: How many persons were in the bus?

A: Eight.

Q: Were they all dead?

A: Yes.

Q: Was their death caused by external violence?

A: Probably.

Q: What do you mean by probably?

A: Exactly what I say.

Q: Were there any signs of shooting?

A: Yes.

Q: So all these people had been shot dead?

A: Probably.

Q: So it's really a question of mass murder?

A: Yes.

Q: Have you found the murder weapon?

A: No.

Q: Have the police detained anyone yet?

A: No.

Q: Were the murders committed by one and the same person?

A: Don't know.

Q: How could one single person kill eight people in a bus before anyone had time to resist?

A: Don't know.

Q: Were the shots fired by someone inside the bus or did they come from outside?

A: They did not come from outside.

Q: How do you know?

A: The windowpanes that were damaged had been fired at from inside.

Q: What kind of weapon had the murderer used?

A: Don't know.

Q: It must have been a machine gun or a submachine gun?

A: No comment.

Q: Does the position in which the bus was found indicate that the shooting took place while it was in motion and that it then went up on the sidewalk?

A: Yes.

Q: Did the police dogs get a scent?

A: It was raining.

Q: Where were the bodies found? On the upper or lower deck?

A: On the lower one.

Q: All eight?

A: Yes.

Q: Have the victims been identified?

A: No.

Q: Have any of them been identified?

A: Yes.

Q: Who? The driver?

A: No. A policeman.

Q: A policeman? Can we have his name?

A: Yes. Detective Subinspector Åke Stenström.

Q: Stenström? From the homicide squad?

A: Yes.

Q: Was Inspector Stenström working on any special investigation when this happened?

A: Don't know.

Q: Was he on duty last night?

A: No.

Q: Is it the opinion of the police that the murderer is a madman who wants to draw sensational attention to himself?

A: That is one theory.

Q: Are the police working on the lines of that theory?

A: All clues and suggestions are being followed.

Q: How many of the victims are women?

A: Two.

Q: So six of the victims are men?

A: Yes.

Q: Just a minute, now. We've been told that one of the persons in the bus survived and was taken away in one of the ambulances that arrived on the scene before the police had had time to cordon off the area.

A: Oh?

Q: Is this true?

A: Next question.

Q: Apparently you were one of the first policemen on the scene. What did it look like inside the bus when you got there?

A: What do you think?

Q: Can you say it was the most ghastly sight you've ever seen in your life?

Gunvald Larsson stared vacantly at the questioner, who was a young man with round, steel-rimmed glasses. At last he said, "No, I can't."

The reply caused some bewilderment. One of the women journalists frowned and said lamely and incredulously, "What do you mean by that?"

"Exactly what I say."

Before joining the police force Gunvald Larsson had been a regular seaman in the navy. In August 1943 he had been one of those to go through the submarine *Ulven*, which had struck a mine and had been salvaged after having lain on the seabed for three months. After the war, one of his duties had been to help with the extradition of the collaborators from the camp at Rän-neslätt. He had also seen the arrival of thousands of victims repatriated from German concentration camps. However, he saw no reason to explain himself, but said laconically, "Any more questions?"

"Have the police been in touch with any witnesses of the actual event?"

"No."

"In other words, eight persons have been killed in the middle of Stockholm and that's all the police have to say?"

"Yes."

With that, the press conference was concluded.

IT WAS SOME TIME before anyone noticed that Einar Rönn had come in with the list. Martin Beck, Kollberg, Melander and Gunvald Larsson stood leaning over photographs from the scene of the crime, when Rönn suddenly stood next to them and said, "It's ready now, the list." Although he had lived in Stockholm for more than twenty years he still kept his north-Swedish way of speaking.

"Okay," said Kollberg. "Let's hear."

Rönn put on his glasses and cleared his throat. He glanced through his notes. "Of the eight dead, four lived in the vicinity of the terminus," he began. "The survivor also lived there."

"Take them in order if you can," Martin Beck said.

"Well, first of all there's the driver. He was hit by two shots in the back of the neck and one in the back of the head and must have been killed outright."

Martin Beck had no need to look at the photograph that Rönn extracted from the pile on the table. He remembered all too well how the man in the driver's seat had looked.

"His name was Gustav Bengtsson. He was forty-eight, married, two children. It was his last run for the day and when he had let off the passengers at the last stop, he would have driven the bus to the Hornsberg depot. The money in his fare purse was untouched and in his wallet he had 120 kronor."

He glanced at the others over his glasses.

"There's no more about him for the moment."

"Go on," Melander said.

"I'll take them in the same order as on the sketch. The next is Åke Stenström. Five shots in the back. One in the right shoulder from the side, might have been a ricochet. He was twenty-nine and lived—"

Gunvald Larsson interrupted him. "You can skip that. We know where he lived."

Rönn cleared his throat. "He lived together with his fiancée—"

Gunvald Larsson interrupted him again. "They were not engaged. I asked him not long ago."

Martin Beck cast an irritated glance at Gunvald Larsson and nodded to Rönn to continue.

"Together with Åsa Torell, twenty-four. She works at a travel agency."

Rönn gave Gunvald Larsson a quick look and said, "In sin. I don't know whether she's been told."

Melander took his pipe out of his mouth and said, "She has been told."

"In his right hand Stenström held his service pistol. It was cocked but he had not fired a shot. In his pockets he had a wallet containing 37 kronor, a snapshot of Åsa Torell and a letter from his mother. Also, driving license, notebook, pens and bunch of keys. It will all be sent up to us when the boys at the lab are through with it. Can I go on?"

"Yes, please," said Kollberg.

"The girl in the seat next to Stenström was called Britt Danielsson. She was twenty-eight, unmarried and worked at Sabbatsberg Hospital. She was a registered nurse."

"I wonder whether they were together," Gunvald Larsson said. "Perhaps he was having a bit of fun on the side."

"We'd better find out," Kollberg said.

"She shared a room with another nurse from Sabbatsberg. According to her roommate, Britt Danielsson was coming straight from the hospital. She was hit by one shot. In the

temple. She was the only one in the bus to be struck by only one bullet. She had thirty-eight different things in her handbag. Shall I enumerate them?"

"Lord, no," said Gunvald Larsson.

"Number four on the list and on the sketch is the survivor, Alfons Schwerin. He was lying on his back on the floor at the rear. He was hit in the abdomen and one bullet lodged in the region of the heart. He lives alone at Norra Stationsgatan 117. He is forty-three and employed by the highway department. How is he, by the way?"

"Still in a coma," Martin Beck said. "The doctors say there's just a chance he'll regain consciousness. But they don't know whether he'll be able to remember anything. What about this one in the corner?"

Rönn consulted his notes. "He got eight bullets in his chest and abdomen. He was an Algerian named Mohammed Boussie, thirty-six, no relations in Sweden. He lived at a kind of boarding-house on Norra Stationsgatan. Was obviously on his way home from work at that grill restaurant, the Zig-Zag. There's nothing more to say about him at the moment."

Rönn got up and fished some pictures out of the pile.

"This guy we haven't been able to identify," he said. "Number six. He was sitting on the outside seat immediately behind the middle doors and was hit by six shots. In his pockets he had the striking surface of a matchbox, a packet of cigarettes, a bus ticket and 1,823 kronor in cash. That was all."

"A lot of money," Melander said thoughtfully.

They leaned over the table and studied the pictures of the unknown man. He had slithered down in the seat and lay sprawled against the back with arms hanging and his left leg stuck out in the aisle. The front of his coat was soaked in blood. He had no face.

"It would have to be *him*," Gunvald Larsson said. "His own mother wouldn't recognize him."

Martin Beck had resumed his study of the sketch on the wall. He said, "I'm not so sure there weren't two killers after all."

The others looked at him.

"Look at all the passengers, they never moved from their seats. Someone should have had time to react if there had been only one."

"Two madmen?" Gunvald Larsson said skeptically.

"Shall we go on with the list? We'll find out whether there was more than one killer as soon as we know whether there was one weapon or two," Kollberg said.

"Sure," said Martin Beck. "Go on, Einar."

"Number seven is a foreman called Johan Källström. He was sitting beside the man who has not yet been identified. He was fifty-two. According to his wife he was coming home from the workshop where he'd been working overtime. Nothing startling about him."

"Nothing except that he got a bellyful of lead on the way home from work," said Gunvald Larsson.

"By the window immediately in front of the middle doors we have Gösta Assarsson, number eight. Forty-two. Half his head was shot away. He lived at Tegnérgatan 40, where he also had his office and his business, an export and import firm that he ran together with his brother. His wife didn't know why he was on the bus. According to her, he should have been at a club meeting."

"A-ha," said Gunvald Larsson. "Out carousing."

"Yes, there are signs that point to that. In his briefcase he had a bottle of whisky. Johnnie Walker, Black Label."

The door opened and Ek stuck his head in. "Hammar wants you all in his office in fifteen minutes," he said. "Briefing."

"Okay, let's go on," Martin Beck said.

Rönn glanced at the sheet of paper covered with his scribbling. "Two seats in front of Assarsson sat number nine, Mrs. Hildur Johansson, sixty-eight, widow. Shot in the shoulder and through the neck. She has a married daughter and was on her way home after baby-sitting for her."

Rönn folded the piece of paper and tucked it into his jacket pocket. "That's the lot," he said.

Gunvald Larsson sighed and arranged the pictures in nine neat stacks.

Kollberg tilted his chair and said, "And what do we learn from all this? That on quite an ordinary evening on quite an ordinary bus, nine quite ordinary people get mowed down with a submachine gun for no apparent reason."

"One was not ordinary," Martin Beck said. "Stenström. What was he doing on that bus?"

Nobody answered.

AN HOUR LATER Hammar put exactly the same question to Martin Beck.

Hammar had summoned the special investigation group that from now on was to work entirely on the bus murders. All available facts had been studied, the situation had been analyzed and assignments made. When the briefing was over and all except Martin Beck and Kollberg had left the room, Hammar said, "What was Stenström doing on that bus?"

"Don't know," Martin Beck replied.

"Nobody seems to know what he was working on of late. Do either of you know?"

Kollberg threw up his hands and shrugged. "Haven't the vaguest idea. Beyond daily routine, that is. Presumably nothing."

"We haven't had so much work recently," Martin Beck said. "So he has had quite a bit of time off. He had put in an enormous amount of overtime before, so it was only fair."

Hammar wrinkled his brows in thought. Then he said, "Who was it that informed his fiancée?"

"Melander," said Kollberg.

"I think someone ought to have a talk with her as soon as possible," Hammar said. "She must know what he was up to." He paused, then added, "Unless he—" He fell silent.

"What?" Martin Beck asked.

"Unless he was going with that nurse on the bus, you mean," Kollberg said, "or was out on another similar errand."

Hammar nodded. "Find out," he said.

MOUNTING THE steps to Police Headquarters were two persons in uniform who definitely wished they were somewhere else.

"What do you think they want us for?" Kristiansson asked anxiously.

"To give evidence, of course," Kvant replied. "We made the discovery, didn't we?"

On the third floor they met Kollberg. He nodded to them, gloomily and absently. Then he opened a door and said, "Gunvald, those two guys from Solna are here now."

"Tell them to wait," said a voice from inside the office.

When they had waited for twenty minutes Kvant shook himself and said, "What the hell's the idea? We're supposed to be off duty, and I've promised Siv to mind the kids while she goes to the doctor."

"So you said," Kristiansson said dejectedly.

"Now she'll probably be in a terrible temper again," Kvant continued. "I can't make the woman out these days. And she's starting to look such a fright. Has Kerstin also got broad in the beam like that?"

Kristiansson didn't answer. Kerstin was his wife and he disliked discussing her.

Five minutes later Gunvald Larsson opened the door and said curtly, "Come in."

They went in and sat down. Gunvald Larsson eyed them critically. "Sit down, by all means," he said.

"We have already," Kristiansson said fatuously.

Kvant silenced him with an impatient gesture. He began to scent trouble.

Gunvald Larsson stood silent for a moment. Then he placed himself behind the desk, sighed heavily and said, "How long have you both been on the force?"

"Eight years," said Kvant.

Gunvald Larsson picked up a sheet of paper from the desk and studied it. "This is a preliminary report from the investigation at the scene of the crime. It shows that two persons with size eleven shoes have left behind them footprints all over that bus, both on the upper and lower decks. Who do you think these two persons can be?"

No answer.

"I can add that I spoke to an expert at the lab not long ago, and he said that the scene of the crime looked as if a herd of hippopotamuses had been trotting about there for hours."

Kvant began to lose his temper. He stared stonily at the man behind the desk.

"Now it so happens that hippopotamuses don't usually go about armed," Gunvald Larsson went on in honeyed tones. "Nevertheless, someone fired a shot inside the bus with a 7.65 Walther up through the front stairs. The bullet ricocheted against the roof and was found embedded in the padding of one of the seats on the upper deck. Who do you think can have fired that shot?"

"We did," Kristiansson said. "That's to say, I did."

"Oh, really? And what were you firing at?"

Kristiansson scratched his neck unhappily.

"Nothing," he said.

"It was a warning shot," Kvant said. "We thought the murderer might still be in the bus and was hiding on the top deck."

"And was he?"

"No," said Kvant.

"How do you know?"

"We went up and had a look," Kristiansson said.

Gunvald Larsson glared at them for at least half a minute. Then he slammed the flat of his hand on the desk and roared, "So both of you went up! How the hell could you be so stupid?"

"We each went up a different way," Kvant said defensively. "I went up the back stairs and Kristiansson took the front stairs."

"So that whoever was up there couldn't escape," said Kristiansson, trying to make things better.

"But there wasn't anyone up there! All you managed to do was to ruin every single footprint there was in the whole damn bus! To say nothing of outside! And why did you go tramping about among the bodies? Was it to make even more of a gory mess?"

"To see if anyone was still alive," Kristiansson said. He turned pale and swallowed.

"Now don't start throwing up again, Kalle," Kvant said reprovingly.

The door opened and Martin Beck came in. He looked inquiringly at Gunvald Larsson. "Are you the one who is shouting? It doesn't help much, bawling out these boys."

"Yes it does," Gunvald Larsson retorted. "These two idiots—" He broke off and reconsidered his vocabulary. "These two colleagues are the only witnesses we have. Listen now, you two! What time did you arrive on the scene?"

"Thirteen minutes past eleven," Kvant said. "I took the time on my chronograph."

"I received the call here at eighteen minutes past eleven," Gunvald Larsson said. "If we allow a wide margin and say that you fumbled with the radio for half a minute and that it took maybe fifteen seconds for Radio Central to contact me, that still leaves more than four minutes. What were you doing during that time?"

"Well . . ." said Kvant.

"You ran about tromping in blood and moving bodies and doing God knows what. For four minutes."

"I really can't see what's constructive—" Martin Beck began, but Gunvald Larsson cut him off.

"Wait a minute. Apart from the fact that these nitwits spent four minutes ruining the scene of the crime, they did get there at thirteen minutes past eleven. They didn't go of their own accord but were told by the man who first discovered the bus. Is that right?"

"Yes. The old boy with the dog," said Kristiansson.

"Exactly. They were notified by a person whom we probably would never have known about if he hadn't been nice enough to come here today. When did you first catch sight of this man with the dog?"

"About two minutes before we got to the bus," said Kristiansson, looking down at his boots.

"Exactly. Because according to his statement they wasted at least a minute sitting in the car and shouting at him rudely. Am I right?"

"Yes," mumbled Kristiansson.

"When you received the information the time was therefore approximately ten or eleven minutes past. How far from the bus was this man when he stopped you?"

"About three hundred yards," said Kvant.

"That's a fact, that's a fact," said Gunvald Larsson. "And since this man was seventy years old and also had a sick dachshund to drag along . . ."

"Sick?" said Kvant in surprise.

"Exactly," Gunvald Larsson replied. "The dog had a slipped disk and was almost lame in the hind legs."

"At last I begin to see what you mean," said Martin Beck.

"Mm-m. I had the man do a trial run on the same stretch today. Dog and all. Made him do it three times, then the dog gave up."

"But that's cruelty to animals," Kvant said indignantly.

Martin Beck cast a surprised and interested glance at him.

"At any rate the pair couldn't cover the distance in under three minutes, however hard they tried. Which means that the man must have caught sight of the stationary bus at seven minutes past eleven at the latest. And we know almost for sure that the massacre took place between three and four minutes earlier."

"How do you know that?" Kristiansson and Kvant asked in chorus.

"Inspector Stenström's watch," said Martin Beck. "One of the bullets passed straight through his chest and landed in his right wrist. It broke off the stem on his wristwatch, which according to a watch expert made it stop at the same instant. The hands showed three minutes and thirty-seven seconds past eleven."

Gunvald Larsson glowered at him.

"We know Inspector Stenström, and he was meticulous about time, what watchmakers call a second hunter," Martin Beck said sadly. "That is, his watch always showed the exact time. Go on, Gunvald."

"This man with the dog was walking down Norrbackagatan hill when he was overtaken by the bus just where the street begins. It took him about five minutes to trudge down. The bus did the same stretch in about forty-five seconds. He met nobody on the way. When he got to the corner he saw the bus standing on the other side of the street."

"So what—" said Kvant.

"Shut up," said Gunvald Larsson.

Kvant made a violent movement and opened his mouth, but then he glanced at Martin Beck and shut it again.

"He did not see that the windows had been shattered, but he did see that the front door was open. He thought there had been an accident and hurried to get help. Calculating, quite correctly, that it would be quicker for him to reach the last bus stop than to go back up the hill, he started off along Norra Stationsgatan in a southwesterly direction."

"Why?" said Martin Beck.

"Because he thought there'd be another bus waiting at the end of the line. As it happened, there wasn't. Instead, unfortunately, he met a police patrol car." Gunvald Larsson cast an annihilating china-blue glance at Kristiansson and Kvant. "A patrol car from Solna that came creeping out of its district like something that comes out when you lift up a rock. Well, how long had you two been skulking with the engine idling and the front wheels on the city limits?"

"Three minutes," said Kvant.

"Four or five, more like it," said Kristiansson.

"And did you see anyone coming that way?"

"No," said Kristiansson. "Not until that man with the dog."

"Which proves that the murderer cannot have made off to the southwest along Norra Stationsgatan nor south up Norrbackagatan. If we take it that he did not hop over into the freight yard, there's only one possibility left. Along Norra Stationsgatan in the opposite direction."

"How do . . . we know that he didn't head into the station yard?" Kristiansson asked.

"Because that was the only spot where you wonderboys hadn't trampled down everything in sight. You forgot to climb over the fence and mess around there, too."

"Okay, Gunvald, you've made your point now," Martin Beck said. "Good. But it took a helluva time to get down to brass tacks."

This remark encouraged Kristiansson and Kvant to exchange a look of relief and secret understanding. But Gunvald Larsson cracked out, "If you two had had any sense in your thick skulls you would have got into the car, caught up with the murderer and nabbed him."

Kvant stole a glance at the wall clock and said, "Can we go now? My wife—"

"Yes," said Gunvald Larsson. "You can go to hell!"

Avoiding Martin Beck's reproachful look, he said, "Why didn't they think?"

"Some people need longer than others to develop their train of thought," Martin Beck said amiably.

Chapter Three

"Now WE MUST think," Gunvald Larsson said briskly as he came in and banged the door. "There's a briefing with Hammar at three o'clock sharp. In ten minutes."

Martin Beck, sitting with the telephone receiver to his ear, threw him an irritated glance, and Kollberg looked up from his papers and muttered gloomily, "As if we didn't know. Try thinking yourself on an empty stomach and see how easy it is."

Having to go without a meal was one of the few things that could put Kollberg in a bad mood. By this time he had gone without at least two meals and was therefore particularly glum.

Martin Beck put down the phone. Then he got up, took his notes and went over to Kollberg.

"That call was from the lab," he said. "They've counted sixty-eight fired cases."

"What caliber?" Kollberg asked.

"As we thought. Nine millimeters. Nothing to say that sixty-seven of them didn't come from the same weapon."

"And the sixty-eighth?"

"Walther 7.65."

"The shot fired by that Kristiansson," Kollberg declared.

"Yes."

"It means there was probably only one madman after all," Gunvald Larsson said.

"Yes," said Martin Beck. Going over to the sketch, he drew an X inside the exit doors.

"Yes," Kollberg said. "That's where he must have stood."

"Which would explain . . ."

"What?" Gunvald Larsson asked.

"Why Stenström didn't have time to shoot," Martin Beck said. The others looked at him wonderingly.

Hammar flung open the door and entered the room, followed by Ek. "Reconstruction," he said abruptly. "Stop all telephone calls. Are you ready?"

Martin Beck looked at Hammar mournfully. It had been Stenström's habit to enter the room in exactly the same way, without knocking. It had been extremely irritating.

"What have you got there?" Gunvald Larsson asked. "The evening papers?"

"Yes," Hammar replied. "Very encouraging." He held the papers up and gave them a hostile glare. The headlines were big and black but the text contained very little information. "I quote," Hammar said. " 'This is the crime of the century,' says tough C.I.D. man Gunvald Larsson of the Stockholm homicide squad, and goes on: 'It was the most ghastly sight I've ever seen in my life.' Two exclamation points."

Gunvald Larsson heaved himself back in his chair and frowned.

"You're in good company," said Hammar. "The Minister of Justice has also excelled himself. 'The tidal wave of lawlessness and the mentality of violence must be stopped. The direct investigation force already comprises more than a hundred of the country's most skilled criminal experts, the biggest squad ever known in this country's history of crime.' "

Martin Beck blew his nose quietly. Kollberg sighed.

Tossing the newspapers onto the desk, Hammar said, "Where's Melander?"

"Talking to the psychologists," Kollberg said.

"And Rönn?"

"At the hospital."

"Any news from there yet?"

"They're still operating," Martin Beck said.

"Well," Hammar said. "The reconstruction."

Kollberg looked through his papers. "The bus left Bellmansro about ten o'clock," he said.

"About?"

"Yes. The whole timetable had been thrown off by the commotion in front of the American embassy. The buses were stuck in traffic jams or police cordons, and as there were already big delays the drivers had been radioed to ignore scheduled departure times and turn straight around at the last stops."

"Go on."

"We assume that there are people who rode part of the way on route 47 on this particular bus run. But so far we haven't traced any such witnesses."

"They'll turn up," said Hammar. He pointed to the newspapers and added, "After this."

"Stenström's watch had stopped at eleven three and thirty-seven seconds," Kollberg went on in a monotone. "There is reason to think the first shots were fired at precisely that time."

"Why the first?" Hammar asked.

Turning to the sketch on the wall, Martin Beck put his right forefinger on the X he had drawn a few minutes earlier.

"We assume that the gunman stood just here," he said. "In the open space by the exit doors."

"On what do you base that assumption?"

"The trajectories. The positions of the fired cases in relation to the bodies."

"Right. Go on."

"We also assume that the murderer fired three bursts. The first forward, from left to right, thereby shooting all persons sitting in the front of the bus."

"And then?"

"Then he turned around, probably to the right, and fired the next burst at the four persons at the rear of the bus, still from left to right, killing three and wounding Schwerin, the fourth. Schwerin was lying on his back at the rear of the aisle. We take this to mean that he had been sitting on the longitudinal seat on the left side of the bus and that he had time to stand up. He would therefore have been hit last."

"And the third burst?"

"Was fired forward," Martin Beck said. "From right to left."

"And the weapon must be a submachine gun?"

"Yes," Kollberg replied. "In all probability it's the ordinary army type—"

"One moment," Hammar interrupted. "How long should this have taken? To shoot forward, swing right around, shoot backward, point the weapon forward again and empty the magazine?"

"About ten seconds," Gunvald Larsson said.

"How did he get out of the bus?" Hammar asked.

Martin Beck nodded to Ek and said, "Your department."

Ek passed his fingers through his silvery hair, cleared his throat and said, "The door that was open was the entrance door. In all likelihood the murderer left the bus that way. In order to open it he must first move forward to the driver's seat, then reach over the driver and push a lever." He took out his glasses, polished them with his handkerchief and went over to the wall. "I've had a sketch blown up here," he said, "showing the actual lever. It is to the left of the wheel, below the side window. The lever, as you see from the sketch, has five positions."

"Who could make head or tail out of all this?" Gunvald Larsson said.

"In the horizontal position, or position one, both doors are shut. In position two—"

"Sum up," said Hammar.

"To sum up, the gunman must have moved from his position by the exit doors straight forward along the aisle to the driver's seat, leaned over the dead driver, and turned the lever to position two, thereby opening the entrance door. That is to say, the one that was still open when the police car got there."

Martin Beck picked up the thread at once.

"Actually there are signs showing that the last shots of all were fired to the left while the gunman was moving forward along the aisle. One of them seems to have hit Stenström."

"Pure trench warfare tactics," said Gunvald Larsson.

"Gunvald made a very pertinent comment just now," Hammar said dryly. "That he didn't understand a thing. All this shows that the murderer was quite at home in the bus and knew how to work the instrument panel."

"At least how to work the doors," Ek said pedantically.

There was silence in the room. Hammar frowned. At last he said, "Do you mean to say that someone suddenly went and stood in the middle of the bus, shot everyone there and then simply went on his way? Without anyone having time to react? Without the driver seeing anything in his mirror?"

"No," Kollberg said. "Not exactly."

"What *do* you mean then?"

"That someone came down the rear stairs from the top deck with the submachine gun at the ready," Martin Beck said.

"Someone who had been sitting up there alone for a while," Kollberg said. "Someone who had taken his time to wait for the most suitable moment."

Hammar stood in silence for a few seconds. Then he said, "No. It doesn't hold water."

"What doesn't?" Martin Beck asked.

"The reconstruction."

"Why not?" said Kollberg.

"It seems far too well thought out. A deranged mass murderer doesn't act with such careful planning."

"Oh, I don't know," said Gunvald Larsson. "That madman in

America who shot over thirty persons from a tower had planned as carefully as hell. He even had food with him."

"Yes," Hammar said. "But there was one thing he hadn't figured out."

"What?"

It was Martin Beck who answered: "How he was to get away."

SEVEN HOURS later the time was ten o'clock in the evening and Martin Beck and Kollberg were still at Police Headquarters.

In the course of the afternoon, twenty helpful witnesses had come forward. Nineteen of them turned out to have ridden on other buses. The remaining witness was a young girl who had got on at the start of route 47 and gone to Sergels Torg, where she had changed to the subway. She said that several passengers had got off at the same time as she, which seemed likely. She recognized the driver, but that was all.

Kollberg paced restlessly up and down, eyeing the door repeatedly as if expecting someone to throw it open and rush in.

Martin Beck stood in front of the sketches on the wall. He had his hands clasped behind him and rocked slowly to and fro from sole to heel and back, an irritating habit he had acquired during his years as a patrolman on the beat long ago.

Kollberg stopped his pacing, looked at him critically and asked, "What *is* wrong with you?"

Martin Beck didn't answer.

"Stenström?"

Kollberg nodded to himself and said philosophically, "To think how I've bawled that kid out over the years. And then he goes and gets murdered."

Another silence. Then Martin Beck looked at Kollberg and said, "Well?"

"Well what?"

"What was Stenström doing on that bus?"

"That's just it," said Kollberg. "What the devil was he doing there? That girl, maybe. The nurse."

"Would he go about armed if he was out with a girl?"

"He might. So as to seem tough."

"He wasn't that kind," Martin Beck said. "You know that as well as I do."

"Well, in any case, he had his pistol on him a helluva sight more often than you or I."

"Yes—when he was on duty."

"I only met him when he was on duty," Kollberg said dryly.

"So did I. But it's a fact that he was one of the first to die in that horrible bus. Even so, he had time to undo two buttons of his raincoat and get out his pistol."

"Which means that he had already unbuttoned his coat," Kollberg said thoughtfully. "One more thing."

"Yes?"

"Hammar said something today at the reconstruction to this effect: 'It doesn't hold water. A deranged mass murderer doesn't plan so carefully.' Do you think he was right?"

"Yes, in principle."

"Which would mean?"

"That the man who did the shooting is no mentally deranged mass murderer. Or rather that he didn't do it merely to cause a sensation."

Kollberg wiped the sweat off his brow with a folded handkerchief, regarded it thoughtfully and said, "I think that's nonsense. There's no doubt whatever that the murderer is mad. For all we know he may be sitting at home at this very moment in front of the TV, enjoying the effect. The fact that Stenström was armed and riding that bus means nothing at all, since we don't know his habits. He may have quarreled with his girl and sat sulking on a bus because it was too late to go to the movies and he had nowhere else to go."

"We can find that out, anyway," Martin Beck said.

"Yes. Tomorrow. But there's one thing we can do this very moment. Before anyone else does it."

"Go through his desk out at southern headquarters."

"Your power of deduction is admirable," Kollberg declared. He started climbing into his jacket.

THE AIR WAS RAW and misty, and the night frost lay like a shroud over trees and streets and rooftops. Kollberg had difficulty in seeing through the windshield and muttered dismal curses when the car skidded on the bends. All the way out to the southern police headquarters at Västberga they spoke only once.

"Do mass murderers usually have a hereditary criminal streak?" Kollberg wondered.

And Martin Beck answered, "Yes, usually. But by no means always."

The headquarters building was silent and deserted. They crossed the vestibule and went up the stairs, pressed the buttons on the dial beside the glass doors on the third floor and went on into Stenström's office.

Kollberg hesitated a moment, then sat down at the desk and tried the drawers. They were not locked.

The room was neat and tidy but quite impersonal. Stenström had not even had a photograph of his fiancée on the desk. On the other hand, two photos of himself lay on the pen tray. Martin Beck knew why. Stenström had been lucky enough to be scheduled off duty over Christmas and New Year's and had already booked seats on a charter plane to the Canary Islands. He had had the pictures taken because he had to get a new passport.

In the photos Stenström looked, if anything, younger than his twenty-nine years. He had a bright, frank expression and dark brown hair, combed back. Here, as it usually did, it looked rather unruly.

At first he had been considered naive and mediocre by a number of colleagues, including Kollberg, whose sarcastic remarks and often condescending manner had been a continuous trial. But that was in the past. Martin Beck remembered that once he had discussed this with Kollberg. He had said, "Why are you always nagging at the kid?"

And Kollberg had answered, "In order to break down his put-on self-confidence. To give him a chance to build it up new. To help turn him into a good policeman one day. To teach him to knock at doors."

It was conceivable that Kollberg had been right. At any rate, Stenström had improved with the years. And although he had never learned to knock at doors, he had developed into a good policeman—capable, hard-working and reasonably discerning. In addition he had had certain specialties that had been of great use to them all.

Outwardly, Stenström had been an adornment to the force: a pleasant appearance, a winning manner, physically fit and a good athlete. He could almost have been used in recruiting advertisements, which was more than could be said of certain others. For instance, of Kollberg, with his arrogance and tendency to run to fat. Of the stoical Melander, who in no way challenged the hypothesis that the worst bores often made the best policemen. Or of the red-nosed and in all respects equally mediocre Rönn. Or of Gunvald Larsson, who could frighten anyone at all out of his wits with his colossal body and staring eyes and who was proud of it, what is more. Or of Martin Beck himself either, for that matter. He had looked in the mirror as recently as the evening before and seen a tall, sinister figure with a lean face, wide forehead, heavy jaws and mournful gray-blue eyes.

Martin Beck thought of all this while he regarded the objects that Kollberg systematically took out of the drawers and placed on the desk. But now he was coldly appraising what he knew of the man whose name had been Åke Stenström. The feelings that had threatened to overwhelm him not long ago were gone. The moment was past and would never recur.

Ever since Stenström had put his cap on the hat rack five years before, he had worked under Martin Beck. They had worked together on innumerable investigations. During this time Stenström had matured, overcome most of his uncertainty and shyness, left home and in time moved in with a young woman, with whom he said he wanted to spend the rest of his life.

Martin Beck should, therefore, know most of what there was to know about him.

Oddly enough, he didn't know very much. A nice guy. Ambitious, persevering, smart, ready to learn. On the other hand rather shy, still a trifle childish, anything but witty, not much sense of humor on the whole.

Why did he know so little? Because he had not been sufficiently observant? Or because there was nothing to know?

Martin Beck massaged his scalp with his fingertips and studied what Kollberg had laid on the desk.

There had been a pedantic trait in Stenström, for instance his insistence that his watch show the correct time to the very second. It was also reflected in the meticulous tidiness on and in his desk. Papers, papers and more papers. Copies of reports, notes, minutes of court proceedings, stenciled instructions and reprints of legal texts. All in neatly arranged bundles. The most personal things were a box of matches and an unopened pack of chewing gum.

Kollberg sighed deeply and said, "If I had been the one sitting in that bus, you and Stenström would have been rummaging through my drawers just now. It would have given you a helluva sight more trouble than this. You'd probably have made finds that would have blackened my memory."

Martin Beck could well imagine what Kollberg's drawers looked like but refrained from comment.

They went through the papers in silence, quickly and thoroughly. There was nothing that they could not immediately identify or place in its natural context. All notes and all documents were connected with investigations that Stenström had been working on and that they knew all about.

At last there was only one thing left. A large brown envelope. It was sealed and rather fat.

"What do you think this can be?" Kollberg said.

"Open it and see."

Kollberg turned the envelope all ways. "He seems to have sealed it up very carefully. Look at these strips of tape." He took the paper knife from the pen tray and resolutely slit open the envelope.

"Hm-m," Kollberg said. "I didn't know that Stenström was a photographer." He glanced through the bunch of photographs and then spread them out in front of him. "And I would never have thought he had interests like this."

"It's his fiancée," said Martin Beck tonelessly. He looked at the photographs dutifully and with the unpleasant feeling he always had when he was forced to intrude on other people's private lives. This reaction was spontaneous and innate, and not even after twenty-three years as a policeman had he learned to master it.

Kollberg was not troubled by any such scruples. "She's quite a dish," he said appreciatively. He went on studying the pictures.

"But you've seen her before," Martin Beck said.

"Yes, dressed. This is an entirely different matter."

Martin Beck's only comment was, "And tomorrow we'll be seeing her again."

"Yes," Kollberg replied. "And I'm not looking forward to it." Gathering up the photographs, he put them back into the envelope. Then he said, "We'd better be getting home. I'll give you a lift."

In the car Martin Beck said, "By the way, how did you come to be at Norra Stationsgatan last night? Gun didn't know where you were when I called up and you were on the scene long before I was."

"It was pure chance. After leaving you I walked toward town. On Skanstull Bridge two guys in a patrol car recognized me. They had just got the alarm on the radio and they drove me straight in."

They sat in silence for a time. Then Kollberg said in a puzzled tone, "What do you think he wanted those pictures for?"

"To look at," Martin Beck replied.

"Of course. But still . . ."

BEFORE MARTIN BECK left the apartment on Wednesday morning he called up Kollberg. Their conversation was brief and to the point. "Hi. It's Martin. I'm leaving now."

"Okay."

When the train glided into the suburban subway station,

Kollberg was waiting on the platform. They had made it a habit always to get into the last car and so they often had each other's company into town even when they hadn't arranged it.

"Have you heard how the wounded man is? Schwerin?" Kollberg asked.

"Yes, I called up the hospital this morning. The operations have succeeded insomuch as he's alive. But he's still unconscious and the doctors can't say anything about the outcome until he wakes up."

"Is he going to wake up?"

Martin Beck shrugged. "They don't know."

They found the name TORELL on the list of tenants in the entrance to number 18 Tjärhovsgatan, but above the doorplate two flights up was a card with the name ÅKE STENSTRÖM drawn in India ink.

The girl who opened the door was small and slight.

"Come in and take your coats off," she said, closing the door behind them. Her voice was low and rather hoarse.

Åsa Torell was dressed in a cornflower-blue polo sweater and narrow black slacks. On her feet she had thick gray ski socks that were several sizes too large and had presumably been Stenström's. She had brown eyes and dark hair cut very short. Her face was angular and could be called neither sweet nor pretty; if anything, quaint and piquant.

She stood quiet and expectant while Martin Beck and Kollberg put their hats beside Stenström's old cap on the rack and took off their coats. Then she led the way into a pleasant, cozy living room. Against one wall stood a huge bookcase with carved sides and top piece. Apart from it and a wing chair upholstered in leather, the furniture looked fairly new. A bright red rya rug covered most of the floor, and the thin woolen curtains had exactly the same shade of red.

Åsa Torell sat in the leather armchair and tucked her feet under her. She pointed to two safari chairs, and Martin Beck and Kollberg sat down. The ashtray on the low table between them and the young woman was overflowing with cigarette butts.

"I do hope you realize how sorry we are that we have to intrude like this," Martin Beck said. "But it was essential to talk to you as soon as possible."

Åsa Torell picked up the cigarette that lay burning on the edge of the ashtray and drew at it deeply. Her hand was inclined to shake and she had dark rings under her eyes.

"Of course I do," she said. "It was just as well you came. I've been sitting in this chair ever since . . . well, since I heard that . . . I've been sitting here trying to realize that it's true."

"Miss Torell," Kollberg said, "haven't you anyone who can come here and be with you?"

She shook her head. "No. Anyway, I don't want anyone here."

Martin Beck leaned forward and gave her a searching look.

"Have you slept at all?" he asked.

"I don't know. The ones that were here yesterday gave me a couple of pills, so I expect I did sleep for a while. It doesn't matter. I'll be all right." Stubbing out the cigarette, she murmured, her eyes lowered, "I'll just have to try and get used to the fact that he's dead. It may take time."

Neither Martin Beck nor Kollberg could think of anything to say. An oppressive silence weighed on them all. At last Kollberg cleared his throat and said gravely, "Miss Torell, do you mind if we ask you one or two things about Stenstr—about Åke?"

Åsa Torell raised her eyes slowly. Suddenly they twinkled and she smiled. "You surely don't mean me to call you Superintendent Beck and Inspector Kollberg? You must call me Åsa, because I'm going to say Martin and Lennart to you. You see, I know you both quite well, in a way." She gave them a mischievous look and added, "Through Åke. He and I saw quite a lot of each other. We've lived here for several years."

Kollberg and Beck, undertakers, thought Martin Beck. Pull your socks up. The girl's okay.

"We've heard about you, too," Kollberg said in a lighter tone.

Åsa went over and opened a window. Then she took the ashtray out into the kitchen. Her smile was gone and her face had a set look. She came back with a new ashtray and curled up again in the chair. "Would you mind telling me just what happened?" she said. "I wasn't told much yesterday and I'm not going to read the papers."

Martin Beck lighted a cigarette. "Okay," he said.

She sat quite still, never taking her eyes off him while he related the course of events as far as they had been able to reconstruct it. When he had finished Åsa said, "Why was Åke on that bus at all?"

Kollberg glanced at Martin Beck and said, "That's what we were hoping you would be able to tell us."

Åsa Torell shook her head. "I've no idea."

"Do you know what he was doing earlier in the day?" Martin Beck asked.

She looked at him in surprise. "He was working all day. Surely you ought to know what he was doing?"

Martin Beck hesitated a moment. Then he said, "The last time I saw him alive was on Friday. He was at headquarters for a while in the morning."

She got up and paced about. Then she turned around.

"But he was working both on Saturday and on Monday. We left here together on Monday morning. Didn't *you* see Åke on Monday?" She stared at Kollberg, who shook his head.

"Did you say he worked on Saturday, too?" Martin Beck asked.

She nodded.

"Yes, but not all day. We left here together in the morning and I finished at one and came straight home. Åke got home not long after. He had done the shopping. On Sunday he was free. We spent the whole day together."

She went back to the armchair and sat down, clasped her hands around her drawn-up knees and bit her underlip.

"Didn't he tell you what he was working on?" Kollberg asked.

Åsa shook her head.

"Didn't he usually tell you?" Martin Beck asked.

"Oh, yes. We told each other everything. But he said nothing about this last job. I thought it was funny he didn't talk to me about it. He always used to discuss the different cases. But perhaps he wasn't allowed—" She broke off and raised her voice. "Anyway, why are you asking me? You were his superiors. If you're trying to find out whether he told me any police secrets, then I can assure you he didn't. He didn't say one word about his job during the last three weeks."

"Perhaps it was because he didn't have anything special to tell you about," Kollberg said soothingly. "The last three weeks have been unusually uneventful and we've had very little to do."

Åsa looked hard at him. "How can you say that? Åke, at any rate, had a lot to do. He was working practically night and day."

Chapter Four

RÖNN LOOKED at his watch and yawned.

He glanced at the wheeled stretcher and the person who lay there, bandaged beyond description. Then he regarded the complex apparatus that was apparently necessary to keep the injured man alive, and the middle-aged nurse who was deftly changing one of the rigged-up bottles.

Rönn sighed and yawned again behind his face mask. He had spent far too many hours here at Karolinska Hospital in this antiseptic ward with its cold light and bare white walls.

Moreover, for most of the time he had been in the company of a plainclothes detective called Ullholm, who even to someone with Rönn's uncritical outlook, stood out as a monster of nagging tedium and reactionary stupidity.

Ullholm was dissatisfied with everything, from his salary grade, which not surprisingly was too low, to the police commissioner, who hadn't the sense to take strong measures.

He was indignant that children were not taught manners at school and that discipline was too slack within the police force.

He was particularly virulent about three categories of citizens who had never caused Rönn any headaches or worry: foreigners, teenagers and socialists.

He put the great increase of crime down to the fact that the police were not given proper military training and no longer wore sabers. He thought it was a scandal that police patrolmen were allowed to have beards.

"A mustache at the very most," he said. "But even that is extremely questionable. You see what I mean, don't you?"

Rönn saw only two things.

First: what had happened at headquarters when he had asked the innocent question, "Who's on duty at the hospital?" and Kollberg had said, "Someone called Ullholm." Gunvald Larsson had exclaimed, "Ullholm! It must be stopped! We'll have to send someone to look after him. Someone more or less sane."

Rönn had turned out to be this more or less sane person. Still just as innocently, he had asked, "Am I to relieve him?"

"Relieve him? No, that's impossible. He'll think then that he's been slighted. He'll write hundreds of petitions. Call up the Minister of Justice."

And as Rönn was on the way out, Gunvald Larsson had given him a last instruction: "Einar! Don't let Ullholm say one word to the witness until you've seen the death certificate."

Second: Rönn had seen that he must in some way dam up Ullholm's spate of words. At last he found a solution. It worked as follows:

Ullholm wound up a long declaration by saying, "It goes quite without saying that as a citizen in a free democratic country, I don't make the slightest discrimination among people on account of color, race or opinions. But *you* just imagine a police force swarming with foreigners and socialists. You see what I mean, don't you?"

Whereupon Rönn cleared his throat modestly behind his mask and said, "Yes. But as a matter of fact, I myself am married to a Lapp girl and am one of those socialists, so . . ."

Ullholm wrapped himself in sepulchral silence and went over to the window. He had been standing there now for two hours, grimly staring out at the treacherous world surrounding him.

Schwerin had been operated on three times; both the bullets

had been removed from his body but none of the doctors looked particularly cheerful.

Then about a quarter of an hour ago one of the surgeons had come into the isolation ward and said, "If he is going to regain consciousness at all, it should be within the next half hour."

"Will he pull through?"

The doctor gave Rönn a long look and said, "It seems unlikely. He has a good physique, of course, and his general condition is fairly satisfactory."

Rönn looked down at the patient dejectedly, wondering just how a person should look before his general condition could be regarded as just plain bad.

He had carefully thought out two questions, which for safety's sake he had written down in his notebook.

The first one was:

Who did the shooting?

And the second:

What did he look like?

He had also made one or two other preparations: set up his portable transistor tape recorder on a chair at the head of the bed, plugged in the microphone and hung it over the chairback. Ullholm had not taken part in these preparations, contenting himself with an occasional critical glance at Rönn from his place over by the window.

Suddenly the nurse bent over the injured man and beckoned the two policemen with a swift, impatient gesture.

Rönn hurried over and seized the microphone.

"I think he's waking up," the nurse said.

The injured man's face seemed to undergo some sort of change. A quiver passed through his eyelids and nostrils.

"Yes," the nurse said. "Now."

Rönn held out the microphone.

"Who did the shooting?" he asked. No reaction. After a moment Rönn repeated the question. "Who did the shooting?"

Now the man's lips moved and he said something. Rönn waited only two seconds before saying, "What did he look like?"

The injured man reacted again and this time the answer was more articulated.

A doctor entered the room.

Rönn had just opened his mouth to repeat question number two when Schwerin turned his head to the left, and his lower jaw slipped down.

Rönn looked up at the doctor, who consulted his instruments and nodded gravely.

Ullholm came up to Rönn and snapped, "Is that really all you can get out of this questioning?" Then he said in a loud, bullying voice, "Now listen to me, my good man, this is Detective Inspector Ullholm speaking—"

"He's dead," Rönn said quietly.

Ullholm stared at him and uttered one word: "Bungler."

Rönn pulled out the microphone plug and took the tape recorder over to the window. He turned the spool back cautiously with his forefinger and pressed the playback button.

> *"Who did the shooting?"*
> *"Dnrk."*
> *"What did he look like?"*
> *"Koleson."*

"What do you make of this?" he asked.

Ullholm glared at Rönn and said, "Make of it? I'm going to report you for breach of duty. It can't be helped. You see what I mean, don't you?"

He turned on his heel and strode energetically from the room.

AN ICY GUST of wind whipped a shower of needle-sharp snow against Martin Beck as he opened the main door of Police Headquarters. He lowered his head to the wind and hurriedly buttoned his overcoat. That morning he had at last capitulated to the freezing temperature and put on his winter coat. Pulling the woolen scarf higher around his neck, he started walking toward the center of town.

A car pulled up beside him. Gunvald Larsson wound the side

window down and called, "Jump in." Martin Beck gratefully settled himself into the front seat.

"What horrible weather. You hardly have time to notice there's been a summer when the winter starts all over again. Where are you off to?"

"Västmannagatan," Gunvald Larsson replied. "I'm going up to have a talk with that daughter of the old girl in the bus."

"Good," said Martin Beck. "You can let me off outside Sabbatsberg Hospital."

Minute grains of snow swirled up against the windshield. "This sort of snow is utterly useless," Gunvald Larsson said. "It doesn't even lie. Just flies about blocking the view."

On the way they overtook a double-decker bus on route 47.

"Ugh!" Martin Beck exclaimed. "From now on we'll feel ill at the very sight of one of those buses."

After a minute or so Larsson said, "Are you coming with me to see Assarsson's wife? The guy with the whisky. I'm to be there at three o'clock. It's only one block away from Sabbatsberg. Then I can drive you back afterward."

"It depends when I finish with that nurse."

Martin Beck got out of the car in front of the entrance nearest the maternity ward. As he approached he saw a woman in a sheepskin coat peering out at him through the glass doors. She came out and said, "Superintendent Beck? I'm Monika Granholm, Britt's roommate."

She seized his hand in an iron grip and squeezed it passionately. He almost seemed to hear the bones of his hand crunch and he hoped that she didn't exert the same strength when handling newborn babies.

She was almost as tall as Martin Beck and considerably larger. Everything about her radiated health and strength. The dead girl in the bus had been small and delicate and must have looked very fragile beside this roommate.

"Do you mind if we go to the restaurant just across the street?" Monika Granholm asked. "I must have something inside me before I can talk."

Martin Beck chose a window table, but Monika Granholm preferred to sit farther inside.

"I don't want anyone from the hospital to see us," she said. "You've no idea how they gossip."

She confirmed this by regaling Martin Beck with hospital stories while she set to work on a mountainous helping of meatballs and mashed potatoes. Martin Beck watched her enviously under lowered lids. As usual he was not hungry, only slightly sick. He was about to lead the conversation around to her dead colleague when she pushed her plate away and said, "That's better. Now you can fire away with your questions, and I'll try to answer as well as I can. What do you want to know about Britt?"

"How well did you know her? How long had you two been sharing an apartment?"

"I knew her better than anyone, I should think. We've been roommates for three years, ever since she started here. She was the world's best pal and a very capable nurse. Although she was delicate she worked hard. Never spared herself."

She took the coffeepot and filled Martin Beck's cup.

"Thank you," he said. "Did she have a boyfriend?"

"Oh yes, an awfully nice fellow. I've an idea they were going to get married in the new year."

"Had they known each other long?"

She bit her thumbnail and thought hard. "Ten months at least. He's a doctor. They say girls take up nursing just for the chance of marrying doctors, but it wasn't so with Britt anyway. She was awfully shy, and scared of men, if anything. Then she went on the sick list last winter, she was anemic and generally run-down, and she had to go for a checkup pretty often. That's how she met Bertil Persson. It was love at first sight. She used to say it was his love that made her well, not his treatment."

Martin Beck sighed resignedly. "Did she know many men?"

Monika Granholm smiled and shook her head. "Only the ones she met at the hospital. She was very reserved. I don't think Britt had ever been with a man until she met Bertil."

She drew patterns on the table with her finger. Then she

frowned and looked at Martin Beck. "Is it her love life you're interested in? What's that got to do with it?"

Martin Beck took his wallet out of his breast pocket and laid it in front of him on the table. "Beside Britt Danielsson in the bus sat a man. That man was a policeman and his name was Åke Stenström. What we're interested to know is this: Did Miss Danielsson ever mention the name of Åke Stenström?" He took Stenström's photograph out of the wallet and put it in front of Monika Granholm. "Have you ever seen this man?"

She looked at the photo and shook her head. Then she picked it up and studied it more closely.

"Yes," she said. "In the papers. Though this picture's better."

Handing back the photograph, she said, "Britt didn't know that man. I can almost swear to that. And it's quite out of the question that she would have allowed anyone but her fiancé to see her home. She just wasn't that type."

Martin Beck put the wallet back in his pocket.

"They may have been friends and—"

She shook her head vigorously.

"Britt was very correct, very shy and, as I said, almost afraid of men. Besides, she was head over heels in love with Bertil and would never have looked at another fellow. Neither as a friend nor anything else."

Opening her handbag, she took out her purse.

"I must get back to my babies. I have seventeen at the moment."

She started poking in her purse but Martin Beck put out his hand and checked her.

"This is on the national government," he said. He held out his hand with some hesitation and for safety's sake kept his glove on.

"My regards to the national government and thanks for the lunch," Monika Granholm said and strode out of the restaurant.

GUNVALD LARSSON'S car was parked outside Tegnérgatan 40. Martin Beck looked at his watch and entered the building. The time was twenty minutes past three, which meant that Gunvald

Larsson, who was always punctual, had already been with Mrs. Assarsson for twenty minutes. By this time he had probably found out the main events of her husband's life; Gunvald Larsson's interrogation technique was to begin at the beginning and uncover everything step by step. While the method he used could be effective, often it was merely tiresome and wasted time.

The door of the apartment was opened by a middle-aged man wearing a dark suit with a silver-white tie. Martin Beck introduced himself and showed his official badge. The man held out his hand. "I'm Ture Assarsson, brother of the . . . of the dead man. Please come in, your colleague is already here."

He waited while Martin Beck hung up his overcoat and then led the way through a pair of tall double doors.

"Märta, my dear, this is Superintendent Beck," he said.

The living room was large and rather dark. On a low, oat-colored sofa sat a lean woman in a black jersey coat and skirt, with a glass in her hand. Putting the glass down on a black marble table in front of the sofa, she held out her hand with gracefully bent wrist, as though expecting him to kiss it. Martin Beck took her dangling fingers clumsily and mumbled, "My condolences, Mrs. Assarsson."

On the other side of the marble table stood a group of three low easy chairs, and in one of them sat Gunvald Larsson, looking peculiar. Only when Martin Beck sat down himself did he realize Gunvald Larsson's problem. As the construction of the chair really permitted only an outstretched horizontal position, Gunvald Larsson had more or less folded himself double in order to sit up. He was red in the face with discomfort and glared at Martin Beck between his knees, which stuck up like two alpine peaks in front of him.

Martin Beck twisted his legs first to the left, then to the right, then he tried to cross them and wedge them under the chair, but it was too low. At last he adopted the same position as Gunvald Larsson.

"You'll have a glass of sherry, won't you, Superintendent?"

the brother-in-law inquired. And before Martin Beck had time to protest, Ture Assarsson had filled the glass and placed it on the table in front of him.

"I was just asking Mrs. Assarsson if she knew why her husband was on that bus on Monday night," Gunvald Larsson said.

"And I gave the same reply to you as I did to the person who had the bad taste to question me about my husband only seconds after I had been informed of his death. That I don't know."

She raised her glass to Martin Beck and drained it in one gulp. Martin Beck made an attempt to reach his sherry glass but missed by about a foot and fell back into the chair.

"Do you know where your husband was earlier in the evening?" he asked.

Mrs. Assarsson took a cigarette out of a green glass box on the table. She tapped it several times on the lid of the box before allowing her brother-in-law to light it for her. Martin Beck noticed that she was not quite sober.

"Yes, I do," she said. "He was at a meeting. We had dinner at six o'clock, and then he changed and went out about seven."

Gunvald Larsson took a piece of paper and a ball-point pen out of his breast pocket and asked, "A meeting? Where and with whom?"

Assarsson looked at his sister-in-law and when she didn't answer he said, "It was an organization of old school friends. They called themselves the Camels. It consisted of nine members, who had kept in touch ever since they were at the naval cadet school together. They used to meet at the home of a businessman called Sjöberg on Narvavägen."

"The Camels?" Gunvald Larsson exclaimed incredulously.

"Yes," Assarsson replied. "They used to greet each other by saying, 'Hi, old camel,' so they took to calling themselves the Camels."

The widow looked critically at her brother-in-law.

"It's an idealistic association," she said. "It does a lot for charity."

"Oh?" Gunvald Larsson said. "As for instance?"

"It's a secret," Mrs. Assarsson replied. "Not even we wives were allowed to know."

Feeling Gunvald Larsson's eyes on him, Martin Beck said, "Mrs. Assarsson, do you know when your husband left the meeting?"

"Well, I couldn't get to sleep, so I got up about two o'clock in the morning to take a little nightcap, and when I saw that Gösta hadn't come home I called up the Screw—that's what they call Mr. Sjöberg—and the Screw said that Gösta had left about half past ten."

She stubbed out her cigarette.

"Where do you *think* he was going with the 47 bus?" Martin Beck asked.

Assarsson gave him an anxious look.

"He was on his way to some business acquaintance, of course," Mrs. Assarsson replied. "My husband was very energetic and worked very hard with his firm—that's to say, Ture here is also part-owner, of course—and it wasn't at all unusual for him to have business dealings at night. For instance, when people came up from the provinces and were only in Stockholm overnight . . ."

She seemed to lose the thread. She picked up her empty glass and put it in front of her brother-in-law to be refilled, but he immediately took it to the sideboard without looking at her. She gave him a resentful look, stood up with an effort and brushed some cigarette ash off her skirt. Martin Beck could see now that she was pretty well stewed.

"If Superintendents Peck and Larsson will excuse me, I must retire," Mrs. Assarsson said, walking unsteadily toward the door. "Good-by, it's been *so* nice," she said vaguely and closed the door behind her.

Gunvald Larsson put away his pen and struggled out of the chair.

"Who was he having an affair with?" he asked, without looking at Assarsson.

Assarsson glanced at the closed door.

"Eivor Olsson," he replied. "A girl at the office."

Chapter Five

THERE WAS LITTLE good to be said of this repulsive Wednesday.

Not surprisingly, the evening papers had ferreted out the story of Schwerin, splashing it across the front pages and larding it with details and sarcastic gibes at the police. The police had smuggled away the only important witness to the mass murder. The police had lied to the press and the public. If the press and the public were not given correct information, how could the police count on help? The only thing the papers didn't say was that Schwerin had died, but that was probably only because they had been so early going to press.

Unhappily, too, the mass murder had coincided with a raid—decided on several weeks earlier—on kiosks and tobacco shops in an attempt to confiscate pornographic literature. One of the newspapers was kind enough to point out in a prominent place that while a maniac mass murderer was running amok in town a whole army of Swedish Keystone Cops were plodding about scratching their heads and trying to make out what could be considered offensive to public decency.

When Kollberg arrived at headquarters at about four o'clock in the afternoon, he had ice crystals in his hair and eyebrows, a grim expression on his face and the evening papers under his arm. "If we had as many stoolies as local rags, we'd never have to lift a finger," he said.

"It's a question of money," Melander said.

"I know that. Does that make it any better?"

"No," Melander said. He knocked out his pipe and returned to the papers.

"Have you finished talking to the psychologists?" Kollberg asked sourly.

"Yes," Melander replied without looking up. "The compendium is being typed out."

A new face was to be seen at investigation headquarters. An officer named Per Månsson had arrived from Malmö to help with the investigation. Månsson was almost as big as Gunvald Larsson but he showed a much more peaceable front to the world. He was standing now by the window, gazing out and chewing at a toothpick.

"Is there anything I can do?" he asked.

"Yes. There are one or two people we haven't had time to interrogate yet. Here, for instance. Mrs. Esther Källström. She is the widow of one of the victims."

"Johan Källström, the foreman?"

"Precisely. Karlbergsvägen 89."

"Where's Karlbergsvägen?"

"There's a map on the wall over there," Kollberg said wearily.

Despite all newspaper statements to the contrary, the public was hard at work on the case during the afternoon. Several hundred people called up or looked in to say they thought they had ridden on that very bus. All these statements had to be ground through the investigation mill and for once this tedious work turned out to be not entirely wasted.

A man who had boarded a double-decker bus about ten o'clock on Monday evening said he was willing to swear that he had seen Stenström. He said this on the telephone and he was passed along to Melander, who immediately asked him to come up.

The man was about fifty. He seemed quite sure.

"So you saw Detective Inspector Stenström?"

"Yes."

"Where?"

"When I got on at Djurgården Bridge. He was sitting on the left near the stairs behind the driver."

"Are you sure it was Stenström?"

"Yes."

"How do you know?"

"I recognized him. I've been a night watchman."

"Yes," Melander said. "A couple of years ago you sat in the vestibule of the old police headquarters on Agnegatan. I remember you."

"Why, so I did," the man said in astonishment. "But I don't recognize you."

"I only saw you twice," Melander replied. "And we didn't speak to each other."

"But I remember Stenström very well, because . . ." He hesitated. "Well, he looked so young, and he was wearing jeans and a sport shirt, so I thought he didn't belong at headquarters. I asked him to prove his identity. And . . ."

"Yes?"

"About a week later I made the same mistake. Very annoying."

"Oh, well, it easily happens. When you saw him the night before last, did he recognize you?"

"No, definitely not."

"Was anyone sitting beside him?"

"No, the seat was empty. I remember particularly, because I thought I'd say hello to him and sit there. But then I felt sort of awkward."

"Pity," Melander said. "And you got off at Sergels Torg?"

"Yes, I changed to the subway."

"Was Stenström still there?"

"I think so. I hadn't seen him get off at any rate. Though of course I was sitting upstairs."

"Would you like a cup of coffee?"

"Well, I don't mind if I do," the man said.

"Would you be good enough to look at some pictures?" Melander asked. "But I'm afraid they're not very pleasant."

The man looked through the pictures, turning pale and swallowing once or twice. But the only person he recognized was Stenström.

Not long afterward Martin Beck, Gunvald Larsson and Rönn arrived practically at the same time.

"What?" said Kollberg. "Has Schwerin . . . ?"

"Yes," Rönn said. "He's dead."

"And?"

"He said something."

"What?"

"Don't know," Rönn replied, placing the tape recorder on the desk. They stood around the desk listening.

"Who did the shooting?"
"Dnrk."
"What did he look like?"
"Koleson."
"Is that really all you can get out of this questioning? Now listen to me, my good man, this is Detective Inspector Ullholm speaking—"
"He's dead."

"My God," Gunvald Larsson exclaimed. "The very sound of Ullholm's voice makes me want to throw up."

Martin Beck played back the tape.

"Are the questions your own idea?" Gunvald Larsson asked.

"Yes," Rönn replied modestly.

"Fantastic."

"He was only conscious for half a minute," Rönn said in a hurt tone. "Then he died."

They listened to the tape over and over again.

"What on earth does he say?" Kollberg said.

Martin Beck turned to Rönn. "What do you think?" he said. "You were there."

"Well," Rönn said, "I think he understands the questions and is trying to answer. That he answers the first question in the negative, for instance, 'I don't know.' "

"How the hell do you make that out of 'Dnrk'?" Gunvald Larsson asked in astonishment.

Rönn reddened and shifted his weight from one foot to the other. "Well, I just sort of got that impression."

"Hm-m," Gunvald Larsson said. "And then?"

"To the second question he answers quite plainly 'Koleson.' "

"So I hear," Kollberg said. "But what does he mean?"

Martin Beck massaged his scalp with his fingertips. "Karsson, perhaps," he said, thinking hard.

"He says 'Koleson,' " Rönn maintained stubbornly.

"Yes," said Kollberg. "But there's no one with that name."

"We'd better check," Melander said. "The name *might* exist. Meanwhile . . ."

"Yes?"

"Meanwhile I think we ought to send this tape to an expert for analysis. Sound technicians can separate the sounds on the tape and try out different speeds."

"Yes," Martin Beck said. "It's a good idea."

"But wipe out Ullholm first," Gunvald Larsson growled, "or we'll be the laughingstock of all Sweden." He looked around the room. "Where's that joker Månsson?"

"Got lost, I expect," Kollberg said. "We'd better alert all the patrol cars." He sighed heavily.

Ek came in, stroking his silver hair, a worried look on his face.

"What is it?" Martin Beck asked.

"The newspapers are complaining they haven't been given a picture of that man who is still unidentified."

"You know yourself what that picture would look like," Kollberg said.

"Sure, but—"

"Wait a minute," Melander said. "We can better the description. Between thirty-five and forty, height 5 feet 7 inches, weight 152 pounds, shoe size 8½, brown eyes, dark brown hair. Scar from an appendicitis operation. Brown hair on chest and stomach. Scar from some old injury on the ankle."

"I'll send it out," Ek said and left the room.

They stood in silence for a while.

"Melander has got hold of something," said Kollberg. "That Stenström was already sitting in the bus when it got to Djurgården Bridge. So he must have come from Djurgården."

"What the hell was he doing there?" said Gunvald Larsson. "In the evening? In that weather?"

"I've also got hold of something," said Martin Beck. "That apparently he didn't know that nurse at all."

"Rönn has also come up with something," said Gunvald Larsson.

"What?"

"That 'Dnrk' means 'I don't know.' To say nothing of this guy Koleson."

This was as far as they got on Wednesday, the fifteenth of November.

Of course there was no one called Koleson. At least not in Sweden.

On Thursday they didn't get anywhere.

WHEN KOLLBERG got home to his apartment on Thursday evening the time was already past eleven o'clock. His wife sat reading in the circle of light under the floor lamp. She was dressed in a housecoat that buttoned in front, and sat curled up in the armchair with her bare legs drawn up under her.

"Hello," said Kollberg. "How is your Spanish course going?"

"To the dogs, of course. Absurd to imagine you can do anything at all when you're married to a policeman."

Kollberg made no reply to this. Instead he went into the bathroom, shaved and took a long shower, hoping that some stupid neighbor wouldn't call up to complain of the water running so late. Then, putting on his bathrobe, he went into the living room and sat down opposite his wife. He regarded her thoughtfully.

"Haven't seen you for ages," she said without raising her eyes. "How are you all getting on?"

"Badly."

"I *am* sorry. It seems odd that someone can shoot nine people dead in a bus in the middle of town just like that."

"Yes," Kollberg said. "It is odd."

"Is there anyone else besides you who hasn't been home for thirty-six hours?"

"Probably."

She went on reading. He sat in silence for some time, perhaps ten or fifteen minutes, without taking his eyes off her.

"What are you goggling at?" she asked, still without looking up but with a note of mischief in her voice.

Kollberg didn't answer, and she appeared to be more deeply engrossed in her reading than ever. She had dark hair and brown eyes, her features were regular and her eyebrows thick. She was fourteen years younger than he was and had just turned twenty-nine, and he had always thought she was very pretty. At last he said, "Gun?"

For the first time since he came home she looked at him, with a faint smile and a glint of sensuality in her eyes. "Yes?"

"Stand up."

"Why, certainly."

She shut the book and laid it on the arm of the chair, then stood up and let her arms hang loosely, her bare feet wide apart. She looked at him steadily.

"Strip," he said.

Raising her right hand to her neckband, she undid the buttons, slowly and one by one. Still without taking her eyes off him she opened the thin cotton housecoat and let it fall to the floor behind her.

"Turn around," said Kollberg.

She turned her back to him.

"You are beautiful."

She turned around and looked at him with the same expression on her face as before.

Kollberg looked at her thoughtfully. "Supposing I wanted to take your photograph like that?" he said. "What would you say?"

"What do you mean by like that? Naked?"

"Yes."

"You don't even have a camera."

"No, but that's neither here nor there."

"Of course you can if you want to. What are you going to do with the pictures anyway?"

"That's just the question."

She went up to him. Then she said, "And now do you mind if I ask what the hell this is all about?"

"Stenström had a bundle of pictures like that in the drawer of his desk."

"At the office?"

"Yes."

"Of whom?"

"His girl."

"Åsa?"

"Yes."

She looked at him and frowned.

"The question is, why?" he said.

"Does it matter?"

"I don't know. I can't explain it."

"Perhaps he just wanted to look at them."

"That's what Martin said."

"It seems much more sensible, of course, to go home and have a look now and again."

"Of course. Something doesn't add up," Kollberg said.

"Why? You know how men are. Was she attractive in the pictures?"

"Yes."

"So far as Stenström is concerned, he probably wanted to show them to his pals. To boast."

"It doesn't add up. He wasn't like that."

"Why are you worrying about this?"

"Don't know. I suppose because there are no other clues left."

"Do you call this a clue? Do you think someone shot Stenström because of these pictures? In that case why should he kill eight more people?"

Kollberg looked at her intently. "Exactly. That's a good question."

Bending over, she kissed him lightly on the forehead.

"Let's go to bed," Kollberg said.

"A brilliant idea. I'll just make a bottle for Bodil first. It only takes thirty seconds. According to the directions on the package."

She went out into the kitchen. Kollberg got up and turned off the floor lamp. He watched his wife through the half-open kitchen door. She was standing at the counter by the sink, impatiently stirring the saucepan. His wife was exactly what he wanted, but it had taken him over twenty years to find her and another year to think it over.

"Thirty seconds," she muttered to herself. "Liars."

MARTIN BECK had met his wife seventeen years ago, married in haste and repented at leisure. Now she was standing at the bedroom door, a living reminder of his mistake, in a crumpled nightdress and with red marks from the pillow on her face.

"Why do you lie there smoking and coughing in the middle of the night?" she said. "Your throat's bad enough as it is."

Stubbing out the cigarette, he said, "I'm sorry if I woke you."

"Oh, it doesn't matter. The main thing is that you don't go and get pneumonia again. Besides, you should be asleep and not reading those old reports. You'll never clear up that taxi murder anyhow. It's half past one. Leave that old pile of papers alone and put the light out. Good night."

"Good night," Martin Beck said mechanically to the closed bedroom door.

Frowning, he slowly put the report down. It was quite wrong to call it an old pile of papers; it was a copy of the postmortem reports handed to him just as he was going home the evening before. It was true, however, that a few months earlier he had lain awake at night going through the investigation into the murder of a taxi driver twelve years before.

He lay still for a while, staring up at the ceiling. When he heard his wife's light snoring from the bedroom, he got up swiftly and tiptoed out into the hall. He hesitated a moment with his hand on the telephone. Then he shrugged, lifted the receiver and dialed Kollberg's number.

"Kollberg," Gun said breathlessly.

"Hi. Is Lennart there?"

"Yes. Closer than you'd think."

"What is it?" Kollberg muttered.

"Am I disturbing you?"

"You might say that. What the hell is it now?"

"Do you remember last summer, just after the park murders?"

"Yes, what?"

"We had nothing special to do then and Hammar said we were to look through old unsolved cases. Remember?"

"Of course, I damn well remember. What about it?"

"I went through the taxi murder and you worked on that old boy at Östermalm who simply disappeared seven years ago."

"Yes. Are you calling up just to say that?"

"No. What was Stenström working on? He had just got back from his vacation then."

"I haven't the vaguest idea. I thought he told you."

"No, he never mentioned it to me."

"Then he must have told Hammar."

"Yes. Yes, of course. Yes, you're right. So long then. Sorry I woke you up."

"Go to hell."

Martin Beck heard him bang the receiver down. He stood with the phone to his ear for a few seconds before putting it down and slouching back to the sofa bed. He lay down again feeling he had made a fool of himself.

CONTRARY TO ALL expectations, Friday morning brought a hopeful scrap of news.

Martin Beck received it by telephone and the others heard him say, "What! Have you? Really?"

Everyone in the room dropped what he was doing and stared at him. Putting down the receiver, he said, "They're through with the ballistic investigation."

"And?"

"They think they've identified the weapon."

"Oh," Kollberg said listlessly.

"A submachine gun," Gunvald Larsson said. "The army has thousands lying about in unguarded military depots. Might just as well deal them out free to the thieves and save themselves the trouble of putting on new padlocks once a week."

"It's not quite what you all think," Martin Beck said, holding the slip of paper he had scribbled on. "Model 37, Suomi type."

"Really?" Melander asked.

"That old kind with the wooden butt," Gunvald Larsson said. "I haven't see one like that since the forties."

"Made in Finland or made here under license?" Kollberg asked.

"Finnish," Martin Beck said. "The guy who called up said they were almost sure."

"M 37," Kollberg said. "With 70-shot ammunition drum. Who is likely to have one today?"

"Some mad Finn," Gunvald Larsson growled. "Out with the dog wagon and round up all the crazy Finns in town. A helluva nice job."

"Shall we say anything of this to the papers?" Kollberg asked.

"No," said Martin Beck. "Not a whisper."

The door was flung open and a young man came in and looked about him in curiosity. He had a brown envelope in his hand.

"Whom are you looking for?" Kollberg asked.

"Melander," the youth said.

"Detective Inspector Melander," Kollberg said, a reprimand in his tone. "He's sitting over there."

The young man went over and put the envelope on Melander's desk. As he was about to leave the room, Kollberg added, "I didn't hear you knock."

The youth checked himself, his hand on the door handle, but said nothing. There was silence in the room. Then Kollberg said slowly and distinctly, as though explaining something to a child, "Before entering a room, you knock at the door. Then you wait until you are told to come in. Then you open the door and enter. Is that clear?"

"Yes," the young man mumbled, staring at Kollberg's feet.

"Good," Kollberg said, turning his back on him.

The young man slunk out of the door, closing it silently behind him.

"Who was that?" Gunvald Larsson asked. Kollberg shrugged. "Reminded me of Stenström actually," Gunvald Larsson said.

Melander put down his pipe, opened the envelope and drew out some typewritten sheets bound in green covers. The booklet was about half an inch thick.

"What's that?" Martin Beck asked.

Melander glanced through it. "The psychologists' compendium," he replied. "I've had it bound."

"A-ha," Gunvald Larsson said. "And what brilliant theories have they come up with? That our poor mass murderer was once put off a bus during puberty because he couldn't pay his fare and that this experience left such deep scars—"

Martin Beck cut him short. "That is not amusing, Gunvald," he snapped.

Kollberg gave him a surprised glance and turned to Melander. "Well, Fredrik, what have you got out of that little opus?"

Melander emptied his pipe. "We have no Swedish precedent," he said. "Unless we go back as far as the Nordlund massacre on the steamer *Prins Carl*. So they've had to base their research on American surveys that have been made during the last few decades." He blew at his pipe to see if it was clear, and filled it again.

"Mass murders seem to be an American specialty," Gunvald Larsson said.

"Yes," Melander agreed. "And the compendium gives some plausible theories as to why it is so."

"The glorification of violence," said Kollberg. "The career-centered society. The sale of firearms by mail order."

"Among other things," Melander said.

"What do your psychologists have to say about the mass murderer's character?" Kollberg asked.

Melander turned the pages to a certain passage and read out:

"He is probably under thirty, often shy and reserved but regarded by those around him as well behaved and diligent. It is possible that he drinks liquor, but it is more usual for him to be a teetotaler. He is likely to be small of stature or afflicted with disfigurement or some other physical deformity that sets him apart from ordinary people. He plays an insignificant part in the community and has grown up in straitened circumstances. In many cases his parents have been divorced or he is an orphan and has had an emotionally starved childhood. Often he has not previously committed any serious crime."

Raising his eyes, he said, "This is based on a compilation of facts that have emerged from interrogations and mental examinations of American mass murderers."

"A mass murderer like this must be stark, raving mad," Gunvald Larsson said. "Can't people *see* that before he rushes out and kills a bunch of people?"

Melander continued reading:

"A person who is a psychopath can appear quite normal until the moment when something happens to trigger off his abnormality. Psychopathy implies that one or more of this person's traits are abnormally developed, while in other respects he is quite normal. And in fact, most of these people who have suddenly committed a mass murder, apparently without any motive, are described by neighbors and friends as considerate, kind and polite, and the last people on earth one would expect to act in this manner. Several of these American cases have told that they have been aware of their disease for some time and have tried to suppress their destructive tendencies, until at last they gave way to them. It is not unusual for the murderer to explain his actions by saying simply that he wanted to become famous and see his name in big headlines. Almost always, a desire for revenge or self-assertion lies behind the crime. He feels belittled, misunderstood and badly treated. In almost every case he has great sexual problems."

Månsson entered the room, a toothpick in the corner of his mouth. "What the blazes are you talking about?" he asked.

"Maybe the bus is some sort of sex symbol," Gunvald Larsson said, reflecting. Månsson goggled at him.

Martin Beck got up, went over to Melander and picked up the green booklet. "I'll borrow this and read through it in peace and quiet," he said. "Without any witty comments."

He walked toward the door but was stopped by Månsson, who

took his toothpick out of his mouth and said, "What am I to do now?"

"I don't know. Ask Kollberg," Martin Beck said curtly and left the room.

"You can go and talk to that Arab's landlady," Kollberg said.

He wrote the name and address on a piece of paper, which he gave to Månsson.

"What's bothering Martin?" Gunvald Larsson asked. "Why's he so sore?"

Kollberg shrugged. "I expect he has his reasons," he said.

IT TOOK MÅNSSON a good half hour to make his way through the Stockholm traffic to Norra Stationsgatan. As he parked the car opposite the terminus of bus route 47 the time was a few minutes past four and it was already dark.

On the door below the name Karlsson were eight cards, fastened with thumbtacks. Two of them were printed, the others were written in a variety of hands and all bore foreign names. The name Mohammed Boussie was not among them.

Månsson rang the bell and the door was opened by a swarthy man in wrinkled pants and a white undershirt.

"May I speak to Mrs. Karlsson?" Månsson said.

The man showed white teeth in a broad smile and flung out his arms. "Mrs. Karlsson not home," he said in broken Swedish. "Back soon."

"Then I'll wait here," Månsson said, stepping into the hall. Unbuttoning his coat, he looked at the smiling man. "Did you know Mohammed Boussie who lived here?" he asked.

The smile was wiped off the man's face.

"Yes," he said. "It terrible. Awful."

"Are you an Arab too?" Månsson asked.

"No. Turk."

"I'm a policeman," Månsson said, looking at the man sternly. "I'd like to look around if you don't mind. Is there anyone else at home?"

"No, only me. I sick."

Månsson looked about him. The hall was dark and narrow. On a table lay a couple of newspapers and some letters with foreign stamps. In addition to the front door, there were five doors in the hall; two of these, smaller than the others, probably belonged to a toilet and a clothes closet. One of them was a double door; Månsson went over to it and opened one half.

"Mrs. Karlsson's private room," the man in the undershirt cried out in alarm. "To go in, forbidden."

Månsson glanced into the room, which was cluttered with furniture and evidently served as both bedroom and living room.

The next door led to the kitchen, which was large and had been modernized.

"Forbidden to go in kitchen," said the Turk behind him.

"How many rooms are there?" Månsson asked.

"Mrs. Karlsson's and the kitchen and the room for us," said the man. "And the toilet and closet."

Månsson frowned.

"Two rooms and kitchen, that is," he said to himself.

"You look our room," the Turk said, holding open the door.

The room measured about 23 feet by 16. It had two windows onto the street with flimsy, faded curtains. Along the walls stood beds of various types and between the windows was a narrow couch. Månsson counted six beds. Three of them were unmade. The room was littered with shoes, clothes, newspapers and books. The center of the floor was occupied by a round, white-lacquered table, surrounded by five chairs. The remaining piece of furniture was a tall, dark-stained chest of drawers, which stood against the wall by one of the windows.

The room had two more doors. A bed was placed in front of one of them, which without doubt led to Mrs. Karlsson's room and was locked. Inside the other was a small closet, stuffed with clothes and suitcases.

"Do six of you sleep here?" Månsson asked.

"No, eight," the Turk replied.

He walked over to the bed in front of the door, half drew out a trundle bed and pointed to one of the other beds.

"Two like this," he said. "Mohammed had that one."

"Who are the others?" Månsson asked. "Turks like you?"

"No, we three Turks, two—one Aràb, two Spanish men, one Finnish man, and the new one, he Greek."

"Do you eat here too?"

"No, cooking forbidden. Forbidden to use kitchen, forbidden to have electric hot plate in room. We not allowed to cook, not allowed to make coffee."

"How much rent do you pay?"

"We pay 350 kronor each," said the Turk.

"A month?"

"Yes. I earn lot of money," he said. "One hundred seventy kronor a week. I am truck driver."

"Do you know whether Mohammed Boussie had any relations?" Månsson asked. "Parents or brothers and sisters?"

The Turk shook his head.

"No, I do not know. We were much pals, but Mohammed did not say much. He very shy."

"Shy, uh-huh," Månsson said. "Do you know how long he lived here?"

The Turk sat down on the couch between the windows and shook his head. "No, I do not know. I come here last month and Mohammed—he already live here."

"When will Mrs. Karlsson be back?"

The Turk shrugged. "I do not know. Soon."

Månsson stuck a toothpick in his mouth and sat down at the round table and waited. The Turk threw himself on the couch and began leafing idly through a German magazine. Månsson kept looking at his watch. He had made up his mind not to wait a minute longer than half past five.

At twenty-eight minutes past five Mrs. Karlsson returned.

She placed Månsson on her best sofa, offered him a glass of port and began recounting her trials as a landlady.

"It's not at all nice, I can tell you, for a poor lone woman to have the house full of men," she whined. "And foreigners, what's more. But what is a poor hard-up widow to do?"

Månsson made a rough estimate. The hard-up widow raked in nearly 3,000 kronor a month in rent.

"That Mohammed," she said, pursing her lips. "He owed me a month's rent. Perhaps you could arrange for me to get it? He had money in the bank all right."

To Månsson's question about her impression of Mohammed, she replied, "Well, for an Arab he was quite nice, really. They're usually so dirty and unreliable, you know. But he was nice and quiet and seemed to behave himself all right—he didn't drink and I don't think he brought girls in. But as I said, he owes me a month's rent."

She appeared to be well informed about the private lives of her lodgers; Mohammed had a married sister in Paris, who used to send him letters, but she couldn't read them because they were written in Arabic.

Mrs. Karlsson fetched a bundle of letters and gave them to Månsson. All Mohammed Boussie's worldly possessions had been packed into a canvas suitcase. Månsson took this with him as well. Mrs. Karlsson reminded him once more of the unpaid rent before shutting the door after him.

Chapter Six

MONDAY. SNOW. Wind. Bitter cold.

"Fine track snow," Rönn said.

He was standing by the window, looking dreamily out over the street and the rooftops, which were only just visible in the floating white haze.

Gunvald Larsson glared at him suspiciously and said, "Is that meant to be a joke?"

"No. I was just thinking how it felt when I was a boy."

"Extremely constructive. You wouldn't care to do something a little more worthwhile? To help the investigation along?"

"Sure," Rönn said. "But what?"

"Nine people have been murdered," Gunvald Larsson said. "And here you stand not knowing what to do with yourself.

You're a detective, aren't you?"

"What are you doing yourself?"

"Can't you see? I'm sitting here reading this psychological bilge that Melander and the doctors have concocted."

"Why?"

"I don't know. How can I know everything?"

A week had passed since the bloodbath in the bus. The state of the investigation was unchanged and the lack of constructive ideas was making itself felt. Even the spate of useless tips from the general public had begun to dry up.

The consumer society and its harassed citizens had other things to think of. Although it was over a month to Christmas, the advertising orgy had begun and the buying hysteria spread swiftly and ruthlessly along the festooned shopping streets. The police stations downtown had frequent visits from the outriders of the great family festival, in the shape of Santa Clauses who were dragged blind drunk out of doorways. Two exhausted patrolmen dropped a drunken Father Christmas in the gutter when they tried to get him into a taxi.

During the ensuing uproar one of the patrolmen lost his temper when a lump of ice landed in his eye and he resorted to his baton. He hit out at random and struck an inquisitive old-age pensioner. It didn't look pretty and the police-haters were given grist for their mill.

"There's a latent hatred of police in all classes of society," Melander said. "And it needs only an impulse to trigger it off."

"Oh," Kollberg said, with complete lack of interest. "And what is the reason for that?"

"The reason is that the police are a necessary evil," Melander explained. "Everybody knows that they may suddenly find themselves in situations in which only the police can help them. But so long as such situations don't crop up, most people react with either fear or contempt when the police interfere in their existence or disturb their peace of mind."

"Well, that's the last straw, if we have to regard ourselves as a necessary evil," Kollberg muttered despondently.

"The crux of the problem is, of course," Melander went on, quite unconcerned, "that the police profession in itself calls for the highest intelligence and exceptional physical and moral qualities but has nothing to attract persons who possess them."

"You're horrible," Kollberg said.

Martin Beck had heard the argument many times before and was not amused.

"Can't you carry on your sociological discussion somewhere else?" he said grumpily. "I'm trying to think."

And the telephone rang.

"Hello. Beck."

"Hjelm here. How's it going?"

"Between ourselves, badly."

"Have you identified that unknown passenger?"

Martin Beck had known Hjelm for many years and had great confidence in him. Hjelm was considered to be one of the cleverest forensic technicians in the world. If he was handled in the right way.

"No," Martin Beck said. "Nobody seems to miss him." He drew a deep breath and went on. "You don't mean to say you've produced something new?"

Hjelm must be flattered—that was a well-known fact.

"Yes," he said smugly. "We've given him an extra look-over. Tried to build up a more detailed picture. That gives some idea of the living person. I think we've managed to give him a certain character."

Can I say: "You don't mean it"? thought Martin Beck. "You don't mean it," he said.

"Yes, I do," Hjelm said delightedly. "The result's better than we expected."

What should he pile on now? "Fantastic"? "Splendid"? Just plain "Fine"? "Great," he said.

"Thanks," Hjelm replied enthusiastically.

"Don't mention it. I suppose you can't tell me—"

"Oh, sure. That's why I called up. We took a look at his teeth first. The fillings we have found are carelessly done. I don't think they can be the work of a Swedish dentist. I won't say any more on that point."

"That in itself is a good deal."

"Then there's his clothes. We've traced his suit to one of the Hollywood shops here in Stockholm. There are three, as you may know."

"Good," Martin Beck said laconically.

He couldn't play the hypocrite anymore.

"Yes," Hjelm said sourly, "that's what I think. Further, the suit was dirty. It has certainly never been dry-cleaned, and I should think he's worn it day in, day out for a long time."

"How long?"

"A year, at a guess."

"Have you anything more?"

There was a pause. Hjelm had kept the best till last. This was only a rhetorical pause.

"Yes," he said at length. "In the breast pocket of the jacket we found crumbs of hashish, and some grains in the right pants pocket derived from crushed Preludin tablets. The autopsy confirms that the man was a junkie."

Martin Beck finished making his notes, said thank you and put down the phone.

"Reeks of the underworld," Kollberg declared.

He had been standing behind the chair eavesdropping.

"Yes," Martin Beck said. "But his fingerprints are not in our files."

"Perhaps he was a foreigner."

"Quite possibly," Martin Beck agreed. "But what shall we do with this information? We can hardly let it out to the press."

"No," Melander said. "But we can let it circulate by word of mouth among stoolies and known addicts."

"Mm-m," Martin Beck murmured. "Do that then."

Not much use, he thought. But what else was to be done? During the last few days the police had made two spectacular raids on the so-called underworld. The result was exactly what they expected. The raids had been foreseen by all except those

A NO-NONSENSE BEST-FOR-LESS MONEY-SAVING OFFER!

TV GUIDE TV GUIDE TV GUIDE TV GUIDE TV GUIDE TV GUIDE

Now – let us put your name on the cover of TV GUIDE – and Canada's favorite TV Magazine will be delivered right to your door each week. Save as much as $9.76 - 29% **off** single copy price.

Just check the subscription term you prefer, fill out and mail. We'll even pay postage . . . . and bill you later.

YES! DELIVER TV GUIDE TO MY HOUSE AS FOLLOWS:

☐ **35 WEEKS – $23.49**

I save $9.76 off the single copy price

☐ **26 WEEKS – $17.49**

I save $7.21 off the single copy price

J831B

PLEASE PRINT

NAME _____

ADDRESS _____

CITY _____ PROV. _____ CODE _____

GUARANTEE
If you are not satisfied with TV Guide for any reason simply cancel and receive a full and immediate refund on all undelivered copies.

Offer subject to change without notice.

who were most broken-down and destitute. The majority of those who had been picked up by the police—about one hundred and fifty—had been in need of immediate care and could be passed on to various institutions. The detectives who handled the contacts with the dregs of society said they were convinced the stoolies really didn't know anything about the mass murderer. Everything seemed to bear this out. No one could reasonably gain anything by shielding this criminal.

The only thing the police could do was to work on the material they already had. Try to trace the weapon and go on interrogating all who had had any connection with the victims. These interviews were now carried out by the reinforcements—Månsson from Malmö and a detective inspector from Sundsvall by the name of Ulf Nordin. But it really didn't matter; everyone was pretty sure that these interrogations would lead nowhere.

THE HOURS DRAGGED past and nothing happened. Day was added to day. The days formed a week, and then another week. Once again it was Monday. Monday, December 4. The weather was cold and windy and the Christmas rush grew more and more hectic. The police reinforcements got the blues and began to feel homesick. Neither of them was used to a big city and they both felt miserable in Stockholm. A lot of things got on their nerves, mainly the rushing and tearing around, the jostling crowds and the unfriendly people.

"It beats me how you guys stand it in this town," Nordin said.

He was a stocky, bald man with bushy eyebrows and squinting brown eyes.

"We were born here," Kollberg said. "We've never known anything else."

"I just came in on the subway," Nordin said. "Just in a short ride, I saw at least fifteen persons the police would have nabbed on the spot if it had been at home in Sundsvall."

"We're short of men," Martin Beck said.

"Yes, I know, but . . . People are scared here. Ordinary decent people. If you ask for directions or ask them for a light, they practically turn and run. They're plain scared. Feel insecure."

"Who doesn't?" Kollberg said.

"I don't," Nordin replied. "But I expect I'll be the same before long. Have you anything for me just now?" he asked Melander.

"We have a weird sort of tip here," Melander said.

"What about?"

"The unidentified man in the bus. A woman in Hägersten. She called up and said she lives next door to a garage where a lot of foreigners collect."

"Uh-huh. And?"

"It's usually pretty rowdy there, though she didn't put it like that. 'Noisy' is what she said. One of the noisiest was a small dark man of about thirty-five. His clothes were not unlike the description in the papers, she said, and now there hasn't been any sign of him."

"There are tens of thousands of people with clothes like that," Nordin said skeptically.

"Yes," Melander agreed, "there are. Moreover she didn't seem at all sure. But if you've nothing else to do—" He left the sentence in midair, scribbled down the woman's name and address on his notepad and tore off the sheet. The telephone rang and he lifted the receiver as he handed the paper to Nordin.

"Okay," Nordin said. "I can take a run out there." He went out.

"He didn't seem particularly inspired today," Kollberg remarked.

"Can you blame him?" Martin Beck replied.

"Hardly," Kollberg said with a sigh. "Why don't we let these guys go home?"

"Because it's not our business," said Martin Beck. "They're here to take part in the most intensive manhunt ever known in this country. I'm merely quoting the Minister of Justice," Martin Beck went on. " 'Our keenest brains'—he's referring of course to Månsson and Nordin—'are working at high pressure to corner and capture an insane mass murderer; it is of prime importance to both the community and the individual that he be put out of action.' "

"When did he say that?"

"For the first time seventeen days ago. For the umpteenth time yesterday. But yesterday he was given only four lines on page 22. I bet that rankles. There's an election next year."

Melander had finished his telephone conversation. He poked at the bowl of his pipe with a straightened paper clip and said quietly, "Isn't it about time we took care of the insane mass murderer, so to speak?"

Fifteen seconds passed before Kollberg replied. "Yes, it certainly is. It's also time to lock the door and shut off the telephones."

"Tell them to put all calls through to Gunvald," Martin Beck said.

Melander reached for the phone.

"Tell them to send up some coffee, too," Kollberg said. "And some sweet rolls, please."

The coffee arrived shortly. Kollberg locked the door.

"The situation is as follows," Kollberg said with his mouth full of roll. "The working hypothesis is this: A person armed with a Suomi M 37 submachine gun shoots nine people dead on a bus. These people have no connection with each other, they merely happen to be in the same place at the same time."

"The gunman has a motive," Martin Beck said.

"Yes," Kollberg said. "That's what I've thought all along. But he can't have a motive for killing people who are together haphazardly. Therefore his real intention is to kill one of them."

"The murder was carefully planned," Martin Beck said.

"One of the nine," Kollberg said. "But which? Have you the list there, Fredrik?"

"Don't need it," Melander said.

"No, of course not. Let's go through it."

Martin Beck nodded. The conversation that followed took the form of a dialogue between Kollberg and Melander.

"Gustav Bengtsson," Melander said. "The bus driver. His presence on the bus was justified, we can say."

"Undeniably."

"He seems to have led an ordinary, normal life. No marital troubles. No convictions. Conscientious at work. Liked by his colleagues. We've also questioned some friends of the family. They say he was respectable and steady-going. Forty-eight years old. Born here in the city."

"Enemies? None. Influence? None. Money? None. Motive for killing him? None. Next."

"I'm not following Rönn's numbering now," Melander said. "Hildur Johansson, widow, sixty-eight. She was on her way home from her daughter's, in Västmannagatan. Daughter questioned by Larsson, Månsson and . . . ha, it doesn't matter. She led a quiet life and lived on her old-age pension. There's not much more to say about her."

"Well, just that she presumably got on at Odengatan and only went six stops. And that no one except her daughter and son-in-law knew she would ride that particular stretch at that particular time. Go on."

"Johan Källström, who was fifty-two. Foreman at a garage on Sibyllegatan. He had been working overtime and was on his way home, that's clear. He too, happily married. His chief interests were his car and summer cottage. Earned good money but no more than that. Those who know him say he probably took the subway to Central Station, where he changed to the bus. Should therefore have boarded the bus outside Åhléns department store. His boss says he was a skilled workman and a good foreman. The mechanics at the garage say that he was—"

"—a slavedriver to those he could bully and a bootlicker to his bosses. I went and talked to them. Next."

"Alfons Schwerin was forty-three and born in Minneapolis in the USA of Swedish-American parents. Came to Sweden just after the war and stayed here. He had a small importing business but he went bankrupt ten years ago. Schwerin drank. He had two spells in an alcoholic clinic and was sentenced to three months in jail for drunken driving. That was three years ago. When his business went to pot he became a laborer. He was working now for the highway department. On the evening in question he had been at Restaurant Pilen and was on his way home. He hadn't had much to drink, presumably because he was broke. His lodgings were mean and shabby. He probably walked from the restaurant to the bus stop on Vasagatan. He was a bachelor and had no relations in Sweden. His fellow workers liked him. Say he was pleasant and good-tempered."

"And he saw the killer and said something unintelligible to Rönn before he died. Have we had the expert's report on the tape?"

"No. Mohammed Boussie, Algerian, worked at a restaurant, thirty-six, born at some unpronounceable place. I've forgotten the name."

"How careless."

"He had lived in Sweden for six years and before that in Paris. He had a savings account at the bank. Those who knew him say he was shy and reserved. He had finished work at ten thirty and was on his way home. Decent, but stingy and dull."

"You're sitting there describing yourself."

"Britt Danielsson, nurse. Age twenty-eight. She was sitting beside Stenström, but there's nothing to show she knew him. The doctor she was going steady with was on duty that night at Southern Hospital. She presumably got on at Odengatan together with the widow Johansson and was on her way home. There are no time margins there. She finished work and went to the bus. Of course we don't know for sure that she was not together with Stenström."

Kollberg shook his head.

"Not a chance," he said. "Why should he bother about that pale little thing? He had Åsa at home."

Melander looked at him blankly but let the question drop.

"Then we have Assarsson. A respectable exterior but not so pretty underneath."

Melander paused and fiddled with his pipe. Then he went on: "Rather shady figure, this Assarsson. Sentenced twice for tax evasion at the beginning of the 1950s. He was ruthless in business and in everything else. A lot of people had reason to dislike

461

him. Even his wife and his brother thought he was pretty nasty. But one thing is clear. His presence on the bus had a reason. He had come from some sort of club meeting and was on his way to a mistress by the name of Olsson. He had called her up and told her he was coming. We have interrogated her several times."

"Who questioned her?"

"Gunvald and Månsson. On different occasions. She says that—"

"Just a moment. Why did he take the bus?"

"Presumably because he'd had a lot to drink and didn't dare to drive his own car. And he couldn't get hold of a taxi because of the rain."

"Okay. What does the mistress say?"

"That she thought Assarsson was a dirty old man. She put up with him to keep her job."

Martin Beck broke into the conversation for the first time. "So that leaves only Stenström and the unknown man?"

"Yes," Melander said. "As regards the unidentified man, we know that he was a narcotics addict and between thirty-five and forty. Nothing more."

"The moment has come for the already classic question: What was Stenström doing on the bus?" Kollberg said.

Kollberg and Martin Beck looked at each other for a long time. Neither of them said anything, and at last it was Melander who broke the silence.

"Well? What was Stenström doing on the bus?"

"He was going to meet a girl," Kollberg said unconvincingly. "Or a pal."

"You're forgetting," Melander said, "that we've been knocking at doors in the Norra Stationsgatan district for ten days. And not found a single person who has ever heard of him."

"That proves nothing. That part of town is full of odd little hideaways and shady boardinghouses. At places like that the police are not very popular."

"All the same, I think we can dismiss the girlfriend theory as far as Stenström is concerned," Martin Beck said.

"On what grounds?" Kollberg asked quickly.

"I don't believe it."

"Okay, dismiss it then. For the time being."

"The key question therefore seems to be: What was Stenström doing on the bus?" Martin Beck said.

"Wait a minute," Kollberg objected. "What was the unknown man doing on the bus?"

"Never mind the unknown man at the moment."

"Why? His presence is just as remarkable as Stenström's. Not only did he have crumbs of hash and pep pills in his pockets. He also had more money than all the passengers put together."

"Which, incidentally, excludes all possibility of murder for the sake of robbery," Melander put in.

"Furthermore," added Martin Beck, "as you yourself said, that district is full of hideouts and shady boardinghouses. Perhaps he lived in one of those fleabags. Now, back to the basic question: What was Stenström doing on the bus?"

They sat silent for at least a minute. In the next room the telephones kept ringing. Now and then they could hear voices, Gunvald Larsson's and Rönn's. At last Melander said, "What was Stenström's specialty?"

All three knew the answer to that question. Melander nodded slowly and answered himself. "Stenström could shadow."

"Yes," Martin Beck said. "He was skillful and stubborn. He could go on shadowing a person for weeks."

Kollberg scratched his neck and said, "I remember him with that murderer from the canalboat four years ago. Stenström drove him mad."

"Baited him," said Martin Beck. "He had the knack even then. But he had learned a lot since then."

"By the way, did you ask Hammar about that?" Kollberg said suddenly. "I mean about what Stenström did last summer when we went through unsolved cases."

"Yes," Martin Beck replied. "But I drew a blank. Stenström had discussed the matter with Hammar, who made one or two suggestions—which ones he didn't remember."

Kollberg looked at him and said, "Who's going to see Åsa?"

"You. It's a one-man job and of us two you're best fitted for it."

Kollberg made no answer.

"Don't you want to?" Martin Beck asked.

"No, I don't. But I will all the same."

"This evening?"

"I have something to attend to first. But call her up and say I'll be along about seven thirty."

Chapter Seven

OUTSIDE A HOUSE in Hägersten a snowy man stood looking thoughtfully at a scrap of paper. It was sopping wet and was coming apart; he had difficulty in making out the writing in the whirling snow and the dim light from the streetlamps. However, it seemed as if he had at last found the right place. He shook himself like a wet dog, went up the steps and rang the doorbell.

The door was opened a few inches and a middle-aged woman peeped out. She wore an apron and had flour on her hands.

"Police," he said raucously. Clearing his throat, he went on, "Detective Inspector Nordin."

The woman eyed him anxiously. "Can you prove it?" she said at last. "I mean . . ."

With a heavy sigh, Nordin transferred his hat to his left hand, unbuttoned his overcoat and jacket, took out his wallet and showed his identification card.

The woman peered at it shortsightedly through the crack in the door. "I mean you can't be too careful nowadays. You never know . . ."

The snow was falling thickly and the flakes were melting on Nordin's bald head. He came from a part of the country where it was customary to invite all strangers into the kitchen, offer them a cup of coffee and let them warm themselves by the stove. Perhaps it wasn't done in big cities. Collecting his thoughts, he said, "When you called up you mentioned a man and a garage, didn't you?"

"I'm awfully sorry if I disturbed you . . ."

"Oh, we couldn't be more grateful. Er, that garage—"

"It's over there. Some foreigner has it. All sorts of queer characters hang about there."

He followed her gaze and said, "And this man?"

"Well, he seemed funny. And now I haven't seen him for a couple of weeks. A short, dark man."

"What was strange about this man?"

"Well . . . he laughed."

"Laughed?"

"Yes. Awfully loud."

Nordin sighed. "Well, I'll go and make inquiries," he said. "Thank you, madam."

She opened the door a few inches, gave him a quick glance and said graspingly, "Is there any reward?"

"For what?"

"Er . . . I don't know."

THE GARAGE, a small building standing by itself, had cement walls and a corrugated iron roof. There was room for two cars at the most. Above the doors was an electric light.

He opened one half of the double doors and went in.

The car standing inside was a green Skoda Octavia, 1959 model. It might fetch 400 kronor if the engine wasn't too worn out, thought Nordin, who had spent a great deal of his time as a policeman on shady car deals. It was propped up on low trestles and the hood was open. A man lay on his back under the chassis, quite still. All that could be seen of him was a pair of legs in blue overalls.

Dead, thought Nordin, poking the man with his right foot.

The figure under the car started as though at an electric shock. The man crawled out, got to his feet, and stood with a hand lamp in his right hand, staring in amazement at the visitor.

"Police," Nordin said.

"My papers are in order," the man said quickly. He was about thirty, slender, with wavy dark hair and well-combed sideburns.

"Are you Italian?" Nordin asked. He was not much of an expert at foreign accents.

"Swiss. From German Switzerland."

"You speak good Swedish."

"I've lived here for six years. What is it you want?"

"We're trying to get in touch with a pal of yours."

"Who?"

"We don't know his name. He's not quite as tall as you. A bit fatter. Dark hair, rather long, and brown eyes. About thirty-five."

The other shook his head. "I've no pal that looks like that. I don't meet many people."

"But I've heard there are usually a lot of people out here at the garage."

"Guys come with cars. They want me to fix them when there is something wrong." He thought hard, then explained: "I am a mechanic. Work at a garage in Ringvägen. Now only in the mornings. All these Germans and Austrians know that I have this garage. So they come out and want repairs free. Many I do not know at all."

"Well," Nordin said, "this man we want to get hold of might have been dressed in a black nylon coat and a beige suit."

"That tells me nothing. I do not remember anyone like that. That's certain."

"What's your name?"

"Horst. Horst Dieke."

"Mine's Ulf. Ulf Nordin."

The Swiss smiled, showing perfect white teeth. He seemed a pleasant, steady-going young man.

"Well, Horst, so you don't know who I mean?"

Dieke shook his head. "No. I'm sorry."

Nordin was in no way disappointed. He had simply drawn the blank that everyone expected. But he was not prepared to give up yet, and besides he didn't fancy the subway with its horde of unfriendly people in damp clothes. The Swiss was evidently trying to be helpful, for he said, "There is nothing else? About that guy, I mean?"

Nordin considered. At last he said, "He laughed. Loud."

Dieke's face brightened at once. "Ah, I think I know. He laughs like this." He opened his mouth and emitted a blasting sound, shrill and harsh as the cry of a snipe.

Nordin waited expectantly.

"I know now who you mean. Little dark guy," Dieke said. "He has been here four or five times. Maybe more. But his name, I do not know it. He came with a Spaniard who wanted to sell me spare parts. But I did not buy."

"Why not?"

"Too cheap. I think stolen."

"What was this Spaniard's name?"

Dieke shrugged. "Don't know. Paco. Pablo. Paquito. Something like that."

"And this man who laughed?"

"Don't know at all. He was just in the Spaniard's car."

"Was he Spanish too?"

"I think Swedish. But I don't know."

"How long since he was here last?"

"Three weeks ago. Perhaps two. Exactly I do not know. He seemed a bit drunk."

Nordin paused to consider. "Do you think he might have had a fix?"

A shrug. "Don't know. I think he had been drinking. But— dope? Well, why not? Nearly everybody here gets high."

"You've no idea what his name is or what they call him?"

"No. But a couple of times a girl was in the car. With him, I think. A big girl. Long fair hair."

"What's her name?"

"I don't know. But they call her Blonde Malin, I think."

"How do you know?"

"I have seen her before. In town."

"Whereabouts in town?"

"At a café on Tegnérgatan. Where all foreigners go. She is Swedish."

"Blonde Malin?"

"Yes."

Nordin couldn't think of anything more to ask. He looked doubtfully at the green car and said, "Is that your automobile?"

"Yes. I pay only 100 kronor for this car. But I get it fixed up by Christmas, so I can drive home and see my parents. I'm good mechanic."

"When are you coming back?"

"Never. Sweden bad country. Stockholm bad city. Only violence, narcotics, thieves, liquor."

Nordin said nothing. With the last he was inclined to agree.

"Misery," the Swiss said, summing up. "But easy to earn money for foreigner. Everything else hopeless. I have saved money. I'm going home, I get my own little garage and marry."

"Haven't you met any girls here?"

"Swedish girls are not worth having. Maybe students and the like can meet nice girls. Ordinary workmen meet only one sort. Like this Blonde Malin."

Nordin shook his head. "You've only seen Stockholm. Pity."

"Is the rest any better?"

Nordin nodded emphatically. Then he said, "I hope you get home all right." He shook hands and left.

Under the nearest lamp post he stopped and took out his notebook.

"Blonde Malin," he murmured. "Junkies. Stolen goods. What a profession to have chosen."

It's not my fault, he thought. The old man forced me into it.

Then, putting pen and paper in his pocket, he sighed and trudged away out of the circle of light.

KOLLBERG STOOD outside the door of Åsa Torell's apartment. The time was already eight o'clock in the evening and he felt worried and absentminded. In his right hand he held the envelope they had found in Stenström's drawer out at southern headquarters.

The bell didn't seem to be working and, true to habit, he pounded with his fist on the door. Åsa Torell opened it at once.

She stared at him and said, "All right, all right, here I am. Don't kick the door down."

"Sorry," Kollberg murmured.

It was dark in the apartment. He took his coat off and switched on the hall light. Åke's old police cap was lying on the hat rack, just as before. The wire of the doorbell had been wrenched loose and was dangling from the jamb.

Åsa Torell followed his gaze and muttered, "A horde of idiots kept intruding. Journalists and photographers. The bell never stopped ringing."

Kollberg said nothing. He went into the living room and sat down in one of the safari chairs.

"Can't you put the light on so that at least we can see one another?"

"I can see quite well enough. All right, if you like, sure I'll put it on." She switched on the light but did not sit down. She paced restlessly to and fro, as though she were caged in and wanted to get out.

The air in the apartment was stale and stuffy. The ashtrays had not been emptied for several days. The whole room was untidy and didn't seem to have been cleaned at all, and through an open door he saw that the bedroom too was in a mess. In the kitchen, dirty plates lay piled up in the sink.

Then he looked at the young woman. She walked up to the window, swung around and walked back toward the bedroom. She stood for a few seconds staring at the unmade bed, turned again and went back to the window. Over and over again.

Åsa Torell had changed during the nineteen days that had passed since Kollberg last saw her. She still had thick gray ski socks on her feet, and the same black slacks. But this time they were spotted with cigarette ash and her hair was uncombed and matted. Her gaze was unsteady and she had dark rings under her eyes; the skin on her lips was dry and cracked. She could not keep her hands still and the insides of the forefinger and middle finger of her left hand were stained with nicotine. On the table lay five opened cigarette packs.

"What do you want?" she asked gruffly. Then she said, "Nothing, of course. Just like that idiot Rönn, who sat here mumbling and rolling his head for two hours."

"Aren't you working?" Kollberg asked.

"I'm on sick leave. The firm has its own doctor. He said I was to rest for a month in the country or preferably go abroad. Then he drove me home."

She drew deeply at her cigarette and tapped off the ash; most of it fell beside the ashtray.

"That was three weeks ago," she said. "It would have been much better if I could have gone on working as usual."

She swung around and went over to the window, looked down into the street and plucked at the curtain.

"As usual," she said to herself.

Kollberg squirmed in his chair, ill at ease. This was going to be worse than he expected. Somehow he must break the isolation. But how?

He got up and went over to the big carved bookcase. He looked at the books and took one out. It was *Manual of Crime Investigation* by Otto Wendel and Arne Svensson, printed in 1949. He turned over the title page and read:

This is a numbered and limited edition. This copy, No. 2080, is for *Detective Lennart Kollberg*. The book is intended as a guide for policemen in their work on the scene of the crime. The contents are of a confidential nature, and the authors therefore request everyone to see that the book does not fall into the wrong hands.

Kollberg himself had written in the words "Detective Lennart Kollberg" long ago. It was a good book and it had been very useful to him in the old days.

"This is my old book," he said.

"Take it then," she replied.

"No. I gave it to Åke a couple of years ago."

He dipped into it as he considered what ought to be said or done. Here and there Stenström had underlined certain passages. In two places Kollberg noticed a stroke in the margin made with a ball-point pen. Both were under the chapter heading *Sex Murders*.

> The sex murderer (the sadist) is often impotent and his violent crime is in that case an abnormal act for the attainment of sexual satisfaction.

Stenström had underlined this sentence. Beside it he had drawn an exclamation point and written the words "or the reverse."

In the paragraph a little farther down the same page that began with the words "In cases of sex murder the victim can have been killed," he had underlined two points:

4) after the sex act in order to prevent accusation
5) because of the effect of shock.

In the margin Stenström had made the following comment: "6) to get rid of an unwanted partner, but is it then a sex murder?"

"Åsa," Kollberg said.

"Yes, what is it?"

"Do you know when Åke wrote this?"

She came up to him, glanced at the book and said, "No idea."

"Åsa," he said again.

She plunged her half-smoked cigarette into the overflowing ashtray and remained standing beside the table with her hands loosely clasped over her stomach.

"Yes, what is it?" she asked irritably.

Kollberg looked at her searchingly. She looked small and wretched. Today she was wearing a shortsleeved blue overblouse instead of the knitted sweater. She had gooseflesh on her bare arms and the blouse hung like a loosely draped cloth over her thin body.

"Sit down," he commanded.

She shrugged, took a cigarette and walked over to the bedroom door while she fumbled with the lighter.

"Sit down!" Kollberg roared.

She jumped, and looked at him. Her brown eyes almost glittered with hatred. Nevertheless, she went to the armchair and sat down opposite him, stiff as a poker, with her hands on her thighs.

"We have to put our cards on the table," Kollberg said, stealing an embarrassed glance at the brown envelope.

"Splendid," she said in an icy, clear voice. "It's just that I haven't any cards to put."

"When we were here last we weren't altogether frank with you," Kollberg said.

She frowned. "In what way?"

"In several ways. First let me ask you: Do you know what Åke was doing on that bus?"

"No, no, no and again no. I—do—not—know."

"Nor do we," said Kollberg. He paused. Then, drawing a deep breath, he went on. "Åke lied to you."

Her reaction was violent. Her eyes flashed. She clenched her fists. "How *dare* you say that to me!"

"Because it's true. Åke was not on duty—either on the Monday when he was killed or on the previous Saturday. He had had an unusual amount of time off during the whole of October and the first two weeks of November."

She stared at him without saying anything.

"That is a fact," Kollberg went on. "Another thing I would like to know: Was he in the habit of carrying his pistol when he was not on duty?"

It was some time before she answered. "Go to the devil and stop tormenting me with your interrogation tactics."

Kollberg bit his lower lip.

"Have you cried a lot?" he asked.

"No. I'm not made that way."

"Well then, answer me, Åsa. We must help each other get hold of the man who killed him."

She sat quiet for a while.

"Did he usually carry his pistol?" Kollberg asked again.

"Yes. Often lately at any rate."

"Why?"

"Why not? As it turned out, he needed it. Didn't he?"

He made no reply.

"Though a lot of help it was."

Kollberg still said nothing.

"I loved Åke," she said. The voice was clear and matter-of-fact. Her eyes were fixed on a point behind Kollberg.

"Åsa?"

"Yes?"

"He was away a lot, then. You don't know what he was up to and we don't know either. Do you think he might have been together with someone else? Some other woman, that is?"

"No."

"You don't think so?"

"I don't think anything. I know he wasn't."

She looked him suddenly in the eye and said in astonishment, "Did you get it into your heads that he had a mistress?"

"Yes. We still reckon with that possibility."

"Then you can stop. It's completely out of the question."

Kollberg took another deep breath, as though plucking up his courage. "Was Åke interested in photography?"

"Yes. It was about his only hobby after he stopped playing soccer. He has three cameras. And there's one of those enlarging gadgets in the bathroom. He used the bathroom as a darkroom." She looked at Kollberg in surprise. "Why do you ask that?"

He pushed the envelope across to her side of the table. She put down the cigarette lighter and took out the pictures with trembling hands. She looked at the one on top and went scarlet.

"Where . . . where did you get hold of these?"

"They were in his desk at southern headquarters."

She blinked hard and asked unexpectedly, "How many have seen them? The entire police force?"

"Only three people."

"Who?"

"Martin, myself and my wife."

Her face was still fiery red. Tiny glistening beads of sweat had broken out on her forehead just below her hairline.

"The pictures were taken in here?" he asked.

She nodded.

"When?"

Åsa Torell bit her lip nervously. "About three months ago."

"I presume he took them himself?"

"Naturally. He has . . . had all kinds of photography gadgets. Self-timer and tripod and whatever they're called."

"Why did he take them?"

She was still flushed and perspiring but her voice was steadier. "Because we thought it was fun."

"And why did he have them in his desk?" Kollberg paused briefly. "You see, he didn't have a single personal thing in his office," he said, explaining. "Apart from these photographs."

A long silence. At last she shook her head slowly and said, "I don't know."

Time to change the subject, Kollberg thought. Aloud he said, "You say he went about with a pistol?"

"Nearly always lately."

She seemed to be thinking something over. Then she got up suddenly and walked quickly out of the room. Through the short passage he saw her go into the bedroom and up to the bed. Sticking her hand under one of the crumpled pillows, she said hesitantly, "I've a thing here . . . a pistol . . ."

Kollberg's phlegmatic appearance had deceived many in various fashions. He was in good trim and his responses were amazingly quick. Åsa Torell was still bending over the bed when he stood beside her and wrenched the weapon from her hand.

"This is no pistol," he said. "It's an American revolver. A Colt .45 with a long barrel. Peacemaker, it's called, absurdly enough. Besides which, it is loaded. And cocked."

He opened the weapon and took out the cartridges.

"With cross-filed bullets, what's more," he said. "Forbidden even in America. The most dangerous small firearm imaginable. You can kill an elephant with it. Where the hell did you get it from?"

She shrugged bewilderedly.

"Åke. He often carried it lately."

"In bed?"

With a shake of her head she said quietly, "No, no. It was I who . . . now . . ."

Slipping the cartridges into his pants pocket, Kollberg pointed the revolver at the floor and pulled the trigger. The click echoed in the silent apartment.

"The trigger has been filed," he said. "To make it quicker and more sensitive. Horribly dangerous. You'd only have had to turn over in your sleep to—"

"I haven't slept much lately," she said.

"Hm-m," Kollberg muttered to himself. "He must have smuggled this away when he was confiscating weapons at some time. Swiped it, in fact." He looked at the big, heavy revolver and weighed it in his hand. Then he glanced at the girl's right wrist. It was as slender as a child's. "Go sit down," he said curtly. "We're going to talk. This is serious."

She looked at him with an entirely new expression; her eyes focused on him now with a clear, direct look. She went straight into the living room and sat down in the armchair.

Kollberg went out into the hall and put the revolver on the hat rack. He took off his jacket and tie, unbuttoned his collar and rolled up his sleeves. Then he went into the kitchen, put some water on to boil and made some tea. He brought the cups in and set them on the table. He emptied the ashtrays, opened a window and sat down.

"First of all," he said, "I want to know what you meant by 'lately.' When you said that lately he liked to go armed."

"Quiet," said Åsa. After ten seconds she added, "Wait."

She drew up her legs so that her feet in the big gray ski socks were resting against the edge of the armchair. Then she put her arms around her shins and sat quite still.

Kollberg waited.

To be precise, he waited for fifteen minutes, and during the whole of this time she did not look at him once. Neither of them said a word. Then she looked him in the eye and said, "Well?"

476

"How do you feel?"

"No better. But different. Ask what you like. I promise to answer. There's only one thing I want to know first. Have you told me everything?"

"No," Kollberg replied. "But I'm going to now. The reason why I'm here at all is that I don't believe in the official version—that Åke merely chanced to fall a victim to a crazy mass murderer. And quite apart from your assurances that he was not unfaithful to you, I do not believe that he was on that bus for pleasure."

"Then what *do* you believe?"

"That you were right from the outset. That he was busy with some police work but for one reason or another didn't want to tell anybody, either you or us. One possibility, for instance, is that he had been shadowing someone for a long time, and this someone at last grew desperate and killed him." He paused briefly. "Åke was very good at shadowing. It amused him."

"Yes, I know."

"You can shadow in two ways," Kollberg went on. "Either you follow a person as invisibly as possible, to find out what he's up to. Or else you follow him quite openly, to drive him to desperation and make him do something rash and give himself away. Åke had mastered both methods better than anyone else I know." He scratched his neck. "But there are several weaknesses in this argument. We needn't go into them now."

She nodded. "What do you want to know?"

"I'm not sure. We'll have to feel our way. Did he change in any way recently?"

She raised her left hand and pressed her fingers through her short dark hair. "Yes," she said at last.

"How?"

"It isn't easy to say."

"Have these pictures anything to do with the change?"

"Yes, they have." Stretching out her hand, she turned the photographs over and looked at them. "To talk to anyone about this calls for a degree of confidence that I'm not sure I have in you," she said. "But I'll do my best."

Kollberg's palms had begun to sweat and he wiped them against the legs of his pants. Their roles had been reversed. She was calm and he was nervous.

"I loved Åke," she said. "From the start. But we didn't suit each other very well sexually. We were different as regards tempo and temperament. We didn't have the same demands." She gave him a searching look. "But you can be happy just the same. You can learn. Did you know that?"

"No."

"We proved it. We learned. I think you understand this."

Kollberg nodded.

"In any case we adjusted ourselves to each other, and we had it good."

She coughed and said in a matter-of-fact tone, "I've been smoking far too much this last week or two."

Kollberg could feel that something was about to change. Suddenly he smiled. And Åsa Torell smiled back, a trifle bitterly, but still she smiled.

"Anyway, let's get this over," she said. "The quicker the better. Unfortunately, I'm rather shy. Oddly enough."

"It's not in the least odd," Kollberg replied. "I'm shy. It's part of the rest of one's emotions."

"Before I met Åke I began to think I was a nymphomaniac or something," she said swiftly. "Then we fell in love and learned to adjust to each other. I really tried hard, and so did Åke, and we succeeded. I forgot that I was more highly sexed than he was. We talked it over once or twice at the beginning and after that there was no need. We made love when he felt like it, we did it very well and never needed anything else. But then—"

"—suddenly last summer," Kollberg said.

She gave him a swift, approving glance. "Exactly. Last summer we went to Majorca on vacation. While we were away you all had a difficult and very nasty case here in town."

"Yes. The park murders."

"By the time we got home they had been cleared up. Åke got sore about it."

She paused, then went on, just as quickly and fluently, "It sounds bad, but so does a lot of what I've said and am going to say. The fact is he got sore because he had missed the investigations. Åke was ambitious, almost to a fault. I know that he always dreamed of coming upon something big that everyone else had overlooked. Moreover, he was much younger than the rest of you and in the early days, at any rate, he often felt pushed around at work. I know, too, that he thought you were one of those who bullied him most."

"He was right, I'm afraid."

"About the end of July or the beginning of August he changed—suddenly, as I said, and in a way that turned the whole of our life together upside down. That's when he took those pictures. There were lots more, dozens of them. We had a sort of routine in our sex life, as I said, and it was fine. Now it was upset all of a sudden, and he was the one to upset it, not I. We made love as many times in a day as we normally did in a month. Some days he wouldn't even let me go to work. There's no use denying that it was a pleasant surprise to me. I was amazed."

"Go on," Kollberg urged.

She took a deep breath. "I thought it was just great. But he himself hadn't really changed and after a while I got the idea that he was trying out some sort of experiment on me. I asked him, but he only laughed."

"Laughed?"

"Yes, he was in a very good mood all this time. Right up to . . . well, until he was killed."

"Why?"

"That's what I don't know. But one thing I did understand, as soon as I'd got over the first shock."

"And that was?"

"That he was using me as a kind of guinea pig. That basically he wasn't particularly interested, other than now and again."

"How long did this go on?"

"Until the middle of September. That's when he suddenly had so much to do and began to be away such a lot."

"Which doesn't at all fit in." Kollberg looked steadily at her, then added, "Thanks. You're a great kid. I like you." She gave him a surprised and rather suspicious glance. "And he didn't tell you what he was working on?"

She shook her head.

"And you didn't notice anything special?"

"He was out a lot. I mean, out of doors. I couldn't help noticing that. He would come home at all hours wet and cold." Kollberg nodded. "But, as I told you, he didn't tell me what he was doing. The last case that he talked to me about was one that he had in the first half of September. A man who had killed his wife. I think his name was Birgersson."

"I remember it," Kollberg said. "A family tragedy. A very simple, ordinary story. Unhappy marriage, neuroses, quarrels, money troubles. At last the man killed his wife more or less by accident. Was going to take his own life but didn't dare to and went to the police. But you're right, Åke did have charge of it. He did the interrogating."

"Wait—something happened during those interrogations."

"What?"

"I don't know. But one evening Åke came home very cheerful. During the interrogations this man said something to Åke."

"What?"

"I don't know. But it was something he considered very important. I asked the same as you, of course, but he only laughed and said I'd soon see."

"Did he say exactly that?"

" 'You'll soon see, darling.' Those were his exact words. He seemed very optimistic."

They sat in silence for a while. Then Kollberg shook himself, picked up the open book from the table and said, "Do you understand these comments?" Åsa Torell got up, walked around the table and put her hand on his shoulder as she looked at the book. "Wendel and Svensson write that the sex murderer is often impotent and attains abnormal satisfaction from committing a crime of violence. And in the margin Åke has written 'or the reverse.'" Kollberg shrugged and said, "He means, of course, that the sex murderer may also be oversexed."

She took her hand away suddenly. Looking up at her, he noticed to his surprise that she was blushing again.

"No," she said. "He means the very opposite. That the woman—the victim, that is—may lose her life because *she* is oversexed."

"How do you know that?"

"Because we once discussed the matter. In connection with that American girl who was murdered on the Göta Canal."

He thought for a moment, then said, "But I hadn't given him this book then."

"And that other comment of his seems rather illogical."

"Yes. Aren't there any pads or diaries in which he used to write things down?"

"Didn't he have his notebook on him?"

"Yes. We've looked at it. Nothing of interest there."

"I've searched the apartment," she said. "He wasn't in the habit of hiding things. He was very tidy. He had an extra notebook, of course. It's over there on the desk."

Kollberg got up and fetched the notebook. It was of the same type as the one Stenström had had in his pocket.

"There's hardly anything there," Åsa Torell said.

Kollberg looked inside the notebook. She was right. There was almost nothing in it. The first page was covered with jottings about the poor wretch of a man called Birgersson who had killed his wife.

At the top of the second page was a single word. A name. Morris.

Åsa Torell looked at the pad and shrugged. "A car," she said. She was standing by the table. Her eye caught the much-discussed photographs. Suddenly she slammed her hand down on the table and shouted, "If at least I'd been pregnant!" Then she lowered her voice. "He said we had plenty of time. That we'd wait until he was promoted."

Kollberg moved hesitantly toward the hall.

"Plenty of time," she mumbled. And then: "What's to become of me?"

Turning around, he said, "This won't do, Åsa. Come."

Whirling around, she snarled at him, "Where? To bed?"

Kollberg looked at her.

Nine hundred and ninety-nine men out of a thousand would have seen a pale, thin girl who held herself badly, who had a delicate body, thin nicotine-stained fingers and a ravaged face. Unkempt and dressed in baggy, spotted clothes.

Lennart Kollberg saw a physically and mentally complex young woman with blazing eyes, provocative and interesting and worth getting to know.

Had Stenström also seen this, or had he been one of the nine hundred and ninety-nine and merely had a stroke of luck?

Luck.

"Come home with me," Kollberg said. "Gun and I have plenty of room. You've been alone long enough."

She was hardly in the car before she started to cry.

Chapter Eight

NORDIN SHOOK his head at the cloakroom attendant who came forward to take his loden-cloth coat and his Tyrolean hat, stood in the entrance to the restaurant and looked around. He caught sight of her almost at once.

She was big-framed but didn't seem fat. Her fair hair, bleached by the look of it, was piled up on top of her head. Nordin didn't doubt for a moment that this was Blonde Malin.

She was sitting on a wall seat with a wineglass in front of her. Beside her sat a much older woman, whose unruly black curls didn't make her look any younger.

He observed the two women for a while. They were not talking to each other. Blonde Malin was staring at the wineglass, which she twiddled between her fingers. The black-haired woman kept looking around the room, now and then flinging her long hair aside with a coquettish toss of the head.

Nordin turned to the cloakroom attendant. "Excuse me, but do you know the name of that blonde lady sitting over by the wall?"

The man looked across the room. "Lady!" he snorted. "No. I don't know her name, but I think they call her Malin. Fat Malin or something like that."

Nordin gave him his hat and coat.

The black-haired woman looked at him expectantly as he came up to their table.

"Pardon my intrusion," Nordin said. "I'd like a word with Miss Malin if she doesn't mind."

Blonde Malin looked at him and sipped her wine. "What about?" she asked.

"About a friend of yours," Nordin said. "Perhaps we could move to another table and have a quiet talk?"

The black-haired woman filled her glass from the carafe on the table and got up. "Don't let me disturb you," she said huffily. "I'll go and sit with Tora. So long, Malin." She picked up her glass and went over to a table farther down the room.

Nordin drew out a chair and sat down. Blonde Malin looked at him expectantly.

"I'm Detective Inspector Ulf Nordin," he said. "It's possible that you can help us with something. We'd like some information about a man you know."

Blonde Malin's look changed to contempt. "I'm not squealing on anybody," she said.

Nordin took out a pack of cigarettes and offered it to her. She took one and he lighted it for her.

"It's not a question of being a fink," he said. "A few weeks ago you rode with two men to a garage in Hägersten owned by a Swiss named Horst Dieke. The man who drove was a Spaniard. Do you remember that occasion?"

"Supposing I do," Blonde Malin said. "What of it? Nisse and I only went with this Paco so Nisse could show him the way."

She drained her glass and poured out the rest of the carafe.

"May I offer you something?" Nordin asked. "A little more wine?"

She nodded and Nordin beckoned to the waitress. He ordered half a carafe of wine and a stein of beer.

"Who's Nisse?" he asked.

"The guy with me in the car, of course. You said so yourself just now."

"Yes, but what's his name besides Nisse? What does he do?"

"His name's Göransson. Nils Erik Göransson. I don't know what he does. I haven't seen him for a couple of weeks."

"Why?" Nordin asked.

"Eh?"

"Why haven't you seen him for a couple of weeks? Didn't you meet quite often before that?"

"We just went together sometimes. Maybe he's met some gal. How do I know? I haven't seen him for a while at any rate." The waitress brought the wine and Nordin's beer. Blonde Malin immediately filled her glass.

"Do you know where he lives?" Nordin asked.

"Nisse? No, he sort of didn't have anywhere to live. He lived with me for a time and then with a pal on the South Side, but I don't think he's there now. I don't know, really. Even if I did, I'm not so all-fired sure I'd tell a cop."

Nordin took a draft of beer and looked amiably at the large, fair girl opposite him. "Pardon me, but what's your name besides Malin?" he asked politely.

"People call me Blonde Malin because I'm so blonde. My name's really Magdalena Rosén." She stroked her hair. "What do you want Nisse for, anyway?" she asked. "I'm not going to sit here answering a lot of questions if I don't know what it's all about."

"No, of course not. I'll tell you what it is you can help us with," Ulf Nordin said. He finished his beer and wiped his mouth. "May I ask just one more question?"

She nodded.

"How was Nisse usually dressed?"

She frowned and thought for a moment.

"Most of the time he wore a suit," she said. "One of them light beige-colored ones with covered buttons. And shirt and shoes and shorts, like all other guys."

"Didn't he have an overcoat?"

"Well, I'd hardly call it an overcoat. A thin black thing—nylon, you know. Why?" She looked inquiringly at Nordin.

"Well, it's possible that he is dead."

"Dead? Nisse? But . . . why . . . why do you say it's possible?"

Ulf Nordin took out his handkerchief and wiped his neck. It was very warm in the restaurant and his whole body felt sticky.

"The thing is," he said, "we've a man out at the morgue we haven't been able to identify. There's reason to suspect that the dead man is Nils Erik Göransson."

"How's he supposed to have died?" Blonde Malin asked suspiciously.

"He was one of the passengers on that bus, that you've no doubt read about. He was shot in the head and must have been killed outright. Since you're the only person we've traced who knew Göransson well, we'd be grateful if you'd come out to the morgue tomorrow and see if it's him."

She stared at Nordin in horror. "Me? Come out to the morgue? Not on your life!"

BLONDE MALIN, pale and quiet, sat beside Nordin in the back of the taxi on the way back from the morgue to Police Headquarters. Now and then she mumbled, "How awful. Poor Nisse!"

At headquarters Martin Beck and Ulf Nordin treated her to coffee and sweet rolls and after a while Kollberg and Melander and Rönn joined them. She soon recovered and it was obvious that not only the coffee, but also the attention shown her, had cheered her up. She answered their questions obligingly and before leaving she pressed their hands and said, "Imagine, I never would have thought that co— policemen could be such sweethearts."

When the door had closed behind her they considered this for a moment. Then Kollberg said, "Well, sweethearts? Shall we sum up?"

They summed up:

Nils Erik Göransson.

Age: 38 or 39.

Since 1965 or earlier, no permanent employment.

March 1967–August 1967, lived with Magdalena Rosén (Blonde Malin), Arbetargatan 3, Stockholm K.

Thereafter and until some time in October lived with Sune Björk on the South Side.

The weeks prior to his death whereabouts unknown.

Drug addict, smoking, swallowing and mainlining whatever he could get hold of.

Possibly also a pusher.

Last seen by Magdalena Rosén November 3 or 4. Then in same suit and coat as when killed on November 13.

Usually had plenty of money.

OF ALL THE MEN who were working on the bus murders, Nordin was thus the first to show something that, with a little goodwill, could be called a constructive result. But even on this point, opinions were divided.

"Well," Gunvald Larsson said, "now we know the name of that bum. So what?"

"Mm-m . . ." Melander murmured thoughtfully.

"What are you mumbling about?"

"He was never picked up for anything, that Göransson. But I seem to remember the name."

"Oh?"

"I think he cropped up in connection with an investigation at some time."

Melander stared abstractedly out into the room, puffing at his pipe. Gunvald Larsson waved his big hands in front of his face. He was opposed to people using tobacco and was irritated by the smoke.

"I'm more interested in that swine Assarsson," he said.

"I expect I'll think of it," Melander said.

"Not a doubt. If you don't die of lung cancer first."

Gunvald Larsson got up and went into Martin Beck's office. "Where did this Assarsson get his money from?" he asked.

"Don't know."

"What does the firm do?"

"Imports a lot of junk. Anything that pays, from cranes to plastic Christmas trees."

"I took the trouble to find out what these gentlemen and their firm have paid in taxes during the last few years."

"And?"

"About one third of what you or I fork out. And when I think of what it looked like at the widow's apartment . . ."

"Yes?"

"I've a damn good mind to ask for permission to raid their office."

Martin Beck shrugged. Gunvald Larsson walked toward the door, stopped and said, "An ugly customer, that Assarsson. And his brother is probably no better."

Shortly afterward Kollberg appeared in the doorway. He looked tired and dejected, and his eyes were bloodshot.

"What are you busy at?" Martin Beck asked.

"I've been playing back the tapes from Stenström's interrogation with Birgersson. The guy who killed his wife. It took all night."

"And?"

"Nothing. Nothing at all. Unless I've overlooked something."

"It's always possible."

"Kind of you to say so," Kollberg snapped, slamming the door behind him.

Martin Beck propped his elbows on the edge of the desk and put his head in his hands.

It was already the eighth of December. Twenty-five days had passed and the investigation was getting nowhere. In fact, it showed signs of falling to pieces. Everyone was clinging to his own particular straw.

Melander was puzzling over where and when he had seen or heard the name of Nils Erik Göransson.

Gunvald Larsson was wondering how the Assarsson brothers had made their money.

Kollberg was trying to puzzle out how a mentally unbalanced wife-killer by the name of Birgersson could conceivably have cheered up Stenström.

Nordin was trying to establish a connection between Göransson, the mass murder and the garage in Hägersten.

Ek had made such a technical study of the red double-decker bus that nowadays it was practically impossible to talk to him about anything except electric circuits and windshield-wiper controls.

Månsson had taken over Gunvald Larsson's diffuse ideas that Mohammed Boussie must have played some sort of leading role because he was Algerian; he had systematically interrogated the entire Arab colony in Stockholm.

Martin Beck himself could think only of Stenström, what he had been working on, whether he had been shadowing someone and whether this someone had shot him. The argument seemed far from convincing.

Rönn could not tear his thoughts away from what Schwerin had said at the hospital during the few seconds before he died.

On this very afternoon he had had a talk on the phone with the sound expert at the Swedish Broadcasting Corporation who had tried to analyze what was said on the tape. The man had taken his time, but now he seemed ready with his report.

"Not very copious material to work with," he said. "But I've come to certain conclusions. Like to hear them?"

"Yes, please," Rönn said. He transferred the receiver to his left hand and reached for the notepad.

"You're from the North yourself, aren't you?"

"Yes."

"Well, it's not the questions that are interesting but the answers. First of all, I've tried to eliminate all the background noise like whirring and dripping and so on."

Rönn waited with his pen at the ready.

"As regards the first answer, referring to the question as to who it was that did the shooting, one can clearly distinguish four consonants—*d, n, r* and *k.*"

"Yes," Rönn said.

"A closer analysis reveals certain vowels and diphthongs between and after these consonants. For example, an *a* or an *i* sound between *d* and *n.*"

"Dinrk," Rönn said.

"Yes, that's more or less how it sounds to an untrained ear," the expert said. "Furthermore, I think I can hear the man say a very faint *oo* after the consonant *k.*"

"Dinrk oo," Rönn said.

"Something like that, yes. Though not such a marked *oo.*" The expert paused. Then he went on reflectively, "This man was in pretty bad shape, wasn't he?"

"Yes."

"And he was probably in pain."

"Very likely," Rönn agreed.

"Well," the expert said lightly, "that could explain why he said *oo.*"

Rönn nodded and made notes. Then he poked at the tip of his nose with the pen, listening.

"However, I'm convinced that those sounds form a sentence, composed of several words."

"And how does the sentence go?" Rönn asked, putting pen to paper.

"Very hard to say. Very hard indeed. For example 'dinner reckon' or 'dinner record, oo.' "

" 'Dinner record, oo'?" Rönn asked in astonishment.

"Well, just as an example, of course. As to the second reply—"

" 'Koleson'?"

"Oh, you thought it sounded like that? Interesting. Well, I didn't. I've reached the conclusion that there's an *l* before the *k,* and that he says two words: 'like,' repeating the last word of the question and 'oleson.' "

" 'Oleson'? And what does that mean?"

"Well, it might be a name . . ."

" 'Like Oleson'?"

"Yes, exactly. You have the same thick *l* in the word 'Oleson' too. Perhaps a similar dialect." The sound technician was silent for a few seconds. Then he went on: "That's about the lot then. I'll send over a written report, of course, together with the bill. But I thought I'd better call up in case it was urgent."

"Thanks very much," Rönn said.

Putting the receiver down, he regarded his notes thoughtfully. After careful consideration he decided not to take the matter up with Martin Beck. At any rate not at present.

ALTHOUGH THE TIME was only a quarter to three in the afternoon, it was already pitch-dark when Kollberg arrived at the Långholmen Prison. He felt cold and miserable, the bare visitors' room was shabby and bleak, and he paced gloomily up and down while waiting for the prisoner he had come to see, Birgersson, the man who had killed his wife.

After about fifteen minutes the door opened and a prison guard admitted a small, thin-haired man of about sixty. The man stopped just inside the door, smiled and bowed politely. Kollberg went up to him. They shook hands.

"Kollberg."

"Birgersson."

The man was pleasant and would be easy to talk to.

"Inspector Stenström? Oh yes, indeed, I remember him. Such a nice man. Please give him my kind regards."

"He's dead."

"Dead? I can't believe it. . . . He was just a boy. How did it happen?"

"That's just what I want to talk to you about."

Kollberg explained in detail why he had come.

"I've played back the whole tape of his questioning you and listened carefully to every word. But I presume the tape recorder was not going when you sat talking over coffee and so on."

"That's right."

"But you did talk then, too?"

"Oh yes. Most of the time, anyway."

"What about?"

"Well, everything really."

"Can you recall anything that Stenström seemed specially interested in?"

The man thought hard and shook his head. "We just talked about things in general. On this and that."

Kollberg took out the notebook he had brought from Åsa's apartment and showed it to Birgersson. "Does this mean anything to you? Why has he written 'Morris'?"

The man's face lit up at once. "We must have been talking about cars. I had a Morris 8, the big model, you know. And I think I mentioned it on one occasion."

"I see. Well, if you happen to think of anything else, please call me up at once. At any time."

"It was old and didn't look like much, my Morris, but it went well. My . . . wife was ashamed of it. Said she was ashamed to be seen in such an old rattletrap—"

He blinked rapidly and broke off.

Kollberg quickly wound up the conversation. When the guard had led the prisoner away, a young doctor in a white coat entered the room.

"Well, what did you think of Birgersson?" he asked.

"He seemed nice enough."

"Yes," the doctor said. "He's okay. All he needed was to be rid of that woman he was married to."

Kollberg looked hard at him, put his papers into his pocket and left.

THE TIME WAS eleven thirty on Saturday evening and Gunvald Larsson felt cold in spite of his heavy winter coat, his fur cap, ski pants and ski boots. He was standing in a doorway, as still as only a policeman can stand. He was not there by chance, and it was not easy to see him in the dark. He had already been there for four hours and this was not the first evening, but the tenth or eleventh.

Shortly before midnight a gray Mercedes with foreign license plates stopped outside the door of the apartment house across the street. A man got out, opened the trunk and lifted out a suitcase. Then he crossed the sidewalk, unlocked the door and went inside. Two minutes later a light was switched on behind lowered venetian blinds in two windows on the ground floor.

Gunvald Larsson strode swiftly across the street. He had already tried out a suitable key to the street door two weeks ago. Once inside the entrance hall, he took off his overcoat, folded it neatly and hung it over the handrail of the marble staircase, placing his fur cap on top. Unbuttoned his jacket and gripped the pistol that he wore clipped to his waistband. He had known for a long time that the door to the lighted room opened inward. He looked at it for five seconds and thought, If I break in without a valid reason, I'll probably be suspended. But it doesn't matter because I can always go to sea.

Then he took out his pistol and kicked in the door.

Ture Assarsson and the man who had alighted from the car were standing one on either side of a desk. To use a hackneyed phrase, they looked thunderstruck. They had just opened the suitcase and it was lying between them.

Gunvald Larsson waved them aside with the pistol, lifted the telephone and dialed Police Headquarters with his left hand without lowering his service pistol. He said nothing. The other two said nothing either. There was not much to say.

The suitcase contained 250,000 tablets of a brand of dope called Ritalin. On the black market they were worth about one million Swedish kronor.

GUNVALD LARSSON got home to his apartment at three o'clock on Sunday morning. He was a bachelor and lived alone. As usual he spent twenty minutes in the bathroom before putting on his pajamas and getting into bed. He picked up a novel he was reading, but after only a minute he reached for the telephone and dialed Martin Beck's number.

Gunvald Larsson made it a rule never to think of his work

when he was at home, and he could not recall ever before having made an official call after he had gone to bed.

Martin Beck answered after the second ring.

"Hi. Did you hear about Assarsson?"

"Yes."

"Something has just occurred to me."

"What?"

"That we might have been making a mistake. Stenström was of course shadowing Gösta Assarsson. And the murderer killed two birds with one stone—Assarsson and the man who was shadowing him."

"Yes," Martin Beck agreed. "There may be something in what you say."

Gunvald Larsson was wrong about Assarsson. Nevertheless, he had just put the investigation onto the right track.

FOR THREE EVENINGS in succession Ulf Nordin trudged about town trying to make contact with Stockholm's underworld, going in and out of the beer halls, coffeehouses, restaurants and dance halls that Blonde Malin had given as Göransson's haunts.

Those expeditions did not provide one new fact about the man Nils Erik Göransson. In the daytime, however, Nordin managed to supplement Blonde Malin's information by consulting the census bureau, parish registers, seamen's employment exchanges and the man's ex-wife, who said she had not seen him for nearly twenty years.

On Saturday morning he reported his lean findings to Martin Beck. Then he sat down and wrote a long, yearning letter to his wife in Sundsvall, now and then casting a guilty look at Rönn and Kollberg, who were both hard at work at their typewriters.

He had not had time to finish the letter before Martin Beck entered the room. "What idiot sent you out into town?" he asked Nordin fretfully.

Nordin quickly slipped a copy of a report over the letter. He had just written ". . . and Martin Beck gets more peculiar and grumpy every day."

"You sent him out yourself," Kollberg said.

"What? *I* did?"

"Yes, you did. Last Wednesday after Blonde Malin was here."

Martin Beck looked disbelievingly at Kollberg. "Funny, I don't remember that. It's idiotic all the same to send out a northerner who can hardly find his way around on a job like that."

Nordin looked offended but had to admit to himself that Martin Beck was right.

"Rönn," Martin Beck said, "you'd better find out where Nils Göransson hung out, whom he was with and what he did. And try and get hold of that guy Björk, the one he lived with."

"Okay," Rönn said.

He was busy making a list of possible interpretations of Schwerin's last words. At the top he had written: "Dinner record." At the bottom was the latest version: "Didn't reckon."

Each was busier than ever with his own particular job.

Chapter Nine

MARTIN BECK got up at six thirty on Monday morning after a practically sleepless night. He felt slightly sick and his condition was not improved by a cup of cocoa. He sat in the kitchen with his daughter. There was no sign of any other member of the family.

"What are you thinking about, Daddy?" Ingrid asked.

"Nothing," he said automatically.

"I haven't seen you laugh since last spring."

Martin Beck raised his eyes from the Christmas brownies dancing in a long line across the oilcloth on the table, looked at his daughter and tried to smile. Ingrid was a good girl, but that wasn't much to laugh at either. She went to get her books. By the time he had put on his hat and coat and galoshes she was standing with her hand on the door handle, waiting for him.

Nine years ago he had carried Ingrid's bag on her first day at school, and he still did so. On that occasion he had taken her hand. A very small hand, which had been warm and moist and trembling with excitement. When had he given up taking her hand? He couldn't remember.

"On Christmas Eve you're going to laugh, anyway," she said.

"Really?"

"Yes. When you get my Christmas present."

"What would you like yourself, by the way?"

"A horse."

"Where would you keep it?"

"I don't know. I'd like one all the same."

"Do you know what a horse costs?"

"Yes, unfortunately."

They parted.

At headquarters, Gunvald Larsson was waiting, and an investigation that didn't even deserve to be called a guessing game. Hammar had been kind enough to point this out two days ago.

"How is Ture Assarsson's alibi?" Gunvald Larsson asked.

"Ture Assarsson's alibi is one of the most watertight in the history of crimes," Martin Beck replied. "At the time in question he was making an after-dinner speech to twenty-five persons."

"Hm-m," Gunvald Larsson muttered darkly.

"What's more, if I may say so, it's not very logical to imagine that Gösta Assarsson would not notice his own brother getting on the bus with a submachine gun under his coat."

"Yes," said Gunvald Larsson. "If he wasn't carrying the gun in a case, that is."

"You're right, there," Martin Beck said.

"It does sometimes happen that I'm right."

"Lucky for you," Martin Beck retorted. "If you'd been wrong the night before last we'd have been sitting pretty now." Pointing his cigarette at the other man he added, "You're going to get it one of these days, Gunvald."

Gunvald Larsson stumped out of the room.

KOLLBERG WENT over to the window and looked out.

"Is Åsa still staying with you and Gun?" Martin Beck asked.

"Yes," Kollberg replied. He stood silent for a while, then

added doubtfully, "I doubt if I can get anything more out of her. Åsa, I mean."

"Well, never mind, we know what Stenström was working on," Martin Beck said. "The minute you told me about his sexual-psychological experiments with Åsa Torell, I knew what he had been working on."

Kollberg gaped at him. "Did you?"

"Sure. The Teresa murder. Hadn't you realized that?"

"No," Kollberg said. "I hadn't. And I've thought back over everything from the last ten years. Why didn't you say anything?"

Martin Beck looked at him and bit his ball-point pen thoughtfully. They both had the same thought and Kollberg put it into words: "One can't communicate merely by telepathy."

"No," Martin Beck said. "Besides, the Teresa case is sixteen years old. And you had nothing to do with the investigation. I forgot that you didn't know as much about that murder as I did. I think Ek is the only one left here from that time."

"So you've already gone through all the reports?"

"By no means. Only skimmed through them. There are several thousand pages. All the papers are out at Västberga. Shall we go and have a look?"

"Yes, let's. My memory needs refreshing."

In the car Martin Beck said, "Perhaps you remember enough to realize why Stenström took on the Teresa case?"

Kollberg nodded. "Yes, because it was the most difficult one he could tackle."

"Exactly. The most impossible of all things impossible. He wanted to show what he was capable of, once and for all."

"And then he went and got himself shot," Kollberg said. "How stupid. Can the Teresa case be solved? Now?"

"Shouldn't think so for a moment," Martin Beck replied.

KOLLBERG SIGHED unhappily as he listlessly turned the pages of the reports piled in front of him.

"It will take a week to wade through all this," he said.

"At least. Do you know the actual circumstances?"

"No, not even in broad outline."

"I can give you a rough idea."

Martin Beck picked out one or two sheets and said, "The facts are clear-cut. Very simple. Therein lies the difficulty."

"Fire away," Kollberg said.

"On the morning of June 10, 1951, that is to say more than sixteen years ago, a man who was looking for his cat found a dead woman in some bushes near Stadshagen sports ground here in town. She was naked, lying on her stomach with her arms by her sides. The forensic medical examination showed that she had been strangled and that she had been dead for about five days. The body was well preserved and had evidently been lying in a cold-storage room or something similar. Examination showed that the body could not have been lying there for more than twelve hours at the most. Further, fibers were found indicating that she had been transported there wrapped in a gray blanket. It was therefore quite clear that the crime had not been committed in the place where the body was found, and that the body had just been slung into the bushes. Little attempt had been made to hide it. Well, that's about all. . . . No, I was forgetting. Two more things: She had not eaten for several hours before she died. And there was no trace of the murderer in the way of footprints or anything."

Martin Beck turned over the pages of the typewritten text.

"The woman was identified the very same day as one Teresa Camarão. She was twenty-six years old and was born in Portugal. She had come to Sweden in 1945 and the same year had married a fellow countryman called Henrique Camarão. He was two years older than she and had been a radio officer in the merchant marine but had gone ashore and got a job as a radio technician. Teresa Camarão was born in Lisbon in 1925. According to the Portuguese police she came from a good home and a very respectable family. Upper middle class. She had come to study, rather belatedly because of the war. That's as far as her studies got. She met this Henrique Camarão and married him. They had no children. Comfortably off. Lived on Torsgatan."

"Who identified her?"

"The police. That's to say the vice squad. She was well known there and had been for the last two years. On May 15, 1949—circumstances were such that it was possible to determine the exact date—she had completely changed her way of life. She had run away from home—so it says here—and since that time she had circulated in the underworld here. In short, Teresa Camarão had become a prostitute. She was a nymphomaniac and during these two years she had gone with hundreds of men."

"Yes, I remember," Kollberg said.

"Within the space of three days the police found no less than three witnesses who, at half past eleven the evening before, had seen a car parked on Kungsholmsgatan by the approach to the path beside which the body was found. Two of them had passed in a car, one of them on foot. The two witnesses who had been driving had also seen a man standing by the car. Beside him on the ground lay an object the size of a body, wrapped in something that seemed to be a gray blanket. The third witness walked past a few minutes later and saw only the car. The descriptions of the man were vague. It was raining and the person had stood in the shadow; all that could be said for sure was that it was a man and that he was fairly tall. Pressed for what they meant by tall, they varied between 5 feet 9 and 6 feet 1 inch, which includes ninety percent of the country's male population. But—"

"Yes? But what?"

"But as regards the vehicle, all three witnesses were agreed. Each said that the car was French, a Renault model 4 CV, which was put on the market in 1947 and which turned up year after year with no change to speak of."

"Renault 4 CV," Kollberg said. "Porsche designed it while the French kept him prisoner as a war criminal. They shut him up in the gatekeeper's house at the factory. There he sat designing. Then, I think, he was acquitted. The French made millions out of that car."

"You have a staggering knowledge of the most widely differing subjects," Martin Beck said dryly. "Can you tell me now what connection there is between the Teresa case and the fact that Stenström was shot dead by a mass murderer on a bus four weeks ago?"

"Wait a bit," Kollberg said. "What happened then?"

"The police here in Stockholm carried out the most extensive murder investigation ever known in this country. It swelled to gigantic proportions. Well, you can see for yourself. Hundreds of persons were questioned who had known and been in touch with Teresa Camarão, but it could not be established who had last seen her alive. All trace of her case came to an abrupt end exactly one week before she was found dead. Every single Renault 4 CV was tracked down. First in Stockholm, since the witnesses said that the car had an A license plate. Then every car in the whole country of that make and model was checked, with the idea that it might have had a false license plate. It took almost a year. And at last it could be proved, actually proved, that not one of all those cars could have stood at Stadshagen at eleven thirty on the evening of June 9, 1951."

"Hm-m. And at that moment . . ." Kollberg said.

"Precisely. At that moment the entire investigation wound up. The only thing wrong with it was that Teresa Camarão had been murdered and it was not known who had done it. The last twitch of life in the Teresa investigation was in 1952, when the Danish, Norwegian and Finnish police informed us that the car could not have come from any of those countries. At the same time the Swedish customs confirmed that it could not have come from anywhere else abroad."

"And the three witnesses . . ."

"The two in the car were friends from work. One was foreman at a garage and the other a car mechanic. The third witness was also very well informed in the matter of cars. By profession he was a police sergeant. Specialist in traffic questions.

"These three men were made to undergo a series of tests. One at a time they were asked to identify silhouettes of different types of cars, projected on slides. All three recognized every current model, and the foreman even knew the most exotic makes. They couldn't even trick him when they drew a car that didn't exist. He said, 'The front is a Fiat 500, and the back is from a Dyna Panhard.' "

"What did the guys in charge of the investigation think? Privately?" Kollberg asked.

"The inside talk was something like this: The murderer is to be found among all the papers, it's one of the countless men who went with Teresa Camarão. The investigation collapsed because someone bungled over the checkup of all these Renault cars. So let's check them once again. And once again. Then they thought, quite rightly, that after all that time the scent had grown cold. They still thought that at some point or other the rundown of the cars had slipped up and that it was too late to do anything about it. And on the whole I agree."

Kollberg sat silent for a while. Then he said, "What happened to Teresa on that day you mentioned that her life suddenly changed? In May 1949?"

Martin Beck studied the papers and said, "She received a kind of shock, which led to a mental and physical state which is comparatively rare but by no means unique. Teresa Camarão had grown up in an upper-middle-class Catholic family. She was a virgin when she married at the age of twenty. She lived for four years with her husband in a typical Swedish manner, although both were foreigners. She was reserved, sensible and had a quiet disposition. Her husband considered the marriage a happy one. She was, a doctor says here, a pure product of strict Catholic upper-class parents and a strict Swedish bourgeois environment, with all the moral taboos inherent in each.

"On May 15, 1949, her husband was away on a job in the north. She went to a lecture with a woman friend. There they met a man whom the friend had known for years. He accompanied them back to the Camarãos' apartment, where the friend was to spend the night. They sat talking about the lecture over a glass of wine. This guy was feeling a bit down because he had fallen out with a girl—whom incidentally he married not long afterward. He thought Teresa was attractive, and started making a pass at her. The woman friend, who knew that Teresa was the most moral person imaginable, went off to bed—she slept on a sofa in the hall, within earshot. The guy kept trying with Teresa, but she kept saying no. At last he simply lifted her out of the chair, carried her into the bedroom, undressed her and made love to her. Apparently it was the first time sex had been a pleasure for her. Next morning the guy said 'so long,' and off he went. She called him up ten times a day for the next week, and after that he never heard from her again. He made it up with his girl and married her, and got on very well."

"And Teresa started running around?"

"Yes. She left home, her husband would have nothing more to do with her, and she was dropped by all her friends and acquaintances. For two years she lived for short periods with a score of different men and had relations with ten times as many. She was, as I said, a nymphomaniac, ready for anything. Of course, she never met anyone who could put up with her for any length of time. She tumbled right down the social ladder. Within six months the only people she mixed with were those who belonged to what we then called the underworld. The vice squad knew of her but could never quite keep up with her."

Pointing to the bundle of reports, Martin Beck went on.

"Among all these papers are a lot of interrogations with men who fell prey to her. They say she never left them alone and was impossible to satisfy. Most of them got scared to death the very first time, especially those who were married and were just out for a bit of fun on the side. She also knew a large number of shady characters and semi-gangsters, thieves and con men and black-market swindlers and the like."

"What happened to her husband?"

"Not unnaturally, he considered himself scandalized. He changed his name and became a Swedish citizen. Met a girl of good family, remarried, had two children and lived happily ever after. His alibi was watertight. . . . If you look through this folder you'll understand where Stenström got some of his ideas."

Kollberg looked inside it.

"My God! Who took these pictures?"

"A man interested in photography who had a perfect alibi and who had nothing to do with a Renault car. But unlike Stenström, he sold his pictures at a fat profit. As you remember we didn't have the same profusion of naked women then as we have now."

They sat silent for a while. At last Kollberg said, "What possible connection can this have with the fact that Stenström and eight other people are shot dead on a bus sixteen years later?"

"None at all," Martin Beck replied.

"Why did Stenström say nothing—" Kollberg began and then broke off.

"All that is explained now," Martin Beck said. "Stenström was going through unsolved cases. As he was very ambitious and still rather naive he picked the most hopeless one he could find. If he solved the Teresa murder it would be a fantastic detective feat. And he said nothing to us because he knew that some of us would laugh at him. When Teresa Camarão lay in the morgue Stenström was twelve and probably didn't even read the newspapers. He considered he could look at it in quite an unbiased way. He combed right through this investigation."

"And what did he find?"

"Nothing. Because there's nothing to find. There's not one loose thread."

"How do you know?"

Martin Beck looked gravely at Kollberg and said, "I know because I did exactly the same thing eleven years ago. I didn't find anything either. Except I didn't have an Åsa Torell to carry out experiments with."

"So that's why we found those pictures in his drawer? He was trying out a kind of psychological method?"

"Yes. That's all there is left. Find a person who resembles Teresa in some respect and see how she reacts."

"But this doesn't tell us what he was doing on the bus."

"No. It doesn't tell us a damn thing."

"I'll check a couple of things anyway," Kollberg said.

"Yes, do," Martin Beck said.

KOLLBERG SEARCHED out Henrique Camarão, who now called himself Hendrik Caam, a corpulent, middle-aged man who sighed and stole an unhappy glance at his blonde upper-class wife and a thirteen-year-old son with a Beatles hairdo, and said, "Am I never to be left in peace? Only last summer there was a young detective here and . . ."

Kollberg also checked Caam's alibi for the evening of November 13. It was faultless.

He also tracked down the man who had taken the pictures of Teresa eighteen years earlier and found a toothless old alcoholic in a cell in the long-term pavilion of the central prison. The man, who had been a burglar, screwed up his mouth and said, "Teresie. I'll say I remember her. Funny thing, there was another cop here a few months ago and . . ."

Kollberg read every word of the report. It took him exactly a week. On Tuesday, December 18, 1967, he read the last page.

There's no missing part in this, Kollberg thought. No loose ends. All the same, tomorrow I'll make a list of all the people who were interrogated or who are known to have been with Teresa Camarão. Then we'll see who all are still left and what they're doing now.

A MONTH HAD PASSED since the shots were fired on the bus on Norra Stationsgatan. The mass murderer was still at large.

The police commissioner, the press and the general public were not the only ones who showed their impatience. There was yet another category of people who were particularly anxious for the police to find the guilty man as soon as possible. This category is popularly known as the underworld. So long as the police were on the alert, it was best to lie low. There was not a thief, junkie, pusher, mugger, or pimp in the whole of Stockholm who didn't hope that the mass murderer would soon be seized so that the police could once more devote their time to Vietnam demonstrators and parking offenders and they themselves could get back to work. One result was that most of them had no objections to helping in the hunt for the murderer.

Rönn's work in his search for the pieces of the jigsaw puzzle named Nils Erik Göransson was made easier by this willingness. He had spent the last few nights searching out people who had known Göransson in restaurants, beer bars, billiard parlors and rooming houses. On the evening of December 15, he met a girl who promised to put him in touch with Sune Björk, the man who had let Göransson share his apartment for a time.

The next day he sat down at the kitchen table of his apartment with paper and pen. He laid Nordin's report and his own notebook in front of him, put on his glasses and began to write.

Nils Erik Göransson.

Born in the Finnish parish, Stockholm, October 1929.

Parents: Algot Erik Göransson, electrician, and Benita Rantanen.

Parents divorced 1933, mother moved to Helsinki and father given custody of the child.

G. lived with father till 1945.

Went to school for 7 years, thereafter 2 years at trade school learning house-painting.

1947 moved to Göteborg, where he worked as painter's apprentice. Married Gudrun Maria Svensson in Göteborg 1948. Divorced 1949. From June 1949 to March 1950 deckhand on boats of the Svea Steamship Company. Moved in the summer of 1950 to Stockholm. Employed as a house painter until November 1950, when he was dismissed for being drunk at work. From then on he seems to have gone downhill. He got odd jobs, as night porter, errand boy, porter, warehouseman, etc., but probably made a living mainly out of petty thieving and other minor crimes. Was never apprehended, however, as suspected of any crime but on several occasions was charged with being drunk and disorderly. For a time he called himself by his mother's maiden name, Rantanen. Father died 1958 and between 1958 and 1964 he lived in his father's apartment. Evicted 1964 because he was three months in arrears with rent.

He seems to have started using narcotics some time during 1964. From that year until his death he had no fixed residence. In January 1965 he moved in with Gurli Löfgren. Löfgren was registered with the vice squad but considering her age and appearance she cannot have earned much from prostitution during this time.

THE LAUGHING POLICEMAN

Löfgren too was addicted to drugs. Curli Löfgren died of cancer at the age of 47 on Christmas Day, 1966. At the beginning of March 1967 he met Magdalena Rosén (Blonde Malin) and lived with her until August 1967. From beginning of September until middle of October this year he had a temporary domicile with Sune Björk. Rosén says that Göransson was never without money and that she doesn't know where this money came from. To her knowledge, he was not a pusher and did not carry on any other form of business.

Rönn read through what he had written. His handwriting was so microscopic that it all fitted on less than one sheet of legal-sized paper. He put the paper in his briefcase and the notebook in his pocket, and went off to see Sune Björk.

Sune Björk was younger than Rönn had expected, not more than twenty-five. He had a blond beard and seemed nice enough. There was nothing about him to indicate that he was an addict, and Rönn wondered what he could have had in common with the much older and seedier Göransson.

Björk's apartment consisted of one room and kitchen and was poorly furnished. The windows looked onto an untidy courtyard. Rönn sat down on the only chair and Björk sat on the bed.

"I heard you wanted to know about Nisse," Björk said. "I must confess I don't know much about him myself, but I thought you could perhaps take care of his things."

He bent down and fished out a shopping bag from under the bed and gave it to Rönn. "He left this when he cleared out. He took some stuff with him—that's mostly clothes. Worthless junk."

Rönn took the bag and placed it beside the chair. "Can you tell me how long you knew Göransson, where and how you met and how you came to let him stay here with you?"

Björk settled down on the bed and crossed his legs. "It was like this, see. I was down at Zum Franziskaner having a beer and Nisse was sitting at the next table. We started talking and he stood me a drink. I thought he seemed a nice guy so when they closed and he said he had no pad, I brought him back here. This must have been the third or fourth of September."

"Did you notice he was an addict?" Rönn asked.

Björk shook his head. "No, not at once. But after a couple of days he gave himself a fix in the morning as soon as we woke up and then, of course, I realized it. He asked if I wanted one, by the way, but I don't dig that sort of thing."

Björk had rolled his sleeves up above his elbows. Rönn cast a practiced eye at the bends of his arms and noted that he was evidently telling the truth.

"You haven't much room here," he said. "Why did you let him stay here for so long? Did he pay for his keep, by the way?"

"I thought he was okay. He didn't pay any rent, but he had plenty of money and always brought home grub and liquor and so on."

"Where did he get his money from?"

Björk shrugged.

"I dunno. He didn't have any job, I know that."

Rönn looked at Björk's hands, which were black with in-grained dirt.

"What's your job?"

"Cars," Björk replied. "I've got a date in a while, so you'd better get a move on. Anything more you wanted to know?"

"What did he talk about? Did he tell you anything about himself?"

Björk rubbed his forefinger quickly to and fro under his nose and said, "He said he'd been to sea, though I think that was years ago. And he used to talk about dames. Especially one he'd been living with who had kicked the bucket not long before. She was like a mom, he said, only better."

"When did he clear out of here?"

"On the eighth of October. I remember because it was a Sunday and it was his name day. He took his things, all except them there. He didn't have many, they all went into an ordinary bag. He said he had got himself another pad but that he'd come by and say hello in a day or two."

He paused and stubbed out his cigarette in a coffee cup that was standing on the floor.

"After that I never saw him again. Was he really one of those on the bus?"

Rönn nodded. "Do you know where he went to from here?"

"Haven't a clue. He never looked me up and I didn't know where he was. He met several of my mates here, but I never met any of his."

Björk got up, went over to a mirror hanging on the wall and combed his hair. "I have to change now," he said. "My dame's waiting."

Rönn stood up, took the shopping bag and walked toward the door. "So you've no idea what he did with himself after the eighth of October?" he said.

Björk took a clean shirt out of the chest of drawers and tore off the laundry's paper strip.

"I only know one thing," he said.

"What?"

"He was as nervous as hell for a week or two before he cleared out. Seemed to have something on his mind."

"But you don't know what?"

"No, I don't."

WHEN RÖNN got home to his apartment he went into the kitchen and emptied the contents of the shopping bag onto the table. Then he picked the objects up cautiously and studied them before dropping them back into the bag, one at a time. A spotted, threadbare cap, a pair of undershorts, a wrinkled tie, an artificial leather belt with a yellow brass buckle, a pipe with a chewed stem, a wool-lined pigskin glove, a pair of yellow crepe nylon socks, two dirty handkerchiefs and a crumpled light blue poplin shirt.

Rönn held the shirt up and was just going to put it back in the bag when he noticed a scrap of paper sticking out of the breast pocket. He put the shirt down and unfolded the paper. It was a bill for Kr. 78:25 from Restaurant Pilen. It was dated October 7, and according to the sums stamped by the cash register, it was for food, liquor and soda water.

Rönn turned the bill over. In the margin on the back someone had written with a ball-point pen:

October 8, from bf	3000
Morph	500
Owe ga	100
Owe mb	50
Dr. P	650
	1300
Bal	1700

Rönn took the jottings to mean that Göransson, on the eighth of October—the same day he left Sune Björk—had gotten 3000 kronor from somewhere, perhaps from a person with the initials B.F. Out of this money he would buy morphine for 500, pay 150 in debts and give a Dr. P 650, for drugs or something else. That would leave him 1700. When he was found dead in the bus over a month later he had had over 1800 kronor in his pocket. So he must have received more money after the eighth of October. Rönn wondered whether this, too, had come from the same source, bf or B.F. It needn't be a person, it could just as well be an abbreviation for something else.

Brought forward? Göransson didn't seem the type that would have a bank account. The most likely thing after all was that bf was a person. Then he went to bed and lay wondering where Göransson had got his money from.

Chapter Ten

A WEEK LATER, on the morning of Thursday, December 21, Rönn stood in the wind gazing at a hole in the ground and a tarpaulin; some of the highway department's trestles had been placed around about. The hole was quite uninhabited. Not so the service truck that was parked over fifty yards away. Rönn knew the four men who sat inside fiddling with their thermos flasks and merely said, "Hello, there."

"Hello. Shut the door. Like some coffee?"

"Thanks, I don't mind if I do."

After a while one of the men said, "Want anything special?"

"Yes . . . A man named Schwerin—he was born in America. Was it noticeable when he talked?"

"Was it! He had an accent and when he was drunk he spoke English."

"When he was drunk?"

"Yes. And when he lost his temper. Or forgot himself."

Rönn took a bus back to headquarters. It was a red double-decker, packed with people who stood clutching for support with one hand and grasping Christmas packages with the other.

He thought hard all the way. Then he sat down at his desk for a while. Went into the next room and said, *"Drnk,"* and then in English, "Didn't recognize him," and went out again.

"Now he's gone crazy too," Gunvald Larsson growled.

"Wait a second," Martin Beck said. "I think he's got something there." He got up and went after Rönn. The room was empty. His hat and coat were gone.

Half an hour later Rönn once again opened the door of the highway department truck. The men who had been Schwerin's co-workers were sitting in exactly the same place as before. The hole in the road looked untouched by human hands.

"You scared me," one of them said. "I thought it was Olsson."

"Olsson?"

"Yes. Or 'Oleson,' as Schwerin used to say."

Rönn did not produce his results until the next morning, two days before Christmas Eve.

Martin Beck stopped the tape recorder and said, "So you think it should go like this: You say, 'Who did the shooting?' And he answers in English, 'Didn't recognize him.' "

"Yes."

"And then you say, 'What did he look like?' and Schwerin answers in English, 'Like Olsson.' "

"Yes. And then he died."

"Splendid, Einar," Martin Beck said.

"Who the hell is Olsson?" Gunvald Larsson asked.

"A sort of inspector. He goes around between the different working sites and checks to see that the men aren't loafing."

"And what *does* he look like?"

"He's next door in my office," Rönn said modestly.

Martin Beck and Gunvald Larsson went in and stared at Olsson. And went out. Olsson stared after them, mouth agape, in puzzlement.

When Martin Beck returned from lunch, Rönn had put a sheet of paper on his desk.

Olsson.

Olsson is 48 years old, an inspector for the highway department.
He is 6 feet tall and weighs 170 pounds stripped.

He has ash-blond wavy hair and gray eyes. He is lankily built.

His face is long and lean with distinct features, prominent nose, rather crooked, wide mouth, thin lips and good teeth.

Rather dark complexion, which he says is due to his work, which forces him to be so often out of doors.

Clothing: neat, gray suit, white shirt with tie and black shoes. Out of doors at work, wears a waterproofed, knee-length raincoat, wide and loose-fitting. Color, gray. He has two such coats and always wears one of them in winter. On his head he has a black leather hat with narrow brim. He has heavy black shoes with deep-ribbed rubber soles on his feet. In rain or snow, however, he usually wears black rubber boots.

Olsson has an alibi for the evening of November 13. At the time in question, from 10 p.m. to midnight, he was at premises belonging to a bridge club of which he is a member. He took part in a competition and his presence is confirmed by the competition scorecard and the testimonies of the three other players.

Regarding Alfons (Alf) Schwerin, Olsson says that he was easy to get on with but lazy and given to strong drink.

"Do you think Rönn stripped him and weighed him?" Gunvald Larsson said.

Martin Beck did not answer.

"He had the hat on his head and the shoes on his feet. He

wore only one overcoat at a time," Larsson went on. "What are you going to do with that?"

"Don't know. It's sort of a description."

"Yes, of Olsson."

"What about Assarsson?"

"I was talking to Jacobsson of the drug squad just now," Gunvald Larsson said. "Even he admits that Assarsson was the biggest wholesale dealer in dope they've ever laid hands on. They must have made money by the sackful, those brothers."

"And that foreigner you took in with him?"

"He was just a courier. Greek. An addict himself. Assarsson thinks he was the one who squealed." He paused briefly. "That Göransson on the bus was also an addict. I wonder . . ."

Gunvald Larsson did not finish the sentence, but he had given Martin Beck something to think about.

Kollberg plodded away with his lists but preferred not to show them to anyone. He began more and more to understand how Stenström had felt while he was working on this old case. The work with the list of men who had associated with Teresa Camarão was by no means easy. It was amazing how many people managed to die, emigrate or change their names in sixteen years. Others were in prison or mental hospitals or in homes for chronic alcoholics. A number had simply disappeared, either at sea or in some other way. Many had long since moved to distant parts of the country, made a new life for themselves and their families and could in most cases be written off after a quick routine checkup. By this time Kollberg had reduced his list to twenty-nine persons who were at large and still lived in Stockholm or the vicinity of the city.

Kollberg sighed as he looked at the list. Teresa Camarão had included all social groups in her activities. She had also operated within different generations. When she died the youngest of these men had been fifteen and the eldest sixty-seven. On this list alone there was everything from bank managers in Stocksund to alcoholic old burglars at the Högalid institution.

"What are you going to do with that?" Martin Beck asked.

"Don't know," Kollberg replied despondently but untruthfully. Then he went in and laid the papers on Melander's desk.

"You remember everything. When you have a moment to spare will you see if you recall anything extraordinary about any of these men?"

Melander cast a blank look at the list and nodded.

On the twenty-third Månsson and Nordin flew home, missed by nobody. They were to return immediately after Christmas.

Outside, the weather was cold and horrible.

On his way home that evening, Martin Beck thought that Sweden now had, not only its first mass murder, but also its first unsolved murder of a policeman.

The investigation had stuck fast. And technically—unlike the Teresa investigation—it looked like a pile of rubbish.

CHRISTMAS EVE arrived. Martin Beck got a Christmas present from his daughter, Ingrid, which, despite all speculations to the contrary, did not make him laugh.

He woke up early but stayed in bed reading until the rest of the family began to show signs of life. Then he got up and pulled on a pair of jeans and a sweater. His wife, who thought people ought to be dressed up on Christmas Eve, frowned as she eyed his clothes but for once said nothing.

While she paid her traditional visit to her parents' grave, Martin Beck decorated the tree together with Rolf and Ingrid. The children were noisy and excited, and he did his best not to dampen their spirits. His wife returned from her ritual call on the dead and he gamely joined in a custom that he didn't care for—dipping bread into the pot in which a ham had been cooked.

After a colossal Christmas Eve dinner came punch and ginger cookies. Ingrid said, "Now I think it's time to lead in the horse."

As usual they had all promised to give only one present to each and as usual they had all bought a lot more. Martin Beck had not bought a horse, but as a substitute he gave Ingrid riding breeches and paid for her riding lessons for the next six months.

His own presents included a model construction kit of the clipper ship *Cutty Sark* and a scarf two yards long, knitted by Ingrid. She also gave him a flat package, watching him expectantly as he unwrapped the paper. Inside was a 45 rpm record. On the jacket was a photograph representing a fat man in the familiar uniform and helmet of the London bobby. He had a large, curling mustache and knitted mittens on his hands, which he held spread out over his stomach. He was standing in front of an old-fashioned microphone and to judge from his expression he was roaring with laughter. His name was apparently Charles Penrose and the record was called *The Adventures of the Laughing Policeman.*

Ingrid fetched the record player and put it on the floor beside Martin Beck's chair. "Just wait till you hear it," she said. "It'll kill you." She took the record out of its jacket and looked at the label. "The first song is called *The Laughing Policeman*. Pretty appropriate, eh?"

Martin Beck knew very little about music, but he heard at once that the recording must have been made in the twenties or even earlier. Each verse was followed by long bursts of laughter, which were evidently infectious, as Inga and Rolf and Ingrid howled with mirth.

Martin Beck was left utterly cold. He couldn't even manage a smile. So as not to disappoint the others too much he got up and turned his back, pretending to adjust the candles on the tree.

When the record was finished he went back to his chair. Ingrid wiped the tears from her eyes and looked at him.

"Why, Daddy, you didn't laugh," she said reproachfully.

"I thought it was awfully amusing," he said as convincingly as he could.

"Listen to this, then," Ingrid said, turning the record over. "*Jolly Coppers on Parade.*"

Ingrid had evidently played the record many times and she joined in the song as though she had done nothing else but sing duets with the laughing policeman.

The candles burned with a steady flame, the fir tree gave out its scent in the warm room, the children sang and Inga curled up in her new dressing gown and nibbled the head of a marzipan pig. Martin Beck sat leaning forward, his elbows propped on his knees and his chin in his hands, staring at the laughing policeman on the record jacket.

He thought of Stenström.

And the telephone rang.

SOMEWHERE INSIDE him Kollberg felt far from content. But as it was hard to say exactly why, there was no reason to spoil his Christmas Eve with unnecessary brooding. He therefore mixed the punch with care, tasting it several times before he was satisfied, then sat down at the table and regarded the deceptively idyllic scene surrounding him. Bodil lying on her stomach beside the Christmas tree, making gurgling noises. Åsa Torell sitting with crossed legs on the floor, playfully poking at the baby. Gun sauntering about the apartment with a soft, indolent nonchalance, barefoot and dressed in some mysterious garment that was a cross between pajamas and a tracksuit.

He helped himself to a serving of fish, prepared especially for Christmas Eve. He sighed happily at the thought of the large, well-deserved meal he was about to gobble up, and tucked a napkin into his shirt and draped it over his chest. He poured out a big drink of aquavit, raised the glass, looked dreamily at the clear ice-cold liquid and the mist forming on the glass. And at that moment the phone rang.

He hesitated a moment, then drained the glass at one gulp, went into the bedroom and lifted the receiver.

"Good evening, my name is Fröjd, from Långholmen Prison."

"Well, that's cheering," said Kollberg, in the secure knowledge that he was not on the emergency list and that not even a new mass murder could drive him out into the snow. Capable men were detailed for such things. Gunvald Larsson, for example, was on call, and Martin Beck had to take the consequences of his higher rank.

"I work at the mental clinic here," the man said. "And we

have a patient who insists on talking to you. His name's Birgers-son. Says you questioned him and he promised to tell you—"

Kollberg frowned. "Can he come to the phone?"

"Sorry, no. It's against the rules."

Kollberg's face took on a sorrowful expression. "Okay, I'll come," he said, and put down the phone.

His wife had heard these last words and stared at him wide-eyed. "Have to go to Långholmen," he said wearily. "How the hell do you get a taxi at this hour on Christmas Eve?"

"I can drive you," Åsa said. "I haven't drunk anything."

They did not talk on the way. The guard at the entrance peered suspiciously at Åsa. "She's my secretary," Kollberg said.

Birgersson seemed even more gentle and polite than he had been two weeks earlier.

"What do you want to tell me?" Kollberg said gruffly.

Birgersson smiled. "It seems silly," he said. "But I just remembered something this evening. You were asking about my car, my Morris. And—"

"Yes? And?"

"Once when Inspector Stenström and I sat having something to eat, I told him a story."

Kollberg regarded the man with massive disapproval.

"A story?" he asked.

"A story about myself, really." He broke off and looked doubt-fully at Åsa Torell.

"Well, go on," Kollberg growled.

"My wife and I, that is. We had only one room and when I was at home I always used to feel nervous and restless. I also slept badly."

"Uh-huh," Kollberg grunted. He was very thirsty and above all hungry. Moreover, his surroundings depressed him and he longed for home. Birgersson went on talking, quietly but long-windedly.

". . . so I used to go out of an evening, just to get away from home. This was nearly twenty years ago. I walked and walked the streets for hours, sometimes all night. After a while I'd calm down, it usually took an hour or so. But I had to occupy my thoughts with something, you see, in order to keep from worrying about everything else. So I used to find things to do. To divert myself, you might say, and keep myself from brooding."

Kollberg looked at his watch.

"Yes, yes, I see," he said impatiently. "What did you do?"

"I used to look at cars."

"Cars?"

"Yes. I used to walk along the street and through parking lots, looking at the cars that stood there. Actually I wasn't at all interested in cars, but in that way I got to know all the makes and models there were. After a time I became quite an expert. I could recognize all cars forty to fifty yards away from in front or from behind or from the side, it made no difference."

"And you told Inspector Stenström about this?" Kollberg asked.

"Yes. He said he thought it was interesting."

"I see. And this is what you brought me here to say? At nine thirty in the evening? On Christmas Eve?"

Birgersson looked hurt.

"Yes," he replied. "You did say I was to tell you anything I remembered . . ."

"Yes, sure," Kollberg said wearily. "Thank you."

He stood up.

"But I haven't told you the most important part yet," the man murmured. "It was something that interested Inspector Stenström very much. It occurred to me since we'd been talking about my Morris."

Kollberg sat down again.

"Yes? What?"

"Well, it had its problems, this hobby, if I may call it that. It was very hard to distinguish between certain models in the dark or if they were a long way off. For instance, Moskvitch and Opel Kadett."

"What has this to do with Stenström and your Morris 8?"

"No, not my Morris," Birgersson replied. "What interested the inspector so much was when I told him that the hardest of all was to see the difference between a Morris Minor and a Renault 4 CV from in front. Not from the side or the back, that was easy. But from straight in front or obliquely in front—that was very difficult indeed. Though I learned in time and seldom made a mistake."

"Wait a moment," Kollberg said. "Did you say Morris Minor and Renault 4 CV?"

"Yes. And I remember that Inspector Stenström gave quite a jump when I told him. All the time I was talking he had just sat there nodding, and I didn't think he was listening. But when I said that he was terribly interested. Asked me about it several times."

"From in front, you said?"

"Yes. He asked that too, several times. From in front or obliquely in front. Very difficult."

When they were sitting in the car again, Åsa Torell asked, "What's this all about?"

"I don't quite know yet. But it might mean quite a lot."

"About the man who killed Åke?"

"Don't know. At any rate it explains why he wrote down the name of that car in his book."

"I've also remembered something," she said. "Something Åke said a couple of weeks before he was killed. He said that as soon as he could take two days off he'd go down to Småland and investigate something. To Eksjö, I think. Does that tell you anything?"

"Not a thing," Kollberg replied.

The city lay deserted. The only signs of life were two ambulances, a police car, and a few Santa Clauses staggering about, handicapped by far too many glasses in far too many hospitable homes. After a while Kollberg said, "Gun told me you're leaving us in the new year."

"Yes. I've exchanged the apartment for a smaller one. I'm selling the furniture and buying new stuff. I'm going to get a new job, too."

"Where?"

"I haven't quite decided. But I've been thinking it over."

She was silent for a few seconds. Then she said, "What about the police force? Are there any vacancies?"

"I'll say there are," Kollberg replied absently.

Then he started and said, "What! Are you serious?"

"Yes," she replied. "I am serious."

Åsa Torell concentrated on her driving. She frowned and peered out into the whirling snow.

When they got back Bodil had fallen asleep, and Gun was curled up in an armchair reading. There were tears in her eyes.

"What's wrong?" he asked.

"The dinner," she said. "It's ruined."

"Not at all. With your appearance and my appetite you could put a dead cat on the table and make me overjoyed."

"And that hopeless Martin called up. Half an hour ago."

"Okay," Kollberg said jovially. "I'll give him a buzz while you're getting the grub."

He took off his jacket and tie and went to the phone.

"Hello. Beck."

"Who's doing all that howling?" Kollberg asked suspiciously.

"The laughing policeman."

"What?"

"A phonograph record."

"Oh yes, now I recognize it. An old music hall tune. Goes back to before the First World War."

A roar of laughter was heard in the background.

"It makes no difference," Martin Beck said joylessly. "I called you because Melander called me."

"What did he want?"

"He said that at last he had remembered where he had seen the name Nils Erik Göransson."

"Where?"

"In the investigation concerning Teresa Camarão."

Kollberg unlaced his shoes. He thought for a moment, then said, "Then you can tell him from me that he's wrong for once.

I've just read the whole pile, every damn word. And I'm not so dumb that I wouldn't have noticed a thing like that."

"Have you the papers at home?"

"No. But I'm sure. Dead sure."

"Okay. I believe you. What did you do at Långholmen?"

"Got some information. Too vague and complicated for me to explain now, but if it's right—"

"Yes?"

"Then you can throw away every single sheet of the Teresa investigation. Merry Christmas."

He put down the phone.

"Are you going out again?" his wife asked suspiciously.

"Yes. But not until Wednesday. Where's the aquavit?"

Chapter Eleven

IT TOOK A LOT to depress Melander, but on the morning of the twenty-seventh he looked so miserable and puzzled that even Gunvald Larsson brought himself to ask, "What's with you?"

"It's just that I don't usually make a mistake."

"There's always a first time," Rönn said consolingly.

"Yes. But I don't understand, all the same."

Martin Beck had knocked on the door and before anyone had time to react he was in the room, standing there tall and grave, coughing slightly. "What is it you don't understand?"

"About Göransson. That I could make a mistake."

"I've just been going over the papers," said Martin Beck, "and I found something that might cheer you up."

"What is that?"

"There's a page missing from the Teresa investigation. Page 1244, to be exact."

At three o'clock that afternoon Kollberg was standing outside an automobile salesroom. He had already got through a lot this day. He had made sure that the three witnesses who had observed a Renault 4 CV at Stadshagen sports ground sixteen and a half years earlier must have seen the vehicle from the front or possibly from obliquely in front. He had supervised some photographic work, and rolled up in his inside pocket he had a dark-toned, slightly retouched advertising picture of a Morris Minor 1950 model. Of the three witnesses two were dead, but the car expert—the workshop foreman—was still hale and hearty. He now sat in an office, talking on the phone. When the call was finished Kollberg went in, without knocking and without in any way saying who he was. He merely laid the photograph on the desk in front of the man and said, "What make of car is this?"

"A Renault 4 CV. An old job."

"Are you sure?"

"Bet your life, I'm sure. I'm never wrong."

"Positive?"

The man glanced again at the picture.

"Yes," he said. "It's a 4 CV. Old model."

"Thanks," Kollberg said, reaching for the photograph.

The man gave him a puzzled look and said, "Wait a sec. Are you trying to trick me?"

He examined the picture thoroughly. After a good fifteen seconds he said slowly, "No. This isn't a Renault. It's a Morris. A Morris Minor, 1950 or 1951 model. And there's something wrong with the picture."

"Yes," Kollberg said. "It has been touched up and made to look as if it were taken in a bad light and in the rain, for instance on a summer evening."

The man stared at him.

"Look here, who are you anyway?"

"Police," Kollberg replied.

"I might have known it," the man said. "There was a policeman here early last fall who . . ."

SHORTLY BEFORE five thirty the same afternoon Martin Beck had assembled his immediate colleagues for a briefing at investigation headquarters. Nordin and Månsson had returned from Christmas leave, and the investigating force was complete except for Hammar, who had gone away for all of Christmas week.

"So there's a page missing from the Teresa investigation," Melander said with satisfaction. "Who can have taken it?"

Martin Beck and Kollberg exchanged a quick glance.

"Does anyone here consider himself a specialist in house-searching?" Martin Beck asked.

"I'm good at searching," Månsson said listlessly from his seat. "If there's anything to be found, I'll find it."

"Good," Martin Beck said. "I want you to comb through Stenström's apartment."

"What shall I look for?"

"A page out of a police report," Kollberg said. "It should be numbered 1244 and it's possible that the name Nils Erik Görans-son occurs in the text."

"Tomorrow," Månsson said. "It's always easier in daylight."

"I'll give you the keys in the morning," Kollberg said. He already had them in his pocket but wanted to remove one or two traces of Stenström's photography before Månsson set to work.

AT TWO O'CLOCK the next afternoon the phone on Martin Beck's desk rang.

"Greetings. It's Månsson."

"Well?"

"I'm in Stenström's apartment. The sheet of paper isn't here."

"Are you sure?"

"Sure?" Månsson sounded deeply offended. "Of course, I'm sure. But are *you* sure he's the one who took that page?"

"We think so, anyway."

"Oh well, I'd better go on looking somewhere else."

"There must be a copy of the investigation in the central files," Gunvald Larsson growled.

"Yes," Martin Beck said, pressing a button on the telephone and dialing an interoffice number.

In the room next door, Kollberg and Melander were discussing the situation.

"I've been looking through your list," said Melander.

"Did you find anyone on it whose name is familiar?"

"Yes, several. But I don't know whether it's of any use."

"I'll soon tell you."

"Several of those guys are crooks who have been sentenced dozens of times. They're too old to work now."

"Go on."

"Johan Gran was a fence then and no doubt still is. He did time only a year ago. And this Valter Eriksson killed his wife with a kitchen chair during a drunken brawl. Was convicted of manslaughter and got five years."

"I'll be damned."

"There are other troublemakers besides him in this collection. Bengt Fredriksson has been sentenced for assault and battery no less than six times. A couple of the charges should have been for attempted manslaughter, if you ask me. I remember Björn Forsberg, too. He was up to quite a few crooked dealings as a young fellow. Then he turned over a new leaf and made a nice career for himself. Married a wealthy woman and became a respected businessman. Hans Wennström also has a first-rate list of crimes, everything from shoplifting to safecracking. And Bo Frostensson is a third-rate actor and notorious junkie."

"Didn't this girl ever take it into her head to sleep with any decent guys?" Kollberg said plaintively.

"Oh yes, sure. You have several on this list. Married too, all of them."

"Had a bad time, I expect, explaining this to their wives," Kollberg said.

"On that point the police were pretty discreet. When it comes to the youngsters, who were about twenty or even younger, there was nothing much wrong with them. Do you want me to start rooting seriously in these people's pasts?"

"Yes, please. You can weed out those who are over sixty now. Likewise the youngest, from thirty-eight downward."

Melander consulted the list. "That leaves fourteen. The field is shrinking. All these men, of course, have an alibi for the Teresa murder."

"Bet your life they have," Kollberg said.

NEW YEAR'S EVE and 1968 arrived before the search for copies of the report showed any results, and not until the morning of January 5 was there a dusty pile of papers lying on Martin Beck's desk. He didn't need to be a detective to see that it had come from the innermost recesses of the files and that several years had passed since it had last been touched by human hands.

Martin Beck turned over quickly until he came to page 1244. Kollberg leaned over his shoulder. The text was brief.

> Interrogation of salesman Nils Erik Göransson, August 7, 1951.
>
> Regarding himself, Göransson states that he was born in the Finnish parish in Stockholm on Oct. 4, 1929. He is at present employed as salesman by the firm of Allimport, Stockholm.
>
> Göransson owns to having known Teresa Camarão, who periodically moved in the same circles as he did, though not during the months immediately prior to her death. Göransson owns further that on two occasions he had intimate relations with Teresa Camarão, when several other persons were also present. Of these he says he remembers only one Karl Svensson-Rask. Göransson says he does not remember the exact dates but thinks the events must have taken place at an interval of several days at the end of November and/or beginning of December the previous year, i.e., 1950. Göransson says he knows nothing of Mrs. Camarão's acquaintances otherwise.
>
> At the time of the murder Göransson was in Eksjö, to which he drove for the purpose of the sale of clothes for the firm where he is employed. Göransson is the owner of automobile A 6310, a 1949 model Morris Minor. This statement read out and approved.
>
> (Signed)
>
> It can be added that the above-mentioned Karl Svensson-Rask is identical with the man who first informed the police of Göransson's relations with Mrs. Camarão. Göransson's account of his visit to Eksjö is confirmed by the staff of the City Hotel at that place. Questioned in detail about Göransson's movements on the evening of June 10, Sverker Johnsson, waiter at the said hotel, states that Göransson sat the whole evening in the hotel dining room, until this was closed at 11:30 p.m. Göransson was then the worse for liquor. Sverker Johnsson's statements are confirmed by items on Göransson's hotel bill.

"Well, that's that," Kollberg said. "So far."

"What are you going to do now?"

"What Stenström didn't have time for. Go down to Eksjö."

"The pieces of the puzzle are beginning to fit together," Martin Beck said.

KOLLBERG ARRIVED in Eksjö on the morning of Monday, January 8. He had driven down during the night, 208 miles in a snowstorm and on icy roads, but did not feel particularly tired even so. The City Hotel was a handsome, old-fashioned building that blended perfectly into the idyllic setting of this little country town. The waiter called Sverker Johnsson had died, but a copy of Nils Erik Göransson's hotel bill still existed. It took several hours to fish it out of a dusty cardboard box in the loft.

The bill seemed to confirm that Göransson stayed at the hotel for eleven days, ate all his meals and did all his drinking in the hotel dining room. One item, however, caught Kollberg's eye. On June 6, 1951, the hotel had paid a garage bill on Göransson's behalf, for "towing and repairs."

"Does this garage still exist?" Kollberg asked the hotel owner.

"Oh, sure it does, and the same owner the last twenty-five years. Just follow the road out toward Långanäs and . . ."

Actually the man had had the garage for twenty-seven years. He stared incredulously at Kollberg and said, "Sixteen and a half years ago? How the hell can I remember that?"

"Don't you keep books?"

"You bet I do," the man said indignantly. "This is a properly run place."

It took him an hour and a half to find the old ledger. He turned the pages slowly until he came to the day in question. "The sixth of June," he murmured. "Here it is. Picked up from hotel, that's right. The throttle cable had gone haywire." Kollberg waited. "Towing," muttered the man. "What an idiot. Why didn't he hook up the cable with something and drive here?"

"Have you any particulars about the car?" Kollberg asked.

"Yes. Registration number A . . . A 67 . . . something. I can't read it. Someone's put an oily thumb over the figures. Evidently a Stockholmer, anyway."

"You don't know what sort of car it was?"

"Sure I do. A '49 Ford Vedette."

"Not a Morris Minor?"

"If it says Ford Vedette here, then a Ford Vedette it damn well was," the garage owned said testily.

Kollberg took the ledger with him. When finally he got back to the hotel it was evening. He was hungry, cold and tired, and instead of starting the long drive north he took a room at the hotel. He had a bath and ordered dinner. While he was waiting for the food he made two phone calls. First to Melander.

"Will you please find out which of the guys on the list of fourteen had cars in June 1951? And what makes?"

"Sure. Tomorrow morning."

"And the color of Göransson's Morris?"

"Yes."

Then a call to Martin Beck.

"Göransson didn't bring his Morris here. He was driving another car."

"So Stenström was right."

"Can you put someone on finding out who owned that firm where Göransson was employed, and what it did?"

"Sure."

"I should be back in town about midday tomorrow."

He went down into the dining room and had dinner. As he sat there it suddenly dawned on him that he had in fact stayed at this same hotel exactly sixteen years ago when he was working on a taxi murder. If he had known then what he knew now he could probably have solved the Teresa case in ten minutes.

ON TUESDAY morning Rönn got an idea and as usual when something was weighing on his mind he went to Gunvald Larsson. Despite the far from cordial attitude they adopted toward each other at work, Rönn and Gunvald Larsson were friends. Very few outsiders knew this, and they would have been even more surprised had they known that the two had in fact spent both Christmas and New Year's Eve together.

"I've been thinking about Göransson's restaurant bill with the letters bf written on the back," Rönn said. "On that list that Melander and Kollberg are messing about with are three persons with those initials. Bo Frostensson, Bengt Fredriksson and Björn Forsberg."

"Well?"

"We could take a cautious look at them and see if any of them resembles Olsson."

"Can you track them down?"

"I expect Melander can."

Melander could. It took him only twenty minutes to find out that Forsberg was at home and would be at his office downtown after lunch. At twelve o'clock he was to have lunch with a client at the Ambassadör. Frostensson was at a studio out at Solna playing a small part in a film.

"And Fredriksson is presumably drinking beer at the Café Ten Spot. He's usually to be found there at this hour of day," Melander said.

"I'll come with you two," Martin Beck said, to the surprise of Rönn and Gunvald Larsson.

Sure enough Bengt Fredriksson, artist and brawler, was in that café. He was very fat, had a bushy, unkempt beard and lank gray hair. He was already drunk.

Out at Solna the production manager piloted them through long, winding corridors to a corner of the big film studio. "Frostensson is to play a scene in five minutes," he said. "It's the only line he has in the film."

They stood at a safe distance but in the mercilessly strong spotlights they clearly saw the set evidently meant to be the interior of a little grocery store.

"Stand by!" the director shouted. "Silence! Camera! Action!" A lean, bald little man with a nervous twitch around his mouth, dressed in a white cap and coat, came into the stream of light and said, "Good morning, madam. May I help you?"

"Cut!"

There was a retake, and another. Frostensson had to say the line five times.

Half an hour later Gunvald Larsson braked the car twenty-five yards from the gates of Björn Forsberg's mansion. Martin Beck and Rönn crouched in the back. Through the open garage doors they could see a black Mercedes of the largest model.

"He should be leaving now," Gunvald Larsson said, "if he doesn't want to be late for his lunch appointment."

They had to wait fifteen minutes before the front door opened and a man appeared on the steps together with a blonde woman, a dog and a little girl of about seven. He kissed the woman on the cheek, lifted the child up and kissed her. Then he strode down to the garage, got into the car and drove off. The little girl blew him a kiss, laughed and shouted something.

Björn Forsberg was tall and slim. His face, with regular features and candid expression, was strikingly handsome, as though drawn from the illustration for a short story in a woman's magazine. He was suntanned and his bearing was relaxed. He was bareheaded and was wearing a loose-fitting gray overcoat. His hair was wavy and brushed back. He looked younger than his forty-eight years.

"Like Olsson," Rönn said. "Especially his build and clothes. The overcoat, that is."

"Hm-m," Gunvald Larsson murmured.

NOT ONLY DID Kollberg oversleep, but the weather was worse than ever. By one thirty he had still got only as far as a motel just north of Linköping. He stopped for a cup of coffee and called up Stockholm.

"Well?" he asked Melander.

"Only nine of them had cars in the summer of '51," Melander replied. "A new Volkswagen for—"

"Stop. Did anyone have a '49 Ford Vedette?"

"Björn Forsberg had a '49 Ford Vedette."

"Then that'll do."

"The original paintwork on Göransson's Morris was pale green. He could, of course, have had it repainted."

"Fine. Can you switch me over to Martin?"

"One more detail. Göransson sent his car to the scrapyard in the summer of '51. It was removed from the car registry on August 15, only one week after Göransson had been questioned about Teresa."

Kollberg put another coin into the phone and thought impatiently of the 127 miles still ahead of him. In this weather the drive would take several hours.

"Hello, this is Superintendent Beck."

"Hi. What did Göransson's firm do?"

"Sold stolen goods, I should think. But it could never be proved. They had a couple of traveling salesmen who went around the provinces peddling clothes and the like."

"And who owned it?"

"Björn Forsberg."

Kollberg thought for a moment and then said, "Tell Melander to concentrate entirely on Forsberg. And ask Hjelm if either he himself or someone else will stay at the lab until I get up to town. I've something that must be analyzed."

AT FIVE O'CLOCK Kollberg had still not returned. Melander tapped at Martin Beck's door and went in, pipe in one hand and some papers in the other. He began speaking at once: "Björn Forsberg was married on June 17, 1951, to a woman called Elsa Håkansson. She was the only child of a businessman who dealt in building materials and was the sole owner of his firm. He was considered very wealthy. After his marriage, Forsberg immediately wound up all his former commitments. He worked hard, studied economics and developed into an energetic businessman. When Håkansson died nine years ago his daughter inherited both his fortune and his firm, but Forsberg had already become its managing director."

Martin Beck blew his nose.

"How long had he known the girl before he married her?"

"They seem to have met while skiing in March '51," Melander replied. "It seems to have been so-called love at first sight. They kept on meeting right up to the wedding and he was a frequent guest in her parents' home. He was then thirty-two and Elsa Håkansson, twenty-five."

Melander changed papers.

"The marriage seems to have been a happy one. They have three children, two boys who are thirteen and twelve and a girl of seven. He sold his Ford Vedette soon after the wedding and bought a Lincoln. He's had dozens of cars since then."

Melander was silent and lighted his pipe.

"What else have you found out?"

"One more thing. Important, I should think. Björn Forsberg was a volunteer in the Finnish-Russian War in 1940. He was twenty-one and went off to the front straight after he'd done his military service here at home. His father was a warrant officer in the Wende artillery regiment."

"Okay, it seems to be him."

"Looks like it," Melander said. "Shall we look at his alibis?"

"Exactly," Martin Beck said.

KOLLBERG DIDN'T reach Stockholm until seven o'clock. He drove first to the forensic laboratory with the garage ledger.

"We have regular working hours," Hjelm said sourly. "We finish at five."

"Then it would be awfully good of you to—"

"Okay, okay, I'll call you before long. Is it only the car number you want?"

"Yes. I'll be at headquarters."

Kollberg and Martin Beck hardly had time to begin talking when the call came through.

"A 6708," Hjelm said laconically.

"Excellent."

"Easy. You should almost have been able to see it yourself."

Kollberg put down the phone. Martin Beck gave him an inquiring look.

"Yes. It was Forsberg's car that Göransson used at Eksjö. No doubt of that. What are Forsberg's alibis like?"

"Weak. In June '51, he had a bachelor apartment in the same building as that mysterious firm. At the interrogation he said that he had been in Norrtälje on the evening of the ninth. Evidently that was true. He met some person there at seven o'clock. Then, still according to his own statement, he took the last train back to Stockholm, arriving at eleven thirty in the evening. He also said that he had lent his car to one of his salesmen, who confirmed this."

"But he was careful not to say that he had exchanged cars with Göransson."

"Yes," Martin Beck said. "So he had Göransson's Morris, and this puts a different complexion on things. He made his way comfortably back to Stockholm by car in an hour and a half. There was parking space in the rear courtyard of his apartment building, and no one could see in from the street. There was also a cold-storage room in the yard. It was used for fur coats, which officially had been left for summer storage but which in all probability were stolen. Why do you think they exchanged cars?"

"I expect the explanation is very simple," Kollberg said. "Göransson was a salesman and had a lot of clothes and junk with him. He could pack three times as much into Forsberg's Vedette as into his own Morris." He sat in silence for half a minute, then said, "I suppose when Göransson got back he realized what had happened and that the car might be dangerous. That's why he had it scrapped immediately after the interrogation."

"What did Forsberg say about his relations with Teresa?" Martin Beck asked.

"That he met her at a dance hall in the fall of 1950 and took up with her for a while. Then he met his future wife in the winter and lost interest in Teresa altogether. Why do you think he killed her? To get rid of an unwanted partner, as Stenström wrote in the margin of Wendel's book?"

"Presumably. They all said they couldn't shake her off. And it wasn't a sex murder."

531

"No, but he wanted it to look like one. And then he had the unbelievable stroke of luck that the witnesses got the cars mixed up. That meant he could feel pretty well safe. Göransson was the only worry."

"Göransson and Forsberg were pals," Martin Beck said.

"Nothing happened until Stenström started rooting in the Teresa case and got that tip about the resemblance between Morrises and Renaults from Birgersson. He found out that Göransson was the only one who had had a Morris Minor. The right color, what's more. He started shadowing Göransson and soon noticed that Göransson was getting money from someone and assumed that it came from whoever had murdered Teresa Camarão."

Martin Beck nodded.

"Stenström figured out that sooner or later Göransson would lead him to the murderer, and so he went on shadowing him day after day, and presumably quite openly. It turned out that he was right. Though the result for his own part was not a success. If he had hurried up with that trip to Eksjö instead . . ." Kollberg paused.

"Yes, it seems to fit," Martin Beck said thoughtfully. "Psychologically as well. Forsberg had to get rid of Stenström and Göransson, both of whom were extremely dangerous by this time. There were still nine years before the Teresa murder case would have lapsed and the period of prosecution expired. And a murder is the only crime sufficiently grave for a more or less normal person to go to such lengths in order to avoid discovery. Besides, Forsberg has unusually much to lose."

"Do we know what he did on the evening of November 13?"

"The only thing we know at present is that he had an opportunity to commit the murders."

"How do we know that?"

"Gunvald managed to question Forsberg's German maid. The thirteenth, she said, was her night off and she spent it with her boyfriend. She also told Gunvald that Mrs. Forsberg was out at a ladies' dinner that evening. Consequently, Forsberg himself was presumed to be at home. On principle, they never leave the children alone."

"Where is she now? The maid?"

"Here. And we're keeping her overnight."

"What do you think about Forsberg's mental condition?" Kollberg asked.

"Probably very bad. On the verge of collapse."

"The question is, do we have enough evidence to take him in?" Kollberg asked.

"Not for the bus," Martin Beck replied. "That would be a blunder. But we can arrest him as a suspect for the murder of Teresa Camarão."

"When?"

"Tomorrow morning."

"Where?"

"At his office. The minute he arrives. No need to drag his wife and children into it, especially if he's desperate."

"How?"

"As quietly as possible. No shooting and no kicked-in doors."

Kollberg thought before asking his last question. "Who?"

"Myself and Melander."

Chapter Twelve

WHEN MARTIN BECK and Melander entered the reception room of Forsberg's office it was only five minutes past nine. They knew that Forsberg did not usually come until about nine thirty.

"If you care to, please sit down and wait," the receptionist said.

On the other side of the room, out of sight of the receptionist, some armchairs were grouped around a low glass table. The two men hung up their overcoats and sat down.

The six doors leading out of the reception room had no nameplates. One of them was ajar. Martin Beck got up, peeped in the door and vanished inside the room. Melander took out his pipe and tobacco pouch, filled his pipe and struck a match. Martin Beck came back and sat down. They sat in silence, waiting.

It was close to ten when Forsberg arrived.

He was dressed in the same way as the day before and his movements were brisk and energetic. He was just about to hang up his overcoat when he caught sight of Martin Beck and Melander. He checked himself in the middle of the movement for a fraction of a second but recovered himself quickly, hung the coat on a hanger and went toward them.

Martin Beck and Melander stood up together. Björn Forsberg raised his eyebrows questioningly. He opened his mouth to say something, and Martin Beck put out his hand and said, "Superintendent Beck. This is Detective Inspector Melander. We'd like a word with you."

Björn Forsberg shook hands with them. "Why, certainly," he said. "Please come in."

The man appeared quite calm and almost gay as he held open the door for them. He nodded to his secretary and said, "Good morning, Miss Sköld. I'll be engaged with these gentlemen for a little while."

He preceded them into his office, which was large and light and tastefully furnished. The floor was covered from wall to wall with a deep-pile gray-blue carpet, and the big desk was shining and empty. Two telephones, a dictaphone and an intercom stood on a small table beside the swivel chair covered in black leather. On the wide windowsill stood four photographs in pewter frames. His wife and three children. The room also contained a cocktail cabinet, a conference table, a sofa and two easy chairs, some books and china figurines in a case with sliding glass doors, and a safe discreetly set into the wall.

All this Martin Beck saw as he closed the door behind him and watched Björn Forsberg walk toward his desk with deliberate steps.

Laying his left hand on the top of the desk, Forsberg leaned forward, pulled out the drawer on the right and put his hand into it. When his hand reappeared, the fingers were closed around the butt of a pistol.

Still supporting himself against the desk with his left hand, he raised the barrel of the pistol toward his open mouth, pushed it in as far as he could, closed his lips around the shiny blue-black steel and pulled the trigger. He looked steadily at Martin Beck the whole time. His eyes were still almost cheery.

All this happened so quickly that Martin Beck and Melander were only halfway across the room when Björn Forsberg collapsed sprawling over the desk.

The pistol had been cocked and a sharp click had been heard as the hammer fell against the chamber. But the bullet that was to have rotated through the bore and shattered Björn Forsberg's brain never left the barrel. It was still inside the cartridge that lay in Martin Beck's pocket, together with the other five that had been in the magazine.

Björn Forsberg lay with his face pressed against the smooth desk top. His body was shaking. After a few seconds he slipped to the floor and began to scream.

"We'd better call an ambulance," Melander said.

So RÖNN WAS sitting once more with his tape recorder in an isolation ward at Karolinska Hospital. This time not in the surgical department but at the mental clinic, and as company he had Gunvald Larsson instead of the detested Ullholm.

Björn Forsberg had been given various treatments with tranquilizing injections and a lot of other things, and the doctor concerned with his mental recovery had already been in the room for several hours. But the only thing the patient seemed able to say was, "Why didn't you let me die?"

He had repeated this over and over again, and now he said it once more. "Why didn't you let me die?"

"Yes, why didn't we?" Gunvald Larsson mumbled, and the doctor gave him a stern look.

They would not have been here at all if the doctors had not said that there was a certain risk that Forsberg really would die. They had explained that he had been subjected to a shock of enormous intensity, that his heart was weak and his nerves had gone to pieces; they rounded off the diagnosis by saying that his general condition was not so bad. Except that a heart attack might make an end of him at any moment.

"Why didn't you let me die?" Forsberg repeated.

"Why didn't you let Teresa Camarão live?" Gunvald Larsson retorted.

"Because I couldn't. I had to get rid of her."

"Oh," Rönn said patiently. "Why did you have to?"

"I had no choice. She would have ruined my life."

"It seems to be pretty well ruined in any case," Gunvald Larsson said.

The doctor gave him another stern look.

"You don't understand," Forsberg complained. "I had told her never to come back. I'd even given her money though I was badly off. And still—"

"What are you trying to say?" Rönn said kindly.

"Still she pursued me. When I got home that evening she was lying in my bed. She knew where I used to keep my spare key and had let herself in. And my wife . . . my fiancée was coming in fifteen minutes. There was no other way."

"And then?"

"I carried her to the cold-storage room where the furs were."

"Weren't you afraid that someone might find her there?"

"There were only two keys to it. I had one and Nisse Göransson the other. And Nisse was away."

Rönn nodded to himself. This was going well.

"Where did you get the submachine gun from?" Gunvald Larsson asked out of the blue.

"I brought it home from the war."

Forsberg lay silent for a moment. Then he added proudly, "I killed three Bolsheviks with it."

"Was it Swedish?" Gunvald Larsson asked.

"No, Finnish. Suomi model 37."

"And where is it now?"

"Where no one will ever find it."

"In the water?"

Forsberg nodded. He seemed to be deep in thought.

"Did you like Nils Erik Göransson?" Rönn asked after a while.

"Nisse was fine. A good kid. I was like a father to him."

"Yet you killed him?"

"He was threatening my existence. My family. Everything I live for. Everything I had to live for. He couldn't help it. But I gave him a quick and painless end. I didn't torment him as you're tormenting me."

"Did Nisse know that it was you who murdered Teresa?" Rönn asked. He spoke quietly and kindly the whole time.

"He figured it out," Forsberg replied. "Nisse wasn't stupid. And he was a good pal. I gave him 10,000 kronor and a new car after I was married. Then we parted forever."

"Forever?"

"Yes. I never heard from him again, not until last fall. He called up and said that someone was shadowing him day and night. He was scared and he needed money. I gave him money. I tried to get him to go abroad."

"But he didn't?"

"No. He was too down. And scared stiff. Thought it would look suspicious."

"And so you killed him?"

"I had to. The situation gave me no choice. Otherwise he would have ruined my existence. My children's future. My business. Everything. Not deliberately, but he was weak and unreliable and scared. I knew that sooner or later he would come to me for protection. And thereby ruin me. Or else the police would get him and force him to talk. He was a drug addict, weak and unreliable. The police would torture him till he told everything he knew."

"The police are not in the habit of torturing people," Rönn said gently.

For the first time, Forsberg turned his head. His wrists and ankles were strapped down. He looked at Rönn and said, "What do you call this?"

Rönn dropped his eyes.

"Where did you board the bus?" Gunvald Larsson asked.

"Outside Åhléns department store."

"How did you know which bus Göransson would take?"

"He called up and was given instructions."

"In other words, you told him what he was to do in order to be murdered," Gunvald Larsson said.

"Don't you understand that he gave me no choice? Anyway I did it humanely, he never knew a thing."

"Humanely? How do you make that out?"

"Can't you leave me in peace now?"

"Not just yet. Explain about the bus first."

"Very well. Will you go then? Promise?"

Rönn glanced at Gunvald Larsson, then said, "Yes. We will."

"Nisse called me up at the office on Monday morning. He was desperate and said that that man was following him wherever he went. I realized he couldn't hold out much longer. I knew that my wife and the maid would be out in the evening. And the children always go to sleep early, so I . . ."

"Yes?"

"So I said to Nisse that I wanted to have a look myself at the man who was shadowing him. That he was to entice him out to Djurgården and wait until a double-decker bus came and to take it from there about ten o'clock and ride to the end of the line. Before he left he was to call my direct number at the office. I left home soon after nine, parked the car, went up to the office and waited. I did not put the light on. He called up as agreed and I went down and waited for the bus."

"Had you decided on the place beforehand?"

"I picked it out earlier in the day when I rode the whole way on the bus. It was a good spot—I didn't think there would be anyone in the vicinity, especially if the rain kept up. And I figured out that only very few passengers would go all the way to the last stop. It would have been best if only Nisse and the man who was shadowing him and the driver and one more were on the bus."

"One more?" Gunvald Larsson remarked. "Who would that be?"

"Anybody. Just for the sake of appearances."

Rönn looked at Gunvald Larsson and shook his head. Then, turning to the man on the bed, he said, "How did it feel?"

"Making difficult decisions is always a trial. But when I've once made up my mind to carry something out—" He broke off. "Didn't you promise to go now?" he asked.

"What we promise and what we do are two different things," Gunvald Larsson said.

Forsberg looked at him and said bitterly, "All you do is torture me and tell lies."

"I'm not the only one in this room telling lies," Gunvald Larsson retorted. "You had decided to kill Göransson and Inspector Stenström weeks before, hadn't you?"

"Yes."

"How did you know that Stenström was a policeman?"

"I had observed him earlier. Without Nisse's noticing."

"How did you know he was working alone?"

"Because he was never relieved. I took it for granted that he was working on his own account. To make a career for himself."

Gunvald Larsson was silent for half a minute. "Had you told Göransson not to have any identification on him?" he said at last.

"Yes. I gave him orders about that the very first time he called up."

"How did you learn to operate the bus doors?"

"I had watched carefully what the drivers did."

"Whereabouts in the bus did you sit? Upstairs or down?"

"Upstairs. I was soon the only one there."

"And then you went down the stairs with the submachine gun at the ready?"

"Yes. I kept it behind my back so that Nisse and the others sitting at the rear wouldn't see it. Even so, one of them managed to stand up. You have to be prepared for things like that."

"Supposing it had jammed? Those old things often misfire."

"I knew it was in working order. I was familiar with my

weapon and I had checked it before taking it to the office."

"When did you take the submachine gun there?"

"About a week beforehand."

"Weren't you afraid that someone might find it there?"

"No one would dare go through my drawers," Forsberg said haughtily. "Besides, I had locked it up."

"Where did you keep it previously?"

"In a locked suitcase in the attic, with my other trophies."

"Which way did you go after you had killed all those people?"

"I walked eastward along Norra Stationsgatan, took a taxi, fetched my car outside the office and drove home."

"And chucked the submachine gun away en route," Gunvald Larsson said. "Don't worry. We'll find it."

Forsberg didn't answer.

"How did it feel?" Rönn repeated gently. "When you fired?"

"I was defending myself and my family and my home and my firm. Have you ever stood with a gun in your hands, knowing that in fifteen seconds you will charge down into a trench full of the enemy?"

"No," Rönn replied. "I haven't."

"Then you don't know anything!" Forsberg shouted. "You've no right to speak! How could an idiot like you understand me!"

"This won't do," the doctor said. "He must be given treatment now." He pressed the bell. A couple of orderlies came in. Forsberg went on raving as he was rolled out of the room.

Rönn started packing up the tape recorder.

"How I loathe that bastard," Gunvald Larsson muttered.

"What?"

"I'll tell you something I've never said to anyone else," Gunvald Larsson confided. "I feel sorry for nearly everyone we meet in this job. They're just a lot of scum who wish they'd never been born. It's not their fault that everything goes to hell and they don't understand why. It's types like this one who wreck their lives. Smug swine who think only of their money and their houses and their families and their so-called status. Who think they can order others about merely because they happen to be better off. There are thousands of such people and most of them are not so stupid that they strangle the girls they pick up. And that's why we never get at them. We only see their victims. This guy's an exception."

"Hm-m, maybe you're right," Rönn said.

They left the room. Outside a door farther down the corridor stood two policemen in uniform, legs apart and arms folded.

"Huh, so it's you two," Gunvald Larsson said morosely. "Oh yes, of course, this hospital is in Solna."

"You got him in the end, anyway," Kvant said.

"*We* didn't," Gunvald Larsson said. "It was really Stenström himself who fixed it."

ABOUT AN HOUR later Martin Beck and Kollberg sat drinking coffee. "It was really Stenström who cleared up the Teresa murder," Martin Beck said.

"Yes," Kollberg said. "But he went about it in a silly way all the same. Working on his own like that. And not leaving so much as a piece of paper behind him. Funny, that kid never grew up."

The phone rang. Martin Beck answered.

"Hello, it's Månsson."

"Where are you?"

"I'm out at southern headquarters at the moment. I've found that sheet of paper."

"Where?"

"On Stenström's desk. Under the blotter."

Martin Beck said nothing.

"I thought you said you'd looked here," Månsson said reproachfully. "And—"

"Yes?"

"He's made a couple of notes on it in pencil. In the top right-hand corner it says: 'To be replaced in the Teresa file.' And at the bottom of the page he has written a name. Björn Forsberg. And then a question mark. Does that tell us anything?"

Martin Beck made no reply. He just sat there with the receiver in his hand. Then he began to laugh.

The
Black Curtain

The
Black Curtain

A CONDENSATION OF
THE BOOK BY

Cornell
Woolrich

ILLUSTRATED BY RICK McCOLLUM

Frank Townsend suddenly recovers
from three years of amnesia. There is no
solid clue to how he spent those years —
nothing but a nagging feeling
someone is following him, and cold
dread when he tries to turn his
mind toward the missing years. He must
learn the truth about his past,
or be forever haunted by it.

Painstakingly, he tracks back
and begins to pick up the faint trail of his
other self, "Dan Nearing." As the
trail becomes clearer, it leads to a murder.
To Townsend's horror, he finds that he,
as "Dan Nearing," is accused of the crime.
He doesn't feel like a killer, but
unless he can find some flaw in the
overwhelming evidence, there is little
doubt he will be convicted.

Cornell Woolrich, one of America's
favorite mystery writers, also wrote, under
the name of William Irish, the story
Rear Window, made into a classic
Alfred Hitchcock film.

Chapter One

AT FIRST EVERYTHING was blurred. Then he could feel hands fumbling around him, lots of hands. They weren't actually touching him, they were touching things that touched him—flinging away small loose objects like chunks of mortar or fragments of brick that seemed to be strewn all over him.

Dimly he heard an unfamiliar voice say, "Here's the ambulance now."

Another answered, "Bring him over here, where we can get at him easier."

He felt himself being moved, set down again. He tried to open his eyes, but a lot of grit and dust settled into them and stung them shut again. The second time he tried, he got a blinding flash of light blue sky. Faces were peering down at him, upside down, around the perimeter of it.

He felt his coat and shirt being spread open and then pressure being applied along his sides. Someone flexed his arms and legs. "No broken bones. Just that nasty bump on his head and the scrape on his forehead." He was righted to a sitting position.

"Okay, brother," the intern said, "we'll dress this for you, and that ought to take care of it." He dabbed something on the scrape that burned and then plastered something over it. "All right, you can stand up now."

They helped him to his feet. He reached out and steadied himself against one of them for a moment, and then was able to stand by himself.

"You want to take a ride in with us and have yourself checked over?" the intern asked.

"No, I'm all right," he said. He wanted to get home. Virginia would be waiting for him.

A cop shoved forward with poised notebook and said, "Let me have your name and address."

"Frank Townsend," he answered unhesitatingly. "Eight Twenty Rutherford Street North."

That was all. The ambulance clanged off and the cop turned away. A pile of rubble on the sidewalk and a jagged rent in the roof coping of the building beside it were the only remaining signs of what had just happened. The thick cluster of onlookers began to fan out and disperse, and Townsend began to worm his way through them.

A youngster of twelve or so called out, "Hey, here's your hat! I picked it up for you."

Townsend took it from him, dusted it off sketchily, then stopped and stared down inside it. The hat had *DN* initialed on the sweatband.

He shook his head at the kid. "This isn't mine—"

"Sure it's yours! I seen it roll off you when you went down!"

Townsend cast his eyes doubtfully over the sidewalk, but there was no other hat in sight. The kid was eying him askance. "Don't you know your own hat, mister?"

Some of the grownups standing around laughed. Others turned and gaped at him. Still shaky from the accident, Townsend wanted to get away, to get home. He tried the hat on and it fit him to a T. It had that telltale feeling of having been on his head a hundred times before. So he left it on and made his way up the street, but he knew that he was wearing somebody else's initials on his head.

Looking around him now, he couldn't understand what he was doing in this neighborhood, what had brought him here in the first place. It was a slum, swarming with humanity and vendors' pushcarts. Was he on some mission from the office? Some errand for Virginia? Whatever it was, the shock of the accident had knocked it completely out of his mind. He turned the corner, passing under a street sign that read TILLARY STREET, and reached absently into his pocket for a cigarette.

Instead of the cheap, crumpled pack he was used to carrying around with him for days at a time, he brought up a wafer-thin black enamel case banded in gold, flashing at him with malignant brilliance. He dropped it as though it had bitten him and stared at it where it lay for long minutes. Finally he stooped, picked the case up with an unsteady hand and examined it. The cigarettes inside weren't even his own brand. And there was nothing on it to show whose it was or where he had got it.

He put it back in his pocket and forced himself to go on. He was afraid to let himself think too much. A strange terror darted in and out of the air just over his head, like lightning, and he was afraid to attract its full force. Now he wanted to get home more than ever.

He had to take a bus, he was so far out of his way. When he got off and the familiar reaches of Rutherford Street opened before his gaze, he trudged down it toward his apartment. Just a few doors more now and he'd be inside. But familiar as the street was, there was something a little different about it. Details seemed to have altered here and there. He saw the same familiar kids playing around, but they all looked bigger to him.

When he reached his apartment building, he stopped suddenly and stood rigid, looking at his own two ground-floor windows. What had happened here since this morning? The curtains were gone from the windows. The panes were cloudy, as though they hadn't been washed in weeks. Virginia always kept them crystalline. How could they have got into such a state since this morning?

He went into the hall, palpitating from the shock his nervous system had just received. He seemed to have lost his key, probably at the scene of the accident. He didn't waste time looking for it; he wanted to get inside, away from all this strangeness. He knocked and rattled the doorknob hectically, but Virginia didn't come to the door. He went back to the entrance and rang for Mrs. Fromm, the janitor's wife.

She came right up, but showed an inordinate surprise at seeing him. "Mr. Townsend! What are *you* doing around here?"

"What am I—?" he repeated dazedly. So she was going to be part of the strangeness, too.

"You thinking of taking your old apartment back? Just say the word. The last tenants moved out six weeks ago."

"My old apartment?" He felt his hackles rising, as if in the presence of some chilling, unfathomable mystery. He tried to get a tight grip on his mental equilibrium. *I'm Frank Townsend. I've come home like I do every day from work. Why is this happening to me?*

But instinctively, he knew that neither Mrs. Fromm nor any other outsider could help him in this. They would only involve him in all sorts of delays, maybe even haul him off to confinement. There was only one person he could go to, only one person he could fully trust: Virginia, wherever she was. But where was she?

He said, trying to sound casual, "Could you tell me where I can find my wife? Some falling plaster hit me on the head just now, and I guess I got a little dizzy and came here by mistake—"

She paled but gave him what he was hoping for. "Your wife's living on Anderson Avenue now, Mr. Townsend—two blocks down, the second house from the corner."

"Thanks," he said, backing away. "Isn't it funny how I—uh—got balled up?"

He went outside and walked rapidly down the street, his heart going like a trip-hammer. He was more than just frightened now. The terrifying mysteries were mounting. First, initials on his hatband that didn't match his name. Then a cigarette case in his pocket that he'd never seen before, full of a brand of cigarettes he'd never smoked. Now his home changed, without warning, between morning and evening. He began to run toward Anderson Avenue.

He found the place, and it was with a feeling close to horror that he read the name beneath one of the bells: MISS VIRGINIA MORRISON. What was she doing living in this strange apartment under her maiden name? Whatever it was that had happened, he knew he was about to have it explained to him. But that was no solace. He dreaded the explanation almost as much as the mystery.

He rang the bell and went into the hallway, to the door that bore a number matching the one beneath the bell. He stopped before it and waited. Minutes of deliriumlike strangeness passed, minutes tense with waiting for something to happen and wondering what it would be. Then the knob turned and the door opened a little, and there they were, looking at each other. He and she. Frank Townsend and his wife, Virginia.

He'd called her his rag doll. She'd always reminded him of a rag doll, the pert kind—maybe because she had a way of flinging herself into chairs sideways, over their arms. Then, too, she wore her hair cut in a straight line above her eyes. But now the rag doll was just a little faded, a little toned down.

He thought she was going to fall on the floor at his feet, but her grip on the door held her up. She leaned her forehead against the door frame for a minute, then suddenly she was in his arms and breathing against him as though she couldn't get enough air. He couldn't breathe very well himself; it was sort of catching.

"Virginia, honey, let me come in," he said. "I'm frightened. Queer things have been happening. I want to be inside with you."

She drew him inside, holding onto him with both hands, and closed the door. Then he was in the bedroom, sitting on one of their familiar twin beds. The other bed, stripped down and shunted against the wall, held an accumulation of boxes and other nondescript paraphernalia. He lay back and she sat down beside him, took his hand between both of hers and pressed it to her cheek. She didn't say anything. He could tell she was afraid, just as he was.

He kept staring at her questioningly. Finally he blurted out, "Virginia, I feel funny, like I'm lost. I don't understand it. Maybe it's only that clout on the head. But I've got to hear it from you. What made you do it? What made you move so suddenly without telling me? Why, when I left this morning to go to work—"

Her hands flew to her mouth in a vain attempt to stifle a cry. He reached up to her and pulled her hands down. "Virginia, speak to me!"

"Oh, Frank, what are you saying? *This morning*—? I moved to this apartment over a year and a half ago!"

He held his skull tightly pressed with both hands, as if to keep it from flying apart. "But I remember kissing you good-by at the door!" he said helplessly. "I remember you calling out after me to remind me, 'Sure you've got your muffler? It's cold out.' "

"Frank," she said, "the weather alone should tell you—it's warm out, you're not even wearing a coat now. You left me in the winter, and now it's spring. You left me on January 30, 1938. I never forgot that date. How could I? And today is— Wait, I'll let you read it for yourself."

She staggered out of the room and came back with that evening's newspaper. He scanned the dateline feverishly. "May 10, 1941."

He dug the heels of his hands desperately under the bony ridges of his eye sockets. "My God! What happened to all that time? Over three years! I can remember everything perfectly, every last detail, up to that morning. I can even remember what we had for breakfast. And just now, the molding of a building fell on me, on Tillary Street, and after they helped me up, I simply came on home, where I belonged. But what happened to those years between?"

"Don't you remember *any*thing at all?"

"No. They're gone. As though they never were."

"I've read about cases like this," she tried to reassure him. "Amnesia, I think they call it. Somewhere, after you left that morning, something must have happened to you—some accident, like what happened to you tonight on Tillary Street. And whatever it was, you picked yourself up, outwardly unhurt, but you didn't know who you were anymore. You forgot where you were going, forgot to come back home to me. And none of the people that saw it happen were any the wiser. The suit you were wearing that morning had just come back from the cleaner's, and you left in kind of a hurry, without taking time to transfer the personal things you usually carried around in your pockets from the old one to the new one. Any one of them—an address on an old envelope, a bill—would have helped you. But without them you were cut off completely."

He felt less starkly frightened as the hours wore on and they talked it over. Presently she said, "Frank, you're back now. That's all that counts. Let's forget about it." But deep within him he was still greatly troubled. He had lost his identity for three years, and the mystery of those years was still impenetrable, yawning behind him like an abyss. One misstep and—

In the still of the night, long after they'd put out the lights, he suddenly started upright, cold sweat needling his forehead. "Virginia, I'm scared! Put on the lights, I'm frightened of the dark! Where was I? *Who* was I, all that time?"

Chapter Two

HE HAD HIS old job back. Or at least, one with the same employers. In the weeks following his disappearance, Virginia had told them that he had suffered a nervous breakdown and had had to go away for a rest. Pride had made her do it. She couldn't bear to have anyone think she didn't know what had become of him. So when he had presented himself at the office, room had been made for him with the fewest possible questions asked. The old familiar routine was beginning to reclaim his daily life, and the blank was beginning to recede into the past.

The days were long now, and he emerged onto a street bright with sunlight as he left his place of work. He bought a paper, walked to his usual place for boarding the bus and began scanning the news.

He had been there at the street corner perhaps two minutes when something made him raise his eyes and peer over the paper. It was a feeling of being looked at intently. A man was about to pass him in the crowd streaming along the sidewalk, and Townsend's face seemed to have caught his attention. The roving glance became a fixed stare; the fixed stare became a searching scrutiny; and then the starer broke his headlong stride and faltered to a full stop.

The lens of Townsend's mind photographed, developed and printed an image of the man—all in one instantaneous process. He was sturdily built, a little below medium height, wearing a gray suit and hat. Beneath the low hat brim, his eyes were also gray, and agatelike under thick dark brows. Hard eyes. The kind that don't laugh.

Townsend didn't know him, thought he had never seen him before in his life, but an alarm bell started ringing in his heart. People don't stop and scrutinize you exhaustively on the street for no reason. This man recognized him, or thought he did. And whatever prompted his actions, it was obviously not an innocent social acquaintanceship.

Belatedly now, the man seemed to realize that he was attracting attention to himself and putting Townsend on his guard by staring so overtly. So he tried to undo the damage by abruptly continuing on his way along the bustling sidewalk. But he didn't go far. A nearby shop window seemed to attract his interest. He came to a halt before it, and with his back to the sidewalk, he peered in intently. Windows make good reflecting surfaces, Townsend knew.

The alarm bell within Townsend was a din by now. *I've got to get out of here!* he told himself grimly. He weighed the possibilities. The bus would be a four-wheeled trap if this unknown man chose to follow him aboard. Yet if Townsend returned to his office building and waited for a later bus, the stalker might still be lurking around when he came out again—and then he would know where Townsend worked, which he didn't seem to know as yet. But if Townsend simply took a walk around the block— well, two could walk around the block as well as one, at a spaced distance.

A hunted thing, whether two-legged or four-, instinctively seeks cover in a hole in the ground. And the next street over, there was a subway. He'd never used it before, because it was not the best route home, but he decided now that some action was better than the threat of this veiled surveillance.

That window was certainly holding the stranger a long time. Too long. Townsend readied himself. He waited for the traffic light to change, and then he made a break for it—not in full flight, but at a brisk walk.

While he was in the open, crossing to the other side, he didn't look back, although he felt an awful compulsion to do so. When he reached the opposite curb and the corner building line knifed across their mutual line of vision, he instantly changed his brisk walk to a long, loping run that ate up ground without being harried enough to arouse suspicion in the passers-by.

The clean-cut, oblong gap of the subway entrance ahead of him was his goal; he gained it and started down, his heels clicking on the steel-rimmed steps with a sound a little bit like dice being shaken. It was a chance; he had no choice but to take it.

When he was halfway down, he stopped and looked back, his eyes on a level with the street. What he saw sent him hurtling the rest of the way down. The man was careening up the street after him full tilt. He meant business.

Townsend arrived at the station level just as a surging roar exploded into a razzle-dazzle of illuminated car windows streaming the length of the platform. He dove for a turnstile. He might be able to lose himself in the crowd aboard the train. Seconds would decide the outcome, he knew, and he blessed the meticulous habit that made him always have a nickel ready in his pocket, separate from the rest of his change, to use as bus fare.

He cracked through the turnstile. He'd made the gamble, and he couldn't back out now. He sprinted for a car far down at the rear of the train, out of sight of the steps, and sandwiched himself inside just as the doors were starting to slide closed. He'd won. Or had he? The train was effectively sealed off from the station now, though it hadn't moved an inch. But if his pursuer had had sense enough to plunge into the nearest car, he might have made it; he might be somewhere on the jammed train at this very moment.

Townsend felt sick at the thought, but he was to be spared the agony of uncertainty, of not knowing when he might feel the sudden clutch of a heavy, restraining hand falling on him from out the anonymous crowd, or of being kept steadily in view without his knowing it by agate-hard eyes under a shading hat brim, to be followed off the train and overtaken in more isolated surroundings. Just as the train started to glide out of the station, he saw his pursuer on the platform. Something must have gone wrong with his timing. Any one of countless things. Most likely, the outgoing surge of passengers—which Townsend had been just in time to avoid—had prevented him from getting down the stairs until it was too late. Townsend had won the gamble.

The man was running now, pacing the train but falling steadily behind it, his eyes peering hawklike in through the lighted windows as they outdistanced him, one by one. When Townsend's window caught up with him, their stares met eye to eye for the second time that day. Townsend felt terror at the grim inflexible purpose he saw in those agate eyes.

His pursuer didn't try to dissemble now. He'd lost Townsend that way the first time. Without a change in his frozen expression, without a flicker of emotion lighting his cold gray eyes, he reached back to his hip pocket and drew a gun. Townsend was too paralyzed with horror at the incredible action to move. But the man didn't fire, as Townsend thought for a crazed moment he intended to. Instead he swung his arm up and slashed at the glass panel with the gun handle. It cracked with a dull thud, white veins streaking through it, and it sagged inward. But it held; none of the pieces fell out.

The man was trying to break the glass and reach in to snag the overhead emergency cord and bring the train to a stop. It was maniacal, but not impossible. But outside forces interfered to prevent him. The serge-sleeved arms of a station guard suddenly twined about him from behind, grappled with him and pulled him back.

He could have shot me, Townsend thought as the train sped on unimpeded, but he seemed to want me alive. The thought did not relieve his terror.

He didn't tell Virginia any of it. What was there to tell? A man on the street had pursued him. He didn't know who the man was, what he wanted with him, or even who it was that *he*, the one wanted, was supposed to be! He only knew that the black abyss of his anonymous past had just emitted a blood-red lick of flame, as if seeking to drag him back into its depths and consume him.

A DAY WENT BY, as he held his breath; then another, and he began to breathe more easily. But on the third day, the wind was knocked out of him again. He saw it once more—that face in the crowd.

An accident saved him, a trivial thing. On his way out of the building where he worked, he tripped over a loosened shoelace. At that moment he saw Agate Eyes go by outside. They were only a few feet away from each other; if it hadn't been for the shoelace, Townsend would have emerged just in time to cut across his path and practically tread on his toes. He knew he wasn't mistaken, it was the same man—the bulky shoulders, the same clothes and hat, and the same eyes, cold and hard and gray.

Townsend's first impulse was to turn and plunge back into the depths of the building. Instead, he found himself irresistibly drawn to see where the man was going.

Midway between Townsend's building and the corner—and

in an excellent position to watch the bus stop—there was a shoeshine stand. As Townsend watched, the gray-clad figure stepped up on the rickety structure and sat down in one of the two chairs. Screening his face with a newspaper, he became just an anonymous pair of legs with his feet on the footrests of the shoeshine platform.

Apparently Agate Eyes had only two fixed points to work from so far: the bus stop, which might be Townsend's usual embarkation point; and the time of day—about now—that might be Townsend's habitual time for taking the bus. He was right on both counts, and this meant that the bus stop was lost to Townsend for good. He'd have to use the bus line on the next avenue over and detour a block out of his way at each end.

He went back into the building and left by another exit, and all the way to the new bus stop he kept looking behind him. Every gray suit was an enemy until the pink oval above it came into focus.

At home, drawing false courage from the security of his own walls, he thought, Why don't I go up to him the next time I see him and demand to know what he wants with me? But he knew he wouldn't do that.

The next time Townsend saw the stranger, he realized the pace of the chase was growing quicker and the coils contracting around him were growing tighter. Agate Eyes had found his office building and entered it. Again Townsend avoided blundering into him by a hair's breadth. It was morning, and he had stopped in the cut-rate drugstore on the ground floor to buy cigarettes. As he looked out idly into the building lobby, he saw Agate Eyes talking to the lobby attendant.

The attendant nodded, his lips pursed judicially. The pantomime was as clear to Townsend as if he'd been able to overhear the actual words: "Yeah, I have seen someone like that coming in and out of here."

The agate eyes buried themselves deeper behind their lids with baleful calculation and the mouth beneath asked something. The attendant shook his head, waved a hand toward the unending trickle of humanity going by them and shrugged. His meaning was plain: "So many people pass, you can't keep track of every one of them."

Townsend turned quickly and walked out of the drugstore into the street. Then, haunted, he looked back. There was no gray-eyed visage behind him. He'd made it. But he knew this meant the end of his job. He hurried away—fleeing before the unknown.

Easy enough to say to himself, Face it! Find out what it is, once and for all! Make sure, at least, that there's something to be avoided before you avoid it. But he couldn't face it. It would be like jumping off into space from a great height. You might land safely, or you might not; the one certainty was you couldn't get back on your perch again. If he accosted this pursuer, if he once put himself within his reach, he'd never get away from him again. There was a deadly tenacity about him. This was no halfhearted pursuit; it was a manhunt in every sense of the word.

The thought of Virginia was an added anxiety. Should he tell her that he must give up his job?

Why not wait? Why burden her with another worry? He could just get another job, and then he wouldn't have to go into his reasons for chucking this one. Anyway, he didn't have to tell her right away. He'd stay out of the apartment today during working hours—he'd find a park somewhere and sit in it, killing time.

HE SAT ON a park bench beside a winding path, surrounded by green spring grass dappled by sunlight. But the peace of the setting did little to relieve the knotted tension within him. For the most part, he just stared wanly down at the ground as the hours slowly passed.

The problem had no answer. He comes from That Time, he thought. He must, there's no other explanation. It's not a mistake in identity. He really knows me. But I don't know him. He's someone from the three forgotten years.

And that, he knew, was why he was afraid. This man had come out of the shadows of the past, and there was a terrible remorselessness about his pursuit. Townsend could not bring himself to meet the challenge. He had just experienced a deep-reaching psychic shock, and he hadn't had time to get over it. He needed peace; he needed safety. His lacerated psyche required time to knit itself together again before it was called on to meet fresh tests of spiritual courage.

No one noticed Townsend sitting on the park bench all that day. A quiet figure, desperately trying to pierce the curtain that hid the past.

It grew late. The children began to hurry out of the park, followed by a random nursemaid or two. The whole world was leaving the scene, and the park became hushed with a sort of macabre expectancy. The daily death of light was about to occur.

The things of the night began to slink into view. Blue shadows, like tentatively clutching fingers, started to creep slowly out from under the trees toward Townsend. Deepening, advancing furtively when they weren't watched closely, pretending to be arrested when they were. One, the longest and boldest of them all, as if trying to trap him fast where he was, pointed itself straight across the path and advanced upon him by crafty, insidious degrees, like a slithering octopus tentacle. He drew his foot hastily back out of its reach.

He wanted to get out of here. He got up and moved along the winding path in urgent awareness of the unseen. Only the slow dignity of his outer step was adult; inside he was a lost child moving through an array of goblin trees, with a lighted cigarette for protective talisman instead of crossed fingers.

Chapter Three

HE DIDN'T LIKE having to fool Virginia like this. He wanted to tell her. Several times he almost did, but then checked himself. She'd had so much trouble already. Three years of it. As he looked across the dinner table at her, he could still see the traces of it. Her eyes were sad, and she still didn't laugh as she had before he went away. So he didn't tell her.

Then with a soundless flash he was aware of a danger that had escaped him until now. His name, his address and other pertinent information about him were on file in the office where he had worked, accessible to the most casual inquiry.

For Agate Eyes, that would be the inevitable next step. Today he had found the building. By tomorrow he would know the exact floor. Then the right door on that floor, and after that he would painlessly extract Townsend's address. Then the pursuit would strike suddenly here at home. And here there was no easy retreat. Here there was Virginia, and here he was rooted fast. All he had done until now had merely postponed the inevitable. He had gained a day or two at the most.

But there might still be time—time, the ally of all frightened things. Maybe he could persuade the office to withhold his address and shield him. He would have given anything to be able to get in touch with them right away, but he'd have to wait until morning. There was one good thing about that, though: if he couldn't reach them at night, neither could Agate Eyes.

In the morning it was the first thing on his mind as his eyes opened—*phone them fast, get to them before* he *does!* He could hardly wait to gulp his coffee, grab his hat and get out.

"But you're not late," Virginia tried to reassure him.

He threw her a half-truth across his shoulder. "I know, but there's a call I've got to make the very first thing!"

He did it right away from the corner booth, and after a few rings the phone was answered by the familiar voice of the switchboard operator.

"Hello. That you, Beverly? This is Frank Townsend."

"Oh, hello. What happened to you yesterday, Frank? Weren't sick, I hope?"

"I'm not coming in anymore, Bev," he said.

"Ah, I'm sorry to hear that, Frank. We'll all miss you."

"Look, Beverly," he went on hurriedly, "I want you to do something for me, will you?"

"Sure, Frank."

"Please, under no circumstances, give out my home address. I mean, just in case anyone happens to inquire. I don't say anyone will, of course, but just in case they do—you don't know my whereabouts, see?"

She wasn't curious enough to ask any questions. "I understand, Frank. You can rely on it. And I'll tell Gert. We're the only two who know where to look for it in the files. Wait a minute, I'll make a note of it." He could tell she was jotting something down as she spoke. " 'In future, don't give out Townsend's address if you are asked for it.' "

In future! He didn't like that! "No one's asked *already*, have they?"

"Yeah, there *was* somebody in here yesterday—"

The world—and the phone booth with it—went plunging into darkness, as though it were a train passing through a tunnel.

She was saying, "A man came in at the very last moment yesterday, as we were all getting ready to go home. We couldn't lay our hands on your address right away—you know five o'clock down here. So Gert gave it to him from memory, but she wondered later whether she got it right or not."

A shaft of silver pierced the leaden pall around him. Very slender, very fragile, but struggling through. "Find out if she remembers just what she said."

In a few minutes Beverly was back on the line. "Frank, Gert couldn't remember, so we looked it up. It's Eight Twenty Rutherford North, right?" She laughed contritely. "Well, Gert got you mixed up with Tom Ewing, sent the guy all the way to— He'll have a fit when he finds out!"

So they did have his old address. And *he* had one that was totally wrong! He was safe; he was out of reach. Relief shot through him in an exquisite flood.

"Have we the right address, Frank?" Beverly went on, trying to be helpful. "They'll be sending you a paycheck for half a week on Friday, and you want to make sure of getting it."

"Yes," he said firmly, "it's right." He'd stop by and pick up the check at the old place. Mrs. Fromm would hold it for him.

As he hung up, he felt as if he'd been saved again from the

menacing stranger. An unfastened shoelace had rescued him the first time. A pack of cigarettes the second time. And a switchboard operator in a hurry to get home had saved him the third time. But from what? What had he ever done to be so endangered?

The answer was immediate and inevitable. Three years is a long time. In three years it's possible to do lots of things that bring danger in their train. And now, somewhere in this city, there's a man who is looking for me, looking up one street and down another, minute by minute, hour by hour. Sooner or later, since I am a more or less fixed object and he is in constant motion, he is going to find me.

THEIR OLD APARTMENT was still tenantless, he noticed when he went there the following Saturday to pick up his paycheck. He rang for Mrs. Fromm and stood waiting in the street entrance for her to come up from below. Someone else looked out at him inquiringly, some other woman. "I'm looking for Mrs. Fromm," he said.

"She doesn't work here anymore."

For a minute he didn't recognize the fact for what it was worth. Then realization swept in on him. This meant that without his having to say a word or lift a finger, he was safe at this end. This newcomer, whoever she was, did not know his present address. She couldn't pass it on to anyone, even if she wanted to. He was cut off, beyond reach for good now. Well, barring any mishaps, of course. His relief knew no bounds.

With his retrieved paycheck in his pocket, his homeward tread had a lilt to it that had been missing since his shadowy nemesis had first descended on him. Fear was gone. Self-confidence was back. He even caught himself humming a little under his breath. A man in a gray suit, with a gray hat aslant over his eyes, went by, almost grazed him, and he didn't even remember to be wary. Maybe it was all over now and he was safe—out in the sunlight at last.

Barring any mishaps, of course.

He had to do a certain amount of juggling to conceal from Virginia that he had quit his job. The check wasn't payment for a full week, so he added a proportionate amount out of his small reserve to make the correct total. He couldn't do this a second time; he didn't have sufficient funds. But Monday he'd look for another job, and possibly by week's end he'd have a bona fide paycheck again.

Monday he looked. Tuesday he looked again. Wednesday, Thursday and Friday. He looked in a way that applicants seldom do, by geographical location, disregarding potential employers within the danger zone, applying only to those with addresses a considerable distance away.

Several jobs that he might have had slipped through his fingers for lack of credentials. He needed references, and he was unwilling to refer them to his last place of work lest he reopen a means of tracing him. By the end of the week he was finally faced with the necessity of telling Virginia the thing he'd been trying all along to spare her.

When he returned home on Saturday, his supposed payday, all primed to confide in her, he could see something was troubling her. "Frank, did your paycheck come today?" she began immediately, before he had a chance to say anything.

"No—"

"Then it's been lost in the mail!" She rushed on. "It wasn't received at our old address either. I was just over there—"

His body tensed. "You were over there?"

"Only this morning I happened to pick up the envelope of last week's check—I came across it in the back of the bureau drawer—and I noticed our old address on it big as life! You never told me you had to go over there and claim it. Well, I went over to see whether it would be forwarded here if it went there again by mistake—" She stopped when she noticed the look on his face.

"And you gave the new woman our address *here?*"

"Why, yes, I wrote it down for her."

Barring any mishaps, he reflected bitterly.

Chapter Four

HE COULDN'T SLEEP. Although he had dozed off for a short time immediately upon touching the pillow, it had been only a half-sleep, troubled by a dream. A peculiarly grueling dream, though there were no distortions in it, no traumatic goblin shapes. Nothing, in fact, but a pair of feet and a patch of pavement.

They kept moving forward, toward him, toward the dreamer's eye, and the pavement they trod kept slipping past beneath them, like a treadmill. It was as though the dreamer were moving backward, away from the feet, and the latter were following remorselessly.

In the dream the feet kept coming toward him, never at a run, always at the same even, persistent walk. And there was more undiluted horror in that pair of black-shod feet than in all the ogres, monsters and menaces of dream plasma put together. It was their quiet implacability, their incessant fall upon the pavement: *pat—pat—pat—pat*. The sound you hear at night when the streets are still, when someone is coming toward you in the distance. The feet never faltered, never missed a step. It was as though they knew they needn't hurry, for nothing, no one, could escape them. And slowly they began to gain on him. The crevice between sole and pavement, opening and closing, was like a hungry maw now, threatening to trap and crush the dreamer. Then the dream shattered into unbearable light at the moment of their finally overtaking him, and he woke up.

In the slow reintegrating process of psychic cohesion, he realized where the ominous vision had come from: that pair of feet on the footrests of the shoeshine stand. As for their dogging him so relentlessly—wasn't that what they *had* been doing? Or was it the portent of the dream that they were somewhere outside on the surrounding streets right now, coming toward him, drawing nearer, footfall by footfall, at this very minute?

He touched a match to a cigarette, and Virginia's face, opposite him in the other bed, stood out for a minute, a pale golden oval.

Thank God at least one of us can sleep, he thought contritely. She had earned her repose.

He couldn't go back to sleep and felt like moving around. He didn't own a robe, so he put on his trousers and shirt and felt his way toward the bedroom door. In the living room he turned on a small light. Then he walked to the window and looked out, drawing on the cigarette.

How long is this going to keep up anyway? he asked himself. What am I going to do about it? I've got to do *something* about it sooner or later. I can't just—

Suddenly the cigarette fell from his lips. He jumped over to the wall, killed the light and approached the window again, stealthily, edging up to it sideways along the wall until he could look out at what he thought he'd seen.

There did indeed seem to be someone standing out there, directly opposite him, facing these windows, someone in the black silt of a shadow that filled an indentation in the wall. But as he peered out, a faint flow of motion altered the silhouette and the image disappeared into the heart of the shadow.

He had to get out of here, fast. He tiptoed to the apartment door and listened. There was a low voice murmuring somewhere beyond. *He* had others with him. They were all around the place, getting ready to rush it. Any minute now.

He looked toward the bedroom that contained all he loved in the world. I've got to get her out of here, too, he thought distractedly. I don't want it to happen in front of her—whatever it is.

He went into the darkened bedroom and leaned over her, trying not to startle her too much. "Virginia, can you hear me?"

She sat up. The soft perfume of her hair was around him.

"We've got to get out of here. I want you to come with me right now. No, don't turn on a light, they may be able to see us through the back window."

"They? Who?" She was on her feet now.

"Just put on your coat," he said, grabbing up his own jacket. "Put your feet into your shoes the way they are. There's no time—"

"Don't," she whimpered, a silken shadow beside him, "you're frightening me."

He sought her lips with his, to give her courage. "Do you love me?"

"How can you ask?" Her voice was a frightened whisper.

"Then trust me enough to follow me without asking any questions. Ready? Come on."

They went to the apartment door, Virginia still only half awake, her hair awry within the towering circle of the red-fox collar of her coat. Outside there was a sort of swelling quiet, like a balloon about to burst.

"I don't think we can make it this—" he started to say.

The shock ran right through the two of them, as though a volley of blank cartridges had been fired off under their noses. The door seemed to explode and the light bulbs jittered in the ceiling. They were using something heavier and harder than fists to break down the door.

She huddled against him, terrified. "Who's doing that?"

"This is what I wanted to get you away from," he answered bitterly.

To get her to safety was his only concern now. He drew her away from the door, an arm circled protectively about her shoulder, and like a pair of blundering dancers in half-embrace, they went this way and that, looking for a way out that wasn't there. They took three steps toward the hopelessly blocked front windows, then doubled back toward the kitchen window and the rear court. The telltale grate of feet on the cement outside reached them. "There must be some way, there's got to be—!" he said desperately.

And then it came to him. He threw open a high wooden door set in the kitchen wall and brought up a dumbwaiter. "Our building and the one next to it have a single basement between them. I may be able to get you out through the other house. See if you can squeeze into this thing. I'll hold the ropes so you don't shoot down too fast."

She backed into the dumbwaiter and huddled there, looking

ridiculous in her fur collar. "Frank, you're coming after me? You're not staying behind?"

"The minute you get off, honey. Wait down there for me," he said as he wondered to himself if there'd be time for a second trip. The wood of the front door was beginning to splinter now; they must be using hatchets on it.

The pulleys whirred as he paid out the rope, and her face went down out of sight, almost as if she were being entombed alive. He heard the dumbwaiter strike bottom and he leaned over the opening. A loose swaying told him she had gotten off. He brought the dumbwaiter up again fast, climbed awkwardly in and went down jerkily. The crash of forced entry above, as the remnants of the door finally flattened before the onslaught, blended with the crash of the dumbwaiter as he struck bottom with a thud that jarred his teeth.

She was standing there holding the door of the shaft open for him. He came tumbling out on hands and knees to the basement floor.

He struck matches to guide them through the cellar darkness. With an eery sensation of unreality, they could hear the scurry of searching footsteps overhead, scattering through the apartment. There were at least a half dozen of them, to judge by the sound.

"They'll know," he murmured. "Your bed must still be warm. They'll be down here in a minute. Quick, darling, quick!"

They found the door that led into the other building. He got it open and they trod warily up the cement steps, he in the lead, to still another door. He opened it slightly and listened carefully for sounds of activity in the hall beyond. Silence. The hunt hadn't reached this building yet. They came out together like two wraiths, their hands linked defensively.

He broke hands, leaving her where she was, and crept toward the street entrance. Then he motioned her forward. "You go first. You have a better chance alone than with me. They don't know what you look like. Don't look back—just walk toward the corner, minding your own business."

She took one step outside, within the guiding circle of his arm.

The street seemed empty of figures at the moment. He urged her gently forward. "Go on, honey, quick. In another minute it may be too late—"

With a plaintive sob, she struck out by herself, her shoes making a nervous little ticking along the pavement. He lingered until he gauged she was halfway to the corner. No one had gone after her, no shout of discovery had been raised. He drew in a breath and edged out the door.

For a moment he looked up at the pale oblongs of light cast by his own apartment windows. Then he turned and started off in the direction Virginia had walked. Rigid with fear, he kept his neck muscles locked against the impulse to look back. But the street was very dark, and just before rounding the corner, he did allow himself to glance back. He couldn't help it: that had been their home, that place so suddenly set upon and warred against. He could still make out the faint gleam of its windows. Then he turned the corner, and the present became the past, the past became the present.

Virginia had found a driverless cab parked in front of an all-night lunchroom, and was inside it with the door open, waiting for him. He went up to it and closed the door from the outside.

"No, honey, I'm not coming with you," he said quietly. "Go out of the city, to your mother's, and stay there until you hear from me. That way, whatever happens to me, I'll know that you're safe. They won't connect you with the apartment because you rented it in your maiden name. If they find you, just say you're Mrs. Townsend, whose husband disappeared three years ago, and you haven't seen him since. Don't try to reach me or get in touch with me in any way, for your own sake. I'll see you again—someday. And whatever you hear, whatever it turns out this is all about—give me a break in your own mind, like you always have before."

She seized his wrist with both hands. "No! Let me take my chances with you! Frank, I'm not afraid! What's a wife for? What's marriage for?"

He disengaged her hands gently. "Honey, when a guy falls

into a sewer, he doesn't reach up and pull those he loves best down with him. Good-by for now, and do as I tell you if you love me."

Their lips met hungrily, almost furiously, through the open cab window. Then he drew back. "I'm going over that way now. When I'm out of sight, sound the horn for the driver. Good-by, darling."

He shoved off into the anonymity of the night. In a few minutes a taxi horn beeped querulously once or twice behind him. He'd never thought a taxi horn could hurt so.

He looked back: a dwindling red mote of taillight was all that was left of his marriage. He'd never known how fiercely he loved her until now. He looked back once more; even the taillight was gone. Now there was just himself and the night and the past.

He kept going, ticking off crossings as the factor of distance secured a slight edge of safety for him, if only for a while. He continued to stride on until the gray dawn appeared and his future course of action slowly but immutably began to take form in his mind. Since the present held no safety, he must go back into the past to find out why. Back into the past that had done this to him, to force it to retract or else let it engulf him. Back into the past—if he could find it.

So far, the past was only a small chink, like the secret entrance to a bewitched garden in a child's fairy tale. It had only one street on it, Tillary Street. But if he could find his way to the past through that gate, he could push back its boundaries and widen them out all around him, until they took in his whole world again. Tillary Street. The past would become the present on Tillary Street.

But would it? Perhaps he had just been passing through Tillary Street at random that day, from somewhere to somewhere else? Or had he lived on it, or around it? There was only one way to find out. He would go back and haunt it, like the ghost he was, until it gave him the answer.

It was lighter now, but it was also chillier. A wind as homeless as he was himself blew out across the steel-blue city. He turned his collar up around his neck and set his face toward Tillary Street—and yesterday.

Somewhere along its reaches there must be someone who knew him. He would travel it every day, up one side, down the other, over and over, until at last some pair of eyes lit up in recognition, some voice said hello, some person stopped to greet him. Back he would go into the limbo from which he had come, a man looking for his forgotten self.

The street sign at its entrance was just like any other, dark blue enamel and white capitals. TILLARY ST., he read, ONE WAY ONLY.

Chapter Five

THE ROOM WAS a relic of some long-buried yesterday. "You going to be here long?" the wizened old rooming-house keeper asked.

Townsend didn't really know. It might be only an hour or two before they found him again. Or it might be days or weeks. No, not weeks, unless he found a job to keep him going. He'd had exactly eight dollars and seventy-nine cents in the pockets of the suit he was wearing when those blank-cartridge-like blows had exploded against his door. "That depends on what you charge me," he replied.

The gnarled old man chafed his hands. "For a room like this, it's four dollars."

Townsend moved toward the doorway. "Four dollars is too much."

"Look, *every* week you got clean sheets on the bed. And fresh running water, even." He went over to a corroded faucet and turned its encrusted handle with difficulty. A trickle of reddish-brown fluid issued from it. "Must be using it downstairs," he said and forced it shut again.

"I'll give you two and half for it," Townsend said.

"All right, take it, take it."

Townsend clapped two bills and a coin ungraciously into the old man's eager hand. "Gimme a key."

His new landlord grumbled at such a luxury. "A key he wants. What next?" But he took one from his pocket, put it in the door and left.

Alone now, Townsend went over to the bleary window and stood looking down at the street. Sunlight came in through the gap at the side of the shade, making a bright chevron on his sleeve. So that was the new world down there. He'd already walked once to the end of the world and back, before coming up here. Tillary Street wasn't very long; it only extended four blocks, from Monmouth to Degrasse.

The people down below were swarming every which way, forming black clumps around each of the pushcarts that rimmed both curbs in a nearly unbroken line. The street had very little vehicular traffic, but an occasional agonized motor conveyance threaded its way through at a snail's pace, its horn sounding every moment of the way.

Townsend thought he'd rest awhile first and then go out again. He'd had almost no sleep the night before. He loosened his tie, took off his coat, hung it across the back of the chair and lay down on the bed. Before he knew it, he had slept his first sleep of the new life. When he awoke, it was afternoon. He tried the stubbornly resistant faucet over in the corner, and after several minutes of steady leakage the rusty trickle became colorless enough to use.

As he set out, he locked his door behind him, more as a reflex than anything else. In the hall he found himself assailed by the odor of cooking. It reminded him he was hungry. Even ghosts have to eat.

One thing that he noticed on his way down the stairs was a happy augury: the horrible sense of guilt he had felt last night had vanished. If this was the "feel" of the past, it suggested that either he had been guiltless then or he had had an unusually impervious conscience. There was a continuing sense of danger, but it was the exhilarating, not the depressing, kind. It had a lacing of adventure in it. Perhaps it was because Virginia was out of the picture, and he had only his own fate to work out.

He walked a block down from his rooming house, which was near the Degrasse end of the street, and chose a lunchroom. At this time of day, of course, there was no one in it. Tillary Street didn't have enough per capita wealth to indulge in between-meal snacks.

As he perched on one of the tall stools, he wondered if he'd ever eaten in here before. The counterman's glance swept over him and nothing happened. But Townsend realized that people like the counterman had many faces before them day after day.

Finally he asked him, "How long you been working in this place?"

"Couple of weeks now, chief," the man said.

Well, Townsend thought grimly, there goes my first chance.

He mapped out the preliminaries of his campaign while he ate. For every meal, he would patronize a different eating establishment along Tillary Street, hoping for recognition from an employee or a customer. That would be one line of attack. The second would be to enter every store and shop on the street, on some excuse or other, and linger haggling, hoping for recognition from a storekeeper.

Both of these plans were secondary, however; they were unlikely to turn up anyone who knew important details about him. He was pinning his main hope of discovering a close personal acquaintance on a random encounter on the pavement. But any sort of recognition would be better than none; it would be a beginning. He would no longer be suspended, as he was now, in a complete vacuum.

As he came out onto the sidewalk, he pushed his hat back on his head to expose his upper face so it couldn't fail to impinge on an onlooker's line of vision. Then he started toward the Monmouth end of the street, three blocks away. He moved slowly, so that anyone glancing at him and in doubt the first time would have ample time to look twice and verify his identity.

In any case, rapid progress along Tillary Street would have

required exhausting dexterity. The customers doubled up before the pushcarts clogged one side of the already inadequate sidewalk. And gossiping groups and doorway loungers blocked the other side. Only a tortuous lane of clearance was left between. He didn't time himself, but it must have taken him a full thirty minutes to traverse the three blocks. Then at the Monmouth Street end, he crossed over to the opposite sidewalk and began to work his way back.

The sun was starting to crimson now and go down. Vacancies appeared along the curb as pushcarts broke ranks. Women leaned from windows high aloft and screeched down to their children to come inside. By the time Townsend found himself back at Degrasse again, Tillary Street had definitely thinned out, although it was the sort of slum street that was probably never lifeless at any time of the day or night. He recrossed to what he considered his own side of the street and stopped in front of his rooming house to rest awhile and try his luck from a motionless position.

Presently it grew dark and the lights of Tillary Street came on. There was an amber glow behind many of the upper windows, and the naked-glass display bulbs in the shop fronts shone brilliantly. The street took on a sort of holiday guise, almost gay, if you didn't look too closely.

He stayed on awhile, hoping he'd have better luck after dark than during the daylight hours. Like a mendicant begging alms, Townsend stood begging a donation of memories. But the obliviousness of those around him only increased rather than lessened.

Finally he turned and went upstairs to his room. He raised the shade, and the lights from below cast a luminous repetition of the window square on the other side of the room, bent in two, half flat upon the ceiling and half upright on the wall. He sat down on the edge of his bed, a dejected, shadowy figure. Once, at some break in his inner fortitude, his head suddenly dropped into the coil of his arms. Then he raised it again, and that didn't happen anymore. But it wasn't easy to start life over at thirty-two. Particularly when it was a life doomed even before you took it over, and its time limit was subject to call without notice.

He took off his shoes and lay back, and Tillary Street dimmed, like a lantern slide, into the blankness of sleep.

His first day in the past hadn't paid off. He was still lost between two dimensions.

IT HAD BEEN on a Monday morning that he had taken the room on Tillary Street. Tuesday passed and Wednesday. After that, the days began to telescope into one another, and it was harder to keep track of them. The blurring monotony of the routine he had set for himself might have had something to do with it. Then came a day when his landlord accosted him at the foot of the stairs on his way out, and he knew he had been there a full week, and it was Monday again.

He had been eating only irregularly, but even so, he had only two dollars and some change left. He handed over the two bills and said, "I'll have the other fifty cents for you by tonight or tomorrow," wondering to himself at the same time how he'd manage to.

But he did have it, by that very night, and handed it over with fingertips puckery and red from a long session washing dishes in the place where he'd eaten a week before. Luckily, the lunchroom had had a temporary need for a dishwasher. And there was enough left from his earnings to tide him over the next day or two.

He'd already finished his casing of the shops, but nowhere had he gained the impression that any of the proprietors had seen him before. And now his clocklike pacing of the street, day after day, up one side, down the other, was undoubtedly making him familiar to dozens of the denizens of Tillary Street. Eventually, when they became used to seeing him, he would no longer be able to differentiate recognition born in the immediate past from that of the more distant past that he was trying to reenter. But that point hadn't quite been reached yet.

At times, alone in his barren room at night with the eerie

window square cast by the streetlights wavering on the wall, he was haunted by a looming sense of failure, of the futility of what he was attempting. Perhaps his plan was based on a faulty premise. He might just have been traversing Tillary Street at random on that day when the curtain had suddenly been drawn on his past. In that case, how was he ever to find out where he had been going or where he had come from? Or supposing his premise was correct and Tillary Street really had played a fixed part in his past life, even so, he was relying on the laws of chance, wasn't he? If the one or two people who could have reoriented him had drifted away themselves by now, then he might stay here a thousand years without getting a glimpse into that unknown past.

Meanwhile time was running out. Although his rent was paid for a while yet, now the dishwashing money was all gone. His stomach was starting to feel hollow as he prowled his beat. He still had that flashy-looking cigarette case that had turned up in his pocket after the accident, however, and he decided to try to raise something on it.

Strangely enough, there was no pawnshop anywhere along Tillary Street, but he found one about a block and a half down on Monmouth. He pushed his way into its camphor-reeking interior, empty at the moment, and took out the case.

The pawnbroker came out of a storage room at the back. He gave Townsend the sharply appraising look of his kind as he advanced along the inside of the counter to where he stood. "Well?" the broker said noncommittally.

Townsend passed the case to him through the small orifice in the wire mesh that separated them. But the broker made no effort to test it, weigh it or examine it in any way. He just said, in a casual tone, words that had explosive implications for Townsend: "This again, hm?"

Townsend wasn't expecting it. Caught off guard, he blinked as the meaning hit him. Then he paled a little and gripped the edge of the counter. *This again. Again.* He must have been in here before, with this same cigarette case.

His voice shook a little, but he tried to sound plausibly forgetful. "Oh, uh, was this the—the same place I brought it to before? All hockshops look alike to me."

The broker sniffed disdainfully. "I ought to know this case by heart already. Three times you been in here with it now." He was holding it extended, as if in rejection. Then, after a time lag, he made his offer. "All right, four dollars for it."

Townsend saw an opening and clutched at it desperately. "That wasn't what you let me have on it before."

The broker immediately took professional umbrage. "So you're going to argue? Four dollars is what it's worth."

Townsend's voice was tense. "Do you keep the—the ticket stubs after the article's been redeemed? I mean the part that the customer signs?"

"Sure. You want me to look it up? Why? I know this case. I tested it for you before. Look at that." He showed him a little mark made by the drop of reagent acid. Townsend had thought it was a worn spot. "You were raising a big holler, remember? Fourteen carat gold, you tried to tell me. It's silver, gilt. Four dollars."

Townsend was pleading almost abjectly now. "Well, just to convince me, please see if you can dig up the old ticket."

The broker went into the back of the shop and Townsend had a long, agonizing wait.

"April eighteenth," the broker said suddenly from the back. "Silver-gilt black enamel cigarette case—*four dollars*. Am I right?"

"Bring out the canceled ticket, I want to see it," Townsend called, urgency in his voice.

The broker came back with it and looked at him curiously. "Here. Now is this you, or isn't it?"

Townsend cocked his head to match the angle at which the pawnbroker was holding the stub. The name was George Williams, and he knew at first sight that it was spurious. Not that there weren't people named George Williams, but *he* hadn't been named that. His hatband had been initialed *DN*. The address on the stub was 705 Monmouth Street. Was that also fictitious, like the name?

"Well? You want to turn it in now or not?" the broker called after Townsend sharply as he started for the door.

"Be back later," he said, and gave the half-doors a fling that must have kept them banging in and out for minutes.

He hustled up Monmouth Street toward the seven-hundred sector. Pretty soon now. He came to a halt, then went on a few faltering steps and stopped again. There was no 705. There was a 703. The one after it was 707.

The door had slammed shut, and the room was dark again.

THREE DOLLARS and seventy cents later—thirty cents away from destitution with nothing left to pawn—Townsend was walking his beat when Tillary Street was suddenly drained of people: the usual afternoon crush on the sidewalk was siphoning off around the corner ahead of him into Watt Street. The jangle of fire apparatus a moment earlier had started it; now the whole population was streaming en masse in one direction. The emptiness of the street robbed it of any usefulness for Townsend, so he turned and strolled slowly in the wake of the crowd, detached, unhurrying.

There was a haze of bluish-gray smoke visible a block up Watt Street, but he couldn't get any nearer than that. For this neighborhood, a fire was a joyous event, a means of self-expression, almost a social occasion. A solid mass of humanity stretched from one side of the street to the other. Townsend remained on the outskirts of the crowd, craning his neck to see over the heads of those in front of him.

All the windows in every house along the street were brimming with hopeful onlookers. He had stopped in front of a house where at a top-floor window a kid was mangling an orange. Someone happened to jostle the kid from behind, and something viscous fell, hitting Townsend on the shoulder and then glancing off and landing with a soggy splat on the ground before his feet.

Skittishly he shied away and turned to look up to identify the culprit. A face upturned in a crowd attracts the eye from above, even an eye fixed elsewhere. Suddenly a voice keened out from somewhere in the building above, a voice thin against all the hubbub and commotion but audible as a flute just the same: *"Dan!"*

The past had opened to admit him at last.

Chapter Six

HE QUICKLY corrected his angle of vision, bringing it down window tier by window tier, but all he found was a sudden blank spot. The face had gone before he could locate it, and the surrounding faces quickly pressed in to fill the gap.

He knew the cry had been meant for him, by sheer instinct alone. It had been "thrown" directly at him, not to the right and not to the left; the intensity of vibration caught by his eardrum told him that. He stayed right where he was, rooted, rigid, as a crushing sense of irony overcame him. This was undeniably recognition, and recognition that had been lurking *one block off* Tillary Street all the time he had been pacing there.

Almost certainly he was about to be accosted. Would it be by friend or enemy? What was he to say? How was he to find out what he might be expected to say? A warning inner voice adjured him, Keep cool now, whatever you do. Make sure you don't miss anything. Say very little. As little as possible. *Feel* your way, like a blindfolded man walking a tightrope.

It seemed like hours since that despairing cry had winged down to him. Suddenly the door of the house discharged a careening figure like a shot out of a sling, and she was up to him, eye to eye. He couldn't take her in in any perspective. His visualization of her had to spread outward in concentric, radiating circles from those eyes staring into his at such close range. Brown eyes. Bright brown eyes. Overflowingly tearful bright brown eyes. At last a handkerchief came up to cover them for a moment, and he was able to steal a full-length snapshot of her.

She was young, slim and a little more than medium height. The part in her hair came up to the lobe of his ear. Her hair was brown with a bronze shimmer, and she wore it down the nape of her neck in a waterfall. She wasn't pretty, but she was anything but plain. Her face was vibrant with animation and warmth, to take the place of conventional beauty. She was— But that was it, who?

The handkerchief was gone, and the inventory was over. Her first words were, "Danny! I never thought I'd see you again!"

She was as close to him as she could possibly be, so she had made no mistake. He was Danny, that was his name in the living past, the *present* past. Irrationally, he thought that he'd always hated that name.

"Oh, you fool! You crazy fool! What are you doing out on the open street like this! Have you lost your mind?"

He spoke for the first time, beginning life all over again with her—whoever she was. "Watching the fire," he said quietly. Not saying too much, not too little.

She looked up one way and down the other; she looked around in a sweeping half-circle. She was plainly worried—for him. "What's the matter with you? Don't you know scenes like this are the worst places for you? You never can tell when one of *them* will be in a crowd, looking for just such people as you!"

One of them. Just such people as you. She must know about it. Something about it, anyway. He had to find something neutral to say; he couldn't just stand there dumb. He let his eyes flick upward toward the window from which her voice had come. "You've sure got good eyesight."

"I ought to know you by now, from any distance." She said it in a scathing sort of way, as if with remembered hurt.

"Yes, I guess you ought to," he said evenly.

"Well, what are you going to do, stand out here in full sight until someone comes along and picks you up?" In her concern, she began to pull him toward the doorway. "Come in! Come into the hallway, at least!"

He followed her into a narrow passage leading back to stairs, and they stopped, facing each other. He took a chance, slithering a foot out along the tightrope to see if he couldn't make a little headway. "You—you seem kind of worried about me."

Her hand switched up and slapped him across the mouth. The question, evidently, had inflamed some hurt or grievance. She pummeled him on the chest with her fists. "You devil! Oh, you low-down devil! Why do I love you like I do?"

Suddenly she rested her head forlornly against him. Just for a brief moment. Then she raised it again. "Oh, Danny, why'd I ever meet you? Why'd I ever have to know you at all?"

What is this I've run into? Townsend wondered, appalled. What have I been doing to this girl?

"You're no good," she said. "You never will be—" And then, without a change in inflection, at the sound of a descending footstep on the stairs: "Quick! Come back this way—where everyone coming in and going out of the building won't bump into you!"

They waited in silence in the hallway until the tread had gone out into the open. Then she turned back to him again and said, with heightened solicitude, "Where are you staying now, Danny?"

He took a chance and told her. "I've got a room around the corner, on Tillary Street."

"Well, get back there, for heaven's sake!" She went to the door, peered through and returned. "Look, the crowd's starting to break up. Mingle with them, and you can make it. I'll go up and get my things, then I'll slip over there after you."

"I'll wait for you right here," he suggested.

She wouldn't hear of it. "No! No, Danny, I'm afraid! Please get back where you belong. It's just begging for something to happen to you if you hang around like this!"

He gave a jerk of his head upward. "Who's up there?" he said. Even if he was supposed to know what the place was, whom it belonged to and what she was doing there, the question was still valid.

But her answer wasn't enlightening, except that it indicated

he was supposed to know. "The whole darn bunch! It'll take me a few minutes to break away; I don't want them to tumble to anything. I'll tell them I'm taking an earlier train. You *can't* wait down here!"

If she was going to betray him, he was giving her a big, wide opening. But there was no way of avoiding that under the circumstances, he supposed. It would simply have to be risked. "All right," he agreed. "It's Number Fifteen, the second-floor front."

"Danny, *be* there. Don't run out on me again." She half tilted her face with an air of expectancy. He brushed his lips past hers rather than be guilty of an overt omission.

There had evidently been more wholehearted kisses exchanged in the past. "Don't overtax your strength," she commented sulkily. And then with more immediate urgency: "Danny, be careful getting back."

He nodded and left her. As he went down the passage toward the street, he heard the light tap of her shoes on the stairs behind him.

Who was she? What was she? She was obviously aware he was hunted, but did she have any direct connection with the reason? Question marks, nothing but question marks.

He turned into Tillary Street—and for the first time his walk was brisk, purposeful; no more dilly-dallying along the sidewalks, that much at least was over. Tillary Street couldn't have anything more than this to give him.

The payoff had been delayed, but it had been well worth waiting for.

IT HAD BEEN dark for hours. He had lit the single lamp long ago—that was the most he could do for her in the way of hospitality. And still she didn't show up. It must be over three hours by now. No, four. What was taking her so long? Was this going to be a washout? Or worse, was a net, guided by her, being carefully disposed around him? Was that what was taking so long? He harbored this last thought only at intervals. The whole thing would have been over by now if treachery had been the cause of delay. It was too long a time for anything but a plain, old-fashioned stand-up.

He kept roaming back and forth on the gently undulating floorboards. Intermittent suspicions, like fire tongues, darted up and down in his brain. How do I know who she is? Evidently I treated her shabbily in the past; how do I know she won't take this chance of paying me back? Maybe she's the last one I ought to trust—

Wait a minute. Was that a rustle out there on the stairs? He took a quick, catlike jump over to the door, put his head down and his ear close. A breath of silk came threading through the keyhole.

"Dan."

First he was going to open it right away. Then he thought, Make her say her name. Find out what it is. "Who is it?" he insisted in a low voice.

"Me."

He grimaced with disappointment, turned the key.

She came in, a little spark of jealousy glinting in her eyes. "You must be having quite a few girls up here if you have such a hard time telling them apart."

He answered with the literal truth. "You're the first person that's been in this room, outside of the landlord, since I've been here."

"Don't make me laugh," was all the belief she gave him on this. "You'd never be lonely very long, no matter where you were. Wait a minute, don't close the door. I've got my things out there."

She hauled in a small battered suitcase and two or three paper parcels. Just what had they been to one another, anyway? He carefully ignored the name "Virginia" trying to form at the back of his mind.

"I can go straight from here to the train," she said. "In the morning. I'll take the six o'clock up there."

His mind asked, The six o'clock up *where?*

"It'll get me in at seven ten," she said.

One hour and ten minutes away. One hour and ten minutes away from the city was a place he called X. But in which direction? He didn't dare ask the name of the place. But there was something he could ask that might help him to get it for himself, later, without her. He formulated a question, and carefully reserved it in his mind for later, when the right opportunity offered itself.

She had been glancing around the room. "Oh, Danny, this is a sha-ame." Then she drew him under the light of the lamp. "Let me look at you."

He let her. She traced the outline of his face, as though trying to get the feel of it. She didn't seem altogether satisfied. "Danny, there's something different about you. I wonder what it is."

Townsend didn't risk an answer. He sat down on the bed.

She sat down beside him, still evidently missing some sort of harmony between them. "You sound so, so sort of cagey. What's happened to you, Danny? You act like you were afraid of saying the wrong thing."

I am, he thought. Oh, if you only knew how I am!

She opened the parcels she'd brought in. Groceries. "I don't want you to have to budge outside from now on. You've got everything you need right here." She was bending down now, with her back to him, placing the groceries along the baseboard of the wall, the only storage place in the room. "They never give up," she went on. "Don't forget that. You've got to watch your step."

They. Who were *they*?

Her handbag was lying on the bed behind him. As he lay back, he could feel its bulk partly beneath him. Surreptitiously he opened it and then closed it again. There wasn't anything in it to tell him what he wanted to know. No shortcuts in this, it seemed.

She came over to the bed, stretched out alongside him and began to play with the wing tip of his collar. "What're you going to do, Danny? Have you thought?"

"I wish I knew," he answered, carefully evasive.

"It's a losing game, isn't it? Why didn't you think of that before?"

"There's no jackpot in it." You could say that about anything, so it was safe enough to say it now.

She gave a mournful little laugh. "For me there isn't, that's a cinch." Her cheek came to rest upon his chest. Her hair was soft under his chin. Thoughtfully he stared over her head, listening to what she said. "It's funny, though. I wouldn't change places with any girl who has her fellow forever. Who knows no one's going to come and take him away from her any week, any day, any minute. I'd rather have you, Danny, than anyone else, even if I know I could lose you anytime. A knock on the door, and no more Danny."

"No—no," he drawled reassuringly, "we'll find a way." He knew he mustn't jolt her out of this kind of talk, with its infinite promise of revelation.

"I wonder if they smelled a rat over there," she said, and he knew she meant the Watt Street apartment.

"Do you think they did?"

"I don't know," she said dubiously. "Luckily, my sister was in the kitchen giving one of the kids a bath when I hollered out your name. I could have bitten my tongue off a minute later. But it popped out before I could stop it."

Her sister's apartment, then. Her married sister's apartment. She was visiting it from one hour and ten minutes away.

"When I came back upstairs again later, she said, 'Didn't I hear you holler out "Dan" a little while ago?' and gave me kind of a suspicious look. I laughed and told her that I had hollered 'Scram!' to some kid that was teasing a dog. I only hope she believed me."

The conversation showed signs of lagging. She stirred a little. "It must be getting late. I don't want to miss my train in the morning."

He reached up to the wall behind them and turned the switch on the lamp. The room went dark except for that ghostly window thrown upward from the lights in the street. Her mention of the train was the opening he'd been hoping for, the opening for that question he'd held carefully in reserve until now. "What track does it leave on?" he asked, as casually as he could.

"You ought to know, you took enough of those trains yourself. Track seventeen, lower level."

One hour and ten minutes away, track 17, lower level, six a.m. That was enough to get the name of the place.

She had put tracks and trains out of her mind now. Out of both their minds. "You kiss me like you're thinking of something else."

As a matter of fact, he had kissed her from one hour and ten minutes away. He brought his thoughts back and kissed her again.

He had been wondering how he could find out her name. In almost every sentence he addressed to her, there was an awkward letdown at the end, where her name should have rounded it out. The tongue expected it. The ear expected it, too. He rigged up a little trap to see if he could snare it out of her. His voice was low now, beside her ear. "If you could change your name, what would you rather have it be?"

It got him a name—his own. "That's a pushover—Mrs. Daniel Nearing."

Dan Nearing. Another key to the past. He took a chance and suggested, "That would make it longer than it is now."

She had to figure it aloud, as he'd hoped she would. "Let's see. D-i-l-l-o-n, six. N-e-a-r-i-n-g, seven. Only one letter." Then with a little burst of petulance: "Say, what is this anyway, a spelling bee in the dark?"

"I was just talking," he tried to pacify her. "You know how it is—it's been a long time since we talked together. I like to talk to you."

"Sure, talking's all right, but there are other things."

He didn't say anything more for a while. "How's this for not talking?" he asked her presently.

"For my part, you should never say another word."

In the morning he found his arm curved around nothing, giving emptiness a hug where she had been. But she'd be back again, the note said so.

Danny Darling,
   I had to make that six-o'clock train, and I didn't have the heart to wake you. Until next Thursday, and please be careful in the meantime.

Ruth

Her name was Ruth Dillon, the place she trained to and from was one hour and ten minutes away, the train that took her there left on track 17, lower level—and he felt as if he'd been pulled through a wringer.

HE KNEW HE WAS taking a chance. Stations are dangerous places for those in hiding. He entered with chin ducked to shirt front, to conceal at least the lower part of his face.

He was here at the hour she had departed the day before. He worked his way along the gates. There it was, gate 17, with the stops made by the six-a.m train conveniently posted alongside it. He studied the list of stops, and went over to the gateman. Picking a name from the board, the middle one, the halfway point of the trip, he asked, "What time does this train get to Meredith?"

"Seven five."

Too near. It must be the next one. "How about New Jericho?"

"Seven ten," the gateman said gruffly.

Townsend turned away. He'd hit the place. New Jericho was where she went. He was one step farther on the way.

THURSDAY AGAIN. Two voices in the dark again. The game of love and tightrope walking again. The things he'd already found out filled him with an insatiable passion to lift the curtain higher now, and there were two main things to be elicited from her tonight. *Where* had it happened? And *when* had it happened? The place. The date. Once he had these two factors of the equation, he could work out the rest. He must get them. Even as his lips touched hers, his mind kept going: where and when?

She got up and crossed the room to lower the shade. When she came back, she hesitated a moment before rejoining him, as though some spark of resentment had fanned itself alight during her brief absence. He could tell. Couples are almost telepathic at such times. "What're you sore about?" he murmured.

"Who's Virginia?"

He swallowed. "I don't know. Where'd you get that name?"

"From you."

"You're hearing things."

"Is she somebody you horsed around with up at New Jericho?" she went on resentfully. "Or somebody you dug up while you've been hiding out down here in the city?"

"I've been undercover the whole time down here—"

"Well, you weren't undercover up there!" she flashed back.

That gave him one answer. Up there was where. New Jericho. Now when?

She was still aggrieved. "Let her buy your groceries for you, then, if she's so hot! That's a fine thing! I've got to hear somebody else's name in my ear, even—"

"Shh! They'll hear you around this dump. Listen, I don't know any Virginia. To me Virginia's a state—"

"*You* weren't thinking of geography just now!"

He reached out and caught hold of her hands, and she came back to him by stages, finally relapsing in full forgiveness, her head on his shoulder once more. When had it been? When? He lit a cigarette.

"Light one for me, too, Danny. Like you used to. . . . No, don't blow out the match! I want to make a wish. . . . There. . . . What was it? You ought to be able to guess. That they'll never catch up with you; that they'll let me keep you to myself like this forever."

Forever. A time word. There it was. Better grab it quick, he might not get another chance that night.

"Forever is a long time. How long has it been—like this with me now? Any idea? I'm not good at keeping track of time . . ."

"Ten months now, isn't it? Let's see: August, September . . . yeah, it was ten months on the fifteenth."

So whatever it was, it had happened on August 15, the year before.

Where, plus when, equaled the past.

Chapter Seven

HE WAS AS timorous about entering the reading room of the library as he had been about venturing into the station, and he kept his head down as he approached the information desk. "Do you keep the back numbers of newspapers from New Jericho on file here?" he asked.

The librarian looked it up for him. "No, I'm sorry, we don't."

Maybe there were no newspapers published there. He didn't know how small a place it was. "Have you any idea, offhand, what the nearest large town to New Jericho is?"

"I believe Meredith would be about the closest."

"Have you any back-number Meredith papers?"

The librarian looked it up. "We have the Meredith *Leader*."

He requested the issue of August 16, 1940—that would be the day after it happened. But when the paper was brought to him, he wanted to drop it, never to look inside it. The past was here in his hands now, and he was afraid of it. Frank Townsend and Dan Nearing were together at last. What had Dan Nearing done?

Finally, with desperate resignation, he took the newspaper over to one of the tables, sat down and opened it. The name "Daniel Nearing" leaped out at him. He began to read.

MAN KILLS BENEFACTOR
BRUTAL SLAYING AT SUBURBAN ESTATE

New Jericho, Aug. 15th—Turning on the man who had given him shelter and employment during the past two years, Daniel Nearing shot and killed Harry S. Diedrich, member of a well-known local family, at his country estate near here early this afternoon.

The victim's wife, Alma, his younger brother, William, and a neighbor, Arthur Struthers, were eyewitnesses to the crime, having returned unexpectedly after leaving a few minutes before. They only narrowly escaped sharing Mr. Diedrich's fate. The enraged assailant pursued them from the house when he caught sight of them, but they managed to regain the highway in their car and telephone for help from Mr. Struthers' house.

By the time police under the direction of Constable E. J. Ames reached the scene, the slayer had made good his escape. The weapon used, a shotgun, was found at the scene, lying where the killer had discarded it. The slain man's father, Emil Diedrich, a helpless invalid, was found unharmed in his wheelchair in another room of the house.

Nearing, whose antecedents are unknown, had been taken in and given work by the murdered man, against the advice of other members of the household. Originally, he worked as handyman about the premises and looked after the grounds. For the past few months, however, Nearing had been placed in charge of Mr. Diedrich's invalid father and had occupied a room within the house itself, replacing a former attendant who had been dismissed.

Other members of the household at the time of the tragedy were Mr. Diedrich's sister, Adela, secluded in an upstairs room due to a nervous disorder; a cook, Mrs. Mollie McGuire; and a housemaid, Miss Ruth Dillon. The two servants were not in the house at the time of the shooting.

According to the story pieced together by Constable Ames, Mrs. Diedrich during luncheon had expressed a wish to go to the city on a shopping trip. Her husband suggested that his brother drive her to the New Jericho train station, and they set out shortly before 2:00 p.m. Mr. Diedrich, meanwhile, retired to the conservatory, where he habitually took an afternoon nap, and Mrs. McGuire and Miss Dillon, having the afternoon off, left a few moments afterward and took the bus together. Nearing, when last seen, was sitting beside his invalid charge, apparently dozing.

Mrs. Diedrich and her brother-in-law, on their way to the station, encountered a neighbor, Mr. Struthers, and offered to take him with them. A moment later Mrs. Diedrich discovered she had left her train tickets behind, and they turned back to get them. As they drove up to the house, they heard a gunshot, and before they could get out of the car, they saw Nearing rush from the conservatory, brandishing the still-smoking shotgun. Horrified, they drove down to the highway again, pursued by him.

Mr. Diedrich, when the police arrived on the scene, was found to have been killed instantly, his head partly blown off by the blast. A small safe in the library had been forced open and its contents scattered about on the floor. Whether any money was missing could not immediately be learned. Mr. Diedrich had complained of missing small sums in cash from time to time over the past several weeks, and the police speculate that he set a trap for the thief, discovered Nearing in the act of ransacking the safe, attempted to call for help, and was driven back into the conservatory by the enraged malefactor and shot to death there.

The killer is described as of medium height, about thirty or thirty-one years of age, with light brown hair and eyes, and a deceptively mild appearance. He has a small blue anchor tattooed on the back of his left wrist.

The police are watching all main roads leading into the city.

Townsend let his cuff slide forward, and the little blue anchor ebbed from sight under it.

Murder! It lit up his mind like a rocket. He brushed the back of his hand across his mouth, as if to wipe off some sort of foul taste. He was an outcast now. He could be hunted down. He could be killed by law. There was no refuge for him, no mercy. He was a murderer.

Now he knew, now he understood: the meaning of the man in gray, the silent grim pursuit, that raid in the dead of night on his home. It was no private enemy stalking him out of the miasmas of the past, seeking personal vengeance. His pursuit had been organized by society itself. That man must have been a policeman. Who else would have dared to draw a gun on a crowded subway platform and shatter a car window?

The black curtain had lifted at last.

A hand fell on him lightly, and the touch of it went to his heart like electricity. "No sleeping in here, please," a voice murmured tactfully.

He raised his head from between his arms. His eyes were haunted. He'd been watching a man thirty-one years of age, of medium height, come rushing out of a room, holding a smoking shotgun in his hands.

THERE WAS a difference now. They weren't alone anymore. There was a ghost in the room with them, in the very bed. And when he tried to kiss her, he was kissing its cold, grinning face instead.

"Why are you so quiet tonight, Danny? What's the matter?"

He knew he had to do one of two things. Go to the police and say, "I'm Dan Nearing," or . . . He knew he couldn't live anymore with the question in his mind.

"Ruth, do *you* believe I did it?"

She hid her face against him. "Three people saw you with their own eyes. I've *tried* not to—"

"But if I said I didn't, would you believe me and try to help me prove I didn't? Would you help me find out who really did?"

"Oh, Danny, I'd do anything! But how?"

"I'm going to go back there. Right where it happened. That's the only way to clear myself. And you've got to help me."

She bounded out of bed and stood there, aghast, in the dark. "To the Diedrich place? D'you know what they'll do? No, Danny! Please! It would be like sticking your head into a trap. They'd turn you in so fast—"

"*If* they see me. That's where you come in."

"Danny, it can't be done. We'd never get away with it—"

He cut her short. "My mind's made up. If you don't help me, then I'm going anyway, on my own. It'll be just that much tougher. *I know I didn't do it.* I know three people saw me. I know it's in the papers, and on the cops' blotters. I don't care. I don't care if the whole world says I killed that man. *I* say I didn't. And I won't let them tell me different—not while there's a breath left in me. I'm going back there. It's going to end where it began, one way or the other. Now, will you help me or will you let me go hang?"

She bent toward him in the dark, her hair rippling over his shoulders like soft, warm rain. Her lips sought his, and just before they met in a kiss that was a pledge, she murmured, "You don't have to ask me that. Don't you know I'd help you, Danny, even if it was the last thing I ever did?"

Chapter Eight

THIS WAS THE night set for his return to the past, on the last train out, at eleven. All the necessary details had been arranged between them on her visit the week before. She was to bring clothes that would alter his appearance as much as possible. She was to come straight to his room from the station. On the estate, she had remembered, there was an unused lodge nobody ever went near. It would do to conceal his presence.

Darkness had fallen on Tillary Street, and the ghostly square flickered once more on the room wall. It seemed to mock him as he waited and she became longer and longer overdue, as if it were saying, "You'll never make it. You'll never get out of here."

Finally he couldn't stand it. He jerked down the shade to kill the blasted mirage of a window where there was no window, of a way out where there was none. But that didn't bring her any faster. He craned his neck, peering out around the side of the shade. She should have reached the city hours ago.

He needed her more than she realized. She thought he'd been up there before. And his body had, but his mind hadn't. He couldn't move an inch without her. He would be as helpless as a blind man trying to cross a street without a guide.

She wasn't coming, he decided, or she would have been here by now. She'd let him down—not purposely, he knew, but that didn't help. There was no question of treachery or disloyalty. She was all for him, just as Virginia herself would have been if she'd been called on to play this part. Some unforeseen slipup must have occurred.

He heard chimes now, coming from some little church steeple hidden among the tenements. He counted them, although he knew what they were going to add up to. *Clong, clong, clong*—eight, nine, ten. One hour left. Just enough time, if he left almost at once, to catch that last train.

But how could he make it without her? How could he possibly hope to run the gauntlet of recognition? They must know him well up there. The very first person he approached to ask directions—and he would have to ask directions—might turn him in. Even walking around down here in the city was risky. That was why she'd been bringing in concealing clothes for him. To tackle the undertaking alone was more than inviting arrest—it was making certain of it. But—

He was going to do it.

There must be something he could do to give himself a fighting chance to pass unnoticed. He couldn't put on a wig or dye his face. But wait a minute—there was that old fur repairer down on the ground floor, the one who salvaged scraps of worn-out, discarded fur and patched them together with shears and glue and then went peddling them around the neighborhood.

A moment later he was looking in at the old fellow through the open door. "Listen, I want to play a trick on my girl. You know, just for fun. Put a dab of glue on me here, on each side, just in front of my ears. And one on each eyebrow. Then take a few thin pieces of dark fur—ends you don't need—and see if you can make them look like they're growing there."

The furrier waved his arms, outraged. "Funny business I got no time to make."

"Listen, here's a quarter. You can do it. You're good at anything you do."

The peddler sounded the quarter against the bare floor, and then accommodatingly poised his glue brush near Townsend's face. "The way this glue makes you smell, your girl ain't going to like you so much," he warned.

They got a halfway natural effect. He pulled his hat down low so that only the thinned-out sealskin sideburns and eyebrows showed beneath it. He turned up his coat collar. It was the most he could do. Anyone who knew him well would recognize him at once. This was just for those who mightn't be sure at first sight.

He went back to his room again for a minute, hoping against hope that she had come, but the room was empty. He'd have to strike out on his own. He took a deep breath. "Well—here goes." He reached up and tweaked out the light.

Tillary Street sank from sight, returning into that past from which he'd so patiently dredged it.

As HE ENTERED the station's main waiting room, the symptoms of agoraphobia struck him full blast. He felt as though he were walking alone across this immense expanse of marble and cement, with a spotlight focused squarely on him, and all around him an unseen circle of faces scanning, scrutinizing, staring at him.

It was nearly eleven. He hurried over to a ticket window. "Gimme a ticket to New Jericho."

"Dollar eighty-four."

He kept looking around while he scooped the money out of his pocket. Ticket in hand, he got to the gate and squeezed through as they were closing it. He careened down the ramp and caught the train just as it began to move.

It was the last train of the night, and it was full. In the car he'd boarded, there wasn't a seat to be had, so he started forward, toward the locomotive, trying to find a place to sink down out of sight. In the third car up, he nearly blundered into catastrophe.

Two things saved him. All but one of the seats in the third car faced forward. *All but one.* And the occupant of that one seat facing toward him was Ruth Dillon.

She knew him instantly, despite the fur eyebrows and sideburns, and her eyes dilated with horror. He stopped moving in mid-footfall, the car door just newly closed at his back, as she made a fleeting warding-off gesture with her palms that could have only one meaning: "Don't come in here. Don't come near me." Then she deflected her eyes toward the aisle, swiftly, urgently. The message was clear: "Look over there."

He did. Two seats away, on the opposite side, was that same profile, under the same gray hat, of the man who was hunting him. A tensing of the man's neck cords indicated that he was about to swing his head around; perhaps he had heard the opening and closing of the car door just now. On Townsend's left was another door, marked LAVATORY. He shouldered it open and bolted through.

All the rest of the way, he rode in uncomfortable confinement, his back firmly to the washroom door, one foot up against the opposite wall to brace himself.

He counted five stops and three unsuccessful door tries. The ease with which the three people were discouraged showed, at least, that none of them was his nemesis in the gray hat. Still, the mere fact that a number of people were being denied admittance to the washroom might bring about a shattering investigation. And now he wouldn't know which stop was New Jericho; the station calls of the conductor didn't penetrate the washroom.

At the sixth stop, there was a sort of scuff down near the bottom of the door. Its repetition in a matter of seconds showed it to be a signal, not the careless tread of someone going by. Ruth must have found time to do it on her way past with the heel of her shoe.

He opened the door instantly. She was lingering there, her back to him, pretending to powder her nose. She didn't turn but spoke to him into the pocket mirror she was using. "Ames," she breathed hurriedly. "He got off at the other end of the car just now, to try to keep out of my sight. He's out there, someplace in the station. Count ten, slowly, from the time I leave, then get off. Now listen closely. There's a baggage truck against the station wall, just a little way down. I saw it through the car window. Get over to it and hide behind it, and wait for me there. If I can't come to you right away, I'll come back for you later—as soon as I'm sure I've shaken him off. Now, remember: count ten, slowly."

He came out into the aisle just as her figure disappeared.

He heard the click of her descending heels on the car steps and started to count . . .

" 'Bo-o-o-ard!" echoed dismally outside.

The train was moving by the time he hit ten. Just as he jumped off, he heard a wailing scream wrenched from her, somewhere behind him on the concrete platform. It was a slick piece of timing.

He had sense enough to keep going straight for the baggage truck, but he did catch a glimpse of the vignette she was artfully producing. Every head on the platform had turned her way. A pretty girl turning her foot like that and floundering down on one hand and knee, with a scream to advertise her plight, couldn't help but monopolize every eye—even a detective's. A small knot of people gathered around her to help her up. Then they all straggled off at one end of the platform while the hum of the train receded at the other. The station was suddenly silent and empty.

A good quarter of an hour later he heard the tap of her heels coming toward him. He looked out from his niche as she reached him. "All right now?"

"Yes. I stopped in at Jordan's drugstore across the square and had a spot of iodine put on the palm of my hand. I had to have an excuse to hang around, so I had a soda at the counter. Ames went straight into the constable's office; I saw him through the drugstore window. That's one good thing about these hick towns that have just one main street—you can spot everything that's going on."

"How do you know he isn't still watching you?"

"He's not interested in me once I'm back here. It was only in the city that he kept breathing down my neck. Probably the only reason he got on the same train coming back was that there isn't any other until six a.m. What a day he gave me, though! I just avoided giving myself away by the skin of my teeth! Another minute and I would have led him straight into your lap! I already had one foot on the bus to Tillary Street when I saw him." She sighed with remembered fright. "Lucky he didn't catch on that I saw him. Well, I went right ahead and got on the bus. I had to. I couldn't back out because he would have caught on that I was trying to throw him off the scent, and that was the one thing I didn't want him to think. So I got off at Watt Street, and spent the afternoon at my sister's place and had supper with them. I knew I couldn't go near you for the rest of the night. I couldn't take the chance."

Townsend said, "That was smart work, Ruth."

She flushed at his tribute, then went on. "You can imagine how I felt. It's hard letting yourself be followed without letting on you know it's being done. But I never actually saw Ames again from the time I got on the bus until I came through the train looking for a seat coming home. He must have a hunch I've been seeing you. God knows why! Don't let anyone tell you they're not *good*. They're *good*, all right. They're mind readers and magicians all rolled up in one."

"No, they're not," he scoffed. "They can be wrong. They think I killed Diedrich, and I say I didn't."

"If you say that, I say that, too. But now the thing is, how're we going to get you away from here and out to the estate?"

"How do you usually go yourself?"

"I take the bus from the square here, and it brings me right to the Diedrichs' driveway. But obviously that's out for you." She looked around, in search of inspiration. "Wait a minute. There's a truck standing out in front of the station—the driver must be in Joe's Lunch getting a meal. If he's going the right way, we could ask him to give us a lift. He wouldn't know us, he's not from around here, just passing through. Come on." He followed her out of the station to the street, where she stopped and pointed. "See? There it is."

He squeezed her arm admiringly. "You think of everything, Ruth."

"You have to when you're looking out for someone you love," she said with the utmost simplicity. "There's the driver now, coming out. Stay here until I find out where he's going. If it's okay, I'll wave you on. Cut straight over to the truck fast. Don't stay out in the open any longer than you have to. Ames will probably be in the constable's office half the night making out his report, but you never know—"

He watched her go over to the driver and stand there a moment talking. Then he saw one white-gloved hand go up in a signal, and he walked fast across the exposed space to the welcome shadow cast by the truck.

"It's all right, *Jimmy*," she shrieked above the din of its warming-up motor. "The driver says he'll give us a lift, but we'll have to ride in the back."

He pantomimed his thanks to the shadowy figure in the cab of the truck, and they scrambled up onto the rear apron. They settled down as far inside as they could, in a protective triangle of shadow. They rumbled off and New Jericho quickly receded behind them. Then a long, tapelike country highway started to unroll, with a black tracery of roadside trees on both sides, an occasional house and up above a sky full of stars.

A good thirty or forty minutes went by, or so it seemed, without incident. Then a passenger car, coming up from behind and overtaking them, gave him a bad moment as its headlights swept the inside of the truck. He cocked his knees and ducked his head, as though he'd fallen asleep in a sitting position, and the car swerved out around them and went past.

About five minutes later the truck shuddered to a halt. Ruth got out and her piercing tones filtered back to him. "Thanks a lot. You're a lifesaver. Jimmy, are you clear?"

He vaulted down off the truck, and a moment later they were standing all alone by the roadside in a little haze of gasoline exhaust.

"Did you recognize who it was that went by awhile back? My heart was in my mouth."

"No, I ducked my head."

"Bill and Alma Diedrich! I recognized the car. So that's what they've been doing whenever I have a night off! They're supposed to stay home and keep an eye on the old man. Why, that's criminal, Dan! D'you know that there's not another living soul in the house with that helpless old fellow except the crazy sister, Adela, and if she ever got out of her room, there's no telling what she'd do to him. Anything could happen. A short circuit could start a fire or—"

Maybe they wouldn't be too sorry, he thought.

She pointed back to an asphalt driveway, dimly discernible a short distance behind them. "That's the way I usually go in. Hurry up, let's get away from here before we're seen."

He couldn't help looking back in that direction, lingeringly. So that was the way in to murder. There was a white signboard swaying midcenter over the drive, strung from some invisible support. He imagined it would read, PRIVATE PROPERTY, NO THOROUGHFARE.

They moved off in the opposite direction along the roadside, Indian file, she in the lead. "There's a much shorter way than this," she said over her shoulder. "Do you remember? Along the path that leads to the lodge from the house itself. But I don't want to bring you that near if I can help it. If Alma and Bill only just got back, one of them might still be up and see you from the windows."

The main driveway was far behind them now, and still she kept going. If the property was equal in depth to its length along the highway, it was some private estate!

She stopped finally. "There's the boundary marker, that white circle painted around the trunk of the tree. We'll cut in through here now. We'll have to feel our way through the rough. Then that path from the house makes a sharp turn, and we can get on that and follow it the rest of the way."

"How is it they don't have the estate fenced in?" he asked. "Leave it open like this for anyone to trespass—"

"Too tight-fisted, I guess. They've owned it for centuries. You know these old families—they don't live much better than my sister does on Watt Street. Won't spend a red cent for improvements. Maybe the old man would, though, if he could tell what he wanted."

They came out onto a little dirt path, untended and barely visible beneath a patina of leaves and twigs. They followed it to an unused caretaker's lodge, with a lower story of rough-edged boulders cemented together and an upper one of logs. The windows were all broken and the door opened flush with the ground.

"Come in and close the door, Danny. I left a candle inside when I was out here today."

Darkness smothered them like a feather bolster. Then a star of matchlight twinkled and widened into a candle flame that sketched in the ground-floor room in dusky-yellow wash. He could see the black patch of an open trapdoor at one end of the ceiling. "How do you get up there?"

"You don't. There's no ladder around, and I'm not sure the flooring up there would hold you anyway. You'll have to stay down here, Danny."

"How about the windows?"

"I tacked some green felt that I found over the ones facing the main house. The ones in back I had to leave the way they were. You're not in direct sight of the house from here anyway, but the thing to watch out for is someone prowling around in the open over that way and catching sight of a chink of light from inside. I've been busy here all week long, smuggling things out underneath the old man in the wheelchair." She smiled a little. "Sometimes he sat six inches higher in it than usual, but luckily no one seemed to notice. I've been wheeling him out here every day and reading to him. As long as he's out of their sight, they don't give a damn where he is. That's as much as they care about him."

She motioned to a double layer of blankets spread over a foundation of potato sacking, flat on the floor. "That was the best I could do for you, Danny. I gave you the blankets from my own bed."

He took her in his arms, and they stood there together, silent. He found no words to say, but she seemed content.

"I'd better be getting back now," she said finally.

"Can you get in, or will you have to wake them?"

"I've got my own latchkey."

"I'd better go part of the way with you. That lane out there looked darned lonely."

"After all my trouble to get you in here safely without being seen? I guess not! I'll be all right; there's never anyone around out this way. But kill the candle until you're ready to close the door again."

He went outside a few steps with her. "When will I see you again?"

"I wheel him out for air about eleven. I'll slip over then."

"Don't take any more chances than you have to," he said, and watched her out of sight down the path. Then, after closing the door and relighting the candle, he took off his coat and rolled it up for a pillow. *"Home is the slayer,"* he parodied grimly, *"home from the sea."*

Chapter Nine

HIS SENSATION, on waking up, was that of opening his eyes inside a grotto. All blue dimness. His bones ached from the plank floor and his neck felt as if it had a permanent kink. He unrolled his pillow and put his arms through its sleeves, then took the green felt down from the windows and went out to find some water.

There was a sort of meadow outside, brimming with hot sun, white butterflies supplying the only motion. The main house was well out of sight. He finally found what he was looking for, a small stream with water that was clear and cold. He washed his face in it and then filled up an empty can for his coffee and took it back inside.

Ruth seemed to have thought of everything; there was coffee, canned milk, bacon, beans, even sugar. He got a little twig-and-straw fire going for his coffee in the cobbled fireplace at one end of the room. He was afraid to use large pieces of wood lest the smoke coming from the chimney betray him.

He was shaving over a tin can of slightly warm water, with the razor he'd brought from Tillary Street, when he caught a rustling sound outside. He jumped over to the door and crouched, peering out through a crack. It was the rubber-tired wheels of an invalid chair that Ruth was pushing up the path.

He stepped outdoors and stared. In the chair sat an inert thing that looked like cleverly molded pink dough shaped in the likeness of a human form. Only the eyes were alive. Townsend and the eyes gazed at one another in tense silence until Ruth, speaking with that slightly monotonous intonation used only toward children, said, "See? Look who's here. Your old friend back again. Aren't you glad to see him?"

It didn't seem those eyes could get any brighter than they already were, but they managed to.

Then, in a more lifelike tone, she said, "How is it going, Danny?"

"Not a hitch, Ruth. You took care of everything."

"I could hardly close my eyes all night, I was so worried."

"Why?"

"Bringing you this close. You talked me into it last week, but—it seems such a scatterbrained chance to take. This is the last place on earth you should be hanging around!"

He smiled but didn't answer. He was seeing her in her work outfit for the first time. It wasn't actually a uniform, rather the suggestion of one . . . a dress of some crisp yellow stuff, and over it two white strips that crossed her bosom grenadier-fashion.

She bent forward to look at her charge. "Ah, look, he's waiting for you to say hello. Don't disappoint him, Danny!" she urged. "I know what he wants. Don't you remember those swearing sessions you used to go into with him when there was no one around? Not because you were sore or anything, just in a kind of a lazy, good-natured way. But such language!" She chuckled reminiscently. "It was like a code between the two of you. He enjoyed it. I guess it was a kind of reverse way of showing you liked him. Go ahead, say hello to him. I'll clear out until it's over."

She turned and strolled aimlessly away. The eyes above the chair glinted.

It should have been a funny situation, but it wasn't. To Townsend, it was poignant, almost tragic. He felt helpless, filled with a nameless sorrow, but he pulled down his collar with two fingers, swallowed hard and began in a halting, labored voice that picked up fluency as it went along. By the time he had finished, it had become a good performance. The old man's eyes were dancing with sheer joy when Ruth returned, and Townsend was wiping his forehead.

Afterward, as they sat, one on each side of the chair, Townsend suddenly noticed something and asked, "Why does he keep blinking like that?"

"The sun must be bothering his eyes." She shifted the chair a little, leaned forward to look. "He's not doing it now."

Townsend watched the motionless head in silence for a moment or two. "He's at it again," he said presently in an undertone, when she had regained her original position. "He stops whenever he catches you looking at him. He only seems to do it when I'm watching him."

"Maybe he's just trying to show you how happy he is to have you around again."

"He's *not* happy," Townsend insisted. "There are tears in the corners of his eyes."

"That's right, there are," Ruth said, taking a handkerchief from the side pocket of the chair and touching it delicately to both sides of the old man's nose. "What does he want from you?"

"I don't know," Townsend said helplessly. "There must be something I've let him down about."

There must be, he thought, but who could tell him what it was? The only one who knew couldn't speak.

"I don't like to see him cry. Now stop it, you hear, Mr. Emil? It's been a long time since Danny was last with you; he can't be expected to repeat every last thing just as it was before. . . . They get to be like children," she added in a pitying aside. "Did you used to give him things, like jelly beans or cough drops or something, out of your pockets?"

"I can't remember," he said with utter, forlorn truthfulness.

THAT NIGHT, WELL AFTER DARK, there was a light unexpected tapping at the door that threw a short circuit into him. He palmed the candle out with a flat downward sweep of his hand, reared up from the packing case he'd been sitting on and stood tense and silent.

"Dan," the night seemed to breathe outside. "It's me."

He went over to the door, removed the chair barricade he'd tilted against it and put down the iron crowbar he'd armed himself with.

"They went out about three quarters of an hour ago. I'd already put Mr. Emil to bed, and I just had to slip over for a minute to see how you were. Besides, I sneaked some more supplies for you."

"How is it I didn't hear you coming?" he asked, helping her to carry the large carton inside.

"Maybe because I'm wearing sneakers. Dan, listen, I want to warn you. You'll have to be more careful about that candle. I could distinctly see a wink of yellow showing as I came down the path; there must be a crack underneath a window—"

He seemed to be thinking of something else. "Where'd they go, have you any idea?"

"I don't know, I didn't hear them say. Why?"

"I want you to let me into the house while they're out, Ruthie."

Immediately she was aghast, filled with unreasoning terror on his account. "No, Danny, no! There's no telling when they'll come back. Suppose they suddenly walk in on you? Please, Danny, don't."

With a quiet determination that brooked no argument, he said, "I want to see it, Ruthie. If you won't take me over, then I'll go without you."

"You crazy fool," she mourned, following him falteringly out of the lodge and down the path. "You ought to be a thousand miles away, instead of hanging around here," she scolded. "I don't know why I bother my head about you anyway!"

"I don't know either," he agreed, "but thank God you do."

All at once he saw the outline of a house set against a luminous silver-clouded sky, with indirect lighting furnished by a hidden moon. "So that's it," he breathed. She gave him a questioning look of surprise. She didn't know that he was seeing it for the first time.

He followed her up to the front door, a peculiar quivery feeling cascading down his spine. At last he was reentering the very heart of the past.

She opened the door with her key, looking fearfully back over her shoulder. "Get in first and over to one side, where you can't be seen through the glass, before I put the lights on."

He obeyed, and for the first time he was looking down the halls of murder. For the first time he, Frank Townsend, was seeing the place where Dan Nearing was accused of committing murder.

The house must have been as old as the hills. It had a brooding, depressing quality, as though there hadn't been much laughter in it down through the generations. There was a teasing trace of gardenia on the air, so faint that when you tried to catch it, you couldn't; it assailed you only when you had forgotten it was there.

Ruth turned the lights on in a room to the left. "This was Mr. Harry's library and study—remember?" He saw her eyes come to rest on a painted iron plaque set into the paneling, then drop quickly in embarrassment, and he realized that it must be the wall safe he was supposed to have burgled.

She turned off the lights and they crossed the hall. "Here's the living room; it's just the same as when you were here."

They went deeper into the house. "*He's* in here." She turned on the lights, and Townsend saw the old man lying in a tremendous bed with the wheelchair drawn up close beside it. His eyes were shut, and his face looked more natural in sleep than it did awake. "We leave him down here at night now, in this little sitting room. His chair is too heavy to manage up and down the stairs twice a day."

"Do you put him to bed?"

"Well, I don't undress him; Mr. Bill does. But I lift him in and out of the bed. He doesn't weigh much. It's so cruel when you're helpless, at the mercy of other people."

As Ruth's hand reached out to the light switch, Townsend received a momentary impression that one of the peacefully-lidded eyes had opened and was peering craftily at them. But the light went out before he could confirm it.

Outside the room, at the foot of the stairs, he hesitated. "What's that? I thought I heard somebody tiptoeing around above us."

"*You* know, that's Miss Adela, the—" She made a little circle with her finger close to her forehead. "She's always creeping around and listening at her door, even when there's nothing to hear. I don't know why they've left her here in the house, instead of shipping her off to an institution. Mr. Bill always carries the key to her room on him, won't let anyone else have it. Just like Mr. Harry used to."

"Has she ever been examined by any outsider? How do they know she's actually—"

"They say they had it done years ago. They say there's no use now anymore."

"They say," he repeated laconically. "For all anybody knows, they may be getting away with murder. White murder."

"I used to try to make believe to myself that it was *her* who did the killing—you know, to try to find an out for you in my mind. She was the only other person here in the house at the time, except the poor old man, of course. But"—she let her arms drop forlornly—"the key to her room was still on Mr. Harry's body and her door was still locked from the outside when they came back."

They walked through a wide entrance into a dining room. Beyond it, Townsend saw double glass doors, closed. Ruth seemed anxious to leave now, he noticed. "Come on, Danny, let's go. You've seen everything," she said. Instead, he went on toward the double doors. "What do you want to go in there for?" she whispered. "What good will that do?"

But he already had the doors open and the lights on inside. It was a sun parlor.

Reluctantly she followed him. The glass doors were lined on the inside with dark blue roller shades, one to every three panes of width. There was also a shade that spread across the ceiling like an awning and was controlled by a drawstring from below. All the shades were patched and mended in places, but one had a neat little diamond-shaped rent that had not been repaired.

The room had an old-fashioned mosaic floor that was once colorful but was now gray with encrusted dust. It was furnished with two wicker armchairs and a wicker settee, and opposite the settee was a low tile-topped table that had evidently held many potted plants and flowers in the old days. The whole enclosure now had only a couple of dried-out greenish wisps still lingering in pots in the corners.

"Is this where he was sitting?" Townsend asked, nodding at the settee.

Her face creased. "Dan, don't talk that way! As if you didn't know! Don't look at it!"

"Oh, I thought those stains were just rust streaks from the nails in it."

"I don't know why they didn't throw it out long ago," she went on more quietly. "But no one ever comes in here anymore. It's the first time I've been near it myself since that day—"

"It's the first time I have, too," he murmured bitterly.

They turned away, and as she reclosed the blue-shaded glass doors behind them, he stood there, lost in thought. She came up close to him and buried her face against his chest. "Danny, Danny, why did you have to do it? You must've gone nuts when he said you'd been stealing from the safe. If we could only undo that one afternoon! I loved you so. I still do, but I can't have you now."

He let her mourn it out. There was nothing he could say to comfort her. At last she raised her head. "Come on, Danny, you'd better go now. You've been here long enough."

They walked down the hall past the stairs. He fell behind a

moment to light a cigarette, so that she reached the front door ahead of him. When she opened it narrowly to look out, a big golden light seemed to beat in at her. The sound of brakes being thrown on punctuated the glare. She reclosed the door hurriedly. Disjointed, breathless warnings flew from her as she ran back to him. "I told you! The car—they're back!"

She pushed him around the side of the stairs and into the dark dining room. "The back! Get out the kitchen door!" Then she took sudden root where she was, paralyzed by a noise at the far end of the hall: a key was pecking at the keyhole from outside.

He just had time to take a floundering step forward before the front door opened, but the edge of the dining table caught him at the waist and blocked him. He moved around it, found a door and started through it into what he thought was the kitchen. Suddenly shelving bit into him in ridges from his forehead all the way down his body, and something that was glass or china pinged complainingly.

He managed to back out without knocking anything over, but the dining table edge caught him again. He got down on his haunches and clung to it with one hand, hopelessly trapped. He was afraid to move again, lest he collide with something and give himself away.

In the hall a raspy contralto voice was asking, "Wasn't that you, Ruth, peeping out at us just now? Why the hell didn't you leave the door open so I wouldn't have to go hunting for my key? What're you acting so spooky about?"

Ruth said, "I guess I must have fallen asleep, Miss Alma. And the lights of the car dazzled my eyes for a minute."

"We'll have to get you a pair of smoked glasses," the voice said ungraciously.

The whine of the car had shifted around to the garage and broken off short. And the contralto voice was nearer now; she must be coming down the hall to the back. A shadow flicked across the dimly lighted entrance to the dining room. "The picture was lousy. We settled for a couple of beers at the tavern." She was obviously unsteady, and he heard her mutter on the way up the stairs, "Pretzels and beer! Beer and pretzels! With thousands of bucks in the kitty! I did better for myself when I was free-lancing in Shanghai!" A bedroom door slammed above.

For tonight it was all right. Her perceptions were a little blurred. But in the morning would she remember the slight dissonance in Ruth's reception of her? Would she start wondering about it?

The front door slammed and the latch went on. Someone else had come in. Townsend heard a brief scuffle and heard Ruth say sharply, "That'll be all of that!" Then there was a snigger and a heavy tread going up the stairs.

Townsend straightened up, came out around the table and met Ruth as she was edging her way through the dining room to the kitchen. She gave a start. "Danny! Why didn't you go? What if one of them had come back here for a drink of water or something?"

"I couldn't find the way out. I got all balled up in the dark."

"*This* way, what's the matter with you!" She urged him toward a screened door, unseen until now. "Please go now, Danny."

As he stepped out into the darkness, she whispered after him reproachfully, "I can't for the life of me understand how you could get mixed up like that and not be able to find the way out."

He made no answer to that until he was at a safe distance, and then only to himself: "Because I was never in there before."

Chapter Ten

THERE WAS a certain tree near the turn of the footpath that they had agreed would mark the safety zone beyond which he ought not to venture. They called it their meeting post, and he used to go down and wait beside it for her to come along the path with the old man. He amused himself by watching her progress. She would come along a mottled tunnel of light and shade, one minute yellow disks of sunlight falling on her through the leaves, the next cool blue shade. From way up ahead, she'd see him standing there. Then she'd always go through the same little performance. First she would give a guarded look backward to make sure she wasn't being followed; then she would greet him with a slow wave of her hand, two or three times, a little over her head. She could make waving her hand like that seem as tenderly adoring as a kiss. Finally, she'd reach him.

Today he scrutinized the old man carefully. The eyes were flickering up at him again. "He's still doing it," he said to her, with relief in his voice.

"And he doesn't do it at the house. I've been watching him ever since you called my attention to it."

At the door of the lodge, he asked, "Did you get me those things I asked you for?"

"Yes. I went to the village this morning, and I've got them here in the side of the chair." She passed them over to him. "A steno pad and pencils."

"Now I'm going to take him inside with me. You stay out here and keep your eye on the path. Let me know when it's time for you to go."

She had a disappointed look. "What are you going to do?"

"I'm going to try something," he said, "and if it works out, I'll tell you about it afterward."

He wheeled the chair inside, and from then on, there wasn't a sound from within the lodge. How could there be? Whatever the means of communication he was trying to open up with this mute old man, it had to be a silent one.

SHE STEPPED inside the door about an hour and a half later and stood watching the two of them for a puzzled moment. Townsend had turned the old man's chair around so that the light from outside fell full on his face, and with the steno pad open on his knee, he was rapidly making marks on the page, his eyes attentively on the old man's eyes.

"What're you doing, Dan, trying to take down his winks in shorthand?" she exclaimed.

"I'm just noting them down as they come."

"But isn't every wink just like every other one?"

"That's what I'm hoping to find out. If it is, then I'm just wasting my time. But he keeps on sending 'em; he hasn't stopped once since he's been in here. So there must be some coherent message in them. I'll work on this tonight, when I'm alone—"

"You'll have to let me have him now. I'm overdue for lunch, and I don't want them to get suspicious."

He got up and wheeled the chair outside for her. "Try to get back with him this afternoon if you can."

Townsend stood by the tree, watching her hurry down the leafy tunnel. Now the disks of sunlight and patches of shade didn't gently alternate on her; they streaked in one continuous blurred line like a striped tiger pelt, she was moving so fast. Suddenly the end of the tunnel showed blank and she was gone.

When Ruth returned that afternoon, he could tell at first sight that she was frightened.

"What's the matter? Did something happen?"

"I don't like the way Miss Alma's acting. I'm afraid. I could swear she's caught on that there's something up."

"Why? Did she say anything?"

"She doesn't have to. I know her well enough by now. I wouldn't have dared come back here, only I heard the shower going upstairs, and by the time she gets through putting the last coat of shellac on her face afterward, it'll be another two hours. Danny, you better clear out of here—"

"Just what makes you think she's suspicious?"

"She was already eating her melon by the time I got him to the lunch table. I told her my watch was slow, and she didn't say a word. Then when she got up from the table, she stopped by Mr. Emil's chair and picked up that damn book I've been packing back and forth with me, pretending to read aloud to him all these days. The book is long and has one of those old-fashioned ribbon markers in it—you know, the kind you put between the pages to keep your place. Well, she opened it and looked. Then she said, 'You're a slow reader, Ruth. A remarkably slow reader.' Like a fool I'd let the marker stay in the same place for days. She fixed her eyes on me, and honestly, Dan, they were like daggers."

"That's not so good," he said slowly.

"What're we going to do? I don't think I can bring him out here anymore."

"All right, I'll work fast and see if I can finish up what I'm doing this afternoon."

But he had barely touched pencil to pad, his eyes on the old man's face, when she came floundering in again, almost incoherent. "Danny, she's coming! Straight for here! I caught a flash of her through the trees! Give him to me, quick!" She wrenched the chair out of the lodge, backward. He started after her. "No, you haven't time to get out, she'll spot you through the trees—"

He funneled up the litter of loose sheets of paper with a great double sweep of his arms, then opened his coat and buttoned it over them, holding them in place with both hands on the outside, as though he had a cramp in his middle. Then he stepped behind the door, which was folded back almost against the wall.

Ruth had just time enough to fling herself onto the campstool she had with her and open the book before the intruder was upon her. "Oh, here's Miss Alma, see?" she cooed for her patient's benefit, with just the right note of impromptu casualness. "Coming to find out what we're doing all the way over here."

There was a brief silence, then that scratchy contralto voice sounded. "Well, what *are* you doing, now that you mention it?"

"Oh, I found this place quite by accident one day, weeks ago," Ruth answered, "and I've been coming back ever since. When it gets too hot, I wheel him inside to get him out of the sun."

"There's plenty of shade outside." The contralto voice was toneless. It waited a moment, then added, "What's the inside like?" It was an obvious challenge intended to test the girl's reaction, and it worked. He heard a dull thwack as the book suddenly toppled to the ground.

"Oh," Ruth began, "there's nothing to see—"

The threshold creaked slightly, as if under the pressure of a single step. Then nothing more. The woman was looking in, but she already knew enough not to come in very far.

Ruth was still talking to her back, trying to minimize the discovery that was imminent. "I've been fixing myself little snacks in there with things I brought out from the pantry." Her deprecating laugh sounded hopeless. "I don't know why I get so hungry between meals! I must have a tapeworm."

"Yes, I've heard of that," the voice said, deadly level. "That's when one person eats enough for two, isn't it?" She was still standing there, her eyes taking in everything.

A whiff of gardenia filtered through the seam of the reversed door. The back of the door was flattening his nose now, but he didn't dare try to evade the pressure. She was so close it was a wonder she couldn't hear him breathing. Why was she standing there so long? Wasn't she ever going to move?

She spoke again. "Quite homey. You seem to have gotten quite a kick out of playing house out here by yourself."

Ruth's voice was completely self-possessed, even though she must have known her answer sounded absurd. "It's sort of fun to fix up an old place and make believe it's your own—"

"Like Marie Antoinette at Trianon." And then with an almost imperceptible change of key: "I always did wonder whom she used to meet there."

Neither Ruth nor the woman said anything more. Only the breathing told him she was still there. Then suddenly a pinkish scallop adhered to the door's edge, within a hair's breadth of his face. It was four of her five fingers, curled about the door, the nails like scarlet daggers. He couldn't get his head any farther away from them; the angle of the door where it joined the frame was too narrow. And when the time came for her to flex her fingers and withdraw them, there was a very good chance they would touch his cheek.

But they didn't. They opened and missed touching him by sixteenths of an inch. If he'd needed a shave, they might have contacted the stubble on his face, that was how close they were.

She had seen something that had drawn her away. "Shouldn't these things get rusty?" she said, and he heard a little *plink* as she tossed something down that she had picked up. It was his razor blade, which he had left on a scrap of paper to dry. He cursed inwardly.

The threshold creaked now in reverse passage, and the awful propinquity was over. He released his breath and felt perspiration tracking down the side of his nose.

Her next remark sounded from outside. "I tell Bill he should have this property fenced in. Left open the way it is, on all sides, anyone at all could hide out in it. I never feel safe, even in the daytime, living on this place. At least, not while that man's still at large."

"What man?" he heard Ruth ask guilelessly.

The answer was bursting with accusation. "*You* know what man I mean. Dan Nearing. The man who murdered my husband."

Ruth didn't answer.

"Well, I'll be getting back now. I was just curious to see the attraction that keeps drawing you out here day after day—I've noticed more than once that the tracks of Father's chair led off in this direction. I suppose you'll be sticking around awhile longer, my dear."

Ruth played out her part with beautiful consistency. She jumped up. "Oh, no, wait for me, Miss Alma! You've got me so frightened now, I wouldn't stay here alone another minute, not on a bet!"

He heard the hiss of the chair wheels fade away down the path. The last sound he heard was the contralto voice, already a distance away. "Your hands *are* clammy—for some reason or other." She must have found an excuse to touch one of Ruth's hands.

When all was quiet, Townsend came out of his hiding place, feeling like a bath towel three people have used. Unless Alma was a whole lot dumber than she sounded—and he didn't think she was—she'd caught on that somebody had been hiding out in the lodge lately, even if she didn't know he'd been there at the same moment she was.

He released his compressed burden of papers and started to pry at one of the warped floorboards, using the saw-toothed lid of a can for a lever.

NEED FOR FOOD drew him back to the lodge. He'd been out of it all day, hiding among the trees, to avoid any possible surprise raid. He intended to sleep out, too: it was a clear warm night, and he would roll up in one of Ruth's blankets. But first he had to get something into his stomach.

No Indian brave ever stalked a lone cabin in a clearing more craftily than Townsend approached the lodge. He worked his way toward it from the rear, then huddled motionless for a long time behind a tree, listening. Reassured, he crept toward the front wall, bending low to make as little outline as possible, even in the gloom. Again he stopped and listened. The dirt path ahead was lifeless, the lodge empty. Quickly he covered the short remaining distance to the doorway.

The door was slanting inward now, whereas he'd left it closed. That worried him for a minute, but maybe the wind had done it. He moved carefully into the room, and then he saw the white square pinned to the inside of the door. He could make out lines of writing on it, even in the dark. He took it down, closed the door and struck a match. The lines on the paper sprang into legibility.

Dan—
    I've found out something terribly important. You will have to see it with your own eyes. Come over to the house at nine. I'll fix the door so you can get in. They won't be here, they're going into the city, so don't worry.
                                                                                Ruth

He studied it carefully. He'd had only one other piece of writing from her, the note she'd left for him at Tillary Street. He still had it, stuck away in his rear trouser pocket with little clots of wool dust sticking to it. Funny that he should have kept it until now. Not so funny, maybe. Lucky, darn lucky that he should have kept it until now.

He put the two notes side by side, struck a fresh match and held it over them. When the match went out, he put the two pieces of paper back in his pocket. He had a few things to do before his rendezvous at nine.

Chapter Eleven

THERE WAS a blurred moon up, and it spilled a platinum-gray wash over the house. He came out from under the trees and stood looking across the lawn at it for a while, thinking things over. To go in there was final. He couldn't afford to be wrong. One way or another, this was the story's end.

His thoughts were a little like those of a man about to enter an execution chamber. He thought of the rag doll with the piquant face, Virginia, and of Dan Nearing's sweetheart, Ruth. He thought of the strange story he'd lived, his own story. The first placid, uneventful twenty-eight years. The three lost years; not fully visualized even yet, even with the aid of Ruth's eyes. Then the dismal, fugitive life made up of a blending of the two. And tonight—either the end or the beginning of a fourth life. Four lives in thirty-two years. Whatever happened, he'd never be quite like other people again.

The house waited for him, dark on all sides, not a light showing. It was nine o'clock now. He started across the lawn to keep his rendezvous. The short grass hissed under his feet, and a wavering black shadow like running water followed him, for he was going toward the moon.

As he went up the two low flagstone steps to the door, his shadow stood up against it like a paper cutout. It was a doorway to the past and to the future.

The knob felt cold under his touch. *Here I go* sparked in his mind as the door gave way; the latch had been fixed for him, just as the note had promised. Inside, the darkness lay as thick and palpable upon him as a drift of black feathers. It all but tickled his nostrils. He reached over to the left, found the electric switch, pressed it. Nothing happened. The bulb in the fixture must have burned out. Or been removed.

He started forward, arm half bent before him to guard against collision. A dark form moving to one side of him made the hair on his neck rise up, but he realized it was only his own reflection flitting across a mirror. He remembered seeing a mirror hanging at just about that place the night he'd been in here.

He went on, stopped at the foot of the staircase, and gave a short interrogative whistle: two notes, one up, one down. You hear it a lot on the streets. It means: Hey, there! Where are you?

He repeated it, and the second time it got results. He heard a cautious tread in the upper hall. It was very soft, stealth implicit in every scuff. At the upstairs railing, directly over his head, it stopped.

"It's me, Ruth," he whispered huskily.

The answer came down blurred with an excess of caution. "Shh! I'm coming right down."

The tread started down the stairs. As it came near, he could make out the two white cross strips of Ruth's outfit, as if they were outlined in faintly luminous paint.

The apparition stopped about four steps above him, and the white of an arm reached out toward him. A voiceless whisper went with it. "Give me your hand—"

"Wait a minute, I'll light a match—"

"No, don't! Give me your hand, I'll lead you."

She seemed stubbornly determined that he take the steps that would close the short gap between them. Her hand stretched out demandingly toward him. He clasped it with his own. Her second hand came out and joined the first, and he felt them both sidling around his wrists.

He started up and she began to tug at him to make him come faster. The warning scent of gardenia touched his brain, and suddenly, treacherously, the outstretched arms drew him in close and fast with unexpected clinging strength. He lurched off balance and a taut rope, stretched from banister post to banister post, caught him just below the knees, so that he went floundering helplessly down at nearly full length. A shattering shriek rent the air. "He's down, Bill! Get him, quick!"

Something crushingly heavy flung itself upon him from behind, pinning him flat as he tried to wrench his hands free.

"Have you got him, Bill? Hurry up, it's killing me to hold him!"

A male voice spoke for the first time, winded with effort and so close behind his ear that he could feel its warmth. "Gimme his hands! Bring them together—over this way—"

He kept trying to thrash free, but the dead weight resting on him crushed resistance.

She crossed her arms, thus bringing his wrists together. "Here, take them—quick!" A leather strap twined around, cruelly, crushingly tight, so that the wrists pancaked over one another in tormented compression.

"There, now." The crushing weight lifted from his back and was replaced by a thick, powerful hand holding him down.

The female voice—and only now that it was neither whispering nor screaming could he recognize it as Alma Diedrich's raspy contralto—said, "Oh, Bill! What he did to my poor hands!"

The man, still breathing heavily, said, "Got the bottle?"

"It's up there by the top step."

"Bring it down. It'll make things a lot easier."

The woman went up and came treading deftly down again. "Can they tell afterward when you've used this stuff on them?" she asked.

The man didn't answer that. "Give me a little light, so I can see what I'm doing."

The man sat down now, across Townsend's shoulders, holding his head between sinewy thighs as in a vise. A flashlight clicked on and found Townsend's face, dazzling him after the long darkness. There was a tiny gurgle of liquid.

The man said, "Hold his head up off the step."

His head was suddenly bent upward from the neck. She had

him by the hair, the whites of his eyes showing against the flashlight beam. The liquid gurgled again.

A freezing horror percolated through Townsend's veins, the horror that comes of not knowing what's going to be done to you. A cloying reek swirled around his head, and a soaked pad closed in over his mouth and nose. He tried to get his nose out of the way by jerking his head from side to side, but the pad just followed his jerks. For a moment or two, he saw a pair of eyes staring into his with pitiless clinical interest. Then they started to blur. He could still hear, even after sight had dimmed, but then hearing went, creeping away into the distance.

Feeling went last of all. Then it was all jerked out from under him, like something on a rug: hearing and seeing and knowing.

The anesthetic wore off sometime during the next quarter of an hour and left a brief nauseated reaction that reminded him of the time he'd had his appendix out years before. Only this time, he knew, the operation was still to come.

He found himself in a sitting position, his arms bent back around a straight-backed chair. Something thick and braided, like the cording used with draperies, was holding him fast. He felt it through the insulation of stiff leather; his hands had been rebound over driving gloves, presumably to leave no telltale traces of chafing on his wrists.

The shades of the room were drawn, but there was enough of a gap at the bottom for a glimmering of moonwash to spill across the windowsill. For the first moment or two he thought he was alone, although something that sounded like labored breathing faintly caught his ear once or twice. But as the moon climbed up in the sky, a bar of reflection on the wall opposite the gap began to move, and in a few moments it struck the top of a sofa and began to billow downward over its convex surface. A turmoil of hair that it silvered, like a squashed-down halo, told him that Ruth was in the room with him. But the glimmering head made no move.

"Ruth!" he whispered urgently across the darkness. "Ruth!" She didn't answer. Why? What had they done to her? He'd have to wait for that bar of moonlight to climb down to her eyes.

When it had, he saw that her eyes were wide open, staring at him in helpless, limpid appeal. He knew that she must be gagged. More than likely, she had already been bound up in here when he had edged into the trap, and they had gagged her to make sure she couldn't warn him.

People in peril don't make memorable remarks to one another. At first he could think of nothing to say but, "Hello, Ruthie." Then he tried desperately to think of phrases that might comfort her, but nothing came to his mind. He forced himself to speak to her anyway, while the moonlight lingered on her eyes. Things like, "It'll work out all right. Something'll turn up." Simply to keep her going, take her mind off their danger. He must keep her going a little while longer.

It was pathetic when her eyes started to disappear into the darkness as the bar worked its way lower down her face. It was like watching someone drowning in reverse. She lowered her head, to keep this window of visual communication open between them another half minute, but finally her eyes were gone and the gag across her lips came into view.

A door opened somewhere upstairs, softly in the silence, and his skin prickled. A man's tread was coming down the stairs. It hit floor level and came on toward the closed door. The door opened, a switch snapped and the room shot into unbearable, blinding brightness. When his eyes began to function again, he got his first good look at Bill Diedrich, who was standing motionless in the doorway.

He was squat and thickset, with the yeasty look that light-haired people get when they've pushed dissipation beyond a certain point. His hair was straw-colored, with a nasty tight little crinkle in it. He had on a plum-colored bathrobe over blue rayon pajamas, although Townsend knew he hadn't been either sleeping or bathing. The costume must be part of the act. He'd undressed for the murder, for reasons best known to himself. He had brought a revolver down with him and was holding it negligently now, muzzle pointed to the floor. He grinned at

Townsend, then turned and called, "Alma, are you ready? Hurry it up. I want to get this over with."

Another step sounded on the stairs, and the woman's form appeared at the door, bringing the gardenia fragrance with her. Townsend kept his eyes on the man.

Diedrich put down the gun and stabbed a hand impatiently at her coiffure, rumpling it. "Lookit your hair, like you just came out of a beauty parlor! Get a little realism into this, will you! What's the idea of the hat and coat?"

"I'm going out, you fool, to get the police! With the phone wires cut, what other way is there?"

"Yeah, but you're not going like that—looking like you just came out of a bandbox. Remember—we were in our beds when this guy tried to murder us. And when you run out of a house for your life, after you've just seen what you're supposed to have seen, you don't stop to put on a hat and coat!" He tried to control his fury. "Put on a robe over that nightgown. And bring the knife when you come back. There's something I want you to do before you go."

They were both so matter-of-fact about it they might have been discussing what clothes to wear to a show. Well, as a matter of fact, they were.

So that was what it was going to be. A murder staged as self-defense. Well, they had the law on their side. He was a wanted killer. Not too many questions would be asked. And Ruth would have to go with him, to shut her up.

The woman came back holding a long-bladed kitchen knife. She was more appropriately attired now, as the man had demanded. "What d'you want this for?" she asked. Townsend thought he could detect a note of nervousness in her voice, as if she didn't mind Diedrich's committing a murder, but didn't want to see it happen in front of her eyes.

"This guy's supposed to mark me up before I drop him. I can't get away without showing any wounds. You do it for me."

"For the love of—!" she gasped.

"It's gotta be done! Come on—this is no time to be finicky.

Just don't dig in too deep, that's all." He tensed his forearm, like someone about to have a blood sample taken. "One across there, the back of it. Not the inside. Easy, now."

As she did it, her back was to Townsend, so he couldn't see the act itself, but across her shoulder he could see the man's face looking absorbedly down. It twitched slightly.

"Now try one on the chest," he instructed coldly. "Don't close your eyes like that. You're liable to bungle it."

Her elbow moved slightly.

"Whew!" He sucked in breath with the sting. "Now a thin one across the forehead. Just with the point. Careful now."

That time Townsend could see the blade move, tracing across the forehead. She stood back.

Diedrich was blowing along the upraised side of his arm, trying to cool the sting. "All right, get the car. Hurry up, we haven't got all night."

It was their cold-blooded matter-of-factness that lent such grisly horror to the situation. They were talking as if she were going on an errand to the grocery store and he were promising to repair some household gadget for her while she was gone.

They went out into the hall together, stopping just short of the front door, where he gave her last-minute instructions, impressing upon her what had already been arranged between them. "It's nine twenty now. It'll take you thirty minutes in and back, even doing sixty. Don't bring them back sooner than that, whatever you do! I'm going to need a good half hour to get rid of the cords and fix those two the way they should look. If you find that you've gotten to the police too soon, throw a faint or something—tack on another five minutes that way. But make sure you do it before you tell them what's happened. Once you've told them, you won't be able to control their speed getting back here. Those state highway cars are fast. Remember, *thirty minutes*."

The front door opened, and Townsend heard her parting remark. "Bill, will we ever be able to sleep again?"

Then he heard the sound of a kiss, and the answer that went

with it. "I'll stay awake nights from now on for the two of us. You can buy a lot of sleep with a dollar sign. This is on me."

So there was love in it. Love of a sort. It hadn't been only for money that they had wanted Harry Diedrich out of the way.

The door closed. Townsend heard the car engine start up, open up into an even hum, then finally fade out down the driveway. She had gone to get help—for something that hadn't happened yet. The murderer and the murdered-to-be were left alone together.

Diedrich came back along the hall, but his destination was not yet this room, this execution chamber. He stopped in it a moment to pick up the knife and went out again and on up the stairs. He was very quiet about the whole thing. But then, murder doesn't need to make much noise.

First the sound of a key in a keyhole somewhere up above. Adela, the woman they said was insane—kept locked in her room for years. A dollar sign, he'd said just now to Alma at the door. This Adela must be a beneficiary of the estate, insane or not. And this was her own brother, standing at the door, the knife—probably—behind his back.

Townsend heard Diedrich's voice, in casual, treacherous salutation. "Still awake, Addie? I thought you'd be in bed long ago. Cook wants to know what you'd like for dessert tomor—" The door closed, cutting the rest of it off.

There was a moment of utter stillness. About as long as it takes a person to cross a room. Townsend could feel Ruth's distended eyes burning into his face from the sofa opposite. He didn't have the heart to meet them; he ignored the mute appeal. There was something obscene about having to sit and look at one another while such a thing was happening.

Suddenly a scream of animallike unreason sounded, a scream that belonged in a slaughter yard. It stopped. Then there was a gurgling, slavering moan of dissolution. Then nothing.

Diedrich stayed in there awhile. Then Townsend heard a chair or a bench go over. Not with a clatter, but with a careful, deliberate sound. More stage setting, Townsend thought. The

chair would look as though it had been overturned in the course
of a hand-to-hand struggle.

He heard the tread on the stairs again, and Diedrich appeared
in the doorway. It was a terrible moment for Townsend: he was
seeing what a man's face looks like right after he's committed
murder. It was parchment yellow and satiny with sweat. In it
was the racial heritage of fear and awe that always accompanies
violent death. Diedrich still had the knife in his grasp, and he
was the killer steaming from the kill. He was murder, on two
legs and in the flesh.

Not a word had passed Townsend's lips since Diedrich and
Alma had first descended on him. He had known that it would
be hopeless to plead or try to reason with them. But now a raging
resentment simmered up in him, boiled over, and he began to
swear in a hissing, monotonous litany. All this horror at the man
who stood there was translated into inadequate language.

Diedrich smiled as he closed the door behind him. "That's
what I call real big talk," he murmured. "It's a shame to have to
deprive the world of such a vocabulary." He came close, and for
a minute Townsend thought, This is it. But he only touched
Townsend lightly about the face a few times with the flat of the
blade. He was daubing Townsend with telltale traces of a crime
that wasn't his.

Then he wiped the knife handle carefully with a bit of gauze
and put it down. It lay there waiting for Townsend's hand to
close around it—after death.

Diedrich picked up the gun, shot the clip back to make sure it
was fully loaded and closed it again. Then he moved over into a
straight line with the man on the chair, slowly paced backward
six steps and sighted the gun at Townsend without a tremor of
the hand.

"You'd better shut your eyes," he said grimly. "That'll make it
easier on you."

The little round black bore, centering on Townsend, seemed
to expand, to widen, and a pulse in his cheek, up near the ear,
started to pound. But he didn't speak. Instead he smiled thinly,

way over at one side of his mouth, and forced the smile to stay on his face.

There's something about such a smile that troubles the beholder, that makes him wonder, What's he got to smile about at such a time? The challenge worked.

Diedrich said, "What's funny?"

"You never heard about the angle of fire, did you?" Townsend had to moisten his lips to make them articulate. "I'm in a chair and you're on your feet. You're firing *down* at me. That's going to look great for self-defense. D'you think they won't notice that? Don't kid yourself." It was hard to keep the smile from wavering, but he did it by force of will.

The way the gun went abruptly vertical, muzzle to floor, showed he'd made his point. A minute gained? Forty-five seconds? Time was Diedrich's enemy now.

Diedrich dipped one knee under him, trying to correct the discrepancy. But it was no good; the bullet's course would now be slightly upward. And the midway position, which would have been the right one, was a half-crouch and too awkward to maintain for any length of time. He couldn't be sure of his shot taking effect from such an unsteady stance.

The method he hit upon at last was almost ludicrous. Diedrich slung out a vacant chair and placed it in a straight line with the one that held his prisoner. Then he sat back in it and raised the gun once more.

But he didn't fire it. He was unsure now. The subtle objection Townsend had managed to insert into his mind must have kept on unfolding postscripts—other things to be considered. In addition to the bullet's trajectory, there was the position of the bodies afterward. If the bullet entered in a certain way, then they must be found lying in a certain way.

He couldn't take any chances. So he rose, strode impatiently across the room and threw open the top of a writing desk. He pocketed the gun and took out paper and a pencil. Then he pointed—to Ruth, to Townsend, to the floor. He was arranging them ahead of time, measuring the arcs of their body falls from the positions in which he wanted it thought that they had met their deaths. Townsend could glimpse his markings, hasty broken lines on the paper.

He worked quickly, like a director mapping out a stage plan for a crime supposed to be impromptu, a crime committed in the heat of self-defense. Once he went so far as to murmur raptly, with a stab of the pencil toward Ruth, "You—over there." A sadistic demon out of Dante's hell could not have improved upon it. The girl was almost cataleptic. Beads of sweat began forming at the roots of Townsend's hair.

Finally Diedrich closed the desk, tacked his blueprint to the desk front for ready reference and consulted his wristwatch. He gave a last comprehensive look around, to make sure everything was in order. No details of the general scenic effect could be overlooked. With his foot he hooked a chair that would presumably have impeded him in fighting for his life, allowed it to crack over on its back, then painstakingly stepped over it in order not to disturb its prone position.

He rubbed his hands together a couple of times, like a surgeon about to perform a delicate operation. He was ready for it at last.

He went over to Ruth and fumbled with one of the cords that bound her to the sofa. Her eyes made a concentric swirl in their sockets and her head looped over. She had fainted away. He seemed not to notice, or if he had, not to care. He freed her, picked her up in both arms, and staggered out a ways into the middle of the room, where he set her down on the floor with a gentleness that was hideous.

A sudden fit of coughing interrupted him before he could draw his arms out from underneath her. He swayed over her, racked, for a minute. At last he stopped and got his breath back.

Then Townsend began to cough. There was something the matter with the air in here. The linings of his eyelids began to smart, water formed, and he saw Diedrich through the tears, as if in a trick mirror—one minute tall and skinny, the next squat and bloated. He heard him go over to the door, coughing

again, and stand there a moment listening. Then Diedrich reached out and opened the door.

What followed was as though a giant eraser had been rubbed across his figure: he all but disappeared, fading into gray half-tones, as a great gust of dirty, flannel-thick smoke mushroomed in. It must have been accumulating out there in the hall for some time to have acquired such density. Instantly it diffused itself everywhere, yet it scarcely thinned at all as it did so. The whole room was filled with a sort of swirling twilight.

Townsend could glimpse Diedrich's gray ghost-form weaving its way back from the door, one purpose still uppermost in its mind, retching up its insides as it came. Diedrich's foot must have struck Ruth, for he suddenly went down in a full-length fall, his gun ricocheting almost to Townsend's feet. Townsend could see it lying there, outlined like a black T square, through the stratified haze that was still thinnest down by the floor. Then a hand came out along the floor, groping blindly for it.

Townsend tried hectically to reach the gun with his own foot and push it beyond the hand's reach. But he couldn't; the tip of his shoe just missed it. Then the crawling, buglike white fingers found the gun, closed hungrily on it and drew it back into the pall of smoke.

There was a fitful wink of orange light down close to the floor, and the room thudded with the detonation.

A long moment of grisly expectancy followed. Then a face suddenly thrust out at Townsend from a low level, as though the body under it were traveling on its knees, unable to lift itself erect anymore.

A hand pointed waveringly toward him, its index finger black and thicker than the rest, with a hole at the tip. It swayed from side to side, missing him by whole feet in either direction. Then the light sparked again and what felt like hot sand stung his cheek, and something thudded into the Chinese folding screen behind him.

But he didn't need a bullet to finish him; he was going fast enough. Every breath was red-hot agony, ripping the lining from his windpipe. His eyes were sizzling coals extinguished in their own fluid.

He was hardly aware of what was happening anymore. There was a heavy thud on the floor right in front of him, and then somebody's head landed on his knee, slid off it, hit his foot and stayed there. His own head was straining apart, ready to fly into pieces.

The last thing he heard was a far-off tinkle of glass breaking somewhere.

Chapter Twelve

THE OXYGEN going down his throat felt good. He was angry when it stopped. When they took the tent off him, he saw that he was lying on his back someplace out in the open, with white shafts of light crisscrossing the grass here and there, and against them a motionless frieze of black legs standing around him in a half-circle.

One pair of legs telescoped into a face that came down close to his. He took a good long look at this face, and it took a good long look back at him. He knew it intimately, this inscrutable, wooden-Indian face that never smiled. It had stopped and stared at him in the crowd and glowered balefully at him through a dusty subway-car window. It had been reflected through a store window, and it had started to turn and look at him in the aisle of a day coach. And here it was; it had caught up with him at last. It had him flat on his back on the ground, pinned to the mat.

He spoke to it finally, with languid unconcern. "You're Ames, aren't you?"

"That's me," the face said challengingly. "And you're Dan Nearing, aren't you?"

"Like hell I am," he said. "I'm Frank Townsend."

They helped him up to a sitting position. He found the oxygen had left him a little light-headed. "Don't you ever change that hat?" he heard himself say to Ames, who did not reply.

On his feet again, he looked around. The Diedrich house was in the background, with interlocking circles of light, like big white poker chips, against it. An occasional whiff of pungent smoke drifted over from it on the breeze. There were people and fire-fighting apparatus on the lawn, and cars galore, all parked on the grass at various angles. There was also an ominous-looking black vehicle with its back standing open. A small crowd watched something on a slab being pushed into it. Something that was covered up, with two peaks at one end that suggested uptilted shoes.

They started to walk him, Ames on one side and a deputy on the other, giving him a hand. Townsend asked the question that he'd been thinking about ever since his awakening. "What happened to the girl?" he said, trying hard to keep his voice calm. "He got her, didn't he? I heard a shot through the smoke."

Ames nodded, his face expressionless.

Townsend uttered a savage epithet.

"Save your breath. He's been fumigated, like the rat he was."

"She was a great kid," Townsend said. "Without her . . ." His voice trailed off and the three men said nothing more.

A group just ahead of them shifted to admit them as they came up. He could see another covered slab on the ground, and the black car that had swallowed up the first slab was backing up to this one now. "Who's this—Ruth?" he faltered.

"No, we've got her down in the village already. This is the guy that saved your life."

"I don't get it. Who's that?"

Ames squatted down and tipped back the edge of the tarpaulin. "The guy that gave up his life for yours."

"The old man!" Townsend said contritely. "I forgot him for a minute! So he went too."

The visible effects of the dead man's disability had been obliterated now and he looked like any other man in death. They'd closed the eyes, and the face looked placid, satisfied— yes, almost triumphant. Townsend looked down in silence. What was there to say?

636

"Did you know he'd retained the slight use of one hand?" Ames asked.

"Yes, I caught on to that a couple of days ago, when Ruth had him over at the lodge. He could move a couple of the fingers a little and pivot them slightly from the elbow, that was all."

"That was enough. Enough for him to get hold of a weapon."

"A weapon?" Townsend looked at the detective.

"That's what it amounted to. The only kind of weapon he could handle. An ordinary everyday sulphur-tipped kitchen match. What d'you suppose all that smoke was, spontaneous combustion? There must have been a box of them within his reach somewhere, on the edge of the range maybe, like in most kitchens. I guess he was wheeled in there at times, and his chair accidentally left standing close to it. And each time he stole one or two of those matches. God knows what he thought he'd do with them."

Townsend said, "He had good ideas."

Ames shrugged and said, "He clawed a little rent in the mattress under him. We found it stuffed with charred matchsticks when we carried it out just now. It tells the whole story. He faced that death, not the easiest kind there is, to try to attract attention from the highway in time to save you. It wasn't much of a chance, but it was the only one he had, and he was willing to take it."

"And he did save me," Townsend said. "My own message would have gotten you here too late. Diedrich would still have had time to put a shot into me. It was the smoke, not you fellows, that dropped him. As a matter of fact, he did snap off a shot at me, but he was too far gone by that time to aim straight."

"Was that you who phoned in the tip saying that if we wanted the killer of Harry Diedrich, we should close in here no later than quarter to ten tonight?"

"That was me," Townsend said dryly. "And if you've got any doubts, I asked to speak to you yourself, and you tripped over something getting to the phone. I heard it over the wire. The foot of a chair or a desk, something like that."

"It was you," Ames conceded.

"I couldn't time it any closer than I did. If I'd gotten you here too soon, they would have pulled their punches and it would have been your hands I'd have walked into instead of theirs. They would have been just innocent third parties to the arrest of a wanted murderer in their house. But if I timed it too late—bingo, you saw what nearly happened. It was a gamble: I took it, and I lost. But the old man called my bet off and gave it back to me."

"How'd you know they'd play into your hands at just such and such a time tonight?"

"I got a decoy note from them, which I was supposed to think came from the girl. They'd caught on I was hiding out around here, but they didn't want me turned in alive—they knew damn well I hadn't killed Harry Diedrich; they had. So they tied up the girl and then laid a trap for me. I caught on to it, but I walked right into it of my own accord with just one slight variation—tipping you people off about coming out here."

"Well, you sure messed up the dame's timing," Ames admitted. "We were already on our way out here, a little below the Struthers house, when we met her on the road. For a person in search of help, she didn't seem too happy about meeting us, but she went into her spiel anyway and she took a hell of a time telling us about it. She was so damn explicit, too, that was the trouble. Too damn explicit. We were going to find you both dead: she was sure of it. He'd had to do it, in self-defense, she said. She even gave us a sound track on it."

"I saw them planning it," Townsend said.

"The only thing was"—Ames came pretty close to smiling—"by the time we got here, some people from a passing car had broken the windows and gotten you out. And you were certainly not dead, even if the girl was. The giveaway was that you were still trussed up, hand and foot. Self-defense can be stretched pretty far at times, but tying a person up first and *then* shooting him to protect yourself is going too far. And then, when the smoke had cleared enough for us to look around, a couple of other little things turned up. F'rinstance, this. Above all, this."

He took out the chart Diedrich had tacked onto the desk front. "Guys that shoot in self-defense don't usually have time to draw pictures of it ahead of time."

Townsend said, "I suppose you still think I killed Harry Diedrich?"

"As a matter of fact, I don't, after what's happened. But what I think or don't think has nothing to do with it. I'm just the arresting officer in the case. There are charges outstanding against you, there's a warrant out for you, and if you didn't kill him, have you any proof you didn't? That's what you're gonna need."

"Yes. I've got proof. Solid proof, twofold. And one's an eyewitness account."

"What eyewitness? You were alone in the house with him—"

"Oh, no, I wasn't! Aren't you forgetting—?" He nodded toward the still form at their feet.

"*Him?*" The detective gave a start. "Now, wait a minute—"

"His eyes were all right, weren't they? And his chair was in that side sitting room that whole afternoon, wasn't it? He couldn't see all the way across into the sun parlor, of course—for one thing, the doors were closed. But he could hear everything. And he could see whoever went in there and whoever came out."

"Suppose he could—and did? He's dead now. And even if he weren't, he couldn't speak a word; his tongue was paralyzed along with the rest of him. How'd you get it out of him?"

"You go back to that lodge where Ruth hid me out. Count back six floorboards from the door, and pull the sixth one up. It's loose. Under it you'll find a pad and some loose papers. That's his testimony, taken down by me firsthand."

"How?" said Ames skeptically. "By mental telepathy?"

"Through the eyes. In ordinary Morse code, the way they tap out messages in every telegraph office in the country. A short blink was a dot, a long blink was a dash."

"Well, I'll be—! Why the hell didn't he try a little of that on me when I was out here working on the case at the time?"

"You mean why the hell didn't you keep watching him long enough to figure it out for yourself. He practically broke his heart winking at you every time you came near him—he says so himself in his account—and you wouldn't stand still in one place long enough to dope it out. You probably just took it for part of his sickness."

"Yeah," Ames admitted, lowering his head thoughtfully, "something like that. And what's the second proof you've got?"

"I'll show you that. I'll let you see it for yourself around midday tomorrow, weather permitting."

Two men came forward to pick up the inanimate form lying on the ground under the tarpaulin and put it in the back of the black car.

"Wait a minute," Townsend intervened. "Let me say good-by to him first. We had a special way of talking together. It isn't usually heard at a time like this, and it might shock you, but I want to sign off in the way he'd want."

Ames motioned at the men and they all wandered off a short distance.

The man who had been Dan Nearing gazed down at the still face on the ground before him. Ames could hear his voice in a steady murmur. Only the last sentence was loud enough for words to be distinguished. "This is your friend, Danny, saying thanks—and so long."

Chapter Thirteen

AT NOON THE next day, the weather permitted. It was bright and hot and still. The Diedrich place was drowsing in the sun as the official car pulled up, as though all that had happened there had long been forgotten. A cop posted at the door to keep away the curious was the only incongruous note.

Townsend entered first, with Ames beside him and the others behind them. He opened the doors of the sun porch and they all went in.

"This is where Harry Diedrich was killed," Townsend said. "I'll show you now just how it was done, by Bill and Alma Diedrich—his brother and his own wife—while they were miles away from the house."

Ames folded his arms and tapped his fingers on his biceps with an air of saying, "Go ahead, that's what I'm here for."

"The way it is now is just the way it was that day. Wicker chairs, a settee and a low table with a tiled top opposite it that they used to keep plants on when this was a conservatory. I'd like to have something to mark the place of Harry Diedrich on this settee. It isn't really necessary, but it might help us get the whole picture."

"All right, one of the fellows here will—" Ames began.

"I think it had better be something inanimate, unless you want to be minus a member of your force."

One of the policemen brought in a medium-sized glass-domed table lamp and stood it upright in one corner of the settee, against the back cushions. The greater part of the dome showed above the wicker edging at the top.

"That's about the right height," Townsend said. "Harry Diedrich came in here every day after lunch and napped for about an hour. All right now, that's him there, napping on the settee, head showing above it in that corner. He slept with those dark blue shades all drawn full length, to keep the light out of his eyes."

"D'you want 'em down?" Ames grunted.

Townsend smiled a little. "We need the exact details."

One of the men got busy.

Townsend said, "I want you to keep your eyes on this tile-topped table as the place darkens."

As shade after shade was drawn, the tiles went from brilliant yellow-white to yellow-green, to greenish-blue, to indigo. And on the table, with every eye in the room drawn to it, a diamond-shaped scar of light leaped to life, cast by a matching rent in the shade above.

The shades were frayed and threadbare in places, and all over the floor and table and wicker furniture there was a vague pattern of streaks and dabs of reflected light. But the diamond-shaped scar was the most distinct, the largest. It was the only one with a clean-cut shape. So clean-cut it might almost have been scissored out deliberately.

Townsend said, "He was in here napping, but he was in a deeper sleep than usual that day. The old man figured Harry had been doped. I think I must have been given dope myself, and I dozed off in the little side room across the hall, where I usually wheeled the old man.

"Ruth and the cook were finishing up the lunch dishes, fast and noisy, in the kitchen at the back. Both of them had a half day off and they planned to catch the two-o'clock bus into the village. And the murderers knew it, so they weren't taking any chances when they left first; they were making things look as plausible as possible. Harry was a grouch and a tyrant; none of the help would dare come near the sun porch to disturb him once he closed himself in for his afternoon nap. And naturally his brother and his wife knew that, too.

"So they came down the stairs, ready to leave. She got the car out and brought it around to the door, and he—here's what he did."

Townsend reached toward one of the motionless figures standing around him. "Give me the shotgun now. Has it been loaded?"

"I reloaded it before we came out."

Townsend took it over to the door with him, turned the knob, opened and closed the door without moving from it, then came forward again, shotgun in hands. "By this, I mean that Diedrich stepped quickly aside to the storage closet behind the stairs, after he'd followed Alma down, and got out this gun. It was always kept there. It was all readied and primed; he'd seen to that. He stepped quickly in here with it. Only one pair of eyes saw him, and he didn't give a hang about them, because they were set in a head that couldn't talk.

"He came in here with the gun, cocked it so that the charge

was exposed—like this—and laid it down across the table this way."

He lowered it carefully so that its muzzle pointed straight at the lamp propped in the corner of the settee.

"There were marks on this table to guide him. Not the kind you might have found when you looked around later. But marks just the same. These crevices between the tiles were like lines of latitude and longitude. To make them workable, all he had to do was adjust the feet of the table on the floor and shift it slightly forward or back, so that this diamond of light would be sure to fall on and follow the lengthwise seam between the tiles for a considerable distance, before it finally curved off it. And the crosswise seams, they were like the hands of a clock. He'd already timed it carefully and found out just how long it would take the light mote to travel along from one tile to the next. Say it was ten minutes—one and a half tile widths then would give him a quarter of an hour. Much the same basic principle as a sundial.

"All right. He didn't put the gun immediately under the light mote. That wouldn't have given him any lead time. Instead he set what amounted to a time bomb. He placed the gun a certain distance to the right of the diamond of light, but in a straight line along which it was bound to pass in a given number of minutes. Say I foreshorten the distance for our purposes and make it a half square."

He did so and stepped away from it, motioning his gallery to do likewise.

"All this didn't take him as long as it has taken me to tell it. Then he stepped out again and closed the doors behind him. Alma, at a prearranged signal, called inside to him at the top of her lungs, 'Hurry up, Bill. We'll miss that train!' This was for the benefit of the two in the kitchen. Then he got into the car with her and they drove away.

"That was all he did. Brought the gun out of the closet, stepped in here with it, laid it down on this table and aimed it at his sleeping brother. He certainly didn't fire it. But that, gentlemen, explains the murder of Harry Diedrich, of which I was accused.

"You can take out your watches and time it now, if you care to. Or just stand quietly a few minutes and wait for it to happen."

One of them timed it as Ames watched. The diamond was crawling slowly along the line but too slowly for the eye to detect the motion. Ames said—perhaps to break the tension of waiting—"But how could they be sure of picking up this Struthers from the next estate down the road, so they'd have a witness?"

Townsend shrugged. "Hard to know. But I'd guess that the woman did a little checking in the morning to find out what neighbor was planning to go to town."

The sun had hit the exposed powder magazine of the gun now. It lay across it like a vivid yellow leaf, luminous where all else was cool blue shade.

Minutes went by slowly. The sun diamond didn't seem to move, but it was moving all the time. They could tell that by checking its relation to the things around it. Finally it began to slip off the magazine on the opposite side.

They watched in silent intensity. Once or twice a face turned to Townsend, questioningly, then turned back again without saying anything. A thread of black unraveled from the open magazine; then freed itself, broke off short and went up into nothingness. No more followed.

"I get what you were trying to show us," Ames said at last, "but it looks like this time it's not going to pay off—"

There was a malignant little flash that made them all jump. Then a jet of red-orange shot out the opposite end of the barrel, an angry roar rattled the tiled table and the windowpanes on three sides of the room, and a great broil of acrid, sickening smoke huffed out.

Only the base of the lamp remained, nestled in the lower inside corner of the settee. The dome, the bulbs, had been shorn off clean.

"That dome," Townsend said, "was Harry Diedrich's head."

"So that's how it was," Ames said.

"That's how it was," Townsend concurred.

"Could be," Ames said. "But don't forget: one honest witness saw you running out of the room with the gun in your hand."

"Lucky for me the old man saw that, too," Townsend said. "I was asleep in the chair next to him. The shot woke me up and I ran in to see what had happened. Evidently I picked up the gun and ran out of the house holding it in my hand. I must have seen the car driving up, and I was shouting with excitement." Townsend shrugged. "Naturally the murderers played that for all it was worth. It was a cinch for them to convince Mr. Struthers that I was running out with the gun in my hand to kill them too. Alma probably let out a couple of good loud screams so Struthers couldn't hear what I was shouting."

"Nice setup," said Ames, a grudging respect in his voice.

They all filed out of the house, past the cop on duty, and got into the car. The Diedrich house faded out behind them like something that had never been. Trees got in the way, and it was gone. Somebody looked back, but it wasn't Townsend.

"Where do I stand now?" he asked Ames.

Ames fingered the edges of the briefcase holding an official transcript of Emil Diedrich's optical telegrams. "I'm turning the old man's account in to the public prosecutor's office, and of course I'm making my own report, which'll include what you just showed us. Technically, it won't be in my hands from that point on. But"—he gave Townsend an encouraging look—"I don't think you've got much to worry about. They'll put you through the formality of having the murder charges against you dismissed, and then you'll probably be remanded into my custody as a material witness against Alma Diedrich. You'll have to stick around until the trial's over with, but I'll do what I can to make it easy on you."

He began forthwith, as soon as they reached the constabulary, which was in the same building as the jail. "The prisoner's having his meal with me in my office," he informed the guard. "I'll send him back to you later." Then he had their dinners and two bottles of cold beer sent in from the restaurant across the square.

"Gee, this must feel funny to you," Townsend said at length, "sitting here having a quiet meal with me, of all people—the guy you were trying so long to get."

"Yeah," Ames admitted. He finished the beer in his glass. "Let's let it go at this: I was after a guy named Dan Nearing. I lost him someplace along the way, between here and Tillary Street. I don't think he'll ever show up again—there or any-where else." He grinned.

Townsend saw that the gray eyes were friendly.

Chapter Fourteen

THE TRAIN WAS coming into New Jericho now, the train that would take him back to the present, back to Virginia. It hissed and rumbled and fanned by, only stopping after he had given up hope and thought it was going to pass the station. Ames, and the man who was now merely a material witness in the forthcoming case against Alma Diedrich, and the deputy who was to accompany the witness had to chase up the platform to keep abreast of it.

The deputy swung aboard first. Townsend put his foot on the bottommost step, then swung around to say good-by to Ames. The latter poked a finger of reminder into his arm. "Come back no later than Wednesday, now—that was as long as I could get you. Did you let her know you're coming?"

"No, I'm going to walk in on her from nowhere—like I did once before. Only this time it's for keeps. I'd like to bring her back with me, only I hate to get her mixed up in all the publicity there'll be once the trial begins."

"I'll take care of that," Ames promised. "I'll get her a room in my boardinghouse."

The train started to move. Townsend preceded the deputy into the car and sat down by a window. New Jericho was starting to slip backward when suddenly he caught sight of something out of the corner of his eye that made him shy away, as if in memory of past danger. Ames was running alongside the train window, holding up something that flashed metallically.

Townsend threw up the window and Ames thrust the thing in at him—it was the cigarette case that he had once pawned on Tillary Street. "You left this in the office last night and I forgot to give it back to you. What're you laughing at?"

"Life is like a circle, isn't it? I'm thinking of the last time you were pacing me like that outside a moving window, trying to get in at me."

Ames fell behind, and then vanished as the train gained speed. When it shrieked past the sprawling moss-grown cemetery just outside the village, Townsend caught a fleeting glimpse of a familiar mound and the small headstone that had been his only gift to Ruth Dillon. Ruth, who had given him so much, the past and the future. He raised two fingers to his temple and brought them out in a salute. Salute and farewell.

The locomotive up ahead gave a long, wailing whistle of unutterable sadness. After it died away, it hummed in Townsend's eardrums for a second or two, like a playback. Then that went too. And with it, he knew, was gone more than the echo of a lonely train whistle over the countryside.

With it, the past was gone.

Forever.

ACKNOWLEDGMENTS

The condensations in this volume have been created by
The Reader's Digest Association, Inc.,
and are used by permission of and special arrangement
with the publishers and the holders of the respective copyrights.

The Tiger in the Smoke, copyright 1952 by Margery Allingham Carter,
renewed © 1980 by Emily Joyce Allingham,
is reprinted by permission of Doubleday & Co. Inc., New York,
and Chatto & Windus Ltd., London.

The Uninvited, copyright 1942 by Dorothy Margaret Callan Macardle,
renewed © 1969 by D.F. Macardle,
is reprinted by permission of Doubleday & Co. Inc.,
New York, and Curtis Brown Ltd., London.

The Laughing Policeman, copyright © 1968 by Maj Sjöwall & Per Wahlöö,
translation copyright © 1970 by Random House, Inc.,
is reprinted by permission of Pantheon Books, New York,
and Victor Gollancz Ltd., London.

The Black Curtain, copyright 1941, by Cornell Woolrich,
renewed © 1968 by Cornell Woolrich.
Copyright assigned in 1974 by Chase Manhattan Bank, N.A.,
as executor for the Estate of Cornell Woolrich
to Sheldon Abend d.b.a. Authors Research Co. of NYC.
Reprinted by permission of
Scott Meredith Literary Agency Inc., New York.

The Strange Case of Dr. Jekyll and Mr. Hyde by Robert Louis Stevenson,
first published in 1886, is reprinted in its entirety,
with minor modernizations of vocabulary.

Reader's Digest Fund for the Blind is publisher of the Large-Type Edition of *Reader's Digest*. For
subscription information about this magazine, please contact Reader's Digest Fund for the Blind, Inc.,
Dept. 250, Pleasantville, N.Y. 10570.